THE PROMISE OF A GENTLEMAN

THE COUSINS OF THE ARISTOCRACY

LINDA RAE SANDE

Twisted Teacup
PUBLISHING

The Promise of a Gentleman

ISBN: 978-0-9915075-4-2

V1.5

Cover photographs © PeriodImages.com

Cover art by KGee Designs.

PRINTED IN THE UNITED STATES OF AMERICA

A LADY TAKES HER LEAVE OF MERRIWEATHER MANOR

A prelude set in 1777

One of the preeminent homes of the aristocracy, Merriweather Manor could be found on a twelve-thousand acre estate about seven miles west of London. Besides the large multi-wing structure that made up the manor, the estate also included stables, a carriage house, three gardens, and a large pond. The brick structure hosted several generations of Merriweathers until a few years after the untimely death, in 1777, of Roger, the youngest son of Mary Margaret Merriweather Grandby, Dowager Countess of Torrington.

The countess had been especially pleased when Roger Grandby married Lady Sophia, the youngest daughter of William Burroughs, Duke of Ariley. Her oldest son and the current Earl of Torrington, George, was already married to the duke's oldest daughter, Sarah. Although it had taken a few years to produce an heir from that merger, the two were the proud parents of Milton, who was proving at the age of one to be a rather mischievous little boy.

But more about him later.

Roger's death from pneumonia left his wife, Sophia, with a young boy, Gregory, an inheritance of ten thousand pounds for her, and a twenty-thousand pound trust for the son that would make him one of the wealthiest men in England when he reached twenty-one years of age.

"You will stay here, of course," the countess insisted once the reading of the will had taken place.

Sophia regarded her mother-in-law for only a moment. *Where else*

"""

would I go? There was her son to consider. She supposed she could return to her family—the Burroughs had a country estate in Derbyshire, a house in London, a cottage in Brighton and a townhouse or two in Bath—but she had no desire to leave Merriweather Manor. "Of course, we'll stay," she answered with a wan smile.

Mary Margaret gave her a nod and turned her attention to the other family members, acting as if she hadn't done anything more than give a servant an order.

Sophia placed her arm around her young son's shoulders. How could she leave when his entire family—aunts, uncles, cousins—lived at the manor?

So it was quite a shock when only a few years later, on the last day of 1781 to be precise, Lady Sophia Grandby found herself packing her own trunks in the middle of the night. With one last kiss on her son's forehead and a whispered promise she would see him everyday and speak with him when she could without being seen, Sophia took her leave of the estate and disappeared.

Once flush with the funds from her inheritance, her account at the Bank of England, set up on her behalf by her brother, Sir William Burroughs III, was suddenly empty. When inquiries were made, Sophia's brother assured the Dowager Countess of Torrington that no withdrawals had occurred until just a few days before Sophia's departure from Merriweather Manor. An agent representing Sophia had cleaned out the account, explaining to the bank teller that Lady Sophia wished to change banking institutions.

Her brother, who would have seen to the transfer of funds had Sophia asked him to do so, was on Christmas holiday at the Burroughs' family estate in Derbyshire at the time. In fact, Sir William claimed he didn't learn of the missing funds and his sister's disappearance until his return to London in mid-January.

Given the amount of money involved and Lady Sophia's standing in London society, William assured the family it wouldn't be long before he could ascertain what happened to his sister.

After all, ten thousand pounds was difficult to hide.

He met with the account representatives of England's other banks, asking that he be contacted should any sizable deposits be made by Lady Sophia under her married or maiden names.

But he never was.

And William's attention was already diverted to the rather sizable acquisition of rows of townhouses along a section of Kingly

Street, so the importance of tracking down the fate of his sister faded to an occasional comment about her supposed whereabouts.

In the meantime, it was suggested perhaps Sophia had run off to the Continent with a secret lover or, since the war was over and the Colonies had won their independence, she could have embarked on a trans-Atlantic trip to the States and taken up residence there.

Had Sophia's relatives pursued the search a bit closer to home, they would have been surprised to learn Sophia did no such thing. A simple marriage proposal on Christmas Day 1781 changed her life, for it was the promise of romantic love with a man of a lower class that drove Sophia to leave Merriweather Manor for a modest but comfortable townhouse in London's West End.

Although it pained her to leave her son behind, Sophia knew Gregory would be raised properly by the nurses and educated by the governesses and tutors who were in charge of all the children of Merriweather Manor. She was close enough to see him should she require assurance of his health and well-being. Once he was in private school in London, she made frequent trips to see the boy and was pleased when he matured into a tall, well-educated, and very smart man with a head for business and a heart for natural sciences.

And had anyone bothered to ask the butler just why he was leaving Merriweather Manor when he resigned from his position at the beginning of February 1782, well, he might have admitted he did it to marry the love of his life.

CHAPTER 1
A TRIP TO THE BANK

anuary 15, 1802, Threadneedle Street, London

Emma Fitzsimmons stood just inside the large doors of the Bank of England, grateful to be out of the bitter cold. The hackney she had hired to bring her from Warwick's Grammar and Finishing School had been equipped with a brazier, but there hadn't been any coal in the coach.

"Sorry, miss," the driver had said with a shrug when she stepped out onto Threadneedle Street, white clouds surrounding her with every breath she took. "I didna ha' the coin to buy any yesterday," he said by way of an apology.

Emma simply nodded in his direction, glad he had discounted her trip for the inconvenience. To keep her mind off the cold, she had spent the half-hour reviewing her class notes from the previous evening's lecture. The guest speaker, Thomas Wellingham, had been a rare treat for the students enrolled in Alexander Spoke's course on a newly invented form of accounting.

The importer's speaking style, one that mixed a self-assured manner with some self-effacing humor, was certainly a welcome change from the monotone delivery and pompous attitude of their regular instructor.

Wellingham was actually involved in the day-to-day operations of a business and, given what Emma knew of Wellingham Imports, he was quite successful.

She had expected he would talk about contract negotiations, trade agreements, and tariffs, but he instead discussed his company

—how it was founded, who it employed, the kinds of products he procured for his clients, and from where in the world they came.

Emma admired his confident demeanor as he spoke in his clear, tenor voice, his attention seeming to be on everyone and no one all at the same time. He was quite relaxed in front of the large audience, his hands occasionally waving in the air as he emphasized a point in his speech.

The gas light above him illuminated his navy superfine topcoat and a loosely tied cravat. As he talked, Emma found herself listening more closely to the cadence of his voice. Although it wasn't the refined speech a member of the *ton* might employ, it was pleasant and quite engaging.

She spent the entire ninety minutes in a state of high anxiety, sure the cousin to the Earl of Trenton would ask Mr. Stokes for an introduction to her.

Emma was his sister's roommate at Warwick's Grammar and Finishing School, after all, and she had been for over a year.

So, Emma was a bit surprised when, at the end of his talk, Thomas Wellingham fielded just three questions from the audience and then begged forgiveness as he claimed he had a meeting to attend. There was a murmur in the crowd in response to his comment. At the sound of a nearby snicker, Emma's cheeks grew hot as she realized how his comment had been interpreted. *He has a mistress, no doubt,* she thought. *Or a favorite Cyprian in the theatre district.*

Suddenly aware of his eyes aimed in her direction, Emma shifted in her seat and felt a rather pleasant flutter pass through her. A pool of heat had formed deep inside her abdomen by the time his gaze drifted elsewhere.

Emma allowed a quick gasp, realizing she had been holding her breath far too long. She quickly glanced down at her bodice. Relieved her corset was hiding her sudden arousal, she dared to take another breath before turning her attention back to the stage. But Thomas Wellingham had moved off to the side and was shaking hands with the instructor. By the time the man dismissed the class, the importer had left the building.

Even thinking of him just then in the hackney, Emma felt her entire body fill with welcome warmth and wondered at her reaction. She hurried to pay the driver.

Now she relished the warmth of the bank's lobby while she

waited for a footman to open the interior doors. She would have opened the bronzed door herself, but her gloved fingers were so chilled she didn't trust them to grip the polished handles. The overworked footman hurried to the door in front of her, quickly opening it and bowing as she entered.

The receptionist, a very young gentleman dressed in traditional attire and sporting a powdered wig, acknowledged her with a nod and a smile of what seemed like recognition. Despite the crush of men who stood waiting in front of him, he said, "Sir William will see you, miss," his attention on her as he pointed toward the offices down a long corridor off the main lobby.

"Thank you," Emma responded with a nod, her face reddening even more than it was from the cold when she realized several eyes had turned to see who had been privileged enough to gain the receptionist's favor.

"A comely woman can get in right away, then, eh?" one nattily dressed man commented with a raised eyebrow, his manner suggesting he didn't really begrudge Emma the quick service. Women were rarely seen within the premises, their banking usually arranged by a male relative or a solicitor.

"Anyone with an *appointment* can be seen right away," the receptionist replied sardonically, turning his attention to the next man in line.

Emma hurried to the corridor, her half boots barely making any noise on the marble floor. Embarrassed at not having to wait like the rest of those in line, she had to remind herself she *had* made an appointment. The note she had written the morning before had been dispatched with a courier, and the return note was delivered mere hours later to her residence, Gamma House of Warwick's.

In his reply, Sir William seemed most pleased about the prospect of seeing Emma again. Although not technically his ward, Emma had been left an orphan when her father, George Fitzsimmons, had died four years before. Through an arrangement made by George prior to his death, Sir William Burroughs II was put in charge of her finances. Having assured her late father he would see to Emma's education and living arrangements using the modest inheritance left to Emma, Sir William made investments on her behalf and set up a five percenter with the remaining funds.

. . .

*E*mma's half-sister, Samantha, was a different story. The product of George's *affaire* with the woman who was promised to his brother, Samantha was born to a life of privilege. Told her real parents had died in a carriage accident—the couple who perished were actually her aunt and uncle—Samantha was being raised in the household of Matthew Fitzsimmons, Viscount Chamberlain, and his wife, Caroline. As his supposed niece and, at seven years of age, the oldest child in the household, Samantha was coddled by the viscountess. If she grew up to look anything like Emma, she would have no trouble landing a suitable spouse after her come-out.

Sir William briefly wondered if Emma knew anything about her half-sister.

And if she didn't?

Was it his place to inform her? Perhaps. Or perhaps he would leave it to the Fitzsimmons, should the issue ever become a topic of conversation.

Sir William stood up from the mess of papers on his desk to regard the twenty-year-old standing in his doorway. "Do come in," he motioned, a large grin splitting his broad face. "It's been some time since I've seen you. October, wasn't it?"

An older man who still wore wigs and traditional trousers from the century before, Sir William bowed as much as his pot belly would allow. As the youngest son of a duke, he probably shouldn't have accepted the offer of employment he had received from the bank more than twenty-five years ago, but Sir William had developed an understanding of financing and a penchant for earning money for his father's duchy that he thought could be put to good use for others. Despite the disapproval of several members of the *ton*, Sir William rather enjoyed working at the bank.

He took in the sight of Emma in a quick glance, careful not to allow her to notice his perusal. Blonde, comely, and taller than most women, Emma carried herself with poise and confidence. Although her deep green morning gown and matching pelisse were not of the latest cut, they were clean and pressed.

She was maturing nicely, he decided, a particularly important point since Sir William was about to broach the subject of finding a husband for his charge.

Emma curtsied and returned the smile. "You have an excellent memory. I trust you're well, Sir William?" she asked as she took the seat across from his desk, removing her gloves and pulling a sheaf of papers from her reticule. "And Lady William?"

"Yes, very, thank you," he replied with a dismissive wave of his hand. "And I understand from a friend of mine that you are doing quite well in school," he countered, settling into the large leather chair and pulling it up to the massive mahogany desk.

Surprised by the comment, Emma wondered who would have spoken to him about her schooling. "Yes, I believe so. As we discussed last October, I should complete Mr. Stokes' course in accounting in May." She settled deeper into the leather chair, glad there was a thick Aubusson carpet in which to plant her cold toes.

Sir William nodded and clasped his hands together over his belly. "And Warwick's, too?" he queried, an especially hairy eyebrow lifting to the edge of his wig. "Your father was quite clear in his desire to see you complete finishing school," he said with a hint of warning.

Her eyes darting to one side, Emma sighed. "From Warwick's, too, I assure you," she said with a wan grin. "Although I'll never understand why it was so important I attend such an expensive school."

She did know that if she hadn't attended the boarding school, alternative living arrangements might not have been as comfortable —or as safe. If Sir William hadn't taken on her modest estate, she might well have ended up at a workhouse or an orphanage or had her funds bled dry by an unscrupulous foster parent.

Sir William considered telling her the reasons George Fitzsimmons had put forth when he demanded his daughter be sent to Warwick's. At the time, the man knew he didn't have long to live. His oldest sister, Christine, who would become Emma's guardian upon his death, wasn't one to trust with managing money.

Given the circumstances, George insisted his daughter be enrolled in the finishing school so she would be introduced to the level of society George had given up when he had left his family to start his business—designing and making hats of a quality much higher than was generally available.

Most of the girls at Warwick's were daughters of barons and viscounts and captains of industry. As a middle-class hat maker, George Fitzsimmons wanted the same opportunities for his own daughter—she was the granddaughter of a viscount, after all— especially the opportunity for her to meet the brothers of those daughters and the well-to-do of British society.

Even if he didn't expect her to end up married to a member of the *ton*, George was quite sure Emma could marry well given her part ownership of the hat shop he would leave behind. Sir William had agreed, assuring the hat maker he would see to it there would be funds to cover her tuition and living expenses until such time as a suitable marriage could be arranged.

Emma had other plans, though.

In an effort to secure her own financial future, she had arranged to sell her father's business to his young partner and use some of the funds from the sale to attend the accounting course. Having done her father's books for many years, she found she enjoyed working as an accomptant and wanted to pursue it as an occupation.

When she had explained her plan to Sir William last October, however, he was dumbfounded. "An occupation?" he had repeated in surprise, sitting up as straight as he could given his girth. "But... but, you're a... gel," he stammered. "Whom do you expect will hire you to be an *accomptant*?" he asked, trying hard not to be angry with the willful girl. "And what of a companion? You shouldn't be in public without the benefit of a chaperone."

Emma's shoulders slumped as she considered her banker's words. "If I do well in school, it shouldn't matter if I'm of the fairer sex," she countered naïvely. "I must have a fallback, after all," she had explained quickly. "What if I'm not able to find a suitable husband? I must be able to see to my own finances. Have my own place to live. Hire a companion. When I'm done at Warwick's, of course," she had added, seeing the look of consternation on her banker's face.

She hadn't mentioned her desire to be as independent as possible. And she didn't want to enter into what could be an unhappy marriage just for the sake of being married. There were too many girls at the school who had done just that and were now bemoaning their domestic situations.

A marriage was not in her immediate future.

But she wasn't about to tell her banker that.

Sir William sat in silence for a moment, remembering her words from their last meeting. Impressed by Emma's comments and a bit smitten by the young woman, he had allowed her expenditure. If he wasn't already happily married, and if he were twenty years younger, he would have proposed marriage right then and there.

A woman who wants to see to her own finances! And could! The young woman had already shown remarkable restraint, spending money only on tuition and a few necessities—rarely on gowns and frippery. Once she had her own townhouse, she would take possession of the household goods and furnishings, currently in storage, from her parents' home above the hat shop, making it unlikely she would have to spend funds in that regard.

With her father's name in every hat sold from his shop in Oxford Street by the new owner, his legacy of producing "Hats that make the gentleman" might continue for many years to come.

Any man should be glad to have her, Sir William thought proudly.

It was at that moment Sir William decided he would see to it Emma Fitzsimmons had a townhouse and a very suitable husband.

Even if he had to be the one to find her both.

CHAPTER 2
A DAY IN THE LIFE OF AN IMPORTER

January 21, 1802, Puddle Dock, London

Thomas Wellingham regarded the red brick building that housed the import business he had inherited from his father and took a deep breath.

Two sides of the lower story now included large doors that could be opened to admit loaded drays while the other sides were made up of a series of horse stalls. From the ground, a passerby wouldn't give it a second look. However, with its row of sleek windows circling the second story, Wellingham Imports appeared more sophisticated than the surrounding warehouses and businesses along Puddle Dock.

With the building renovation complete, Thomas could proceed with more important matters—growing the business. In the few years since Graham Wellingham's death, he had managed to expand the reach of his company. The import-export concern dealt in as many products native to the British Isles as it did with goods from other lands.

Thomas was careful in his selection of items to import, ensuring they had buyers or markets in London. He was even more careful in selecting the captains of ships with whom he contracted for importing from the Continent as well as the new United States.

As opposed to his competitors' grueling and dangerous working conditions and filthy warehouses, his employees enjoyed two days off each week after toiling ten hours a day in a warehouse kept as clean as was possible. As a result, he had gained a reputation as a fair businessman and was well liked by those who served him.

His latest project, a large network of overland transports made up of horse-drawn coaches, was just about complete. Following schedules meant to seem irregular to those that might be tempted to rob them, the coaches were a reliable means of transporting goods from all over England to his warehouse near the River Thames as well as distributing imported goods to customers as far north as Scotland.

Unlike most of the London importers, Wellingham Imports was located near the Blackfriars Bridge. His office and those of the support staff—clerks, brokers, and buyers—were inside the very warehouse that stored the bounty for which they were responsible.

"Mr. Wellingham, may I have a word?" Stephen Bingham asked as he approached the owner of Wellingham Imports.

Thomas paused and allowed the warehouse manager to fall in step next to him. "Of course. What is it?" he asked as he brushed dust off his long great coat with one gloved hand while holding his hat in the other. Although it was the middle of winter, the weather was kind enough to allow him to drive a gig the six miles to the warehouse from his home west of London.

The warehouse manager held out a manifest. "We received this crate this morning. I have an order for the contents, but the buyer, or rather, the shop in this case, doesn't seem to be in business any longer," he explained as he pointed to a name on the paper.

Thomas took the manifest and studied it. "Damn!" he cursed under his breath as he recognized the name. "Worthington Drapers doesn't exist anymore. I overheard someone at Boodles say he went bankrupt last month," Thomas continued in explanation, shaking his head as he entered his office.

Stephen followed him in, a scowl on his face. "Can we find another buyer?" he asked, hoping to get rid of the crate to make space for another shipment.

Sighing, Thomas replied, "I'll see what I can do, but finding a buyer for two-hundred and fifty yards of brocade will be next to impossible. No one makes gowns out of the stuff anymore," he added. "Drapes for windows, maybe," he murmured.

He hadn't done business with Harding, Howell and Company in the past. Perhaps it was time he approach the fashionable draper. "This is exactly why I prefer dealing with the cotton factories," he added as he regarded the manifest. How different importing would be if Richard Arkwright hadn't invented the water frame and made it possible to spin yarn and make cotton and silk fabrics in England.

After a long pause, he returned his attention to Stephen and said, "Move the crate to the back corner, and I'll see what I can do." *And if I can do nothing?* How might an expense like this be handled in the new kind of accounting his friend Mr. Stokes was teaching? *What was the man calling it?*

Cost accounting.

What little of it he knew seemed to make sense. Include not just the expenses of payroll and raw materials to make products, but also account for the costs of the building in which the products were made and the expenses associated with getting them to where they needed to go once they were finished.

Nodding, Stephen seemed about to take his leave but turned back to face his employer. "There's one other issue," he said with some hesitation.

Having removed this great coat and top coat, Thomas loosened his cuffs and began rolling up his sleeves. "Of course. What is it?"

The manager hesitated a moment. "I may have simply read the ledger wrong, but I think some of the numbers from last week's shipments were..." He paused, uncertain of how to put voice to his concern.

"Damn it, man, what is it?" Thomas asked, his brows furrowing in concern.

"I think the amounts were entered incorrectly. The addition was all wrong."

Thomas stiffened. If Stephen Bingham had noticed the very same errors Thomas had discovered the night before while reviewing the latest ledger, then someone in the clerking office had made a mistake. "Off by ten pounds?" he whispered, giving the open door to his office a quick glance.

Stephen's eyes widened. "Yes. How—?"

"I took the ledger home last night." After a pause, Thomas shrugged. "It may be nothing, but don't speak of it to anyone else."

The warehouse manager nodded. "Yes, sir." He took his leave of the office, pulling the door shut behind him.

Thomas moved to his desk and regarded the piles of papers— manifests and orders, receipts and bills—that required he give them enough notice so his clerks could do their jobs.

At five-and-twenty, Thomas was as handsome as any pale, brown-haired, brown-eyed Brit could be. Not quite six feet tall, he took pride in his appearance, he bathed regularly, he kept regular hours, and he was married to his work.

With a younger sister he was determined to properly raise, educate, and see married before he would consider matrimony, Thomas often dined with friends or spent time at Boodles to keep up with the social scene of London.

His preference, though, was to spend the late afternoons and evenings at his estate home west of London.

Woodscastle, at one time an unentailed property of the Trenton earldom, had been given to his father, Graham, as a wedding present. Since the younger brother of the Earl of Trenton had apparently disappointed his family by marrying a commoner, the earl bestowed him with what had been the house he used for trysts and hunting parties.

Once a brick jewel just off Burlington Lane near Chiswick, Woodscastle had suffered a great deal of neglect and had stood empty for the five years before his father and mother moved in. They began renovations when he was a small child, using every bit of the profit his father made off the import business to pay for a new roof over the east wing and for a few rooms to be renovated.

Although the rooms along the east wing and front of the home were livable, the entire upper west wing was still uninhabitable. Although Thomas had intentions of completing the upgrades to the estate, he had instead concentrated on upgrading Wellingham Imports by reinvesting his profits into the business.

Horses and coaches were expensive.

He continued to employ the staff his father had hired for Woodscastle—a butler who was also his valet, a housekeeper, a maid, a cook, and two grooms. With his sixteen-year-old sister in a private girls' boarding school in London for eight months of the year, he was able to take her to dinner or dine with her at the boarding house when time permitted. Depending on how the day progressed, dinner with her seemed like a good prospect for that evening.

"Master Overby," he called out to a young boy who came running up when he heard his name.

"Yes, sir," the youth replied with a bow, his face smudged with soot.

"Do you remember how to get to Warwick's in Glasshouse

Street? To Gamma House?" Thomas asked. He wished the boy would wash occasionally and often wondered if William Overby had a mother.

"Yes, sir," the boy replied with a lopsided grin. He was missing one front tooth and at least two on the bottom, and his stained clothes were common to those children who called a tenement in the Seven Dials area home.

"Please deliver the message that I will be taking my sister out to dinner this evening. I plan to be there to collect her at seven o'clock sharp," Thomas stated. "Once you've delivered the message, come straight back here. No detours." Thomas reached into his waistcoat pocket and found some farthings. "But buy some sallop on your way back," he added as he handed the startled boy the coins.

The youth nodded. "Thank you, Mr. Wellingham," he said happily and hurried off.

After several stops at various offices to check in with his employees, Thomas finally took a seat at his desk and began the task of wading through piles of contracts, manifests, and inventories.

At two o'clock, he set off for the nearby Crown and Anchor for a mid-day meal, hoping he'd find a friend with whom to share his luncheon. He was not disappointed when Todd Vandermeer of the East India Company entered the inn just after Thomas was seated.

"Mr. Vandermeer," he said as he waved to a chair at his table. "Please, join me."

The very tall, thin man grinned and nodded as he placed a hand on the back of the chair across from Thomas. Tan pantaloons, a white blouse and a white cravat only exaggerated his height. But his tail coat, made of bath coating, was dark blue and suited his pale complexion and angular features. Except for the mud smears on his brown tasseled Hessians, Todd Vandermeer was impeccably dressed. "Mr. Wellingham, it is very good to see you again. I trust you are well?" he asked as he sat down and placed his walking cane against the edge of the table.

Of all the men Thomas knew to carry canes, Todd was the only one who actually required a cane to help him walk. "Yes, thank you for asking," Thomas replied as he leaned back in his chair. "And you?"

The dark-haired man shook his head. "My knees ache terribly in this weather," Todd complained. "But, otherwise, I'm well," he added as he placed his beaver on the chair next to him. "It is fortuitous that I find you here today."

Thomas straightened. "Indeed?" He regarded the man who had been his friend since their days as caddies—Thomas for his father and Todd for a trader at the East India Company.

The tall man nodded. "I have news," he said quietly. "East India has just formed a company to build their own docks on the Thames," he whispered, glancing around the room as he said it. "You cannot speak of this with anyone just yet."

Thomas nodded and leaned across the table. "This is, indeed, great news. Perhaps the city leaders will now approve my request for building my own dock," he replied with a genuine smile. Thomas had submitted the request months before, but the topic never seemed to come up at city meetings, and with so many political bodies involved in London's planning decisions, it could be several more months before he would receive an approval. As a result of his request, though, several other companies had followed suit by putting in their own applications.

The London docks were simply too crowded to accommodate all the ships making deliveries to London, and the traffic on the river was too congested to allow for import businesses to bring in more shipments. The only solution seemed to be to locate an import business on the river and to have a dock directly adjacent to the company warehouse.

"When will you start construction?" Thomas asked, but when he noticed the server approaching to take their order, he sat back. He nodded to Todd to order first.

"Shepherd's pie and an ale for me," Todd said, his tone suggesting his boredom with the offerings.

"I will have the same," Thomas added with a bit more enthusiasm. The waiter bowed and disappeared into the kitchen.

Todd leaned over the table. "It will be at least four years before they're ready for use, though," he said with a frown. "They will be built between Blackwall Reach and Bugsby's Reach, and I believe our current facilities at Blackwall will be merged with new docks," he said, referring to the docks used for fitting out and repairing ships. "The West India Docks intended for unloading inbound ships will be complete on the Isle of Dogs later this summer," he added as he rolled his eyes. "But the docks they intend to use for loading *outward bound* ships won't be complete for several years."

"Several *years*?" Thomas questioned, concern etching his face. "Why so long? I plan to have mine built within a month or two of approval. At least, that's the amount of time I've been told it will take to build one," he said quietly.

Sighing, Todd sat back and spread his arms. "You are building but one dock to accommodate one ship," he said as he held up a forefinger. "We are building enough to moor two-hundred and fifty ships."

His shoulders dropping, Thomas shook his head. He had never considered the East India Company to be a direct competitor in the import business since his selection of goods didn't match what they were bringing into the city. But the resources available to the John Company, money as well as political power, far exceeded any that would be available to Thomas and his small business. "Perhaps I should have requested two docks," Thomas said with mock amusement.

Todd smiled as he caught his friend's meaning. "Perhaps. But you have done a remarkable job building up your business without having your own dock space. Companies like mine need companies like yours to do the part of the business we do not want. Who would have ever thought to set up an overland transportation business with as many coaches as you must be operating? And just how many horses do you own now?"

Thomas considered Todd's comments before replying. "I have ninety-four," he stated, figuring he would have at least that many by the end of the year. "Most are Cleveland Bays, but we use some Friesians for the northern routes."

"Damnation," Todd replied with a shake of head. "I guess having your own stables was the best decision you made when you built onto that box," he said with a grin, referring to the building that housed Wellingham Imports.

Nodding, Thomas leaned back as he noticed the waiter returning with their food. The youth set their plates on the table along with two tankards of ale.

Thomas lifted his ale and Todd followed suit. "To the import business," Thomas said with a grin.

"Aye," Todd replied and took a drink. "'Tis a good business. Our financials were just released to us. On the first of March last year, the debts of the John Company amounted to about five-and-a-half million pounds and our effects were nearly fifteen-and-a-half million pounds. Our sales were up over seven=and-a-half million pounds. We nearly doubled sales in just eight years!" he exclaimed quietly, his tone suggesting that even he was surprised by the numbers.

Thomas' eyes widened. "And these would be the same eight years you have been a broker," he said as he smiled and slapped Todd across one arm. "Congratulations."

Todd shrugged his shoulders, not having considered the information in that context. "Thank you," he replied with a nod, obviously uncomfortable with the compliment. "So, what are you doing to enjoy life these days?" he asked, no longer wanting to talk about business.

Eyebrows arched, Thomas had to think about the question. "Not much, really," he finally replied. "A good ride on my horse and an occasional book. And you?"

Todd started to eat but stopped with his fork in mid-air. "I am thinking it is time I find a wife," he answered matter-of-factly. He didn't seem pleased at the thought, if only because he was overwhelmed at the thought of how he should go about finding one.

Having spent the better part of the morning reading a women's journal from Paris, Todd had decided women were fickle. But he was determined to discover which fashion trend could make its way to England and be successful with the women of Great Britain.

The contents of the journal had him slightly frightened and very confused.

Startled by the comment about finding a wife, Thomas angled his head. "And what made you start thinking this?" he asked, crossing his arms and grinning. He had known the broker since he was five years old, and he had never heard the man speak of an interest in courting—or even in women. For several years, Thomas had figured the man to be a molly.

Staring into his shepherd's pie, Todd shook his head. "I'm six-and-twenty... and I'm lonely, Mr. Wellingham. Every night I go home to an empty house..."

Thomas guffawed. "Empty?" he chided with an amused expression. "You must have at least twelve servants working at your mansion." The man's three-story abode took up an entire corner where it was located in the tony portion of the West End called Cavendish Square.

Todd shook his head and leaned over the table. "Eleven, actually. Eight of them are younger women. And there isn't a one I'd want to spend an evening with in the library... or the bedchamber," he replied with a raised eyebrow. He had heard talk that the former owner had taken advantage of his status as master of the house, personally seeing to it that no virgins were left on the staff by the time Todd held the title to the house. "You see, I wish to find a woman who has a... a *brain* and an interest in the world. Someone with whom I can have a conversation that doesn't involve the latest scandal or gossip or what frippery she should acquire for a ball or soirée. Unfortunately, our society does not seem to allow the fairer sex to display such qualities, so I'm at a loss as to how to find such a woman."

Silent for a moment, mostly because he was incredulous at what he was hearing, Thomas realized Todd Vandermeer was quite serious. Had he not decided to see his sister married before he would begin courting, perhaps he, too, would be looking for a wife. "Do you have your eye on anyone in particular?" Thomas asked carefully.

The tall man shook his head. "No. But I suppose I should ask you about your sister. Does Miss Christiana have any prospects? If you haven't already arranged something for her, I mean," he asked. Last he had seen the girl, she was developing into an attractive young woman who carried herself as if she were much taller and older than she was.

Thomas dropped his fork. "She's only *sixteen*," he replied, rather stunned Todd Vandermeer would even ask about Christiana. "And she's less than half as tall as you are," he added, trying to bring back some of the humor they had shared only a few moments before.

Todd slumped in his chair. "You would have to bring up the height problem, now wouldn't you?" he accused with mock disgust. He took a deep breath and let it out slowly. "I swear, where does a man such as me find a Long Meg in this town?" he asked rhetorically.

Taking a swig from his tankard, Thomas swallowed and thought a moment. "Well, I have never met the woman, but my sister's roommate at Warwick's is supposed to be rather tall. At least, according to Christiana."

It was Todd's turn to guffaw. "Everyone is tall compared to Miss Christiana," he countered. "But how old is this roommate of your sister's?"

Thomas suppressed a grin, glad he had piqued his colleague's interest. "Well, she is due to finish Warwick's this spring, and I know she is at least two years older than Christiana. Eighteen, maybe more?" he guessed. "Would you like me to arrange a meeting? I'm actually taking my sister to dinner tonight—"

"No," Todd quickly replied. "Not yet. I am... just thinking about this," he said with conviction. "And I'm a bit dubious about courting girls from wealthy families," he added, his brows furrowing in disgust at the thought. "She is rich, isn't she?" he asked. "It's just that, I do not need to marry a rich girl. I have made a small fortune working at East India, and I really don't think I want to deal with the hubris that comes with marrying into a wealthy family," he explained, still shaking his head.

As an orphan, he had no inheritance or family connections to offer in a marriage deal, and he wasn't looking for any in a possible bride. "But I'd also prefer to marry a woman who feels affection for me rather than for my pocketbook." He took a long draw on his ale and set down the tankard.

Thomas finished a bite of the pie. "I rather think all the girls who attend Warwick's come from wealth to some degree. I don't know how their fathers could afford the tuition and room and board if they did not," he said as he considered Todd's comments. "But you must know that not all rich girls come from wealthy families," he added with amusement.

Cocking his head to one side, Todd gave the comment a moment of consideration. "And just what the hell is that supposed to mean?" he asked, annoyance in his voice.

Thomas placed his open palms on the table. "Were you born to a wealthy family, Mr. Vandermeer?"

The tall man shook his head. "You know that I was not," he replied with a frown, giving Thomas a suspicious glare.

"And neither was my sister," Thomas countered quietly as he leaned forward to make his point.

Todd thought about Thomas' statement. "I see what you mean," he finally admitted, his expression changing. "All right then. But I still want to think about this some more," he said before he took a bite of his pie. After a moment of contemplation, he said, "So...," before deciding his line of questioning might not be appropriate. When Thomas indicated he should continue, Todd asked carefully, "If not a wife, then what is it you find yourself wanting these days?"

Thomas grinned at his friend's query. "Besides my own dock, you mean?" he answered playfully. He paused in thought for a moment. "I suppose I should be wanting a new roof for the west wing of Woodscastle," he murmured as he continued to ponder the odd question. At Todd's upraised eyebrows, Thomas added, "The entire west wing is in disrepair. My father was barely able to complete repairs on the east wing, and I've not had the interest to even start on the west side of the house. I'm more interested in my company, I suppose," he explained before taking another bite of his pie.

"Hmm," Todd replied simply. "I see your point, though. I wasn't interested in where I lived or what I lived in until after I'd come to some sort of comfort, I suppose one could say, with my profession. Now I find myself hardly caring about my work and more interested in my house and having a wife to go home to every night," he said quietly.

Thomas gave a 'humph' and stared at Todd in disbelief. "My God, man, what has gotten into you?" he teased as he allowed a large smile.

Returning the broad smile, Todd replied, "I'm getting old, I suppose."

The smile on Thomas's face slowly disappeared as he considered his friend's words. "Ask your colleagues about the availability of their sisters," he suggested.

Todd nodded and a thought struck him. He leaned over the table again. "When it comes to our fairer sex here in Britain, do you suppose they would wear the latest gown from France?" he whispered, an eyebrow raised in question. One hand reached into a waistcoat pocket and pulled out a folded piece of paper.

Frowning, Thomas leaned over his plate. "What gown might that be?" he asked, wondering if he should consider importing such an item.

Todd unfolded the page from a women's journal and held it out toward Thomas. He glanced around to be sure no one was listening. "Transparent gowns," he said simply, giving the paper a shake as he said the words.

Convinced he hadn't heard the word correctly, Thomas' eyebrows knitted together before his eyes took in the drawing of a lithe Parisian woman apparently wearing such a gown. "Transparent?" he repeated, his face taking on a redder shade. "As in... one can see through to their... " His question trailed off without him finishing as he studied the artwork and realized, that, indeed, the transparent gown allowed one to see right through to a woman's undergarments. And stockings. *And garters.*

Nodding his head, Todd replied in a whisper. "Pantaloons and corsets, yes. It seems it is the latest rage in Paris."

Thomas sat back and considered the idea. Would a self-respecting British woman be seen in Hyde Park wearing a gown that displayed her corset for all to see? His face screwed up as he considered the thought. "No, I don't believe they would be very popular here," he replied finally. "Although, perhaps the more well-to-do courtesans might be convinced to wear them when their gentlemen come calling," he added with a teasing grin.

A large smile split Todd's face as he considered that those very men would probably be the ones to purchase the gowns for their mistresses. "Thank you for your input, my friend. I think I shall forget the idea," he said as he fished some coins from his pocket and placed them on the table. "I will pay for luncheon today," he added as he pushed away from the table.

"Well, thank you, Mr. Vandermeer, but are you leaving so soon?" Thomas asked, his face taking on a look of concern as he noticed the nearly full plate of food in front of Todd. "You have barely touched your pie."

The importer frowned and shook his head. "I have no appetite these days," he replied sadly. "And the only times I eat well are when I'm in the company of women," he added with a quirked lip.

Thomas regarded his friend. "Then perhaps you really do need a wife," he said with a grin. "But in the meantime, if you would like, we could arrange a mistress for you, or you could hire a harlot..."

"Never!" Todd replied sternly, keeping his voice low. "I was probably born to one, and I have no intention of ever using their services."

Thomas stiffened. "I apologize," he offered quietly, just then remembering he should have known better than to broach such a suggestion to Todd.

Although the man had been orphaned, there had been nothing to suggest he was a bastard. Over the years, though, Todd Vandermeer had convinced himself his origins were most likely similar to those of Master Overby's.

"I don't employ their services, either. It was untoward of me to suggest that you should," Thomas explained quickly.

In fact, it was nearly impossible to find a man in London who didn't employ a whore on occasion. Some did so on a daily basis. Keeping a mistress, despite the high costs involved, had become *de rigeur* for the wealthy single as well as married men in town.

The tall man smiled and nodded at Thomas. "Apology accepted, of course. Now, I really must be going. Give my regards to Miss Christiana, won't you?"

Thomas drained his tankard. "I will. Thank you for luncheon, Mr. Vandermeer. And thank you, too, for the news."

"My pleasure, Mr. Wellingham." With that, Todd limped out the door with the help of his cane.

Thomas was left thinking about docks and marriage.

When Thomas returned to the office, he dispatched Master Overby to Woodscastle to request that one of his grooms, Mr. Allen, come to town with the town coach. The youth took off on a horse and was back within two hours with word that Mr. Allen would be there at six o'clock. Thomas then sent the youth to make a reservation at Reagan's, a restaurant suitable for a member of the fairer sex in the West End.

By the time Mr. Allen arrived, Thomas had managed to clear most of the papers from his desk and had begun reviewing the ledgers for the current week. Grateful for the interruption, he set them aside, donned his topcoat, great goat, and hat, and stepped into the town coach.

CHAPTER 3
DINNER WITH A SISTER

"*I* am beginning to think this roommate of yours doesn't exist," Thomas said, his tone suggesting he was annoyed when Christiana informed him Emma Fitzsimmons was not in residence.

"She is in accounting class," Christiana explained when she joined Thomas in the parlor. She reached up and kissed her brother on the cheek. Dressed in her whitest muslin gown, she looked as if she were about to attend her first ball. She had decorated the top of the skirt with a bright blue ribbon. Egyptian style earbobs hung from her ears, and an ornate comb decorated her strawberry blonde hair. She was pulling on long gloves as Mrs. Streater, the headmistress of the school, entered the parlor.

"It is so good to see you again, Mr. Wellingham," the elderly lady enthused as she curtsied to Thomas' bow.

"And you, Mrs. Streater," Thomas replied. "I hope taking my sister to dinner tonight is not an inconvenience," he said politely, knowing the headmistress would never say if it were.

"Not at all," Mrs. Streater replied with a toothy smile. "However, you must know you are invited to dinner anytime you would wish to join the young ladies here," she added, her hands wrung together in front of her considerable bosom. "They can always use the practice of dining in the company of a gentleman."

Thomas nodded. "I shall consider it for next month," he replied quickly. Turning to his sister, he asked, "Are you ready?"

Christiana handed over her redingote and slipped her arms into the sleeves as Thomas held it open. "I am now," she said before she led him to the vestibule.

Mr. Allen bowed and assisted Christiana into the small coach. "'Tis very good to see you, Miss Christiana," the coachman said in his thick accent.

"Are you well, Mr. Allen?" Christiana asked.

"Indeed. Mrs. Werthers says to give you her regards. She was asking if you would be home before your school ends for the summer."

Christiana gave her brother a hopeful glance. "You should come home for Easter, at least," he suggested.

Christiana's disappointed sigh was missed by her brother. "I was hoping to come home more often this spring. Maybe for Sundays?" she suggested, wishing her brother would arrange for the extra trips between Woodscastle and Warwick's. Although it wasn't a long distance to the estate in Chiswick, it did require travel by horse or carriage and one of the only two groomsmen available at Woodscastle.

"I don't believe it will be feasible, Christiana," Thomas replied. "Despite the season, my work has kept me from home far more than I expected," he explained as he took her hand and squeezed it gently.

How many miles had he covered while visiting coaching inns? Making the initial arrangements for his drivers and horses to be housed during their delivery treks had him traveling more than expected, but there was no one else he could send in his stead. If the current routes proved profitable, there would be more such trips in the spring.

Given how dark it was, Christiana didn't bother trying to hide her disappointment. To Mr. Allen she said, "Please give Mrs. Werthers my love, and let her know I will be home for Easter." She slumped in the seat and folded her gloved hands in her lap, keeping Thomas' hand between them.

"Very good, miss," Mr. Allen replied with a tip of his hat. He waited for Thomas to be seated before he closed the door and climbed onto the driver's seat.

The trip to Reagan's didn't take long this time of the evening. Most warehouse workers would have left their places of employment and been home by now, while the shops on the nearby Strand generally stayed open until ten o'clock at night.

As the coach bumped along the cobblestones toward the restaurant, Thomas Wellingham studied his younger sister. She had matured considerably over the course of the past year. At sixteen, she could look like a little girl with her strawberry blonde ringlets and simple bun atop her head. Tonight, she appeared much older with her hair in a more elegant roll outlined with a braid and a ringlet on either side of her face. "You look very beautiful this evening. Did one of the lady's maids do your hair?" he asked as he spread a quilt over their legs to ward off the evening chill.

"Goodness, no," she replied. "Miss Emma did it for me before she left for class tonight." She didn't add that the Gamma House had only two abigails for the six girls who lived there, so most dressed themselves and only vied for the abigails' time when it came to their corsets and hair.

Thomas shook his head, snorting in the process. "I don't suppose I'll have the pleasure of meeting her later tonight then, shall I?"

Emma Fitzsimmons and his sister had been roommates at Warwick's Grammar and Finishing School for nearly three terms, and he had yet to meet the girl. When Christiana's first roommate left Warwick's to elope with a soldier, Christiana was moved into Emma's room. Ever since, she had extolled the virtues of the older and much taller girl. Although Thomas was anxious to meet Emma —and to thank her for looking after his sister so well—he was beginning to think she was avoiding him.

Deliberately.

Christiana shrugged and pulled up the quilt to cover her shoulders. "I don't expect so. When she is done with class tonight, she will have homework. I think she was awake past midnight doing accounting," she commented, her nose wrinkled in disgust.

Thomas furrowed his brows. "Accounting? Are you quite sure?" he asked, wondering if his sister had said the right word.

"I am. She takes a class at night and won't be finished until the late spring," she said as she watched her brother's backlit profile in the cold night. She wondered at his sudden interest in her roommate.

Thomas thought a moment. "And what does she intend to do

after she finishes Warwick's and this accounting class?" he asked. "She cannot expect to gain a position, can she?" he asked rhetorically. "She is a woman, after all."

Christiana turned to gaze on her brother. "But she does plan to gain a position," she argued. "She has no prospects for marriage, and I'm quite sure she has no intention of being kidnapped by a fat broad," the young girl added, referring to the generally overweight women who ran the brothels in London.

Shocked at the comment, Thomas gasped and stared at his sister. "I'm quite certain Miss Emma is safe from a life of prostitution," he said in a lowered voice. "After all, she must come from money or she wouldn't be attending Warwick's," he stated with certainty.

Her eyes rolling at her brother's stubbornness, Christiana replied, "Her late father saw to the cost of finishing school, of course. But what is she to do after school is over in the spring? When her funds run out?"

Thomas considered his sister's words. What indeed?Genteel women weren't allowed to work, really, although he knew many who were in charge of businesses or who were quite involved in their family's trade. "I hope she is able to find a position suited to her education, then," he said doubtfully, wondering how a woman in London could expect to find employment other than that as a servant, seamstress, milkmaid or street vendor. A governess, perhaps?

"I know you will like her when you finally meet her. She thought your lecture on importing was quite interesting," Christiana said matter-of-factly. "I can't imagine what you said, but she was quite taken with the topic."

Thomas sat up straight and stared at his sister. "She was in that lecture hall?"

As a favor to Alexander Stokes, Thomas had agreed to speak to the class about Wellingham Imports. He remembered thinking he had seen a women among the students, but the hall was filled to capacity, and a gas light above his head had made it difficult to see those in the audience.

Christiana nodded her head. "We're here," she said with some excitement as she pointed to the restaurant.

"Indeed," Thomas replied as Mr. Allen steered the coach to a space near the entrance and halted the horses.

"You will need to inform me on everything that has happened at Warwick's," Thomas said as he helped Christiana out of the carriage. "You are my only source of gossip these days," he said with a nod in Mr. Allen's direction.

Once inside, a host seated them in a banquette near the back of the room and left Thomas with a menu board. He barely glanced at the offerings but asked Christiana what she wanted. "The fruit tray here is very delicious," she suggested, hoping he would order it as a first course.

"Very good, then," Thomas replied. He placed orders for the both of them. When the waiter left them, he leaned forward. "So, tell me the news. What has happened since Christmas?" he asked with a wicked grin.

Christiana knew her brother enjoyed gossip as much as anyone, but it still surprised her when he seemed to take joy in the not so good news of aristocrats. Had he been born a generation earlier or had his uncle as a father, he might have been an earl!

A waiter brought wine and water. "I will do so. But where to start?" she asked, thinking back to the beginning of the month. "The Beta House is short two girls. Miss Katherine and Miss Katy —they are twin sisters, you remember—they were married over the holiday to some boys from Kent. Brothers, actually, but not twins," she began in earnest. "Their parents were most happy since there was some concern they would be old maids if they didn't marry by the time they reached eighteen."

Thomas raised an eyebrow and took a sip of wine. "A girl cannot even be married without parental consent until she is twenty-one, for goodness sake," he countered, a confused expression on his face. "Old maids, indeed."

Christiana smiled and shrugged, deciding not to press the issue. "In our house, Miss Elizabeth came back from holiday betrothed to a much older man from Sussex. She will marry in June. I believe her parents arranged it since she was most upset at first, but the man sends her letters nearly every day, and gifts, too. I think she rather likes the attention," she said as the waiter brought them a tray of honey-glazed fruits.

Mostly cubed apples, dates, and raisins, the dish varied according to the season. Noticing Thomas' appreciative eye, she said, "Please, do try some."

Tom stabbed an apple with his fork and thanked her. "Did Miss

Elizabeth say what her betrothed does for employment?" he asked before tasting the fruit.

"I don't think he works, Thomas. He is a wealthy man with an estate near Shipley," she replied. "Perhaps he is a viscount or some such."

Thomas thought a moment. Most of the girls would never actually complete four years of elocution, art appreciation, French, music, dancing, drawing, painting, theatre, grammar, sewing, and social intercourse classes at Warwick's—because most married before they completed three years. "Besides Miss Emma, are there any other very *tall* girls at the school?"

Christiana finished a date and replied suspiciously, "Pray tell, why do you ask?"

Thomas sighed and helped himself to a date. "I had lunch with Mr. Vandermeer today."

"Oh," Christiana replied, sitting back in the banquette, her shoulders drooping. "As much as I wish to be married before I am eighteen, please don't arrange a marriage for me with *him*," she pleaded, her face screwing up in an expression of pure disgust.

"Christiana..." Thomas started to reply and then stopped. "I promise, I won't arrange for you to marry him. And it's doubtful I will allow you to marry before you are twenty," he added. "And just what is it about Mr. Vandermeer you find so—?"

"Repulsive?" she finished for him.

Mortified, Thomas was tempted to slap his sister across the face. "What a horrible thing to say about my friend!" he whispered hoarsely as his face took on a reddish cast. "How dare you? And when did you adopt this snobbish attitude?"

Christiana rolled her eyes and sat up straighter as she scowled at her brother. "Mr. Vandermeer lacks *social graces*. I find it difficult to spend time with him because he... he offends without even knowing it," she said in her own defense. "And he is... *awfully tall*," she added in an exasperated whisper.

Thomas inhaled and let the breath out slowly. "He does lack some social graces, I will give you that," he replied quietly, still rather annoyed by his sister's comments. "However, he is endeavoring to learn from his mistakes, and he tries very hard. I was merely wondering if there might be someone for him at Warwick's, is all. I believe he will begin looking for a wife very soon."

Eyes wide, Christiana thought for a moment. Certainly there was a tall girl at school she disliked, one that might suit the man. But when she considered the girls from the various houses, she could think of no one taller than Emma and certainly no one near as tall as Emma she would wish to suffer with Mr. Vandermeer. A few of the shorter ones, to be sure... "I cannot think of anyone who is tall," she said with a frown.

Sighing, Thomas put his hands together. "Just how tall is Miss Emma?"

"She is five-foot-nine inches," Christiana replied with a firm nod. "We just measured each other last week," she added proudly. "And I am five-feet and one inch!"

Trying hard not to, Thomas began chuckling. "She is shorter than me, and you have grown an entire inch since summer," he said happily. "From the way you described Miss Emma, I thought perhaps she was six feet tall!"

Christiana rolled her eyes. "Goodness, no," she said. "But she has a friend who is," she added, her eyes widening. "Though, Miss Deborah is a stick. And Emma is not a stick. She is very... well, she has...." Her hands waved in the air to indicate a bosom, "And, well,... let us just say that she has a better figure than the statue of Diana at the British Museum. And much longer legs," Christiana added after careful consideration. With that, she flushed red as she watched her brother's reaction.

"Indeed?" he replied carefully, imagining the nude statue and deciding he rather liked the figure he was imagining. "What color is her hair?" He immediately regretted the question.

"Blonde. But golden, not red, like mine," Christiana replied as she watched her brother more closely. Her eyes widened again and she grinned. "*You* would really like her, Thomas," she said quietly. "She is really very comely."

Clearing his throat, Thomas sat up straight as the waiter delivered their dinners. "Thank you," he said as platters and plates were put down between them. "Yes, I probably would, if I were ever to actually *meet* her," he replied in an exasperated whisper.

Christiana smiled. "Then come to the Gamma House for dinner on a Wednesday night in February," she suggested, her eyebrows dancing suggestively. "She does not have classes on Wednesday nights, so she eats dinner with the rest of us."

Shrugging, Thomas agreed. "I will do that," he promised, eating his dinner while Christiana regaled him with stories of her classmates and schooling.

It was nearly two hours later when they left the restaurant and headed back to Warwick's.

CHAPTER 4
A DAY IN THE LIFE OF A
MIDWIFE

ebruary 1, 1802, Newport Street, London
Deborah stepped carefully over the uneven cobble-stones, a basket of fruits and vegetables hanging from her bent arm. Even though it was early in the morning, steam rose from the drying stones as the summer sun warmed the muggy morning air.

Contemplating the high prices the produce commanded and wondering how much longer inflation could last, she didn't immediately notice the call of "Freak!" Perhaps it was the second or third time, when the source of the word was right in front of her, when she looked up to find a middle-aged man snarling at her.

Clad in filthy black trousers and a tattered cape coat, the man seemed to sway with each step, as if one leg might have been shorter than the other. His facial features were hidden by the brim of a partially crushed top hat. Holding out a gnarled finger, he pointed at her. "You are a *freak!*" he accused, menace in his voice. There could be no mistaking the anger he aimed in her direction.

Startled, Deborah stepped to the side and attempted to walk around him, thinking perhaps he was drunk or a candidate for Bedlam. It was not the first time she had heard the word 'freak' used to describe her. At six-feet, she was unusually tall for a woman. But her brunette hair was wound into a bun and covered with a white bonnet, and her dark blue kerseymere walking gown was long enough to graze the tops of her half boots. Her porcelain skin was flawless, her facial features pleasant to look upon. From a distance, she looked like any other girl who had been to market. To this man, though, her height made her a freak.

She didn't realize just how incensed he was until she was suddenly flung to the cobblestones, the odor of an unwashed body assaulting her nostrils before the air was knocked out of her lungs when her back hit the cobbles. Pain radiated from her cheek as she felt a blow across her face. She tried to inhale as another fist punched into her stomach.

Her vision graying, she saw only floating dots as she tried to scream and found she could not. Air had not yet filled her lungs. The sound of tearing fabric, the sensation of gloved hands on her legs, the pain of her maidenhood tearing, the repeating mantra, "You are a freak" in her ear... panic finally set in, but her efforts to move were thwarted by the heavy body and the hot breath against her neck.

And as suddenly at it had started, it was over.

When the weight lifted from her body, she tried to curl herself into a fetal position and found she could barely move. Once her vision cleared, she could see only a clump of grapes and several potatoes wedged into the spaces between the cobbles.

*D*eborah White sat up straight in bed, gasping for breath. Despite the chilled air, sweat dribbled in rivulets from her damp hair while tears streamed down her face.

Perhaps it was better I didn't see his face, she thought.

"Are you ill?" she heard Anna ask from the other bed in the tiny room. It was still dark outside. The single window, bare of curtains and shutters, was black.

Taking a deep breath, Deborah shook her head. "I... I just had a bad dream," she whispered, not wanting to admit that everything she had seen in the nightmare had actually happened.

"Oh," Anna replied, obviously displeased her sleep had been interrupted by anything less than an emergency. Within a moment, she was snoring softly.

Deborah listened to Anna's breathing for a few moments, using the steady rhythm to help calm her nerves and slow her own breathing. Exhausted, she finally fell asleep.

At half-six in the morning, the chill of the gray February

morning finally seeped into her room on the second story of the Home for Unwed Mothers. Deborah, nearly fully dressed under the single quilt, shivered and blew into her hands. Rubbing them together, she knew she wasn't going to feel warm unless she moved to a room with a fire.

Puffs of white air hung in clouds above Anna as her roommate continued to slumber in the other cot. The girl, barely sixteen, was in her eighth month of pregnancy. Once Anna gave birth to her baby, Deborah would have the room to herself again.

The overcrowded condition of the Home was common during the winter months. Many of the denizens were "girls of the town." Pregnant prostitutes couldn't easily ply their trade with their regular customers, so they sought a room in which to stay at the Home in Newport Street until they gave birth. If the babies were not welcome, they would end up in an orphanage. Those girls not wishing to part with their newborns could continue to live at the Home in a small room and expect a hot meal or two every day until they were able to arrange some other accommodations.

Anna had arrived a few months before. Unwed and unwilling to name the father of her baby, she was forced out of her home when her swelling abdomen became too noticeable to hide from neighbors and other family members. Deborah knew Anna planned to leave her baby at the Foundling Hospital so she could return home.

A facility devoted solely to raising first-born illegitimate children, the Foundling Hospital was not an ideal institution. The orphans housed there were malnourished and brutalized by their care-givers. Although they wore uniforms and attended school, they didn't have a life outside of the facility until they reached the age of twenty-one.

Shuddering at the thought of a newborn being left in the care of such a large orphanage, Deborah forced herself out of her cot, stood up slowly and worked the kinks out of her sore back and her aching knees. She stretched as much as she could, allowing the muscles to slowly warm as she regarded Anna's sleeping form.

Instinctively, she held a hand against her own abdomen. There had been a babe there two years before, conceived during the rape but lost to a miscarriage a few months later. She had come to the Home for the same reason as Anna.

Now she was one of its midwives.

Deborah made her way to the lobby of the Home for Unwed Mothers. A roaring fire warmed the waiting area and the corridor leading to it. Holding her hands over the flames, Deborah breathed in deep and allowed the warmth to penetrate her bones.

"Mornin' sleepy 'ead," Mrs. Dawes said dryly as she entered the lobby. She was dressed in a clean hospital uniform and seemed in good spirits.

Smiling sheepishly, Deborah nodded to the founder and proprietor of the Home. "Good morning, Mrs. Dawes." For at least the tenth time, she wondered if there was a "Mr. Dawes," but she never had the courage to ask the woman.

The stout midwife regarded Deborah, just now noticing the dark circles under the girl's eyes. "Oh," she murmured. "One of those nights, eh?" she commented, a frown replacing her amused expression.

Shaking her head, Deborah retained the sheepish smile. "I have not yet washed or combed my hair. But I didn't hear anyone arrive in the night, nor did I hear any sounds of labor," she said in defense of her later-than-usual waking. "Did I miss anything?"

The older woman smiled and shook her head as she reviewed the list of girls staying at the Home. "Not a thing," she replied. "Ye'll pro'bly 'ave to deliver one soon, though. Miss Sophia up in one-oh-four is due any day, and I 'ave to be meetin' with the parish clerk this week."

Deborah nodded. Mrs. Dawes was rarely gone from the Home, but law required the parish be given a list of live births and details for their records. Should the Home need money, there was the possibility Mrs. Dawes could obtain it from the parish.

The woman prided herself on running a clean and safe haven for pregnant girls and unwed mothers and their small children. When it came to funding the enterprise, however, she despised having to solicit funds from the parish or to seek patrons to pledge monies.

Their one regular patron, Mr. Todd Vandermeer, had been their sole source of funding for most of the time Deborah had been at the Home. His contributions couldn't begin to cover the cost of running the Home in the winter months, though, when so much more coal was required. Mrs. Dawes occasionally sought help from the Ministry of the Poor to help tide them over.

"If I must," Deborah nodded, finally feeling warm enough to seek a bowl of porridge and a cup of coffee.

The mess hall was not yet set up for serving breakfast, but Deborah hurried to the kitchen and helped herself. The girls on breakfast duty acknowledged her with nods and went about their work preparing the morning meal. Soon, a crowd of hungry young mothers would begin arriving with their babies and toddlers in tow.

Deborah took her usual seat in the dining hall. Within minutes, she had downed the porridge and was drinking the weak coffee when Anna, wearing only her night rail, waddled into the room. Her eyes red from crying, Anna held one hand under her belly as if to hold it up.

At first, Deborah didn't realize the source of Anna's distress, but the girl who followed Anna into the dining hall certainly did. At her ear-piercing screech, Deborah glanced down to see a trail of blood drops on the wood plank floor.

On her feet in an instant, Deborah rushed to Anna's side and led her to the delivery room, barking orders to the girls just arriving. Alerted to a problem by the sound of the screech, Mrs. Dawes joined Deborah and Anna as they made their way to the delivery room.

"Something tore," Anna said between sobs. "I could feel it," she whispered.

"Did your water break?" Deborah asked as she motioned for Anna to lie on the delivery table. She pushed up the night rail and then moved to the head of the table to push a pillow under Anna's head.

"No. I don't think so," Anna replied uncertainly.

Mrs. Dawes shook her head as she felt Anna's belly, pushing and prodding here and there while she made quiet comments. "Baby's alive. Ya may just be spottin'," the midwife announced. But at the surge of red-stained liquid that sprang from between Anna's legs, Mrs. Dawes looked up to give Deborah a worried look. "'Tis broke now," she said, trying to remember how far along the girl was in her pregnancy.

"Eight months," Deborah whispered as she turned to look at Anna for confirmation. The girl nodded, her face white with fright. "'Tis all right," she cooed to the girl. "Are you having contractions? Did your back hurt you at all last night?"

Anna's eyes widened. "Yes, all night," she replied. "After you woke up from your nightmare." She grunted and nearly sat up as a contraction took hold.

"Steady, girl," Mrs. Dawes said as she rubbed oil on the girl's nether region, dabbing away blood as she did so. "I don't think we'll be needing Bobby today," the midwife whispered as she gave a look of warning to Deborah.

Stiffening at the mention of Bobby, a young boy who occasionally volunteered his services as a nipple chewer, Deborah let go of Anna's hand and nodded to Mrs. Dawes.

She knew that look. Something was *wrong*.

Deborah left the delivery room and raced out of the Home, not bothering to stop for a coat or to put on a bonnet and boots.

The traffic was heavy this time of the morning. She dodged between window shoppers and men on horseback, all the while wincing at the pain she felt in her knees.

Arriving at a doctor's home nearly three streets away, she was breathless and wild-eyed as she burst through the door. The doctor's wife, normally seated at a small desk in the front room, had just come from the surgery. She put her hand to her mouth as Deborah entered.

"Is he here?" Deborah asked as she hurried to the woman.

Mrs. Talbot finally recognized her and stepped back. "Yes, but he's with a patient—"

"We need him. Now!" Deborah hissed, ready to walk into the surgery herself if need be.

Shaking her head, Mrs. Talbot retreated another step and then turned to get her husband. "Dr. Talbot!" she called out as she left the waiting area. "Mrs. Dawes needs you."

Although it felt like an eternity, Dr. Maurice Talbot stepped into the waiting room only moments later, his medical bag in one hand and his coat draped over one shoulder. "Miss Deborah," he nodded in greeting, his wire-rimmed spectacles perched on his hooked nose.

"Good morning, Dr. Talbot," Deborah said as she curtsied. "Thank you for... being available," she said with a nod.

They left the office with Mrs. Talbot standing in the doorway, a worried look on her face. Mrs. Dawes rarely sent for the doctor, but when she did, it was always an emergency, and, most importantly, she always paid the bill.

"Give me the particulars," the middle-aged doctor ordered as he took large strides down the path back to the Home for Unwed Mothers.

Deborah took a deep breath as she matched his stride. "Sixteen-year-old female. Eight months pregnant. Experienced back pain and contractions since about two or three o'clock this morning. Woke up bleeding at nine. She said something tore," Deborah recited as they hurried along. "We got her to the delivery room, her water broke, and Mrs. Dawes was preparing for her for birth when she..." She stopped, not sure how to describe the look Mrs. Dawes used to indicate a mother's life was in peril.

Dr. Talbot nodded as he walked quickly. "How far apart are the contractions?" he asked as he glanced over at Deborah, noting her limping gait and the winces on her face as she walked.

Shaking her head, Deborah chided herself for not having timed the contractions. "I don't know. She only had one in the minute we had her on the table."

The doctor remained silent for a moment and then asked, "Is she a lightskirt?"

Deborah inwardly cringed. For those that made their living on their backs, the doctor seemed less willing to provide his services, although he never voiced aversion or hesitated to do what was necessary to deliver a baby.

The doctor caught Deborah's facial expression and rolled his eyes. "I only ask because she may have a disease that can be passed to the baby during delivery," he said in his own defense. "Syphilis, for example," he added, hoping he correctly interpreted her sudden tight-lipped expression.

Inhaling sharply, Deborah paused in mid-step and realized he witnessed her reaction. "The French pox can be passed to a baby?" she half-whispered as she resumed her quick walking, wincing with each step.

"Indeed. I believe it is usually the cause of their blindness, should they contract it during childbirth," he explained quickly. He noted her pained expression as they quickened their steps. "And how long have you been experiencing such discomfort, Miss Deborah?"

Nearly stumbling in her surprise at the question, Deborah shrugged. "I have felt pain in my knees for several years, sir," she replied between gasps for air. "Ever since I grew... tall," she added with a weak smile.

"You should wear better shoes," he commented as he motioned

to her feet. "Slippers don't provide enough support. And you need a good night's sleep. I understand the latter may not be possible given your occupation, but you must have a day of rest now and then."

Deborah considered his words. He was right, of course. The next time she received any payment from the Home, she would use it to buy new shoes even though she also needed a gown and stockings and a corset and a night rail. "Yes, sir," she replied. They rushed into the Home, and Deborah allowed the doctor to precede her into the delivery room.

Anna, crying and grunting, was nearly sitting up and in the middle of a contraction when the doctor put a reassuring hand on her shoulder and then moved to Mrs. Dawes' side. "Good morning, Mrs. Dawes," he said, his tone very business-like as he peered at the patient's nether region.

Mrs. Dawes nodded to the doctor. "Thank you for coming so quickly, Dr. Talbot. She wants to push, but I told her to 'old off."

Deborah prepared a basin with water for Dr. Talbot to wash his hands, and he did so before beginning his examination. Unlike other doctors the Home occasionally used for difficult births, Dr. Talbot was a stickler for cleanliness and didn't resort to using leeches or laudanum on his patients. He poked and prodded much like Mrs. Dawes had done, but he noted the amount of blood loss and considered the options. Although the baby had not yet crowned, it would do so with another push or two. If he did a Caesarian section, he would have to do it immediately. "Probably a placental tear," he said quietly. To his patient, he asked, "Do you feel like pushing now?"

Mrs. Dawes gasped and whispered, "Isn't she hemorrhaging too badly?"

The doctor shook his head. "Not necessarily. If she can deliver before she loses her strength, she'll be fine. I don't want to cut her open if I don't have to," he whispered back.

Nodding, Mrs. Dawes gave a nod to Deborah. Taking Anna's hand in hers, Deborah spoke quietly but firmly. "When the next contraction starts, you push as hard as you can. And yell as much as you need to," she added, knowing the girl would do so anyway. They almost always did. Even before she finished the instructions, Anna set her teeth and curled up. Deborah supported her shoulders as the girl pushed with the contraction.

"She's crowning," Dr. Talbot announced. "One more push, please."

Deborah let Anna relax before she told her to push again. When the contraction started, Anna, suddenly weak, could barely muster the strength to push. Dr. Talbot's hand pushed on her belly, and a moment later, Mrs. Dawes held up a tiny baby boy.

The doctor left the baby to the midwife's care as he saw to Anna. The girl had indeed been hemorrhaging, but the blood flow had stopped with the birth.

Deborah squeezed Anna's hand, but found the girl unresponsive. "Doctor Talbot—"

"She'll be fine, Miss Deborah. She's just weak and needs some rest," he assured her.

Once the baby boy's mouth and nose were clear of fluids, he let out a wail that filled the delivery room.

Mrs. Dawes wrapped the baby in a flannel cloth and brought him to Anna's side. "You have a baby boy," she said as she held the bundle next to Anna's face.

The girl finally opened her eyes and stared at her son. She turned her head toward Deborah and then back to the baby before she finally smiled. "I can go home now," she whispered, making no move to take the child from Mrs. Dawes. Within a moment, she was fast asleep.

Deborah took the baby from Mrs. Dawes and sat down with it in the small chair in the corner, hoping Anna wouldn't give the baby to the Foundling Hospital. She held the bundle on one shoulder, covering its bald head with one hand as she watched Mrs. Dawes begin cleaning and Dr. Talbot complete his work on the new mother. The floor beneath his patient was awash in fluids, but after a few moments, Mrs. Dawes had the evidence of the birth cleaned away. Patting the baby absently on its back, Deborah marveled at how heavy such a tiny thing could be. And how warm!

Within moments, she and the baby were sound asleep.

"She needs better shoes," Dr. Talbot stated with a nod in Deborah's direction.

"Don't we all?" Mrs. Dawes replied with a frown, throwing a towel into a canvas bin next to the door.

"I mean it, Margaret," he said quietly. His stern features formed a more serious expression, and Mrs. Dawes stopped what she was doing to give him her full attention. The doctor rarely called her by her first name.

"What would you have me do, Maurice?" she whispered hoarsely.

"I cannot pay her a regular wage. I don't know when contributions will come in. This damn winter has nearly exhausted our supply of coal, and the Ministry for the Poor canno' give me more right now," she complained, her eyes occasionally glancing in the direction of Deborah and the tiny baby she held.

"There is a man...," Dr. Talbot started to say before Mrs. Dawes' eyes flashed a warning. "He's not looking for a Cyprian," he went on quickly, knowing immediately what the midwife had imagined. "He is an artist. From France," he explained in hushed tones. "I met him at my club, and he says he's in need of a girl to model for him. A very tall girl."

Margaret Dawes regarded the doctor for a moment, suspicion evident in her eyes. "Model?" she repeated. "You mean, to be in a painting?"

Dr. Talbot nodded quickly, closing up his black bag. "Exactly. He's been commissioned to do a painting for a client in France and has been searching for the perfect woman." He motioned toward Deborah. "She might be the one. If she is, she could pose for him and earn the money for the shoes."

Looking doubtful as she watched Deborah, Mrs. Dawes shook her head. "I do na' know, Maurice. Do you trust this Frenchman?" she asked as she returned her attention to the doctor.

"Seems like a good man. But he is an artist, so he's a bit... *different* from the rest of the men at the club," he admitted, an eyebrow cocking at an odd angle. "May I tell him about Miss Deborah?"

Margaret Dawes regarded the doctor for some time, wondering if what he was suggesting would be in the best interest of the Home's other midwife. Finally nodding, Mrs. Dawes said, "Agreed. But she can only pose in the days. No nights," she insisted. At the doctor's nod of agreement, she asked, "How much do I owe you for the visit?"

The doctor shook his head. "We're even, Mrs. Dawes," he said with a grin. "You got me away from a most unpleasant patient." With that, the doctor picked up his medical bag and took his leave of the Home for Unwed Mothers.

Deborah awoke when she felt Mrs. Dawes lift the baby from her shoulder. The doctor was long gone, and Anna was awake and asking for her son. "You go on up to bed," Mrs. Dawes ordered quietly. "Doctor Talbot says you 'ave to sleep, and you 'ave to get new shoes."

Smiling weakly, Deborah nodded and made her way to her room. Now that Anna had given birth, the room was back to being her own again.

CHAPTER 5
A YOUNG LADY IN LOVE

February 10, 1802, Glasshouse Street, London

"A post came for you today," Ann-Marie said as she held out a salver toward Christiana Wellingham. A bright white envelope sealed with wax lay on the silver tray, and Christiana reached for it immediately. The initial 'G' was pressed into the red wax, and Christiana smiled as she fingered the embossing.

"Thank you, Ann-Marie," she said as she took the envelope. The maid curtsied and continued with her feather dusting in the vestibule of the Gamma House of Warwick's Grammar and Finishing School.

Christiana hurried up to her bedchamber and tossed her spencer and reticule onto her bed. Her yellow muslin empire gown, adorned with a bright blue ribbon, was already wrinkled from sitting in grammar class. Emma was still in art class and wouldn't be home for another hour. From the lack of noise in the boarding house, Christiana guessed she was the first one to arrive from a long day of classes.

Opening the envelope, she smiled and recognized the cursive script of her beloved. *My dearest Christiana*, it began, and Christiana quickly sat down on the bed.

I hope this letter finds you of Good Health and Happiness. It has been far too long since I last saw you at Christmastide, and I find myself planning a trip to London just so that I may gaze upon your Countenance once again. I simply cannot wait until the Hornsby ball to see you. If it is Agreeable to you and Not an Inconvenience, I shall call upon you at Your House the First moment I'm able on the ninth of April. I look most forward to your Favorable Reply, and as always, I am Very Truly Yours.

Christiana bit her lip and wanted to cry out in joy. Instead, she folded the letter and returned it to its envelope. Sitting at her desk, she took a pen and paper and carefully wrote her reply.

My dearest beloved, I am well, indeed, and hope that you are as Healthy and Happy as I am having received your most Welcome Letter. I'm Overjoyed at the news it contained. I shall very much Look Forward to your arrival in April. You didn't say as to the length of your stay, but I'm Hoping it will be a Very Long Time indeed. If you have not already been offered hospitality in London, please be assured that you are welcome to stay in your bedchamber at Woodscastle. My Brother would be most pleased to see you. However, since I find myself most certainly in Love with you, I will always be more pleased to see you than even your Best Friend. You are in my Heart and in my Dreams. Yours, most truly, Christiana.

Using her small embroidery scissors, she snipped off a lock of her red hair. Rereading the letter before folding it and adding the hair, she wondered if it was too soon to admit she loved her brother's best friend.

When the man had stayed at Woodscastle over the Christmas holiday, he had spent hours with her walking in the thin snow blanketing the grounds around the estate. On more than one occasion, he had taken her hunting for deer in the woods and promised he would one day teach her how to shoot the hunting gun.

Despite wearing a winter bonnet on those days, Christiana's nose displayed an array of freckles that usually appeared in the summertime. And, although he claimed he rather liked them, he teased her mercilessly, threatening to buy her a bottle of Gowland's Lotion so she might erase them and not suffer the indignity of displaying the supposed sign of a sexual disease.

When they rode into London in his small carriage, he wrapped them both in a blanket and pulled her close to help keep her warm in the chilly air.

Once in town, they had eaten at a small inn, just the two of them, with no chaperone in sight, and spent an hour talking about everything and nothing. Later, as they shopped in Oxford Street,

Christiana stopped to admire a bonnet in a milliner's shop. They went in to get warm, or so he said, and he bought the bonnet for her.

Then, one day, while he was tugging on her strawberry blonde ringlets, he leaned over and kissed her on the cheek. When she turned to face him, to admonish him for messing her hair, he kissed her on the lips. It was a soft kiss, she remembered, but not at all the innocent kiss of a man pretending to be an older brother.

Left speechless, she felt her face redden, and she turned away. After a short pause, she took one of his hands in hers, squeezed it, and kissed its palm in return.

The following day, as he was about to climb into his coach for the trip back to his estate, he started to admit his love for her when Thomas interrupted them to say his 'good-byes'. Christiana was so surprised by his confession, she was unable to reply and simply blushed and smiled as he disappeared down the road toward Burlington Lane.

Less than a week later, a post arrived from Gregory with his full confession of love and honor.

"*Y*ou are home early," Emma said as she strode into the bedchamber. Her arms were full of books and papers, and she stopped at her desk to set them down as Christiana completed folding her letter. "Are you well?" Emma asked lightly, surprised when Christiana didn't immediately reply with some kind of greeting.

"Indeed, thank you for asking," Christiana said with alacrity. "I was just completing a letter to a friend," she explained as she held up the note. Her eyes widened. "Is that your homework?" she asked, a frown on her face as she regarded the stack of books on Emma's desk. "Oh, my."

Emma sighed. "'Tis. But I have a few hours before I have to be in class, so I expect to get some of it done right now," she said, pulling out her chair to work at her desk. "And do you have homework, too?" she asked, hoping Christiana wouldn't want to spend the afternoon in conversation.

"No, but I should practice piano-forté," the younger girl replied, moving away from her desk as if she were going to leave the room.

She stopped, though, and sat on the edge of her bed. "Have you... have you ever been in love, Emma?" she asked, her voice very quiet.

Emma's back went rigid, and she carefully turned to stare at her roommate. No one had ever asked her the question, at least not quite so directly. Realizing Christiana was serious about the inquiry, she carefully considered her response. "I thought I was once," she finally admitted. "There was a man who used to come to my father's shop to buy hats for the drivers in his livery service. He was so handsome, and he used to greet me and watch me while I completed his receipt. I was sure he was going to ask to call on me, but he never did. And I have not seen him since Mr. Smith took over the shop."

Christiana sighed. "So you have never been called on by a man?"

Emma regarded Christiana for a long moment. "Well, I was once asked by an older gentlemen if he could call on me, but I knew Mr. Morton was married, so, of course, I refused."

Besides the embarrassment she had felt, she thought Mr. Morton was old enough to be her father.

Mortified, Christiana put a hand to her mouth. "How simply awful of him!" she whispered hoarsely. She leaned in closer to Emma. "Have you ever been kissed?"

"Of course not!" Emma replied quickly, stunned by the question. "Although, I suppose I could mention the peck I received from my cousin when I was ten. He wanted to learn how to kiss, and he thought I would teach him. I did not," she said with a mischievous grin.

Christiana smiled.

"Why the questions?" Emma asked as she placed her arms on the top of the chair back. "Has someone asked to call on you?" It was a possibility, she realized. Although Christiana would have her formal coming out during the upcoming Season, she was of an age to attract suitors even now.

Christiana's smile turned to a look of shock. "No! I'm only sixteen, and my brother wouldn't allow it just yet," she replied, a bit too indignantly. "I just... I wondered when I might expect such queries is all."

Emma eyed her roommate. "Anytime now, I expect. You are a very pretty girl. You said you have a good inheritance. You are certainly attending the best finishing school in London. It won't be long before the young men are lining up to call on you."

At twenty, Emma feared her own window of opportunity had closed. Her next best choice was to seek employment and, after she turned one-and-twenty, hope she might meet an older gentleman or perhaps a widower. There was no shame in a marriage of convenience, but she could hope that she might grow to love a man once a marriage was arranged. With no living parent and parental consent required for those marrying before the age of twenty-one, she didn't know if the rules applied to her.

"If I do have someone call on me, must I tell my brother?" Christiana asked as she bit her lip. She realized almost immediately she should not have broached the question.

Taken aback, Emma thought for a moment. "I suppose you could see what comes of it before you tell Mr. Wellingham anything. Just because a boy calls on you does not mean he is courting you," she added. "But if he makes it clear he wishes to marry you, then you must tell your brother. He is your guardian. You really must have his blessing in order for a marriage to take place before you are one-and-twenty."

Nodding, Christiana considered her options. Her beloved had said he loved her. He had not asked for her hand in marriage. She decided to keep him a secret for a while longer.

"I understand," Christiana finally replied. "I will be in the music room," she said as she hopped off the bed and, taking her letter with her, left the room.

Emma shook her head, glad she was no longer sixteen years old. She turned around in her chair and started her homework.

CHAPTER 6
A DAY IN THE LIFE OF A
BROKER

February 18, 1802, Mayfair, London

Todd Vandermeer regarded his reflection in the large mirror and frowned. "Are these really supposed to be this... tight?" he asked as he tried to adjust the leathern breeches and found he could barely bend over.

"Indeed, sir," replied the maker-of-breeches as he studied his work with a critical eye. "You will require the assistance of your valet to pull them on, of course. And I would advise you not to wear them on a rainy day, or you will require assistance in getting them *off*."

Sighing, Todd shook his head. "And how do I undo the buttons?" he asked, finding his fingers couldn't force the fastenings through the tooled holes in the leather.

The other man stood and walked around the broker, all the while studying his creation. "There is a special instrument. I will provide one." He used a finger to indicate he wanted his client to turn around.

Todd obeyed and then saw the reflection of his rear in the mirror. "Now, that is not so awful, I suppose," Todd admitted as he noticed how the breeches displayed his best feature. Despite his lean, tall body, the three things he could boast were a rump, muscular arms, and a decent head of hair perfectly suited to the Titus style he had adopted the year before. "I could get used to these," he said with a satisfied smile.

"Very good, sir," the maker said with a nod.

Todd left the leather shop with his new breeches and hurried to the waiting town coach. "To my meeting, Mr. Stevenson," he ordered as he climbed into the coach. Noting the lateness of the hour, he berated himself for having taken too long at the shop.

Randolph Hughes, a rather nosy and unpleasant colleague at the East India Company, had requested an audience with him that afternoon. Since it was the man's custom to do business in places other than his office—Todd had overheard other colleagues complain on several occasions that Hughes could only be found in a men's club, a chocolate shop, or with a prostitute—it was a relief his presence had been requested at one of the many corner coffee shops near the river.

Todd had considered turning down the man's request, but Randolph Hughes had made arrangements for his sister to meet with Todd for tea later that day. Not wanting to undermine a potential courtship opportunity, Todd agreed to the meeting.

Mr. Stevenson brought the coach to a halt in a space near the corner of Lower Thames Street and Fish Street Hill. The London Bridge loomed in the background as Todd climbed down from the coach with the help of his cane. "I hope I shan't be too long," he said to his driver as he headed toward the coffee shop.

Todd was about to enter the shop when Randolph Hughes walked up to him.

"Good day, Mr. Vandermeer. So good of you to join me," Hughes greeted his colleague as he reached for the door and allowed Todd to enter before him.

"And good day to you, Mr. Hughes. To what do I owe the honor of your request today?" he queried as they took a seat in the crowded shop. Todd removed his top hat. In such close proximity, a waft of a most unpleasant odor reached Todd's nose, and he remembered another reason why he found it hard to be in Hughes' company. Like many others in the city, Hughes believed bathing was bad for his health and so only did it a few times a year.

Todd did his best not to breathe deeply and leaned back in his chair.

A server was quick to place menu boards on their table and stood waiting patiently as the men considered their options. "Tea and Dutch biscuits will do me," Todd said when he realized Randolph was waiting for him to order first.

"Coffee with milk. There will be extra coin for you if you make it quick, lad," Hughes said as he passed the menu to the server.

The boy hurried off through the crowded coffee shop and Hughes leaned over the table. "Have you ever wanted something so much, you cannot think of anything else until you get it?" he asked, his eyes darting about the room.

Todd's eyebrows drew together, wondering where Hughes was going with the conversation. "I... I have not found myself in such a situation, no," he replied uncertainly. The leathern breeches were not something he *had* to have, but they were attainable—at a price—and within reason for an unmarried man of his age and income.

"I find myself wanting a tumble at the moment," Hughes said matter-of-factly. The server set down two tea cups on saucers along with a small plate of biscuits. "And I was hoping you could share some information with me," he said without further preamble.

Startled, Todd leaned toward his colleague. "Of course. If I can," he replied carefully.

Hughes looked anxious as he scanned the room. "I would prefer we speak in less crowded quarters," he explained, "One never knows who might be listening."

Todd didn't recognize anyone when he took a quick glance around the shop, but he nodded. "Perhaps we could discuss matters on a walk outdoors?" he suggested, wincing at the thought of the pain in his knees and wishing instead they could just conduct business at the table.

"Very good," the man replied as he stood up to go, dropping a coin onto the table. "Let us be on our way then." Hughes took his cup and saucer and headed for the door.

Todd sighed and stood up slowly. It was not unusual for patrons to drink their coffees outside the crowded coffee shops, but sporting a cane while balancing a cup and saucer and a couple of the biscuits proved challenging for the tall man. "You have me quite curious, Mr. Hughes. What is this about?" he asked as they walked toward the river.

Hughes sighed audibly. "I was hoping you would allow me to work with you on whatever your next venture might be," he finally said, only looking over at Todd when he had completed the sentence. He took a drink from his cup, his expression suggesting he was pleased with the drink.

Todd worked hard to hide the amusement he felt at the man's

request. Hughes had been with the John Company for over twenty years, but his ability to negotiate deals and to guess what the public might want next in the way of imported products had long ago diminished. As a result of his negotiations with a textile company in the Netherlands, the import company would be receiving crates of now-unwanted brocade fabric for at least another two years. The man could only hope that someone would come up with a use for the fabric now that most fashionable gowns were being made of domestic cloth.

"You see, it has come to my attention that your background," he said with some hesitancy, "seems to have favored you with a knack for choosing products the middle class... *desires*," Hughes continued, awe in his voice, "And it seems that I am still in the last century."

The man didn't add that his upbringing as the fourth grandson of a viscount insulated him from those very people who Todd seemed to understand so well, or that his excessive gaming and thirst for wine and women had cost him most of his inherited fortune.

Todd regarded Hughes with a sympathetic smile. "I have had a bit of luck," he admitted without a hint of pride in his voice. "And it helped that those products were things *I* desired," he added.

Hughes nodded as he walked towards the bridge. "I could use your help. And your luck," he said with a grin.

Amazed by the normally unpleasant fellow's humble attitude, Todd considered what product he might allow the trader to take on as his own project. Their walk had taken them onto the bridge, where a line of prostitutes called out to them and every other passing man who appeared to have coin. Much to Todd's surprise, Hughes motioned to one of the taller, younger girls.

"Care to join me?" Hughes suggested to Todd as he nodded to the harlot. "How much, love?"

The disheveled woman, who at one time was probably very handsome, looked over her potential clients. "Six pence for the both of you," she replied, her accent suggesting she was Welsh. She reeked of rosewater mixed with the same stench that surrounded Hughes.

Todd quickly shook his head and took a half step backwards, hoping for fresher air. "I am not interested," he replied, trying to keep his embarrassment from showing when he realized that when Hughes said he wanted a harlot, he meant right away.

Hughes looked surprised at his colleague's response, but unbuttoned his breeches. "You sure, Vandermeer?" he asked as he gave the prostitute a coin. She hiked up her skirt and positioned herself in front of the trader. Hughes gave his cup and saucer to Todd, who nearly dropped his own in the exchange.

"Quite," Todd replied, biting back his anger when he realized the trader was going to conduct his business right then and there in broad daylight on the bridge. He stacked the cups and saucers in one hand. "Have you forgotten that I am to meet your sister this very afternoon?" he asked rhetorically, checking his pocket watch as he said so. "In an hour, in fact," he added, finding it hard to keep annoyance out of his voice.

The other trader repositioned one foot and nodded in Todd's direction. "Of course. I find it's rather noble of you to give up an opportunity such as this for the sake of my sister," he said, his admiration apparently genuine.

Todd averted his eyes and considered the man's earlier request. "Mr. Hughes," he began, not at all concerned about divulging the married man's name to the interested ears of the prostitute. "Would you be interested in taking on a new fashion from Paris?" He pretended to study his fingernails as he held the cups and saucers.

The prostitute, who was barely able to balance herself while Hughes pushed his member into her, turned her attention to the taller man. "I might," she said, boredom evident in her voice.

"He's speaking to me, love," Hughes said between grunts. "What kind of fashion might it be?" he asked, keeping his attention on the prostitute.

Smiling, Todd replied, "Transparent gowns."

Hughes didn't respond immediately, but the prostitute's eyes widened. "Transparent?" she repeated happily. "Does that mean you can see right through them?" she asked, her sudden excitement causing Hughes to pound into her with a bit more force.

Todd grinned at her enthusiasm for what he—and Thomas Wellingham—had figured to be a fashion trend destined to fail in England. "Indeed," he replied, trying hard to keep from staring at the coital encounter going on in front of him.

"Sounds like you have a gold mine, Mr. Vandermeer," Hughes said, his face straining before he emitted a loud grunt and pulled the girl hard against his body. The prostitute gave a disgusted groan but allowed Hughes to hold her for a few more seconds before she stepped away, stuffed a kerchief between her legs, and shook her skirts back down around her legs.

"Very good, Mr. Hughes. I will provide you with more information in the morning," Todd said as he passed the man's coffee to him. "In the meantime, I really must be going," Todd said. When Hughes looked surprised—he hadn't yet finished buttoning his breeches—Todd added, "Remember, I am hosting your sister for tea this afternoon, and I don't wish to be late."

Hughes nodded and waved him away. "Of course. One cannot keep a lady waiting," he said as he tried to catch his breath. "And thank you for the business idea. I shall look forward to this product more than any other," he added as he headed off toward the south side of the bridge, one hand holding up his breeches.

Todd turned around to head back to the coffee shop and was relieved to find Mr. Stevenson parked at the end of the bridge. A quick look at his pocket watch showed they had very little time to get to Cavendish Square.

Todd thought about Hughes' earlier question. *Have you ever wanted something so much, you cannot think of anything else until you get it?* After his conversation with Thomas Wellingham about courting, Todd decided he really did want something—a wife.

He had set about finding suitable possibilities almost immediately. His inquiries among peers at the East India Company provided the most promising unpromised ladies, the first of whom was scheduled to pay a call to his home for tea at four that afternoon. He found her suggestion to come for tea at his house rather surprising, but then thought she would probably bring along a chaperone—a lady rarely called on a gentleman at his home, after all. Todd's plan had been to bathe and dress before she arrived. Now he would barely have time to change his clothes.

After arriving at Grace Park, his four-story, seventeen-room brick mansion with carriage house and stables, Todd rushed to his room.

"May I be of assistance?" his valet, Winston, asked as he watched his master unwrap his new breeches.

"I believe I shall require it, yes," Todd replied as he removed his woolen breeches. "These are quite tight, but the maker claims they are made correctly," he said as he held out the leathern breeches.

Winston nodded his head and regarded the breeches. "You will want to use the facilities before putting these on," he suggested with a raised eyebrow. "Did he provide you with a special tool to help get the buttons undone?"

Todd nodded as he fished the instrument out of his pocket. "You are familiar with these, then?" he asked hopefully, not sure he knew what the maker had done to get the damn things fastened.

The valet sighed. "Yes," he admitted, not the least bit happy about it. "Promise me, sir, that you will not wear them in the rain."

Standing to his full six-foot, six-inch height, Todd stared at his valet. "I shall only wear these for special occasions, I promise," he assured the man as he headed for the private bath. When he returned, he asked, "How much time do I have? And does my hair—?"

"If Miss Hughes is typical of women in her class, she will be late. Which means she will not arrive for about another ten or more minutes. And your hair is quite acceptable," he replied dryly, giving his master a cursory glance.

When Todd Vandermeer had first purchased Grace Park, fully furnished with a staff of servants, Winston had his doubts about the man. He wasn't a member of the *ton* but seemed to have the money and position usually afforded those of the peerage, including invitations to the very best soirées, balls, and dinner parties. His apparent wealth was obviously earned, for his manner was not the attitude of entitlement usually associated with aristocrats. His master seemed beholden to him for advice when it came to his choice of clothing and topics of conversation.

But Todd Vandermeer's very best reference came from an unusual source, for one of Winston's assignments was to deliver the man's frequent donations to Mrs. Dawes' Home for Unwed Mothers. Mrs. Dawes spoke very highly of Vandermeer, even on the rare occasions when, on his days off, Winston merely paid social calls on the midwife.

After a great deal of exertion expended by Winston and by his master, the leathern breeches were pulled up and fastened. The valet stepped back and studied Vandermeer with a critical eye. "I will get you a different waistcoat," he offered as he stepped into the dressing room.

Todd struggled to pull on his best riding boots. Since he was unable to bend much, he ended up on the bed with a leg in the air and a boot barely over his foot when there came a knock at the front door.

Winston returned with a brocade waistcoat and topcoat. "Mary will get the door," he said, referring to one of the housemaids. He came to a halt when he saw his master's predicament. He immediately hurried to the bed and managed to get the full boots onto Vandermeer's feet and then finished dressing him. "And she will see Miss Hughes to the parlor. I will bring tea and chocolate biscuits straight away."

Exhausted from the effort of looking presentable, Todd gladly accepted Winston's hand of assistance in getting up and off of the bed. "Thank you, Winston." Grabbing a cane at the last moment, Todd was off, walking crookedly for several steps until the breeches had adjusted themselves around his rear and long thighs.

Going down the stairs to the parlor was easier than sitting, but not by much. Todd's knees had begun to ache, and his nervousness increased with each step. When he finally entered the parlor, he smiled and tried to bow before his guest, finding it nearly impossible to do so. "Miss Hughes, 'tis so good of you to come," he remarked as he greeted his guest. A quick glance around the room suggested the woman had come without a companion or a maid. "Todd Vandermeer, at your service."

Miss Charlotte Hughes, younger sister to Randolph Hughes and third granddaughter of a viscount, regarded her host with a practiced smile and a curtsy. She even managed to suppress her gasp of surprise at his height. "Mr. Vandermeer, 'twas so good of you to invite me," she replied as she allowed the importer to take her gloved hand and brush his lips over the back of it.

"Please, do take a seat," Todd offered as he walked to a tall-backed chair next to the settee. He waited for her to spread her skirts over the settee before seating himself.

Or, at least, trying to do so.

The leather breeches were not yet forgiving enough to allow him to sit completely, and he struggled to get comfortable. His guest tried hard not to notice, but he could tell from her quick glance away that she had witnessed his difficulty. "May I say, you are a very lovely lady," he commented as he tried but then decided not to cross his legs.

"Why, you are kind to say so, Mr. Vandermeer. You have a very lovely home," the woman replied as she surveyed the sage green and crimson fabrics and Axminster carpets in the parlor. "Have you lived here long?" She pulled a fan from her reticule and opening it with a practiced snap of her wrist.

Todd couldn't help but notice the pink feathers in the fan perfectly matched her pink batiste gown, pink reticule, and the pink ostrich feather arcing up and out of her ornately styled blonde hair. Her earrings were even more ornate and had probably been shipped from France or Egypt.

Charlotte began fanning herself, although the room was not overly warm.

"Not long at all," Todd replied carefully. "I moved in just a few months ago, in fact."

Bearing a tray laden with teapot, cups, saucers, a sugar-pot, cream pitcher, and chocolate biscuits, Winston appeared in the doorway. Once he determined it was safe to enter, he did so, setting the tray on the low table in front of the settee.

"Sugar and milk, miss?" Winston asked as he poured her tea. He half expected the visitor to take over the tea service, but she made no move to do so.

"Just the sugar," she replied with a curt nod. Her gaze continued to dart about the room as if she were taking inventory of the place. "You really must tell me who your decorator is," she commented as she accepted the cup and saucer from the butler.

Todd bit his lip. "I'm afraid I cannot, Miss Hughes. I bought the house in this state and have no idea who did the design," he admitted, surprised she took so much notice. "My only contribution has been these chairs," he added as he indicated the tall, high-backed chairs next to the settee. The legs and backs of the chairs were much higher than normal, and they allowed him to sit comfortably. Their damask fabric had been carefully chosen to match the fabrics already in the room, though, so they didn't appear as later additions to the decor.

"A shame," Charlotte replied as she helped herself to a biscuit. "A girl such as myself is always looking for a good decorator."

His eyebrows raised, Todd asked, "Have you recently purchased a home, Miss Hughes?"

The woman eyed her host with surprise. "Not at all. It is just that when I do accept an offer of marriage, I'm sure I will have to have my husband's house redone to suit me," she said matter-of-factly.

"Oh, of course," Todd replied, wondering if she already made up her mind about him. "Tell me, do you attend school?" he asked, deciding to change the subject.

Charlotte's eyebrows shot up. "Not for several... a couple of years now," she stammered. At four-and-twenty, she wasn't yet on the shelf, but if she didn't land a husband soon, she might be considered a spinster by some. "I completed finishing school, of course," she said, "and I continue to practice elocution and piano." Bored with the direction of the conversation, she changed the subject. "When my brother asked if I would have tea with you, he didn't say why it was you wished to meet me, Mr. Vandermeer." There was the slightest widening of her eyes followed by a couple of quick bats of her eyelashes.

Todd sat up straighter in the chair, at least as much as he could given the reluctance of his breeches to follow suit. "Well, I was hoping we could meet and engage in lively intercourse," he answered, hoping she had enough education to participate in an intelligent discussion.

Having seen Todd's hips move about as he made the comment, Charlotte Hughes' mouth dropped open and she suddenly stood up, her pink feather fan closing in a quick twist of her wrist. "How *dare* you?" she huffed as her eyes turned to daggers. "Filthy man!" she spat out as she nearly ran from the parlor, leaving Todd struggling as he tried to get up from his chair.

"But...," he started to say when he realized the front door had already opened and slammed shut. Glancing out the window, he watched as Charlotte Hughes hurried down the stairs and climbed into a small chaise. The driver, surprised at her sudden appearance, hastened to get into the driver's seat before the startled horse could pull away without him.

"Oh, dear, Mr. Vandermeer," Winston said from the parlor door. "Whatever did you do?" he asked with a sigh, his eyes rolling heavenward.

His mouth open and closing like a fish, Todd simply shook his head. "I... I said I was hoping we could meet and engage in lively intercourse, is how I put it, I believe," he said with a shrug, obviously perplexed by the woman's sudden departure.

"Perhaps you should have said 'social intercourse'," Winston offered. "Or, better yet, you may want to avoid the term 'inter-course' completely. At least until you are wed," he added wryly.

Todd scrubbed his face with his hands as he realized his mistake. "She was rather lovely, too," he said quietly. "And as much as I wanted them, I may never wear these breeches again."

CHAPTER 7
A MIDWIFE MODELS FOR A PAINTER

February 17, 1802, London
A fortnight after his last appearance, Dr. Talbot returned to the Home for Unwed Mothers and brought with him a short, round man who bore a pencil-thin mustache above swollen lips. Following the doctor into the lobby, the man surveyed the scene, his eyes flitting about as he took in the sight of several pregnant women.

"None of these will work, *monsieur*," he said in a thick French accent, annoyance coloring his speech.

Dr. Talbot paused in mid-step. "Of course not. We seek the girl named Deborah White," he explained as much to his companion as to one of the girls who looked interested enough to give him Deborah's whereabouts.

"She's in the dining room," the girl said as she looked up from a tattered book. "Through that hall and to the left," she added as she motioned down a nearby corridor.

Dr. Talbot nodded his thanks and led the Frenchman to the mess hall.

Deborah White sat at a long table in the back of the empty room, her head propped up with one arm as she stared into space. "Miss Deborah," he said as he bowed in greeting.

Startled from her reverie, Deborah stood up from the table and executed a clumsy curtsy, her knees not allowing more. "Dr. Talbot," she replied, her expression one of surprise.

The Frenchman gasped and hurried to stand in front of Deborah. He then walked around her as if he were seeing a ghost. "She is perfect," he announced happily, reaching out to grab Deborah's hand. He kissed the back of it before she had time to react and pull her hand away, cringing as she did so.

"Miss Deborah, allow me to introduce you to Jean Claude Perot," the doctor stated formerly. "Monsieur Perot is an artist from France. He would like you to pose for him for a painting he has been commissioned to create," he explained. "He will pay you for your services, of course," he continued, noting the girl's less than cordial response to the odd Frenchman. "Enough to buy a pair of shoes," he added when she didn't seem to change her expression.

Deborah regarded the artist for a moment and then returned her attention to Dr. Talbot. "Pose?" she repeated, her brows furrowing.

"Ah! You are perfect. Your skin is so beautiful. So fine. Like a doll," Perot was saying as he circled his subject. "Allow me to see your hair," he ordered, motioning for her to undo the tight bun atop her head.

Reluctantly, Deborah reached up and pulled out the two pins that held the tightly wound hair in place.

"Your arm... your shoulder... *oui!* You are what I have been searching for, *mon cherié*," the artist exclaimed as he watched Deborah take down her hair. "You will pose for me, no?" he said as his head bobbed enthusiastically.

Giving Dr. Talbot an uncertain glance, Deborah turned her attention to the Frenchman. "*Oui,*" she replied quietly. "I will pose for you," she said, sighing in resignation.

*M*odeling for Jean Claude Perot turned out to be a rather dull and boring experience. His sole expectation of Deborah was that, while wearing only a sleeveless gown, she lean against a whitewashed wall in a particular pose with her head turned just so, one arm bent slightly at her side, and the other pressed against the wall. And for several hours over the next few days, Deborah White did as she was instructed, unaware that the French client for whom the artist was doing the painting had requested a nude woman.

At the end of her work, Perot promptly gave her a modeling fee of three pounds—an enormous sum when compared to her earnings at the Home.

When Deborah stole a peek at the painting, she visibly swallowed as her face blushed pink. "But... I wore a *gown*," she whispered when she finally had Perot's attention. The likeness of the woman in the painting was definitely her, but the body, slightly more voluptuous with fuller breasts and a slightly rounded belly, was definitely not.

"Ah, but I have an *imagination*," Perot replied, tapping his bald head with the end of a paintbrush. "And, I promise, *mon cherié*, no one in England will see this painting," he added, noting her sudden distress. He pulled out another coin and pressed it into her hand. "Go buy yourself some shoes."

And so Deborah took her leave of Jean Claude Perot and promptly used the modeling fee to purchase a proper pair of shoes. As a reminder she should never pose for a painter again, she kept the extra sovereign with her meager savings.

CHAPTER 8
A GENTLEMAN ARRANGES A
TRIP TO LONDON

February 22, 1802, Cherrywood in Derbyshire

Gregory Grandby looked up from reading *The Times* when he noticed his butler stood expectantly on the threshold of the library. "Yes, Foster?" he asked as he dropped the newspaper to his lap.

Bored with the week-old business information in the paper, he welcomed the interruption. He had been at Cherrywood far longer than usual, conducting his business by post and courier, and the time it took for replies to arrive made the process tedious. For a man who traveled extensively and was rarely in the same place for more than a month, Gregory was growing restless.

"Pardon me, sir. A post just arrived for you," the butler replied as he came forth with the white folded paper.

Gregory reached for the missive and grinned when he recognized the feminine script. "Thank you, Foster," he said with a satisfied grin. "Could you get me a cup of coffee, please? I think I will skip tea today," he said as he broke the wax seal embossed with the cursive 'CW'.

"Right away, sir," Foster replied before leaving the library. The large room, which featured a twenty-foot high coffered cherry ceiling, smelled of leather and tobacco. Clad in amber-colored paneling, matching moldings, and deep red carpets and drapes, it was decidedly masculine.

Gregory found he was spending more time in the library since the furnishings had been updated with leather chairs and brocade-upholstered sofas in golds and greens. During the winter months, a fire was always lit in the massive stone fireplace on the north wall. Even now, late in the afternoon, occasional pops and crackles emanated from the only source of heat in the room.

Gregory gave the painting above the fireplace a quick glance and smiled. The odd portrait of his mother, painted before she had given birth to him, had caused him great embarrassment when he was a young teenager. Now he found it winsome and a reminder of what he could look forward to seeing everyday when he finally took a wife.

He often wondered what his mother had been thinking to pose for such a painting. One day, he would have to ask her.

Perhaps it was a reminder to his late father that he need not take a mistress. Lady Sophia Burroughs Grandby was a beautiful woman, and the provocative pose displayed her in a manner that left very little to the imagination.

Gregory had never heard her voice regret at having had the painting done. Her current husband, who worshiped her in a way that his real father would never have done, certainly seemed to appreciate the painting when he was in residence. "I've a mind to steal it away from you," his stepfather had warned one afternoon on their latest visit. "But since I've the privilege of seeing her every day, I suppose I shall allow you to keep it."

Finally opening the letter, Gregory grinned at the salutation and sat up straighter when a lock of strawberry blonde hair spilled out onto his desk. He continued to grin as he read the letter. He was in the middle of reading it a second time when his butler returned with the coffee and a tray of Dutch biscuits.

"Good news, sir?" Foster inquired as he set down the tray and positioned it on a low table for his master.

"Indeed," Gregory replied, giving his manservant a sideways glance. "It looks as if I'll be taking that trip to London in a fortnight, Foster," he said, the grin still very much in evidence. "I'll need the coach and a driver. And I'll need to send letters to Mr. Vandermeer and Sir William in tomorrow's post."

The butler bowed. "I'll see to the coach, Mr. Grandby. Will you require more than five sheets of parchment for your letters, sir?"

"Two will be enough," he replied cautiously. "Have I already used all the rest?" he asked. Apparently, he had written so many letters, he had used the entire supply of stationery he had purchased on his last trip to London in December.

The butler nodded. "Indeed, sir. Shall I order more?"

The younger man shook his head. "I will buy some in town when I'm there," he said as he stood to his full six-foot, one-inch height. "And I'll see if I can't get into Schweitzer and Davidson for a new tail coat and buckskin pantaloons," he added, annoyed at not having visited the tailors during his last trip to London.

He took his coffee and the lock of hair to the elegant ebony desk in the corner of the library. The butler used a long match to light the lamp on the corner of the desk and removed the cork from the ink bottle. A rather expensive metal nib pen was already on the desktop.

"You could use a new beaver, as well, Mr. Grandby. I understand they're getting taller every year," the butler suggested.

"I think a seven-inch tall hat is quite high enough for me," Gregory countered. "But another quality hat would be good for the rainy season," he reasoned, thinking his list of errands to do in town would be quite long before the day was out. "I'll plan a trip to Fitzsimmons' shop."

"Will there be anything else, sir?" the butler asked as he did one last survey of the desktop.

"No, thank you, Foster." Gregory set aside the lock of hair, stroking it absently for a moment. Taking a deep breath, he set to writing the first letter to Todd Vandermeer, making sure to keep his cursive clean and neat. He knew the importer sometimes had a hard time reading long hand, but Gregory didn't have the patience for printing his letters.

Having spent the last year reviewing his business dealings, bank accounts, and housing situation in an effort to determine what to do next in his life, Gregory had come to an impasse. When he had turned one-and-twenty, his inheritance made him one of the richest men in England. The investments made on his behalf prior to his coming-of-age allowed him a generous allowance of five thousand pounds a year. Since then, his savvy business dealings had earned him another twenty-thousand pounds.

Now six-and-twenty, he lived in the Burroughs family country house in Derbyshire. Although any family member was welcome to use it at any time, Gregory had adopted it as his home. Since he had to travel so frequently, he arranged to be absent when other family members were in residence.

His frequent travels, though, had become a curse and a blessing to his reputation.

As a bachelor with funds to spend, he would frequently wine and dine businessmen and their consorts or mistresses, leaving most to suspect he kept several mistresses of his own. He found the mistaken impression helpful on more than one occasion. Extremely lucrative business opportunities would present themselves when his guests were gastronomically satisfied and drunk. He would simply take advantage of the information he gleaned from such meetings and excuse himself, claiming there was someone at his hotel who needed his attentions. The assumptions made about him were almost always wrong, but they served his purposes.

By the time he was five-and-twenty, even he was telling the gentlemen at Boodles, "My needs are few. A girl in every port, and port after dinner." If anyone had bothered to notice, he rarely traveled to port cities, nor did he ever order port after dinner.

At the ripe age of twenty-six, though, Gregory discovered he was in love. Not the lust-love of having met a new young woman who turned his head because she was pretty and long of limb. Indeed not, since the subject of his ardor was a full foot shorter than he. Nor was his love sudden or unexpected. This was a love borne from years of friendship and familiarity with a girl he had known since her birth.

Over the years of Christmases and summer holidays and occasional visits to London, he had watched Christiana Wellingham mature from an impetuous, spoiled child to a more mature, caring woman. Knowing a girl her entire life and then suddenly seeing her in a whole new light gave him pause.

When had she grown up? When had the playful teasing turned into flirting? Was it wrong if a chaste kiss on her cheek was followed by a kiss on her lips?

Will I be allowed to make her my wife?

Gregory understood why those in love tended to keep their feelings a secret from those around them, especially family members. Those same family members tended to be the ones who would most object to their union. He feared that would be the case in this situation.

His attention returned to the letter he held in his hand.

She loves me, he thought wistfully as he fingered the lock of hair. He wanted desperately to hold her in his arms, to provide protection for her, and to give her anything she wanted. And he could, given his vast fortune. *Soon.*

When he felt his loins stir, he shook himself out of his reverie and tried to concentrate on the remainder of his letter to Todd Vandermeer.

I Humbly request your Hospitality whilst in London and wonder if I may Impose upon your House?

He paused in his writing and smiled, thinking that if he didn't inform Vandermeer he was planning to take advantage of his hospitality, it was doubtful his host would even know he was in his house.

The man's mansion was that large.

Although the Cherrywood estate was large and included enough sleeping rooms for most of a village, it was in the country. Vandermeer's house was in town and boasted many amenities that could be found only in the most modern of homes.

Deciding he was merely jealous of his friend's situation, Gregory returned his attention to the letter.

I should arrive on the Nineteenth of March and plan to spend Three Weeks as I have Business and Banking issues with which to dispatch. I look forward to your most Favourable Reply and remain yours in service,
   G. Grandby.

Leaning back in his chair, he remembered a comment Vandermeer had made in his latest letter. He took up the pen again and wrote,

P.S. Have you found a Woman to call your Wife? I should think a man of your Means would have a bevy of Beautiful Women from which to choose. I expect to receive a Wedding Invitation in short order.

Folding the letter, Gregory wondered if the postscript would be offensive to his friend. Todd Vandermeer was well-to-do, but what he possessed in wealth and home, he lacked in social graces. Although the man had traveled to India twice, his friend had no formal education and no exposure to the life of a gentleman prior to his position with the John Company.

Should the man actually find a woman agreeable to marriage, would she be true to him? Or merely a fortune hunter intent on spending his earned wealth on jewelry and gowns and carriages? This was this very fear that led Gregory to believe his own choice in a woman was a good one. He was sure Christiana had no inclinations to spend his money on frivolity and expensive gowns.

Sighing loudly, Gregory folded the letter and sealed it with wax. Sitting back in the desk chair, he drank his coffee and considered other business matters, all the while holding the lock of hair between his fingers.

His letter to Sir William could wait until later.

CHAPTER 9
MAKING A CAKE OF
MAKING DINNER

ebruary 24, 1802, Glasshouse Street, London
"And just what is going on here?" a harsh voice called out from behind a group of young women crowded into the kitchen of Gamma House.

Six girls turned in unison to find Mrs. Streater on the kitchen door's threshold with her hands on her hips and a most displeased expression on her face. They curtsied in unison and all looked to Emma Fitzsimmons to answer the headmistress.

"I'm so glad you've come, Mrs. Streater," Emma said with as much enthusiasm as she could muster, wiping her hands on the apron she had found in the pantry. She stepped forward and gave a curtsy. "Miss Younger took ill when she returned from market today. Indeed, I believe she has been ill for several days, but she fainted after her errands. We moved her to her room and sent for a doctor," she explained.

Emma had known that the residents of Gamma House would receive a visit from the headmistress of Warwick's Grammar and Finishing School at some point during the evening, but she had rather hoped the woman wouldn't appear until after dinner was served. Now her attempt at preparing the evening meal was quite obvious to the stern woman.

Mrs. Streater's harsh glare softened, and she dropped her arms to her side. "Then I must find another cook at once," she declared and started to turn away. "If Lady Pettigrew finds out, I will surely have to resign. This just cannot be happening. We cannot have you girls missing a meal. You'll *starve!*" she said.

The headmistress didn't actually believe this to be the case, but it was important for her to show as much concern for her charges as possible. These were the daughters of some of England's wealthiest families, after all. "And, oh, my," she clutched her chest with her hand as she remembered why she had even come to Gamma House in the first place. "I'm truly vexed. You have a *guest* coming for dinner tonight!"

The other girls gasped in unison, and Emma turned to glare at them.

"Since it may be too late to have you arrange a replacement cook, I have taken the liberty of preparing dinner," Emma said as she motioned to the roast and potatoes on the counter. "They have all been kind enough to help," she said as she motioned to the five girls who stood with her, their gowns dusted with flour and all manner of foodstuffs from their attempt to help. "I expect we will have dinner at eight as usual. And there will certainly be enough to feed all of us and our guest," she added with a nod toward several whole fruits still on the counter waiting to be sliced into some sort of concoction.

The headmistress eyed her suspiciously and then noticed the trussed beef roast and peeled potatoes. "You can cook, Miss Emma?" Mrs. Streater asked, her eyes turning to slits.

Emma nodded and stepped to the headmistress. "I used to watch our cook when I should have been practicing piano-forté," she whispered, acting as guilty as she could under the circumstances. Her claim was a lie, of course, but Mrs. Streater didn't need to know that her family rarely employed a cook.

Mrs. Streater's eyes widened. For a moment, Emma thought she had made a mistake by taking the older woman into her confidence. But the headmistress smiled and whispered back, "It is good for any girl to know how to prepare a meal. You just never know when your cook will take ill."

Emma nodded and turned to glance back at the girls. "And we shall not say a word of this to Lady Pettigrew," she said in a louder voice. "There is no need for her to find out our cook took ill," she added, hoping the girls would understand that, should Lady Pettigrew discover anything amiss at the boarding school, they would probably all suffer some sort of fallout from the busybody's gossip.

Mrs. Streater straightened as she saw the girls shake their heads and murmur in agreement. "Very good, then. Carry on," she ordered. With that, the headmistress turned and headed down the corridor.

Emma closed her eyes and sighed in relief, her deep breath turning to a gasp when she remembered Mrs. Streater had said something about a guest. "Mrs. Streater," Emma called out. "Whom shall we expect for dinner?"

The headmistress whirled in the vestibule as she continued her exit. "Why, Miss Wellingham's brother, Mr. Wellingham, of course," she replied as if they should have all guessed the identity their dinner guest. Before anyone could respond, she was out the front door.

Emma whirled around to stare at Christiana. The expression on the younger girl's face told her all she needed to know—until Mrs. Streater's announcement, Christiana had no idea her brother was expected for dinner.

"He didn't send me a post," Christiana whispered in her defense as Emma returned to the stove and placed the roasting pan into the oven.

Emma moved aside as a wave of hot air escaped. "Perhaps he is just in town on business and wishes to see you," Emma considered, realizing there would be no way for her to avoid finally meeting the man in person. It wasn't as if she had been deliberately avoiding her roommate's brother. There just hadn't been an opportunity for her to be present when he was there to see his sister.

"Perhaps, but his business is almost always in town," Christiana countered. "It has been four weeks since I last saw him, though," she added, her brow furrowing. And then she remembered it was Wednesday night, the night of the week she had told him Emma would be in residence.

Emma surveyed the kitchen. "Ladies, we have much work to do," she announced as she returned to the counter. "We are going to prepare the most delicious meal Mr. Wellingham has ever eaten."

A round of giggles filled the room as they returned to their meal preparation, most using the unfamiliar utensils for the first time in their lives.

At seven o'clock, Emma removed the roast from the oven and pierced it with a long fork. The juices were still red, but the potatoes were nearly tender, and the carrots were bubbling away in their molasses and sugar glaze. Dinner rolls were rising under a tea towel and wouldn't have to go into the oven for some time.

The apple tart, a project that required the help of no less than five of them, was just going into the oven. With luck, it would be done by eight-thirty. A bottle of cream and two bottles of claret were just outside the back door. A cup of fresh butter had been placed on the dining table, and a tomato-based soup made with cream and seasoned with basil was beginning to simmer. The fruits could be cut up and sprinkled with lemon juice just before dinner was served.

"Our serving maid still hasn't arrived, but the table is set and the candles are lit," Christiana announced as she returned to the kitchen. "What should I do next?"

Emma stirred the soup and offered a spoonful in Christiana's direction. "Taste this," she ordered, "and tell me what it needs."

Gingerly, Christiana sipped the liquid and carefully swallowed. Her eyes widened but she didn't cough or otherwise seem displeased. "It tastes very good," she said finally. "Really, it does," she added when she noted Emma's look of disbelief.

"Then go change into a dinner gown Your brother will be here shortly, and we surely don't want him to see us dressed like this." She had already sent the other residents of Gamma House to change into their dinner gowns. She hoped they would see to removing the flour from their faces. At least their manner had been most happy, as if making a meal were a novelty.

Emma attempted to clean up the spilled flour and potato and carrot peelings. She didn't want the new cook seeing their mess when she finally arrived.

When Emma turned to find Christiana back in the kitchen, she stopped her work. "Oh my, what is it?" she asked, noticing the distress on the younger girl's face.

Tears pricked the corners of Christiana's eyes, and the young girl's shoulders shook. "The doctor just said Miss Younger is dead."

Emma caught her breath and covered her mouth with a hand. "Oh, dear. Does everyone else know?" she asked, her voice betraying fear.

The younger girl shook her head. "He just spoke with me in the dining room. I think I was the only one he could find to tell."

Taking a deep breath, Emma turned off the heat under the soup and hurried to the dining room. The doctor, already in the vestibule, was donning his cloak.

"Doctor," she called out as she hurried to confront him. "What's to be done about... about the *body*," she asked in a lowered voice.

The doctor paused in the doorway and picked up his bag. "I will send the mortician, but it may be after his dinner before he comes for her. Good evening." With that, he took his leave.

Emma and Christiana stood opened-mouthed. "Oh, dear," Emma breathed as the door opened again. The serving maid, Fletcher, entered and removed her coat, surprised to find the two girls staring at her.

"Am I so very glad to see you," Emma said as she hurried to the maid's side.

"What is it, Miss Emma?" Fletcher asked as she stepped back, noticing the dirty apron and disheveled hair of the two roommates.

"We need your help this evening, if you would be so kind?" Emma replied as she took the maid's arm and led her to the dining room. "Miss Younger died today." She didn't allow the maid even a moment to react, but continued, "The coroner will come for her body sometime this evening, but in the meantime, we have a guest coming for dinner at any moment."

She proceeded to tell the servant about the dinner they had prepared and when items would be ready or need to go into the oven. "Now, I really must be changing for dinner. Do you have any questions?" she asked, making her voice sound as neutral as possible.

Fletcher simply stared at Emma. "If Miss Younger died, then who made the dinner?" she asked quietly.

Christiana started to answer, but Emma held up a hand to silence her. "When you see the state of the kitchen, you will know," she answered in an apologetic tone.

Fletcher was left open-mouthed as the two hurried off to their room to change gowns.

CHAPTER 10
A GENTLEMAN ATTENDS
DINNER AT WARWICK'S

"*Y*ou will be sure to introduce your brother to all of us, won't you?" Emma encouraged as she and Christiana entered their bedchamber.

"Of course," Christiana replied. "I will introduce you first since you are the oldest in the house, and then I will introduce him to everyone else as they enter the parlor. But, you realize, of course, he has already *made* everyone else's acquaintance," she added as she frowned at her roommate. "You are the only one in Gamma House he has not yet met."

Emma sighed as she cleaned her face with a linen. "I have always been in class," she replied in her own defense. She glanced at Christiana's reflection in the looking glass. "It's not as if I have been avoiding him," she added when she caught Christiana's attention.

Not exactly, anyway.

What would a proper gentleman think should he find out she had no intention of hiring a companion when she was finished with school and had no close relatives with whom to live?

Christiana pulled her dinner gown over her head. Although it had an empire waist and square neckline, the gown was slimmer through the torso than most empire gowns. She turned so Emma could do the buttons. "I want you to like him," she said. "He is very handsome. He has a business that is doing very well, and we have a beautiful house in the country."

Staring at her roommate's reflection in her looking glass, Emma regarded Christiana with alarm. There may have been nearly four years' difference in their ages, but there was sometimes a generation of difference in their maturity levels. "I have every intention of *liking* him," Emma replied with a smirk, wincing when she realized she might not like him. "He is your brother, after all."

How was one to know?

The night he had guest lectured her class still left her unsettled. Although she expected him to be pompous and self-absorbed, he was quite interesting and not the least bit condescending toward the class. Even when asked questions at the end, he was gracious and answered them despite frequent glances at his pocket watch. And she had hung on his every word. According to Sir William, she owned stock in his company, and she was determined to learn as much about his import business as possible during his talk.

Then there was the odd reaction she had experienced deep inside when she was sure he was staring at her. "And, I already know he has a pleasant appearance," she added, remembering Christiana's arguments.

The sound of a knock at the front door had the two giving a start. "Should I be the one to let him in?" Christiana asked as she checked her strawberry blonde hair in Emma's looking glass. "Elly is playing dresser for the other girls," she added when Emma's eyebrow shot up at her question. Usually the housekeeper answered the door in the evenings.

"Anna-Marie will show him to the parlor. Are you sure you are ready to be seen?" Emma asked as she motioned for Christiana to turn around. "Do you have a necklace or brooch you could wear?"

Christiana completed her turn and hurried to her dressing table. "Yes, I have several here," she said as she pulled out a long chain of tiny gold loops and pulled it over her head. "Thomas always brings me gifts when he comes to visit," she added with a smile. Although the comment could have been construed as a boast, it was more of a statement about her brother's thoughtfulness.

Emma took one last look at her roommate and nodded. "Be off with you," she ordered as she pulled her own dinner gown over her head. "I will join you shortly." She smoothed out the pale yellow batiste skirts and added a ribbon at the empire waist. Threading tiny gold earrings through her pierced ears, she put on her gloves and took one last look in the mirror.

Fairly sure there was no longer any flour in her hair, she removed all the pins, brushed it out, and twisted and pinned it up in the quickest chignon she could manage. The ringlets she'd ironed into the hair at her temples that morning were wilted, but they would have to do. There wasn't enough time to heat the iron.

Before heading to the parlor, Emma consulted with Anna-Marie about dinner. Rolls were in the oven, the meat was ready to slice, and, with one quick reminder about the cream for the apple pie and the wine, Emma took her leave of the kitchen.

With a great deal of trepidation, she finally arrived at the parlor to find her roommate and Mr. Wellingham having an animated discussion about the upcoming Season.

She smiled as she watched Christiana interact with her brother. Despite the difference in their ages, the two were obviously comfortable with one another. Even in the relaxed atmosphere of the parlor, Emma could sense his protective nature. Their parents long deceased, Thomas and Christiana only had each other. Thomas seemed to take his role of older brother and guardian very seriously.

The strange fluttering sensation filled Emma's belly even before Thomas Wellingham's attention was fully on her. Instinctively, she placed a hand on her abdomen as if to settle the flutterbies and then nervously used the motion to smooth the skirts of her gown.

When Christiana was aware of her presence, she jumped up, nearly bouncing as she told her brother that she wished to finally introduce him to her roommate. "Miss Emma Fitzsimmons, please allow me to introduce you to my brother, Mr. Thomas Wellingham," she stated confidently. Thomas stood quickly, apparently surprised by Emma's appearance.

Emma couldn't help but smile at Christiana's enthusiasm as she curtsied and then entered the room. "It is so very good to finally meet you, Mr. Wellingham," Emma commented as she held out her right hand. "I have heard so much about you."

At first glance, she found the man more handsome than she remembered him from class. The lighting in the parlor was far kinder to the planes of his face, and his rich brown eyes made him seem warmer and more approachable. The wavy brown hair was trimmed short but not plastered to his head as some men were wont to do given the latest styles.

. . .

homas bowed and regarded Emma with a tentative smile. "And I of you," he replied as he took her gloved hand and raised it to his lips. *She was the one,* he thought with some excitement as he remembered seeing, very briefly, a young woman amongst the male students in his friend's class. She wasn't as old as he had first thought, but then the parlor lighting was far kinder than the gas lamps had been that night.

"My sister was just telling me about the untimely death of your cook and everything you had to do to prepare dinner," he said as he studied the tall woman. He thought her pretty—not just handsome as he had first thought— and the way in which her honey blonde hair reflected the light from the fireplace made her glow.

He was sure Todd Vandermeer would find her very suitable.

Emma's face reddened. She secretly wished she had asked Christiana to keep quiet about what had happened that afternoon. "I can assure you, sir, none of us will have our homework finished this day," she said as she took a seat in the rose damask settee.

"I didn't realize Warwick's required homework," Thomas replied, attempting to determine Emma's age. From the way she carried herself, she could be twenty or even older.

"There is always English and grammar homework," Christiana countered as she took a seat and motioned for her brother to sit in an adjacent chair. "But not every day. Miss Emma always has much more homework because she has her accounting class in the evenings."

Curious, Thomas turned his attention to Emma. "What made you decide to take a course in accounting?"

"I'm hoping to gain employment as an accomptant when I'm finished here at Warwick's," Emma replied. She wanted to ask if he knew of someone who needed a bookkeeper. The men in her class would have no trouble landing positions straight out of the respected class. As the only woman, she would have a harder time without strong references. "May I say, Mr. Wellingham, I very much enjoyed your guest lecture last month. I only wish there had been more time for you to describe your company's transportation methods and what it is you do there."

Thomas sat up straighter, surprised she would bring up the lecture and more surprised at being asked about his work. "Indeed. I own and run the company," he acknowledged. "We have a warehouse on the west end of town. Very near the river. We also have several offices in port towns around England. Although we specialize in shipments by sea, I have been working to increase our overland transport options." He paused for a moment when he noticed Christiana's expression. "Oh, I... I apologize, I must be boring you," he said as he nodded his head in his sister's direction.

"Oh, not at all," Emma replied quickly. "Do you own your own ships, or do you hire ships on consignment?" It hadn't been her intention to display her décolletage in the process of leaning forward, but she noticed Mr. Wellingham's glance at her bosom before he quickly returned his gaze to her face. Color reddened his face at the same moment she felt own face bloom with color.

Before Thomas had a chance to answer, several female voices sounded form the corridor as the dinner bell chimed. Breathing a sigh of relief at the interruption, Thomas was sure Emma had noticed his wandering gaze and realized he hadn't paid attention to her question. *Something about ships,* he thought absently. *Vandermeer will certainly think her comely.*

Reluctantly, Emma stood up and nodded at Thomas while Christiana took her brother's arm. "Perhaps we can continue this conversation later," Thomas suggested as they left for the dining room.

"That would be lovely," Emma replied, stifling a sigh of disappointment.

*C*hristiana's brother was most charming and, if the odd interruption provided by the mortician had upset him in any way, he was certainly good at hiding his reaction from the girls of Gamma House.

"May I have a word with you before I depart, Miss Emma?" Thomas asked as he pushed away from the mahogany dining table.

Remembering his earlier comment about continuing their conversation, Emma smiled and replied, "Of course, Mr. Wellingham. Shall we go to the parlor?"

Some of the other girls departed for their bedchambers while a couple of them remained at the dining table to continue their conversations over tea.

Emma preceded Thomas into the parlor. He waited until she had taken a seat and then sat in the chair opposite her. Leaning forward, he began in a very quiet voice, "I must compliment you again on your cooking skills and assure you that, if my cook were to ever take ill, I should certainly want for your services in his stead." He paused a moment as if in thought. "In fact, he wouldn't even need to take ill..."

Surprised by the topic of his conversation, Emma blinked. "Why, it is very kind of you to say so, sir. But I must also apologize to you for what happened during dinner. To have the mortician arrive was most unfortunate."

Thomas suppressed a smile. For the girls of Gamma House, this day had certainly been an adventure of sorts, and yet, the superb dinner and company of no less than six women for dinner had left him in good spirits. "I rather thought it made the evening that much more interesting," he replied, and found he had to chuckle. He sat back in the chair. "I say, the look on that man's face."

No longer suppressing her own embarrassment, Emma nodded in agreement. "I'd invite you to join us for breakfast, but I'm not sure Mrs. Streater will have found us a cook by then, and I rather doubt I could have the girls up soon enough to dress and help in the preparations."

Thomas held out a hand and shook his head. "Thank you for considering it, but I will take breakfast near the club where I am spending the night," he explained quickly. "In the meantime though, I wanted to give you my heartfelt thanks for looking after my sister."

Emma sat up straighter. "Oh, I assure you, no thanks are necessary, Mr. Wellingham. Miss Christiana is a joy to be with, and she is a very good student. And quite an accomplished player."

Thomas angled his head as he recalled his sister playing cards with his best friend. He tried to squelch the bit of rising panic he felt. "Playing... what, exactly?" he asked finally, his brows furrowing as a frown took over his features.

"Why, piano-forté, of course," Emma replied, surprised by his reaction. "She is very good. She practices at least an hour a day, and she has the uncanny knack for being able to play a piece without looking at the music after she has played it through only once with the sheet music. I believe she has been spending most of her pin money at Birchall's," she added, referring to the music seller in New Bond Street.

Thomas was not averse to showing his surprise, and he did so by sitting up straight and allowing a look of shock to cross his face. "I had no idea." After a moment, he added, "I will see to it there is a piano-forté in the music room when she comes home for the summer." He stood up. "Miss Emma, thank you again for a wonderful meal."

Emma curtsied to his bow and led him to the vestibule, where Christiana was there to see him off. "Come visit again soon," his sister said as she angled her cheek so that he could give her a kiss. "I miss you."

"And you," Thomas replied, donning his hat and great coat. With that, their dinner guest was gone.

After shutting the door, Christiana turned to Emma. "That was rather odd," she said with a frown, her back leaning against the door.

"Whatever do you mean?" Emma asked as she locked the door and made sure the gas light on the outside of the house was still lit.

"He didn't give me a gift," Christiana replied. "He almost always brings me *something*." Shrugging her shoulders, she headed up the stairs to their bedchamber.

Emma followed so she could retrieve her homework. "Perhaps he simply forgot to give it to you," she offered in the man's defense, although there had been no outline of a box in the fabric of the man's dinner attire. "With all that happened this evening, it would have been easy for him to do so."

Christiana shrugged. "Did you like him?" she asked as she removed her necklace and earrings and placed them in her velvet-lined jewelry box, her face once again bright.

"Very much," Emma replied, her expression as neutral as she could make it. Inside, she was berating herself at having allowed Mr. Wellingham to take his leave before she'd had a chance to bring up the topic of one Mr. Ambrose Smith.

A month ago, she had stood in front of her late father's hat shop and watched as two men hoisted a new shingle above the door. *Fitzsimmons and Smith*, it read in stylish lettering. The smaller shingle it replaced had read simply, *Fitzsimmons*, and had hung in the same location for over twenty years.

The front window of the shop now displayed an array of artfully arranged hats on carved wooden heads.

At one time, a series of black and white vertical stripes, about two feet tall, had been painted on the inside of the window, an indication of the shop's appeal to the male persuasion. Now, a few pink stripes could be found amongst the black and white, and there was a white background against which the black beavers stood out in sharp contrast.

The entire display was eye-catching and, Emma had to admit, elegant. To compete with the other shops in the fashionable West End, though, it had to be. Every shop in Oxford Street had appealing window displays no matter the time of day. Given the late hours kept by the well-to-do and members of the peerage, some of the most lucrative purchases were made just prior to the ten o'clock store closings.

Ambrose Smith, the partner George Fitzsimmons had acquired when he knew he was too sick to continue working, had come from inside the shop to stand with Emma in the bleak January cold.

"Good morning, Miss Emma," he had greeted her as he bowed. Dressed impeccably, with striped trousers and a waistcoat to match, a navy topcoat, a walking cane, and a hat, Emma was sure Ambrose was too young to own a shop such as this without some kind of financial backing from a wealthy relative. Although business was good, Emma doubted he could make enough of a living to support a wife and two children and make the payments on the business. But his payments for the shop had been prompt and for the full amount every month since her father's death. In only six more months, he would own the shop free and clear.

Emma curtsied and smiled as she absently twirled her parasol. "Good morning, Mr. Smith. I must admit, I am surprised to see my father's name still on your shop," she said as she indicated the shingle. The sign in the window had been changed the day before to add the 'Smith' name.

"'Fitzsimmons' is the name that discerning gentlemen remember," Ambrose replied as he removed his hat and pointed at the label inside. "It has cachet. It was very kind of you to allow me to continue using it," he added as he returned the top hat to his head. The man, in his mid-twenties, stood nearly as tall as Emma and sported a trimmed mustache and long sideburns.

Emma nodded and replied, "Of course. And I want to thank you for your payment last week," she said as she took the arm he offered. "You have been most prompt every month. As I am still in school and not yet employed, I cannot tell you how good it is to be able to count on the money you send." Although Emma had used part of her inheritance to invest in Wellingham Imports, she didn't yet know how well the investment would pay, and she didn't want to depend on any income from it.

"You are most welcome. I have come to discover that exporting is the key to a successful business," he remarked in an off-hand manner.

Furrowing her brow, Emma asked, "What's this you said?"

Ambrose leaned in closer. "I started exporting hats to the Continent about two years ago," he explained quietly, his eyes bright with excitement. "They sell very well, even in France, so I had to add two more employees to help me make enough to fill all the orders. I could make even more if I could just acquire enough beaver skins and wool, but that's for another day, I suppose." He paused a moment and took a deep breath. "I am hoping to work out a royalty agreement with you so I may continue to use your father's name in the hat labels."

Stunned, Emma could think of nothing to say. Although her father had built a good business with a loyal following in London and the surrounding area, this young man had taken the business to another level. "I am sure we could reach a fair royalty agreement," Emma finally said.

She could certainly use the money. Her inheritance had covered the tuition and board at Warwick's Grammar and Finishing School and the cost of the accounting class. She was using the funds from the sale of his business to pay the rest of her way in life. With no marriage prospects and the need to take an apartment in May when she finished at Warwick's, money would be tight until she found a position.

"Allow me to work out some numbers and make a proposal to you, say with next month's payment?" Ambrose offered. He glanced toward the store before returning his attention to her. "If you would join me in the shop, I have a gift for you."

"A gift?" Emma repeated. She was about to decline the offer out of a sense of propriety—Ambrose Smith was a married man, after all —but the twinkle in his eye suggested he was not about to bestow her with an improper gift.

Ambrose nodded and opened the door for her. The newly hung shingle was now in place overhead, its fresh paint bright despite the clouds. "We started a line of women's bonnets and hats," he announced proudly. "My wife, Penelope—she's a milliner—has been helping with the designs and construction."

Emma closed her parasol and walked into the store. It was brighter and seemed larger than when her father had run it by himself for so many years. The displays of hats were creative—some stacked on neat shelves while others hung on curved hooks—while small looking glasses hung at various heights on all the black, white, and pink-striped walls. "This is very elegant, Mr. Smith," she gushed as she took in all the changes. "My father would be so proud of you."

The hat maker beamed as he led her to a wall of women's hats and bonnets. "This is for you," he said as he took down a bright white poke bonnet made of eyelet and decorated with a broad velvet ribbon.

Emma carefully took the bonnet from Ambrose's hands and studied it inside and out, admiring the workmanship. In the inside at the back of the bonnet, a white label reading, 'Fitzsimmons for Women' caught her eye.

"This is beautiful," Emma said as she continued to study the bonnet. "And it is very well constructed."

Ambrose nodded excitedly. "We just started selling them this week. That is why I asked you to stop by if you could. My wife was very anxious to learn if you would approve."

Emma took off her winter hat and placed the bonnet on her head. Seeing her reflection in a nearby mirror, she smiled. "Tell her she has done a remarkable job," Emma breathed as she adjusted the ribbons. "I love that the front is not so large. Bonnets can be far too deep in the front sometimes," she commented as she studied her reflection. "I will tell all the girls at Warwick's about these," she promised, knowing the daughters of London's wealthiest would want new bonnets for the spring.

"I would be in your debt," Ambrose started to say as Emma allowed a grin. "I mean, I would *continue* to be in your debt," he corrected with a matching grin. After a pause, he added in a quiet voice, "I nearly forgot to mention it, but a gentleman made an inquiry about you last week."

Intrigued, Emma arched an eyebrow. "Indeed? Did he... give his name?" She felt her heart skip a beat.

Ambrose frowned as he said, "It was Samuel Morton." The manner in which he said the name proved he had little regard for the man or his intentions.

Rolling her eyes, Emma could feel her cheeks flush with embarrassment. "Oh." It wasn't the first time the married man had asked about her. His inquiries would no doubt affect her reputation as a genteel woman if they were allowed to continue.

Noting her discomfort, the hat maker leaned forward. "Although he has been a customer for a very long time, I told Mr. Morton that you would never consider his overtures…" Ambrose stopped in mid-sentence and caught his breath as he realized the impertinence of his comment. "Please, accept my apology."

But Emma gave him a knowing smile in an effort to put him at ease. "Thank you, Mr. Smith," she said with a sigh. "You hardly need to apologize for having defended my virtue. Perhaps now Mr. Morton will no longer ask about me in polite company." After a pause, she added, "It is odd that such a meek man would be so obvious in his pursuit of a mistress in polite company, don't you think?"

Mr. Smith's eyebrows popped up and then he frowned, not quite sure how to respond. "I should think Mr. Morton would be dead by the hands of Mrs. Morton should she ever find out he is even *thinking* about taking a mistress. And I believe Mr. Morton knows as much," he added, his expression suggesting he was amused by the thought.

Replacing the eyelet bonnet with her winter hat, Emma whispered, "To think, I could cause the death of a man through no action on my part!"

Understanding her comment was made in jest, Ambrose Smith grinned. "Indeed."

Satisfied the issue with Mr. Morton was safely dispatched, Emma took her leave of the hat shop and hurried back to the boarding school. Giving the eyelet bonnet an occasional glance, she was anxious to tell the other girls about 'Fitzsimmons for Women'.

Exports, she thought as she walked along the cobblestone streets of the West End. *Perhaps purchasing stock in an import company wasn't the best investment, after all.*

*E*mma shook herself back to the present. A few minutes more with Mr. Wellingham, and she would have been able to talk with him about Mr. Smith's need for more raw materials. Perhaps the importer knew of overseas sources, or perhaps he could arrange some shipments for the hat shop.

She was still frowning when she noticed Christiana's attention on her. "What is it?" Emma asked, her eyes widening at seeing her roommate's scrutiny.

"I might ask the same of you," the younger girl teased. "You looked as if you were a million miles away."

Emma blushed but shook her head to hide her embarrassment. "I was... in Oxford Street," she whispered, not wanting to lie. Changing the subject, she asked, "Now, would you like me to help you with your hair for tomorrow?" Elly was no doubt helping another resident with her hair, and there was no telling when or if the older servant would have time to see to Christiana.

Christiana's eyes lit up. "Oh, I'd like that very much," the younger girl replied as she sat at her dressing table and handed Emma her hair brush and comb. Given the amount of time it took to work on her roommate's hair, it would be another half-hour before Emma could begin her homework.

CHAPTER 11
ADVICE

February 24, 1802, Boodles, London

Thomas Wellingham lowered himself into a tufted leather chair and studied the swirling brandy in the rummer he held up to the candlelight. The clear amber liquid would make a perfect ending to the delicious dinner he had just enjoyed at Warwick's Grammar and Finishing School.

Taking a quick glance around the room before sitting back in the chair, he noticed the fire burning low in the grand fireplace. With his arrival, a butler hurried to place a log on the dying embers.

"Thank you, Jackson," Thomas said as he lifted the rummer to take a drink.

"Good night, sir," the butler replied as he left the room.

The club room stank of cheroot smoke and liquor, but most of the men had retired or left for the night. A group of four stalwarts were huddled over a card table in the back corner, their conversation becoming more audible as the room emptied.

Replaying the events of the evening, Thomas smiled as he considered how his younger sister was developing into an accomplished and interesting young lady. Emma Fitzsimmons could certainly be credited with assisting Christiana in that regard, he thought.

The woman was most perplexing, though. Given the standing and cost of the school, only wealthy girls could afford the tuition, room, and board. But Miss Emma Fitzsimmons' behavior was more in line with that of a woman of modest income and a middle class upbringing.

She didn't give off the haughty, superior air so many of the wealthy girls displayed in public settings. Indeed, she seemed most uncomfortable when the other girls flaunted their family names and social standing during their dinner conversation, and she seemed perfectly mortified when the second eldest at the table announced she was going to elope with someone other than to whom a marriage had been arranged unless said man came forth with a proper proposal post-haste.

Yes, she would make a fine wife for Vandermeer, he thought as he took a sip of his brandy.

"I don't understand how you can pine for that chit," one of the card players said in disgust when they were between hands.

Thomas sat up straighter, startled by the comment. He realized almost immediately it wasn't meant for his ears.

"She broke the contract, Mr. Smithson," another player added as he shuffled the playing cards.

Thomas recognized at least two of the gentlemen at the table but decided to remain in his chair and enjoy his brandy. Curious as to what the gentlemen were discussing, he listened intently, not the least bit embarrassed he was eavesdropping.

"She didn't break the contract, Harry," Smithson was saying, his voice betraying his defensiveness and perhaps a hint of sadness. "She simply didn't renew it. And I miss her terribly," he added.

One of the other players huffed. "She didn't renew it because her friends negotiated a better deal for her with that bastard Trent Nelson," the man spat out.

That would be Col. Fitzwilliam, Thomas thought as he recognized the voice of one of the players.

"His friends went too far, I say. The man agreed to buy Liza a townhouse in the West End, pay for a private modiste, and pay her two-thousand pounds a year for her exclusive services," he explained in anger. "Now, I know you are a man of some means, Mr. Smithson, but there is simply no way we could have countered that offer with anything better on your behalf," he added in a softer voice. The other gentlemen around the table nodded their heads and murmured in agreement.

Thomas rolled his eyes as he realized the topic of the conversation—a mistress. Apparently Mr. Smithson's mistress, who the man had come to love over his year with her, had been dealt to a higher bidder.

The contracts for the services of a mistress were rarely worked out directly between the two parties but rather involved the best friends of the man negotiating with the best friends of the mistress. If a suitable arrangement could be worked out, usually involving a provided apartment or townhouse and some amount of pin money, the parties would agree and an arrangement to meet would be worked out.

The rest was up to the man and his mistress.

I cannot imagine having to pay the cost of an apartment and pin money toward keeping a woman—in addition to the costs of keeping a wife and family, Thomas thought when he remembered that Smithson was married and had a brood at his estate home north of London.

"I gave up on the idea of a mistress when I met that hat shop girl years ago," one of the other men was saying.

That would be Samuel Morton, Thomas thought. Although he was rich beyond his ability to handle it, the man would be far too timid to have a mistress.

Besides, it was doubtful his wife would allow such an arrangement.

"I wanted her to be my mistress. I still do, actually. I once asked if I could call on her, but she declined," Morton said sadly. "She was polite about it, though. And so very pretty," he added wistfully.

"That is because she knew you to be *married,*" Smithson countered with a hint of anger in his voice. "Besides, a genteel girl would never agree to become a *mistress,*" he continued before stuffing his mouth with the last bit of his cheroot.

"Now, now, gentlemen," Fitzwilliam interjected. "Back to the cards, shall we?" he said with a hint of annoyance. "I must be home by midnight or you will be arranging a mistress on my behalf, for my wife will not allow me entry into my own home," he added as he dealt cards around the table. The conversation returned to the game at hand, and Thomas returned his attention to his brandy.

"Why, Thomas Wellingham, what a surprise to find you here this evening," a low, booming voice broke into his reverie. As Thomas started to get up to acknowledge Sir William F. Burroughs, the man pushed down on his shoulder. "Please, do not get up on my account. You look positively relaxed, as you should be," the heavyset balding man said. He took the tufted chair next to Thomas and lifted his brandy rummer in the younger man's direction. "Cheers," he offered with a smile.

"Cheers, Sir William. Are you spending the night here, too?" Thomas asked the investment banker. Despite his having a mansion in London proper, Sir William seemed to be at the club nearly every night of the week. Although a man of his position and wealth could afford a mistress, the banker remained steadfastly faithful to his ailing wife.

"No, no, I just came for a drink," Sir William replied, settling into the chair as he tugged on his waistcoat. "I had a very good day today. And you?"

Thomas smiled and set his rummer on the occasional table that separated them. "I can say the same for myself," he replied with a nod. "Business is going very well, and I have just returned from a wonderful dinner with my sister."

Sir William raised his bushy eyebrows. "Over at Warwick's?" he asked politely. "With all those wealthy young women?" he added playfully, his one hand swirling his brandy as he regarded Thomas.

Embarrassed at the man's comment, Thomas admitted, "Indeed. I have been there on several occasions, of course, but this was the first time I had occasion to meet my sister's roommate."

Sir William grinned and set down his rummer. "And that would be Miss Emma Fitzsimmons, no doubt," he stated proudly. "Smart girl. One of my clients, she is."

His curiosity piqued, Thomas sat up straighter in his chair. "Really? A woman of some fortune, I suspect?" he queried without trying to seem too interested. Vandermeer had said he didn't want to marry a rich girl, but Miss Emma seem to lack, *what had Vandermeer called it?*

Hubris, he had said.

"Not at all," the banker replied matter-of-factly. He took a cigar out of one waistcoat pocket and expertly snipped the end off of it with a knife.

Not necessarily surprised by the comment, Thomas listened more intently.

"However, her father was an occasional investor," Sir William said, regarding the cigar with a critical eye. "George Fitzsimmons was a good enough businessman in his own right, but his failing health and death a few years ago meant only a modest inheritance for the girl. He was wise enough to make arrangements on her behalf, and she was wise enough not to squander it away," he explained with an appreciative nod. "Four years ago, she came to me for advise and counsel.

"She knew she had to finish her education. She was the accomptant of her father's business for many years, you see, so she attends Mr. Stoke's course in addition to Warwick's— top of her class, according to Stokes—and she wanted to pay for an apartment when she completed Warwick's in the spring. And despite the fact that she's... a *female*, she figured she could find employment if a marriage wasn't arranged by then," he continued with a hint of amusement. He retrieved his brandy from the table. "We invested her inheritance and saw to it there would be enough to cover her expenses. So far, it's all worked out to plan." He inhaled the scent of the cigar as he drew it across his nose.

Thomas took a sip from his brandy. "My sister could certainly do worse for a roommate," he answered as he put the rummer back down. "So... has a marriage been arranged for Miss Emma?"

The banker lit the cigar and regarded the businessman with an arched brow. "Not that I'm aware," he replied as he scratched the side of his eye with a chubby finger. "But I'm sure when she has completed school, she would consider offers."

Thomas could tell Sir William was eyeing him and then decided the comment was a hint. He was about to say he wasn't in the market for a wife when the banker's next words took him by surprise.

"She has a good deal of her funds in your business, you know."

Thomas tried to control his surprise. "Indeed? I had no idea," he responded. His attempt at seeming uninterested failed.

Why hadn't Emma mentioned it earlier?

Perhaps that was why she had been so interested in learning more about the business.

"You recommend my company for investment then?" Thomas asked, changing the direction of the conversation. His company's stock was privately held, and he wondered if his company would ever draw the notice of the stockbrokers of the London Stock Exchange. Until their building was complete later that year, they were meeting at Jonathan's Coffeehouse to make capital market transactions. Their main focus was to set up joint stock companies to raise the capital necessary for canals, railroads, and other utilities. Given the direction of their investments, Thomas knew it was unlikely his small company's stock would ever be exchanged publicly.

"Of course, Mr. Wellingham. Why you've built that business into a far more profitable venture than your father could have ever done. As a banker, I appreciate how you have created your wealth from nearly nothing—not like these other pompous idiots," Sir William said as he waved his arm in the direction of the four card players who had inherited their fortunes. "And because you built it, you're not likely to squander it like these idiots, either."

Stifling a grin at the banker's assessment of the nearby card players, Thomas took another sip of brandy. "I appreciate your faith in me, Sir William. And I thank you for your confidence." He paused a moment, remembering his recent conversation with his warehouse manager. "May I inquire, sir, about how you might handle a business related situation? I ask you in confidence, and hope you would not change your good opinion of my company given the question I'm about to ask."

The banker regarded him closely as he glanced around the room, wary of eavesdroppers. "Of course. Ask away."

Thomas took a deep breath. "I have yet no proof, but I believe someone on my clerking staff is embezzling funds from the company."

Sir William sat up as straight as his belly would allow. "Do you know who? And to what degree this embezzlement is occurring?" he whispered, once again glancing about the room.

Shaking his head, Thomas at first regretted having brought up the subject. Perhaps he was a fool to enlist advice from his banker, but he knew no one else to ask about the suspicions he had been harboring for the past month. Thomas explained, "Again, I have no proof, I only have a suspicion. And we are talking about one or ten pounds every two weeks or so."

The elder man furrowed his brow. "Then how did you come to be suspicious?" he queried. "With your balance sheet, that could easily be an error in addition or subtraction."

Thomas nodded in agreement. "Or it could be an intentional error. I fear that as my profits grow with the next shipping season, those one and ten pounds will become one hundred or perhaps one thousand pounds."

The banker regarded Thomas for a moment. "Say nothing, but keep a close eye on the ledger. At least you know how to read one. If you still suspect something in the spring, hire an auditor. There will be several new accomptants available in May when Mr. Stoke's class is complete." He paused a moment to take a short drag on the cigar. "Including Miss Emma, in fact," he added as he angled his head. A cloud of smoke filled the air between them.

Eyebrows raised, Thomas started to respond, but Sir William continued with a raised forefinger. "Do not let anyone else in the company know you have hired an auditor, and do not allow the auditor to work in the company offices. Have them work... at your house, or... rent an office on the other side of town for them. Tell no one what you suspect.

"Then, every week, take the auditor all the books from, say, two months ago, or better yet, to when you believe the crime to have started. It may take some time, but if embezzlement is taking place, the auditor will find it."

Nodding, Thomas considered the advice. "And how do we determine who it is?" he asked quietly.

"The auditor will see whose hand the errors are done in. The clerks usually initial or sign each page, so I should think you will be able to determine the name of the guilty party from that."

Satisfied he had made his point, the banker sat back in his chair. "Do let me know how it all comes out, won't you?" he said, an eyebrow arching suggestively. "I do love a bit of scandal now and then."

Thomas smiled in spite of himself. "You will be the only one I tell," he replied, not wanting anyone else to know such information.

Finishing his brandy, he wished the banker a good-night and took his leave of the club.

CHAPTER 12
AND AN OFFER

*E*mma combed out a section of Christiana's hair, rolled it onto her finger, slid the curl off of her knuckle, and then tied it together with a strip of fabric. The rest of the hair on Christiana's head had already been tied up in fabric strips, and now she looked like an overwrapped present at Christmas. "There," Emma said as she handed Christiana a looking glass. "You should be all set for tomorrow."

"Thank you, Emma," Christiana replied, all smiles. "Now, as long as it doesn't snow or rain, I should have curls."

Emma glanced at the timepiece and shuddered. She had at least an hour of accounting homework yet to do and it was already ten-thirty. "You get to sleep. I will be down in the dining room. I must complete my homework," she said as she gathered some books, a pen and an ink pot, and ledger paper from her desk. "Good night," she said as she left the room.

Several candles were still lit in the dining room along with those in the overhead chandelier. She took a glance into the kitchen and found Anna-Marie finishing the dishes. The room was immaculate. "You are to be commended," Emma breathed as the mess they had created earlier that evening was all but erased. "Thank you for your help tonight," she said to the maid.

Anna-Marie curtsied. "Of course, Miss Emma. I will be leaving for Delta House when I'm done here. Do you need anything before I go?"

"Thank you, the leftover tea will be fine," Emma replied. Not really wanting to drink tea, she helped herself to the last of the claret and settled at the table to start her assignments.

When she was nearly finished, Emma was startled by the sound of the knocker on the front door. She walked quickly to a window to look out, thinking perhaps Anna-Marie had returned. A coach was parked out front, and a well-dressed man was at the door. She opened it to find Mr. Wellingham, top hat in hand, looking very apologetic.

"Good evening, Mr. Wellingham," Emma said quietly as she stepped aside. "Do come in out of the cold." She took his hat as he entered and placed it on the hall tree.

"I apologize for the lateness of the hour. I know this is wholly inappropriate," he said in greeting, keeping his voice low.

"Not at all. I'm still doing homework," Emma replied with a wan smile, glad to know someone else was still awake. She noticed the faint odor of cigar smoke and brandy and decided he must have been at a men's club. "Your driver is welcome to come in. It must be freezing out there."

Startled by her suggestion, Thomas stepped back. "How very kind of you," he commented, an eyebrow raised. He opened the door, leaned out so his voice wouldn't be heard in the house, and called out to the driver, "Mr. Allen, come in from the cold." In a moment, the lanky man entered the vestibule, obviously chilled to the bone.

"Please, have a seat in the parlor, sir," Emma said as she motioned to the room off the vestibule. "I will get you a cup of tea." She hoped the stove would still be hot enough to make tea.

"Much obliged, miss," Mr. Allen said with a nod, rubbing his hands together and bowing.

She turned to Thomas and said, "If you'll excuse me, I'll go up and wake Miss Wellingham."

Thomas shook his head. "No. I do have something I intended to give to her earlier this evening, but I was actually hoping to speak with you."

About to lead the men to the parlor, Emma paused and allowed her surprise to show.

"The dining room would be fine, Miss Emma," he said as he headed in that direction. "I would prefer to talk in private," he added, nodding at Mr. Allen.

Emma changed her direction and cautioned, "Then you must

excuse my books and such." Once she was in the room, she asked, "May I get you a glass of wine or tea or some pie perhaps?" She wasn't sure how to receive a guest directly into the dining room.

"No,... it's tempting, but no," he replied as he waited for Emma to get the tea for Mr. Allen and then take her seat at the table.

He sat down across from her and interlaced his fingers. "I just had an impromptu meeting at Boodles with Sir William Burroughs," he began without preamble. "I understand you are well acquainted with the man."

Emma's eyes widened at the statement. She leaned forward. "Why, yes. I have sought his advice on several occasions," she responded with some hesitance, not quite sure how much to admit. "My accounts are with the Bank of England," she added, as if that might be explanation enough.

"It is possible... probable, rather," Thomas stammered, "That I will require an auditor for my company's books this spring. I need someone who can work at my house or here in town, but it has to be private. No one at my company can know about the audit. I will pay a fair wage, of course, and I expect the employment will last at least three, possibly four months." Truth be told, he had no idea how long such an exercise would take. Sir William hadn't mentioned a timeline, and Thomas hadn't known to ask.

Intrigued, Emma sat up straighter. "And you would like me to recommend someone for the position?" Her immediate thought was to recommend Benjamin Cunningham, a man with whom she attended the accounting class. She knew he would appreciate landing a position prior to graduation. He had a family he was trying to support on a warehouse job that paid very little.

"Not exactly," Thomas replied. "You see, I have already received a recommendation. I was hoping *you* would accept the position," he explained as he leaned forward. "With my sister being home from school, I think it necessary I employ someone who can act as her chaperone if circumstances require it," he added with an arched eyebrow.

Surprised, Emma put her hands together on the table in an effort to still them. She tried her best to suppress a smile. The idea of becoming Christiana's chaperone seemed ludicrous. She was hardly old enough not to require one for herself.

But then she remembered the rest of the comment. He needed an auditor, and she had been recommended. If Sir William, of all people, had mentioned her for a position, perhaps she didn't require other references. But just in case, she tentatively asked, "If I perform the work well and complete the audit in a timely fashion, would you provide me with a character reference?"

"Well, of course," he answered with a nod, somewhat surprised by the request. Apparently, she really was serious about obtaining a position. But if she married Vandermeer, she certainly wouldn't have to work.

He wondered if the broker would tolerate a wife with an occupation.

"Then I accept your offer," Emma replied quickly. She put out her right hand. Thomas leaned over and shook it, surprised by the firm grip. A warming tingle shot up his arm.

"Splendid," he said with a nod. "I will provide more details in May, but in the meantime, if you could see to it Christiana gets this, I would be in your debt," he added as he held out a small black box.

Emma took it from him. Even though she remembered Christiana's comment from earlier that evening, she asked, "Is there a special occasion I may have forgotten?" Despite shops being open until ten o'clock most nights, it was doubtful he had just purchased the gift this evening.

"Oh, not at all," he replied. "I'm just doing my brotherly duty by spoiling her rotten," he said with a sly grin as he pushed away from the table.

Remembering her conversation with Ambrose Smith the month before, Emma held out a staying hand. "Mr. Wellingham?" she said before Thomas could stand up. "If I may, I know it is late, but could I ask a question about your overland transport business?"

An expression of curiosity passed over Thomas' face. "Certainly," he said as he sat back down.

"The gentleman who bought my father's hat shop is having difficulty acquiring enough wool and beaver skins from the northern districts with which to make hats. He has become very successful exporting to the Continent, you see, and although he can find additional sources for wool, he does not have the means to get it here to town," she explained.

"Indeed?" Thomas replied, his raised eyebrow indicating his interest. "We may be able to help. We operate overland transports from several ports, and there is one north-south line from just south of Scotland. That particular coach is not always... fully utilized," he hedged. Raising the other eyebrow, he eyed Emma. "Who did you say this chap was?"

Emma leaned forward. "His name is Ambrose Smith. Of *Fitzsimmons and Smith*, in Oxford Street."

Thomas grinned as he recognized the name and remembered the comment made by Sir William earlier that evening. "So George Fitzsimmons was your father?" he half-asked as he rested his arms on the table and leaned forward.

Nodding, Emma smiled. "Yes. Did you know him?"

"Well, I didn't know him beyond being a customer, but I have certainly purchased enough hats from that shop over the years," Thomas replied. "'Tis not too terribly far from my warehouse," he added as he reminisced for a moment. "What was it he called that one hat?" he asked as he tried to remember the slogan for his favorite model.

"The hat that makes the gentleman?" Emma offered, recalling her father's advertising slogan for one of his most popular styles.

"That's it," Thomas replied with a grin as he pointed a finger in the air. "'Tis my favorite hat," he added. He paused for a moment when he suddenly recalled a comment he had heard earlier in the evening. *What had Samuel Morton said about a hat shop girl?* "*I gave up on the idea of a mistress when I met that hat shop girl years ago...*"

Thomas angled his head as he regarded Emma Fitzsimmons and wondered if she were the one who had declined Morton's impertinent offer to be his mistress. *What an ass,* Thomas thought as he recalled the man's comment at the gaming table. Emma Fitzsimmons was obviously a genteel woman. And she was certainly comely, he noted once again, with her expertly coiffed blond hair looking almost amber in the dimly lit dining room.

He noted the way she placed her hands on the table, so her long, slender fingers barely touched the surface. Perhaps some men would find her height intimidating where Thomas found it perfectly suited to the way she carried herself—as if she were the mistress of Gamma House rather than one of its residents. It stood to reason that one day she would be mistress of her own house. *Vandermeer's house,* he thought. Once she was married to him, of course.

If she hadn't already had her come-out, perhaps she would this Season, he thought as his gaze lingered. Despite her attendance at a finishing school that boasted a few daughters of the aristocracy, was it likely she would receive an offer of marriage from a member of the *ton?* As the daughter of George Fitzsimmons, could she expect to win the hand of a baron's son or a young viscount? Especially when her dowry was probably being drained just to pay the tuition at Warwick's?

Probably not, he reasoned. *All the more likely she would make a good match for Vandermeer.*

When Thomas realized he had paused too long in responding, he recovered his composure and smiled. "I will contact Mr. Smith tomorrow and see what we might be able to work out on his behalf," he promised.

"That is very kind of you," Emma replied as she stood up, realizing Mr. Wellingham was dismissing her and intended to leave.

"If this business pans out, I may be in *your* debt," Thomas stated as he headed for the vestibule. "Mr. Allen," he called out quietly. "I am ready." He turned to address Emma. "Thank you, Miss Emma. And, thank you again for a lovely dinner."

He donned his hat as Emma opened the door for him and his driver. "Thank you, Mr. Wellingham. You cannot know how much the auditing position means to me."

She curtsied as the two gentlemen bowed and took their leave.

*W*hat had Thomas Wellingham been thinking as he watched her so intently a few moments earlier? She had been left unnerved by his gaze, sure he was studying her hands.

Holding them to the lamp light, Emma took a moment to study them, assuring herself she had managed to clean off the ink stains that frequently darkened the tips of her fingers on both hands. Indeed, they were clean.

Lowering her gaze to her cleavage, Emma was afraid her lack of a fichu might have exposed more of her bosom than was appropriate. But, no, her square neckline was high enough not to reveal the tops of her breasts. So, why had he stared at her? Had he been undressing her in his mind's eye?

An odd sensation passed through her body, leaving a pool of heat deep within her. Her hand moved to her belly as she inhaled sharply. Surprised by the sensation and even more embarrassed by her carnal thoughts, Emma shook her head and took a deep breath. Certainly Mr. Wellingham was merely contemplating options for Mr. Smith, she considered.

And he's to be my employer! she thought happily.

Returning to the dining room, she carefully lifted the black box Mr. Wellingham had left for Christiana. Opening it, she stared at an emerald pendant on a gold chain, the square cut gem sparkling with the nearby lamp light. Shaking her head in disbelief, Emma closed the box and smiled to herself. *Spoiling her rotten, indeed,* she thought.

Emma fingered the short stack of papers that made up her homework and looked them over. Given she already had a position lined up, she decided she could, just this once, not finish her homework assignment. Instead, she gathered up her papers and went up to bed.

CHAPTER 13
CHARITY BEGINS AT THE HOME

ebruary 27, 1802, Newport Street

As she had every Saturday at nine o'clock in the morning for the past two semesters, Emma Fitzsimmons reported to Mrs. Dawes at the Home for Unwed Mothers to perform her work for charity. Warwick's Grammar and Finishing School required all their students to choose a charity and spend at least three hours a week doing whatever tasks were deemed reasonable by the person in charge. The school's headmistress, Mrs. Streater, found it difficult to fill the opening at the Home since most of her students refused to associate with harlots and pregnant girls. Prostitutes, after all, were the lowest of the classes of London, and there were other, more visible and socially acceptable charities with which her students could be associated.

Emma found the stout and jovial Mrs. Dawes in the front waiting room. She was speaking with a very frightened looking girl of no more than twelve who stood with a satchel and blanket draped over her arm. The bump pressing against the front of the girl's gown told Emma the girl was at least five months along. The lack of a ring on her left hand also indicated the girl was unmarried.

"Ah, there you are," Mrs. Dawes said as she noticed Emma waiting. "Come 'ere and help this wee one, will you?" she asked as she motioned to the girl. "There's a room upstairs at the end of the 'all that just opened yesterday. Could you take 'er thar and get 'er situated?" The sound of a wailing baby startled even Mrs. Dawes as she glanced down one corridor. "Miss White 'as just delivered another one, it seems," she said as she hurried to provide assistance.

"Of course, Mrs. Dawes," Emma replied with a curtsy. She knew she wouldn't receive the same courtesy from the midwife. Mrs. Dawes had long ago explained there just wasn't time to practice the finer points of civilized society when running a facility such as this one.

Emma hoped there had not been any complications with the baby Deborah White had just delivered. She counted Deborah as one of her few close friends and knew the midwife would take it hard should the baby have difficulty.

Emma turned and smiled at the girl. 'Wee' was certainly an appropriate term to describe the poor waif. She was shorter than even Christiana and was slight of body. Her hair was not even pinned up and hung past the middle of her back.

"I am Miss Emma. May I help you carry something?" Emma asked as she stepped forward. The girl, obviously not one to easily trust, pulled away and said, "No, thank you, miss."

Angling her head, Emma said, "I apologize. I didn't hear your name."

The girl's eyes were downcast. "Mary," she said simply.

"It's very nice to meet you, Miss Mary," Emma said as she motioned for the girl to follow her up the stairs and to the room at the end of the corridor. It hadn't yet been cleaned, but its previous tenants, a young mother and newborn, had not been there long. The malnourished mother died a few hours after childbirth, and the premature baby had not lasted much longer. Emma straightened the bedding on the small cot and repositioned the one chair in the room. Motioning to the hooks on the wall, Emma said, "You can hang up your satchel there, if you would like," she suggested. The small bundle wasn't large enough to hold much. "I see you've brought your own blanket. It does get chilly in here some nights."

The girl unwrapped her satchel and pulled out a brown lawn gown and a nightgown and hung them on the hooks. Other than the blanket, there wasn't a pelisse or mantle or a warm wrap of any kind. "Mrs. Dawes said breakfast would be served soon," Mary said in a small voice.

Realizing Mary had settled in as much as she was going to, Emma replied, "Yes. I'll take you down to the dining hall." She led the way down the hall to the stairs. "How did you find out about our facility?" Emma asked, trying to strike up a conversation with the girl.

"My father brought me," she replied as she held a hand over her belly. "He said I was bringing shame on the house. He said I could go to the country to live with my aunt or come here."

Emma pulled out a chair in the dining room for Mary and offered it to her. "I'd have thought spending time in the country would be good," she said, surprised Mary would choose the Home. The accommodations were sparse, the meals were limited in both quality and nourishment, and there wasn't enough coal to keep the place adequately heated in the winter.

"My aunt doesn't like me," Mary replied, her eyes finally making contact with Emma's. The dour expression on the girl's face told more than her simple words. For her to choose the Home over living with a relative suggested she really believed life would be better at the Home. Emma could only hope that would be the case.

Nodding, Emma said, "All right. Well, there are some rules here at the Home," she started to say, but paused until she was sure she had the young girl's full attention, "You must be in for dinner at six, and there is no going out after dinner. You must help in the kitchen for a few meals each week—"

"Cooking?" Mary interrupted, showing a hint of excitement, the only emotion she had shown since arriving.

"Yes, or going to market or washing dishes... whatever skills you might have in that regard," Emma explained. "Supper is at one, breakfast is usually about now," she said as she glanced around and noticed more girls with their babies and toddlers coming into the room. "You will have an opportunity to meet other mothers and their children whilst you are here," she added as she indicated the growing line.

"How long may I stay?" Mary asked when she realized none of the children seemed older than two.

Emma sighed. "That depends on our patrons. As long as there are contributions and there is space, you can stay until your baby is two or three. If the money runs out, you will be forced to marry or seek employment and find another place to live," Emma explained carefully. She didn't add that if Mary's child was given up for adoption or put into an orphanage, Mary would need to seek housing elsewhere almost immediately.

Emma noticed one of the kitchen workers motioning to everyone. "You can go up for breakfast now," she told the girl. "They serve it over there by the kitchen."

Mary thanked her and joined the line of other young girls and their children waiting for food.

Deborah White, looking as if she had been up all night, limped into the room and smiled when she saw Emma. "Miss Emma!" she said as she hurried to hug her friend. "It is so good to see you. I'm always amazed at how quickly the week goes by," she said as she took a seat across from Emma and stretched her long legs out under the table, reveling in the sensation of finally be off of them.

"Except for the fact that you look like you've been up all night, and the fact that you are limping, I would say you are looking well, Miss Deborah," Emma said in a teasing voice. "Really, how are you?" she asked as she placed a hand over one of Deborah's. At one time, Deborah's hands, with their long, slender fingers and perfectly manicured nails, had been the envy of others. Now, they were dry and reeked of alcohol.

"Except for my knees, I am well, really," she answered with a wan smile. "It's been a horrible week for babies though. We lost three out of the five deliveries. One was stillborn," she said. "The mother didn't arrive until the day before her labor, and she was so weak from not having eaten. I just need to be off my feet for a few hours," she added.

At six feet tall in stocking feet, Deborah was the only girl Emma knew who was taller than she was. With her brunette hair, which was now mostly out of its bun, and her pale porcelain skin, Deborah could also turn heads—if she could afford a decent gown and good night's rest. "I was very well yesterday," she added, her smile broadening to show off her straight teeth. "A patron came through with a huge contribution. Mrs. Dawes says we have enough money to operate two months or more with what he gave," she said with a grin.

Emma smiled. "And who was the patron this time?" she asked, knowing that sometimes the money came in anonymously and sometimes the patron delivered it in person or by courier. If the Home was ever in dire need, Emma knew the parish would help, but so far, Mrs. Dawes had been able to raise funds to keep the Home open without having to ask for much money from the Ministry of the Poor.

"Mrs. Dawes said it was her dear Mr. Vandermeer," Deborah said with a teasing smile. "It is amazing that a man she delivered twenty-five years ago would continue to support her cause," she commented, referring to the Home.

The older midwife often spoke of her 'dear Mr. Vandermeer' as if the gentleman were her own son, or, as Emma originally assumed, her lover. Emma was surprised when Deborah explained the man had been an orphan. Her friend claimed to know little of the man's parents or how it was he came to be an orphan, but Emma was sure Mrs. Dawes knew the full story, for the midwife had seen to the care of the boy, arranging for him to stay at hospital, where she was a midwife, until he was weaned. With the help of friends, Mrs. Dawes had him placed in one of the better orphanages, and using contacts she had at the East India Company, she arranged for him to be hired as a caddie, a sort of message boy, when he was old enough. After that, it was up to the boy to determine his own fate.

Given the frequency of his contributions, Deborah decided he must have done well with the John Company.

"So does this mean you were paid?" Emma asked hopefully, knowing a contribution from a patron generally meant some pin money for Deborah.

"Yes!" Deborah said excitedly. "One of these days, I am going to kiss that man!"

Mortified, Emma's eyes widened in surprise. "Shush!" she said, glancing about to be sure no one had heard Deborah's declaration. She couldn't help but smile broadly at her friend's good fortune, though. "Let's go out tonight, then, shall we?" she suggested. "I have good news of my own."

It was Deborah's turn to look shocked. "You are betrothed?" she half-asked, her excitement growing as she watched Emma.

"No!" Emma replied with a firm shake of her head. The taller woman had always teased her about being betrothed.

Although Deborah had given up on the notion of romantic love and marriage for herself, she seemed to enjoy imagining it for her best friend. "So, if not word of a betrothal, then what is your good news?"

"I accepted an offer of employment. I'm going to be an auditor," Emma said in a whisper, just then remembering what Mr. Wellingham had said about keeping the details of her employment a secret. "'Tis only for a few months, but if I do a good job in the position, my employer said he will give me a character reference."

Deborah's excitement waned considerably. "Oh," she said as a frown formed. Slumping in her chair, she caught her lower lip with a tooth. "And when do you start this position?"

Emma's brows furrowed. "In May, when I'm done with class and Warwick's," she replied, wondering why Deborah didn't seem happy for her.

"So, I probably won't see you as often," Deborah said with a sigh, the comment coming out as almost a question.

"Why ever not? I will be done with finishing school and done with accounting class, and I won't have any more dreadful home-work!" she exclaimed with a grin. "Oh, please Deborah, wish me happy," Emma implored as she leaned over the table to place a hand over Deborah's.

Deborah thought for a moment. "All right. I'm happy for you, then. And we really must go to the theatre tonight. But only if I can borrow a gown. And some slippers," she added with a hopeful look.

"Done," Emma replied. "We shall go to the theatre."

Deborah nodded. "We shall, as long as no one goes into labor this afternoon," she added quietly. "But first, let's get breakfast. I'm starving."

With that, the two friends joined the line for porridge and coffee.

CHAPTER 14
A GENTLEMAN CALLS ON
HIS BELOVED

April 9, 1802, Mayfair

On a cool, clear evening, a rather nervous Gregory Grandby instructed his driver to take him to Gamma House at Warwick's Grammar and Finishing School. His host, Todd Vandermeer, was having dinner with associates and would be gone most of the evening. Having sent word ahead that he would call on Christiana for dinner at seven, the man rather hoped she would be ready and that he wouldn't be subjected to a wait in the parlor and the curious glances and questions of the other residents of the house.

He wondered about a chaperone and hoped she had lined up a maid that might attend in the capacity. He had no wish to set tongues wagging should the two of them be seen dining together by town gossips.

As it turned out, Gregory had no cause to be concerned. Christiana Wellingham was the only one in Gamma House at the time of his calling.

Christiana opened the door to find her suitor, the very handsome and tall Gregory Grandby, standing on the stoop with a handful of daffodils and a top hat in hand. "Mr. Grandby, do come in!" she said in happy greeting as she stood on her toes. She wrapped her arms around his chest and hugged him hard, a rather inappropriate way to greet a gentleman caller, she knew, but her enthusiasm couldn't be contained. "It has been far too long," she gushed as she continued to hold him. "How was your trip? Are you well?" she asked, her words nearly lost in the fabric of his waistcoat.

Startled by the sudden physical and most improper contact, Gregory, holding the flowers in one hand and his hat in the other, couldn't return the hug until he at least dispatched the hat. He did so on the hall tree and placed an arm around Christiana's shoulders. "Yes, it has been, my love," he whispered as he bent down to kiss her strawberry blonde hair. It was knotted in an elaborate bun and surrounded by tiny braids and ringlets. "And my trip was swift, and I am quite well." Glancing around nervously, he pulled her away from his body and stole a quick kiss on the lips. "We probably should not be doing this, Miss Wellingham," he whispered, afraid they could be seen by another member of the household. He held out the flowers between them and said, "These are for you."

Christiana's face lit up with a smile, an infectious, sweet smile that displayed her perfect teeth and bright green eyes. Gregory found he couldn't help but smile in return. "Thank you, Gregory. And 'tis all right," Christiana added as she placed a gloved hand along the side of his face. "The servants have left for the night, and I'm the only one home this evening," she explained, taking his hand in hers.

"Indeed?" he replied, still nervous but glad she had used his first name. Having grown up in a house of aristocrats, he found he preferred informality. "So, I suppose this means I shan't be meeting your roommate or your house mates this evening?" he asked, a wave of relief passing over him. Not knowing how far his reputation preceded him, he feared someone in the household might have heard of him and accuse him of improprieties of which he wasn't guilty.

Christiana shook her head. "Not tonight, unless you are still here when they return from the play at San Souci Theatre," she said with a mischievous grin and a raised eyebrow. "The theatre usually does not end until about midnight."

Gregory's eyes opened wider as he took Christiana's meaning. Although she was dressed for dinner in a yellow batiste gown adorned with dark green ribbons, she didn't wear a spencer. With the cap sleeves of her gown pulled down to the tops of her arms, he couldn't help but notice her shoulders were bare. Not yet a fully developed woman, her décolletage was still apparent in the low neckline of the gown. Her collarbones traced the slight curve to the hollow of her throat, where Gregory was sure he could see her pulse. "We can leave for dinner when you are ready..."

"We are having dinner here," Christiana countered as she led him to the dining room. "Or, a picnic, I suppose, would be a more suitable word for it."

There, on the dining room table, was a basket filled with linens, meat and vegetable pasties, fruits, cheese, Dutch biscuits, a bottle of red wine, and two glasses.

Gregory surveyed the selections and nodded his satisfaction. "And just where are we going to have this picnic?" he asked as he sat down in one of the dining room chairs and pulled Christiana into a hug. Her skin smelled of French milled soap and lavender. He gently kissed her earlobe.

"In my room," she answered, whispering seductively in his ear.

Gregory pulled away and regarded his beloved. "When I was attending school here in London, I recall that gentlemen callers were not allowed to visit the rooms of students here at Warwick's," he said, his demeanor rather serious.

"I built a fire, and no one else will know. Please?" she replied, her lower lip protruding into a pout.

Unable to suppress a grin, Gregory finally nodded. "All right, but if your house mates return, you had better hope I can get out of your bedchamber by some means other than the window," he replied, trying to sound cross. He couldn't imagine having to escape from a second-story window, although he was sure other illicit callers had probably done it many times in the past.

Rolling her eyes, Christiana shook her head. "I'm going to put these into a vase," she announced as she picked up the daffodils and removed a cut crystal vase from the china cabinet. She disappeared into the kitchen for a few moments and returned with the flowers. Placing them in the middle of the dining table, she turned to Gregory as he stood up. She wrapped her arms around him again, and he leaned over to hug her.

"Are you well? Truly?" he asked as he lifted her chin with his finger.

"Yes, now that you have come," she replied as she rested her head against his chest and looked up at him. "You have mutton chops!" she said, her voice pitched to emphasize her surprise. "Whenever did you acquire those?"

Gregory placed a hand against the side of his face and remembered his sideburns were a bit longer than they had been at Christmastime. "Do you like them?" he asked as he turned his face first to one side and then the other. "I cannot decide if I should keep them or have my valet shave them off," he admitted as he sighed and finally wrapped both his arms around her shoulders.

"Are you getting enough to eat?" he asked, feeling the bones of her shoulders beneath his hands, the blades sharp under her skin. He ran a hand down her side and pressed it against her body as he did so, feeling her ribs and the top of her hip and around her bottom.

Squirming at the sensations his hands created, Christiana giggled and her eyes widened in shock. "What ever are you doing?" Delightful shivers were coursing through her belly, not unlike those she had experienced when she'd spent time with him at Christmas.

Gregory stood up and frowned as he looked down at her. "Really, Christiana? Are you eating enough?" he asked again, his demeanor very serious.

"Yes!" Christiana answered, a worried expression appearing on her face. "Why ever do you ask?" Although he had always shown concern on her behalf—for as long as she could remember, at least —Gregory hadn't yet proclaimed to be her protector. Perhaps...

Shaking his head, Gregory knelt down on one knee and angled his head to see her in the light from the dining room window. He took her face in his hands and looked into her eyes, one at a time, and then felt the sides of her neck. Pressing gently, he ran his fingers along her jawbone and then placed his hands on her shoulders. Next, he placed his ear to her chest and listened. "Take a deep breath and hold it," he ordered.

Startled, Christiana did as she was told.

"Now let it out slowly through your mouth. Between your teeth," he said as he continued to listen.

The exhaled breath whistled as it passed out of her mouth, and she stood still as he continued to press his ear against her chest.

"Well, your lungs are clear, your color is good, your eyes are clear, and your glands are not swollen," he stated as stood up and put his arm around her shoulder. "Your pulse is a bit fast..."

Christiana grinned demurely. "I expect so after such an improper examination."

Gregory raised his chin. "From a doctor's perspective, it wasn't improper in the least. And, I say, you are in perfect health."

Christiana tilted her head to look up at him. "And when did you become a doctor?" she asked with a grin, realizing he very well could be a doctor. He had never talked much about his work or his education.

"I used to watch my uncle, Harold Merriweather, who really was a physician. He would do that to all the children in the household when I was younger. We would have to line up at his study door every month so he could test us, much like I just did with you. He taught me what to listen for, what to... to touch," he explained as his face flushed red. "I suppose he is why I took an interest in science in school, although I have not used that knowledge in any applied way," he added with a disappointed glance. "Until now, of course," he added as his eyes darkened. *My sweeting*, he thought as he gazed at her upturned face, a face he wished he could gaze upon every morning upon waking.

Christiana lifted the basket in one hand and took Gregory's hand in the other. "You really must tell me more about your work," she said as she led him up the stairs and into the bedchamber she shared with Emma.

Once in the room, she shut the door and locked it. Pointing to a tall chair located between the fireplace and the bench at the end of her bed, she said, "Please, do take off your coat and have a seat. I wish for you to be comfortable."

The tall man nodded and sat down, happy he wouldn't have to sit on the floor as he had expected. The fire warmed the room, but its heat wasn't enough to make sitting close to the hearth uncomfortable. Whilst he removed his cape coat, Christiana set the basket down and pulled out a cloth to spread over the bench. She placed a napkin over his lap and gave him the bottle of wine. The cork, which had already been pulled, was barely in place. He easily jerked it out and poured wine for the two of them, setting the glasses on the bench between them.

"So, if you are not a doctor, then what do you do for an occupation?" Christiana asked. "Or are you in trade?"

Gregory sighed. "I make business deals, I suppose you could say," he said finally. "I invest my money in companies or products or people, and then I collect part of the earnings when they make money."

Christiana stared at him for a moment. "And from where do you get the funds to invest in the companies?" she asked, realizing she really was interested in this aspect of his life. She pulled the pasties out of the basket and gave him one.

"Well, originally, I inherited it," he explained as he eyed her, heartened she showed such interest in his work. "Thank you," he added as he took the pasty.

Christiana angled her head. "From whom? Certainly not Mary Margaret Merriweather," she mused, remembering from her youth that he lived at Merriweather Manor with a number of cousins and other relatives.

At the mention of his grandmother, Gregory frowned and wondered what she knew of the tyrannical matriarch. "My father," he replied simply. "He died when I was... three, I think. And when I was twenty-one, I suddenly had a big bank account I could squander on anything I wanted."

Christiana's eyes widened again. "Indeed? And what did you squander it on?" she asked, mortified by the thought he would do such a thing.

Gregory laughed at that. "Well, now, *squander* is probably not the correct term. I invested some of it and made even more money, and I just keep making more money every year." Gregory took a tentative bite of the pasty, and was surprised by its flavor. "Who made this?" he asked as he indicated the pasty. "'Tis very good."

"Miss Emma helped me make them," Christiana admitted before she took another bite of hers. After she swallowed, she added, "It is our cook's night off, since everyone had to attend tonight's play at the theatre."

A quizzical glance appeared on Gregory's face. "And you are not one of *everyone?*"

Christiana smiled and shrugged. "I won't have theatre arts class until next year. I'm the youngest in the house," she added as she angled her head playfully.

"Were you *invited* to join them, at least?" Gregory inquired as he leaned forward in the chair. He found he couldn't take his eyes off of her, and he realized he was glad they hadn't gone to a public inn for dinner.

Blushing, Christiana nodded. "Of, course. But I feigned illness, and Emma... Miss Emma, took pity on me. That is why we are having this picnic," she explained, and took another bite of her pasty. Changing the subject back to his investing, she asked, "Miss Emma said she invested money in a company. Is it like gambling? When you invest, I mean?" she asked, her demeanor once again very serious.

Impressed by her insight, Gregory nodded. "Indeed, that is a most appropriate way to look at it," he agreed. "Tell me, what is Miss Emma's investment?"

Christiana shook her head. "She said it was with an import company, but she wouldn't tell me the name of it." Her brow furrowed then. "What happens if an investment doesn't work?"

Gregory took a sip of wine and swallowed hard, his mirth at her question apparent. "You lose your money," he answered with a shrug, his hand waving in the air.

Christiana's eyes widened. "Have *you* lost money?" she queried, her consternation increasing.

Gregory shook his head and tried to contain his amusement. "Not yet. In my case, I seem to win nearly every time, so I have not squandered the money away. Not like my second eldest cousin, at least."

Christiana sat up straight at the comment. "You mean Michael?" she inquired, trying to remember just who was the oldest of all the cousins who had lived in the Merriweather estate.

"Yes, the poor bastard," Gregory replied with a frown. "Filthy rich at twenty-one and dirt-poor by twenty-five. Mary Margaret Merriweather Grandby wouldn't have anything to do with him, and she wouldn't allow anyone in the family to help him, either. So he is in debtors' prison, last I heard," he explained.

Staring at Gregory, Christiana swallowed. "How did he squander the money?"

Gregory sighed. "Gambling. The kind with cards and dice," he added quickly when he noticed her quizzical expression. "He was a member at White's," he added, referring to the men's club. "Brandy and women. A huge house in Cavendish Square. He spent it all and even more he didn't have," he said sadly, continuing to shake his head as he considered his cousin's plight.

"Do you ever gamble?" she asked then, "I mean, the kind with cards and dice?" she added quickly, her eyebrows dancing.

Gregory sighed, not sure how much to admit. Of course he gambled, but usually as part of a business negotiation. "I do with your brother and Mr. Vandermeer. But only when the stakes are a few pounds," he added with a smile. He didn't admit to having occasionally participated in bets that took place at men's clubs, and he often wondered if there were any in which he were subject of the bet.

"Do you drink brandy?" Christiana asked between bites of her pasty.

Amused at her line of questioning, he grinned. He supposed if she were to be his wife, he may as well answer her questions. "Not to excess, but two or three times a week, I suppose. Like your brother, I actually prefer a brandy before bedtime," he added with a shrug.

"And women?" she whispered as she leaned in closer. "Do you *really* have a girl in every port?" she asked with a mischievous grin as she studied his face. Although she had never felt envious of the women he might consort with—she knew gentlemen employed mistresses and whores—she felt a sudden pang of jealously at the thought of him in someone else's bed.

Gregory's eyes widened in shock. "No!" He sat up straight in the chair. "Oh, my God," he whispered as he regarded her in surprise. "I swear, Christiana," he said as he turned his body to face her. "I don't have any other women in my life but you. And wherever did you hear that awful phrase about me?" he asked as he stared at her in shock.

Shrugging, Christiana wrung her hands together. "You said it. When you were in the library. With my brother. You used to say it..."

Gregory rolled his eyes and let out a breath. "Oh, damn," he said under his breath. *Little pitchers have big ears*, he considered. Taking a deep breath, he asked, "Have you ever heard anyone *else* describe me using that phrase?"

Christiana considered his question. "No," she replied carefully.

He let out the breath he was holding. "It is possible that over the course of the next year or so, you will hear things about me. And women. But, please, Christiana, you must believe me when I tell you I do not consort with women. Indeed, I have been most chaste since I... since Christmastime," he stuttered as he tried to sort when his elder cousin, Rebecca, had last insisted on bedding him. *A couple of years ago, at least.* He was certain half his male cousins had lost their virginity to the cruel woman. She'd had an insatiable appetite for sexual intercourse and younger men, and she employed a riding crop on those who didn't obey her every command.

"Indeed?" Christiana answered, a small pout appearing on her face. "And you don't keep a mistress?" she inquired, not sure she wanted to hear about her if he did.

"Not even a mistress, my sweeting," he claimed. "I have known for some time ...," he looked to the fire for a moment before continuing, "... I have been waiting for you," he finally said.

He would have admitted feeling lust for her. Especially now, given the way she gazed at him, her clear green eyes suggesting she might be feeling the same way about him. Then she looked away, her attention back on the picnic foods.

Gregory took a deep breath and allowed a small smile. "I cannot tell you how very pleased I was to receive your letter two weeks past," he said as Christiana gave him a slice of cheese and a chunk of bread. "I feared time might have changed the way you felt toward me."

Christiana's eyes widened. "Not in the least. If anything, time has made me... I love you even more," she said as she watched him closely. "And you?" She took a sip of wine and watched him over the rim of the glass.

Gazing at her, Gregory sighed. "No, I'm happy to report. I have felt affection for you for at least a year, and I do believe I shall love you for the rest of my life."

Leaning her head to one side, Christiana's mouth opened in surprise. "A *year?*" she repeated, her face turning a bright shade of pink. She lowered her head and looked at him from beneath her eyelashes. "You... you didn't mention *that* at Christmastime. Or in your letters."

Gregory felt his face flush as he heard her words. In the darkening room, he felt his loins stir as he regarded the girl. Holding up his right hand, he displayed the rather large square-cut ruby on his ring finger. Christiana's lock of strawberry blonde hair was looped around the finger and set around the ruby. "Your hair makes a rather beautiful ring, don't you agree?" he asked as he watched her reaction of surprise.

"It is beautiful," she breathed in reply, swallowing hard. "Do you wear it often?"

Watching her face flush, Gregory grinned. "Every day." After a moment, he leaned in her direction. "Come, sit with me," he said quietly.

Broadening her smile, Christiana stood up from the bench and moved to sit on Gregory's knee. Swinging her legs over his other leg, she leaned against his body as he held her with one arm, his chin resting on the top of her head. "Has your brother talked of arranging a spouse for you?" he asked quietly.

Taken aback by the question, Christiana shook her head against his shoulder. "You know better than anyone his attitude toward arranged marriages, Gregory," she replied. She took an interest in his ear and gently drew her finger around his earlobe. "He has refused to arrange one for me and insists that when I marry, I do so for love."

Gregory looked up from his food and took a deep breath. In a quiet voice, he said, "Since I have professed my love for you, and you have done the same to me, may I request of you to forsake other gentlemen callers?" he asked, finding it hard to concentrate on the topic at hand with her finger tickling his ear.

Nodding her head, Christiana replied, "I shan't accept any gentlemen callers but you," she agreed. Would he propose this very evening? Her heart started to pound in her chest, and she was sure he could feel it.

"Have you told Miss Emma about us?" Gregory asked. He leaned around Christiana and took a cluster of grapes out of the basket. "Or your brother, perhaps?"

Shaking her head, Christiana replied, "No. I have told no one," before she took another sip of wine.

Gregory nodded and was silent for a few moments. He wasn't sure what he would have done had she told her brother. At some point, he would have to discuss the girl's future with his friend. "I want so very much to tell the whole world I'm in love with you," he said in a quiet voice. "It is very difficult to keep you a secret."

Blushing again, Christiana turned her eyes away. When she looked back up at him, she did so from beneath lowered lids. "I share your difficulty sometimes. But it is very exciting to have this secret, don't you agree?"

Gregory didn't reply, nodding instead. "Please understand. I cannot ask for your hand in marriage until I have your brother's permission," he explained as took her hand in his.

Christiana pressed her eyes shut and did her best not to react. On the one hand, she was thrilled to learn he intended to ask her, but on the other, she was annoyed he would require Thomas Wellingham's permission. "I understand," she responded finally, allowing a small smile to appear. "I wish we didn't have to wait to marry, though," Christiana said quietly as she reached into the basket. She gave him an apple and took one for herself.

Still hungry, Gregory took a bite of the apple and chewed while he considered her words. "If Thomas allows me to ask you, he will probably make me wait until you are seventeen," he said thoughtfully. He took another bite and stared into space.

"July fourteenth is just three months from now," Christiana replied. She took a bite of her apple. "I suppose I can wait that long, but I certainly don't wish to," she added as she leaned her head into the small part of his shoulder.

Gregory rubbed his hand along her arm as he held her. "I think I should let you know that, as an only child raised in a house of many, I'd very much like children."

Sitting up straighter on his knee, Christiana turned and smiled at her suitor. "Five or ten?" she countered as she put down her apple.

Eyes widening, Gregory finished his apple and considered her offer. "I was thinking of ten, actually," he admitted as he continued to stroke her arm. "So... you would be willing to give me children then?" he asked quietly. He pulled her against him.

"Of course," she replied with a smile.

Gregory playfully tugged on one of her ringlets as she fed him a grape. Giggling, Christiana pulled away and placed a hand in his hair. As she ruffled the dark locks, he leaned forward and kissed her. It was a quick, chaste kiss, but Christiana took a deep breath and kissed him, gently at first, tasting grapes and wine on his lips, and then harder as he returned the kiss. Her lips, soft and tasting of wine, were playful as they took purchase on his again, and Gregory took the opportunity to kiss her harder.

The hand on her arm slid down to her side, where his thumb caressed the side of her breast. Feeling no corset under her gown, his other hand moved to the front of her breast and felt a nipple poking through the fabrics of her camisole and gown. *What am I doing?* he wondered, the last shred of self-control nearly gone.

Gasping, Christiana broke away from the kiss for just a moment as a wave of pleasure shot through her body. Placing a knee between his thighs and raising herself up on the chair, she pulled down one sleeve of her gown until a small, round breast popped over the top the neckline. The taut pink nipple gracing the orb hovered between them as she offered it to Gregory. He gave her a startled glance before taking the nipple between his lips. He suckled it gently at first, and then took her breast into his mouth, using his tongue to caress it to a ruched bud. Laving the edge of his tongue across the hardened nipple, he groaned as felt his groin tighten.

Her head tilted back, Christiana spasmed as he pulled down the other side of the gown and did the same for the other nipple. When they were hard and red, he continued kissing her chest and shoulders.

"Take me," Christiana whispered as she leaned down and nibbled on his earlobe. "I am yours in love and for life."

Breathing heavily, Gregory considered her words and fought an inner battle. *I cannot! She is but sixteen!* He took a deep breath. *She will be my wife one day. If I ruin her now, she will be mine*, he reasoned. They would be married soon. *But if I take her virtue now and she changes her mind before her birthday, what then?*

"I've never..." He paused to take another deep breath as he tried to maintain control. His cock had been rigid since she'd bared her breasts to him, and now it strained against the front of his breeches. "I have never bedded a virgin," he whispered, his breaths becoming labored.

Despite his cousin Rebecca's insistence she no longer bedded every cousin in their family, Gregory knew he wasn't the first to bed her. Or, rather, to allow her to have her way with him, on her terms and in her bed.

"My virtue is my gift to you, Gregory. Please take it willingly," Christiana whispered, her eyes locked on his.

Swallowing hard, Gregory regarded her, knowing he would have to give in to the lust he felt for her. His body demanded it. Every fiber of his being wanted her. He would take her virtue this night, but in doing so, he would ensure she would be his wife. "Then... I accept," he whispered hoarsely. "But please know, Christiana, I cannot give it back should you change your mind about us," he said quietly as he held his hands on either side of her face. It was golden in his hands. With the sun completely set, the only light in the room was that of the fire.

A beatific smile appeared, and Christiana shook her head. "I won't change my mind." She stepped off of the chair and held out a hand to Gregory. He took it and stood up. As he placed his hands on her back, he slid them under her gown and chemise and down to her hips. Christiana pulled her arms out of the sleeves, and the gown dropped to the floor in a puddle of batiste and ribbons.

Gregory's breath caught as he gazed at her nearly naked body, his pulse pounding in his ears and his engorged cock.

Christiana, busy with unfastening all the buttons on his topcoat and waistcoat, didn't notice his attention until she pushed the garments off of his body. Hesitating, her hands stilled where they were about to pull his shirt from his breeches.

"Are you disappointed?" she whispered, conscious of her exposed breasts.

His breaths harsh, Gregory shook his head. "God, no," he replied, taking her mouth with his in an urgent kiss that left her lips swollen. "You're so beautiful," he managed to get out before he bent to remove his boots.

As Christiana reached for the buttons on his breeches, her quick gaze down the length of his body took note of his arousal and her breath caught. When he stayed her hands to undo the buttons himself, she slid her hands under his shirt. Running them up the sides of his body, she barely touched the skin over his ribs as she did so.

Gregory hissed and bent forward, surprised when Christiana used the opportunity to kiss his neck. He felt her lean closer when the round buds of her breasts brushed against his belly. *Rebecca never offered herself like this*, he remembered, his breaths becoming more labored. *She was always the one in charge, the one deciding what would happen next.*

Holding his hands on either side of her body, he drew them down as his thumbs brushed her nipples and then touched together when they reached her waist. Lifting her in his arms, he took her to the bed and lay her down. Hurrying to the bath, he found a small linen towel and returned to place it beneath her hips.

Pushing her pantaloons down her thighs, Christiana turned to one side as she watched his gaze pass over the length of her body. She fought down her panic. Was it merely lust she saw in his eyes as he took in the sight of her? Or was it adoration? If she thought too much about what they were about to do, she feared she would lose all the confidence she had mustered for this evening.

"I knew you would be beautiful," Gregory whispered between his quickened gasps for air. "But you are even more so than I imagined." He climbed onto the bed and positioned his body over hers. Still on his knees, he pulled his shirt over his head.

Christiana held her breath as she took in the sight of her

beloved. In the firelight, his skin was golden, the hair dark on his chest and belly ending just above where his manhood emerged from a separate mass of dark curlies. "You are more handsome than even David," she murmured, a hint of delight in her voice. Although she had only seen male genitals in statuary and paintings, she found herself in awe over what protruded from the top of his thighs.

Eyebrows arching in surprise, Gregory swallowed. "David?" he croaked, his face screwing up at the thought of her with another man.

"Michelangelo's David," she replied with a coy smile. She reached for his manhood, tentatively running a forefinger down the full length of his erection, grinning when she heard his breath catch. Her fingers slid under and around his balls while she tried hard not to stare at the hardened shaft. It was much larger than she expected, given the descriptions she had read in the Minerva Press books she had taken to reading while Emma was at class.

She tore her gaze away from his cock and glanced back up to find Gregory staring at her.

Gasping, Gregory leaned forward and supported himself on one hand. With the other, he stroked the front of her body from above a nipple, over her ribs, past the hollow between her hip bones and through the curly red hairs at the top of her thighs.

Even before he had parted the creamy folds of her cleft, he felt her wetness, heard her sudden whimper and gasp of surprise. His middle finger probed her entrance, seeking the engorged bud of her womanhood. Determined to impart some pleasure before he induced what he feared would be excruciating pain, Gregory teased the red flesh, aware of how her entire body seemed to shiver at his every touch. Her whimpers turned to pleas, her legs spreading in invitation as he continued his ministrations.

Christiana cried out and lifted her torso nearly off the bed. Gregory dropped to one elbow, wrapping his arm beneath her so he could better support her as he rubbed the source of her sudden pleasure. Christiana reached up and kissed him hard on the lips, wrapping her legs around his back. "Take me," she begged, her hips rising rhythmically with his every touch.

Gregory's hand stilled. He slowly smoothed it around the back of her thigh and then held his body over hers. Christiana sensed his tentativeness and ran her hands as far down the sides of his body as she could. His breaths, short and shallow, excited her. She felt his manhood again, her thumb rubbing the wet tip ever so lightly. Running her hands back up his body, her wet thumb leaving a trail as she did so, she rubbed her thumbs over the tops of his nipples and he hissed again. "I... love you," he whispered and then plunged into her.

The pain was sudden and intense, and although it was over in a moment, Christiana couldn't help but wince. Knowing he had hurt her, Gregory placed an arm along the side of her head and leaned down to kiss her forehead. "I'm so sorry," he whispered. He felt her tighten her legs around his back as he carefully pushed into her. Surprised at how wet and tight she was around his manhood, he moaned and began the rhythmic motion of pushing his hips against hers.

Arching her back, Christiana gasped as his lips took purchase on a hardened nipple and his teeth nipped it. Gasped again at the sensation of fullness deep within her.

He straightened his upper body as he pushed into her again and again. Reaching up with her head and neck, she kissed his chest and nipples. Holding himself up on one arm, he used the other to cradle her head as she continued to kiss him and glide her fingers over his skin. He lowered her head to the bed and ran his hand down the front of her body, sliding his fingertips down her chest and belly as he pushed into her again.

When his thumb reached her belly, Christiana arched her back and gasped loudly. She allowed the shivers of pleasure to take her as her fingers held onto Gregory's shoulders.

Watching her in ecstasy, Gregory found he could do nothing but allow the release his body demanded. Groaning loudly, he buried his face in the quilt above Christiana's head as she kissed his neck and shoulders.

Their bodies trembled for several minutes as their breathing slowed, and Christiana allowed her legs to slide down around his buttocks and the back of his thighs. Wrapping her arms around his chest, she whispered, "I love you, Gregory."

When he could no longer hold himself up on his arms, he gingerly pulled out of her and rolled onto his back, nearly falling over the edge of the small bed as he did so.

Christiana moaned and turned her face towards him as she languidly lifted her arms above her head and stretched. Gregory eyed her appreciatively, sorry for what he had done but well aware he couldn't have maintained control. *I've left my seed in her*, he thought. *I've never done that with Rebecca. How could I be so careless? So selfish?*

Sliding an arm under her shoulders, he pulled her body against his side, his other arm wrapping around her in a protective hold. Resting her head in the small hollow between his arm and chest, Christiana wrapped an arm over his stomach. "I'm so sorry I hurt you," Gregory whispered, kissing the top of her head.

Christiana repositioned her head so she could see the side of his face. "The pain didn't last but the slightest moment," she whispered. "But the rest of it was divine," she said with a satisfied smile. "Is it like that every time?"

Gregory nodded. "I do believe we shall enjoy making babies," he whispered between his gasps for air. Christiana nodded into his chest and pressed her body against his.

For nearly an hour, he held her as they whispered to one another about anything and everything. When a shiver passed through her body, Gregory lifted himself on one elbow. "Are you cold?" he asked. "I should put you under the covers," he offered as he started to get up.

"No," Christiana answered as she placed a hand on his shoulder and pushed him down. "I just want to lay here with you a few minutes more. Before you must take your leave," she said quietly.

Gregory considered her words. "I'm going to put more wood on the fire, and then I'm going to put you under the covers, and, if you are very good, I will get into bed with you for a few more minutes," he countered in a teasing voice. He knew he sounded like a scolding parent, but a good deal of time had passed since his arrival. He was sure the residents of the house would soon return from the theatre.

He pushed off the mattress and did what he set out to do. Finding his pocket watch, he checked the time and decided he could stay another half-hour or so before the theatre would likely end.

Lifting her in his arms, he noticed the blood on the towel and took her into the bath. Fumbling in the dark, he found the matches and lit a candle.

"What are you doing?" Christiana whispered as the room filled with the light from the flame.

"Washing up," he replied, matter-of-factly. "We cannot have your roommate find you…" He started to say 'ruined' but thought better of it.

"Oh!" Christiana replied, seeing her reflection in the mirror. "I… I can do this myself," she added, embarrassed at having him see her naked.

His nakedness didn't seem to bother her, though, and Gregory grinned at her sudden modesty. He was also keenly aware of how much his body appreciated her nakedness. He stepped to the side of the bed and removed the bloody towel.

My virtue is my gift to you, she had said.

Folding it up into a small bundle, he left it next to his clothes. Satisfied there was no other evidence of their lovemaking, he pulled down the covers.

Christiana emerged from the bath and quickly covered her breasts with one arm. Biting his lip, Gregory gazed at her candlelit silhouette. She was small, but she had a comely figure and pretty features. He imagined her with a babe—his babe—at her breast, and his breath hitched as his chest tightened. Smiling, he took her in his arms. "I love you," he said quietly. "And I hope you shall never regret this night," he added in a whisper.

Her face flushed, Christiana wrapped both of her arms around his shoulders and pressed the front of her body against his. "I shall never regret this night. I promise," she stated as she hugged him harder.

"Thank you," Gregory whispered as he held her.

"You are most welcome," Christiana replied, her voice muffled against his chest.

Kissing the top of her head, he asked, "Where do you keep your nightrail?"

Reluctantly, Christiana backed away from Gregory and moved to the bed, pulling her gown from under her pillow and shrugging in embarrassment.

Gregory took it from her and grinned. "I keep my nightshirt in the same place." He opened it and held it over her head. She pulled it on and smoothed the wrinkled fabric down her sides. He nodded in her direction. "When we are married, perhaps on warmer nights—"

"When we're married, I should think I won't want to wear a nightrail," Christiana stated, her tone suggesting he shouldn't argue.

Gregory smiled and arched an eyebrow. "Then I know I won't

want to wear a nightshirt," he admitted as he regarded her. Lifting her in his arms, he placed her in the bed and covered her with the sheets and counterpane. "I know you don't have a proper chaperone, but may I take you to dinner tomorrow evening?" he asked as he took her hand in his.

"I'd like that very much," she replied, her eyelids nearly closed.

"I'll come for you at seven," he said quietly. He kissed her mouth. He continued to kiss her for several minutes, but finally realized she had fallen asleep. Plucking the hairpins out of her bun and braids, he set them on the dressing table and kissed her one last time on the forehead.

Gregory dressed quickly, collected the wine bottle and glasses into the basket with the rest of the food, grabbed his gift, and left the room. In his haste to leave the house, he nearly forgot his hat. Putting it on as he pulled the front door shut, he walked calmly to his chaise. The driver, who had fallen asleep, jerked awake as his master climbed in.

"Take us back to Grace Park, please," he said as he sat back in the seat.

"Right away, sir," the coachman replied.

When they were about to turn the corner to head toward Cavendish Square, a large group of young women appeared from Marylebone Street, talking and laughing as they followed several link boys carrying lanterns to light their way. Seeing clusters of them break off in front of each house along Glasshouse Street,

Gregory let out a loud sigh of relief. "That was a bit too close," he said to no one in particular.

CHAPTER 15
A TOWNHOUSE TO
CALL HOME

April 23, 1802, Gamma House

The note was written on rather expensive parchment, folded neatly into its own square envelope, and sealed with wax. A double-S was stamped into the near-perfect circle of scarlet wax. Given the impression in the wax was as fine as gold filigree, Emma wondered if the seal had been made by a jeweler rather than a stationer.

"Who is your letter from?" Christiana asked as she held her latest post in both hands, secretly excited when she realized who had penned it.

"Whom," Emma said absently, almost unaware she had corrected her roommate's grammar. She carefully loosened the wax seal and unfolded the parchment.

"Whom is your letter from?" Christiana tried again, opening her own but turning so her missive wasn't visible should Emma's attention be diverted from her own.

"I'm not sure," Emma murmured, awed by the beautiful shape of the handwriting she found inside.

Christiana quickly perused her own letter, her heart rate increasing with each line she read. *He's coming back for the ball!* she thought with joy. Just a few more months and her beau would be back in London.

Before she finished reading, she glanced back at Emma and watched as her roommate's expression changed from a look of bewilderment to stunned awe.

"I may have a place to live," Emma breathed. "And not far from here."

Frowning, Christiana refolded her note. "Whatever do you mean?" she asked, moving to stand next to Emma. She glanced at the parchment still held open in Emma's fingers and was startled to see a feminine script with not a single crossed out word nor errant ink smear. "Someone obviously had Mrs. Pendergast for penmanship," she said as she admired the script.

Emma's brows furrowed. Although she, too, had admired the handwriting, she hadn't noticed its similarity to their instructor's hand.

"Possibly," Emma murmured as she continued to read. When she finished, she lifted her head and stared at her reflection in the dressing table looking glass. "It seems Sir William has made a recommendation on my behalf. The letter is from..." She paused as she studied the signature. "Mrs. James Simpson," she finally said. "She and her husband own an entire row of townhouses in Kingly Street. One of their tenants has recently died, and so a townhouse is available to let."

Christiana wrinkled her nose. "Do you suppose he died there?" she asked, not at all impressed with the news Emma might have a townhouse. In less than six weeks, their term at Warwick's would be complete, and they would move out of Gamma House. At least she would return to Woodscastle. And she would still see Emma nearly every day, although she wasn't sure just how much. If her brother was as serious about whatever work he had hired Emma to perform for him as he was with his own work at the warehouse, she was afraid Emma might be locked away in a room at Woodscastle for ten hours a day, and then she would never see her.

"Possibly," Emma answered. "He had no relatives, so there are some furnishings and books left behind, but it sounds as if there is enough room for my mother's furnishings," she said hopefully. Although Ambrose Smith had been generous enough to allow her to leave several pieces of fine furniture and most of her personal effects in the apartment above the hat shop, the couple would soon need the space—a baby was on the way. "Anyway, I'm to call on Mrs. Simpson tomorrow afternoon," she said, her smile fading when she realized she would probably be late for class as a result of the meeting.

"You can finally wear your peacock blue walking ensemble,"

Christiana suggested, her mood lighter despite what she might have first thought of as bad news.

Emma nodded in agreement, folding the note along its original lines and deciding she really must send a reply to Mrs. Simpson as well as a thank you note to Sir William. *Whatever is that man up to?* Mr. Wellingham had mentioned the banker when he had hired her, implying Sir William had recommended her for the position. Now it seemed the man had recommended her for a townhouse. With a wry grin, she wondered if he would also provide a husband.

Although she probably should have asked one of her classmates to join her for the short walk to Kingly Street, Emma set out for her appointment with Mrs. Simpson without a companion in tow. Dressed in her only walking ensemble, a gown of peacock blue muslin topped by a spencer of a slightly darker velvet and a matching parasol, Emma slowly approached the row of townhouses along the east side of the street, her gaze sweeping up and around to the west side, where a similar row of townhouses lined up all the way to Oxford Street.

Made of brick and each sporting a door of a different color, the townhouses appeared fairly new. The pavers making up the walkway next to the cobblestone street were of recent installation, for they were still even, easy to walk on, and *clean*. Nattily dressed gentlemen either strolled by themselves or escorted their well-dressed wives on the pavers. The women wore walking and carriage ensembles of recent design, suggesting a neighborhood of well-to-to residents.

Emma knocked on the forest green door of No. 4. A rather tall man, impeccably dressed and rather handsome, opened the door. From his initial manner, Emma thought he might be the butler, but he seemed to realize her identity right away. "Miss Emma, do come in," he said as he stepped aside. "I am James Simpson," he said as he gave her a deep bow. "At your service."

Emma curtsied and entered the small vestibule, surprised to find marble floors and walls covered in rich forest green silk. "You have a beautiful home," she breathed, allowing him to take her parasol when he reached for it.

"Why, that's very kind of you to say," a woman's voice said from behind her.

Emma turned to find a rather beautiful woman smiling in her direction. "Mrs. Simpson?" she said in a half-question. Dressed in a red round gown with her hair in an elegant chignon, the forty-something woman looked as if she could be a duchess—and given the decor Emma could glimpse from her vantage, she lived like one, too, albeit on a smaller scale.

"Indeed. And you must be Emma. Goodness, you look so much like your aunts, I'd have known you were a Fitzsimmons from a street away," she commented as she held out her right hand in greeting.

Emma shook the proffered hand, stunned by the woman's comments. "You know my aunts?" she asked, feeling a sudden stab of guilt when she remembered it had been far too long since she had paid a visit to the one who lived in town. The others spent their time at their country homes with their husbands, complaining that London was simply too hot in the summer and too damp in the winter.

Her uncle, Matthew Fitzsimmons, had recently inherited the Chamberlain viscountcy, but he and his wife, Caroline, spent their time traveling in the Continent, determined to take in as many of the sites of ancient ruins as they could manage before his duty to the Crown required they return to London.

Sophia waved a hand as she took Emma's arm with her other and led her to a parlor just off the vestibule. "I think I attended finishing school with two of them," she remarked before she led Emma to a floral patterned chair.

Emma took a seat as Sophia inclined her head in her husband's direction.

"Of course, I'll bring the tea, sweeting," James said, his expression of amusement caught by Emma.

Sweeting? The man seemed ever so proper, but his use of a term of endearment in her presence had Emma failing to suppress a sudden grin of embarrassment.

Sophia settled herself in the settee, her face coloring. "You'll have to excuse my husband. I'm quite sure he calls me that just to tease me," she murmured, leaning toward Emma as she made the comment.

From somewhere off down the main hall, Emma heard the man's response. "I'm quite sure I call her that because I love her dearly and have since the moment I met her."

Unable to hide her smile, Emma simply lifted a gloved hand to her mouth. She could certainly understand how a woman could be married to such a man. Not only did he have a sense of humor—

mischief most evident in his dark eyes—but he seemed *distinguished*. His jaw was square, and he had a full head of black hair with but a tinge of gray at the temples. Emma was quite sure she would notice him over any other if he were in a crowd.

Sophia, on the other hand, was beautiful in a manner so common as she could blend into a crowd of other beautiful English women, her blonde hair, blue eyes and pale complexion the norm for those commonly referred to as an English miss. She was memorable to Emma, though, because she seemed so regal in her bearing, as if she'd been born to an aristocratic family.

"He is quite impossible sometimes," Sophia commented with an impish grin. "But I cannot imagine living my life without him, so I indulge his... teasing," she explained with a sigh.

Emma angled her head to one side. "I am of the opinion everyone's marriage should be a love match," she commented. *Like my mother and father's.*

Sophia nodded. "Then let's hope you find a man who will honor your heart as much as he admires your head," she replied. "And, in the meantime, we can at least see to a place for you to live. Would you like to see it?"

Her eyes widening in surprise, Emma inhaled sharply. "Yes, of course." *Not that I'll be able to afford it.* How could Sir William have thought to recommend her for such an expensive neighborhood?

Sophia stood and hurried to the parlor door, peeking around the corner before she waved for Emma to join her. Curious, Emma followed the woman as she walked quickly through the vestibule and out the front door, pausing only to retrieve a key from a small mahogany table in one corner. Then she quietly closed the front door behind them before she allowed a girlish giggle. "You'll have to excuse my indulgence, but Mr. Simpson is making tea and expecting to find us in the parlor," she said as she moved to the red door at No. 3 and inserted the key.

Emma nodded. "And we won't be there when he comes with the tea," she guessed with a wink as she entered a townhouse with a floor plan the opposite of the Simpsons'. A parquet wood floor gleamed as if it had just been waxed, and it extended from the vestibule all the way to what Emma soon learned was the kitchen. The parlor, off to the right, was elegant although mostly unfurnished.

"I understand you already have some furnishings," Sophia said, almost making the comment a question.

"I do, and they will work perfectly in this room," Emma replied. "Are you leaving the carpets?" she asked, her slippered foot sinking into the plush floor covering.

"Of course," Sophia replied, turning to lead her to the library. "Unfortunately, this room has no natural light, which is why the last tenant had some mirrors installed on the south wall. It makes for a brighter room in the evenings." She went onto the next set of double doors and spread them open to reveal a dining room.

Emma gasped. "Oh, it's much larger than I would have imagined," she breathed, her excitement building. She could imagine her mother's dining table and chairs in the middle of the room, and a sideboard set up along one wall.

Sophia had already moved through an adjoining door and into the kitchen. "There's a water pump, of course, and Mr. Simpson had a new stove installed last week." She turned to regard Emma for a moment. "Will you employ a cook, do you suppose?" she asked. "Or a maid? I realize you have to share one at Warwick's," she added as she moved through another door into the main hall.

"I probably shouldn't admit it, but I do know how to cook. I think I shall need a maid on occasion, though," Emma replied, wondering if she could afford the expense. Everything depended on whether or not she could find employment after her position with Mr. Wellingham came to an end.

"Perhaps we can share," Sophia suggested, one eyebrow arching up in query. "My husband is far too efficient at nearly everything a household requires, but I employ one and cannot possibly keep her busy all day long." The woman moved to the stairs and indicated Emma should follow her.

Emma considered the suggestion. "I think I should like that very much," she replied as she openly admired the wide staircase with its polished wood and carpeted runners.

At the top of the stairs were just two doors. "This is where it gets interesting," Sophia said as she opened the first. "A master suite with a bath," she said as she breezed into the rather large room and headed for another door. "The dressing room," she continued, moving through it to another door. "The mistress suite." She paused a moment, her face contorted into a look of disgust. "A rather small mistress suite," she said with a roll of her eyes. "Of course, you'll use the larger bedchamber and hang the mistress suite."

Emma boggled at the woman's comment. "But, it has such large windows, it would make a perfect room for reading," she countered, hurrying to look out. Down below, she spied a mews. "Would I be able to leave my horse in that mews?" she asked, noticing a young boy leading a mare around the stable yard.

"Of course. Mr. Churchill does a fine job. His son is the one you see down there. Do you own a gig?" Sophia asked.

Emma shook her head. "I can barely afford the horse," she replied.

"You can borrow my phaeton when you need it," Sophia said with a wave of her hand. "I hardly use it anymore. James insists on driving me in his curricle if I need to go anywhere."

Once again having to suppress a smile at the woman's use of her husband's given name, Emma realized Sophia already expected her to let the unit. "That's very generous of you, Mrs. Simpson." After a pause, Emma broached the issue of cost. "How much for the lease?" she asked in a lowered voice, prepared to hear a sum far beyond what she could afford.

"Ninety-five pounds for the year," Sophia said with some reluctance. "If it's too much—"

"Oh, no. It's perfect," Emma cried out. "I can write you a cheque right now if you wish."

Sophia regarded her new tenant with a hint of surprise. "If you wish, then simply make it out to James. I let him handle the money, even though I do all the books," she said with an arched eyebrow.

*P*erhaps her brother had been right about Emma Fitzsimmons. She could already tell they would be fast friends, although she knew Emma's schedule would preclude her from being at the townhouse during most days. *William obviously knows what he's doing,* Sophia considered, although she also wondered if his goals were the same as her own—find a suitable wife for her son.

From down below, they heard the front door open. "Tea is served, my lady."

Sophia's eyes widened, and she inhaled sharply. "We should be going. If I don't appear at the top of the stairs this very moment, he will come get me and, no doubt, do something rather embarrassing," she whispered. "To me," she quickly clarified.

Emma's eyebrows flew up as she followed Sophia to the top of the stairs. James was already on his way up, his predatory look causing the older woman to shriek in delight. "Too late," she said, handing her the key to the townhouse. "I know this must appear rather... indecorous. Because it is, I know, but... do spend as long you'd like and enjoy your new parlor. You'll have to let yourself out, I'm afraid. It seems I'll be indisposed."

Emma watched as James wrapped his arm around his wife's waist and lifted her over one shoulder. "Good day, Miss Emma," he said with a happy nod. "I've taken the liberty of pouring the tea, and I'll see to its removal later this evening."

And with that, James Simpson turned around and made his way down the stairs with Sophia's arms wrapped around his neck and shoulders. "Do pay a call when you've settled in," the woman called out as she and her husband disappeared through the front door.

*E*mma stood at the top of the stairs and gave her new living quarters another glance, her smile as much for her new landlords as for the townhouse. A frisson shot through her when she imagined what they must be doing.

Sophia had seemed rather *happy* to have been whisked away in her husband's arms, as if she looked forward to whatever James had in mind for her. Emma wondered if he would take the time to undress his wife or...

She shook her head in an attempt to clear the inappropriate images of James' amorous attentions. Just about the time she had done so, she was aware of a very faint giggle on the other side of wall next to which she stood. *The Simpsons' staircase would be on the other side of the wall from this one,* she reasoned. *He's taking her to their bedchamber.*

Or hers.

Emma shook her head and descended the stairs, smiling the entire time. When she returned to the parlor, she found James had, indeed, set up the sea service. One cup was filled, tendrils of steam curling up from the surface. Still grinning, Emma helped herself to the tea and a Dutch biscuit and made her way to the library.

She sipped and nibbled as she perused the books left behind by the prior tenant. The collection was eclectic in both subjects and authors, although some care had been taken in how the books were grouped. Many had leather covers while others still had their original chipboard bindings. Philosophy, art, history, human anatomy...

Emma's gaze stopped to rest on a rather large tome, its spine handwritten with the words, *The Kama Sutra*. Setting her teacup on the shelf, she pulled the book from the shelf and allowed it to open somewhere near the middle.

And she gasped. She was about to close the book when curiosity got the better of her. Where there was text, it was printed in a language she didn't recognize. The margins contained entire paragraphs handwritten in English, what she supposed was the translation of the text. But it was the colorful illustrations that had her mesmerized. Page after page featured drawings of sexual positions, many of which had her angling her head and sometimes the entire book. *Goodness!*

She rifled through the pages toward the front of the book, breathing easier upon finding illustrations of a couple engaged in kissing. After a few moments, though, even those images had her heart racing, her breaths short.

Embarrassed by her reaction to the images, Emma finally closed the book and returned it to its place on the shelf. Finishing her tea, she returned the cup to the parlor and took her leave of the townhouse, locking the door and dropping the key into her reticule before she headed toward Oxford Street.

Class would be starting soon.

CHAPTER 16
TWO LOVEBIRDS IN
THEIR NEST

April 23, 1802, No. 4 Kingly Street

"I wonder what she must think of us," Sophia whispered once her mind had reassembled itself into some semblance of order. Her fingers had managed to find her husband's head of black hair, the nails spreading the silken threads apart as she pulled him down. He finally settled atop one side of her, his head nestled beneath one pert breast. His hands, though, still roamed her body, their simple touches reigniting the frissons of pleasure he had already set off with his earlier lovemaking.

Despite having been married to James Simpson for over twenty years, the man still managed to surprise her with his ill-timed amorous attentions and delightful antics in bed.

"She thinks we're in love," James whispered, his lips taking purchase on the underside of the other breast. "Oh," he murmured. "I don't believe I've been here before."

Sophia giggled as his tongue and teeth captured the soft flesh. "You have, too. Just last week, in fact," she countered, angling her body so he could no longer reach her breasts with his mouth. She pulled a bed linen over her bosom and tucked the edges beneath her arms, thinking to prevent him further access just then.

James lifted himself onto an elbow and regarded his wife with a bemused expression. "She thinks it because we are," he said. Although he was still feeling the effects of having bedded his wife not just once, but twice since they took their leave of No. 3, he was contemplating when he might be ready for a third round.

"Will she help, do you suppose?" she asked, surprised at how much she liked the young woman. Until this afternoon, Sophia hadn't known Emma had connections to the Fitzsimmons—not that those would be of much help for what she was trying to accomplish —but it meant Emma might be more biddable as far as Thomas Wellingham was concerned.

"Sir William is convinced she'll turn his head," James murmured, frowning now that she was denying him access to her bosom. He leaned over and placed a kiss on her shoulder. "But we've got to give it some time, sweeting. She won't even be working for the man for another... five, six weeks?" he added, his lips moving to her neck and down to her collarbone.

"Gregory will be back in a few months," Sophia murmured, one of her hands still sliding through his hair, her fingernails barely scraping his scalp. She had to suppress a satisfied grin when she felt his entire body shiver in response. "I want him to be happy."

"He is happy."

"I want him to be *married*."

James held a kiss on her collarbone and finally pulled away. "He will be" he said. "Why are you so concerned?"

"It's just that, the longer he isn't married, the more likely some barmaid or... or a Cyprian will claim he's the father of their child," she whispered in despair.

That wasn't the *only* reason she wanted Gregory Grandby leg-shackled, but she wasn't about to bring up *grandchildren* just then.

"Whoa!" James sat up and moved to sit with his back to the headboard. He wrapped an arm around the back of her shoulders and pulled her to his chest. "Just what is it you think your son has been *doing?*" he asked.

Sophia shrugged and dared a glance at her husband. "He has a reputation..."

"Which is based on hearsay..."

"As a rake."

"Which he is *not*. I assure you," James said with the same kind of conviction he used when he said he loved her. Although... well, he wasn't about to think the worst of his stepson for what had happened when he was last in town.

The man had been uncharacteristically quiet while they played cards at White's, and after a few losing hands of whist and at James' urging, the two had left the club and taken advantage of the fair weather to walk back to the townhouse. In the course of their conversation, Gregory had let it slip that he had bedded his intended, his manner both sorrowful as well as determined. *She will be my wife*, he had said. *I've seen to it.* Although James had been surprised by his stepson's admission, he found he couldn't find fault with the young man—he would have done the same in the man's shoes.

Sophia gave her husband a look of disbelief. "How can you say that when they say that phrase about him?" she countered.

James allowed a sigh. "A girl in every port, and a port after dinner?" he recited. "My sweeting, when have you ever known him to drink port?"

Shrugging, Sophia angled her head to one side. "He doesn't like port," she whispered. "He says it's too sweet for his tastes."

"And when have you even known him to visit a coastal town? Other than Brighton?" he added quickly.

Sophia shook her head. "I don't think the saying is meant to be taken *literally*," she argued.

Sighing again, James kissed the top of her head. "I believe I know your son a bit better than you in this matter," he said carefully. "He's been rather chaste, if you really must know."

For a moment, Sophia remained resting against the front of his body, but he knew at any moment she would react to his words and probably jump to the wrong conclusion.

She jumped to the wrong conclusion.

"No! He cannot be!" she nearly shouted, her expression of shock causing James to laugh at her expense.

"He's not a molly. He was just snake-bit is all," he murmured.

Her brows furrowing, Sophia stared at her husband. "What do you mean? What happened to him?" Visions of her son, a rather tall, well-built man suffering at the hands of... "Who?"

James stared up at the ceiling. He supposed it was time she knew, especially if he was to convince her one of the wealthiest men of the business world wasn't a rake. "Rebecca Merriweather," he whispered.

Sophia was suddenly out of the bed, taking half the bed linens with her as she wrapped them around herself. "No!" she nearly shouted. "That... that *she-bitch!*" she cried.

Quickly climbing out of the bed, James hurried around to her and took her face in his hands. "It's all right. He... he got away before she could—"

"How many times?" Sophia demanded. She felt her entire body shiver at the thought of her defenseless son in the bed of a cousin with sexual proclivities befitting a man in a whorehouse of deviants.

Brought up short by the question, James shook his head. "I don't... that's not what's important," he countered. "The important thing is he wasn't found with her and forced to marry the she-bitch," he added, rather liking the term his wife had come up with to describe Rebecca. "And despite what happened, he's managed to fall in love with a rather sweet girl."

Sophia shook her head, angry and hurt that her husband knew something about her son and had kept it from her. "Why didn't you tell me? How long have you *known?*" She paused a moment, her eyes widening. "Were you there when it happened?"

"Good God, no," James replied, his head shaking from side to side. "If I had known what was going on in Rebecca's room, I would have..." He stopped, not sure what he would have done to the spoiled chit who made sure none of her male cousins were left virgins. It's not as if he could have gained entry to the house and made his way to her bedchamber. And, what then? One didn't tell Rebecca what she could or couldn't do. She was a force unto herself, a reckless, conceited woman who wasn't about to follow Society's rules when it came to how she behaved.

Had the oldest female cousin just allowed her male cousins to bed her, it might be one thing. But she had practically tortured the poor boys, one minute pleasuring them and the next forcing herself on them, threatening them with bodily harm—James actually winced when he remembered overhearing one of the older boys tell his tale—if they didn't return the favor. Most were too young to understand, he supposed. And some liked the attention, willing to return to Rebecca's bedchamber until she finally tired of them and turned her attentions to someone else.

Having been traumatized by his cousin, Gregory simply avoided any relationships with women, instead using his time and energies to build his already considerable wealth. But now... now he was in love, and it was possible he would propose to a young woman. But given the girl's age and her brother's overprotective nature, it might be some time before they would be allowed to marry.

"He could ruin her," James whispered as he continued to hold his wife, deciding he wouldn't tell her Gregory had already done so.

Sophia shuddered, her head burrowing into the small of his shoulder. "Then he wouldn't be any better than Becky," she whispered back.

James shrugged. "But then they could get married. Hang her brother." He took a deep breath and let it out slowly. "Anyway, you just have to be patient, my little matchmaker." He stopped talking when he realized his wife was glowering at him.

He *definitely* wouldn't tell her of Gregory's transgression.

"I rather like the brother. And I think Emma will, too," she said. "Once he decides he wants to marry her, he'll allow his sister to marry. I'm sure of it."

Nodding, James kissed her on the forehead. "It's a good plan," he assured her.

He didn't add that it would have been a better plan if Thomas Wellingham hadn't also been a victim of Rebecca Merriweather. Better she didn't know that little tidbit of information.

CHAPTER 17
HE'S LATE, HE'S LATE

ay 21, 1802, Puddle Dock
Stephen Bingham trudged up the stairs at the back of the warehouse and knocked on Thomas Wellingham's office door. He waited to hear, "Come in," before opening it. The light from the south-facing window nearly blinded him as the mid-May sun reflected off the river below.

"Mr. Bingham," Thomas acknowledged as he waved his warehouse manager into the room. "What is it?" He could tell from Stephen's furrowed brow something was amiss. "Have a seat," he said as he indicated the chair across from his desk.

"It's about Mr. MacGregor, sir," Stephen began as he hung his head.

Thomas straightened in his chair, a worried expression lining his face. "Was MacGregor late again today?" he asked, knowing the burly Scot they relied on for heavy lifting and moving crates had been late every day that week and a few days the week before.

"Yes, sir," Stephen answered as he met Thomas' gaze. "And he looks terrible. Like he hasn't had any sleep," the manager explained. "He is staying late to make up the time…"

"How late?" Thomas asked as he leaned on his desk.

"Fifteen, thirty minutes at the most," Stephen replied with a shrug.

"Has he said *why* he's been late?" Thomas asked, hoping there was a reasonable explanation.

"No. But I haven't asked," Stephen admitted with a shrug. "Should I?"

Thomas regarded his manager with pursed lips and shook his head. "No, but if it impacts his ability to work, bring it up with me again," he answered with a sigh. "Do you suppose he's staying too late in a pub... or gambling, perhaps?" he asked after a moment. Although he didn't know Sean MacGregor outside of his work at Wellingham Imports, Thomas figured him to be a stalwart employee.

Stephen shook his head. "Wouldn't be like 'im, I don't suppose," he answered, his face screwed up with concern. "And I haven't smelled the drink on 'im."

If it had been anyone else, Thomas might have been tempted to talk to the man directly or dock his pay, if necessary. But Sean MacGregor had been with Wellingham Imports since its beginning, and Thomas wanted to reward loyal employees.

He knew MacGregor lived closer to the London Docks than to Wellingham Imports, and the man could easily gain employment there or at the new West Indies Company's docks. *Perhaps he is working somewhere else*, he considered. "Keep an eye on him. If he's late again next week, I'll speak with him myself," Thomas offered.

"Thank you, sir," Stephen replied and he stood to go. "By the way, has Miss Wellingham finished at school yet?" he asked as he turned to face the desk again.

Thomas raised an eyebrow. "As a matter of fact, Mr. Allen just picked her up from Warwick's this morning. She should be at Woodscastle by now," he said as he checked his chronograph. "Why do you ask?"

Stephen's ears reddened as he hesitated to bring up his concern. "Well, it's just that when she's home, you end up spending less time here, and business is, well,... there is a lot more of it this year than last year," he explained in a halting voice. He shook his head, wishing he could take back the comment.

"Miss Wellingham will have to fend for herself this summer, I assure you," Thomas replied. "I will be here as much as I can stand, if not more," he said wearily. "And I do appreciate your concern. At some point, I will bring in someone to assist us," he added. At the moment, he didn't know anyone he could trust to help run the business.

"Very good, sir," Stephen said with a nod. He left the office and descended the wooden stairs to the warehouse floor below.

Thomas slumped in his chair and gave a sideways glance at the ledger book for the month of April. He dared not look at it, but knew he must at some point. Emma Fitzsimmons would be starting the audit on Monday morning, and, although he didn't expect her to finish for several months, he figured she would find some evidence of embezzlement sooner rather than later.

Reminded to take some ledgers home with him, he made his way to Bingham's office and helped himself to the ledger books for the beginning of the year. When he was sure no one was watching him from the warehouse below, he sneaked back to his own office with the books and dropped them with a thud onto a chair.

Sighing, he returned to the bill of lading he was working on prior to Bingham's visit. A bill of lading featuring five-hundred beaver skins. And every one of them had a buyer—Ambrose Smith of *Fitzsimmons and Smith*.

CHAPTER 18
MOVING IN REVEALS A
SURPRISE

*M*ay 21, 1802, *Kingly Street*

Excitement welled up until Emma felt she would burst. Her last day at Warwick's Grammar and Finishing School was also her first day in her own townhouse. Carrying a valise with some of her clothing and toiletry items, she made her way on foot to Kingly Street. She planned to take another quick tour of the rooms before making arrangements with a drayage company to transfer her furnishings and personal effects.

Ambrose Smith had been ever so accommodating in allowing her to leave her mother's things in the apartment above the hat shop, but it was past time they were moved out.

As she approached No. 3 Kingly, she could see the door was already open. A dray, nearly empty, was parked in front. When a burly man appeared from the townhouse, Emma watched as he moved to the dray and hoisted a trunk over one shoulder. Turning, he was about to reenter when Emma recognized the trunk.

My trunk! she thought with alarm. But how—?

"Ah, Miss Emma!" she heard from above.

Glancing up, she found James Simpson looking out the bedchamber suite window. "Good day, Mr. Simpson," she said with a slight curtsy. She blinked when Sophia appeared next to her husband. "Good day, Mrs. Simpson," she added, her expression of surprise apparent.

"My dear Miss Emma, welcome to your new home," Sophia

called out. She and her husband disappeared from the window, and Emma took a tentative step toward the front door. She leaned in, wondering what was going on.

"We meant to have this all done *before* you arrived," Sophia said as she negotiated the last few steps.

"Indeed, but we are very nearly finished," James added as he joined his wife in the vestibule. "The cart was too small for all of your things, so the men had to make another trip. But this is the last of it," he said as he motioned to the dray parked out front.

A mix of shock and pleasant surprise settled on Emma as she glanced about and realized her mother's things—her things—were already in the townhouse.

"But... how did you know where to find them?" she asked, her brows furrowing before she finally allowed a grin. She dared not allow the Simpsons to think she didn't appreciate their efforts on her part.

James gave a nod. "Sir William Burroughs insisted your home be made ready for you. He made the necessary arrangements, and my gorgeous wife has entertained herself all day by seeing to it these workman put everything where she thinks it belongs."

Sophia placed a hand on her husband's arm. "I do love to order men around on occasion," she said, her lips quirking. "And I know how vexing it can be to move a household," she added, motioning for Emma to join her.

She linked her arm with Emma's and turned them toward the parlor. "You may not agree with the arrangement, so you'll want to take advantage of the muscle whilst the movers are here," she went on, waving a hand as they entered the parlor.

Emma inhaled softly. Her mother's furnishings were arranged in perfect groupings in the long room, the seating taking advantage of the fireplace and the light from the front window. Besides the furniture, several candle lamps had already been positioned as had various items of decor. Even the painting from her mother's parlor was already hung above the fireplace.

Before Emma had a chance to say anything, Sophia whisked her off to the dining room. Her table was positioned just as she had imagined, a beautiful floral arrangement adorning the center. A sideboard was positioned on the wall where she had imagined one should be.

"Oh, there must be some mistake. I don't own a sideboard," she said as she admired the mahogany buffet. The workmanship was exquisite, the wood inlays forming compass patterns on the cabinet fronts and top of the sideboard. The thin legs suggested a design by Thomas Chippendale, but everyone knew his furnishings had to be commissioned months in advance.

"No mistake," Sophia replied with a quick shake of her head. "Sir William bought it on your behalf. As a gift," she said before Emma had a chance to react. She gave Emma a pat on the back of her gloved hand. "For finishing school," she added, realizing the meaning of the gift could be misconstrued. At the sound of a male throat clearing, they both turned.

"Really, my sweeting. You didn't even allow me to take Miss Emma's pelisse," James admonished his wife. He took the steps necessary to join them in the dining room and helped Emma remove the garment.

"Thank you, Mr. Simpson," Emma said with a happy grin, rather liking how the man took on the duties of a butler even when he was in her home.

"You can thank me if we've done everything to suit you," he countered. "Sir William was quite insistent things be perfect for you. He said you would be otherwise engaged in a few days and unable to see to the details of setting up a proper household."

Emma was about to protest, but thought better of it. "It was most kind of my banker to make the arrangements," she acknowledged with a nod. "I can spend the next couple of days sorting everything."

James seemed to rock on his heels. "We haven't opened any trunks," he said with a bit of hesitance, "but Sophia did have the men open a few small crates," he admitted, one eyebrow arching, as if he didn't agree with his wife's actions.

"The china and crystal, of course," Sophia said in her defense. "Vases and the tea set. Things for the kitchen." She shrugged and turned to go through the kitchen door.

Dumbfounded, Emma merely followed, rather enjoying the tour as she recognized items she hadn't seen in several years. She nearly cried when they entered the bedchamber and she found the bed already in place, her favorite counterpane in place. "You have outdone yourself," she murmured, fighting back the urge to cry.

Sophia recognized Emma's reaction, remembering all too well how she had felt the day James had given her a tour of their newly built townhouse, its floors and finishings far finer than anything she could imagine given her station in life. He had seen to it their home was as rich as any Park Avenue mansion and as comfortable as any country estate manor. "I want you to be happy here," she whispered, leaning in as she made the comment. *But not too happy,* she reminded herself.

Nodding, Emma regarded her landlady for a moment. "I don't think I'll change a single thing. You've done a remarkable job," she said quietly, her gaze taking in the rest of the room. Several trunks lined one wall. Unpacking might take her all of a day.

"I'll let James know to release the workmen," Sophia replied with a nod.

"Oh, but I need to pay them," Emma protested, hurrying to the steps. But when she reached the first floor, she could see through the window by the front door that the dray had already gone. "But..."

James joined her in the vestibule. "Sir William—"

"Has already seen to it," Emma finished for him, her lips thinning in an expression of disapproval.

Arching an eyebrow, James shrugged. "I believe he was acting on orders from your father," he offered, hoping the young woman wouldn't be too cross with the banker.

Emma considered his words. *Of course, he was,* she realized, which left her curious as to what else her father had arranged on her behalf.

What other duties had he placed on the man who was essentially her guardian? What secrets had he imparted to Sir William?

Shaking her head as if to clear it, Emma said her thanks and good-byes to her landlords, assuring them she would host them for dinner in a fortnight or two.

Satisfied they had done all they could for their new tenant, James and Sophia Simpson took their leave of No. 3 and entered No. 4, arm-in-arm.

Emma took a deep breath and moved to the parlor, taking a moment to slowly spin around as she took in the familiar furnishings and knick knacks.

An *escritoire,* one she had seen her mother use when writing letters, stood polished and ready for use. Opening the drawers, she was surprised to find sheets of stationery, the paper old and yellowed along the edges. An ink pot, long ago dried up, had become dislodged from its holder. Several folded letters were still nestled in one cubbyhole while a few lengths of red wax and a seal were tucked inside another.

Tugging on the edge of the folded letters, Emma wondered at who might have sent them. Tied with a length of blue ribbon, they appeared to have the same author, the feminine script unfamiliar to her.

Feeling a bit of trepidation, Emma slid one of the letters from the bundle and carefully unfolded the edges. Two sheets of fine paper, slightly yellowed but otherwise in good condition, were covered in the script.

My dearest George, Oh, how I have missed you these past few years! I think of you often—everyday, I must admit—but then how could I not? I see you in Samantha's eyes every moment I'm with her.

Emma gasped, one hand going to her mouth. *Who is Samantha?* She returned her attention to the letter, reading as fast as she could.

She has grown tired of her nurse, and although she claims to dislike her, she is learning everything she must to be a proper aristocrat's daughter. I expect she'll be taller than I, probably as tall as her sister.

You must be so proud of your Emma. I see her occasionally when I walk past the shop. I very nearly went in last week, but thought better of it. What possible reason could I have to go into a man's hat shop? Other than loving the man who owns it and my heart? I hope you still keep me in yours, for I shall love you always. Caro.

Stunned by the words, Emma turned over the sheet to see if she could find any evidence of the date the letter might have been written.

March 31, 1798.

Emma swallowed. Her father had died that year. Was this the last letter he had received? And who was Samantha?

I see you in Samantha's eyes every moment I'm with her.

Rereading the words, Emma moved to sit in the nearest chair. Apparently, her father had been carrying on an *affaire. And I have a sister,* she realized. *Daughter of someone named Caro.*

Caro was Caroline for short, she knew. Given the comment of how Samantha was being raised, Caroline must have been related to an aristocrat. Perhaps she was an aristocrat's wife!

Is the aristocrat's wife, she amended, reaching out to retrieve the bundle of letters. She settled back into the chair and rifled through the stack, realizing the letters were bundled in chronological order.

Beginning with the oldest, she read each one, attempting to glean some hint or names that might help her determine the identity of the woman who had borne her father's child. The woman had obviously loved George Fitzsimmons, for her declarations of romantic love could not be misconstrued.

In the first letter, Caroline's words seemed tentative, as if she were hesitant to admit her affection for him outright. Emma found a mark suggesting the missive had been sent to her father in early 1792. *The year after mother died*, Emma thought with relief. At least her father hadn't taken Caroline as his mistress whilst her mother was still alive. *I was about ten, spending most of the time at Aunt Christine's with a governess*, she remembered.

Her father's oldest sister, a woman who prided herself on being the daughter of a viscount, was not the least bit happy about being saddled with a child, especially when it had become apparent she would spend her remaining days as a spinster. Apparently she wasn't good about managing her money, either. Sir William had implied her father had made arrangements for the banker to handle Emma's inheritance because her aunt couldn't be trusted to do so.

The second letter referred to George's response to the first letter, a reply not made in writing but rather in person, for Caroline's mention of the passion they shared couldn't be a description of anything other than a night spent together.

Although I am betrothed to marry M, I know he will never make love to me the way you did that night, as if your very life depended on my pleasure. I do feel affection for him, but more in the manner of loving a best friend. Unfortunately, he is a best friend with whom I cannot share my joy at having had you in my life. I shall love you always, George. And one day, I will be able to tell the world of my love for you. Until then, C.

Emma took a deep breath, trying to imagine her father with a woman other than her mother.

Was Caroline his only secret?

Or rather, Caroline and Samantha? Emma amended the thought.

She wondered about *M.* Although Caroline couldn't tell him of her love for the hat maker, she obviously intended to marry the man when she wrote the letter.

Who is M? Did he know his intended had borne a child?

The third letter contained the most damning information—and the most shocking.

I haven't yet told M I bore Samantha, and I rather doubt I will. Since Liza and her husband died in that awful carriage accident just after Sam was born, I have allowed M to believe Sam to be Liza's babe. He's quite taken with her. When I asked if she could be our ward after we are married, he was most accommodating, saying we must do right by her.

When I spoke with him about traveling to Yorkshire to visit Liza's family, he encouraged me to do so, insisting I should go as he would be spending more time at Horse Guards. I believe he was even more concerned for Sam, however, as he has a rather poor opinion of the family of Liza's husband. How a Harrington girl could have ended up married to a commoner is beyond my comprehension (I do not mean for that to include you, of course, but then you are as much a member of the ton as any of us—even if you will not acknowledge it).

I shall be gone from London for at least two months. I will miss you terribly. I will write to let you know of my safe arrival, and I wish for the day I can introduce you to our child.

My love always and forever, Caroline.

Emma gasped, stunned by the ruse Caroline had devised to keep her identity as the true mother of Samantha from her husband.

Poor *M.*

Poor Samantha, for the girl could never be told of her true parentage.

Setting aside the letters, Emma realized she had spent far too much time ruminating. She would begin her position with Thomas Wellingham in two days. She had much to do to get her new home in order.

Wanting to take advantage of the daylight hours, she decided she would read more of Caroline's letters before retiring, perhaps while in bed.

Although she hadn't considered her father's *affaire* as anything involving her—if he had wanted her to know, he would have told her, she decided—she still felt sorrow.

Does Samantha know about me?

Emma made her way to her bedchamber and began unpacking the trunks, tears finally falling when she realized she had no idea who her sister could be.

CHAPTER 19
FIRST DAY ON THE JOB

ay 24, 1802, Woodscastle

"Good morning, Mr. Wellingham," Emma said brightly as she allowed Humphrey to take her riding cloak. She added a quick curtsy when she could. A covered basket hung from one arm as she stood in the vestibule of Woodscastle.

Thomas smiled and bowed. "Good morning, Miss Emma. Have you had breakfast?" he asked as he took in the sight of his newest employee. "It's rather early." Although he had not set a start time for her first day of work, Thomas hadn't expected her to show up at eight o'clock in the morning.

"Yes, thank you," Emma replied. "I hope I'm not too early. I remember you saying you liked to get to your office before nine."

Thomas clasped his hands behind his back. "Not at all. But I'll just go to town for a few hours later today. I wanted to take the opportunity to familiarize you with the business and the books, and to be available in case you had questions." He motioned for her to follow as he led the way to the library, a well-lit room on the front of the house. Before he took the turn to go through the doors, though, he held up one finger. "Before we start, there is something I must show you," he said, a grin appearing.

He continued walking down the broad corridor to the far west room of the house. Large portraits lined the otherwise unadorned walls of the gallery, giving Emma the impression she was being watched as she followed her employer. Stopping inside the arched doorway, Thomas held out his arm to indicate the piano-forté in the middle of the music room. "I must thank you for informing me of Christiana's abilities on this instrument. She really can play," he said enthusiastically.

Emma smiled at his comment. Would Christiana ever put voice to her love of music? "You are most welcome, Mr. Wellingham. 'Tis a beautiful instrument," Emma remarked as she noted the piano's inlaid wood and gold trim. "Did you have it imported?" she asked as she studied the finish, careful not to touch the surface.

"Actually, no," Thomas replied. "Ganer makes them in the West End," he said happily. "In Broad Street," he added as he held his hands together behind his back.

Emma recognized the name and recalled the display of harps they kept in their stylish window. "I wonder if Miss Wellingham will still practice an hour every day," she commented, hoping Christiana would continue the routine she had developed while at school.

"Indeed, at least an hour or two everyday," he replied with a nod. "You are, of course, welcome to use it during your break for luncheon, if you should so desire," he offered. *She has the fingers for it*, he thought as he noticed her hands.

"It is very kind of you to offer," Emma replied as she turned to follow Thomas back to the library. "I must warn you, though, that I don't play nearly as well as your sister," she said. She entered the library ahead of him as he stood aside for her. While marveling at the dark oak moldings and trim, coffered ceiling, banks of shelving filled with leather-bound books and scrolls, and the rich furnishings, she nearly walked into a library table.

"You'll work here," Thomas said as he pulled out a leather covered desk chair that matched the exquisite library table.

"Thank you. It may take me some time to adjust," Emma replied with a grin, thinking of how much more pleasant it would be to work at such a large table compared to the small writing desks she had been using at school. The surface of this table was smooth—no ruts or gouges from years of abuse by students. Glancing around the table, she noted a candle lamp and matches, a pen and inkwell, and piles of leather-covered ledger books.

The short edge of the library table was placed against the wall with all the windows, so there was plenty of natural light in which to work. Another chair faced hers. Once she was seated, Thomas sat across from her. "I use this room frequently during the day. Please don't be interrupted by my comings and goings," he said as he pulled a book off the pile. "If I need your attention, I will address you directly," he explained as he opened the ledger book.

"I understand," Emma replied with a nod.

"Miss Emma, the first night we became acquainted, I recall you asking about the shipping practices of my company," Thomas began in preamble. "Wellingham Imports don't own any of their own ships. We have contracts with captains who own their own ships, and then we consign them to pick up and deliver from a variety of ports."

Emma nodded. "I imagine captains who own their own vessels are less likely to take unnecessary risks than their independent counterparts," she reasoned.

"Exactly," Thomas replied, surprised she had come to the conclusion without needing to be told. "And we pay them in cash just as soon as their ships are emptied and the merchandise is satisfactorily inventoried. That usually requires a few days or more," he added in explanation. "We have one ship on consignment that can handle a much larger inventory, so it can take up to a week to inventory its cargo, but the captain is a good man and trusts us with the extra time."

Turning a page of the ledger book Thomas had opened, Emma noticed a few line items. "What about overland transport?" she asked. "It appears that perhaps you own some coaches and use company employees to drive them?"

Thomas leaned over the table and noted the entries. "Ah, yes. For routes from London north to as far as Scotland, we have a total of sixteen coaches that follow the postal routes to pick up and deliver goods, mostly textiles, yarns, wool, and such. We own those as well as four others that travel east-west routes to port towns. The drivers are employees who live along the routes. They trade off with the other drivers as the coaches arrive in their villages. For the most part, the system works well. We have one driver, though, who must be on the road about twice as much as the others due to the length of his route."

Emma looked over the page with the payroll list. "That would be Mr. B. Browning?" she asked as she read through the list of names and noticed his higher pay.

Impressed at how quickly she had figured out the person to whom he referred, he nodded. "That is correct. We are working to add another driver to the route, or perhaps we will change it to even out the distances."

Emma glanced at a few more pages, carefully turning the large sheets. "How many accomptants work on these?" she asked as she noticed a variety of signatures on each page. The same two accomptants seemed to work on the overland transport numbers while a variety worked on the shipping numbers and taxes. Only one did the payroll.

"There are ten clerks in all. They work in the west London warehouse," Thomas explained quickly. "I hired them all myself. They all came with references or were recommended to me by friends or business associates," he added, trying not to sound too defensive. He had employed the same care in hiring his warehouse and dock workers as he did the clerks in the accounting department. "They're all of exceptional character," he added, realizing even as he said it, that if Emma did find evidence of embezzlement, then one of his accomptants was not of good character.

"Are there blank ledgers I might use to check this work?" Emma asked, looking around for blank paper or ledger sheets.

Thomas nodded and pulled two large books to the center of the table. Both were new books, but they had dark red leather covers as opposed to the brown leather covers of the completed ledgers. "There are more where these came from, should you need more," he offered. "Just let me know a day or so in advance so that I may bring one home with me."

Continuing to look through the ledgers, Emma said, "I believe I have all I need. May I ask about your expectations of my workday?"

Thomas angled his head to the side. "What expectations should I have?"

Straightening in her chair, Emma asked, "What time would you like me to start each day? Do you want me to work Saturdays? When and how long may I take luncheon? What time do you want me to leave each evening? And are there any days you would prefer me to *not* be here?"

Thomas considered her queries. "Eight o'clock is certainly early enough. Saturdays... perhaps. You are certainly welcome to take luncheon with Christiana and me when we are here. That is usually at two o'clock. Six o'clock is late enough—I wouldn't want you returning to London in the dark." Pausing a moment, he asked, "And what was your last question?"

Emma smiled. "Are there any days that you would prefer me—?"

"Oh, yes," Thomas remembered. "Not that I can think of at this time. I will give you notice if something should arise, though. Humphrey can always let you in, of course." He paused as he considered what else to cover. "I will see to it you get paid at the end of each week. By the way," he asked, "Just how *are* you getting here?"

Relieved he couldn't guess she had ridden a horse by the odor she was sure permeated her clothing, she replied, "I rode my horse."

Taken aback, Thomas said, "Indeed. Then Mr. Allen will see to its care during the day."

It was Emma's turn to be surprised. "That is very kind of him," she commented. "Thank you."

Thomas nodded but displayed a look of concern. "Did you ride here... alone?"

Stiffening, Emma gave the man a slight shrug. "I might have, but one of the grooms from the mews behind my townhouse insisted he escort me. He made some excuse about a horse needing to be exercised."

Straightening in his seat, Thomas regarded the young woman. Was she always this headstrong? "A groom will escort you home, as well," he stated with some finality, thinking Mr. Allen would probably welcome the opportunity to get out of the stables. "What will you do when it rains?" he queried. "You'll catch your death!"

Emma had to suppress a grin. How many times had she heard that comment as she made her way to classes in the rain? "I can come by phaeton when necessary," she assured him, remembering Sophia Simpson's offer to use her equipage. Or she could rent a post chaise, if need be.

"Perhaps it would be a better idea for you to pack a trunk or bring a valise with enough clothing for a few days. You will stay in the guest bedchamber. In the event of rain, you will, of course, spend the night here," he stated evenly. "I will let Mrs. Werthers— she's the housekeeper—know to prepare the bedchamber."

Stunned at his offer of hospitality, Emma could only say, "That's very kind of you, sir."

The enigmatic Mr. Wellingham seemed generous, gracious, and certainly more tolerable of the lower classes than she had experienced with other people of wealth. Despite having met the man the two times prior to this meeting, she still expected him to exhibit a degree of snobbishness, but instead found him merely... demanding.

Thomas remembered his conversation with Stephen Bingham the previous Friday and bit his lip. "Miss Emma, did your father ever employ others to work in his shop? Besides you, of course," he asked as he gave her an expectant look.

Emma angled her head. "Of course," she replied, her curiosity piqued by his question. "Sometimes as many as five or six. Why do you ask?"

Leaning back in the chair, Thomas crossed his arms. "I have a long-time employee who has suddenly taken to being tardy every day for the past couple of weeks," he began in explanation. "And, from the looks of him, he is not getting much sleep. I'm concerned he might be... gambling or staying too late at the pub or..." He shook his head, not sure what to think of the sudden change in Sean MacGregor.

"Or perhaps his wife has just had a baby," Emma offered as she leaned on the table. "'Tis common for the entire household to be kept awake by a colicky newborn," she explained as she noted his look of disbelief. The residents of the Home of Unwed Mothers certainly knew first-hand how difficult it could be to get sleep when just one baby was up all night crying.

Thomas leaned forward and considered her comment. "I suppose that could be," he replied, still lost in thought.

"So, no one has asked him why he is late?" she asked in a hoarse whisper.

Shrugging helplessly, Thomas shook his head. "My warehouse manager said he tried to draw him out, but the man wouldn't say."

Emma regarded her boss for a moment. "Perhaps if you spoke with him in private, he might be more... forthcoming," she suggested. "You said he was a long-time employee. He's probably very embarrassed at what's been happening. And if it's something besides gambling or the drink, such as a baby or... another position, then perhaps his hours could be changed to accommodate his schedule."

Thomas sat up straight at the comment, a look of annoyance briefly crossing his face. *"Accommodate his schedule?"* he repeated, his brows furrowing.

Aware she had angered her new boss, Emma stiffened. "I was under the impression you wished to retain his services," she responded meekly.

"Well, of course! He's a valuable employee," Thomas answered defensively. Realization dawned on him then. If it were just a new baby, at some point, the man's life would return to normal, and he would no longer be tardy. But if he had taken a second job, either because he had been lured away by another company or because he just needed the extra income, then it would make sense to do whatever he could to accommodate him. "Very good then. I will leave you to your books," Thomas said as he stood up.

Startled, Emma stood up and curtsied. "Thank you again for this opportunity, Mr. Wellingham," she said with a nod.

"Thank you for your insight, Miss Wellingham," Thomas replied as he bowed and left the room.

When Thomas returned from town at five o'clock, he found Emma where he had left her that morning. Several ledgers were arranged on the library table, and he noticed ink stains on the fingers of both hands. "Do you write with both hands, Miss Emma?" he asked as he stood over the table.

Emma gasped and started to stand up. "Pardon me, sir, I didn't hear you come in," she said as tried to compose herself.

Thomas attempted to suppress a smile and found he could not. "Pardon me for interrupting your work. I didn't realize how deep was your concentration."

Her ears turning pink with embarrassment, Emma nodded. "Yes, I do write with both hands," she admitted. "Notes with my right, numbers with my left," she added.

"Efficient, then," Thomas replied as he took the chair across from her. "And have you questions or… concerns?" he asked, not sure how far she would have progressed in just a few hours.

"Not yet, Mr. Wellingham. So far, it is very straightforward," she replied. "I have found a few questionable entries, of course, but the errors are small and are most likely unintentional errors in addition or subtraction." After a short pause, she added, "I do wonder, though, about the lack of numbers for overhead costs for the operation."

Thomas frowned at the comment. "Overhead? Whatever do you mean?"

Emma straightened and considered the cost accounting she had learned in Mr. Stoke's class. It was far more thorough in determining the true profit or loss of a company because it considered all the costs of overhead in running the business, not just the salaries of the employees. "Are you familiar with Josiah Wedgwood?"

Thomas straightened and regarded Emma as if she were mad. "Well, of course. He was a well-known potter, as is his son."

Nodding, Emma said, "Yes. His firm was the only pottery factory to survive the depression of seventy-two, despite the fact that his head clerk was embezzling from him."

Thomas' eyebrows reached his hairline. "Indeed?" he replied, now quite interested in the story.

"The reason he was able to continue his operations is because he invented cost accounting," she explained quickly. "It's a method of determining the true cost of being in business by tracking overhead costs. In addition to including the salaries of his employees, Mr. Wedgwood figured out what costs were associated with his buildings, the machinery, the materials, transportation, breakage—everything that contributed a *cost* to his operation.

"When he realized certain products cost more to produce, he charged more for them. Other products were cheaper to manufacture, so he could charge less for those. And some lent themselves to volume production, so he could maximize profits on those products."

Thomas followed her explanation, trying to figure out how it could apply to his business. "I own my own building and the land on which it is built, so there is no leasing cost to me or my company," he reasoned.

"But there should be maintenance costs," Emma countered. "And costs to heat and light the building. Coal, gas, wood. None of those costs are showing up in the ledgers. And I cannot find any reference to feed or care for the horses that are not in your stables, nor for the coaches and their upkeep."

Rolling his eyes, Thomas sat back and regarded Emma for a moment. "And that would be because the drivers pay for all of that themselves. That is why their salaries are so much higher than those of our dock workers," he explained simply.

Emma pursed her lips, not wanting to seem argumentative. "But... there is no *accounting* of those expenses here. How can you be sure they're spending the money on feed and maintenance and not using it for personal gain?"

Thomas was about to argue on behalf of his drivers, but decided he couldn't find fault with her reasoning. *She has a point.* Scrubbing

his face with a hand, he considered her words. "I cannot," he admitted, more concerned for the horses in the field than the effects of a
few pounds lost to embezzlement. "I shall work with the clerks to
determine these... overhead costs, did you call them?" he asked with
a furrowed brow.

"Yes," Emma replied.

"To get these costs figured. These will be considered liabilities, I
suppose?"

"That's correct," Emma replied as she nodded. "But if you buy
enough of something to last longer than a month, you can carry it
over to the next month," she added. "Spread out the liability, so to
speak."

But Thomas' attention was on other considerations. "I'm
supposing that the costs in the winter will be higher for the
building due to heating and higher for the stables because more
horses are kept in town in the winter. Costs will be higher for
transportation in the summer since we run far more overland
transports in good weather," he murmured as he continued to
think out loud. "Come to think of it, the products that come
from farther away really should be priced higher than the same
products that come from areas closer to London... textiles,
wool..." His voice trailed off as he considered the other costs of
running the business. When he finally returned his attention to
Emma, he nodded. "I'll see to it tomorrow morning," he
announced.

"Very good, sir," Emma replied with a quiet sigh, glad to get the
first order of business out of the way. "I realize it may not look like
it, but I have made a bit of progress today," she said as she indicated
her place in the first ledger book.

Thomas shrugged and realized from the looks of the ledgers
spread out on the table that she had, indeed, become familiar with
his business. "Very well, then." Remembering their earlier conversation, he added, "By the way, I spoke with the tardy employee. Who
was, by the way, tardy again today," he said as he leaned back in the
chair, obviously ready to share his information as if it were gossip.

Although it was really none of her concern, Emma realized
Thomas expected her to ask the obvious question. "Did he explain
why he was late yet again?" she asked as she angled her head.

Thomas nodded and allowed a mischievous grin to cross his
face. "You were right. Our Mr. MacGregor is the father of a two-

week-old baby boy who apparently doesn't sleep at night," he said with some amusement.

Emma shook her head in sympathy. "First baby?" she guessed.

"Indeed. The man has been an employee so long, I rather thought his children, if he had any, would be grown and having their own by now. But he only married for the first time last year," he said in disbelief. "I cannot imagine starting a family at his age! He's nearly forty!"

Smiling, Emma regarded her employer and agreed with his comment. "So, has he been oversleeping?" she asked.

At that, Thomas shook his head. "No, poor man. It seems he doesn't wish to leave his wife and baby alone. His sister comes to stay with them during the day, but she works nights as a maid and cannot get to his house until five, and he won't leave until she arrives. By the time he gets to the West End, he's bound to be late for a six o'clock start. So, I changed his schedule so he starts at seven."

From the manner in which he described the situation and his solution, Emma thought he felt a hint of triumph at having solved the problem. "Very good, sir," she said with a curt nod.

So, Mr. Wellingham can be an accommodating man, she thought happily.

"Can't say Mr. Bingham is very happy about it, but, as you said, it's only temporary," Thomas added with a smile.

Emma leaned forward. "At least, until his wife has another baby," she said with a wink.

Thomas' look of triumph faded. "I cannot understand why anyone would want a *baby*," he said under his breath.

"Neither can I," Emma replied in a whisper, the topic reminding her of another baby, a baby that would now be around eight years old. "Mr. Wellingham, I wondered if you might know any ... aristocrats in London. An aristocrat whose wife's name might be Caroline?"

Thomas arched an eyebrow, surprised by the question. "Well, I don't know Lord Chamberlain personally, but he's a viscount. A relation, is he?"

Emma's eyes widened. "Relation?" she repeated.

"Matthew Fitzsimmons," Thomas countered, wondering at Emma's look of surprise. "I'm not sure of Lady Chamberlain's name, though." He stood up and moved to the bookshelves. "Unfortunately, I don't I have an updated DeBrett's here."

Forcing her mouth to stay closed, Emma considered the information. "He is my uncle," she acknowledged as she realized his first name started with an '*M*.' And her aunt's name was Caroline.

She closed her eyes, hoping beyond hope her father hadn't had an *affaire* with his brother's wife. *Although they weren't married at the time Samantha was born*, she remembered.

Thomas gave a start and turned from where he stood next to a shelf of books. He moved back to the couch and regarded Emma for a moment. "You're the granddaughter of a viscount?" he half-asked, one eyebrow nearly into his hairline. "What was your father doing making *hats?*" he asked in surprise when Emma nodded.

Giving her employer a shrug, she thought for a moment. "He was... fascinated with hats, but he hated the way they fit. And he despised their poor construction," she explained. "So he learned to make them the way he thought they should be made, and then he went into trade."

Trade. Thomas nodded, realizing his father had done much the same thing in escaping a family of aristocrats. "Black sheep?" he asked in a quiet voice.

"Very," Emma replied with a nod, suddenly noticing the late afternoon sun. "And with that, I should be going," she said as she stood up.

Thomas saw her to the vestibule, leaving her with Humphrey to see about her horse and a groom to escort her back to London.

Shaking his head, he marveled at the day's discoveries.

My bookkeeper is a viscount's granddaughter.

CHAPTER 20
SPLITTING LOGS

June 4, 1802, Woodscastle

By the end of her second week at Woodscastle, Emma had settled into a comfortable routine in her work on the ledgers. When she found a mistake, she transcribed the ledger onto a new sheet, noting her findings. If a page was free of errors, she simply added her initials to those at the bottom of the sheet and moved to the next page.

With the warmer weather came a busier shipping season. Thomas spent the first four workdays in London but returned home by four o'clock for tea, sometimes bringing a new book for Emma to audit. He usually took his tea in the library as he read a newspaper or sat at his huge oak desk and wrote letters. Emma, who always accepted a cup of tea, worked through teatime, content to continue her work while Christiana practiced piano-forté in the music room down the hall.

It was on Friday of that second week when Thomas, who had elected to spend the entire day at home, viewed the good weather as an opportunity to prepare for winter. Dressed only in trousers, boots, and a loose shirt, he was in the yard behind the house chopping wood. Having been at it for over an hour, he had worked up a sweat, but paused only to take a drink of the lemonade Humphrey had brought out the moment before. Placing another log on an old tree stump, he raised the ax and brought it down on the end of the log, creating a loud 'thunk' before the wood neatly split into two pieces.

Christiana and Emma, about to take their luncheon on the back terrace, had just come out of the house. Emma turned to discover the source of the sound, and then watched as Thomas raised the ax and brought it down again on another log. The damp fabric of his shirt clung to him, outlining every muscle of his arms and upper torso. Even the muscles of his thighs appeared in relief through the breeches he wore.

At that very moment, a most intense and pleasurable frisson coursed through Emma. She felt her face flush bright red, sure anyone looking in her direction would have noticed... something.

Stunned, she quickly turned around to face Christiana. Had the younger girl noticed anything untoward? Placing her hand against her belly, Emma stared at Christiana for a moment and then sighed audibly.

"Are you all right?" Christiana asked when she finally noticed the awestruck look on her friend's face.

"Quite," Emma replied, forcing herself to take a seat at the small iron table. "I... I just... thought of something I need to correct in a ledger," she said lamely, realizing the girl knew nothing of what had just happened. Indeed, Christiana simply continued the conversation she had started when they were still in the house, arranging small plates on the table as she did so.

Wondering if it was possible to recreate the sensation she had felt, Emma dared another glance in Thomas' direction. She was forced to wave when he acknowledged her from where he stood, and the only sensation she felt was embarrassment at seeing her employer without his topcoat or waistcoat.

Deciding whatever she had felt was merely a fluke, Emma simply ate her lunch and willed herself not to look again as Thomas continued to split wood.

*T*homas regarded the last log from the pile. After more than an hour of splitting logs, he was exhausted and drenched in sweat. The physical activity felt necessary, though, since he had been spending far too much time behind a desk.

He hadn't considered his lack of attire while he wielded the ax. His sister had many times seen him split logs while he wore nothing more than a shirt and breeches. But Miss Emma...

Had she been offended by his appearance when she caught sight of him as she and Christiana moved to the table to take their luncheon? He thought her expression one of surprise or... he couldn't quite put his finger on it.

He knew what he had thought upon seeing her, though. A sudden and most unexpected feeling of *desire* had struck him. Primal and fierce in its intensity, the urge to...

To what? He had been so stunned by the feeling, all he could think to do was give her a nod and resume his work, hoping his sudden arousal wasn't evident.

What the hell? He hadn't felt urges such as these in years. A couple of afternoons with Rebecca Merriweather had been enough to ensure he wanted nothing to do with young women. But he couldn't imagine Miss Emma doing the unnatural acts Rebecca did to those she bedded. He could imagine her doing some of the natural acts... Thomas shook his head as if to clear it before bringing the ax down on another log.

Thunk.

Realizing he had no more logs to split, he sighed. A shower-bath was in order.

A cold one.

CHAPTER 21
A BUSINESS MEETING OF
THE MINDS

June 7, 1802, Woodscastle

At the start of the third week, Thomas entered the library just as Emma opened a ledger. "Several gentlemen will be joining me for a meeting here tomorrow," he stated as he moved toward his desk. "Will our discussions disturb you?" he asked. "I can arrange for you to work in a different room if you prefer," he offered when Emma turned in his direction.

"I shouldn't think I will even notice their presence, Mr. Wellingham," she replied and returned her attention to the ledger, thinking the voices of a few men would be easy to ignore. But Thomas' next comment surprised her.

"Miss Emma, if any of these men should ask you what it is you're doing here, simply say something about keeping the household books. They cannot know you are working on my business accounts," he stated quietly, obviously bothered by the secrecy in the request he was making.

"Of course, Mr. Wellingham. I'll see to it the ledgers I'm not working on are put away," Emma assured him

"Very good," he said with a nod. "And I've asked Christiana if she'll lunch with you on the back terrace tomorrow. I do hope that's not an inconvenience," he added, noting her look of surprise.

"Not at all," she replied. She and Christiana had been taking their luncheon on the back terrace nearly every day. "I rather like it out there."

When Thomas returned from London that evening, he was

much later than usual. He entered the library just as Emma was closing up ledgers and placing them in cabinets Humphrey had opened for her.

"Mr. Wellingham," she said as she curtsied.

Thomas bowed quickly, obviously out of breath. "Miss Emma, it's most fortunate I caught you before you took your leave," he said. "If you could just stay a moment more, I need to speak with you about tomorrow's meeting."

Emma's eyes widened at his apparent nervousness. "Of course," she replied as she placed another book into the cabinet. Only one book and several ledger pages remained on the library table. Those would be moved to a small desk once Humphrey had rearranged the library furnishings to prepare for the meeting.

Thomas motioned her to sit with him in one of the large leather sofas.

"It is possible that one or more of the gentlemen coming here tomorrow will not have my company's best interests in mind," he began without preamble. The fact that he had to provide hospitality to such men aggravated him more than he cared to admit, but he knew it was for the good of the company in the longer term. "I agreed to this meeting only because three of the gentlemen support my company and want to see it succeed. We'll be discussing long-term strategy for Wellingham Imports. Some... *ideas* for the business may be discussed at length," he explained carefully. "None of what you hear can leave this room," he added sternly.

Emma was beginning to wonder if she should move the books to the music room. "I understand, Mr. Wellingham," she nodded. "I doubt I will even be aware of your meeting, though," she said. A thought struck her. "Unless... unless you *want* me to be," she said in a conspiratorial tone.

Astonished, Thomas jerked his head to look at her directly. It was a moment before he said anything. "What are you implying?"

Emma glanced away for a moment. "Do you need your conversations to be transcribed?"

Thomas thought about her question and shook his head. "I don't take your meaning."

Emma leaned forward. "Do you require a transcript of the meeting?" she clarified. "Who said what, the discussion of the topics, the resolutions, the agreements. I can write shorthand when it is required of me," she said with a nod. When Thomas didn't respond right away, she added, "Sometimes 'tis easier to determine whom your friends are by reading between the lines of what they say."

Thomas sat in silence for several minutes, trying to decide if what Emma was suggesting was a good idea or just an insidious way to spy on businessmen, some of them his direct competitors. "All right," he finally said. "But it must look like you are... writing letters... for the household. You cannot be obvious about listening to us. Half the men will be facing your direction and may notice if you appear to be eavesdropping."

"I understand, Mr. Wellingham." Emma replied as she stood up to go. "I shall make myself nearly invisible to your guests."

To prepare for the men's arrival and their meeting in the library, Humphrey had rearranged the furniture so the largest leather chairs were facing each other instead of the fireplace. He placed bricks under the legs of one high-backed chair so it was taller than the other chairs. The large, low ornate table on which Christiana sometimes played cards was placed in the middle of the setting, and side tables were placed next to some chairs to provide the guests a resting place for their drinks and ashtrays. Humphrey refilled the decanters at the bar and added several crystal goblets and rummers to the collection already gracing the top of the sideboard. Linen napkins were folded and stacked in the event a gentlemen required one before tea was served. A small fire crackled in the fireplace. Although it was June, he knew his master appreciated the ambiance a fire could provide.

The library table Emma usually used was placed up against the wall of windows, and an escritoire and chair were placed next to the window for her use during the day. Although the escritoire didn't provide the same amount of space on which to work, it did provide some privacy.

Prior to her leaving the night before, she had discovered some interesting differences in the ledger balances from week to week, and she wanted to use the early morning to determine what accounts were affected and how much money was involved. An inkwell filled with red ink and a new pen were set to one side in the event she found the problems. The black inkwell and an older pen were also available so she could transcribe ledgers, if necessary. A stack of crisp white parchment in one of the cubbies of the escritoire would be used later as she transcribed the meeting.

Before she had spent more than a few minutes reviewing the

ledgers, a pattern of embezzlement became clear in three months of numbers. One account, inventory, was consistently off when it came to beginning and ending values. Otherwise, the numbers were correct in every other journal entry. Once she had documented all the instances in the first book, she stood up to retrieve another ledger from the cabinet when she heard noises out front. A large carriage bearing four gentlemen of various heights and ages pulled up to Woodscastle. A few moments later, another smaller coach with two gentlemen stopped behind the first carriage. Mr. Allen assisted the riders of the carriage while Humphrey hurried to assist those in the coach. When all the men were on their feet, the contingent made their way to the front door.

Emma hurried to get the other ledger and be seated at the desk before the men made their way to the library. When Humphrey led them into the library, she stood and curtsied to the entire contingent as Thomas introduced her. Most of the men bowed in return or at least gave her a nod. Emma took her seat and pretended to ignore them as they took seats around the low table. Mrs. Werthers delivered trays of biscuits, cakes, pastries and a tea and coffee service, seeing to it each man had been served before she took her leave of the room. Apparently, hospitality required several minutes be devoted to food and drink before a meeting could begin.

Once the meeting finally started, Emma wrote as many comments as she overheard, amused that those who drank alcohol were more likely to share their company secrets or admit to some scandalous wrongdoing than those who only drank the tea. Occasionally, their voices would rise as they argued, and Thomas would have to quiet them. By the time Humphrey announced luncheon was served, Emma sensed her employer's impatience with the proceedings and could tell he was relieved to have the gentlemen adjourn to the dining room.

As he was getting up to leave the library, Todd Vandermeer of the East India Company paused in mid-step and glanced in Emma's direction. She casually closed the ledger book and slipped her notes into one of the desk cubbyholes, acting as if she were clearing the desk.

"Why, you are as quiet as a church mouse over here in the corner," he commented as he approached her. Emma quickly stood up and curtsied as he bowed.

Nearly a foot taller than Emma, the man was also very thin and walked with a cane. Remembering the chair with the bricks under the legs, she realized Humphrey had prepared it for this man.

"I am Todd Vandermeer, at your service. Have you been here the entire time?" he asked as he angled his head.

Emma started at hearing his name. Todd Vandermeer, the patron of the Home for Unwed Mothers.

The man Deborah threatened to kiss should she ever meet him!

The girl certainly wouldn't have to bend down to do it. Todd Vandermeer had at least six inches on her!

Emma struggled to regain her composure, realizing the man had been sitting with his back to her and may not have been in the library when Thomas introduced her to his guests. "Yes, since nine o'clock, in fact. I've been working on the household accounts," Emma replied as she motioned to a ledger book on the desk, hoping he wouldn't ask too many questions. "I'm Emma Fitzsimmons. I'm very honored to meet you," she said as she held out her right hand, intending to shake his hand.

The tall man instead captured the tips of her fingers with his and raised them to his mouth, his lips brushing over her knuckles in a move that at once startled her and impressed her.

No man had ever kissed the back of her ungloved hand before!

In the moment it took him to release her hand, Emma noticed his stylish clothing and the front-combed curls of his dark hair. Although there were few men who could achieve the Titus hairstyle without a great deal of work, Mr. Vandermeer's seemed to be natural.

Emma swallowed, realizing the man hadn't made any response. "I know of you from your patronage of the Home for Unwed Mothers," she blurted. "It was my charity work when I attended Warwick's," she added quickly, sure her cheeks were flushed red from his surprising move.

"Indeed?" he replied as he regarded her, his raised eyebrow indicating an interest that seemed to increase with each comment she made. "I give where I think it helps most," he said with a nod. "I do hope our conversations didn't disturb you," he added with a nod in the direction of the meeting space.

Emma dared a glance to where the men had been sitting. "Oh, not at all," Emma said with a wave of her hand. "Once I'm working in numbers, I'm hardly aware of anything else. I had several letters to write for Mr. Wellingham, as well."

The other gentlemen were making their way to the library door. A few took note of her presence. "Mr. Wellingham, you really must invite this young lady to lunch with us," William Bottoms commented as he indicated Emma. A few others nodded in agreement.

Startled he had noticed her, Emma smiled nervously. "Thank you, sir, but Miss Wellingham is expecting me to take luncheon with her today," Emma said with a nod and a curtsy in their general direction.

"Oh, come now, we could use a reminder to be civil," the mustached Walter Binger said with a frown. He had raised his voice at least a few times in their morning discussions and didn't seem at all happy with the meeting's proceedings.

"I do believe Mr. Binger has the right idea," Todd Vandermeer said in agreement.

Emma couldn't help but notice the comment was directed to Thomas. *So, is Mr. Vandermeer a friend or a foe?*

Thomas nodded to the importer. "Would you do us the honor of joining us for luncheon then, Miss Fitzsimmons?" he asked, his manner almost apologetic.

Friend, she decided. Emma blushed and smiled demurely at all the men. "However could I refuse an invitation to lunch with so many handsome men?" she replied, making sure she said the word 'handsome' as she looked directly at Todd. She took his arm even before he could offer it and kept her steps in line with his slower gait.

In the dining room, she made sure to sit next to Mr. Binger and allowed a smile when Mr. Vandermeer sat directly across from her. If Thomas' goal at this meal was to keep his friends close but his enemies closer, he had succeeded in the seating plan. Binger sat to her left, and the two gentlemen who had been rather vocal towards the end of the morning session sat to her right. Those to Vandermeer's left were also rather cantankerous, she remembered, leaving Richard Wodehouse, on Vandermeer's right, as the one who had barely said a word. Thomas' earlier introduction of the man hinted Wodehouse was an ally of Wellingham Imports, though.

As the maid, Dahlia, served soup, several of the men began taking up conversations about various topics, and Emma relaxed. She overheard something about a band of housebreakers terrorizing estates west of London and a snippet about an actor being shot by his mistress. But several eyes turned to her when Mr. Vandermeer spoke up. "Miss Emma, I understand you are a recent graduate of Mr. Stoke's accounting course in London," he stated as he lifted his wine glass.

Caught off-guard, Emma lowered her soup spoon. "That's right, Mr. Vandermeer. I found it quite challenging and very informative," Emma replied with a nod, hoping the conversation would end there. Then she realized it was her turn to ask something of the importer. "Have you taken his course?" Out of the corner of her eye, she was aware of Thomas slumping in his chair.

"Unfortunately, no," Todd replied with a wave of his wine glass. "I have been working at East India since I was but six years old," he explained, a hint of pride entering his voice. "I learned the business of importing by doing it, I suppose you could say." Changing the subject back to the accounting class, he said, "I understand that every class must do a practicum of some sort in order to complete their study. May I ask what your class did to fulfill the requirement?"

At this point, all eyes were on Emma, and she was sure the tops of her cheeks were bright red. "Of course, Mr. Vandermeer," she nodded. Taking a deep breath, she said, "Our supposition was that any business involved in the importation of goods to England needed to employ the most efficient cargo transport and ship off-loading practices in order to stay price competitive, even if they had monopolies on certain goods. Since the London docks are too crowded, we looked at locating an importer directly at a port on the channel side of England." Emma paused in her explanation when several of the men made noises of amusement.

"Please continue," Mr. Vandermeer encouraged her, giving the man next to Thomas a look of annoyance.

"As these gentlemen are already aware," Emma said with a nod to the ones who had reacted with amusement, "The overland transport costs of getting the goods to London and into another warehouse proved too expensive, even if the up-front costs were generally less to ship to a channel port. So we proposed that import companies locate their warehouses directly on the River Thames and then build private docks directly adjacent to their warehouses..."

If anyone at the table had not been listening up until that point, she now had everyone's attention. Todd suddenly looked very nervous, as did a few others, including Thomas, who sat staring at her with a blank expression.

"Private docks?" Binger repeated, awestruck. "But the city would never allow such a thing!"

Emma turned her head to look at the man and shook her head. His comment made Emma wonder if he were unaware of what merchants were willing to do to have more dock space built. Just seven years earlier, the plans and estimates done by Daniel Alexander for the new London docks at Wapping were laid before a general meeting of merchants where they were unanimously approved. To ensure the docks would be built, a subscription of 800,000£ was filled within a few *hours*. However, the merchants' application received a great deal of opposition from the corporation of London and from private interests. Ultimately, however, the merchants triumphed, and the new docks were scheduled to be under construction the following month. It would be two-and-a-half years before the docks would open for business, though.

When Emma realized Binger was referring to the city not allowing individual private docks, she replied, "Well, actually, we were able to prove our supposition correct because when we researched records with the city planners, we found not just one, but four importers had already put in such requests for private docks. East India is creating a company to build and run docks for two-hundred and fifty ships," she said, making eye contact with Todd, "While two smaller importers should be receiving their approval within the month," she added as she looked at Thomas. She desperately hoped she had not said too much, but Todd Vandermeer had broached the subject. What could she do but answer his question?

Binger's jaw dropped while a murmur went up around the table. "And just what kind of benefit can an importer expect to enjoy by utilizing such an arrangement, Miss Fitzsimmons?" Wodehouse asked from his end of the table.

Glad to have the opportunity to explain her class's findings, she replied, "We determined that an importer would no longer need to employ small ships to provide freight handling on the water and that the transport costs between the dock and the warehouse would be reduced to such a short distance as to be negligible. Overall, most importers would enjoy a thirty-percent reduction in the costs associated with handling their goods. There was also the consideration of security," she continued when no one moved to interrupt her. "Patrick Colquhoun, the magistrate, estimated that river pirates plunder the West Indian merchants of about a quarter million pounds annually because watermen are in collusion with watchmen. They help arrange the theft of hogsheads of sugar, coffee and tallow. With docks closer to warehouses and the importers employing their own watchmen, it is less likely watermen will be able to assist pirates.

"We were not able to quantify the amount that might still be stolen, however. And, unfortunately, we were not able to quantify the reduction in time that a ship need spend on the river since their crews seem to want to spend *more* time in London, not less," she commented with a raised eyebrow. Quiet laughter ensued as several of the men took her meaning and elbowed one another.

Pursing his lips, Wodehouse nodded his approval. "Indeed. And have you landed a position with an import company, Miss Fitzsim-mons? If not—"

"Miss Fitzsimmons works for me," Thomas interrupted as he sat up straighter, masking his surprise at his employee's knowledge of his business. *She is an investor,* he remembered.

Quickly changing the subject, Thomas stated, "It is my under-standing some of the West India Docks will be built and ready for use within the year. Mr. Vandermeer, how long before the John Company has its own docks open for business?" He knew he would have to apologize profusely to his friend for the question, but at this point, it was public information.

Todd angled his head to the side and smiled. "We should have all two-hundred-and-fifty docks complete in four years," he replied with a nod. The comment was met with a round of murmurs and congratulations.

With Dahlia delivering a tray of sliced meats and cheeses and baskets of steaming hot bread, the men concentrated on food and lighter conversation. Relieved she was no longer the center of atten-tion of the group, Emma relaxed until she realized she was still Todd Vandermeer's center of attention. "Do you live in town, Miss Fitzsimmons?" he asked as he filled his plate with a sampling of the luncheon meats.

"Yes, I do, Mr. Vandermeer. I've let a townhouse in Kingly Street," she replied as she picked a few slices of meat for her own plate. "And you?" she queried, knowing full well exactly where he lived. Anyone who read *The Morning Chronicle* knew of Todd's purchase of No. 1 Chandois Street in Cavendish Square, a huge three-story mansion that boasted its own ballroom, indoor plumbing, and gas lighting. Emma couldn't recall the exact reason the house had been on the market but knew there was a hint of scandal involving the prior owner's gambling debts.

"Me, too!" he replied with a bright smile. "Well, not a townhouse, exactly," he amended, keeping his voice low so as not to attract attention. "I was *encouraged* to buy a house in Marylebone," he said, almost apologetically.

Emma smiled as she wondered just who had encouraged him to buy it and how much of a commission they'd made in the course of the transaction. "And does it suit you?" she asked, about to take a bite of meat and cheese.

Shrugging one shoulder, he replied, "It's a good house, but far too large for me. Someday I hope to have a family, and then I think it shall suit me much better. And your townhouse? Do you like it?" he asked, his attention on Emma and Emma alone.

"Very much so. 'Tis not far from Warwick's and Golden Square, so I'm already familiar with the neighborhood. And my neighbors are good people. At one time, they were servants at an estate very near here," she said lightly.

Todd's brows knitted together as he gave her comment some thought. "Merriweather Manor, perhaps?" he asked finally, his eyes widening.

Emma suppressed a gasp. "Yes, how... how did you know?" she asked, surprised he would be familiar with an estate that no longer housed a family.

Shaking his head, Todd thought for a moment before he said, "I purchased Grace Park from one of the eldest Merriweathers, and I have a friend who spent most of his youth living with the Merriweathers. Mr. Grandby has an estate in Derbyshire now, though, so I don't see him as often as I'd like. He's a very funny fellow, but I fear a woman of Society would find him somewhat of a rake," he commented with a wistful smile.

Emma grinned at his description of his friend. "Indeed?" she replied. "Well, the former butler and his wife are happily married and living off their share of the inheritance," she said with a satisfied sigh. "It was very generous of the Merriweathers to include them in their will."

Todd nodded his head. "'Tis a practice that should happen more frequently," he stated with a thoughtful gaze. "For many of us, our servants are the ones who help keep us humble and alive."

It was most interesting that his comment came just as Dahlia was setting trays of cubed fruit in front of everyone. Emma knew the maid had overheard the remark when she noticed Dahlia's prim smile and the lilt in her walk as she headed back to the kitchen.

"Your servants must adore you, Mr. Vandermeer," Emma replied as she helped herself to some fruit from the tray.

Todd sniffed. "I'm not so sure about that," he said before he bit into an apple cube. "I apparently have the best cook in London, but I don't seem to have much of an appetite these days." At Emma's raised eyebrows, he added, "Well, apparently I do if I am in the company of a woman, it seems," he amended as he realized he had eaten everything offered to him during the lunch.

Emma blushed. She was about to thank him for his comment when Mr. Binger asked him a question.

For the rest of the luncheon, Emma was content to eat and simply listen in on the various conversations that took place around her. When lunch was over, she returned to the desk in the library and dutifully wrote down everything she heard until the gentlemen left at three o'clock. She thanked them for including her in their luncheon and curtsied as they took their leave. When Todd Vandermeer, the last to leave, said his farewell to Thomas, he bade her a separate farewell and bowed and limped out the door, leaning heavily on his cane.

Thomas collapsed into the leather couch and put his head in his hands. "I'm so very relieved that it's over," he said loudly, making sure the carriages and phaetons had all left the grounds before he did so.

"Indeed," Emma replied as she shook out her right hand to ease the cramping.

"Were you truly able to transcribe any of it?" Thomas asked once he lifted his head and regarded her. Despite the amount of time she had spent writing, she still looked as fresh as she had when he found her in the library that morning. He thought of the impression she must have made on Todd—the man had seemed positively smitten with her.

Emma gathered up the pages of transcription. "I was. If I may say, sir, there were three positively insufferable characters in here. I was surprised you didn't make them take their leave before luncheon was served," she said as she brought the pages to the couch and sat down next to her employer. "I must apologize for what happened at lunch. I had no idea Mr. Vandermeer would be so... inquisitive."

Grunting, Thomas sat up straighter and took the pages from her. "No apology required, Miss Emma. Mr. Vandermeer was not raised in a proper home and sometimes does wrong in social settings. I hope he didn't offend you with his questions," he said quietly.

"Oh, not at all," Emma replied, surprised by the comment. "But with such an opportunity to speak with his peers about business matters, I was surprised he would spend time talking with *me*," she said with a quizzical look.

Thomas scratched an eyebrow and wondered how much to tell his auditor. "He speaks with peers about business matters every day. It's a bore to him. He does not, however, get an opportunity to speak with ladies very often. I appreciate that you afforded him so much conversation."

Nodding, Emma replied. "It was my pleasure." Changing the subject, she noticed he was attempting to read her transcriptions. "Can you read short hand? I used initials to indicate who said what, but sometimes I couldn't tell."

Thomas gave it a try, but could only make out a few of the sentences. "I suppose I need a translation," he sighed, curious as to how certain swirled shapes could be whole words.

"Of course," Emma replied, taking the sheets from him. She began reciting the comments, noting how Thomas sat deeper in the sofa and listened intently while watching as her finger kept her place in the recitation.

When she finished, Thomas muttered, "This is very interesting. And very informative."

When he took the notes from her, Emma excused herself and returned to working on ledgers. Humphrey came with tea a few minutes later, and Emma gratefully took a cup as she continued where she had left off that morning—finding errors.

CHAPTER 22
A GENTLEMAN COMES A CALLING

June 9, 1802, Woodscastle

Before leaving for London on Wednesday morning, an excited Thomas Wellingham met Emma as she arrived in the library. "This is brilliant," he said as he held up the meetings transcriptions from the day before. "I'm obviously doing something right, or Bottoms wouldn't be so damned upset," he exclaimed and then paused in his pacing as he realized he had cursed. At Emma's lack of reaction to the curse and her encouraging nod, he continued pacing and added, "And Wodehouse is truly an ally. I wasn't so sure until I read his comments," he said quickly. "I'm convinced an alliance can be struck betwixt several of our companies. I just have to figure out whom to approach first and what enticements will work for each," he added as he stopped pacing and regarded his accomptant.

"I'm very glad you were able to glean so much from the notes, Mr. Wellingham," Emma said with a slight smile. "It's my hope that the time I spend working on the ledgers today will more than make up for the lost time..."

Thomas shook his head, his excitement still evident. "Don't concern yourself with having lost a day, Miss Emma," he assured her before she could finish her thought. "I'll schedule a meal with Vandermeer today, if he'll see me, of course, and review this with him," he said as he held up the notes again.

Mortified, Emma wrung her hands together and bit her lip. "But you won't show Mr. Vandermeer the transcripts, I hope." When she noticed his quizzical stare, she quickly added, "As you wished, he thinks I'm a bookkeeper... that I was writing letters on your behalf." She didn't want it known she eavesdropped on the entire business meeting, especially to the one man she found to be the most interesting in the group. And the one who seemed eligible and most interested in her.

Thomas' brows knitted together. "Oh, of course," he replied as he considered her words. "I'll just infer that I wrote these myself after the meeting was over," he said with a nod. "And I'll get his opinions on how he thinks the meeting progressed. I do think we shall have some formal alliances in place by month's end, though, so the meeting was well worth it," he said with a nod.

"I'm very glad to hear it," Emma replied with a smile. "I'll return to the books now," she added as she hurried to the library table to begin her work.

The next afternoon, Emma was deep in adding inventory amounts when Humphrey interrupted her. "Miss Fitzsimmons," he said, apparently for the second time.

Emma sat up straight and looked at the butler, surprised she hadn't heard him come in. "Oh, my," she said, as she covered her mouth with a hand. "Pardon me for not acknowledging you," she said. "How ever long have you been here?"

The butler was forced to suppress a smile. "I assure you, I only just arrived," he said with a slight bow. In his outstretched hand he held a silver salver, on which was a creamy white pasteboard. "However, there is a gentleman in the vestibule asking for you. Mr. Todd Vandermeer," he stated as he continued to hold out the salver.

Emma frowned as she reached for the calling card. "The very tall man from Tuesday's meeting?" she whispered, trying to figure out how she didn't notice the sound of the horse and phaeton that were now parked in the drive. She tore her gaze from Humphrey so she could read the card.

"Indeed," Humphrey replied with a nod. "Should I send him away?" he asked, a concerned expression on his face. He noted her frown and wondered if he should have turned away Vandermeer, even though the man was a friend of the family and had been to Woodscastle several times in the past.

"No. 'Tis fine, Humphrey. Could you see him to the parlor and bring tea, please? I'll be but a moment," she assured him as she indicated her ink-stained fingers. She set the card next to a ledger, gently brushing a thumb over the elegant script. *I'm being called upon by a gentleman*, she thought, her breath catching as the realization dawned. *Or it could just be business*, she reminded herself, her momentary excitement dissipating.

The butler gave an understanding nod when he noticed her blackened fingers and replied, "Yes, of course," before he bowed and left the library. Emma quickly wrote some notes in the margin of the ledger and went to the kitchen to wash her hands.

The cook, who until Emma's arrival was chopping a large hunk of beef on a wooden cutting board, paused in his work. "Miss," he said as he nodded in her direction.

"Good afternoon, Mr. Tanner," Emma replied, wincing when she noted the condition of his work space and the bloodied apron he wore. "I'll be but a moment," she said as she moved to the sink and pumped water with which to wash her hands. "That's quite a lot of meat. Is Mr. Wellingham expecting company?" she asked as she applied soap to her fingertips.

"No, miss. Some's for dinner tonight and tomorrow's breakfast and the rest is for jerky," he explained as he continued to hack at the beef.

Emma nodded. "Well, if you should ever need a recipe, I have many," she offered, hoping to make friends with the man.

Tanner looked up from the meat. "Much obliged, miss," he said with a nod, neither his voice nor his expression indicating any interest in her or her recipes.

Emma dried her hands on the cleanest linen she could find in the kitchen and hurried to the parlor to find Todd Vandermeer leaning against the fireplace and studying the painting of a landscape hanging above it.

"Good afternoon, Mr. Vandermeer," Emma said as she curtsied. "This is a most pleasant surprise," she said as she smiled brightly.

Todd bowed deeply, which for him was an endeavor. When he stood up to his full height, he cut a most impressive profile. His long, straight nose along with his erect posture suggested he was an aristocrat, an impression that wasn't countered when one noted the impeccable quality of his tailcoat and waistcoat, the shine on his Hessians, and the fit of his Nankeen breeches. On top of it all, he once again wore his dark hair cut short and combed toward the front in a perfect Titus hairstyle.

Emma took in the sight of the broker and decided Todd Vandermeer was either a man who followed fashion or he employed a manservant who did.

"Pardon my intrusion, Miss Fitzsimmons. I understand I've interrupted your work," he said by way of apology as he held a hand over his chest.

Humphrey brought in a tray of tea and biscuits and set them on the table in front of the settee.

"You're not intruding at all, Mr. Vandermeer. Please, do have a seat," Emma said as she indicated a taller chair next to the settee. "Do you take sugar or milk with your tea?" she asked, moving to the settee as Humphrey poured tea. A light citrus scent wafted through the air as the tall man took the proffered chair, making Emma aware the importer had bathed that day.

"No, thank you," Todd answered as he accepted a cup and saucer from the butler. "Thank you, Humphrey," he added quietly.

Emma noted his acknowledgement of the butler and smiled to herself. "Mr. Wellingham is still in town. He'll return by four o'clock, though, if you would care to wait," Emma offered as she stirred sugar into her tea.

Humphrey left the parlor and Todd leaned over the side of the chair. "I didn't come to see Mr. Wellingham," he said, still keeping his voice quiet. "I came to call on you, Miss Fitzsimmons."

Emma set her teacup into the saucer she held with her other hand. "Oh," she replied, trying hard not to blush. It was then she noticed what she had first assumed were heavy-lidded dark eyes were really rather bright blue. Vandermeer's lids merely seemed large when his eyes were directed downward, a common state for a man so tall. When seated, though, his eyes were quite open and, at the moment, seemed to see only her.

Emma tried hard to sit completely still and as upright as she could. When she met his gaze, she felt a blush color her cheeks, and she quickly glanced away. *There should be a chaperone*, she thought. Humphrey had thought so, too, the reason he seemed so hesitant to leave the room.

"You see, I was most intrigued by our conversation during luncheon on Tuesday," Todd said, "But I wasn't able to ask you if it would be acceptable for me to call on you. And although you described your neighborhood to me, I have no idea where you live," Todd continued in a somewhat nervous explanation.

Stunned, Emma blurted, "You came all the way out here, during your work day, no less, to ask me if you could call on me?" Nervous, she swallowed and took a deep breath.

Todd allowed a grin. "It's really not that far, and 'tis a beautiful day for a ride," he countered. "Since I started the day well before dawn, my work was complete before I left town at three."

Emma nodded her understanding, but said, "Still, I am... flattered, Mr. Vandermeer." She allowed a prim smile as she tried to control another flush she felt rising to color her throat.

The tall man nodded, a smile coming to his face. He took a sip of tea. "Mr. Wellingham spoke very highly of you last January, you see, being his sister's roommate and all," he said, hoping to put the young woman at ease. "But when I met you Tuesday, I didn't realize you were Miss Wellingham's roommate at Warwick's. Had I known, I would have made more of an effort to speak with you when our meeting ended."

Emma angled her head as she recalled the first time she had actually met Mr. Wellingham. "That's very odd," she replied, a quizzical expression crossing her face. "I didn't have the privilege of meeting Mr. Wellingham until he had dinner at our school's boarding house in February."

Todd put his empty teacup down on the table and thought for a moment.

"Would you like more tea, Mr. Vandermeer?" Emma asked as she reached for the teapot.

"Yes, thank you," he replied. "I know it was January when he spoke of you. I suppose Mr. Wellingham was passing along what he knew of you from his sister, then," he commented with a shrug.

"Oh, dear," Emma replied with an embarrassed nod as she filled his teacup. She was sure the lobes of her ears were now bright red along with her throat and her cheeks.

Todd couldn't help but grin. "Well, no matter," he said finally. "Perhaps you would agree to come to my home?" he said hopefully. "I'm hosting a dinner," he added quickly, obviously concerned about the wording of his invitation. "If you prefer, you may certainly bring a companion. My house is located in..."

"Oh, I know where your mansion is, Mr. Vandermeer," she interrupted him with a smile, surprised he would be so modest about his huge estate. The three-story brick building was the first along a street where all the houses had beautiful backyard gardens and boasted gas lighting, running water, and fireplaces in nearly every room. "When we spoke on Tuesday, I didn't realize you were the new owner of the Grace Park mansion. My father's shop is very near there."

Todd took a moment to think and then returned his gaze on Emma. "Fitzsimmons?" he said finally. "As in 'Fitzsimmons', the hat shop in Oxford Street?" he half-questioned.

"Yes," Emma replied with a nod, feeling rather proud that a man of his stature would be familiar with her late father's hat shop.

"Was George Fitzsimmons your father?" he asked as he began to grin, putting the pieces together.

Emma nodded. "Yes. Did you make his acquaintance?"

Todd threw his head back to glance at the ceiling. "I do believe every single hat I own is from his shop," he stated happily. Finally at ease with the young woman, he was better able to carry on the conversation. "But now I see the name has changed somewhat. It's... it's Fitzsimmons and..."

"*Fitzsimmons and Smith*," Emma finished for him. "I'm in the process of selling it to my late father's partner, but Mr. Smith wishes to keep the name," she explained.

The tall man nodded. "Capital idea, really," he agreed. "The Fitzsimmons name in a hat is a sign of distinction, you must know."

Emma was so surprised by the broker's words, she had a mind to kiss him. "Thank you for saying so, Mr. Vandermeer," she replied with a smile, sure her face was still flushed red.

"I should think you would be entitled to a royalty on the continued use of your name, however," he said, his expression indicating he was deep in thought.

Emma brightened, remembering what Mr. Smith had said that cold January day. "I believe the new owner is of the same mind. He is to make me an offer very soon."

Todd nodded and took a drink. "I hope he is fair with his offer."

They sat in silence for a moment before Todd leaned forward and placed the cup and saucer on the table before moving his elbows to rest on his knees. "Miss Fitzsimmons, would you do me the honor of joining my dinner party Saturday evening?" he asked, his hands clasped together to hide his nervousness.

Taken aback, Emma tried not to express too much surprise.

"That would be lovely, Mr. Vandermeer. Saturday... Saturday evening would be agreeable," she said with a nod.

The man seemed to say a silent prayer of thanks before he replied, "Splendid. My cook makes a fabulous seven-course meal. I can send a carriage to your townhouse. Let us say, seven o'clock?"

Seven courses. She wondered who else might be attending his dinner. People he knew from his work? Fellow patrons of his favorite charities? *What if I cannot contribute to the conversation?* she wondered, her mind racing as she considered his invitation and all it implied. *Can I attend without a chaperone?* Probably not. "Seven o'clock would be perfect," she agreed as she stood up. "I'll just write my address on a card for you. Pardon me," she said as she curtsied. Already standing, Todd gave her a bow.

As she hurried to the library, Christiana emerged from the music room and hurried up the hall. "Who is here?" she asked in a loud whisper when she spotted the phaeton outside the library windows.

"Mr. Vandermeer from the East India Company," Emma replied in a whisper. "He has just asked me to a dinner party at his home," she added excitedly as she wrote her address on a card. Blowing on the ink to hasten its drying, she noticed Christiana's face screwing into a frown. "Whatever is wrong?" she asked, having seen the same reaction from her roommate when she spoke of disagreeable class-mates at Warwick's.

"And you have accepted?" Christiana asked in a loud whisper, her eyes wide in surprise.

Emma shrugged and wondered why Christiana wouldn't be pleased she finally had an invitation to a social event. "Well, yes," she answered timidly. "The last man who asked me to a dinner was my father." She stared at Christiana for a moment and a horrible thought struck her. "What do you know?" she asked. "Wait, let me finish with him and send him on his way. And then I want to know everything you are thinking this very moment," Emma demanded as she left the library and hurried back to the parlor.

Emma found Todd Vandermeer still standing, although his cane seemed to be holding him up. He managed a bow as Emma entered and she curtsied. "I apologize for having kept you waiting, Mr. Vandermeer," she said as she handed him the card. "'Tis not too far from Golden Square," she said in explanation of the address.

"Not at all," he replied as he studied the address. "Number three in Kingly. You live in a very good neighborhood, Miss Fitzsimmons," he commented with a raised eyebrow. When he redirected his attention from the card to Emma, he found her watching him expectantly.

"Thank you for saying so, Mr. Vandermeer," she said with a nod. "The landlords are quite diligent in maintaining the buildings on that street."

Todd nodded and thought for a moment. He wanted to kiss the woman. Indeed, he had wanted to kiss her since the afternoon they had met, but he instead took her hand in his and kissed the back of it. "I will leave you to your work now, Miss Fitzsimmons. Thank you again for hosting me this afternoon," he said as he left the parlor with Emma walking next to him.

"Thank you for the dinner invitation, Mr. Vandermeer," she said as she opened the front door for him. "I'll see you Saturday evening."

And then, most unexpectedly, Todd leaned down and kissed her on the cheek. "I look forward to seeing you again, Miss Fitzsimmons," he said in a very quiet voice.

For a moment, Emma thought he was going to kiss her on the lips, but he instead took her hand and kissed the back of it again. "Good afternoon," he whispered with a faint smile.

"Good afternoon, sir," Emma breathed in reply, her hand still held in mid-air where he had left it. Her corset suddenly felt too tight, and she was sure her face was flushed again. She knew she should have deduced his character from what had just occurred, but she found she couldn't think of Todd Vandermeer as a rake.

Is he a rake?

His mannerisms didn't suggest an overly confident man, but to kiss her on the cheek on only their second meeting seemed too bold, too calculated. But his intentions seemed so... innocent.

Emma watched as the impossibly tall man donned his hat and limped down the steps, using his cane for balance the entire time.

Each step seemed to cause him great pain, and Emma found herself feeling pity for the man. After the arduous task of descending the stairs, stepping up into the driver's seat of his phaeton seemed easy for him. Emma waved as he set the horse on its way, and, after a moment she sighed and shut the door. Leaning against it and in an effort to calm her breathing, she closed her eyes for a moment.

When she finally pushed herself away from the door, Emma

walked around the corner to the library entrance and gave a start—Christiana stood with her hands on her hips staring at her with a most displeased expression.

"You cannot be serious about attending that man's dinner party," Christiana stated firmly, a scowl on her face. "He is too tall. He has no social graces," the girl insisted. "And he *kissed* you, didn't he?" she accused, her eyebrows arched in anger.

Emma gasped at the accusations. She had never before seen Christiana quite so cross because of a man.

Girls, yes.

"His social graces seemed just fine whilst we were in the parlor and during luncheon on Tuesday," Emma countered defensively, "And he merely kissed my hand," she said, her chin rising while she deliberately chose not to mention the kiss on the cheek. "And the last time I looked in a mirror, *I* was too tall," she added, her voice rising to match Christiana's.

Shaking her head, Christiana crossed her arms. "Promise me you won't accept his offer of matrimony," she demanded.

Mortified, Emma opened her mouth and found she couldn't find words. She clamped her lips shut and took a deep breath. "I'm just attending a dinner party at his house," she said evenly. "He has only asked if he might call on me. He didn't ask if he could *court* me," she added stubbornly, anger creeping into her voice.

"Exactly my point," Christiana countered, rising on her toes as she spoke. "I'll bet you one-hundred pounds he'll propose to you before the evening is over," she stated confidently, one finger poking into the air in front of her.

Shocked, Emma gasped and found it hard to breathe. "Why ever would you say such a thing?"

"Because he probably will," a male voice said behind them. The two startled women whirled around to find Thomas leaning against the corner of the vestibule, holding his riding coat. From his manner, neither could tell if he was angry or amused by their exchange. "And, you, sister, should know better than to gamble in this house, at least anywhere but in the library," he added with a stern look at Christiana. Leaning toward Emma, he whispered, "Don't take the bet."

Embarrassed by their conversation being overheard, Emma was sure her face was bright red. Her ears felt positively hot. "I'm so sorry, Mr. Wellingham. Mr. Vandermeer called on me a few moments ago. Of course, I'll stay late this evening to make up for the lost time," Emma said as she curtsied.

Thomas nodded his head in return and then motioned to the library. "May I have a word with you, Miss Emma?" he asked, pushing away from the wall.

"Of course, Mr. Wellingham," Emma replied, swallowing hard. Her stomach felt as if it were in her throat. She moved into the library and turned around, sure she was about to be fired.

"I'll speak to you later," Thomas said to Christiana, his manner definitely not one of amusement. Then he stepped into the library and closed the door, leaving Christiana in the corridor to wonder about his conversation with Emma.

Thomas sighed heavily. "I spoke with Mr. Vandermeer a few moments ago," he said as he gestured toward the road. "Despite his being in the same business as me—most would consider him a competitor—he is a good friend of mine. I happen to know he very much wants to find a wife, but I feel I must warn you he has a tendency to propose to women with whom he has spent only a few hours." He ignored Emma's sudden inhalation. "There have been two that I know of since this past March," he explained, a pained expression crossing his face.

"I see," Emma replied, not quite sure if her employer's comments were meant as a friendly warning or if he had something else in mind. "So, an invitation to a dinner party is probably one of those situations where..." she started to say and then stopped as she noticed Thomas nodding his head.

"Do you... find him agreeable?" Thomas asked as he tossed his tailcoat onto one of the leather couches.

Emma shrugged and thought for a moment. "To be honest with you, I've not yet formed an opinion of the man," she replied with a bit of hesitance. "I certainly don't find him *disagreeable*," she added quickly, knowing her words were truthful.

Thomas regarded her with a wistful smile. "I rather hoped my sister would grow to appreciate Mr. Vandermeer someday, and then I'd arrange for her to be his bride. But it's become apparent over the past few years that she'll never feel affection for the man and would only resent me for the rest of my days should such a union take place," he explained quietly, knowing full well Christiana was probably eavesdropping on their conversation. "I must tell you one more thing... well, a few more things actually, before I allow you to return to your work," Thomas said as he sat down on the couch. He motioned for her to join him. As Emma sat down next to him, he continued, "Mr. Vandermeer is a very successful businessman who has made a good deal of money in just a few short years. He has no parents. He spent most of his youth in an orphanage or at work at East India, so he has never been educated in the ways of polite society. Everything he knows, he learned outside of school. As such, he is bound to say or do things you will find... offensive."

Emma started to shake her head. "But I have only found him to be a perfect gentleman—"

"He will offend you at some point. Trust me," Thomas continued as he held up a hand to stop her interruption. "Probably around the fourth or fifth course. When he does, you must tell him you are offended," he explained carefully. "Get up and leave if you must, but know he will ask you to explain why you find him disagreeable. Please do him the courtesy of explaining the offense before you depart. He really does want to improve his social graces," Thomas said with a pointed finger. "And learning from his mistakes is the only way a man in his situation will improve."

Nodding, Emma considered her employer's comments. "I understand. I give you my word I will do so. Although," she said and then paused as she remembered a comment Todd had made. "May I ask why you recommended he call on me?"

A look of consternation crossed Thomas' face as he thought for a moment. "Oh, good God," he murmured. "This is all my fault, isn't it?" he admitted. He had been the one to mention Emma to Todd before he had actually met her.

Emma shrugged and replied, "We hadn't yet been introduced."

Scrubbing his face with a hand, Thomas sighed. "Well, at the time, it seemed... appropriate," he said lamely. "You see, he actually asked if Christiana was betrothed, and knowing how she felt about him, I told him she was too young and certainly too... *short* for him. And I remembered Christiana saying you were tall, so that's what made me make mention of you to Mr. Vandermeer," he admitted with a hint of guilt.

"But, everyone is tall compared to Christiana," Emma countered, a quizzical expression on her face.

Thomas chuckled then, struck by the familiarity of the comment. "That is precisely what Mr. Vandermeer said," he replied as he turned to look at Emma.

Emma smiled in spite of herself.

"Do let me know how it goes, won't you?" he asked.

"I will, Mr. Wellingham. Thank you for the warnings."

Just as she was about to take her leave of the library, Thomas turned and said, "Oh, by the way, I looked up the name of Lord Chamberlain's wife."

Emma turned and regarded her employer. "Oh?"

Thomas nodded. "Caroline Harrington. She's Lord Mayfield's twin sister."

Stunned at the information, Emma blinked. And blinked again.

Caroline. Sister of Stanley Harrington, Earl of Mayfield.

"Indeed?" was all she could manage.

"Apparently, she was a rather young widow when your uncle took her as his wife," Thomas commented lightly. "Before he inherited the viscountcy and was still an official in the military."

Emma nodded, her attention on her ink-stained fingers.

Aunt Caroline. Uncle Matthew.

Despite Matthew being her father's older brother, she had only ever met the man once in her life, on a dreary winter afternoon when he had come to the hat shop to visit her father. A visit that ended with the two brothers nearly coming to blows.

She had never met his wife. Perhaps it was time she did so.

Thoughts of dinner with Todd Vandermeer were forgotten as Emma said her thanks and took her leave of Woodscastle.

CHAPTER 23
HOUSEBREAKERS

June 11, 1802, Woodscastle

On the Friday of the third week of her work at Woodscastle, Emma was bent over an open ledger book and deep into adding columns of numbers when she was startled by the sound of horses galloping nearby. Too early for Mr. Wellingham's return from town, she looked out the library window to see a chaise drawn by two horses coming up the drive from Burlington Road.

She wasn't particularly troubled by the fact the men in the chaise were dressed oddly, or that two were bearded and wore no hats. She was alarmed that the two in the carriage were standing and brandishing guns, and the driver had slowed the horses to a walk as he studied the front of the estate.

Backing up from the window so she couldn't be seen from outside, Emma swallowed. *Housebreakers*, she thought, remembering a comment she had overheard during the business meeting earlier that week. "Humphrey!" she shouted as she left the library at a run. She nearly collided with the butler in the corridor.

Startled, the man backed up and immediately noticed her horror-stricken face. "Where are the guns? Those housebreakers are out front," she said hurriedly.

But Humphrey had already seen the chaise through the open door to the library. "There are dueling pistols in the library. In a wooden box on the back table. They're loaded, so be careful. I'll get the hunting gun," he said with a nod as he rushed off down the hall.

Christiana, who had been practicing piano-forté in the music room, heard the commotion and stood at the end of the hall. "What's wrong?" she asked, her face betraying her confusion and fear.

"Thieves, I think," Emma replied. "Hide yourself. *Now!*" she shouted as she ran into the library and retrieved the box of pistols. Hurrying to the vestibule, she laid the ornate box on the round table, noticing the "Ryan & Watson" label on the lid. Two identical pistols were nested in the black velvet lining, their barrels over a foot in length and their handles decorated with mother-of-pearl and gold inlay. She carefully removed one and studied it, finally cocking it and lifting it with both hands to check its aim. Although her father had shown her how to cock and aim a pistol—they had kept one under the counter at the hat shop in the event someone tried to rob the store—she had never actually pulled the trigger.

Humphrey ran into the vestibule carrying the longest hunting gun Emma had ever seen. It was nearly as tall as the butler. He stopped short when he saw Emma. "Miss Emma!" he whispered in horror, shocked to see her brandishing a weapon.

"Hide yourself behind the front door!" Emma ordered as she positioned herself square to the front of the door. "And be ready to shoot if you must," she added as she set down the cocked gun, making sure it was within easy reach. With hands that had begun to shake, she prepared the other gun.

Two loud thumps on the front door announced their visitors' arrival. Emma nodded to the butler. When he gave her a questioning look, she motioned for him to open the door. He did so, but stayed hidden behind the door as it opened and then lifted the gun in the event he had to shoot it. Through the space between the edge of the open door and the door frame, he was aware of their visitor, but could make out no details.

But Emma was directly in front of him. And her eyes widened as she stared in fright.

A tall, bearded, brute of a man stood in the center of the doorway, casually holding a gun at his side while the other two ruffians were a few steps behind and on either side of him. His wicked smile, made more so with a missing front tooth and a scar that covered half of his chin, turned to one of shock when he saw the woman aiming a pistol directly at his face.

"Now, lady," he started to say as he lifted the hand that held the gun.

Determined not to allow her growing fright to get the better of her, Emma took the shot. The large, round bullet tore through his neck, knocking him backwards and into one of the other men so he stumbled backwards and to one side of the door. The loud pop startled the horses. They reared and took off, pulling the chaise at an odd angle down the lane, nearly toppling it on its side.

Quickly dropping the used pistol and retrieving the other, she tried to take aim but merely shot in the direction of the other man, who was raising his gun to shoot. The round went into his shoulder, knocking him backwards and down the steps. Emma was aware of screams, but couldn't tear her eyes away from the carnage outside the door.

Seeing Emma's reaction from his place behind the door, Humphrey moved out, took aim, and shot the last man, who had managed to get up from under the leader, his gun left behind on the steps.

Bird shot embedded into one of his arms, and he howled in pain as he turned and ran in the direction of the stables. As the other wounded man tried to get up, the butler flipped the shotgun and beat the man across the head with the stock, sending a spray of blood flying over the steps.

Emma dropped the second pistol and covered her mouth with her hands, the odor of burnt gunpowder the only thing keeping her from fainting. Lowering herself to the floor, her body started to shake when she realized what she had done. *So much blood*, she thought as she remembered the splatter from the first man's neck. If she had bothered to look, she would have seen the droplets of blood lacing the hem of her gown. In the distance, she was aware of a galloping horse, and through the open door, she saw the last man riding away.

Bareback.

On her horse.

"No!" she cried out as she started to shiver uncontrollably.

Humphrey, assured the remaining men were dead, came back into the vestibule to find Emma staring into space, a look of extreme sadness on her face and her body trembling. As he knelt down to check on her, Christiana ran from the music room, tears of fright streaming down her face.

Her screams and the sounds of shots had alerted Mrs. Werthers, who had run to the kitchen and remained with the cook, Mr. Tanner.

Meanwhile, Mr. Allen came running from the stables but stopped short when he saw the bodies on the front steps. "Humphrey!" he called out, his face contorted in a look of agony as he took in the sight of blood and a man with a hole in his neck.

The butler, satisfied Emma wasn't injured, left her on the floor to answer Mr. Allen. "Here," he called out as he stood just inside the front door, the bloodied gun still grasped in his hands.

"A man just took Miss Emma's horse," he shouted as he pointed down the lane toward Burlington Road.

"Yes, we know," Humphrey answered with a short nod. "They were thieves, Mr. Allen, but they won't be robbing this house or any others," he said firmly as he looked over the dead men. "Get the sheriff, Mr. Allen," he ordered.

The groom nodded. "Yes, sir, right away." He took off for the stables and in a moment rode off at a fast gallop.

Humphrey turned to find Christiana on the floor next to Emma, her arms wrapped around the bookkeeper's shoulders. "Ladies, let us get you to the parlor," he said as he reached down to assist them to their feet.

"No," Christiana said as she shook her head. "It's all right. You should check on the rest of the staff," she said as she wiped away a tear.

The butler nodded and stood up. "Very good, then," he replied and he calmly walked in the direction of the kitchen, still carrying the bloodied hunting gun.

*L*ate leaving the office, Thomas Wellingham donned his riding jacket and hurried to the stables. Located on the north side of the warehouse, farthest from the river, the stables were both a convenience and a good business decision. He had long ago purchased a number of horses, knowing Wellingham Imports would require them for drayage. The overland transport group required no less than forty-eight when all routes were employed, and several shires were dedicated to the flatbed wagons used to bring goods from the docks to the warehouse. Owning the stables meant Thomas and other workers had a place other than a public livery stable in which to keep their own horses when they chose to ride instead of being driven to work.

With clear skies and the warmer weather, Thomas decided to exercise his horse and allowed it to take off from London at a full gallop. The horse continued running until Thomas finally forced it to slow down to a more comfortable gate, making it possible for him to enjoy the ride and pay more attention to the rural landscape around him.

About a mile from Woodscastle, Thomas noticed a lone horse standing in the pasture next to Burlington Road. The Cleveland Bay sported reins and a bit, but there was no rider in sight. As Thomas turned his horse to approach, he noticed a body lying nearby. A man, face down and bloody from what appeared to be bird shot, lay sprawled and crooked, his neck obviously broken. Judging from the condition of the corpse, he hadn't been in the field very long. As Thomas dismounted, the horse walked up to his, and the two seemed to exchange greetings. It was then he recognized the horse.

This is Emma's horse, he realized.

Fear gripped him as he considered what might have happened. It was too early for Emma to have left Woodscastle, unless there was a reason she had to leave. If so, where was she? And if not, why was her horse in a field with a dead body?

Thomas mounted his horse and leaned down to take the reins of the bay. "Come on," he said as he sent his horse on a fast walk through the field. He kept his eyes on the horizon and continually scanned the fields hoping against hope he wouldn't find another body.

What he did find confounded him even more. A two-horse chaise with the two horses still in their rigs stood off-kilter in the pasture next to his estate. A wheel had apparently broken, but its owner was nowhere near. The horses were munching on the grass and appeared to be doing so for some time.

As he approached Woodscastle, Emma's horse snorted and jerked on the reins. His own horse seemed spooked, and it took a good deal of prodding to get the two horses down the lane to the estate. Once he was in the clearing in front of the house, he understood why.

He dismounted and looked toward the stables, expecting Mr. Allen or Mr. Larsen to come for his horse. When neither appeared, he took a deep breath and swallowed. "Christiana!" he yelled as loudly as possible, fear gripping him again. "Emma!" He quickly hobbled the horses and ran toward the front door.

Humphrey appeared in the doorway, his hands held out in front of him. "It's quite all right, Mr. Wellingham," the butler assured him. "I've sent Mr. Allen for the sheriff. The women are in the parlor, and the staff is just justifiably uneasy," he explained quickly as Thomas stared at the dead bodies littering the front steps of Woodscastle. He couldn't help but notice two guns and a trail of blood leading toward the stables.

"What happened here?" Thomas asked. The sound of horses on the main road had him turning around.

"That will be the sheriff," Humphrey said with relief. "I didn't want to move the bodies until he had a chance to see this for himself."

Thomas looked toward his butler and nodded. "Who are these men?"

The butler stepped closer to his master. "From what has been written in *The Times*, I believe these are the housebreakers that have been stealing from the homes along this road," he replied quietly, referring to the newspaper article from a few days before. "They have been reported as riding in an open carriage drawn by two horses, just as these men were," he described. "And they carried their guns in the open. They didn't even try to hide them as they came up to the house."

Thomas nodded grimly. "That explains the empty chaise and two horses in the pasture down the road," he said as the sheriff 's horse came to a halt behind him. Mr. Allen and two deputies followed closely, their horses kicking up clouds of dust as they came to a halt.

"Mr. Wellingham," the sheriff called out as he dismounted. The tall man threw his riding cloak off his shoulders and removed his gloves as he approached the house. His riding boots, although dusty, were of recent purchase, but his hat showed signs of wear.

"Sheriff Morgan. It's very kind of you to come so quickly. I have only just arrived myself," Thomas said as he nodded to the lawman. He noticed Mr. Allen retrieving his horse and the look of surprise and happiness on the groom's face when he realized Emma's horse was there, too. "This is my butler, Humphrey. I believe he will be able to answer more questions than I."

The sheriff gave a nod in return and surveyed the carnage. "Did you shoot these men, Humphrey?" he asked, getting right to the point.

The butler shook his head. "No, sir. The bookkeeper did. I merely used the stock of a hunting gun to finish off this one," he said, a hint of anger in his voice as he pointed to the man with a crushed skull and a pool of blood under his shoulder. "Her first shot took out the leader," he explained as he pointed to the man with a hole through his neck. "I was able to get a shot off at the third, but he ran to the stables, stole a horse, and rode away. His arm was full of bird shot, though," the butler said with a proud nod, a scowl on his face.

Startled by the story, Thomas took a deep breath. "Miss Emma did this?" he asked in disbelief. "How? And with what gun?" he added, shocked his auditor was capable of such an act. *Whatever was she thinking putting herself in harm's way like that?* he wondered. *How did she even know the men were housebreakers?*

"Your dueling pistols, sir," Humphrey replied quickly. "She saw the men drive up. They carried their guns in plain sight. She must have realized they were the thieves—the highwaymen they've been writing about in the newspaper. She got the pistols from the library whilst I went for the hunting gun. When I returned to the vestibule, I stayed behind the front door and opened it when they knocked. I barely got the door open before she shot the leader—I could see through the crack he had his gun out. Then she picked up the other pistol and shot this man," he explained as he pointed to the man with the crushed skull. "Then I came from behind the door and shot at the last man. I had to hit this man when he tried to get up."

The sheriff shook his head before planting one hand on his hip. "We've been in pursuit of these men for several weeks," he said as he turned to Thomas. "Do you have anything to add to your butler's story?" he asked as he used the toe of his boot to nudge one of the bodies.

Thomas considered the situation and nodded. "Indeed," he answered with a nod. "I found Miss Emma's horse in a pasture about a mile east of here. And there's a dead man in the same pasture. His neck appears to be broken, and his arm was bleeding," Thomas described cryptically.

Humphrey eyes widened. "That's the third man!"

Cocking his head, Thomas returned his attention to the sheriff.

"In the next pasture east of here, I believe you will find two horses still rigged to a carriage with a broken wheel. I now realize it must have belonged to these men," he said as he pointed to the dead bodies. "Unless they stole it from someone," he murmured.

The butler nodded quickly. "The horses took off when the first shot was fired," he affirmed. "Nearly dumped the carriage on its side trying to get away."

The sheriff turned to one of his deputies. "Go see if you can find that carriage before it gets dark," he ordered, his manner suggesting his impatience with wrapping up the mess. The younger of the two men quickly mounted his horse and took off down the lane toward Burlington Road.

Sheriff Morgan turned around. "Who is this bookkeeper and where can I find her now?" he demanded, a serious expression on his face.

Thomas took a deep breath. "Miss Emma Fitzsimmons is an accomptant in the process of auditing some books for me," he replied, not wanting to give the sheriff too much information. "I don't know where she is at present, though," he added as he looked to Humphrey. *Whatever was she thinking?* he wondered, a feeling of horror rising in him. *She could have been killed!*

"Miss Emma is in the parlor with your sister, sir," the butler replied. "She is rather... distraught, of course."

The sheriff motioned for the remaining deputy to join him, and they headed into the house. Humphrey led them to the parlor. On the front edge of a settee, Emma and Christiana sat with their hands gripped together. Christiana had obviously been crying, but Emma, who was dry-eyed, looked as if she might faint at any moment. Her gaze was directed toward the middle of the room, and, at first, she didn't seem to notice the men come into the parlor. At Christiana's urging, Emma emerged from her reverie, stood up and curtsied as the men bowed in their direction.

Thomas made the introductions as the sheriff sized up the women. Emma kept glancing at Thomas, a pained expression developing on her face. When told to by the sheriff, she sat down. Christiana finally sat down, not sure if she should remain in the room during the sheriff's interrogation.

"Miss Fitzsimmons," the sheriff began uncertainly, "What led you to believe the men you shot were of danger to you?" From the way her body rocked on the settee, he thought she might faint at any moment.

Surprised by the question, Emma looked from the sheriff to Thomas and back again. "It was more they were a danger to the entire household, of course. You see, when they rode up in their carriage, two of them were standing up, and they held their guns out, as if they were looking for someone to shoot. They looked rough, and they didn't wear hats."

Thomas blinked, realizing the absence of hats would have been a decisive clue to a woman who had been raised working in a hat shop. All gentlemen wore hats, after all.

"Also, the man driving the horses made the horses slow down to a walk well before they were close to the house. He was watching the front of the house very carefully."

Nodding, the lawman asked, "And then what did you do?"

Emma swallowed. "I called for Humphrey," she said as she nodded in the butler's direction. "I asked him where the guns were. He told me about the dueling pistols. I found the box and cocked the guns, and that's when Humphrey returned with the hunting gun and hid behind the door. I took aim...There were two loud bangs on the door. I....," she motioned with a finger, "I waved to him to open the door. I saw the men holding guns and when the first one started to speak and bring up his gun, I..." She stopped, her eyes widening in fright. "Pulled the trigger." When the sheriff merely gave her a nod, she added, "I put the gun down and picked up the other gun." She paused again, replaying the events in her head. "I didn't really have time to take proper aim, so I merely shot it in the direction of the last standing man. I think Humphrey took over from there," she explained quietly, her eyes not quite focused on the sheriff. "The last thing I remember was seeing my horse being ridden by a man with a bloody arm," she finished, tears streaming down her face. She began to shiver as she had done just after the shootings.

Ignoring Emma's tears, the sheriff narrowed his eyes. "You must have experience with a gun in order to shoot a man in the neck like that," Sheriff Morgan commented, his voice rather cold with the accusation.

Emma shook her head. "No, sir," she answered, sniffling. "I thought I was aiming it between his eyes," she added.

"Indeed?" he replied in disbelief. "And why was that?"

Shivering, Emma gave the man a shrug. "My father told me if I should ever have occasion to shoot a man, I should aim the gun between his eyes and squeeze the trigger very slowly." She turned her eyes up to meet the sheriff's gaze. "That's what I did."

Eyebrows raised, the sheriff glanced in Thomas' direction. "An *accomptant*, you say?"

Thomas swallowed and finally took his eyes off Emma and directed them at the sheriff. "Yes," he replied simply, removing a handkerchief from his pocket and holding it out for Emma. "She was my sister's roommate at Warwick's these past two years," he added, wanting the sheriff to know she had some history with the family.

"And from where did you get the pistols?" the sheriff asked Thomas.

Surprised by the question, Thomas shrugged. "They were a gift from a friend. I didn't know they were loaded, and when I first received them, I rather doubted they would even work," he added with a quizzical expression.

A commotion at the door had Humphrey scurrying out of the parlor. The voice of the other deputy could be heard as he greeted the butler and made his way to the parlor. "Mr. Wellingham was correct," the young man announced as he entered the room.

Emma and Christiana stood and curtsied, although Emma had to lean on Christiana as she did so. The deputy, surprised by the sight of the women, gave them a clumsy bow in return. "The horses and carriage are very near here, Sheriff Morgan," the man continued, his manner becoming more reserved in the presence of the women. "And one of the wheels is broken."

Sheriff Morgan crossed his arms. "Free the horses, and we'll bring them with us," he said to the young man. Turning his attention to the other deputy, he said, "But first we should remove the bodies from the front steps, and let these people get back to their evening. Mr. Wellingham," he said as he turned and held out his right hand, "Thank you for your cooperation. I won't be pressing any charges against your butler or Miss Fitzsimmons. It's very clear this was a case of defending property and life," he explained as he nodded in the direction of Humphrey and Emma.

Thomas, angered by the thought that his employees might be charged with a crime, begrudgingly shook the sheriff's hand and merely nodded. "There's still the matter of the other dead man in the field," he said in a quiet voice.

The sheriff nodded. "We'll retrieve the body as soon as we leave here," he acknowledged as he pulled on his gloves.

"And I suppose this will be reported in the papers?" Thomas asked, biting his lip as he considered the kind of publicity such an ordeal would create.

The sheriff nodded. "No doubt. This has been a big story for them. I'll file my report when I get back to my office. Sometimes a reporter stops by for the news." He regarded Thomas for a moment before averting his eyes. "Sometimes I send for one." With that, he bowed and left the room before anyone could bow or curtsy in return.

"I will see to it the steps are cleaned," Humphrey said to no one in particular as he left the parlor.

"Thank you, Humphrey," Thomas said as he stood regarding his sister and Emma. He put his hands on his hips. "And where were you during all of this, sister?" he asked with a concerned expression. "Hiding, I *hope*," he added.

Christiana rolled her eyes and crossed her arms. "I was in the music room, crying and screaming like a scared little baby," she replied, obviously embarrassed by her behavior.

"Then you're of good health?" Thomas asked, trying hard to suppress a smile as he bent down to kiss her on the head.

"Yes," she replied with a small smile, knowing her brother was teasing her.

"Why don't you get dressed for dinner and practice on the piano? Perhaps we can have Mr. Tanner get us some tea?" he suggested, hoping the cook was still on the grounds after what had happened.

Christiana nodded her head, happy to be doing something after the past hour of waiting. She hugged Emma, curtsied, and left the parlor.

Thomas sat down on the settee next to Emma. Not sure of what to say, he wondered how to thank someone for defending his property, the lives of his household staff, and especially the life of his sister.

"Mr. Wellingham, I'm so very sorry about what has happened," Emma said quietly as she stared at nothing. Vaguely aware of how close he was, she stayed very still and tried hard not to sob.

Thomas shook his head and took one of her hands in his.

"You have absolutely nothing to be sorry for," he replied quietly, quite aware of how her entire body vibrated. *She must be in shock.* "I'll never be able to thank you enough for what you did this afternoon, though," he commented quietly. "You did a remarkable thing, Miss Emma."

Sniffling, Emma finally turned and gazed at her employer. "Do you think, then, I could leave a bit early today? You see, my horse was stolen, but if I leave now, I think I can make it home before it gets too dark..." As she mentioned her horse, tears began to stream down her face and the shivering worsened.

Putting his arm around her shoulders and pulling her against him, Thomas replied quietly, "I found your horse... about a mile from here," he whispered as he rested his cheek on her hair. The scent of rosewater drifted to his nostrils, and he closed his eyes. "He is quite fine, I assure you."

Stunned by the news, Emma tried to sit up, but Thomas kept her pressed against his side. "Mr. Allen has taken him to the stables where he is going to spend the night. And, no, you cannot leave early, because you are not leaving here tonight. I won't allow it," he said in a manner that suggested no discussion or argument would be tolerated.

"I have killed a man," Emma whispered, a sob nearly interrupting her confession.

Thomas sighed loudly, knowing she spoke the truth. But he didn't want her to feel guilty over the death of a criminal.

As he leaned back, he pulled her to him, his arms wrapped around both her shoulders so her head lay against his chest. He felt the moisture of her tears on his skin as it penetrated the linen of his shirt. "If you hadn't, he might have killed you and everyone else in the house," he whispered softly, a hand stroking her back. "He might have killed Christiana" he added, his voice ouder. "You must have been so frightened," he murmured, tightening his hold on her.

Emma sniffled into the handkerchief she held balled up in one fist. "I wasn't, really," she countered, her voice cracking. "Not until I saw all the blood and my horse..." She began weeping then, her body racked by sobs.

"Shh," Thomas soothed, his lips brushing her hair where it disappeared into its tightly twisted bun. "I had Mrs. Werthers prepare the guest bedchamber for you. You do have a valise here somewhere?" he half-asked, remembering his instructions to her to bring one in case of inclement weather.

"Uh huh," Emma nodded, trying to remember if she had a gown suitable for dinner packed in the valise. *Whatever am I thinking? How important could a dinner gown be?*

"Dinner is at eight. Perhaps you would join me for a drink in the library before dinner? I know I could certainly use one. Or two," he said with an amused expression.

Emma nodded absently. "A drink would be very nice," she agreed, her voice very distant. "Right now, though, I should probably finish the ledger I was working on in the library," she said as she remembered she had several pages spread out on the table in there. "I left things in a bit of a disarray."

Thomas shook his head. "No," he said simply, keeping one arm wrapped around one of her shoulders. "You have done quite enough for one day. It will still be there for you in the morning," he added as he stood up. After a moment, Emma allowed him to help her stand and took his arm. Thomas led her out of the parlor and up the steps to the guest bedchamber. "If you should need anything, please let me or Humphrey know," he offered as he opened the door. "And I will stop by at seven to escort you to the library."

Before Emma could curtsy or say anything in reply, Thomas had closed the door.

Emma leaned against the door, her legs so shaky she was barely able to stand. *I've killed a man*, she thought again, fear gripping her heart. But in the waning light of day, she found she couldn't feel remorse for the dead men. In fact, she realized she felt nothing for the band of housebreakers. *Mr. Wellingham was right*, she figured. She had simply done what had to be done. *Keep busy*, she thought. *Pull yourself together, old girl.*

Emma stood staring at the room for several minutes before realizing her valise was on the bench at the end of the bed.

During the first week of work at Woodscastle, she had been given the opportunity to use her neighbors' phaeton when they insisted it would rain that day. Since Thomas had encouraged her to bring a valise in the event of inclement weather, she used the carriage to transport the valise. At the time, she didn't think she would ever need to accept her employer's offer of hospitality. Now she was grateful he had been so insistent.

Opening it, she pulled out two gowns, a nightgown, pantaloons, and a corset. One of the gowns, made with pastel peach batiste, featured a series of ribbons along the top of the skirt and at the bottom of the long sleeves. *Appropriate for dinner,* she figured.

A knock at the door startled her. She covered the undergarments with the gowns and opened the door to find Christiana standing in the corridor. Already dressed for dinner and sporting a wan smile, Christiana reached up and hugged and kissed Emma on the cheek. "I'm so happy you're staying with us tonight," she said as she let go of her former roommate. "I cannot imagine you thought you were going to walk home after what happened today. Even if you did go home, Thomas would have insisted Mr. Allen drive you," she claimed as she rolled her eyes.

Emma smiled and motioned for Christiana to take a seat by the fireplace. "I don't know what I was thinking. But I didn't have much of a choice in the matter. Your brother was very....," she paused for a moment, trying to find the perfect word to describe his insistence.

"Stubborn," Christiana finished for her. "He likes to have things his way. He's been like that since father died," she added, matter-of-factly.

"I wouldn't have put it quite that way," Emma countered as she removed the gown she was wearing. She tried to ignore the spray of blood stains near the hem, but gave them a cursory glance as she held the gown out in front of her. "Do you think, perhaps, he is that way with you because you're his sister? He's charged with your care, after all," she continued, deciding the gown could be worn in the morning for her ride back to town.

Christiana crossed her arms and shrugged. "Perhaps. I just know I wish to be affianced and be married as soon as possible."

Emma placed the peach gown over her head and pulled it down as she threaded her arms into the sleeves. "When did you decide this?" she asked, startled by the statement. "Or are you already betrothed to someone you've not told me about?"

The younger girl leaned over the arm of the chair. "No, I'm not betrothed to anyone," she stated, deciding to keep her news of her Mr. Grandby from Emma a bit longer. "I plan to marry for love, though. Thomas won't even consider courting anyone until I am engaged," she said, disgust in her voice. "Do you know how long that might be?" she added, remembering her brother's past comments of requiring her to be at least eighteen before she could consider marriage.

"I'd think a man of his wealth and position would already be betrothed," Emma replied as she adjusted the peach gown.

The younger girl sat up straighter in the chair. "Well, I suppose that could be, but not if you ask *him* about it," she replied carefully. Christiana thought for a moment. "Do you think you could feel enough affection for my brother to marry him?" she asked quietly.

In the middle of changing her pantaloons, Emma stopped and stared at Christiana.

"What? He is my *employer*. I cannot be thinking of him... *affectionately*," Emma replied in a hoarse whisper, realizing their conversation might be overheard in the next bedchamber. Besides, she was due to attend a dinner party at Todd Vandermeer's house the following evening. *If the man is still interested in hosting me given the gruesome events of the afternoon*, she thought with a grimace.

Obviously displeased by the answer, Christiana tried again. "So, if he *wasn't* your employer, do you think you would wish to marry him?"

Emma sat down on the bed, a quizzical expression on her face. "Well, he's certainly handsome. The staff seems to like and respect him. Your home is beautiful, although there seems to be something amiss about the west wing. The grounds are impeccable..."

"And he's rich," Christiana added with a wicked smile and a quick nod that appeared almost comical.

"Yes. I rather gathered that from working on his books," Emma agreed as she pulled on a pair of kid slippers.

"So?" Christiana said expectantly. "Would you?"

Emma sighed, walked over to the fireplace, and stared at Christiana. "If I say 'yes', you must promise me you'll never tell him about this conversation. If I say 'no', you must promise me you'll never tell him about this conversation."

Angling her head, Christiana thought for a moment. "So, either way, I cannot tell him about this conversation?" she asked with a frown. Lower lip pushed out, Christiana crossed her arms. "Well, what if he *asks* me about you? May I at least tell him you're... *interested?*" she asked, a mischievous grin on her face.

Emma sighed and shook her head. "He won't ask you.

Besides, you already said he's not going to court anyone until you're engaged." She took a look at her face in the mirror and let out a squeak. "I look as if I've been crying all day," she claimed as she went into the bath for water and a linen.

Christiana followed her into the private bath. Well appointed with a copper bathtub, a fireplace and racks for heating tubs of water, a water pump, and a sink with its own drain, it featured stacks of linens on one shelf while the counter below held an oil lamp and flints. "Well, you *have* been crying," Christiana commented as she watched her roommate clean her face.

"Please don't remind me," Emma replied as she took the pins out of her hair. The long golden blonde locks fell past her shoulders as each pin was removed. She began brushing it out in long, even strokes. "What, pray tell, is really bothering you, Christiana?" she asked, studying Christiana's reflection in the mirror. The younger girl appeared deeply disappointed.

Christiana returned Emma's gaze in the mirrored glass. "It's just that you have finished school, and you'll not be at Warwick's in the fall. I really don't want anyone else for a roommate. I was thinking... if you and my brother were married, he might not make me finish at Warwick's. I could stay here with you. You could finish teaching me elocution and theatre appreciation..."

Stunned, Emma stopped brushing her hair. "You've given this quite a lot of thought, haven't you?" she half-asked, finally understanding Christiana's reasoning.

Nodding, Christiana frowned. "Every day since April," she admitted with a long sigh. "That's why I was so upset you agreed to have dinner with Mr. Vandermeer."

"Oh, my," was all Emma could think to say as she gathered her hair into a roll on the top and back of her head. She started pushing hairpins into place. "So, what possessed you to think your brother would even be interested in *me?* In *that* way, I mean?"

Christiana allowed a small smile. "Well, I suppose it was that night he had dinner with us at Gamma House. He was very impressed with you. But I didn't know for certain until this afternoon. I saw him," she said quietly and then leaned toward Emma. "He was *holding* you," Christiana said excitedly, keeping her voice to a whisper.

Emma spun around, nearly losing her grip on her rolled hair. "What?"

"After the sheriff left. In the parlor. He had his arms around you, and you were... pressed up against him," Christiana stated in a loud whisper. "I think he was kissing your hair."

Emma couldn't tell from Christiana's comment if the girl

thought the act of providing comfort to a distraught woman was scandalous, or if Christiana was delighted her brother had put his arms around her. "He didn't kiss me, I assure you," Emma countered quickly. "And I'm quite sure he merely held me because... because I'm like a sister to you, and he was merely treating me as he would treat you."

Christiana's face screwed up into another frown. "So, you don't wish to marry my brother?"

Suppressing the urge to laugh, Emma continued to put pins in her hair and finally faced Christiana. "I didn't say that," she replied carefully and then turned back to the looking glass. "I have at least another month of work to do on his ledgers. Once this audit is complete, I'll no longer be his employee. Then you can tell him anything you wish," she offered as she turned to look directly at Christiana. "Except, you cannot tell him I want lots of babies, because I don't—not like you," she added as she took one last look in the mirror. In the reflection, she saw Christiana's face brighten.

"Thank you, Emma," Christiana said as she reached up to hug the taller woman. There was a knock on the door and Emma's eyes widened. "What's the matter?" Christiana asked.

"Do you have any earbobs I could borrow? I have absolutely no jewelry with me," Emma said as she touched her bare earlobes.

Christiana smiled. "My bedchamber is next door. I'll get you a pair," she offered as she hurried off to her room. In the hall, she passed her brother, who had come to escort the women to the library. "We're almost ready," Christiana said as she disappeared for a moment and then reappeared in the corridor holding earbobs. "Emma doesn't have any jewelry with her. Actually, she doesn't have much jewelry at all," she added with an arched eyebrow as she disappeared into the guest bedchamber, leaving the door open behind her.

Thomas raised his own eyebrows but didn't comment as he stood in the corridor with his hands behind his back. When Emma emerged from the bath, she was leaning to one side as she put on an earbob. Watching from the corridor, Thomas was taken aback by the transformation his auditor had undergone. Only an hour earlier, Emma Fitzsimmons had seemed not much more than a schoolgirl having a very bad day. Now she looked like a vision in peach—a tall, very elegant lady about to attend a formal dinner.

"You're looking well, Miss Emma," Thomas said, bowing as Emma approached.

"Thank you, Mr. Wellingham," Emma replied with a smile as she curtsied. Thomas held an arm out for her and another for his sister. "Thank you for asking me to stay this evening. This bedchamber seems very comfortable," she added as she took his arm.

"You're most welcome. I wish your stay could have been due to better circumstances," Thomas replied as they made their way down the steps.

"Indeed. Rain will seem like a small inconvenience after today," Emma replied as they made their way to the library.

CHAPTER 24
A HEROINE RETURNS HOME

June 12, 1802, Kingly Street

After a restless night of dreams filled with scar-faced ruffians and the sounds of gunshots, Emma took an early breakfast with Christiana. Anxious to get home, she pulled on a bonnet and riding cloak and headed for the Woodscastle stables.

Her mare, Georgie, seemed not to have suffered as a result of her ordeal. Having spent the night dining on a bucket of oats and several carrots, she proved difficult to coax out of her stall for the ride home.

"You've a fine horse there, Miss Fitzsimmons," Mr. Allen commented as he saddled another horse. "Do ya ha' your own stables in London, then?" he asked, moving a mounting block next to her.

"Just a mews behind the townhouse," she replied, not paying much attention to the groom but inspecting her mare's legs for possible injuries from the incident the day before. She knew Mr. Larsen would have seen to any injury when Thomas returned the horse the day before, but her examination was more for her benefit than for the horse. The busier she kept herself, the less likely she was to think of the events of the day before. "Although the stable boy who sees to Georgie seems reliable enough."

"Georgie?" Mr. Allen repeated.

Her face coloring, Emma gave him a nod. "I was very young when I named her. After my father," she added with a grin.

"Well, Mr. Wellingham's horse has taken a shine to your mare,"

Mr. Larsen, the other groom, mentioned when he had finished securing the saddle strap.

Emma allowed the groom to assist her as she climbed into the saddle and took the reins. "Oh?"

"Indeed. Saw him mounting her out in the pasture late yesterday," he said nonchalantly, turning beet red when he realized what he had said. "Pardon me, Miss Fitzsimmons," he said, his hand coming up to cover his mouth. "I meant no offense."

Emma's eyes widened as she stared at the groom. "None taken," she whispered as she considered what he had just said. "Has it happened before?" she asked quietly, a hint of panic rising in her. The thought that her mare might be pregnant was a source of consternation. Just as she considered she couldn't begin to afford the cost to care for a foal, she wondered if perhaps Mr. Wellingham could use the offspring for his business. The horses were both bays and nicely matched when it came to coloring.

"Not that I recollect," Mr. Larsen replied, his shoulders shrugging as his face returned to its normal color. It was then Mr. Allen informed her he would be seeing her back to town.

"Mr. Wellingham insisted," he explained as he pulled a saddled bay forward. "After what happened yesterday, I'm ta see to your safe delivery home. And I'm to fetch you Monday morning, just as I've been doing."

Stunned by this bit of news, Emma glanced toward the house, about to protest the escort. But considering what had happened, she decided she would be more at ease with a groom, as would her landlady. Mrs. Simpson had been quite critical of her decision to travel without a chaperone and then equally effusive about how accommodating Mr. Wellingham was to supply a groom as an escort to and from Woodscastle.

"If you're up for a run, I know Albert would be willing to race," Mr. Allen added, not about to admit the horse needed more exercise than he had been able to provide the day before.

Although she usually only allowed Georgie to gallop part of the six miles, she thought a race might be just the thing. "Well, if that's the way it's to be, then I do believe we'll take you up on your challenge, Mr. Allen." She dug her heels into Georgie, and they were off down the short road to Burlington Lane.

Mounting Albert from a standing leap, Mr. Allen sounded a curse and rode out after Emma.

A glorious Saturday, Emma thought as her mount galloped into town. Warm but breezy, the early summer air made for an enjoyable ride. The lilacs had bloomed earlier that week, and their scent wafted through the air as she allowed Mr. Allen and his mount to catch up.

"I am well, truly," she said when he asked about her health for the third time. They negotiated the busy intersection at Piccadilly Square. "I slept well and will simply not think on it," she added as the groom pulled along side.

Once he was sure Emma was safely back to Kingly Street, Mr. Allen took off for Wellingham Imports. Emma directed her horse to the mews behind her townhouse, where she dismounted and led the horse to the stable boy. At the sight of her, his eyes opened wide.

"Are you quite aw'ight, Miss Fitzsimmons?" he asked as he took the reins and studied the horse. "We ha' been worried sick about you. And your 'orse," he added, his accent so thick she could barely understand the reference to Georgie.

"I'm fine, Master Churchill," she replied. "My employer insisted I stay the night at his estate, though..."

"I should hope so," the stable boy replied. "After what you did? He should give you a raise in pay!"

Confused, Emma frowned and shook her head. "Whatever do you mean?" she asked, at first not taking his meaning.

Master Churchill hurried over to a stool at the front entrance to the stables. He picked up a folded newspaper and held it out for her. "You're front page news, Miss Emma," he said with a huge grin. "I couldna' read all the words, but from the gist of it, I'd say you and your 'orse were 'eroes. You can keep it if ye'd like," he added as he held out the newspaper in her direction.

"Why, thank you," Emma replied as she unfolded that day's *The Times* and stared at the headline. *Housebreakers killed by book-keeper and butler*, it read. "Oh, good God," Emma breathed as she read the article. Although there was some embellishment in the written account, everything she and Humphrey had described to the sheriff was in the copy, as well as some details Mr. Wellingham had provided about her horse, the third man, and the thieves' carriage.

There was also news about the other estates that had been victims of the housebreakers as recently as the day before. "I had no idea these men had robbed so many homes along that road," Emma said as she looked over the top of the paper to find a very agitated Todd Vandermeer staring down at her.

"Are you quite well, Miss Emma?" Todd asked, his breaths coming in short pants. He had apparently walked quite a distance, and the look on his face was one of deep concern. "I've been so very worried. I came as soon as I read of your ordeal," he said, quickly removing his hat and bowing when he remembered he hadn't done so.

Emma curtsied. "I'm quite fine, Mr. Vandermeer," she assured him, noticing his cravat was tied in a most elegant mail coach style. "It's very kind of you to come all this way to inquire about me, though." She glanced around, not seeing his phaeton or a horse. "Did you *walk* all the way from your house?" she asked in alarm, folding the newspaper and slipping it under her arm.

"I came by carriage. I left it parked in front of your townhouse, but I saw you on your horse only a moment ago and followed you here," he explained, his breaths coming in slower gasps. "Are you quite certain you're in good health? Truly, I've been so vexed."

Grinning, Emma reached out a gloved hand and placed it over the hand that held his cane. Despite the fabric of their gloves preventing her from actually touching him, she was sure she felt a shiver pass through the back of his hand.

Quickly folding her hands together around the strap of her reticule, she said, "Truly, I'm fine, Mr. Vandermeer." A thought struck her, though, and she frowned. "I must admit, though, that I'm a bit surprised a man of your standing would wish to be seen with a woman who has just shot and killed a man and been a party to the deaths of two others.". She glanced to the left and right. "I would certainly understand if you didn't wish me to join your dinner party."

She almost regretted having made the comment. What if Todd agreed and withdrew his invitation? She had been looking forward to the dinner party. With most of the literate populace of London reading about her ordeal in the newspaper, though, she realized she had gained a bit of notoriety, and not necessarily the best kind.

How will polite society treat me now?

Would she be scorned as a murderer? Or celebrated as some sort of hero, as Master Churchill had done? Or given the cut direct, perhaps? And what about her landlords? Would they want her to vacate her townhouse?

The broker vigorously shook his head. "Why, of course, I still want you to come for dinner this evening!" he exclaimed, his eyes quite wide. "Shooting a man in defense of life and property doesn't make you a... a *murderer*, Miss Emma. Far from it," he assured her as he offered her his free arm. "I am most looking forward to this evening, and if it pleases you, I simply won't allow this incident to interfere with our plans," he added as they walked toward her townhouse.

"How very kind of you," Emma replied with relief, hoping the rest of the denizens of London felt the same way.

As they approached her front door, Emma couldn't help but notice the longer they walked, the more Mr. Vandermeer seemed uncomfortable. "Are you ill, Mr. Vandermeer?" she asked carefully, noticing he was grimacing with every step.

Todd sighed and considered how to respond. He couldn't hide his increasing difficulty when walking. The cane he carried, always in evidence, was used to keep him as upright as possible. His upper torso and arms were quite developed as a result, their strong lines occasionally apparent in the bath superfine of his coat. "My knees give me great pain, Miss Fitzsimmons," he finally replied. "But it's an unfortunate side-effect of my height, and nothing can be done. You are kind to ask, though," he added, hoping his response wouldn't lessen Emma's opinion of him.

Emma angled her head to one side and regarded the importer. "So, you've not found relief from salves or ointments?" she asked as she fished her door key from her reticule and slipped it into the lock.

Todd bit his lip. "I have not," he stated with a shake of head.

"We'll see about that," Emma said with a nod as she opened the door. "Will you join me for tea, Mr. Vandermeer?" she offered as she stood aside for him and indicated he should enter.

The importer seemed surprised by her invitation and didn't immediately answer. When Emma raised an eyebrow and asked, "Is something wrong?" Todd shook his head. "Forgive me, but I've never been in this situation before, and I don't know... I don't know what the... *proper* response is for me to make," he stammered as he glanced up and down the street, his embarrassment apparent. *Wasn't it inappropriate for an unmarried woman to request a man enter her home without a chaperone present?*

Emma's eyebrows drew together, and she remembered what

Thomas had said about the importer's lack of social training. Apparently the man had become so fearful of making the wrong decision, he instead made no decision at all.

Although it really *wasn't* appropriate for her to invite Todd into her townhouse—he wasn't family, nor did she have a chaperone—she could hardly leave him on the stoop. "When invited to tea by a woman, and you are unmarried, willing, and able to do so, you accept the invitation. If you don't have the time or don't wish to have tea or the company of the person inviting you, then you may excuse yourself and refuse the offer," Emma explained briefly. "Either response will not offend me, I assure you," she added, not wishing to explain the issue of a chaperone for herself. If she thought she had to have one, she merely had to knock on her landlord's door and request Mrs. Simpson's abigail come in with her.

Todd smiled brightly. "Then, yes, I would very much like to join you for tea," he said as he took a deep breath and let it out. His eyebrows drew together and he looked concerned. "Does this mean a married man cannot accept the offer of tea?"

Angling her head to the other side, Emma gave a slight shrug. "Only if his wife is with him," she replied, deciding not to get into the particulars if the tea was offered as part of a business meeting or among relatives.

At that moment, the door next to hers opened and James Simpson stepped out. He gave a quick glance in Mr. Vandermeer's direction before bowing to the both of them, his expression indicating he recognized Emma's visitor.

Todd returned the bow as Emma curtsied. "Good morning, Mr. Simpson. May I introduce you to Mr. Todd Vandermeer?" she offered. Turning to Todd, she added, "Mr. Simpson and his wife own these buildings."

Todd reached out his right hand, his face lighting up as he recognized the neighbor. "'Tis very good to see you again, Mr. Simpson. It's been a number of years, but I must say, you look in good health."

The elder gentleman vigorously shook Todd's hand and a huge smile broke out on his face. "You're taller than ever, Mr. Vandermeer," James replied happily. "Gads, how many years has it been? Twelve?" he asked, grasping Todd on the arm.

Embarrassed by the comment, Todd nodded and replied, "At least. 'Tis very good to see you again."

Obviously in a hurry, James said his farewells and quickly walked to the end of the street, disappearing around the corner. *He must not read The Times*, Emma thought as she watched him depart.

She motioned with a quick wave of her hand to indicate Todd should enter her townhouse and then led him to the parlor. She suggested he take the high-backed chair. "It'll just take me a few minutes to put some water on for tea," she said as she left the room.

Hurrying to the kitchen, she started the smoldered fire under the stove and filled the teakettle with water from the pump. From the cupboard, she pulled out her finest tea set and a container of Dutch biscuits.

The odor of horse on her gown, more apparent now that she was indoors, had her groaning. The same gown she had worn to work the day before, it was stained with blood and dirt.

Climbing the stairs to the bedchamber above, she quickly changed her gown and found a jar of salve in a box of medicinals. Her father had used the salve for his joint pain. She hoped it would work for her guest.

Rejoining Todd in the parlor, she said, "Please, don't get up," as she entered the room and opened the jar of salve. "I believe this will provide you with the relief from the pain you have been suffering, Mr. Vandermeer," she announced as she held the medicine near his nose.

Todd at first recoiled from the glass jar, but he gingerly sniffed its contents. Not particularly unpleasant nor overly strong, its scent suggested the salve was nothing more than a lotion. Todd took the jar from her and studied the label.

"If you pull up your trouser legs and push down your stockings to the top of your boots, I'll be happy to apply it for you," Emma offered, knowing full well her offer was of the highest impropriety. She wasn't sure Todd would realize it, though.

"Wouldn't that be highly... improper?" he asked as his attention went from the label on the jar to Emma.

Emma shrugged her shoulders and knelt down in front of the importer. "Perhaps. But I won't tell if you don't tell," she answered as she took the jar from him and scooped out some salve on two of her fingers. Waiting expectantly, she urged, "Go on."

Reluctantly, Todd pulled up the leg of his breeches and pushed down on the silk stocking to expose one knee. It was thin and somewhat bony, but Emma was careful as she smoothed the salve over and above the knee bone and around the sides of the knee. Besides the scent of the medicine, she was suddenly aware of the scent of citrus from laundry soap and a hint of sandalwood cologne. *He must bathe frequently*, she realized, remembering the scent of him when he called on her at Woodscastle. "Now straighten your leg," she ordered gently.

Todd took a deep breath and did as he was told, reveling in the gentle touch her fingers provided against his bare skin. He couldn't recall the last time a woman had touched him, and certainly no one had touched him like this.

As Emma's fingers massaged the back of his knee, he let out the breath he had been holding, a slight growl escaping his throat. Did the woman have any idea what her simple ministrations were doing to him? To his manhood? He dared a glance at the placket of his breeches, hoping the evidence of his growing excitement wasn't making itself too apparent.

"Does it hurt when I do this?" Emma asked with concern as she continued to massage the area around his knee.

Todd swallowed. He bent and flexed his knee. "No," he said quietly. "It doesn't hurt at all," he said more forcefully. A warming sensation developed deep in the joint. "The pain... the pain is gone," he said in disbelief as he continued to flex his knee.

Emma smiled and motioned for him to raise the other trouser leg. He did so without argument, and she completed the application on the other knee while Todd studied her hand's motions. He then found his attention had drifted to her cleavage and the slight swell of her breasts above the neckline of her sprigged muslin gown. He swallowed hard as he forced himself to look away. *She is touching me*, he thought. *She is on her knees before me, and she is touching me!*

"Is it acceptable for me to tell you your fingers are most... sensual?" Todd asked as he reveled in the relief of the pain he had been suffering.

Emma paused in her ministrations and looked up at her guest. "No, I rather think not," she replied with a poorly hidden smirk. "But, thank you, nonetheless." She replaced the lid and then handed the jar to him. "Keep this, please," she said, hoping he would take the time to use the analgesic. "You'll probably need to apply it every morning, and possibly before you retire for the night," she added as she accepted his help in standing up. She shook out her skirts.

Todd nodded and put the jar into his coat pocket. "Thank you so very much, Miss Fitzsimmons. I cannot tell you how... how amazing it is not to be in pain." The expression on his face was one of relief and bewilderment, as if he couldn't decide what his next course of action should be.

"You're very welcome, Mr. Vandermeer. As an importer, I should think you'll be able to acquire more when you need it. I've simply no idea from which chemist my father purchased it," Emma said, trying to remember the name of his druggist. "He was in Old Bond Street, though..."

"That would be Thomas Forster," Todd said as his face brightened. "I'm already familiar with his shop."

Emma smiled as she remembered her father espousing the benefits of Forster's various medicines. "Yes, that's his name. Now, please excuse me whilst I wash up and get the tea. There's no need to get up," she added as she left the room, her gown swishing around the door frame as she headed for the kitchen.

His comment about knowing the chemist reminded her of their earlier encounter with James Simpson. Curious to know how Todd knew James Simpson, she decided it couldn't hurt to ask him when she returned with the tea.

When she did return with the tea tray, though, she found her guest sound asleep. He had managed to pull down the legs of his breeches and rebutton the cuffs, at least, but his head was resting comfortably against the top of the padded chair, and he was snoring softly.

Sighing, Emma took a cup of tea and sipped it in the growing quiet as she considered her guest. She found she adored the man and thought a friendship with him would be most interesting—even entertaining—but she knew she couldn't consider him as a possible husband. His height wasn't so much of a problem for her as it would be for him. *He won't be long on this earth*, she thought, a sadness settling over her as she considered his future. Men of his height generally died before reaching thirty-five years of age.

She imagined what a short marriage might be like compared to a lifetime of widowhood, especially in his huge house. *At least I would probably not want for money*, Emma thought to herself. Such a shame when, from what Mr. Wellingham had said, the man was so desperate to be married.

Deborah! Emma thought suddenly, her eyes widening. *Deborah White could certainly use that money more than me.* The midwife at the

Home for Unwed Mothers would make a perfect match for Todd Vandermeer. She was tall, lovely, and skilled at being a nursemaid.

And hadn't she said, 'One of these days, I am going to kiss that man?'

Upon completing her semester at Warwick's, Emma's obligation to perform charity work at the Home had ended. Since starting work at Woodscastle, and despite her promise she would keep in contact, Emma hadn't seen Deborah for nearly a month. *Perhaps today would be a good day to visit*, she thought.

Moving silently to the desk in the corner of the parlor, she pulled out a piece of stationery and sat down to write a letter. She addressed the outside to herself and then on the inside wrote a missive as if it were from Deborah. She wrote of learning of Emma's ordeal with the housebreakers from the newspaper and could she come to Emma's to take her for dinner at six o'clock?

Emma folded the note and sealed it with melted wax, although she didn't stamp her "F" into the warm puddle. When the wax hardened, she checked on Todd to be sure he was still sleeping. Seeing the positively peaceful expression on his face made Emma realize it was probably the first time in a long time he had been able to sleep free of pain.

Feeling a pang of guilt, she walked quietly to the front door, opened it, and then shut it as loudly as she could. Still carrying the note, Emma returned to the parlor to find Todd wide awake. She placed the note on the table and hurried to pour him a cup of tea. As she handed it to him on a saucer, she said, "I apologize the tea took so long." Emma returned to the settee. "And just as I was about to serve, this post arrived. Would you like a Dutch biscuit?" she asked brightly as she held out the tray in front of him.

Todd looked around, his manner betraying his nervousness. "Why, yes, thank you. I do enjoy the flavor of gingerbread," he said as he helped himself to one of the biscuits. "You weren't gone long at all, though," he countered as he noticed the note on the table. When Emma didn't move to open it, he asked, "Aren't you going to read it?" as his hand motioned toward the folded paper, the biscuit acting as a pointer.

Emma made a point of watching his hand and then she shrugged. "Well, I was going to wait until after you had taken your leave, but if you insist..."

"Oh, please do," he encouraged her. He munched on the biscuit while Emma broke the seal and unfolded the note.

"It's from my good friend, Deborah White," Emma said in mock delight as she pretended to scan the letter. She put the letter on her lap, her hands grasping both sides of the paper. "You would simply adore her, Mr. Vandermeer," she said as she glanced at Todd. "Miss White is a gorgeous brunette, very tall, very elegant, and very sweet in nature," she gushed, hoping the 'very tall' would attract his attention. "I believe she's twenty, perhaps one-and-twenty."

His posture suddenly more erect, Todd replied, "Indeed? Miss White is taller even than you?" he asked, his curiosity piqued.

Emma's eyes widened, almost surprised he had taken the bait. "Oh, yes. I believe she stands right at six feet in her stockings. And yet she has a most pleasing figure," Emma added with an enthusiastic nod.

Todd hesitated before asking, "And how is it you are acquainted with this woman?"

Emma decided honesty, to a point, was the best approach in answering his question. "I know her from my charity work at Mrs. Dawes' Home for Unwed Mothers," she explained, pausing a moment to notice his reaction of surprise in how his eyebrows arched up. "When one attends Warwick's Grammar and Finishing School, there is a requirement to work with a charity organization every Saturday. I was assigned to the Home, you see," she added carefully, remembering she had mentioned it to him over lunch the previous Tuesday. "Miss White is a... a midwife there. She delivers babies and provides care for women who are with child."

The importer nodded happily. "I'm familiar with the establishment. In fact, I am a... a patron, I suppose you could say," he mentioned nervously.

"Yes, I remember you saying so last Tuesday," Emma answered, knowing full well Todd Vandermeer had helped support the place with donations for several years. Indeed, when she first started her charity work, Mrs. Dawes had described her association with Mr. Vandermeer. The older woman was rather proud of a man she had delivered in her early days as a midwife.

Embarrassed, Todd nodded. "I was an orphan, you see, and it just seemed the most logical institution in which to place my tithe."

Emma angled her head to one side and smiled at the man. "Then, perhaps you already know Miss White," she suggested carefully. Perhaps they had met when Todd delivered his donations.

The tall man shook his head. "I'm most certain I would

remember a woman matching your description of Miss White," he said with a self-conscious grin. "I shall be sure to give more the next time I am there."

Emma heard the sincerity in his voice and sighed. The more time she spent with Todd Vandermeer, the more she found herself liking the fellow. "You're very kind to do so. They've been desperate for funds. They need a new facility, of course. The man who owns their building has done nothing in the way of repairs, so it's become a bit shabby," she mentioned casually. "Of course, 'tis much too small for the number of mothers they're trying to help."

Leaning forward, Todd displayed a look of concern. "Indeed? Pray tell, what kind of facility would work best for them?" he asked as his eyebrows knitted together.

Shrugging one shoulder, Emma thought for a moment. "Something with a good deal of rooms, of course, a kitchen, and a lobby. Like a... a hotel or an apartment building, I suppose."

Todd nodded and considered Emma's words. "Humph," he finally replied and pointed to the letter. "Pardon my questions, Miss Fitzsimmons. Please, continue reading your letter," he encouraged as he helped himself to another biscuit.

Emma returned her attention to the letter and continued her charade. "Oh, dear," Emma said quietly. When she noticed Todd's attention had him leaning closer to her, she leaned in his direction and continued, "She read this morning's paper and is quite concerned about me. So concerned, in fact, she is coming to take me to dinner at six o'clock this evening." Emma dropped the letter into her lap with a sigh and allowed an expression of disappointment to cross her face. "Well, that simply won't do," she said in mock despair. "Whatever am I to do?"

Todd contemplated the situation. "Well, you must have dinner with her," he replied quickly. "There is no time to get a post back to her, is there?"

Emma slumped her shoulders and gave Todd the saddest expression she could. "But I'm having dinner at your home tonight," she countered.

Todd sat up straight in his chair. "Then you simply must bring her with you. You'll require a chaperone, after all. Miss White is most welcome to join us for dinner tonight," he insisted.

Why didn't I think of that? Emma thought as she berated herself for creating such an involved scenario when she could have simply told him she was bringing a chaperone.

"If she is calling on you at six, then you two can ride together in my carriage at seven. And I will personally see to it you both arrive home safely when dinner is complete," Todd offered with a wave of his hand.

Emma's eyes widened in mock surprise, and she reached over to place a hand over his. This time, she was sure she felt a shiver of something pass through the back of his hand. And she was sure she heard a sharp intake of air. "What a capital idea! You are such a dear," she said with a genuine smile.

Somewhat embarrassed at being touched again by Emma, Todd Vandermeer took a deep breath and let it out slowly. "You are very kind to say so," he replied quietly. After a pause, he added, "Now, regrettably, I really must be going. I must let my cook know that there will be another for dinner," he said as he stood up. Although he had his cane, he didn't use it to negotiate his way to the front door.

Emma hurried to open the door for him and placed a hand on his arm. "Are you still free of pain, Mr. Vandermeer?" she asked as he stepped out the door and turned.

The importer smiled and patted his coat pocket where he had placed the jar of salve. "Indeed, thanks to you," he replied as he took her hand and brushed his lips over the back of it. "I will see you this evening, Miss Fitzsimmons," he said with a genuine smile as he bowed. Then he set his hat atop his head, stepped up into his phaeton, and was on his way.

CHAPTER 25
PREPARATIONS FOR ATTENDING A DINNER

$\mathcal{E}$mma closed the door and took a deep breath as she leaned against it. *What am I doing?* she wondered, realizing how much work had to be done to prepare for dinner at Todd's house. Somehow, she had cover the mile to the Home for Unwed Mothers, talk Deborah into having dinner at Todd Vandermeer's, return to bathe and dress by seven, and hope that fate would put the two of them together.

And she had forgotten to ask the man how it was he knew James Simpson!

Grabbing her reticule and the letter she had written, Emma donned her white eyelet bonnet and hurried out the door. Walking quickly through the streets of west London without benefit of a chaperone or lady's maid, she made it to Newport Street and the Home for Unwed Mothers in a half-hour.

She could hear the sound of crying babies even before she opened the entry door. Mrs. Dawes noticed her immediately, greeting her happily and asking how she was getting on in her position with Mr. Wellingham. Emma assured the stout midwife she was glad to be gainfully employed. "Is Deborah here today?"

"She's in 'er room," Mrs. Dawes replied, her eyes glancing at the ceiling as she said it. "'Tis supposed to be her day off, but she worked all morning, and has been complaining about her knees, so I sent her to her room to lie down."

Shaking her head, Emma thanked the elder midwife and made

her way to Deborah's room. She knocked twice on the door and listened. "Miss Deborah, 'tis Emma," she said quietly.

"Do come in," Emma heard through the door. Opening it, she found Deborah stretched out on her bed, tears streaming down her face. At the sight of Emma, the midwife started to get up, but Emma waved her to stay where she was.

"Deborah, it is so good to see you. I... I have... you see, made dinner plans... You must come... Mr. Todd Vandermeer... we're being sent a carriage... seven o'clock at my townhouse."

Deborah stared at Emma with a look of confusion on her face. "Emma? Whatever is *wrong* with you?" she asked, wiping one side of her tear-stained face with the back of a hand.

Emma took a deep breath. "I apologize. I'm in such a hurry, and I'm being *rude*," she said as she realized Deborah was in distress. The tall girl's red-rimmed eyes made it appear as if she had been crying for some time. "Are you crying because of the pain in your knees?" Emma asked, realizing she had not properly curtsied or asked about Deborah's health.

Sighing, Deborah wiped the remaining tears from her face. "Yes," she replied wearily. "I was standing nearly all day yesterday. I delivered two babies and had to walk several babies to keep them from crying," she explained in exasperation. "The pain is simply *excruciating*."

Emma nodded and bit her lip, regretting having given her only jar of analgesic salve to Mr. Vandermeer. "When I leave here, I will see what I can find at the chemist's. I know there is a brand of salve that will work for you," she claimed. "I just have to find it."

Deborah sniffled. "What was it you said about Mr. Vandermeer?" she asked, trying to remember the gibberish Emma sputtered when she first burst into the room. "Were you speaking of the Mr. Vandermeer who gives us money? Who owns that beautiful mansion in Cavendish Square?"

"Grace Park. Yes, 'tis he. He works for the East India Company." Sitting down on the edge of the bed, Emma began to explain. "Mr. Todd Vandermeer called on me a few days ago and requested I attend a seven-course dinner party at Grace Park this evening. He is sending a carriage at seven o'clock to take me there. In the meantime, I shot two thieves at Woodscastle yesterday and am the front page news story today. Mr. Vandermeer saw the article and rushed to my townhouse this morning to assure himself that I was in good health, which I am, by the way. I asked him in for tea because he was limping so badly and was obviously in a great deal of pain. Like you, his knees ache horribly because he is tall. I put salve..."

Emma stopped when she realized to what she had just admitted and then continued. "I had him put my father's salve on his knees and that gave him relief, but whilst he was sleeping—he fell asleep whilst I was getting the tea, you see—I realized he is an adorable man, and that although I would love to be his friend for life, I don't wish to marry him, and I was led to believe by Miss Wellingham and Mr. Wellingham that Mr. Vandermeer would propose to me, possibly during dinner this evening." She paused to think a moment. "Sometime between the fourth and fifth course, is what Mr. Wellingham said. So while Mr. Vandermeer slept, I wrote this," she paused to pull the letter out of her reticule, "And I faked its delivery by post, and Mr. Vandermeer insisted I read it whilst he was there. So I did, and, of course, I described you to him. Then he insisted *you* must join us for dinner this evening because he is most interested in meeting you. And, now I have come to request that you come to my townhouse and be dressed for dinner and ready for his carriage at seven o'clock."

During Emma's explanation, Deborah had turned on her side and crooked her elbow so she could support her head on her hand. She read Emma's letter and shook her head, a smile finally forming on her face. When she put the letter down, she said simply, "You *shot* two thieves?"

Emma visibly slumped and rolled her eyes in despair. "With Mr. Wellingham's dueling pistols," she replied with a sigh.

Impressed, Deborah nodded. "Indeed? And I can just imagine you doing it, too," she said with a wicked smile as she pantomimed holding a gun with two hands as far out in front of her body as possible and closing both eyes as she pulled the trigger.

"I did not close my eyes," Emma countered defensively, watching Deborah's play-acting with an amused expression. "At least, I don't remember doing so."

"And just how did you describe me to Mr. Vandermeer?" Deborah countered with a frown.

Emma thought for a moment. "I said you were a brunette,... very gorgeous, very tall,... very elegant,... and I said that you had a beautiful figure," she remembered aloud, knowing she didn't get the quotes exactly the same.

Deborah sat up in the bed. "You said all that?" she cried out, a look of disgust on her face. "However am I to live up to that description?" she asked, shocked Emma would be so generous with her adjectives.

"But you are. And you do," Emma insisted as she regarded her friend. "Will you please do this with me tonight?"

Deborah shrugged her shoulders as she contemplated Emma's elaborate plan.

"I'm sure I have a dinner gown you can wear," Emma offered in a quiet voice. "And you can take a bath at my townhouse." This last was said in the manner of the bribe it was meant to be. As Emma expected, Deborah's eyebrows shot up at the offer of a bath.

A bath in a copper tub full of hot water!

Emma leaned closer. "He is rich. And you said you wanted to kiss him," she teased in a playful whisper. "I have every expectation he will propose to you before the end of the evening."

Open-mouthed, Deborah stared at Emma. "Well, why didn't you just say so in the first place?" she asked with a mischievous grin. Standing up carefully, she said, "I need to pack a few things before we leave."

Emma nodded. "I walked here, but now I realize you'll never make it to my townhouse when you're in such pain. I'll go to the chemist and shall return shortly with some medicine," she promised as she left her friend's room.

Hurrying down the street to the next intersection, Emma found a chemist's shop, and although it wasn't Forster's, she thought she might find a product that would work like his analgesic. She quickly perused the store, searching the shelves. When she couldn't find it, she described it to the chemist, mentioning the odd odor and the deep heating quality. The man knew immediately what she sought and pulled a jar from a shelf behind the counter.

"That's it!" Emma exclaimed as she recognized the label. "But why isn't it on the shelves out here?" she asked as she opened her reticule to get some coins.

The chemist shrugged. "It's the only one that works," he explained, "And it's difficult to acquire."

Emma nodded. "Could I refer someone to you should he need to replenish his supply soon?"

Shrugging again, the chemist said, "Of course. But it's costly stuff. Five shillings for one of them jars," he added with a lift of his brow.

A crown!

"Oh, dear," Emma replied. Was the salve usually that price? *He must be taking advantage*. Pulling out every available coin she could find in her purse, she barely had enough to purchase the one jar. But she knew if she didn't, Deborah wouldn't make it the mile to her townhouse. And at this time of the afternoon, there would be no hope of hiring a yellow bounder.

Handing over the coins, she stuffed the jar into her reticule and hurried back to the Home for Unwed Mothers.

Although not pleased with the scent, Deborah gingerly rubbed the salve around her knees. After a few moments, she stood up and gingerly walked around the small room, limping at first and then taking small, even steps. Smiling, she hurried over to where Emma was watching and hugged her. "Relief, finally," she whispered. "Wherever did you get this?"

"The chemist on the next street. He keeps it behind the counter. You must ask for it," Emma replied, not wanting Deborah to know how much it cost. "What can I carry for you?" she asked as she watched Deborah wrap up several items in a bundle. There was no valise in sight, and Emma wondered if her friend still owned a traveling case.

"This is it, I'm afraid to admit," Deborah replied, indicating the small bundle. "I've only the one extra corset and pantaloons. I've no gloves, no jewelry, and just these slippers," she said as she pointed to the black pair on the floor. She wore a pair of lace-up shoes, that, while practical, were not the least bit attractive.

"We'll make do," Emma assured her as they left her room. Pain-free, Deborah's mood lightened considerably as they made their way back to Emma's townhouse. By the time they arrived at two o'clock, Deborah was looking forward to the evening.

Emma made supper while she told Deborah about Woodscastle and Mr. Wellingham. Deborah shared stories about the girls and babies at the home. By five o'clock, both had bathed and were dressed in corsets and pantaloons. By six, their hair was ironed into ringlets, pinned into place atop their heads, and adorned with tiny white flowers. And for the next hour after that, they struggled to find a dinner gown long enough for Deborah to wear.

"I just know I have one that is too long for me," Emma said as she pulled several gowns out of the wardrobe. "My father bought it for me for my first ball. It's white, of course. Here," she said as she plucked a long-sleeved satin and chiffon gown out of the pile on her bed.

Deborah held it in front of her and smiled. Pulling it over her head, she beamed as it dropped around her and ended just inches above the floor. "I think it fits," she said hopefully, noticing the sleeves seemed too short.

"I think it does, too," Emma agreed as she walked around the taller girl. "We can cut the sleeves off up here," she offered, deciding she would probably never wear the gown again. "And then you can wear long gloves," she said as she pulled out a pair and offered them to Deborah. "There's a matching shawl," she murmured as she pulled a long length of fabric from the wardrobe and draped it loosely around Deborah's shoulders. "But you'll need white slippers. Your black ones simply won't do." She leaned down and found a pair of slippers tucked under the edge of the bed. "Try these," she said as she placed the slippers at Deborah's feet. "They're too long for me. Maybe they'll fit you better."

Arching her brow at Emma's unintended cut, Deborah pulled them on and pronounced them perfect. "I'd really rather be comfortable and not be thinking of how tight my slippers are all night," Deborah admitted sheepishly. And if Todd Vandermeer were as tall as Emma claimed, he probably wouldn't see all the way down to her feet.

Emma opened her jewelry box and searched for appropriate earbobs and a hair comb, finally finding a pair of earbobs made of strings of small pearls in a loop and a comb inlaid with mother-of-pearl. The comb was especially fine, the pearlescent finish a stark contrast to Deborah's dark hair. When she finished putting it into place, Emma handed the earbobs to Deborah and began the search for a gown for herself.

Not wanting to appear prettier or more colorful than Deborah, she chose a long-sleeved gold gown of batiste, simple gold earbobs, and a pair of short white gloves. With her golden blond hair nearly the color of the gown, the look was elegant but had the unintended effect of making her seem taller than she was. Next to Deborah's statuesque figure, stunning white gown, pale porcelain skin and dark brunette hair, Emma wouldn't expect a second look in a room full of gentlemen. *And, if Todd Vandermeer is a typical gentleman,* Emma thought slyly, *he'll not give me a second look.*

CHAPTER 26
DINNER AT GRACE PARK

At precisely seven o'clock, a carriage drawn by a matched pair of greys appeared in front of Emma's townhouse. Giggling, Deborah White and Emma Fitzsimmons, with the assistance of the driver, Mr. Stevenson, climbed aboard and sat arm-in-arm for their ride to Cavendish Square. Within a half-hour, they were in the semi-circle drive in front of Grace Park.

Deborah marveled at the sight of the mansion. She and every other Londoner had seen it from the street, but to see it up close in the waning light of day was to see a masterpiece of architectural design. Even the colorful landscaping in front of the house was designed to draw the eye to the pair of forest green front doors and the stained glass transom above them.

The two friends ascended the steps, the doors opening before they could even touch the lion's head knocker. A butler at least ten years younger than Humphrey stood aside as they entered.

Deborah paused a moment as she recognized the man. "Winston?" she said in surprise as she curtsied. "'Tis so good to see you again," she added as the butler bowed in her direction.

From the expression on his face, Emma thought the butler didn't recognize Deborah. She was curious as to why Deborah knew the manservant and was about to ask when she realized they were being watched.

Beyond the vast vestibule stood Mr. Todd Vandermeer. Sans a cane, he was impeccably dressed in cream breeches, a deep blue embroidered waistcoat, and a scarlet superfine tailcoat. Upon their noting his presence, he bowed deeply and then stood still as he seemed to stare in awe.

Emma and Deborah curtsied and approached the importer. "Mr. Todd Vandermeer, may I present Miss Deborah White," Emma stated as she let go of Deborah's arm. She couldn't help but notice Todd's cane was nowhere in sight—and neither were the other guests.

Are we the first to arrive?

Emma watched as Todd and Deborah stood staring at one another, both speechless and both breathless. If she could trust what she saw in Todd's expression, she thought he was seeing the most beautiful woman he had ever seen in his entire life. Here, before him, stood a woman he could actually look upon without looking down.

Deborah regarded their host in awe. The man was on the thin side but more handsome than she had imagined from Mrs. Dawes' descriptions and certainly younger than she expected. She finally spoke. "I'm very pleased to meet you, Mr. Vandermeer."

Todd finally recovered his composure, reaching for Deborah's gloved hand so he could gently kiss the back of it. He marveled at the length of her graceful fingers, and he wondered for a moment how it would feel to have those fingers rub salve into his aching knees.

Have you ever wanted something so much, you cannot think of anything else until you get it?

"The pleasure is entirely mine, I assure you, Miss Deborah," Todd replied as he continued to stare at the tall woman. He finally glanced in Emma's direction. "Miss Emma, your description of your friend simply didn't do her justice," he admonished, finally smiling and holding out his arms for the women.

Emma arched her eyebrows, curious as to which attribute had she missed when describing her best friend earlier that afternoon. She glanced at Deborah with a tentative grin while they each took one of his arms.

The three made their way to the main floor parlor. Decorated in shades of green with accents of crimson, it was perhaps the most beautiful room Emma had ever seen. "What a divine parlor, Mr. Vandermeer," Emma commented as their host led them to a settee. "Did you choose the colors?"

Todd was reminded of the day he had hosted Charlotte Hughes

for tea. "Oh, no, I cannot take credit, I fear. The house was already decorated and furnished when I purchased it," Todd replied as he pointed to a pair of taller wing chairs adjacent to the settee. "Miss White, I believe you will be more comfortable in one of these," he offered as he moved to stand next to the chair in which he usually sat.

Indeed, as Deborah sat down she was amazed at how her feet just reached the floor. Used to having her knees up well above the seat of a chair, she sat back and then straightened herself. "This is the most comfortable chair I have ever had the pleasure of sitting in, Mr. Vandermeer," she commented with a satisfied smile, her gaze showing through her long lashes as Todd watched her admire the chair. With the cut sleeves of her gown still a bit tight, Deborah was forced to hold her elbows back, but the awkward posture also displayed her décolletage to better advantage.

Todd had the best view as he stood above her and looked down. He swallowed hard and averted his gaze, desperate not to offend his guest and well aware his body was responding in a way that might embarrass him.

What had she said? *Chairs.* They were talking about the chairs.

"Indeed, I know what you mean, Miss Deborah. I had them specially made after I purchased the house. The furnishings were all just too short for me," he explained as he walked to a tall stand at the end of the settee. A bottle of champagne, nested in a bucket of ice, had already been uncorked. Todd poured champagne for the three of them and toasted to the evening. "This is a first for me, my ladies. I have never before hosted two of the most beautiful creatures of this earth in my home," he stated. He took a long sip from his glass.

Deborah blushed bright red as she took a sip from the cut crystal glass she held. Not ever having had the chance to drink champagne before, she was amused at the bubbles and found the flavor quite pleasant. "You are too kind, Mr. Vandermeer," she replied as Todd took the tall chair next to hers and gazed at her.

From her vantage on the settee, Emma knew she wouldn't be given more than a cursory glance by the esteemed Mr. Vandermeer for the remainder of the evening. A pang of... *sadness? Loss, perhaps?* She wasn't quite sure how she felt when she realized Todd would no longer regard her as a potential wife.

When the butler announced dinner, precisely at eight o'clock,

Todd escorted his guests to a very large, very elegant dining hall. A massive chandelier of crystal and gas flames hung in the middle, providing enough light so the room was nearly as bright as it was during the daytime. The mahogany table, which appeared to seat at least twenty-four people, was covered with a crisp, white linen cloth edged in Bavarian lace. Three place settings with gold chargers and white china plates and crystal were at one end. In the middle of the table, a round mirror was the base for a sugar-paste sculpture of a cherub, and each place setting featured a mold sugar basket filled with bon-bons.

Three place settings? Emma dared a glance at their host, realizing just then the man probably hadn't invited any other guests, or if he had, they had all declined to attend. If she hadn't brought Deborah along, she would have been dining alone with the importer! If any of his neighbors had paid witness to her arrival, the scandal alone might have forced Todd to offer for her.

Had that been his plan all along, though? Or was he truly so ignorant of Society's rules that he thought it acceptable to host an unmarried woman in his home for dinner?

Emma remembered the comments her employer had made and gave a silent sigh. *Ignorant, then. But apparently eager to learn.*

Despite the evidence of footmen, Todd seated the women on either side of the table. He seemed grateful to see they were impressed by the dining room. Taking the taller chair at the very end of the table, Todd made a simple gesture and three footmen appeared to serve bowls of hot soup, pour white wine into crystal goblets and water into tall glasses.

He noticed as Emma and Deborah exchanged wide-eyed looks. As a novice host, Todd took great delight in watching his guests as each course was served, and even he was surprised when pickles, jellies, puddings, and vegetables seemed to appear from nowhere. They talked about Deborah's work over cheese and wine and Emma's work during the fish course. Todd talked about his business during the meat course only because the two women insisted he do so.

"However did you get into the import business, Mr. Vandermeer?" Emma asked when she had tired of talking about her class and household accounting. The stuffed pork roast suddenly appeared on decorated plates, steaming hot and scented with herbs.

Todd nodded as he thought back to his beginnings. "I was hired by East India to be a caddie, a message boy, if you will," he replied with a smirk as the footmen set the plates down in front of them. "Thank you," he said to his footman before continuing. "I was six years old, but I knew my way around the docks and the bridges, and that's where they sent me with manifests and letters and whatnot," he remembered fondly. "It was the best way to meet the people in the business. In fact, it is how I met Mr. Wellingham. He was a caddie for his father," he added with a nod in Emma's direction.

Deborah looked stunned. "You didn't have to attend university... or a special school?"

Having hoped the topic of his lack of a formal education wouldn't come up, Todd regarded Deborah for a moment. "Not in the formal sense, no, Miss White," he replied. He cut off a piece of the meat and put down his knife. "You see, I was an orphan and didn't have the option to attend school whilst growing up. But I have since learned to read, of course, and I can write when it's required of me," he added with a sideways nod, a frown nearly appearing on his face.

"But you were able to advance at East India?" she half-questioned after tasting the stuffed pork roast. She had to suppress the urge to hum in delight.

"Yes," he replied as he nodded, his frown disappearing. "First as a buyer, and now as a broker," he explained, finding her queries the perfect conversation starters. "The secret to making money in this business is to find a commodity, that is, a product everyone needs, and corner the market on it... become the only company that can trade in that product."

"A monopoly, you mean," Emma commented, not particularly pleased with the idea. Monopolies restricted competition, and inflation was already rampant.

Todd acknowledged her words with a shrug. "If they were not, I rather doubt any other company would pursue acquiring them. Most cannot afford the risk," he explained. "I had great success in semolina, rice, and then in silk until it was possible to manufacture it here in England. We don't import all the spices, of course, but most," he continued, finding the conversation easier as he continued to talk. "My trips to India were most enlightening..."

"You have been to India?" Deborah interrupted, obviously awed by the comment since she had ceased to cut her pork and held her knife in mid-stroke.

Todd nodded enthusiastically. "Yes. Twice, actually. It is a most perplexing country," he said. "I had occasion to stay at the homes of very rich men who live in a country of very poor people," he explained. "But the poor are very rich in spirit, and I do believe they are that country's greatest resource."

Deborah leaned in his direction and lowered her voice. "And are the women as *exotic* as they say?" she asked, her hand reaching out to touch his sleeve.

Aware of how close Deborah was to him, of how her fingers barely made contact with the fabric of his topcoat, Todd held his breath and contemplated how to answer her question. "I suppose some of them are, yes," he replied as he caught his breath. He tried hard not to stare at the hint of her décolletage. "But certainly none are as beautiful as you," he whispered.

The bounder! Emma thought as she quickly covered her mouth with her hand, hoping her look of shock would go unnoticed by her dinner companions. She had nothing to be concerned about. Deborah's eyes were locked in a gaze with Todd's that made it apparent the two were infatuated with one another.

"You are too kind, sir," Deborah breathed in reply, her eyes lowering as she responded. Not finding the courage to return the compliment, she leaned closer. "Did you have occasion to call on any of them?" she asked, trying to hold up her end of the conversation. *And I really do wish to know more about India.*

Todd broke his eye contact with Deborah and shook himself. "I... I did not. Well, not exactly, you see. I was the guest of a raj who had a daughter he wished me to meet. I believe he intended to give her to me as a... a wife... as a gift, you see," he stammered, realizing just then he probably shouldn't be telling the story of how he was almost married. "As it happened, I found out later she had been betrothed to the son of another powerful family, but the boy had died early in his life and another marriage hadn't yet been arranged for the girl. It seems they don't usually marry for love in that country, but you won't find more happily married people anywhere, I assure you."

Sipping wine, Emma listened intently to Todd's story, but nearly choked on his last comment. "They don't marry for love, even among the less fortunate?'

Shaking his head, Todd confirmed the practice and finally turned in her direction. "Nearly all marriages are arranged in that country. So, when I saw his daughter in the company of a young man in the gardens—quite by accident, I assure you—I hid quickly, not wanting to interrupt them and not wanting to be seen, I suppose. But I overheard them admitting their undying love for one another. So when the raj offered his daughter to me, I thanked him profusely but told him her destiny was not with me."

Deborah gasped. "And what did he do? Was he offended?" she asked, thinking any wealthy English father would be most displeased if an offer of a daughter and her dowry were refused.

"Not at all," Todd replied happily. "And his daughter displayed a most relieved expression when I gave my answer. But when the raj asked me what I knew of her destiny, I explained if there was to be a husband in his daughter's life, it must be this other man—the one I had seen with her in the garden. I didn't tell him I had overheard their confession of love toward one another, but I implied I had seen their future and it was a good one. The raj was most impressed and then thanked me for my generosity in not accepting his offer."

Emma sat back in her chair and shook her head. "And what did the daughter do?" she asked, and then chastised herself for taking Todd's attention away from Deborah.

"Oh, she was most thankful," Todd admitted as he merely glanced in her direction. "On my last day at their palace, she requested an audience with me. She gave me an exquisite sculpture that had been crafted by the very man whom she was going to marry. I have it in my library, in fact. She told me she was very happy I had declined her as a gift, but she also admitted she was offended I hadn't readily accepted her father's offer."

He paused to take a drink of wine, and Deborah took the opportunity to touch his sleeve again. "Then, do you suppose she was in love with you, too?" she asked quietly.

Todd's face colored. He shook his head and continued, "When I asked why she would be hurt when my intervention assured she would have what she truly wished for, she said she would always wonder for the rest of her life if I might have been the better husband," he said with a frown. "I thought that very odd," he added after some thought.

Emma watched Todd's face closely while he finished the story. "Did she marry the other man?" she asked as she leaned forward, her curiosity piqued.

Smiling broadly, Todd settled back in his chair. "Indeed, she did.

In fact, at the invitation of the raj, I returned to India to attend the wedding. I had to go again on business anyway, so, of course I included the wedding in my itinerary. It was a beautiful, very strange ceremony. And, I must say, they're a most happy couple," he added as he returned his attention to his meal.

Finishing a bite of pork, Deborah asked, "What else can you tell us of India?" she asked, enthralled by the subject. "What other goods do you import from there? Is there anything I might know?"

Todd shrugged and thought for a moment, rather liking the attention he was receiving from both sides of the table. "Well, we're still importing tapestry and brocade despite the fact that young ladies are not having their modistes make their gowns of the stuff anymore," he admitted with a grin.

"Oh, goodness," Deborah said as she leaned forward. "But what about muslin and batiste and lawn?" she asked. "Where do they come from?"

Emma smiled broadly, and Todd couldn't help but smile with her. "They are very patriotic fabrics, you could say," he replied. Turning to Emma, he said, "I do believe Miss Fitzsimmons's employer has cornered a good deal of that market since he has the best overland transport business in the country." Turning back to Deborah, he added, "Those fabrics are made right here in England."

Deborah bit her lip and smiled at the importer. "I didn't know."

Todd returned the smile and, given the direction of their conversation, decided to broach the topic of transparent gowns. "Tell me, ladies," he began in preamble. "Are you familiar with a recent trend in fashion in France called the transparent gown?" he asked, his arms crossing in front of him as he leaned against the edge of the table.

Gasping, Deborah sat back and turned her attention to Emma. "Have you heard of such gowns?" she whispered, her eyes wide. She hadn't looked at a fashion plate in well over two years and had no idea what styles were considered fashionable in England let alone in France.

"Yes, as a matter of fact," Emma replied as she gave Deborah a surprised look and then turned to their host. "They were featured in a recent *Journal des Dames et des Modes*. It seems some women in France are wearing them as a means to show off their fancy corsets and pantaloons," she said with an arched eyebrow.

Todd visibly swallowed. "I... I am aware of that fact, but I'm wondering if you ladies think such a fashion could make its way to our side of the Channel," he asked carefully, his attention bouncing back and forth between Deborah and Emma. "You see, I have a colleague at East India who is looking to import these gowns, but we're trying to determine if they will sell here in town, and the rest of England, for that matter," he added, his face turning a bright red.

Her eyes downcast, Deborah leaned forward and whispered, "I know there are several ladies of the evening who would probably adore such gowns, Mr. Vandermeer, but I cannot imagine a proper lady wearing them in public."

"Although I'm sure many would wear them in the privacy of their bedchambers," Emma interrupted, an eyebrow arched in amusement. "Perhaps without the pantaloons and corsets, of course," she added in whisper.

Todd gasped and seemed to have a hard time breathing. *Is she implying a woman would be completely naked beneath the transparent gown?* he wondered, hoping the shock of surprise he felt wasn't apparent on his face. "So," he started to ask before Deborah interjected, "Mistresses would wear such gowns, I should think. Especially if their gentlemen buy them as gifts," she added with a prim smile, her embarrassment dissipating.

"So..." Todd started to say before Emma added, "Or they could be worn over a regular empire waist gown. In cases where a gown is slightly stained or the fabric is thinning, it would be possible to prolong the life of the gown by wearing a transparent one over the top of it!"

"Yes!" Deborah agreed happily.

When the two women returned their attention to Todd at the same time, he realized he could finally get a word in. "So, where would you *buy* such a gown?" he asked, his face finally returning to its normal color.

"A modiste," Emma stated with a nod.

Deborah shook her head. "A stay makers, wouldn't you think?" she countered. "Like Nicole's in Bedford Square."

"Yes, that would work, too, I suppose," Emma agreed when she thought about it. "And it would help if a few women of Society were seen wearing them over their gowns. Such as during the fashionable hour in Hyde Park," she suggested helpfully, referring to the daily afternoon parade of the rich and aristocratic members of London society.

Todd nodded enthusiastically. "Thank you, both, for your suggestions. I shall tell my colleague about your recommendations," he promised as he sat back in his chair and regarded his dinner plate.

Emma sighed and put her fork down. "I'm so full," she said sadly, "And everything is so delicious. Is there a chance we could take a walk and stretch our limbs before the next course?" she asked hopefully.

Todd sat up straight and smiled broadly. "Of course," he replied as he started to push back his chair.

"Well, not this very moment," Emma countered as she reached for his sleeve. "Please finish your meat course," she insisted.

Todd glanced over his plate and shook his head. "I, too, am stuffed and simply cannot eat another bite. I know my cook has prepared salads and cheese and sweets for dessert. Let us take a walk and we can enjoy our dessert later," he suggested as he pushed back his chair and quickly moved to the back of Deborah's chair.

"Is there a... water closet we might use first?" Emma asked, knowing full well the house was plumbed for running water and featured Bramah toilets. The devices were still too new to be found in most houses in the city, but she hoped she might see one work.

"Oh, of course," Todd replied as he offered his arms to the ladies. As they made their way to a room near the vestibule, Todd winced in pain with the last few steps. Emma put a hand on his arm. "Has the medicine stopped working, Mr. Vandermeer?" she whispered, a note of concern in her voice.

The broker frowned and took another step. "It would appear so, Miss Fitzsimmons," he replied sadly. "I will apply more whilst you are in the privy. I will be fine," he assured her as he patted her hand, a gesture he realized too late was probably improper.

As Deborah disappeared into the water closet, Emma leaned up toward the importer's ear. "Deborah is a midwife and familiar with medical practices, Mr. Vandermeer," her eyebrow arched in a suggestive manner. "Perhaps... perhaps she could do it for you."

Todd gasped, and he visibly reddened as he considered her words. "Maybe outside, where 'tis darker?" he suggested quietly, deciding he didn't wish Deborah to see his knees in the light. *Oh, but to feel her fingers on me*, he thought. *To be touched by two women on the same day, no less!* "She wouldn't be offended if I ask?" he asked hopefully, his breaths coming quicker as he considered Emma's suggestion.

"She uses the same salve on her knees, too, Mr. Vandermeer," Emma whispered into his ear, making sure her lips barely touched his lobe as she spoke. "Perhaps..." and then she merely angled her head and smiled before disappearing into the water closet.

CHAPTER 27
A WALK IN THE GARDENS

*P*oor Todd Vandermeer was left in the hall in a state of near hyperventilation. Was Miss Fitzsimmons suggesting he offer to put salve on Miss White's knees? His heart hammered against his rib cage. *To touch that pale porcelain skin would be divine,* he thought, his eyes closing so he could imagine rubbing the salve on her knee. Then he shuddered when he realized he didn't know what a woman's knee even looked like.

Having been entertained by the workings of the toilet and fully briefed on the situation of Todd's knees, Deborah emerged from the water closet and hurried to his side. "I wish to offer my services in the treatment of your knees," she said with a half-curtsy.

Todd stared at the brunette beauty before he reluctantly agreed. He didn't wish to appear weak to a woman he had every intention of proposing to before the evening was over. However, the thought of her long, slender fingers on his knees overruled any sense of propriety he might still possess.

Emma joined them shortly, but dropped back as they made their way into the backyard gardens. Despite being in town, the grounds of Grace Park were extensive, and the garden layout took advantage of the land and sloping hill. Gas lights provided illumination for some of the gardens, casting their eerie glow over the floral display.

Emma walked the paved path, passing Deborah and Todd as they took a seat on a stone bench near the house. Deborah opened her reticule and pulled out her jar of salve. Surprised she had it with her, Todd pulled his jar out of a coat pocket. "I have one just like it," he said with a grin as he held it up.

Deborah took his jar, opened it, and used two fingers to scoop out the lightly scented salve. "Place your leg up here, please," she said as she patted her lap with her other hand, "And pull up your trouser leg."

Turning on the bench, Todd took a deep breath and carefully placed a bent leg across Deborah's lap. He pulled up the leg of his breeches to just above the knee and pushed down his silk stocking to expose his bony knee. Deborah carefully rubbed the salve all around the bone and behind the knee, just as Emma had done earlier in the day.

Closing his eyes, Todd reveled in the touch of the massage. Deborah's fingers were gentle but firm as they stroked and circled, forcing the salve deep into his joint. Within minutes, he felt the warming sensation and sighed happily. "You simply cannot know how good the touch of your fingers feels at this very moment," he murmured, his heavy-lidded eyes making contact with hers.

Deborah blushed, but the dim lamp light was enough to hide her embarrassment. "Perhaps when my knees ache again, I can have you do the same for me, and then I will know," she suggested, her voice quiet in the night. She gasped when she realized what she had just said aloud.

Emma had implied she could get away with a bit of impropriety when it came to Todd Vandermeer, but to be so bold by suggesting he touch her as she was touching him? She wondered how many glasses of wine she had drunk.

She found it was difficult not to feel *something* for Todd Vandermeer. He was an enchanting man, rich and yet so humble. Poor, and yet so *thankful*. He seemed to truly appreciate his largess.

A pleasant flutter passed through Deborah as she regarded the man who sat next to her. *Perhaps I already feel affection for him.*

"You would allow me to... to *touch* you?" Todd whispered, his breaths coming faster. He nervously swallowed as he pulled his trouser leg down and straightened on the bench.

Deborah considered his reaction. *I can be daring with him, and I am just flirting*, she told herself. "I would indeed, Mr. Vandermeer," she replied quietly as she placed a hand over his. She got up, walked to the other end of the bench and sat down. When she saw his questioning expression, she said, "I will do your other knee now."

Todd finally took a deep breath and said, "Oh. Of course." He turned and placed his left leg over her lap while pulling the fabric of his trouser over the knee. "May I... may I kiss you, Miss White?" he asked, his question surprising him as much as it might her. "I mean, when you have finished your ministrations, of course."

He blinked, shocked that he would put voice to his desire.

Deborah's fingers hovering over his knee, she froze and wondered how to respond. If she said 'yes,' she might sound immoral to the man. But his question seemed so innocently broached, she reconsidered. "There is something I feel obliged to tell you, but I fear you might form a poor opinion of me once you hear the tale," Deborah replied carefully, watching Todd's face and wishing the gaslight in the garden were brighter so she might see his expression more clearly.

"I assure you, I could not form a poor opinion of you, Miss Deborah," Todd replied, almost too quickly.

Encouraged by the look of anticipation on his face, Deborah took a deep breath and let it out. "On a Saturday last February, Miss Emma came to work at the Home as she always did on Saturdays. That very morning, we received one of your most generous donations, so it meant I was given a bit of pin money. I had not received a payment in a very long time, you see, so I was very happy, and so very excited. I needed clothes, you see, and your donation made it possible for me to get them. I told Emma I could... I could just *kiss* you!" she whispered with an embarrassed smile.

Todd's heart soared as he listened to her confession. *She wanted to kiss me even before she met me!*

"And here you are, asking if you can kiss me. So, yes, I think I'd like that very much," she finally replied with a nod. Her fingers made contact with his knee, and she took extra time in massaging the salve into his skin.

Anxious to kiss her, Todd finally laid a hand over her long fingers, stopping her ministrations. He straightened on the bench, stood up, and helped her to her feet.

Deborah was suddenly aware of how close he stood, aware of how he leaned over her, aware of the scents of citrus laundry soap and sandalwood cologne and of how his eyelashes lowered. Her eyes closed as she lifted her face and let her lips part slightly. When she felt his lips touch hers, she angled her head to one side and molded her mouth to his.

She remembered her vow again. *Someday I'm going to kiss that man.* Even though it was happening, she felt as though she might awaken at any moment to find she had only been dreaming. When Todd's lips lingered for only a moment before he pulled away, she wondered if perhaps she had dreamt it.

Todd studied Deborah in the dim lamp light, his breathing nearly stopped as he took in the sight of her flawless complexion. Her brunette hair piled in a loose bun that threatened to tumble down her long neck. Her dark lashes that lay on top of high, elegant cheek bones. With more force than he intended, he placed a hand at the back of her waist, more to steady himself than to pull her toward him.

But Deborah allowed her body to fall forward as she raised a hand to rest on his shoulder. Sensing no resistance from her, Todd's lips took hers again, the kiss more full as he opened his lips and she followed suit without complaint. When he was aware of the tip of her tongue gingerly touching his teeth, he pulled away and inhaled sharply.

Realizing she had gone too far, an embarrassed Deborah lowered her face and whispered, "I... I apologize. I shouldn't have..." But there was the sound of his walking cane hitting the garden path and then the feel of his hand lifting her chin and his other hand on her waist pulling her closer and the faint whisper of her name before his lips were on hers again.

Deborah molded the front of her body against his, felt the warmth of him and the sensation of her knees weakening. A hardening ridge developed behind the placket of his trousers, pressing into her belly. She quickly slid her other hand behind his shoulder to steady herself.

Todd moaned quietly, his lips hungry for more. This time it was his tongue that touched her teeth and sought her tongue, the movement light and tentative. Deborah dared not allow more than a quiet moan in answer lest he think her in distress. When she did moan softly, it was a plea for more, an invitation for him to continue. He drove his tongue deeper, tasting her, forcing her tongue to respond in kind. When he had to pull away so he could take a shuddered breath, Todd placed a hand behind her head and gently urged it against his shoulder.

He held onto her as if his very life depended on her. *Can this really be happening?* he wondered, the thrill of the kiss and the feel of her body against him so foreign and yet so *necessary*.

She must feel affection for me, surely, he thought, his lips brushing against her rose-scented hair.

Deborah breathed deeply as her cheek lay against the folds of his cravat, her hand still resting on his shoulder. "Is this really happening?" she murmured, almost surprised by the sound of her whisper.

A chuckle of relief bubbled up in Todd. He hugged her tighter to his body. "I was just wondering the very same," he murmured, kissing her hair again, the tip of his nose stroking the edge of her bun. The scent of roses wafted around him, making him smile and breathe more deeply. "Will you be my wife?" he asked then, the words out before he could think of a more suitable proposal.

Deborah stiffened and lifted her head to gaze at him. "Is this really happening?" she repeated, immediately regretting how insipid it made her sound. But Todd's look of affection was quite real, she decided. "I would be honored to be your wife," she said with a nod, the hand on his shoulder moving to his jawline. Her lips were back on his, hungrily kissing him as he cradled her head in his hand.

"You have made me a very happy man," he said between kisses.

"And you have made me a very happy woman," Deborah sighed, her lips moving against his.

He kissed her hair and forehead and murmured, "I love you," into her ear, his lips caressing the lobe. As he moved his kisses down along her jawline and back to her lips, he lost himself in the taste of her and the scent of her and the feel of her body pressed into his.

That is, until he became aware they weren't alone.

Emma, having walked the entire garden path and unsure of what to do when she witnessed the couple in an embrace, slowed her pace. She considered simply strolling around them and allowing herself back into the house, but decided instead to wait for them to notice her.

"Miss Fitzsimmons," Todd called out as he took Deborah's hand from his shoulder. He motioned for Emma to join them, and she hurried to their side, glad she didn't have to wait long. "Miss White has just accepted my marriage proposal," he announced happily as he pulled Emma into a bear hug. "I must thank you so very much for introducing us," he said as he released a very startled Emma from his grip.

Embarrassed by the close contact with Todd, Emma regained her footing and then allowed a broad smile. She winked at Deborah, who simply beamed. "Then let me be the first to say best wishes to you both," Emma said with a genuine smile. "When do you suppose the wedding will be?"

The two exchanged nervous glances and shrugged. "Tomorrow, perhaps?" Todd suggested hopefully.

Emma and Deborah both gasped. "But, I have no gown," Deborah countered.

"And 'tis doubtful you will secure a special license for a wedding on such short notice," Emma said with an amused expression. Did Todd know how expensive such an endeavor could be? "You would have to gain an audience with the Archbishop of Canterbury!"

Todd regarded his intended for a moment. "I shall do what I must," he countered. "Even if it means a trip to Scotland."

Emma gasped, stunned Todd would consider skipping the reading of the banns in order to marry Deborah. She couldn't think he would change his mind about Deborah, though. The two seemed so *perfect* for one another. "I don't think it proper for you to run off to Gretna Green to elope," she said. "It wouldn't be appropriate for a man in your position."

Todd considered his options for a moment. "I simply cannot be without you very long," he said to Deborah. He kissed her hand. "You must come to Grace Park for dinner every night until we are married. Or, even better, you must move into the mistress suite... tonight, if you'd like."

Emma held a hand over her mouth to suppress her shock at the man's offer. "Deborah is staying the night at my townhouse," she countered, sure it wouldn't be acceptable for Deborah to be anywhere near Grace Park before she was legally wed to Todd.

When she saw how crestfallen the man looked at hearing her words, she sighed. "But I'll see to it she joins you for breakfast in the morning, if you wish it," she offered. "You can discuss wedding plans then."

The disappointed expression still on his face, Todd finally nodded. "Do you suppose we could marry Saturday?"

Deborah looked to Emma, who merely shrugged. "We can probably find you a gown by Saturday, perhaps even have one made, but it might be another day or two before alterations are complete," she said doubtfully, knowing that few ready-made gowns would be long enough for Deborah. She gave Todd a nervous look. "The Arch-bishop of Canterbury's office is in Doctors' Common. But I hear a special license can cost upwards of *twenty guineas*," she whispered to Todd.

Deborah's face darkened and tears welled up in her eyes. "I... I cannot do this," she whispered, her head shaking from side to side.

Todd put an arm around her shoulder and a hand along her face. "Whatever is wrong?" he asked, deep concern etched on his face.

"Mr. Vandermeer, I... I've no dowry. I've no money to buy a wedding gown, or morning dresses or gowns for dinners," she explained as a tear escaped and ran down her cheek.

Emma rolled her eyes and visibly slumped. In all her planning, she hadn't considered Deborah's desperate financial situation and her lack of a dowry.

"*I* will buy your gowns," Todd replied firmly, as if he had never intended for her to come with a trousseau. "And your jewelry, and your... shoes, and fripperies and anything else you need," he insisted, his hold on her hand tightening. "I'm not marrying you for a dowry. I don't need... I don't wish to marry for money," he claimed as he pulled her into a hug. "In fact, I wish to spend *more* money on you."

Deborah sniffled and pulled away from his hug. "More?"

"Oh, indeed," he answered with a grin, glancing at Emma as he made the comment. When she gave him a quizzical glance, he said, "On Monday, I'm closing on the deal to buy you the old Cooper Hotel. I made an offer on it today, and the owner accepted."

Stunned by Todd's announcement and immediately under-standing its implication, Emma gasped. The man had obviously been busy since leaving her townhouse earlier that afternoon! The Cooper was in Oxford Street, in a neighborhood considerably better than the neighborhood near the Seven Dials where Mrs. Dawes' Home was currently located.

Deborah, not understanding his mention of a hotel, glanced at Emma, realizing she understood his meaning. When she received a teasing shrug in reply, she turned her attention back to Todd. "Why are you buying *me* a... hotel?"

But even as she asked, realization dawned on her. He had purchased a hotel to replace the near-ruin that currently housed the Home for Unwed Mothers.

Deborah looked stunned. "But, how did you know? What... what if I? Oh,... oh, my." Her face brightened, a smile replacing the look of consternation. "I so wish I could marry you right this very *moment*," she claimed as she hugged him, tears streaming freely down her face. "I love you, Mr. Vandermeer."

Shaking her head in disbelief, Emma watched the happy couple hug and kiss. "We should celebrate," she suggested lightly. "I believe your cook has dessert waiting."

Todd let go of Deborah but put her hand on his arm. He offered his other to Emma and she took it, grinning like a schoolgirl as they made their way back to the dining room. They managed to finish off the bottle of champagne with the rich chocolate dessert and a glass or two of cream sherry before the mantel clock struck one. Todd joined them in the carriage for the ride to Emma's townhouse, inappropriately sitting between them with his arms around both women's shoulders.

As he helped them out of the carriage, he hugged Emma and kissed her on the forehead. "Thank you, truly," he said with a nod. "I would be most honored if I could consider you a friend for the rest of my days," he stated quietly, his arms still on her shoulders in a manner too familiar.

"Of course, Mr. Vandermeer," Emma replied with a grin, hoping her neighbors weren't watching. In a bold move she could hardly believe she was making, she reached up and kissed him on the cheek. "Thank you for a wonderful evening."

Todd gave Deborah another kiss and hugged her quickly. "I will come for you tomorrow..." He paused to check his chronometer. "Rather today at ten, if that is agreeable with you," he said as he released his hold on her but continued to stand very close.

Deborah nodded. "I will be ready. I... I love you," she whispered as she reached up and kissed him again. *And when I awake from this exquisite dream, I think I shall be greatly disappointed*, she thought, marveling at how much had happened in just a few hours.

After another minute, a sudden sense of loss settled over her, for Todd Vandermeer had stepped back into the carriage and was gone.

CHAPTER 28
POST PROPOSAL
CONSIDERATIONS

*E*mma regarded Deborah as the older girl prepared for bed. "So, you do feel affection for him then?" she half-asked as she remembered Deborah's last words to Todd.

Sitting down on the bed, Deborah bit her bottom lip as she wrapped her arms around her bent legs. *So, it wasn't a dream*, she considered. A man had said he loved her, asked for her hand, said he would call on her in the morning.

This was all happening so very fast!

The nightrail she wore was one of Emma's, and the gown she would wear to breakfast with Todd would be borrowed, as well. "I... I don't know for certain," she replied hesitantly, her face showing concern. "Truth be told, I don't know... I don't know what it feels like to *be* in love."

Gasping, Emma turned to face her friend, a linen held to her wet face. "But you feel... *affection* for him, no doubt," she offered hopefully, worried that perhaps Deborah wasn't the woman for Todd Vandermeer. *Did she agree to marry the man for his money?* Emma wondered, a stab of... something... causing her to catch her breath.

Hugging her knees to her chest, Deborah smiled. "Oh, yes," she admitted happily, allowing the fantasy to manifest itself in her mind. "And I am most sure that, with time, I shall grow to truly love him. He has endeared himself to me, to be sure." There was a flash of sudden worry on her face, though, and Emma saw it before it passed.

"What were you thinking just then?" Emma asked, setting the

linen on the wash stand. She moved to the side of the bed and sat down next to Deborah.

Her eyes downcast, Deborah shook her head. "What will happen when he discovers I'm a ruined woman?" she whispered, tears threatening to spill from her eyes.

Emma watched Deborah for a moment, not about to admit she had wondered the same thing. "If he discovers," she amended quietly. "Mr. Vandermeer does not strike me as a man who has much experience with the fairer sex."

Glancing at Emma with a look of disbelief, Deborah shook her head. "He's rich. No doubt, he has a mistress... or a favorite lightskirt."

Wincing at the comment, Emma found she couldn't imagine Todd Vandermeer in bed with a woman. Perhaps she was being naïve, but the man didn't strike her as one who would employ a whore given his patronage of the Home. "You will tell Mr. Vandermeer what happened, and he will... understand," Emma finally said with a nod, hoping the man would indeed be understanding.

Had she made a mistake in introducing the two to one another? *But if not Deborah, then it would be me contemplating a wedding.* And a life with Todd Vandermeer wasn't one she could imagine for herself.

CHAPTER 29
POST PROPOSAL
MISUNDERSTANDINGS

June 14, 1802, Woodscastle

The following Monday, Emma was already on her horse and ready to depart when Mr. Allen rode up on his mount.

"Good morning, Mr. Allen," she greeted the groom as she retrieved a large basket from Master Churchill and perched it on the pommel of her saddle.

"Morning," Mr. Allen responded with a tip of his hat. "I can take that, if ye'd like," he offered as he reached out with a hand.

Emma considered the offer and gave him the basket. "Since it's baked goods for you and Mr. Larsen, it seems appropriate you carry it," she teased. She didn't add the basket also included a picnic luncheon for her and Christiana to share on the front lawn of Woodscastle.

Once there, she grinned as she recalled the events of the past two days and practically waltzed into the library. Unaware Thomas was reading the Sunday edition of *The Times* by the fire, she took her seat at her usual place. Staring at the ledgers still spread out from Friday afternoon, she realized they were exactly as she had left them when the housebreakers arrived.

Emma was about to open the inkwell when she realized Thomas was standing in front of the library table. Smiling brightly, she said, "Good morning, Mr. Wellingham. You're up early."

Thomas stared at her for a moment. "You are positively incandescent." The tone of his voice suggested he was not as pleased as his words might suggest.

Emma sat up straight and regarded her employer. "Why, it's so good of you to say so, Mr. Wellingham. Thank you," she replied happily.

His expression turned dour. He slowly pulled out the chair across from her and sat down, slumping his shoulders as if he didn't have the strength to sit up. "So, I take it there is to be a wedding in your future?" he half-asked, his demeanor suggesting he was most disappointed.

Or perhaps that he disapproved.

Emma angled her head to one side. "Well, yes. Oh, but not *mine*," she answered with a quick shake of her head. "If you can arrange it, you really must take your luncheon with Mr. Vandermeer today," she suggested as she leaned over the table. "The last I heard, which was yesterday morning, the wedding will be two weeks come Saturday. I believe Mr. Vandermeer intends to ask you to stand with him. I will be standing with his bride, Miss Deborah White."

Thomas sat up straight at the news. "Todd Vandermeer is getting married to Deborah White two weeks come Saturday?" he repeated, his tone suggesting disbelief.

"Why, yes," Emma answered brightly. "Do you know her?"

"Never heard of her in my entire life," he replied, his eyebrows making his frown appear almost ominous. "Correct me if I'm wrong, but weren't *you* to have had dinner with him this past Saturday?" he questioned, sure he had heard the details straight from Todd's mouth just last Thursday afternoon.

His accomptant's smile widened, her white teeth gleaming in the morning light from the windows. "Oh, I did attend a dinner party at Grace Park Saturday evening. It was wondrous, by the way. He really does have the best cook in London," Emma commented as an aside. "But, you see, I arranged...," she paused and took a sudden breath. "You cannot tell him I said that," she ordered with a raised finger as she caught herself mid-sentence. Not sure how much Mr. Wellingham would tell Todd, she figured it best to be vague as to how the match was made. "It became *necessary* for him to include a good friend of mine in the dinner invitation. I required a chaperone, you see," she explained coyly. "They fell in love at first sight, and he proposed before the dessert course. A bit later than you said he would, by the way," she added with an arched eyebrow. "I would have won the bet!"

Thomas countered the slight chastisement by raising both his eyebrows as he considered her words. "And just who is this... Deborah White?"

Emma's smile faltered as she wondered how much she should tell her employer about Deborah. The two women had agreed Todd didn't need to know how Deborah first came to be at Mrs. Dawes' Home for Unwed Mothers. If he asked, it would be a matter best handled between the two of them. Enough time had passed that it was unlikely anyone else, excepting her parents, would remember.

"She's a midwife at the Home for Unwed Mothers, where I used to do my charity work," Emma began in explanation. "She delivers babies and provides care for newborns and their mothers. Deborah is six feet tall, brunette, gorgeous, and, as it turns out, the perfect match for Mr. Vandermeer."

Thomas sat shaking his head. "When I dined with Mr. Vandermeer Friday afternoon, he was ecstatic. He was happier than I have ever seen him in the twenty years we have known each other. All because he was planning to propose to *you*," he stated quietly.

Emma leaned back in her chair and crossed her arms. "I am... I'm aware of that," she replied finally, allowing a wan smile. "He was waiting for me when I arrived home Saturday morning. He had read the front page of *The Times* and wanted to be sure I was well," she explained as she rolled her eyes, remembering how he was so out of breath and so relieved to find her at the mews. "And we had a very good discussion over tea. But I realized that, although I adore him as a person and will value his friendship for the rest of my days, I'm not the one who should be his wife. Miss White has that honor."

Swallowing, Thomas looked out the window for a moment and finally turned back to Emma. "So you played matchmaker, did you?" he accused, his demeanor still not suggesting if he was angry with her or not.

Emma shrugged one shoulder and finally admitted, "Yes. Well, somewhat. They still had to do all the work of forming an attachment, though," she said defensively as she remembered how tongue-tied they had both been in the vestibule. When Deborah was dressed up and had her long hair styled into a mass of ringlets and rolls, she could turn any man's head.

"But, tell me, Miss Emma, what if there had been no Miss

Deborah White for our dear Mr. Vandermeer to meet and marry?" he asked as he crossed his arms.

Surprised by the question, Emma felt as if she were being reprimanded. She shook her head. Her first thought was to ignore his question and simply begin working, but Todd was Mr. Wellingham's friend, and she supposed he deserved to know.

She lowered her eyes, unable to make eye contact with her employer. "I... suppose... I would... I would have accepted his offer of marriage,... spent two,... maybe three years with him, and then been a rich widow for the rest of my life," she said sadly as her lower lip began to tremble. She blinked in a effort to stave off the tears that threatened.

Startled by her statement, Thomas leaned forward and stared at his accomptant. "Whatever are you talking about?" he asked in a hushed whisper.

Shaking her head sadly, Emma replied, "Mr. Wellingham, you must know that men who are too tall rarely live past thirty. Mr. Vandermeer already suffers severe pain. He can barely walk on a warm day, partly because of the pain, but mostly because he cannot breathe very well. Winters must be brutal for him. Despite having the best cook in town, he doesn't eat enough. He cannot sleep because of the pain. And the only effective medicine available, which is extremely expensive, doesn't give him relief from the pain for even half a day."

Mortified, Thomas stared at Emma. Somehow, he knew what she was saying to be true, but to hear his friend would die simply because he was too tall seemed a severe assessment.

Emma leaned over the table. "Miss White is a midwife. She knows how to care for those who are ill. She will be able to care for him, probably even help him to live longer than I ever could," she said quietly, her lower lip still trembling. "Please be happy for him. For them."

Thomas shook his head, surprised by her last comment. "I... I think you misunderstand me," he said quietly. "I'm very happy for him. I know how much he has wanted to marry," he explained as he leaned over the table, his voice lowering in volume. "You see, I rather selfishly hoped you wouldn't agree to marry Mr. Vandermeer, although obviously not for the reasons you stated," he continued carefully, not a bit surprised at seeing Emma's arched eyebrows. "I've spent these past two days thinking you might not even come here today, or, that if you did come, it would only be to give me your resignation. And... I suppose... it has made me rather... *cross*," he admitted with a sigh. "Rather selfish of me, I suppose," he added as an afterthought.

Selfish, or was I just a touch jealous?

Offended Thomas would expect her to simply quit her position because she had accepted an offer of marriage, Emma scoffed. The tone of her voice was indignant when she replied, "I assure you, Mr. Wellingham, had this been a regular position, I would have given you two weeks' notice. But I have every intention of completing this audit before I leave your service, no matter my personal circumstances."

Thomas leaned back and crossed his arms as he regarded his auditor. He supposed he should feel just guilt at his reaction, but he found it difficult to do so. Instead, he did his best to hide the sudden good humor he was feeling. "I... I appreciate that," he replied with a nod. "And I... I do apologize for ruining your cheery mood."

Emma regarded him for a moment and found she could no longer be indignant with him. Not this day. "Your apology is accepted, Mr. Wellingham. And please, do go see Mr. Vandermeer. His mood is sure to brighten yours," she teased, making Thomas wonder if she had seen through his attempt to quell her good mood. "Just thinking about him makes me smile," she added as she dabbed at the edge of one eye with a hanky.

"I shall, I assure you," Thomas replied as he stood up. "Good day, Miss Emma."

"Yes, it is," Emma replied happily.

CHAPTER 30
A LETTER FROM A
HAPPY MAN

*A*s Thomas Wellingham dismounted and handed the reins to the groom at Wellingham Imports, he turned to find his message boy waiting for him with a letter.

"Good morning, Master Overby," he said to the caddie as he bent down to take the missive. "And from whence did this come?" he asked when he noticed only his name was written on the outside.

"Mr. Vandermeer, sir," the young boy replied happily.

Thomas frowned and considered the boy for a moment. *The kid has the same smile on his face Emma was displaying earlier!* "And why are you now running errands for Mr. Vandermeer?" he finally asked, concerned about the boy's loyalties.

Todd Vandermeer would probably pay him more for his services.

"I had to take a box to the John Company, and he recognized me, sir. He gave me a pound note to wait whilst he wrote the note!" the boy exclaimed as he pulled the money from this tattered trouser pocket and held it up.

Thomas rolled his eyes and smiled in spite of himself. "Keep that. And save it," Thomas ordered with a nod as he regarded the missive. "I take it he was in a good spirits, then?" he half-questioned as he unfolded the paper and began to read.

"Indeed, sir, and he was walking without his cane and telling everyone he is getting leg-shackled," the boy continued excitedly.

Holding up a finger to quiet the boy, Thomas read the letter. It was a note of apology at first, saying Todd was sorry, but despite his assurances he would ask Miss Fitzsimmons for her hand in marriage, he had instead proposed to a friend of hers who was proving to be the perfect woman for him. Then it went on to ask if Thomas would stand with him at his wedding two weeks come Saturday at eleven o'clock in his backyard garden. The note ended with a most curious recommendation.

Falling in Love has made my Life worth Living again, Thomas. I highly Recommend you find a Woman with whom you can spend the Rest of your Life so you can be as Happy as I am. You must already Know you do not have to look far. I believe She is in your Library.

Thomas gasped, stunned at the broker's supposition. "*Bastard!*" he whispered hoarsely.

"Yes, sir?" Master Overby replied as he continued to stand in front of his boss.

Shaking his head, Thomas said, "I was not talking to you," he said quickly. "And I would never address you by that term," he added with a shudder. He resumed reading the note, which included the postscript,

I wanted Very Much for us to meet for lunch today; however, I am Closing on the purchase of the Cooper Hotel for my Beloved. Perhaps we can meet at the Anchor and Crown for luncheon tomorrow?"

"My God, the man's buying his bride a *hotel?*" Thomas said to no one in particular.

Master Overby nodded. "For the Home for Unwed Mothers," he claimed. "He said they need a bigger building."

Thomas bit his lip and contemplated how to respond to the letter. "Master Overby, go back to the John Company, and tell Mr. Vandermeer the following: Yes, for two weeks come Saturday, and yes, for luncheon tomorrow. Can you remember that?"

The caddie acted offended as he replied, "Of course, sir. I'll be back in two hours." With that, he took off running toward the east.

CHAPTER 31
A BUSY MAN
ACCOMPLISHES MUCH

*I*n the week following his proposal to Deborah White, Todd Vandermeer was a very busy man. Besides performing his regular duties as one of the more productive brokers at East India Company, he began his life as a man on a new mission.

At precisely one o'clock on Monday afternoon, he signed the purchase papers for the Cooper Hotel and shook hands with the real estate broker and former owner. In exchange, he was given title to the property, which included a fully-equipped kitchen and dining room to serve sixty, and a box filled with the keys for every door in the forty-room hotel.

Tuesday morning, he met with the Archbishop of Canterbury to secure a license. His request to have the marriage ceremony performed in his gardens was met with raised eyebrows—ceremonies could only be performed in a church, he was told. But with a special license, and his assurances the ceremony would be completed before noon, the archbishop agreed a special license could be procured. Todd paid the twenty-guinea fee and requested the date of Saturday, July 3rd for the ceremony.

Late that afternoon, he and Deborah met with a paint contractor to choose colors for the hotel rooms, parlor, and lobby for the old Cooper Hotel. The man assured Mr. Vandermeer the work would be completed before mid-July.

Wednesday afternoon, a shingle maker visited him at his office, displaying miniature samples of his signs and shingles for businesses in the West End. Todd chose a style appropriate for the front of the hotel and requested it be in place by mid-July.

While taking his supper at a small pub in downtown London on a very rainy Thursday, he met with the society writer for *The Morning Chronicle*. Despite the unusual request to print an announcement of a betrothal—he had only ever done wedding announcements—the writer hinted he would publish the announcement of Todd Vandermeer's betrothal to Miss White in a most prominent position in the Saturday edition of the paper. Todd paid for their meals, of course, and thanked the writer for his time.

On Friday, June 18th, his cook prepared three samples of wedding cake. Made with dried fruits and several liqueurs, they each had a distinctive flavor and texture. Tasting them all, Todd chose his favorite but asked that a slice of each be made available at that night's dinner so that Deborah might try them. If she approved of one of them, then he would request his cook make that version in the form of a tall cake covered in white sugar frosting. The cook assured him it would be the best cake he had ever baked and there would be enough to send slices by post to all those who couldn't make it to the ceremony.

Now, if the week could only end as well as it had begun, Todd Vandermeer would be the happiest man in the known world.

CHAPTER 32
RAIN, RAIN

*J*une 17, 1802, London

As sometimes happens in southern England in mid-June, a powerful storm of driving rain and wind can force even the most stalwart people indoors. Pubs are stuffed with wet, cold workers, hotels have no vacancies, and inns across the countryside are filled with travelers seeking the warmth of a fire and the comfort of hot food and warm ale.

Thomas Wellingham was at the main warehouse of Wellingham Imports on such a Thursday night. The West End location wasn't particularly convenient considering other import businesses in London, but it was close to shops and businesses that had him transport British products on their behalf. And because it was located next to the River Thames, goods could be loaded onto a cart from a ship down at the docks and be quickly pulled by shire horses to the warehouse for inventory and storage or dispersal by overland transport.

The last of three ships had completed off-loading at the docks, and Thomas was waiting for all of the loads to be delivered before locking down the warehouse and sending everyone home. His warehouse manager usually handled these last tasks of a busy day, but the man had come down with an awful cold, and Thomas sent him home before the luncheon break.

When he finally left after seven o'clock, the rain was coming down hard enough to hurt an uncovered head. He donned his hat, mounted his horse, and took off for Boodles, hoping for a hot meal and a room for the night. When he arrived nearly a half-hour later, his topcoat soaked through to his clothes, his hopes for dinner were dashed—the smoke-filled club was packed with weary and wet businessmen, and the kitchen had used up its available stocks of meat and vegetables while catering to those driven indoors by the rain earlier in the afternoon.

Overhearing several of the men complaining of full inns and hotels, Thomas decided he had no choice but to head for Woodscastle. It was possible the worst of the rain was over. If not, he was sure his Cleveland Bay could handle the wet roads through western London and beyond. With the lower cloud cover and constant rain, it was nearly impossible for him to see the road once he left the city limits of London and its feeble light sources. The horse, which could do no better than a fast walk through the crowded city streets, could now barely walk in the deep ruts and mud of the Great West Road.

When lightning struck a nearby tree, a deafening thunderclap sent his horse rearing and he was forced to dismount. Pulling as hard as he could on the reins, he finally got the bay back onto the road. It was several minutes before he could determine which way to walk, and that was only because an occasional lightning bolt would light the sky and the countryside around him.

The temperature seemed to drop with each step he took, and he started to shiver uncontrollably. With the road turned into a muddy river, he trudged through the pasture next to it, not always sure if he was walking in the right direction. He nearly missed the turn onto Burlington Road, but the horse seemed to know its way as Thomas kept a tight hold on the reins.

When he finally spotted a constant light up ahead and above the trees, he realized he was nearly to the turnoff for Woodscastle. Yellow candlelight glowed brightly from the window of one of the upstairs rooms. *The guest bedchamber*, he realized.

Emma!

Relieved she hadn't tried to make her way back to the city in the rain, he mounted the horse and let it find its way to the front of the estate.

The sound of the rain drowned out his voice as he called for a servant. When none came, he took the horse to the stables on the west end of the estate. Not having the strength to remove the saddle and having a hard time controlling his shivering, he simply closed the stable door and made his way back to the house.

When he opened the front door, Humphrey was not to be found, but Emma, barefoot and dressed in only a nightrail, stood at the top of the stairs holding a lamp from the corridor sconce. In his feverish state, he stared at her, trying to decide if she was real or an apparition.

"Mr. Wellingham? Oh, my God," she whispered as she seemed to float down the stairs towards him. "I was sure I heard someone call out a few moments ago."

Dumbfounded, Thomas stared at her. *I have died, and she is my angel coming to take me to heaven.* He continued to stare at her even as she hurried into the vestibule, left her light on the round table, and took his hand in hers, its tug urging him forward. *We're going now*, he thought in a daze. *I shan't get to say good-bye to Christiana.*

It took a great deal of her strength, but Emma was able to pull Thomas into the vestibule and get the storm-battered door closed behind him. As she undid the fastenings of his coat, she kept her attention on Thomas as much as on her fingers, trying to determine if he was merely too chilled to speak or suffering from the same illness that had gripped most of the household.

She removed his soaked coat, its weight nearly too much for the coat rack in the corner. When she realized Thomas was shivering, she placed a hand against his forehead and felt for a fever. Although his skin didn't feel hot, she realized from his trembling that he was, at the very least, chilled to the bone.

Water dripped from everything he wore. His hat had disappeared long ago, and his wet hair was plastered to his forehead and ears. His once-white cravat was mud-spattered and limp, its tie now a knot of wet linen.

"Where... where's Humph... phr... phrey?" he tried to ask, his shivering making it hard for him to speak. "And why haven't we left yet?" he mumbled, his mind still muddled.

"He had better be asleep by now. He is very ill," Emma replied quietly, taking a moment to be sure Thomas wasn't injured. "Most of the household staff is sick with colds," she whispered as she unbuttoned his tailcoat. "'Tis nearly midnight ...," she started to say, but she realized from his uncontrolled shaking that Thomas was at least as sick as everyone else. "Come. Let's get you to your bedchamber and get these wet clothes off of you."

She wrapped her arm under his shoulder and led him up the stairs while she held onto the lamp with her other hand. Water ran off his clothes in rivulets, leaving small puddles all over the vestibule and on the stairs. By the time they reached the top of the staircase, her muslin nightrail was nearly as wet as Thomas' clothes. The thin fabric clung to her body. Had there been enough light, she would have appeared naked to anyone who saw her.

Once in his room, Emma led Thomas to the fireplace, hoping he could stand in front of it without falling. Humphrey kept the fireplace prepared in case a fire was needed at night. She used the flame from the lamp to light the kindling and then blew gently on the embers until they flared. Then she hurried to the bath and returned with several linens.

Wrapping one around his head and neck, she dropped the others to the floor. Moving quickly, she pulled the bench from the end of his bed to just in front of the fireplace.

Thomas used the linen to dry his hair and face, barely conscious he was doing so. Emma unbuttoned his waistcoat and unwound the soaked cravat while he continued to shiver uncontrollably. Dropping to one knee, she undid the laces of his boots and pulled them off along with his soaked stockings while he balanced himself with one hand on her shoulder.

She considered undoing the buttons on his breeches, thought better of it, and then proceeded to unfasten them as fast as she could. Once the breeches were loose, she handed him a linen to use as cover before she pulled the dripping breeches to the floor. Then she took off his waistcoat and shirt, wrapped the last linen around his shoulders, and sat him down on the bench.

Gathering up the wet clothes, she carried them into the bath and draped them over the copper bathtub.

"Are there any extra blankets?" she whispered loudly as she returned to the room, wincing as she stepped in several wet spots in the Aubusson carpet.

Thomas was staring into the firelight, hypnotized by the flames while he continued to shiver. When he turned to look at her, he saw that her hair was loose and long, framing her face with waves of gold. *My angel is back.* Her nipples, the curves of her breasts, indeed, the entire shape of her body were visible through the wet fabric of her nightgown.

Part of him wanted desperately to kiss those breasts, to fondle them and hold them and gently bite their hardened peaks. To have that body pressed against him promised warmth for his chilled skin, her silken hair a pillow for his hurting head. *A perfect woman.* He wanted her, more than anything else he had ever wanted in his life. But another part of him was so cold and sick, he could only shiver and double over in an attempt to get warm.

When Thomas continued to stare at her but didn't answer her question, Emma finally moved to the bed, pulled aside the counterpane, and removed a quilt. She draped it around Thomas, removing the wet linens from around his head and body and taking them to the bath. Once she had the boots placed near the fire, she surveyed the room to be sure she had picked up all the wet clothes.

"Are you getting any warmer?" she asked quietly as she wrapped the quilt more tightly around his legs and feet.

Thomas nodded but said nothing, his attention back on the flames.

"I'm going to get you some hot tea. Are you hungry?"

Still shivering, Thomas nodded. "Wear... wear my... my dressing gown," he said between chattering teeth as he nodded toward the bath. At her questioning stare, he added, "Your nightgown ...," as he pointed from under the blanket.

Emma looked down and realized for the first time she was nearly as soaked to the skin as he had been. Nodding, she turned and hurried into the bath to find his robe on a hook near the tub. Wrapping it around herself, she was vaguely aware of his scent on it as she took the lamp and rushed out the room. She was careful as she negotiated the stairs. There were puddles on every step and a pool of water near the vestibule.

Once in the kitchen, she found the water kettle more than hot enough for tea. A small fire still burned in the stove from her earlier efforts to make dinner for Christiana and herself. She heated the leftover medallions of meat, gravy, and hunks of potatoes until they were steaming, grabbed a small loaf of bread, and prepared a tray with the teapot, cups, honey, half of a lemon, and the food.

When she was back in Thomas' room, she found him still wrapped in the quilt and staring into the fire. *Perhaps he is not so ill,* she hoped as she moved to his dresser.

At the scent of the food and tea, Thomas sat up straighter and watched Emma as she set the tray on his dresser. After the tea was poured, she added lemon and honey to his, stirred it, and brought it to him.

Thomas gladly took the steaming cup and held it in both his hands, allowing the heat to penetrate his chilled fingers as he sipped the hot liquid. Although he didn't care for the flavor, he knew she intended it as a medicinal drink and said nothing.

Meanwhile, Emma returned to the dresser for his meal. She carried the plate and a fork in one hand and her teacup in the other, taking a seat next to Thomas on the bench. Holding the plate up, she said quietly, "'Tis not much, but it is warm."

Thomas set down his cup on the bench and reached for the plate, his eyes focusing on the steam as it rose from the gravy. "'Tis a veritable feast," he whispered as he took the plate from her. As he tasted the meat, he closed his eyes. "You made this, didn't you?" he whispered, his shaking finally subsiding. He continued chewing as he stared at the fire.

Emma looked at him from over the top of her cup as she took a sip of tea. "Yes. But how did you know?"

Thomas finished another bite. "My cook isn't this good," he said as he stabbed a potato, his attention still on the fire.

"And Mr. Tanner is not very well, either," Emma whispered, wondering if she should mention his sister. Christiana's illness had come on very suddenly during breakfast, but the girl had insisted she felt much better as the day progressed. "Christiana was sick this morning, and before luncheon, nearly everyone else in the house-hold was as well."

News of Christiana made Thomas sit up straight again. The quilt fell from one of his shoulders as he turned to face Emma. "Is she well?" he asked urgently. It was the first time since his arrival that he showed any emotion.

"She is now," Emma assured him as she pushed the quilt back up around his bare shoulder, very aware of how little covered the man. "I didn't finish many ledgers today, I'm afraid, but I will try to catch up tomorrow."

Thomas nodded and returned his attention to the plate. They sat in silence for several minutes while Thomas finished his dinner. After he placed the empty plate on the floor, he held out one side of the quilt. "Come here. You must be freezing," he said as he wrapped the quilt around her shoulders and pulled her against the side of his torso.

The warmth of her body against his was a welcome sensation. At the same time, Thomas sensed a sudden change in Emma.

He took one of her hands in his still-cool hand. "What is it?"

At first, Emma was shocked into silence. It was bad enough to be in a man's bedchamber. It was worse to be in his bedchamber while he sat naked covered only by a quilt. And here she was pressed up against his naked flesh while under the same quilt! Wearing his dressing gown!

Emma finally turned and looked at him, her face mere inches from his. "Other than my father's, I have never before been in a man's bedchamber." She turned to face the fire, panic rising inside. "This is a bit... inappropriate," she whispered, sure he could see how flushed her face had become from her sudden embarrassment.

"No one else need know this happened. No one else *will* know," Thomas replied quietly as he watched her profile. "And it shouldn't have," he added as he leaned forward and used the heel of one hand to scrub his eyes. A sudden weariness settled into his bones, and he found it difficult to hold up his head.

Emma angled her head and turned to look at him. "Whatever do you mean?"

Thomas shook his head as he dropped his hand and then pulled his hand inside the quilt. "I was such a fool tonight," he whispered finally. "The weather was horrible all afternoon. I sent my warehouse manager home because he was sick, and then I ended up staying so late, there wasn't a room at the men's club. All the inns were full. I believed I could make it home on horseback in a blinding rainstorm, and the wind..." He paused for a moment and turned to face her. "If you hadn't had that lamp in your window, I would have walked right past the road to this house," he said, realizing he could have spent an entire night in the cold and wet. "Surely, I would have died," he whispered as he turned to stare at the fire again. A moment later, he pulled her into a hug and clung to her as if his very life depended on it.

At first, Emma gasped and almost resisted. At the same instant, she became aware of something she had been denying to herself.

I want this man, she realized, the scent of him enveloping her senses. The feel of his flesh pressed against her had every nerve ending jumping. A fluttering filled her belly as her pulse pounded in her ears.

What has happened to make me want him so? He was the same man she had met at Gamma House. The same man who employed her to review his books. The same man who had tried to marry her off to Todd Vandermeer.

A thought struck her then.

Because he's wealthy? she wondered, knowing he had amassed a small fortune through building his business.

She quickly put the thought aside. If she wanted a wealthy man, she could have had Todd. Society adored the man. Any wife he took would be as welcome as Todd at their balls and soirées and dinner parties. She could have had that life, but she knew it would be brief and painful in the end.

Thomas was a tradesman—no better than her father as far as Society was concerned. What did they expect of him? *To marry one of his kind,* she considered, although he had improved his station considerably with his business. She would be beneath him now. *Pity,* she thought sadly.

I feel affection for him.

She closed her eyes and allowed herself to mold her body into his shape, to provide warmth for him and comfort for his soul. Deep inside, she could feel him trembling with chills as she wrapped her arms around his shoulders and back.

When Thomas finally let go, Emma placed a hand along the side of his face and pressed her lips against his forehead. As she gauged his temperature, it took a great deal of will not to kiss his forehead. "You have a very bad fever," she whispered as she felt the other side of his face.

Thomas merely nodded at first, he shoulders slumping as if his body were too heavy to hold up. "Will you stay with me?" he asked, his voice sounding very tired. "At least until I..."

"Of course," Emma replied quietly, thinking he meant for her to stay by his bed. "But we should get you into bed." She reluctantly unwrapped her arms from around him and stood up, allowing the quilt to fall from her shoulders.

Moving to the bed, she pulled down the rest of the covers and the bed linens. She found a nightshirt tucked behind one of the half-dozen pillows decorating the bed. Placing the opening of the nightshirt over his head, she helped guide it onto his shoulders as he pulled it down around him. A model of modesty, he struggled to stand and made his way slowly to the bed. Once he had climbed in, she covered him with the linens and blankets and then topped it all with the quilt.

Removing his dressing gown, she left it draped across the side of the bed. With her nightrail dry and the fire having warmed the room, she was about to move to a nearby chair when Thomas caught her hand.

"You're the best nursemaid I've ever had," Thomas said in a tired voice. He kissed the back of her hand and then pulled her hard enough that she lost her balance and fell onto the bed.

Surprised by the strength of his pull, Emma let out a squeak. *I should leave right now*, she thought, panic rising in her as she considered where she was. *I'll be ruined if we're seen like this.* But she saw the expression of pain on his face, felt the vibration of his trembling in the mattress, and decided she had to stay. She allowed him to position her body as he wrapped his arm around the front of her and pulled her back against his chest. Emma felt his chilled skin through the fabric of her nightrail and thought briefly about sending for a doctor.

After a moment to recover from the surprise of what Thomas had done, Emma finally relaxed against him. His bent knees tucked in behind hers as his thighs pressed against the back of her thighs. Her bottom rested against the front of his hips, only the fabric of their gowns separating them. Finally, she felt his face burrow into her hair somewhere near her shoulder.

His entire body trembled as she pulled the blankets and quilts over them both. In the process, his hand brushed over one of her nipples, sending a frisson of pleasure to her very core. Stifling a gasp, Emma lay very still for a moment, aware that his open hand was still close to her breast where it rested on the mattress. She could hear her heartbeats pounding in her ears as her breasts swelled, their nipples becoming tight nubbins.

"Good night, Mr. Wellingham," Emma whispered as she wrapped her arm around his, her fingers intertwining his so the palm of his hand was pressed against her breast. *What will he think of me in the morning?* Any respect he had for her was no doubt gone. *Or perhaps he won't even remember*, she reasoned, relaxing into the soft mattress.

"Good night, Miss Emma," Thomas tried to say. He was asleep before he could finish the thought, though.

CHAPTER 33
RAINING COURTSHIP

June 17, 1802, Cavendish Square

Todd Vandermeer kissed Deborah White one more time before allowing her to close the door to the mistress suite. They had finished dinner only an hour before, but with the driving wind and rain, they had to forego their usual after dinner walk in the gardens. At his invitation, Deborah instead joined Todd in his study for a glass of sherry. The wood paneled room was somehow warm and comfortable despite its massive volume and formal furnishings.

Deborah spent several minutes staring at the walls of books and studying the myriad of objects adorning the tables and desk while she carefully sipped the sherry.

"They're all souvenirs from my trips," Todd commented as he watched her gaze at a collection of East Indian artifacts. "Well, all except that one there," he added as he pointed to a colored glass ball mounted on a metal stand. "A glazer made it for me when I became a broker. Said it would be my crystal ball," he whispered as he waved his hand over the orb.

Deborah gasped and turned her gaze on her betrothed. "Does it work?" she asked in awe, her hand hovering over it.

Todd shook his head as he remembered the day he paid for it. "I don't believe so, no," he answered with a careless shrug. "But I suppose I could claim I've seen the future and the announcement of our betrothal will be printed in Saturday's paper," he said playfully as his hand covered hers and moved it in slow circles above the orb.

A smile brightened Deborah's face as she moved to another set of curios, her hand still captured in his. "Indeed? You have seen this?" she teased as she studied the intricate paintings on a small wooden doll.

A bright flash followed by a loud boom sounded as lightning struck somewhere nearby. Letting out a shriek, Deborah pushed into Todd, nearly knocking him over as she wrapped her arms around his torso. Gasping, she put a hand over her mouth and stepped back, not quite balanced as she did so. "Please accept my apology, sir," she said in a quiet voice, her eyes lowered as if she were ashamed of herself.

Todd reached out and caught her around the waist, steadying her as his look of adoration turned to one of concern. "What is it?" he asked, one hand coming up to cup her cheek and lift her face. *And why is she calling me 'sir'?*

Deborah's eyes, already round with fright, stared at the window and brightened with tears. "I'm deathly afraid of lightning, you see," she explained, breathless, her attention still on the window. She had dropped her head again, although Todd could tell she was still mesmerized by the approaching storm.

Todd suppressed a smile and kissed her forehead before using a finger to gently raise her chin. "No apology is required, I assure you, my sweeting," he replied as Deborah's eyes met his. "Although there is really no need to be frightened, at least according to my friend, Mr. Grandby," he said with a grin, realizing just then that his wife-to-be had rushed to him for safety. "Seems it is a natural phenomenon that can only do us harm if we are struck by it whilst out of doors," he said as he indicated the back gardens with a nod of his head.

Nodding, Deborah glanced back at the window overlooking the gardens. Sheets of rain pounded against the glass as wind hustled through the larger trees in the back yard. "Of course," she replied uncertainly, the color still drained from her face.

Todd angled his head to one side. "So, why are you so frightened of it?" he asked, deciding there must be a reason she feared the jagged white lines in the sky.

Deborah hesitated before replying. "I watched a neighbor's tree *explode*, I suppose one could say," she said as her eyes widened. "It was so loud, and the limbs went crashing to the ground, and a fire started—"

"Oh, my dear!" Todd exclaimed as he wrapped his arms around her shoulders and pulled her against him. "You have seen first-hand the destruction of a lightening bolt. No wonder you are so frightened," he whispered as he kissed her hair and ran a comforting hand down her back.

In that moment, he was aware of how close she was, of the scent of her hair, of her body's trembling, of her heart pounding hard against his chest. And before he could stop himself, he pressed harder against her. His mouth found hers and he kissed her until he had to gasp for air. "If I don't send you to your suite this very moment, I fear I shall do something I will regret," he whispered urgently.

Angling her head to look up at him, Deborah watched as Todd's eyes darkened in the candlelight. Against her hip she felt the hardening ridge of his arousal and the heat he seemed to exude. *He wants me*, she thought, a mix of excitement and fear growing in her belly.

Unconsciously, she pushed her hip harder against him. She watched as Todd closed his eyes. He seemed to fight some inner battle before she was aware of her own body responding to his arousal. Desire swelled in her breasts as the pulsing heat between her thighs made it hard to stand. *Perhaps he'll bed me tonight,* she considered, surprised she didn't feel the same apprehension she had when she agreed to the marriage. *He is to be my husband. And I am already ruined.*

She remembered his comment. "Whatever do you mean?" she asked then, her expression betraying her increasing desire.

"I shall rend your garments from your body and take you right here in the study," he replied as he slowly opened his eyes and let out the breath he'd been holding.

Up until that day, Todd's love for his bride-to-be had been of an innocent sort, where light kisses and flirtatious gestures were as overt as their relationship would allow. Their earlier evenings together had been platonic—almost playful —as they learned more about one another. They teased and commiserated and spoke of their youth, exchanged views on the little bit of politics they each understood, argued about what they would wear to their first public soirée as a married couple, and laughed over tales of life in London.

But with the violent storm and the nearly black skies and the rain beating an incessant tattoo on the roof, an unfamiliar sensation was building in Todd.

Something had awakened in him.

He felt the change happening as he held Deborah and wondered how long it would be before he would kiss her too hard or allow his hands to cup her breasts. *What's happening to me?*

Tonight he wanted her just for himself, not as the object he was proud to put on display for his colleagues and friends as he thought, *Look at what I have. A beautiful woman who loves me.*

Deborah lowered her lashes and then wrapped her arms around his neck. "I would happily allow you to," she whispered in his ear, swallowing hard when she realized she had actually spoken the words aloud.

Todd pulled her harder against his body, but Deborah knew even as he held her he wouldn't give into his desire. "I won't allow myself to become an animal," he said quietly, remembering the concupiscence of Randolph Hughes, who, along with other lustful men, lined the streets near Covent Gardens and completed their transactions with harlots right out in the open for anyone to see.

Before she could reply to his comment, Deborah found herself being whisked up the stairs and into her suite. Todd granted her several good night kisses and then shut the door between them as they exchanged whispered "I love you's".

Allowing a sigh, Deborah leaned against the door and nearly wept. *An animal?* How could he think such a thing? She rather doubted Todd Vandermeer could ever become anything close to an animal. Even his brief forays of holding her to his body suggested he felt guilt at their chaste kissing.

As Deborah moved to undo the fastenings of her borrowed gown, she considered why Todd seemed so reluctant to be with her.

Perhaps he hasn't yet bedded a woman.

Deborah shook her head, removing her gown and nearly giggling at the thought. *Of course, he has bedded a woman*, she argued. *Probably many of them given his station in life.*

Suddenly sober, Deborah moved to the bed and wrapped herself in the linens and counterpane, weeping as she did so.

The sound of a thunder clap brought Todd out of a restless sleep, and he lay motionless as he listened to the rain. He struggled out of his sweat-soaked nightshirt and, deciding he was too exhausted to get another from the dresser, he lay back on the pillows and stared into the darkness. Although he couldn't see anything in his room—the lamp had burned out, he guessed—he was aware he wasn't alone. A familiar scent reached his nostrils, and he gasped when the room was suddenly illuminated by lightning.

For a brief instant, he saw Deborah as she stood with one arm in front of her breasts and another pressed against a thigh, her willowy figure a ghostly apparition. He heard her footfalls as she crept closer to the edge of the bed, heard her shallow breaths punctuated by quiet sobs. "Are you well?" Todd whispered, alarmed at her sudden appearance. *How long has she been in the room? Or am I still dreaming?*

"Please, forgive me. I am... I'm so *frightened*," she stuttered, her voice cracking as if she had been crying.

Todd pulled aside the coverlet on the bed and reached for her hand. He could feel her trembling. "There is nothing to be frightened of, my love," he replied, trying to console her despite his state of undress. Thinking he really was dreaming, his state of undress really didn't matter at the moment.

Deborah climbed in next to him, her entire body shivering. "Please don't think poorly of me," she pleaded, a sob having just wracked her body.

"Of course not, my love," he murmured, his hand stroking her arm as he attempted to gentle her. "But where's your nightrail?" Todd whispered, concern in his voice. Her skin was cool to the touch, a welcome sensation given how warm he had felt just moments before.

Molding her body to the side of his, Deborah rested her left arm over his stomach and burrowed her head into the small of his shoulder. "I don't... I don't have one," she whispered in reply. She hoped he wouldn't realize she could have simply worn her chemise. She usually did so, although the fabric was uncomfortable against her skin while the expensive linens on the bed in the mistress suite were soft and smooth.

There was a brief pause before Todd said, "Oh. You didn't bring one?" He could feel her head twist against his arm as he realized her breasts were pressed against the side of his chest. *Her bare breasts. A* part of his brain still believed he was experiencing a rather vivid dream. *I am never wearing a nightshirt again*, he thought absently, his hand still traveling up and down her arm in an effort to calm her trembling.

"I don't own a nightrail," she said quietly, finally deciding she could no longer hide her poverty. After a long pause, she added, "Where is your nightshirt?" Her voice betrayed a hint of surprise as she moved her fingers over his chest and realized she was touching bare skin.

Todd felt her lips press against the side of his chest as the fingers of her left hand landed lightly on his sternum. "It's here somewhere, but it matters not," he replied quietly. Placing a hand over hers, he caressed it before finally covering it protectively. "Perhaps I shall have to buy you a nightrail," he considered, his words barely audible. "Just so you have one," he added, his voice fading as tiredness crept over him. By the time Todd realized Deborah was, indeed, quite real, her shivering had ceased and she was sound asleep.

And quite naked.

"Lord, have mercy," he whispered as he wrapped an arm around her bare shoulders. The rhythm of her beating heart against his torso was comforting, and the sound of her breathing helped to slow his to an even pace.

Despite his earlier fear of uncontrollable lust, he relaxed into the bed and took joy in the sensation of her skin against his. Kissing her on the head, he allowed sleep to finally take him.

CHAPTER 34
FEVER AND FEAR

*E*mma awoke when she felt the bed shaking beneath her. Still in the same position as when Thomas had pulled her into his bed, she realized he was no longer pressed against her, and the hand she had held was no longer in her grasp. Sitting up, she turned to find Thomas on his back, shivering but sweating profusely and moaning in pain. She placed a hand against his forehead and found his skin hot to the touch. Mortified by his condition, her first thought was to send for a doctor. Rain continued to pelt against the windows, though, and she remembered travel was out of the question. "Your fever is worse," she whispered as she held a hand against the side of his face. He didn't seem to be aware of her or her hand.

Climbing out of the bed, she rushed to the bath. Finding a small linen next to the washbasin, she wet it with the cold water from the pitcher and climbed back onto the bed to place it on Thomas' forehead. She returned to the bath to get a larger linen and used it to dry his face and neck.

When she pulled down the covers, she found his nightshirt soaked with sweat, the fabric clinging to every contour of his hard body. The sudden rush of cooler air chilled him, though, and his shivering increased. Covering him with a single blanket, Emma was at a loss as to what to do. *What do you do to break a fever?* she wondered, panic sweeping over her. *Someone had a fever. What did we do?* One of the girls at the school had suffered such a fever, she remembered, her sleep-fogged brain finally providing some answers.

They had kept the girl wrapped tightly in blankets, but she had nearly died from dehydration.

Water, Emma thought. Picking up an empty teacup from the bench, she filled it with water from the pitcher in the bath. She leaned over the bed and tried to lift Thomas' head. "Drink this," she whispered hoarsely. At first, he resisted until some of it spilled on the side of his face. Then his lips took purchase on the edge of the cup and he drained it in one gulp. "M... more," he gasped, his tongue so swollen he wasn't able to speak.

Emma brought the entire pitcher from the bath, refilling the cup several times as Thomas drank. Exhausted from the effort, he allowed his head to fall back onto the pillows.

She turned over the compress on his forehead, startled at how warm it was where it had rested on his skin. "We have to get you cooled off," Emma whispered as loud as she could. Thomas opened his eyes, but he didn't seem to see her. "Get out of bed," she ordered as she pulled on his arm. The sweat-soaked fabric of his nightshirt clung to his body as he slowly climbed out of the bed. Shivering, he followed as Emma clasped one of his hands and led him to the bench. He sat down hard, moaning as he held his head in his hands.

Although a small fire still burned in the fireplace, Emma placed another log on top of the charred pile and then turned to assess her patient. She could practically see steam rising from his body as his nightshirt dried, but at least he wasn't shivering as much. Standing in front of him, she leaned over and placed her lips against his forehead. Although it was still very warm, it was not as hot as it had been a few minutes before.

"I think your fever broke," she whispered in relief as she held his head in her hands.

Thomas wrapped his arms around her thighs and rested his head against her stomach. "Thank you," he said as he clung to her. His first coherent thought found him hoping she wouldn't remember any of this in the morning. And then he thought that perhaps he was just having a bad dream, and he wouldn't remember any of this in the morning, either.

Her hands cradling his head, Emma stood very still while he rested against her. *This is all very chaste*, she tried to tell herself, even though she found the feel of him through the fabric of her gown more intimate than she should have. Her fingers were woven into his now-dry hair, and it took a good deal of restraint to keep them still when they wanted to caress and stroke him.

When the heat from the fire became too warm for Emma, she unwrapped Thomas' arms from around her thighs. She refilled the teacup and made him drink more water before asking where she could find him a dry nightshirt.

He pointed toward his dresser. "Top drawer," he said quietly, his body so tired he was barely able to hold himself up on the bench.

Emma tentatively opened the drawer and found several nightshirts lined up neatly at the front. When she took one out, firelight reflected from a multi-jeweled brooch and matching earrings. Startled by the unexpected sight of jewelry, she wondered to whom they belonged before realizing they were probably gifts for Christiana. Emma slid the drawer shut and brought the nightshirt to Thomas. She turned away as he removed the wet one and pulled the dry one over his head.

"Come to bed," Emma ordered quietly as she headed back to the guest room through the connecting door.

"Please, don't leave," Thomas whispered as he slowly stood up from the bench.

Emma shook her head. "Your bed linens are soaked," she whispered in explanation. "Now, come to bed."

Startled by her insistent tone, Thomas followed her through the door. The candle in the window, now burned down to a stub, still glowed with warmth and yellow light. "But where are you going to sleep?" Thomas whispered as he climbed into the bed.

"Move over," Emma ordered, pretending she wasn't amused by his question.

"This is most inappropriate, Miss Emma," he replied as he wrapped his arm around her and pulled her against his body.

"Good night, Mr. Wellingham," she whispered as she pressed herself against him. When she didn't hear a response, she turned to find him already sound asleep. Exhausted, Emma fell asleep as she wrapped her arm around his, a slight smile on her face when she realized he had a sense of humor even when he was at Death's doorway. *Silly man.*

CHAPTER 35
A BUTLER CONVEYS NEWS

*J*une *18, 1802, Grace Park*

Sitting up in bed, Todd stared straight ahead and found his butler staring back at him.

"Pardon me, sir. I didn't mean to wake you," Winston stated with a nod. "But it's rather unusual for you to be asleep this late. Are you well?" he asked, his face screwed up in a frown.

Nervous, Todd glanced around the room. His sudden erection was tenting the bed linens, but he did his best to hide it by crumpling the counterpane around his waist. The sun had obviously been up for some time, but his next concern was for Deborah. He pulled up the counterpane and looked beneath it, thinking perhaps she was hiding. But she wasn't in the bed, nor was there any immediate evidence she had been in his bed. "What time is it?" he asked, panic in his voice. *What a vivid dream*, he thought as he recalled the night before. *So pleasant, though.*

The butler glanced at the clock on the massive dresser. "'Tis half-past-eight, Mr. Vandermeer. Are you well, sir?" he repeated as his eyebrows knitted together in concern.

"I believe I am, Winston," Todd replied as he ran a hand through his tousled hair. *Eight-thirty?* He was usually in his office by seven. "Has Miss Deborah been out of her bedchamber yet?" he asked as he moved to get out of the bed. He noticed a long, black hair on the edge of the bed linen, relieved to discover it wasn't a dream. *She really was here. In my bed.*

Winston pulled a topcoat and waistcoat from the wardrobe and returned his attention to his master. "Oh, yes, sir," he replied as he placed the garments on the end of the bed. "She was dressed and ready to walk to Mrs. Dawes' before seven this morning, but I insisted Mr. Stevenson take her in the carriage," he explained before turning to get a pair of breeches from the dresser. "She was very concerned about your knees," he added with furrowed brows.

Todd arched an eyebrow and reached for the jar of salve on the nightstand. "I will be sure to put it on before I leave today," he answered with a sigh, disappointed Deborah wouldn't be doing it for him this morning. "I plan to shop for a few hours. I won't be gone long, though, as my friend Mr. Wellingham is to join me for luncheon today."

"Very good, sir," the butler replied as he paused to regard Todd, obviously wanting to say more but not sure his comments would be welcome.

When his butler didn't offer another comment, Todd angled his head. "What is it, Winston?"

The man gave him a curt nod and finally said, "When Miss Fitzsimmons and Miss White came to dinner, I had the niggling feeling I had the good fortune of meeting Miss White somewhere before. She greeted me by name, in fact. And then, when the subject of Mrs. Dawes came up, I remembered then I had seen her at the Home for Unwed Mothers."

Todd's eyebrows jumped in surprise. "Indeed?" he replied, and then remembered he had, on several occasions, dispatched his butler to deliver his contributions to the Home. Winston would have undoubtedly seen Deborah there on at least one of those visits. But Todd wondered why he hadn't noticed Deborah when he delivered his tithes personally. How could he not notice a woman as tall and comely as she? Perhaps she was in her room. Or delivering a baby. *Or hiding from me.*

Winston nodded and clasped his hands behind his back. "I must admit, my first impressions of the lady were not... complimentary," he said carefully, not sure how much he should admit to his employer. "I thought she was one of the ... *residents* of the Home, you see."

Shrugging, Todd sat up straight on the edge of the bed. "You are not the only one, Winston," he said quietly, "But I find I cannot hold her situation against her. I love her, and she has agreed to be my wife," he stated sharply.

A moment later, and he wondered why he felt the need to be so defensive on her behalf. It wasn't as if he were a member of the *ton* and his choice of wife had repercussions in Society. As far as any of his colleagues knew, Deborah was a midwife, nothing more. "We shall not speak of this again," he added.

Winston drew his eyebrows together in consternation, not quite sure why his master had suddenly grown cross. "I merely wanted to say I think you have made a wise choice for a wife, sir," he stated. "And Mrs. Dawes is quite in agreement." He resumed laying out clothes for his master, hiding his offense at Todd's rebuke.

Taken aback by the comment, Todd stared at his butler. "You do?" he asked with surprise. "She does?" He continued staring and then angled his head. "Then, thank you, Winston," he replied uncertainly.

"You are most welcome, sir," the butler replied with a nod. "I also wish to inform you that I have spoken with Mrs. Dawes about a... courtship," Winston continued, his eyes no longer making contact with his master's. "She has graciously consented to allow me to call on her."

Todd stared at his manservant, his mouth open in surprise. "Courtship?" he repeated, his eyebrows rising again. "You... and Mrs. Dawes?" he asked, awestruck. His butler was courting the woman who had helped bring him into this world! "When did this happen?" he asked, perplexed at how he could have been so blind.

Winston, who looked as if he wanted to crawl into the nearest hole, straightened and replied, "Last Sunday, sir. After church, I escorted Mrs. Dawes to Gunter's Tea Shop. We had a most delightful afternoon. I assure you, sir, that if she agrees to matrimony, we will both continue in our respective positions. I was hoping, sir, you might allow the lady to move into my quarters with me here at Grace Park. Once we're properly married, of course," he added as his resolve began to fade and his face took on a look of sheer terror.

"But, of course," Todd agreed, still stunned by the news. His face split into a huge grin. "Oh, of course she should move in with you," he added, the news making him feel as happy as when Deborah agreed to be his wife. "But we shall have to move you into larger quarters, I should think. We cannot have the two of you in a room barely meant for one," he insisted as he got up from the bed and started to dress. "You know, Winston, I have never understood why the servants' quarters are so small in these large houses," he added as he pulled on his shirt. "You shall take the large suite at the other end of the hall," he stated as he pulled on his breeches. "It has a private bath, and the furnishings are much more suitable for a person of the ...," he paused as he struggled to find the right word. "A woman," he said finally, quickly buttoning up the fly on his breeches. "And you'll have more privacy, of course," he added with a wink.

Awestruck, Winston stared at this master. "'Tis awfully generous of you to offer such large accommodations, Mr. Vandermeer," he stated as he let out the breath he had been holding.

Smiling, Todd arranged the fabric of his shirt around his torso and began tucking it into his breeches. "Nonsense, Winston. Nothing is too good for Mrs. Dawes. I'd be honored to have that woman live in this house. She was practically my mother, you see," he said happily.

Winston nodded. "She once mentioned she was your mother's midwife," he said quietly.

Todd regarded his butler for a moment. What else might Mrs. Dawes have told the man about his mother? Another thought struck him, though, and he considered the irony of the situation. "You realize, of course, that if you and Mrs. Dawes do wed, we will be housing the only two midwives of the Home for Unwed Mothers."

Winston regarded his master for a moment. "Oh, dear," the man replied as his eyes widened. "I do believe I take your meaning," he said as he considered just how many nights would be interrupted by girls pounding on the door and informing them someone was in labor at the Cooper Hotel. "Perhaps I should rethink this courtship," he whispered.

"No need, Winston," Todd whispered back, grinning. "We just need to find a midwife to work the night shift."

The butler smiled broadly. "I shall see what can be done about that, Mr. Vandermeer."

CHAPTER 36
OF WOMEN AND WORK

*J*une *18, 1802, Woodscastle*

The rain stopped sometime before seven o'clock in the morning. Aware he wasn't in his own bed, Thomas opened one eye and tried to remember just where he was. The scent of coffee permeated the air, but the lighter scent of Emma's hair came to him from the pillow next to his nose. He tried to sit up. Immediately regretting the move, he lay back down and groaned.

"Don't even try to get up just yet, Mr. Wellingham," Emma said quietly as she entered the room from the bath. "You must be very thirsty, though. Do you think you could drink some apple juice?"

Keeping his eyes closed, Thomas nodded his head in the pillow. Emma took a full glass from a tray on the dresser and moved to the side of the bed closest to Thomas. "Can you lift your head?" she whispered as she held the glass for him.

He obeyed, drinking nearly half the juice before collapsing back into the pillow. Opening his eyes, he saw she was already dressed in a crisp yellow muslin gown. Her hair was still down around her shoulders, though, and he sighed. "What time?" he asked, his voice croaking with the effort to speak.

"'Tis nearly eight o'clock. You need to sleep some more, though," Emma said as she held a hand on his forehead and decided he no longer had a fever. "I don't believe you'll want to go to town today," she added as she offered him more juice.

Thomas drank the rest of the juice as he held himself up on one elbow. "But... But I must at some point," he said groggily. He fell back into the pillow and was once again sound asleep.

Satisfied he wasn't going to be rising any time soon, Emma wound her hair into a simple bun and secured it with pins before taking her coffee and going to the library.

*A*t precisely noon, Thomas sat up straight in the bed and tried to remember everything that had happened the night before.

He found he could not.

And what the hell am I doing in the guest bedchamber? he wondered as he glanced around and realized everything in the room was backwards. Gingerly stepping out of the bed, he tiptoed through the open door into his bedchamber. His bed was mussed, and a quilt was where his counterpane should have been. When he noticed his bathrobe on the edge of the bed, the memories finally came flooding back.

He pulled the chain to summon Humphrey and then regretted it. Emma had said he was ill—perhaps the poor man was still asleep. Expecting to find evidence of his meal from the night before— plates, cups or the tray Emma had brought up from the kitchen— Thomas was rather surprised to find all evidence of her having been there removed from the room. His clothes, though, were still drying on the edge of the bathtub. Thankfully, his boots, sitting near the hearth, were dry.

"Good afternoon, Mr. Wellingham," the butler said quietly as he entered the room from the hall. He glanced around the room and sighed as he took in the sight of his ill master.

Thomas nodded at his butler and sat down heavily on the bench at the end of his bed. "I understand you were very ill yesterday," he said as he made eye contact with the elderly gentleman. "Are you well today?" he asked, worry in his voice.

"Indeed I am, Mr. Wellingham. Thanks to Miss Fitzsimmons, I must admit," Humphrey said with a nod. "She forced me, against my will, I might add, to go to bed with honey and lemon tea. With the rain, I was sure you would spend the night at the club," he added quickly, hoping his master wouldn't be cross with him. "I must apol- ogize for not being available when you arrived last night. I'm afraid to admit I didn't wake up until an hour ago," he said with a guilty look on his face.

"'Tis quite all right, Humphrey. I managed just fine in your absence," he said, deciding it wasn't necessary to mention Miss Fitzsimmons' assistance on his behalf.

"If I may, sir. You don't look well," the butler said sadly. "Perhaps you would benefit from a cup of hot tea and a day in bed."

Thomas gave the suggestion some thought, but shook his head. "I'm supposed to meet Mr. Vandermeer at Grace Park for a luncheon meeting. I really must be on my way by one o'clock."

The butler nodded and hurried to the bath. "I will prepare your bath at once, sir."

Given the muddy roads and his state of health, Thomas had Mr. Allen take him to town in the small carriage. With an hour of sun and fresh air and a short nap, Thomas arrived at Grace Park feeling much better.

The butler opened the front door before Thomas had a chance to use the brass knocker. The man bowed deeply and stepped aside as Thomas walked into the crowded vestibule. Several parcels and boxes lined the walls, many stacked nearly as high as he was tall. From the number of them displaying feminine names and colors, Thomas realized they probably weren't intended for Todd.

His host was bouncing down the steps from the second story, a big grin appearing on his face when he spotted his guest. He wore breeches, a white shirt, and an ornately embroidered waistcoat, but no topcoat.

"Mr. Wellingham! So glad you could join me today," Todd said loudly as he stepped quickly to the vestibule and gave a bow.

Thomas returned the courtesy. "'Tis very kind of you to have me for luncheon," Thomas replied as he took in the sight of his friend. "You are looking damned well," he commented, amazed at the transformation in his friend. Todd didn't carry a cane, nor did he walk with a limp. And he appeared to have gained at least a stone in weight.

Todd smiled and nodded quickly. "I'm very well, thank you. Being in love has an amazing medicinal quality about it, I think. I do wish Miss White were here today so you could meet her," he added excitedly.

"Is she shopping for the wedding, then?" Thomas asked as they made their way to the dining room.

"No, heavens. She doesn't yet know how to shop," he replied in a teasing voice, rubbing his hands together. "She is working at the Home for Unwed Mothers today. There is one baby due today and another due sometime next week," he said as he motioned for Thomas to take a seat at the dining table. "It is I who has been shopping," he added with a nod. "She has so little. Buying her a few gowns and some fripperies seemed the best thing I could do for her now."

Sitting down hard, Thomas grinned at his friend. "I must admit, I was very perplexed when Miss Emma told me of your plan to wed Miss White. When I saw you last, you seemed to have your heart set on Miss Emma," he accused quietly.

Todd nodded and folded his hands together. A footman entered from the kitchen, poured wine and water and exited, almost before the two gentlemen could thank him. "Miss Fitzsimmons has assured me she takes no offense at my marrying her friend, Thomas. In fact, I'm beginning to believe I may be the happy victim of an elaborate scheme she concocted just so Miss White and I could meet," he said with a grin.

Cocking his head to one side, Thomas tried to remember if Emma had admitted to such a scheme. *I arranged*, she had started to say to him Monday morning before she amended it to something else. "I believe she may have played matchmaker to a certain degree," Thomas agreed with a nod.

"I will thank her again, then," his host said with a nod. A huge grin broke out on his face. "I have news from Gregory," he announced, changing the subject.

Thomas leaned back in his chair and grinned. "And what has Grandby been up to lately?" he asked of their common best friend.

The footman appeared with steaming bowls of thick potato soup. Not having eaten since Emma's quick dinner in the middle of the night, Thomas found he was famished and started eating as soon as the footman disappeared.

"He received my invitation to the wedding and will arrive in time. He says he will be staying with you at Woodscastle," Todd commented. He looked to Thomas for confirmation.

Nodding, Thomas replied, "I was expecting him for a fortnight stay sometime this summer. He plans to attend the Hornsby ball, so the timing of your wedding works out well," he replied between spoonfuls of soup. "Christiana is anxious to see him, too. They get along quite well, despite their age difference. I believe he taught her how to play pontoon over Christmas," he added as he rolled his eyes, remembering how quickly she had learned the card game.

Todd smiled, thinking there was nearly as much difference in their heights as there was in their ages. But it was unlikely Grandby would ever be a suitor for Christiana, he considered. The man had a reputation with the ladies, and most in Society who knew him considered him a confirmed bachelor. "Grandby has offered Cherrywood for Miss White and me to stay after the wedding," Todd said with a smile. "Deborah has never been outside of London and is very excited about the prospect of honeymooning in Derbyshire," he said with a smile. "As am I, truth be told." When he lifted his spoon to begin eating, he visibly winced before flexing his hand.

"What is it?" Thomas asked as he noticed Todd's expression.

Todd shook his head and held up his injured hand. "I punched a man in the nose this morning, Thomas," he stated evenly.

Thomas stared at his friend for a moment, a look of shock on his face. "Indeed?" he replied, rather aghast Todd was capable of such an act. "And why, exactly, did you do that?" he asked, his eyebrows nearly into his hairline.

Todd sat back in his chair and sighed heavily. "One of my colleagues implied that my Deborah was of questionable reputation," he stated with a frown. "Seems a woman cannot work as a midwife at a facility such as the one Mrs. Dawes operates and expect consideration from the more well-to-do of our Society," he said with a frown. "I... I broke his nose," he added with a hint of chagrin.

After taking a sip of his wine, Thomas regarded his friend with a raised eyebrow and tried to imagine Todd Vandermeer raising a fist against someone. "So, I take it you... feel *affection* for this woman?"

Grinning, Todd nodded. "I love her with all my heart, Thomas. I cannot tell you how good it feels to... to feel like this," he said just before he took a spoonful of soup. "She is better educated than me, of course, but she is very patient. We have spent hours in her bedchamber reading." Lowering his voice, he asked, "Are you familiar with the book, '*The Kama Sutra*'?"

Startled by the question, Thomas nearly dropped his spoon. "Well, there is a copy in the library at Woodscastle, but I don't believe I've looked at it since I was a youth," he answered as his face flushed red. Indeed, he had been somewhat frightened by what he saw in the illustrations and realized then there was a reason it was on the top shelf in the library.

"Oh, you really must look at it, Thomas," Todd said urgently. "Although it's written in Sanskrit, I was able to get most of it translated when I was last in India," he explained quickly. "There's an entire chapter on kissing. So Deborah and I read it together, and then we spent hours..."

Thomas held up a hand. "Stop, Todd. I believe you're about to put a picture in my head I don't wish to see," Thomas said firmly, hoping he wasn't offending his friend with the comment. But he wanted Todd to know the topic of the conversation was most improper. He took a long drink of wine and set the glass down as Todd nodded.

"I apologize, Thomas. I didn't think that it's probably inappropriate to be discussing kissing over lunch. It's certainly never been a consideration of mine before, you see." He paused as he realized he was babbling. "I really must speak with you about something that's been troubling me, though," he said firmly. He leaned in closer. "About women."

Having finished his soup, Thomas regarded his friend with a patient grin. "I'm not exactly an expert in the affairs of the feminine persuasion, you must know. I've only the one sister." *Thank goodness*.

Todd leaned toward Thomas and spoke in quiet tones. "I love this woman, Thomas. I adore everything about her. She has these long, slender fingers, and I..." he looked quickly around the room to be sure no one else could hear, "I saw her undressed last night when she didn't know I was... watching," he said, not wishing to admit Deborah had been in his bedchamber. "She has a more beautiful body than even the goddess Diana."

Thomas sat up straighter at the mention of the goddess. Hadn't Christiana compared Emma to the sculpture of Diana at some point in the past? Her assessment was certainly accurate, he considered, when he recalled the vision of Emma in her damp nightrail.

The door to the kitchen opened as the footman brought out a serving platter heavy with china plates lined with gravy and mounded with roast beef, potatoes, and carrots. The two men leaned back and allowed the footman to set the plates in front of them before they resumed their conversation.

"On the one hand," Todd continued, "I want to worship her as I would a goddess," he said quietly. "As a beautiful and pure and virtuous woman. She's all of those things and more," he said with conviction. "But after last night, I find myself wanting to take her to my bed to have my way with her every night. And every morning," he added, his eyes indicating his seriousness—and his confusion. "I want to make love to her in every possible way, and I want her to... I want her to become a... a *wanton* and make love to me... to feel *lust* for me as I do for her." He swallowed hard, his face contorting into a pained expression. "Yet, for her to do so would mean she is no longer a pure and virtuous goddess.

"Whatever am I to do?"

Thomas sighed as he considered his friend's confession. The poor man was obviously in a quandary as to how to treat his bride. Indeed, how would Todd react if his bride treated him as a lover and proved she lusted for him as he apparently lusted for her? Even if she didn't share his desire, would she still play the part of the good wife and allow her husband an occasional conjugal visit?

Thomas found he could be of little help to his friend. "I think you must do both," he said. "If she's to be your perfect woman, you must tell her what it is you expect of her in your bed," he stammered. "And she must do the same for you. She already knows she is to be beautiful and pure to everyone else's eyes, including you, in the light of day. That's the nature of being a woman, I think."

Todd nodded in agreement. "I'll speak with Miss White," he said quietly, swallowing hard. "But I cannot wait to make love to her," he added. "I cannot wait until July the third for those fingers to touch me ...," *Again*, he nearly said, remembering the warmth of her hand on his chest as she lay pressed against him. "I simply cannot. I *ache* for her," he said with conviction, his breath coming in short gasps. "Whatever shall I do?"

Thomas was reminded of the night before, when he had seen Emma in her wet nightrail, her breasts outlined in the clinging fabric, her hardened nipples so evident. He, too, had ached. He had wanted her so badly, wanted her in his bed with her legs spread open for him and her long golden hair fanned out on his pillow. He wanted her lips on his and her fingernails raking his back as he made love to her.

But his sickness had prevented him from saying it aloud, and it had certainly prevented him from doing anything but imagine the possibility. Never before had a woman caused his body to react so. The effect had been so powerful, he had pulled her onto his bed, pulled her body against his and probably held her there against her will.

"Fifty years ago, this wouldn't have been a problem, my friend," Thomas answered firmly. "You could have said your marriage vows to one another without the benefit of the church and been considered legally married. Miss White could have been but twelve years old and the marriage would have been seen as legal and binding," he said in disgust. Why was it necessary to have a Marriage Act that, overnight, sent so many common-law marriages into illegality and caused so many children to become bastards?

Todd sat up straight. "Go on," he said, curious.

"Send your servants on holiday. You and Miss White say your vows to one another. No one need know you're sharing a bed as husband and wife for the two weeks or so before the wedding," he said quietly. "Marry each other in the eyes of the church and all your friends on third of July. Then you can love each other all you want. Although I wouldn't recommend you do so in public places," he added sternly.

Todd stared at his friend, and then a slow smile began to show. "I knew you would be of help," he said quietly. After a moment staring at his plate, he looked at Thomas with concern. "What are the vows?" he asked, his brows furrowed.

Shrugging, Thomas sighed. "I don't think they're cast in stone. You simply tell each other you will love and honor until death." He paused a moment trying to remember what the priest had said at the last wedding he attended, far too many years ago. "You must vow to love her, comfort her, honor her, keep her in sickness and in health, and forsake all others for as long as you live." He raised a forefinger and added, "That means you cannot take a mistress."

Shaking his head from side to side, Todd assured him he would not. "I've never understood why married men have mistresses," he said, his brows furrowed.

Thomas could only shrug his shoulders in reply. He hoped Todd would never come to understand why, indeed, some men had to have more than one woman in their bed. *However could a man expect to please more than one woman? And however do they afford the rent, clothing allowance, and pin money a mistress commands for her services?*

Remembering more of the wedding vows, Thomas added, "She

must vow to obey you, serve you, love and honor you, and keep you in sickness and in health, and forsake all others for as long as you both live," he finished with a nod, shrugging one shoulder and concentrating on the plate of food in front of him.

Todd sat staring into space for a few moments. "So she must obey and serve me, but I don't have to obey and serve her?" he asked, displaying a look of confusion.

Trying to suppress a grin, Thomas sighed. "It would behoove you to do so, even if it's not in your vows," he suggested helpfully. "I remember my father was quite good at obeying my mother," he mentioned, recalling how demanding his mother could be of his father. "It was to his benefit that he did, I assure you."

Smiling, Todd nodded. "I like obeying Deborah," he commented lightly. "She tells me to kiss her, and I do. She tells me to hold her, and I do. What's so hard about that?" he asked, his brows furrowed with concern.

Thomas tried hard not to smile at his friend's expense. "You'll be fine, Todd. My father just said to take it very slow the first time you bed your wife. You'll have your entire lives to try every position in *The Kama Sutra*," he said with a wink.

Eyes widening, Todd shook his head. "I don't think we shall be trying *every* position," he countered. "It would take over two months, and I don't think my limbs will bend in those directions!"

Chuckling, Thomas sliced a potato in half and stabbed a piece with his fork. "Then may you never be bored in bed," he replied with a grin.

Nodding, Todd turned his attention to his lunch. After a few bites, he paused with his fork in mid-air. "Have *you* ever been in love, Thomas?" he asked. "I know you want to wait until Miss Wellingham is betrothed before you go courting, but is there someone with whom you want to share your bed?" he asked, the serious expression returning to his face.

Mortified by the question, Thomas wasn't about to tell Todd he had indeed shared his bed only the night before, although not in the way his friend was implying.

Taking a deep breath, he thought for a moment and finally said, "Last night, I couldn't find a room at the club, and all the inns were full because of the rain."

Todd frowned at the odd reply and put down his fork. "You

should have come here. I'd gladly offer hospitality on a rainy night. Or any night!" he exclaimed. "Wherever did you go?"

Sighing, Thomas chastised himself for not even thinking of Grace Park as a refuge from the storm. "I rode home," he said. "Well, most of the way. My horse was most uncooperative, what with the lightning and thunder," he remembered as he leaned back in his chair. "I'm sure it was past midnight when I arrived at Wood-scastle. I was soaked to the skin. I was freezing. Humphrey was nowhere to be found. He had taken ill, like me. But this... this *angel* appeared at the top of the stairs. She was beautiful, Todd. She was a vision in white with long golden hair holding this giant light. I swear, I thought she was there to take me. I was sure I was dying, and she was there to take me to heaven. So... I climbed up the stairs with her, and she took me to my room, and she built a fire, and undressed me, and dried me, and fed me, and put me to bed, and stayed with me until my fever broke," he said in a faraway voice.

His body started to tremble as it had the night before. "That angel. That is whom I want in my bed," he said as he bit his lip. "She was the best nursemaid I've ever had," he said in a whisper as he put his face in his hands and braced his elbows against the table.

Todd stared at his friend for several minutes as he tried to determine if Thomas' angel was real or a figment of his imagination. "And when you awoke today... was she still there?" Todd asked quietly, his face tinged with worry.

Thomas nodded. "Oh, yes. Offered me apple juice and told me to go back to sleep," he remembered matter-of-factly. "Which, I suppose I did, because I didn't wake again until nearly noon," he added with a grin.

The footman appeared with hot apple tartlets drizzled with caramel, setting one in front of each of them. Thomas looked at Todd in disbelief. "May I please have your cook?" he asked, and not at all in a teasing manner. "Even for just two days a week, perhaps?"

Todd ignored the question and shook his head. "It's fortuitous you had an angel to look after you," he said with a raised eyebrow. "When you arrived, I thought you didn't look well. I apologize for not asking about your health," he offered sincerely.

Thomas shook his head. "I'm fine now," he assured his friend. "I'm certainly feeling much better after such a magnificent meal," he added as he placed a hand over his stomach.

"It isn't over," Todd replied with a smile. "Until you finish your dessert."

Thomas smiled. "All right, but I cannot stay much longer. I want to find a gift for my angel and return to Woodscastle before she leaves," he said lightly as he took a forkful of the tart, unaware of what he had just admitted.

Emma is his angel! Todd realized as his face broke into a broad grin.

Emma was his nursemaid.

She was mine for a day, but now I have my own for the rest of my life. "And what does one buy for an angel who is the best nursemaid you have ever had?" Todd asked lightly as he tried to suppress his knowing grin.

"Jewelry, of course," Thomas replied with a firm nod. "Something symbolic. Gold, surely. Something to go with rain."

Todd frowned. "Rain?" he repeated, perplexed. But then he caught his friend's meaning and smiled. "You can buy teardrop-shaped fobs at Elliot and Miller," he suggested after a moment. "It's not far from here. If you don't like their selection, then we can go to New Bond Street."

Thomas arched an eyebrow. "New Bond Street?" he questioned, surprised by the suggestion.

"Trelegon and Company and Stedman and Vardon are very near one another," Todd commented, mentioning the jewelry stores and goldsmiths he knew on that street.

Furrowing his brows, Thomas asked, "How is it you know where all the jewelry stores are?"

Todd smiled and leaned forward. "I have been hunting for the perfect wedding ring for my Deborah."

Thomas placed his hand on his friend's arm. "We shall do that," he said. "Now, are you ready to exchange vows with Miss White?" he asked as he considered what the next fortnight would hold for his friend.

"Indeed," Todd replied. "Maybe even tonight. It's likely Deborah will arrive home before dinner, and she may not have to be back at the Home tomorrow morning. I'll bring up the matter with her as soon as I'm able, I assure you."

When they finished their desserts, they took their leave of the dining room. "You said you had a business-related concern," Thomas remembered as he and Todd walked through the great hall.

Todd sighed and squeezed his eyes shut. "Yes," he replied, exhibiting a hint of annoyance. "The reason I asked you to have luncheon with me has to do with my future with East India," he said as they headed to the study instead of to the front door.

"Your future?" Thomas repeated.

"Yes," Todd replied sadly as he sat down in a large damask sofa. The room sported an assortment of comfortable chairs, tables and a thin-legged table desk the likes of which Thomas had never seen before. Gold velvet drapes were pulled back and thin sheers revealed some of the backyard gardens. A woven carpet covered most of the wood floor, its gold fibers matching the drapes. Various items from Todd's trips to India were displayed throughout the room.

"You see, I don't believe there is one for me," Todd continued in explanation as Thomas took an arm chair adjacent to the sofa. "You cannot speak of this to anyone, Thomas. Not just yet."

Thomas' eyebrows raised in surprise at the comment. "Whatever do you mean?" he asked.

Shaking his head, Todd frowned and replied, "After our meeting at your home, I spent some time thinking about the import business. It won't be long before East India's status as a monopoly will be rescinded. As you probably know, the company is becoming more important as a political entity than as an import business," he explained quickly. "Oh, we'll have several more years of record business dealings, no doubt, and maybe there will be another product from some obscure eastern country I can locate and exploit as a broker on their behalf, but at some point, capitalism will be allowed to prevail. And I'm not a politician, Thomas. I don't see a future for myself if I stay at East India."

Staring at Todd in disbelief, Thomas considered his comments and made a decision. On any other day, he might have deliberated for several hours or written a letter to Gregory Grandby to ask his opinion, or made an appointment to see Sir William at the bank, but today, he simply made the decision. If he were to take on another broker at Wellingham Imports, then it would be Todd Vandermeer. "Can you afford *not* to work?" Thomas asked first, not meaning the question to sound as personal as it did.

The taller man shook his head. "Only if I no longer supported Mrs. Dawes, and if I were to reduce my staff, and if I stopped buying gifts for Deborah," he grinned as he answered. "Which I have *no* intention of doing," he added with an emphasis on the 'no.'

Thomas nodded and grinned at the comment. "Do you want to continue working in the import business?" Thomas asked carefully. Could he afford to take on the importer? *Can I afford not to?*

Sighing, Todd replied, "It's all I know." He shook his head. "I don't know what else I might do for an honest living," he added, his expression one of fright. "I was hoping you might have... some ideas, a recommendation, perhaps," he said, his uncertainty apparent.

Thomas smiled and took a deep breath. Leaning forward, he said, "I cannot yet offer you a stake in Wellingham Imports. I must first speak with the other shareholders about another stock offering, but... but I would be honored if you would come work for... *with* me," he said with a nod. "After your wedding and honeymoon, of course," he added when Todd didn't respond right away. Indeed, the importer simply stared at him, slack-jawed. "There's an empty office next to mine that has yet to be furnished. It has a window overlooking the Thames," Thomas continued. "You wouldn't have to wear a coat, if you prefer not to," he added, referring to Todd's lack of appropriate attire.

The comment seemed to capture Todd's attention, and he finally looked down at what he was wearing. "Damnation," he murmured as he looked over at his guest. "I'm not wearing a coat," he said in surprise. His face reddening, he added, "Winston has it, of course," he remembered. "It was missing a button." For a moment, he seemed to struggle for air.

"Todd, are you well?" Thomas asked as he studied his friend. "Shall I have Winston send for a doctor?" he asked as he stood up and headed for the hall.

"No!" Todd replied as he stood up and waved a hand in the air. "No. I'm fine," he said, "I just... I certainly wasn't expecting you to offer me a position," he explained as his breathing returned to normal. "I wasn't expecting to leave East India this year or even next. I was just... thinking about the future," he said in a whisper as he moved to his desk and took the chair there.

"As I recall, it was a mere six months ago you told me you were thinking about taking a wife, and here you are, about to be married," Thomas countered with a wan smile.

Todd angled his head to one side as he regarded his friend. "You have a good point, I suppose. But, Thomas, really, can you *afford* to hire me?'

Thomas sighed and leaned forward. "I believe the question is, can I afford *not* to?"

Surprised by the reply, Todd sat up straighter at his desk. "I'm flattered by your faith in my business acumen," the tall man admitted with a slight smile. "As I said, I'm merely thinking about it. By this time next year, I may be a father," he said, his serious expression turning to pure joy. "Can you imagine me? A father?" he asked, his face as happy as when he described Deborah.

Thomas settled back into his chair. "I can, indeed," he replied simply. "Me, no, but you? I believe you would make an excellent father," he added with a grin.

Todd's joyful look changed as he furrowed his brows. "Why can't you imagine yourself as a father?" he asked. "You have already raised Miss Wellingham all these years—"

"And I've done a damned terrible job of it," Thomas interjected. "I put her in a bloody boarding school for eight months of the year so she could spend time with rich snobs and—"

"Emma Fitzsimmons is not a snob!" Todd interrupted, his voice taking on an edge Thomas had not heard before in his friend.

"I don't include Miss Emma in that assessment, of course," Thomas replied quickly, startled by Todd's rebuke. "I was merely referring to every other girl at that damned school. The only person I have to thank for her *not* becoming a spoiled rotten brat is Miss Emma. And it was Miss Emma who informed me my sister was practically a piano virtuoso. *I* certainly had no idea. And now that Emma has graduated and will no longer be Christiana's roommate, I'm at a loss as to what to do with Christiana next fall," he admitted, a sour expression on his face. "She is too old for a governess. Too young to marry..."

One of Todd's eyebrows went up too high as Thomas referred to Emma by her given name. He steepled his fingers as he listened to his friend's tirade, finally snorting at the mention of Christiana's age.

"She *is* too young to marry," Thomas insisted with a frown.

"She's *sixteen*, Thomas," Todd replied quietly. "Seventeen next month, if I recall correctly. You said during luncheon that girls used to marry at twelve," he countered with a nod. "And, since you haven't arranged a marriage for her, then please be accepting to suitors when they begin knocking on her door this summer," he suggested carefully. "Then you won't have to decide what to do with her in the fall."

Thomas gave a 'humph' in reply and considered Todd's words. Changing the subject back to the offer of a position at Wellingham Imports, Thomas asked, "Will you at least think about working with me?"

Todd leaned forward, his elbows on his knees, and regarded his friend. "I have concerns," he said seriously. "I would first have to know if you really could... truly *afford* to hire me."

Thomas leaned forward. "I... I'm almost certain I can," he said, biting his lip and realizing that, at this point, Emma would be the one to answer such a question.

"I would be willing to work on commission for a few years, until we had enough business to generate a salary for me," Todd continued, "I would, of course, want to look at your books..."

"I'll inform Emma. She can show you the books and tell you everything you wish to know," Thomas said with a nod.

Both of Todd's eyebrows went up too high as he stared at Thomas. "Emma?" Todd repeated, surprised once again at Thomas' use of her given name, but even more surprised at the connotation. "What has Emma Fitzsimmons to do with the books for Wellingham Imports?"

Thomas dropped his head into his hands and thought for a moment. "You must not tell anyone what I'm about to say," Thomas said as he turned to Todd and regarded him for moment longer. "Miss Emma is not my household bookkeeper. I hired her to audit my company's books," he stated carefully. "But my clerks don't know, and I wish to keep it that way," he added with a nod. "She should complete the audit in a month or two."

Staring at Thomas, Todd crossed his arms and considered his friend's words, his eyes losing their focus and his face taking on a frown. "She lied to me," he said quietly, sadness in his voice.

"Because she *had* to, Todd," Thomas replied emphatically. "Before we had that meeting at my house, I told her if anyone asked what she was doing there, she was to say she was working on my household accounts. No one was to know about the audit," he explained. "Please, don't think ill of her."

Todd shrugged, murmuring, "Not that I could think ill of her.

But why Miss Emma?" he asked. "Why did you hire *her* to be your auditor?"

Thomas sighed as he spread his hands in front of him. "Her professor mentioned her when I was guest lecturing for him, and then Sir William recommended her when I asked him about an audit last February," he said casually. "And, as it happens, she owns some stock in my company," he added with a shrug, hoping he had appeased Todd with the explanation.

But Todd was lost in thought as he was remembering something else. "Would she have agreed to marry me, do you suppose, had I asked her? If I had never met my Deborah, of course," Todd asked, the frown disappearing from his face.

Startled by the change of subject, Thomas recalled his conversation with Emma the prior Monday morning. "Yes, she would have," he replied with a nod. "But she is, I believe, even more happy you are marrying her friend, since she believes you are perfectly suited to one another," he added quickly, hoping Todd wouldn't feel guilty for having asked Deborah instead of Emma.

Todd smiled then. "I think I will accept your offer after I am married and returned from my honeymoon," he said wistfully. "But I wish to discuss this with Deborah," he added, his smile growing.

Surprised by the comment, Thomas held up a finger. "If I may, why would you discuss your position with your intended?" he asked, a frown appearing on his face. "Can you really expect her to understand what you do for an occupation?"

Not at all surprised by Thomas' comment, Todd leaned back in his chair. "She already does," he replied with a faraway look. "Women are far more clever than we give them credit for, Thomas," he added as he noted the stunned look on his friend's face. "And speaking of women, let's go shop for jewelry, shall we?" he suggested lightly.

Thomas regarded Todd with a quizzical stare. "Perhaps it is because I'm still recovering somewhat from my illness, but are our conversations usually as jumbled as those we are having today?"

"No," Todd stated firmly. "They're usually much more... logical," Todd said with a nod as he stood up. "But we haven't discussed a single logical topic this entire day," he said simply. "And I don't believe you have recovered sufficiently from your illness to be discussing business matters," he added as he led his friend to the vestibule and out the front door.

Once in the Wellingham carriage, the two headed for the goldsmith shops in Ludgate Hill. Their shopping trip would have been a much more enjoyable experience had a certain individual not made his presence known. An odd man, dressed in a black cape coat and a very worn top hat, kept yelling "Freak!" and "You are too tall! You freak!" every time he caught sight of them leaving a shop. Although Todd knew the comments were directed at him, he did his best to ignore the insults and simply continued his shopping excursion.

And much later that afternoon, when Todd returned to Grace Park, he sat down in the study and wrote down the wedding vows as best as he could remember them.

CHAPTER 37
A WOMAN GOES ON A QUEST

June 18, 1802, Horse Guards

Deborah White left the Home for Unwed Mothers only an hour after her arrival. With no impending births and at Mrs. Dawes' insistence, Deborah decided to use her time off to find out more about her future husband's family. She had grilled the midwife for nearly ten minutes about Todd Vandermeer's parents, hoping to learn more so she might find some of his family members before the wedding.

"I can tell you their names, and I can tell you where his father died, but I don't know anythin' more," Mrs. Dawes stated, irritation evident in her voice. They were in the delivery room where Mrs. Dawes was busy unpacking medical supplies.

"So, Mr. Vandermeer knows his parent's names, then?" Deborah countered. Why hadn't he mentioned them in their evening conversations about his childhood? She lifted several bottles and placed them on a shelf, careful to leave them close to the front edge so Mrs. Dawes could reach them.

She regarded her left arm for a moment, remembering the way Todd had stroked it the night before, calming her fear and then holding her against his nude body. She had felt as much fear due to the storm as she had felt when she climbed into his bed. Not knowing how he would react to her sudden appearance, or what he might think of her when he realized her nakedness, she considered returning to her room in shame. But his concern and whispered gentling were genuine, his loving words a comfort to her trembling body.

I love him, she had admitted to herself when she had awakened at dawn to find him still holding her, his lips pressed against her head.

"No, he does not," Mrs. Dawes replied. At Deborah's expression of surprise, she added, "He never asked."

Dumbfounded, Deborah stared at her mentor. "How is it you didn't tell him? He deserves to know from whence he came!" she exclaimed, shocked at Mrs. Dawes' statement. *How could the woman withhold such information from her charge?*

"When he wants to know, he'll ask me," the older woman replied in a quiet voice, her face softening. "'Tis not my place to be telling him things he may not wish to know," she added. She tore open another pasteboard box. When she saw from Deborah's expression that she wasn't convinced, Mrs. Dawes took a deep breath and said, "Mr. Vandermeer made it in this world on his own, child. He didn't rely on his name or the good graces of his relatives to earn his way. He should be proud of himself, and," she paused to take another breath. "And you should be happy he knew enough to want to marry you," she added with a firm nod.

Deborah sat down—hard—on the only chair in the room. "I think... no, I'm quite sure he believes his mother was a prostitute," she said quietly. "And that he was born in a place much like this. Is that much true?"

Mrs. Dawes snorted and nearly dropped a box of bandages. "*What?*" she replied in disbelief as she turned to face Deborah. "Adelyn Tennison was no lady of the evening, I can assure you of that," she stated in a hoarse whisper. "She was a real lady. A very dignified lady. She was a cousin of an earl and an officer's wife, if you must know," the midwife added in a louder voice. "And I delivered Mr. Vandermeer when I worked at hospital!"

Eyebrows raised in surprise at the midwife's outburst, Deborah held her breath and sat up straight. "Adelyn Tennison," she repeated softly. "And his father? What was his name?" she asked as she leaned forward.

Rolling her eyes, Mrs. Dawes moved to kneel next to Deborah. "Colonel William Vandermeer. He was an officer in King George's Army, but he died at the Battle of Bunker Hill in Boston during the war there," she stated evenly. "Seventeen-seventy-five, I believe. Meanwhile, the colonel's young wife..."

"Adelyn Tennison?" Deborah interrupted, wanting to know more.

Mrs. Dawes nodded. "She gave birth to their son and then died a few weeks later." The midwife paused and her face darkened. "I think she died of a broken heart, she did. When she learned of her husband's fate, she just gave up and died," she said softly. "I don't think I have ever seen a woman so distraught at the death of a husband. I know *I* certainly was not," she added with a sad sigh.

Mrs. Dawes related what she knew of Adelyn Vandermeer and then suggested Deborah visit the War Office in Whitehall. "If any place in the world has a record of Colonel William Vandermeer's service in the British Army, it will be Horse Guards," she stated emphatically. Sighing loudly, she stood up to return to her unpacking but paused mid-step. "And Deborah," she added, "Has he asked you how you came to be here at the Home?"

Swallowing hard, Deborah shook her head. "He has not asked. And I have only told him I work here as a midwife," she admitted, understanding the woman's point.

Mrs. Dawes made a 'tsk' sound and leaned against the counter. "He'll be expecting a virgin in his marriage bed, then," she whispered sadly. "Your secret is safe with me, lass. If you do na' tell him and you do na' want him to know the truth, then I can give you a glass vile with a cork and you can see the butcher about some pig's blood," she suggested, her voice very quiet. At Deborah's shocked expression, she added, "It has worked on men a might bit smarter than Mr. Vandermeer, I'm sure."

Shoulders slumping, Deborah considered the older woman's offer. Here she was, engaged to a man who believed he was born to a prostitute and about to marry a woman whom he believed was a virgin. *I am not a harlot, though*, she thought to herself. *I didn't willingly give away my maidenhood. And damn to hell the man that took it!*

She didn't once consider the irony of her situation. For, if she had never had a reason to come to the Home for Unwed Mothers, she never would have met Todd Vandermeer.

Deborah made her way down Newport Street, dreading the long walk to Whitehall and thinking she should have brought along one of the girls from the Home as a companion. Although she had applied salve to her knees just a few hours earlier, she knew the pain would return before she could find her way back to the Home. A yellow bounder paused on its way after dropping off a passenger, and the driver called out to her. "Need a ride toward the west, Long Meg?"

She paused in mid-step, flinching at the driver's slang but curious as to the cost of such a ride in the mid-morning. She knew the drivers could charge much more on busy afternoons and Saturdays. "How much, short sir, to Horse Guards?" she asked in a teasing voice, surprised at how easy it was to respond to the driver's offer.

The driver smiled and secured the reins. "I must be going to Whitehall to pick up a fare. Come along. I'll take you for a pence." He dismounted and opened the door for her. "I'll go as quickly as traffic will allow," he added as he motioned for her to enter.

Hesitating only a moment, Deborah got into the bounder and gave the driver a coin. He lived up to his promise of going fast. The bounder bounced along on the cobblestone streets as they made their way southeast toward St. James Park. Deborah was barely out of the cab when several gentlemen took her place in the bounder and the driver called out his thanks.

When Deborah glanced up and down the street to get her bearings, she found she stood directly across the street from the War Office. Staring at the foreboding structure, her resolve began to fade. With so little information to begin her search, she was unsure if anyone in the War Office would be able to help, or even if she would be allowed to enter the building.

"Would you care for an escort across the street?" a man's voice sounded behind her.

She whirled to find an older uniformed man in a powdered wig, his eyes showing his surprise at her height. He held his left arm out as if expecting her to take it without question. "Yes, thank you, sir," Deborah replied as she curtsied and hesitantly put her arm into his.

"Do you have an appointment at Horse Guards, miss...?" he asked, holding the question so as to discover her name.

"White," Deborah replied with a nod. "I don't have an appointment, sir. Will I be able to make one, do you suppose?" she asked, hoping the man could direct her to the correct department or office for such appointments.

The man smiled. "Colonel Collins, at your service, Miss White," he said quickly. "What is it you seek?" he added as they crossed the busy street and made their way to the front doors of the War Office. Uniformed guards stood on either side of the entry, their guns held in one gloved hand and supported against their shoulders.

"I seek information about my betrothed's late father," Deborah replied hopefully, watching the colonel's face for his reaction.

The man instead returned a salute as a man in uniform stepped out of the building and saluted first. The colonel's expression showed a hint of disappointment. "Do you know anything about this man? Name, rank, regiment, place of service?" he asked as a guard held a door open for them.

"Colonel William Vandermeer died in 1775 at the Battle of Bunker Hill in Boston," Deborah recited as she entered the War Office in front of the colonel. When she stepped aside to allow the colonel to come along side her, she saw a pained expression cross his face.

"We lost nearly every officer in that campaign," he said quietly, his voice matching his expression. "Come. I will escort you to the Records Department," he offered as he held out his left arm for her.

Deborah took his arm again and asked, "Were you there? At Bunker Hill, I mean?"

The officer shook his head, a frown still darkening his face. "No. I was in Jamaica at the time," he replied simply. "My first assignment out of Officer's School," he added. They walked in silence through the massive structure, passing dozens of soldiers and officers and clerks and civilians as they made their way. "If I may ask, how is it you are the one seeking information and not your betrothed?" the colonel asked, his eyebrows drawn together.

Sighing, Deborah shook her head and wondered how to respond. "He... He doesn't know anything about his mother and father. He was an orphan, you see. I'm privy to information supplied by the midwife who delivered him. She knew the mother and not much more," Deborah explained quickly, sure the colonel thought her search a waste of time.

"Do you have reason to believe the information provided by this midwife is accurate?" Colonel Collins asked as they made their way down a wide corridor. His boot heels clicked loudly on the marble floor.

"I do, indeed. I work for her and have for several years," Deborah replied.

"And is your betrothed at least as tall as you are, Miss White?"

he asked with a teasing grin on his face. "If you don't mind me asking."

Deborah blushed and didn't suppress her smile. "Indeed. He is at least a half a head taller than I am," she replied happily. "I don't think he would have noticed me if I was not this tall," she added with a grin.

The colonel's eyebrows shot up to the line of his wig. "He's a very lucky man," he said as he patted her arm with his free hand. "I have a daughter a year or two younger than you. She attended school over at Warwick's until she met a young officer in May. Went off and eloped with the man the last week of school, she did," he commented, his face showing his disappointment. "I cannot say I was pleased with her choice of a military man."

Noticing the colonel's expression, Deborah angled her head to one side. "She must have married for love, then," she offered carefully. "I hope you have given her your blessing?"

Colonel Collins nodded in agreement. "I did, but I must admit, I did so reluctantly. I actually arranged for her to marry the son of one of my best friends, but I've not heard from the Wellingham family in many years, and now I'm led to believe his son wouldn't be happy with my daughter. I know she wouldn't have been happy with a man unless she felt affection for him."

Deborah nodded her understanding. "He was a man of some wealth then?" she half-questioned, thinking arranged marriages were more common among the aristocracy and the wealthy.

"Heavens, no," the colonel replied, shaking his head from side to side. "Which is another reason why I know my daughter wouldn't have been happy with him," he added with a wink. "Here we are," Colonel Collins announced as they approached a set of large wood-paneled, double doors. The engraved plaque next to the entry read, 'British Army Records'. A smaller plaque listed several department names in a long column.

"Oh, Colonel Collins," Deborah breathed as she allowed the colonel to escort her up to the door. "I couldn't have possibly found this without your assistance. You have been so kind," she said.

The colonel nodded in return. "Please believe me when I say it has been my pleasure," he replied with a smile. "I must warn you, Miss White, it could take some time to find what you're seeking," he stated evenly. "We do our best, but in war, not every man lost can be found again."

Deborah's face fell, but she nodded her understanding. "Thank you, Colonel Collins. I am in your debt," she said as she passed through the door he held open for her. A uniformed clerk stood up from a messy desk and hurried to a long counter just inside the doors.

"Sergeant, see to this woman's request at your soonest," Col. Collins ordered before he closed the door behind him and made his way to his own office.

The sergeant immediately turned his attention to Deborah, nodding in response to her curtsy. "Whose record do you seek, miss?" he asked smartly.

Although it did take more than two hours for the sergeant to find the information about Colonel William Vandermeer, Deborah knew it was worth every minute of waiting when he returned with not just a written record of his service in the British Army, but a box of effects owned by the late colonel.

Signing the receipt for the items, Deborah thanked the sergeant more than a few times and left with the small wooden box. And, as she would later regret, she happily walked the entire distance back to the Home for Unwed Mothers.

CHAPTER 38
A LOVE NOT LOST

*J*une *18, 1802, Great West Road*

As Emma and Mr. Larsen rode toward London that Friday evening, they passed the Wellingham carriage as it headed for Woodscastle. Mr. Allen tipped his hat and bade them a good evening while Thomas slept soundly in the back of the chaise. Still suffering from his illness, Thomas was covered with a blanket, and his hat threatened to fall off his head with every bump of the carriage ride. Emma quietly told Mr. Allen to avoid as many ruts as possible. The downpour had made the road nearly impassible in some spots.

Once in town, she marveled at how much better London looked after a cleansing rain. The heady fragrance of lilac filled the air as the bushes were in bloom throughout the town. Despite it being nearly seven o'clock, the sun was still high in the western sky. She approached her neighborhood while humming happily. Her friends would soon be married, the Home for Unwed Mothers was preparing its move into the Cooper Hotel, and despite dealing with sick servants and Christiana the day before, her work for Wellingham was proceeding on schedule.

As she bade farewell to Mr. Larsen, who said he would stop for an ale before returning to Woodscastle, she happened to glance up Kingly Street on her way to the mews. A bundle of white seemed to be leaning against one of the front doors on the east side of the street—her front door, she realized as she continued to stare and nearly walked her horse onto a yard.

Halting her mount, Emma leaned to one side to get a better look, and then simply redirected her bay to trot to her townhouse. It took a long moment before she realized the bundle was Deborah, dressed in Emma's white dinner gown and curled up into a sobbing ball. Some of the pins in her hair were askew, and long locks of brunette hair hung down around her face.

"Oh, my God," an alarmed Emma murmured as she nearly fell off her horse in her haste to dismount. Quickly hobbling the horse, she ran to Deborah's side, kneeling down to take the woman's face in her hands. "Deborah, what has happened?" she asked, breathless. "What's wrong?" She took the woman in her arms and cradled her as best she could. "Are you hurt?"

Once Deborah finally realized it was Emma who held her, she let out a sob. Eyes filled with tears, she couldn't see, and her knees pained her from all the walking she had done that afternoon. "I have lost him," she finally managed to say between sobs. Her fingers clutched the white dinner gown she wore, trembling as if they were cold.

Emma gasped and wondered what could have happened. "Can you stand?" she asked as she reached into her reticule for her key and unlocked the door.

Emma helped get Deborah to her feet. Although the woman could barely walk due to the pain in her knees, she leaned against Emma and hobbled toward the parlor. Emma did her best not to drop Deborah onto the settee but guided her down until she was sitting somewhat upright.

Hurrying back to the front door, Emma looked out to see the horse munching on the flowers in the pot by the door. Deciding Georgie wouldn't go far, she closed the door and rushed back to Deborah's side. "Tell me what has happened. Tell me... tell me *every-thing*," she ordered as she sat next to Deborah and pulled her into a hug.

Sniffling, Deborah sat up and whispered, "I didn't know what to do... or where to go. I just couldn't tell him... I cannot... Now that I know..." New tears streamed down her face, and sobs racked her body.

Emma frowned. *Now that I know?* "Pray tell, what *exactly* happened?'

Deborah sniffled. "I returned to Grace Park from the War

Office. Todd wasn't yet there," she said evenly, scrubbing her face with her hands.

Shaking her head, Emma repeated, "The War Office? Whatever in the world were you doing *there?*" she asked in confusion.

Stifling a sob, Deborah told her of her conversation with Mrs. Dawes and how she came to be in possession of Col. William Vandermeer's personal effects. "I took the box up to my room. I was planning to give it to Todd as a wedding present, you see. After I changed into this gown, I saw from my window that Todd and Mr. Wellingham had returned from town. They must have been shopping, for the carriage was quite full of parcels. I heard the gentlemen bid their farewells, and I saw Mr. Wellingham's carriage leave. And when I heard Todd at the front door, I hurried downstairs to greet him. He was in very good spirits. He even kissed me in front of Winston!" she whispered in shock. "And whilst we were in the parlor, Winston brought three samples of wedding cake for me to try. The cook had made them earlier in the day, but Todd wanted me to taste them and help him choose which one to have for our wedding." Deborah paused a moment, realizing she had just spoken the word 'wedding'.

She was about to burst into tears again when Emma said, "And, so you tried them all and chose your favorite, and then..."

Deborah swallowed hard to stave off the tears and continued, "And then, whilst we were waiting for dinner..." She stopped as she gasped for air. "I have encouraged him to eat dinner earlier since I usually must be back to Mrs. Dawes' before ten o'clock... and I was about to put salve on his knees... and he was telling me about a colleague at his work," she continued, once again sobbing.

Emma took a deep breath. "Go on."

"When Todd—Mr. Vandermeer—told the man that I worked at the Home for Unwed Mothers, the man implied I must be a harlot."

Mortified, Emma sat back. "How rude!" she whispered, surprised any colleague of Todd's would put voice to such an opinion. She had always supposed the men of the East India Company to be gentlemen of good breeding.

"So, Todd punched him. Apparently he broke the man's nose," she said with a glimmer of a smile.

"Bully for him, I say," Emma replied, smiling as she imagined Todd Vandermeer throwing the punch. *He will make a loyal husband,* she thought with satisfaction.

"But the man's comment must have weighed on him, because he asked me from whence I came, and after I told him about my family's home in Cheapside, he asked how I came to be at the Home for Unwed Mothers," she explained. "It was all just in conversation, but ...," and she resumed crying, unable to say what she feared most.

Emma slumped into the settee, knowing Deborah wouldn't have been able to tell Todd about the rape. "So, what *did* you tell him?"

Deborah shook her head slowly. "I didn't. Emma, I panicked. I left Grace Park. I ran here because I didn't know where else to go," she said as she sniffled quietly.

Emma pulled her close and stroked her hair. "Do you love him, Deborah?"

Deborah nodded and wiped away tears with her long fingers. "You know I do, Emma. With all my heart."

Emma nodded and hugged her quickly. "He loves you, Deborah. You will be together. I promise. I'm sure he is worried sick about you this very moment. But I need to know from you..." She thought for a moment about how not to break the girl's trust. Todd deserved to know what happened to Deborah, and Emma was sure it wouldn't change his feelings for her friend. "I may have to tell him what happened to you... but I promised you I would tell no one," she said, her frustration evident as she regarded her friend.

"Oh, Emma," Deborah whimpered as she shook her head.

"If you have lost him as you've said, it won't matter," she offered in a stern voice. "But I believe Mr. Vandermeer to be an understanding man. It cannot hurt to tell him," she quietly assured Deborah, her voice softening. "And it will always weigh heavily on you for the rest of your days should you decide to keep the truth from him."

Deborah finally nodded, a sob shaking her entire body. "You... you may tell him," she agreed in a whisper.

Emma sighed and nodded as she regarded her friend. "Now, I'm going to fetch you some water, and then I will be gone for a time," Emma said as she hurried out to the kitchen. When she returned with a glass of water, she found Deborah crying quietly in one corner of the settee. "It will be all right. I promise," Emma said as she rubbed Deborah's arm. Then she rushed off to find Mr. Vandermeer.

Her horse, having devoured most of the flowers from one of her pots, was working her way through her neighbor's flower pot when she mounted her and took off for the Vandermeer mansion.

Knowing Todd, she figured he might try to find Deborah at the Home, and failing to find her there, he might consider going back to Grace Park or possibly to Emma's townhouse.

Emma made sure to ride the main streets to Cavendish Square just in case he was on his way to her townhouse. Weaving her way in between carriages and other riders, Emma made it to the mansion in less than fifteen minutes. A groom hurried out to meet her as she dismounted. Breathless, Emma asked, "Is Mr. Vandermeer here?"

The groom nodded as he took the reins from her. "He's only just returned, but he is very... *upset*, miss."

Emma took a deep breath. "No doubt," she replied with a nod. She thanked him and climbed the steps to the front door. Ignoring the brass knocker, she banged on the door with her fist. "I must speak with Mr. Vandermeer," she said even before Winston, a relieved look on his face, could greet her.

Emma spotted Todd in the grand hall beyond the vestibule, leaning on two canes and looking miserable. He was dressed in breeches and a shirt, but wore no cravat, waistcoat or tailcoat.

Winston stepped aside and motioned for her to enter. "Miss Fitzsimmons, I fear I may be at fault here," he started to say when he noticed Emma's attention wasn't on him. "I brought up a topic with my master this morning, and it made him rather cross," he started to say, but stopped speaking when he realized his master was behind him.

If only I had continued the comment I made about Miss White earlier, he thought. Mr. Vandermeer had undoubtedly come to the same conclusion he had initially. It was only after Winston's afternoon with Mrs. Dawes that he had discovered Miss White's residence at the Home wasn't because she had been a pregnant prostitute. Now that he knew the nature of her employment there, he chastised himself for ever thinking she could have been one of London's lightskirts.

Emma gave the butler a cursory nod. "None of this is your doing, Winston, I assure you," she whispered as she passed him. She hurried to Todd, and in a most improper move, put her arms around his chest and hugged him hard.

"Emma, I have... I have lost her," Todd said in a quiet, desperate voice as he struggled to stay standing. Emma moved her shoulder so it was under his arm and allowed him to lean on her as they made their way to the parlor. "I must have offended her, but I'm not sure what I said to cause her to leave me," he said. "Whatever do I do?"

"Shh," Emma replied as she helped him to sit in one of the tall chairs. "You've not lost her, Mr. Vandermeer. She is at my town-house, and she is just as miserable as you are," Emma explained as she knelt down in front of him. "Where is your salve?" she demanded quietly, holding out her palm.

Todd gave a sigh of relief at the news of Deborah but then frowned as Emma knelt down in front of him. He reached into his pocket and pulled out the jar. "Deborah was just about to put it on when..." He stopped and swallowed, trying hard to breathe while a sob wracked his body.

"She told me," Emma replied. "And you obviously didn't put any on her, because she can barely walk," Emma accused with a raised eyebrow.

His face coloring to a deep scarlet, Todd swallowed and looked away. "'Tis true," he admitted unhappily. "I don't usually have to put it on her until after dinner," he said sadly as he looked away from Emma's glare. "But I was out shopping this afternoon with Mr. Wellingham, and I could barely walk when I returned, and she had walked a great distance on some errand for Mrs. Dawes."

Emma at first wondered why Mrs. Dawes would send Deborah on an errand that required walking a long distance, but then remembered Deborah's mention of her trip to the War Office. Knowing Deborah as she did, she realized the girl had probably walked both ways. "I have been given permission by Deborah to tell you something I promised never to tell anyone," Emma began carefully, occasionally glancing up at the importer as she massaged the ointment into his joint.

"It matters not to me if she was a prostitute... I love her," Todd replied indignantly.

Mortified Todd would think such a thing of her friend, Emma gasped and slapped him hard across the knee with her open hand.

Stunned at Emma's reaction and now in greater pain due to the impact of her slap, Todd howled and struggled to catch his breath. "Wh...?" he started to say in surprise and then noticed Emma's angry expression.

"How *dare* you?" she replied in a hoarse whisper, wondering how he of all people could have come to such a conclusion. She studied Todd's facial expression and then remembered Deborah's earlier comments. "Deborah has *never* been a prostitute," she stated, trying to keep her voice down. "She came from a good middle class home in Cheapside, and her only crime was... was being too *tall*," she whispered angrily, aware the butler would probably bring tea at any moment.

Brandy would be a more suitable choice.

Todd leaned forward and gave Emma a quizzical look. "What... what are you saying?"

Emma took a deep breath, still angry with him. In quiet measured tones, she said, "When she was but seventeen, Deborah was walking home from the market when a man told her she was a freak,... and he beat her,... and he raped her." She spat out the last words and paused a moment to take another breath, noticing a different kind of pained expression take over Todd's face. "And, several weeks later, when she discovered she was with child, her parents banished her from their home. *That* is how she ended up at the Home for Unwed Mothers, Mr. Vandermeer," Emma stated harshly as she began applying salve to the other knee, although not quite as gently as she had done with the first one.

Todd pressed his lips together and struggled to catch his breath, thinking of the words Emma had just spoken. *He called her a 'freak'.* "Was he... was he wearing all black?" he asked, remembering the man who had yelled at him earlier that day in Ludgate Hill. "A cape coat? Like some coachmen wear?"

Surprised by the odd question, Emma looked up from his knee and nodded her head. "I... I think so. And old black trousers, I recall her saying," Emma added as she leaned back and studied Todd's reaction, one hand still gripping his knee. "With a badly misshapen hat. Certainly not one of my father's. Do you... know the man?" she whispered in horror, her face darkening again.

"No," he whispered, his voice not sounding at all like his own, but his mind was obviously elsewhere. "I must... I must go to her," he whispered as he shook his head back and forth. "She must know it doesn't make a difference to me," he said in a pleading voice. He grimaced as Emma pressed too hard into the back of his knee. "Miss Emma. What of... what of the child?" he asked between gasps for air. "Deborah has never mentioned a baby. Emma, you must know I would gladly take it as my own."

Emma stopped moving her fingers when she heard his words. Leaning forward, she regarded Todd and saw the remorse and fright in his eyes. "She miscarried when she was but three months along," she whispered as she finally made eye contact with the man that might have been her husband.

Todd scrubbed his face with his hands. "But she has stayed on at the Home all this time?" he asked quietly. He pushed down the legs of his pantaloons and fastened the buttons on the cuffs.

"Yes," Emma replied, sorry she had treated the man so poorly. "You must understand, she had no place else to go. She worked as a scullery maid at first, but Mrs. Dawes realized she could assist with delivering babies and encouraged her to stay on."

Resting his elbows on his knees, Todd reached out with a hand to take one of Emma's. "Is she... is she safe now? Truly, I couldn't bear to lose her," he said in a whisper. "I bought her a wedding ring today. I wanted us to say our vows tonight."

Emma finally allowed a wan smile and nodded. "She will be fine when you tell her what you have just told me. Come now," she said as she stood up. She helped Todd to his feet, although the medicine had already started to take effect.

Grabbing one cane, Todd offered Emma an arm and they hurried to the vestibule. The butler, carrying a tray laden with a tea service, immediately turned around, set the tray down on a table in the grand hall, and rushed to open the front door.

"Keep the tea ready, and let the cook know to delay dinner about an hour. I'll return shortly with Miss White," Todd instructed.

As they walked through the vestibule, Emma had to move closer to Todd in order to avoid several stacks of parcels lining the vestibule.

"Very good, sir," the butler replied as he bowed. "Did you wish to take one of these with you?" he asked as he indicated the packages.

Todd slowed his pace and glanced over the stack. "Capital idea, Winston. Could you bring me that large one there?" he asked as he pointed at a box wrapped with brown paper and tied with string.

"Have you been shopping for Deborah?" Emma asked as the butler brought him the package and then opened the door for them.

Todd nodded and glanced back at the stack. "Yes. Some items are from my shopping trip last week and some are from this morning. They were delivered earlier today. And I picked up a few things for her after Mr. Wellingham and I had luncheon this afternoon," he admitted as he surveyed the scene. For a moment, he thought to choose an additional parcel but instead turned his attention back to Emma. "He said something very interesting about gifts. I was... *inspired*," he said as they left the house.

The groom holding Emma's horse hurried over to the steps as they came out the door.

"We'll need the carriage again, please," Todd said, out of breath. He hoped Mr. Stevenson hadn't been too efficient about unhitching the horses after his earlier ride to Mrs. Dawes'. Turning to Emma, he asked, "Did you ride here?"

Emma nodded as she descended the stairs. "Yes. That's my horse," she acknowledged with a wave in the direction of the Cleveland Bay. "Now, tell me, did you leave anything *in* the shops, or did you just buy it all?" she asked rhetorically, her eyebrow rising into a teasing arch.

"Well, I only bought the longest gowns, I assure you," Todd insisted, his demeanor suggesting he felt the need to be defensive. "And some other garments that the shopkeeper recommended... for... underneath," he added in a whisper as he visibly blushed. "Fripperies. A few bonnets. Some ribbons, of course. And gold earbobs..." When he noticed Emma's look of disbelief, he added, "And shoes, of course. Slippers, really."

Both of Emma's eyebrows arched as she listened to his list of purchases. "Oh, my," she replied in awe, remembering for a moment that she might have been the beneficiary of his largesse. "You are a most generous husband-to-be," she commented lightly, deciding not to inform him his gifts were quite inappropriate given his unmarried state.

"Thank you," he replied with an absent nod. "I really just intended to get her a nightrail, you see," he explained as he glanced in the direction of the carriage house. "I discovered last night she doesn't have one," he started to say when Emma's startled gasp stopped him.

Moving in front of him, Emma stared up at Todd. "'Tis true Deborah doesn't own a proper nightrail, but how did *you* come to know that?" she asked, a flash of anger crossing her face.

Todd straightened and ran a hand through his short hair. "Well, there was all the rain and lightning, you see, and I was sleeping and..."

Emma covered her mouth with her hand, remembering how

frightened Deborah could be of thunder and lightning. "Whatever did she do?" she asked in a whisper as she stepped closer to Todd.

Nervous by what he was about to say, Todd took a deep breath. "She sought refuge. In my bedchamber. Please trust me when I say I didn't think she was real when she appeared next to my bed," he pleaded, unsure of how his story would sound to a proper lady. "I thought her a..." He paused as he recalled Thomas' description of his encounter with his angel the night before. "An angel. And she was cold and shivering, so I bid her to join me under the covers."

Her eyes wide, Emma regarded Todd with a glare of disgust. "You *bedded* Deborah?" she started to say, but Todd put a finger to her mouth before she could complete the accusation. "No! We have not yet said our vows," he countered. "I merely held her in my arms, Emma. Yes, she... she *slept* in my bed, but you must believe me, I only allowed her in my bed to provide comfort," he said in a whisper. "And it was a most remarkable evening, for I've never felt so loved or been so in love as I was when her trembling stopped, and she fell asleep in my arms," he explained quietly, his eyes taking on a faraway look as he described the scene from the night before. "You cannot tell me what I did was wrong."

Emma's expression softened as she considered Todd's confession. "She's terribly frightened of lightning," Emma admitted quietly, nodding as she said so. "But when you saw her in your bedchamber like that, you must have thought the worst of her," she murmured sadly. "'Tis no wonder you would believe her to be a harlot, but what must you have thought of me? I introduced you!"

Sighing loudly, Todd shook his head. "Actually, that particular thought didn't cross my mind at all, Miss Fitzsimmons," he said quietly. "I assure you I have had but one ill thought of you, and it had nothing to do with Deborah," he added as he continued to shake his head.

Taking a step back as if she had been slapped, Emma swallowed hard. "What... whatever did I do to earn your ill thought?" she started to ask, an expression of hurt crossing her face.

Todd held up a hand. "It wasn't anything *you* did, I assure you. It's your damned employer," he stated quickly. Leaning on his cane, he regarded Emma with a grin. "You are a remarkable woman, Miss Fitzsimmons," he said as the coachman pulled up driving a large chaise, Emma's horse tethered to the back. "Thomas is only beginning to realize how fortunate he is."

Blushing, Emma shook her head. "Whatever do you mean? What did *he* do?" she added, completely confused by Todd's comments.

Todd held out his hand to assist her into the chaise and climbed in behind her. "Emma," he addressed her with a nod. "You have played matchmaker on my behalf. Now I shall do the same for you," he stated evenly as he moved to take the seat on the same side of the carriage as Emma.

Stunned, Emma sat down and stared open-mouthed at the importer. He finally turned and looked at her. "You do... feel affection for him, do you not?" he asked carefully.

"I am his *employee*," Emma replied, thinking this sounded very similar to a discussion she'd had the week before. "I cannot very well be working for him... and feeling affection for him," she argued. Realizing she had, indeed, had this discussion with Christiana the week before, she gasped. "Have you been speaking with Miss Wellingham about this?" she accused, her brows furrowed.

Todd suppressed a smile and shook his head. "I know I'm not the only one who believes you two would make a handsome couple." Finally grinning, he leaned toward Emma. "But I know his illness opened his eyes," he teased in a whisper.

"How *dare* you?" Emma huffed as she reached out to slap the man across the face.

Todd held out his arm to block the blow and gently restrained her hand. "Your passion for your employer is quite evident, Miss Emma," he accused, his smile widening.

Emma gasped and relaxed her arm, very aware of her hand being held by the man who might have proposed to her. "What... whatever did he tell you?"

Todd took her hand and placed it on his arm. "He said you were the best nursemaid he ever had," he replied quietly, now more amused and even more curious as to what could have happened at Woodscastle the night before. "You must know, Thomas really believed he was going to meet his Maker."

Deciding to be demure, Emma replied simply, "Oh. 'Tis true." She realized she had overreacted to his earlier comment and wondered what Todd thought of her now. After a moment, though, she remembered what had made her slap Todd's knee in the first place. "How did you come to believe Deborah was a prostitute?" she asked in a whisper.

Todd jerked his head back, surprised by the question. He regarded Emma for a moment as his amused expression was replaced with a darker frown. "It made sense at the time, I suppose," he replied, now embarrassed to have come to the conclusion. "I was an orphan, you see, and, over the years, I came to believe I was probably born to a prostitute in a facility much like the one at which Deborah works," he said quietly.

Emma knit her brows together and stared at Todd. "Your mother was not a prostitute," she said in a hoarse whisper, surprised he could think such a thing.

Stunned, Todd half-turned in the seat. "How... how do *you* know this about my mother?" he asked, his amazement evident in the waning light.

"Mrs. Dawes told me about you when I worked at the Home," she replied.

How could he not know anything about his mother when Mrs. Dawes was her midwife? Wasn't that why he was a patron of her Home for Unwed Mothers?

"She was your mother's midwife when you were born at hospital." When Todd still looked stunned, Emma asked, "Isn't Mrs. Dawes the reason you have been a patron of her facility all these years?"

Nodding his head, Todd replied, "Well, to some degree, yes. I have known her all my life, but... who was my mother if not a prostitute?"

Emma recalled Deborah's story from earlier. "Deborah should really be sharing this news, since it was she who discovered it today," Emma responded. "But I suppose it couldn't hurt to at least give you some of the information."

Todd inhaled sharply. "If you know something of my mother, please tell me," he begged.

"She was the young widow of an officer in King George's Army. Apparently your father was killed during one of the early battles in the Colonies," Emma explained quickly. "In Boston." As she studied the changing expressions on Todd's face, she asked, "Didn't you know any of this?"

Shaking his head in disbelief, he murmured, "No. I... I know nothing of my parents."

Emma pondered what her information must have meant to the man. Incredulous, she asked, "Mrs. Dawes never told you?"

Todd shook his head as he stared at the passing carriages and their riders, a wave of relief coupled with surprise washing over him.

I am not a bastard, he thought happily.

"I... I never asked," he said before finally turning his gaze back to Emma.

"You really must speak with Mrs. Dawes, then," Emma suggested in earnest. "I'm sure she was responsible for placing you into one of the better orphanages when she could no longer care for you," she added, curious as to what other history the man might have invented for himself.

Frowning, Todd seemed afraid to ask about his mother, but finally decided he could know the truth. "Do you know what happened to her then?" he asked quietly, swallowing hard.

"I don't know the details. But I'm sure Mrs. Dawes does," she added. Perhaps Deborah would know more than she let on.

Todd sat shaking his head. "I'm the son of an army officer," he said quietly. His face lit up. "I can tell Deborah she is marrying the son of an army officer," he stated excitedly.

Emma was about to say, "She already knows," when the chaise stopped in front of her townhouse.

Todd grabbed his package, jumped out of the chaise and was through the front door before Emma could even stand up.

Pausing at the door to the parlor, Todd took in the sight of Deborah as she stood in front of the settee. Despite her red-rimmed eyes and disheveled gown, Todd thought she was the most beautiful sight he could possibly behold. She curtsied but didn't make eye contact with him as he rushed to her.

Dropping the parcel onto the table in front of the settee, he took her in his arms and hugged her hard against his body. "This past hour has brought me news that is both painful and happy," he whispered, breathless. He kissed her then, his lips pressed against hers in an urgent, forceful kiss as he held her head in one hand.

When at last he pulled away, he whispered, "I'm truly sorry for what happened to you. Soon you'll speak of it with me, but not this evening. I would be very blessed if you'll agree to be my wife. And you must never again leave me as you did this evening," he added as he pulled her down onto the settee, his expression finally softening as he kissed the back of her hand.

Deborah stared at him, stunned at the mix of sorrow and happiness he exhibited. "I will marry you, of course," she murmured.

"Leave you, I will not. I promise," she whispered back as she realized the level of his commitment to her.

The coachman assisted Emma out of the carriage. "Mr. Vandermeer will be inside for a bit. There is a mews just behind these townhouses... just behind this building," Emma said to Mr. Stevenson. "Could you please take my horse there?" she implored, not wanting the beast to eat any more of the flora in front of her townhouse.

"Of course, miss," the coachman replied with a bow. "It would be my honor."

Emma angled her head and thanked the man. Hurrying into the house, she found Todd cradling his beloved bride-to-be and happily sharing his good news. Deborah had spent some time cleaning up, and her hair looked freshly pinned into place. The package lay unopened on the table in front of them, but Deborah didn't seem to notice it as she gazed at Todd.

"I brought you something," he said as he reached over to pick up the package. They nearly fell off the settee as he repositioned her so they were sitting next to one another.

Deborah squeezed the brown paper wrapping and finally untied the string that held it together. Yards of royal blue satin tumbled out around her.

"I would be very honored if you were to wear it for dinner this evening," Todd said as he leaned over and kissed her temple.

Awestruck, Deborah stared at Todd. "I'll return in just a few moments," she said as she gathered the fabric into her arms. Ecstatic, she hurried up the steps as quickly as she could, glad to finally be able to wear something other than Emma's white dinner gown.

She laid out the gown on Emma's bed and spent a moment admiring the cut and the fabric before finally pulling it over her head. The blue gown was the most elegant dress she had ever worn, long enough to cover her ankles and low enough to show off her décolletage and the tops of her shoulders. Feeling very regal, she slowly descended the stairs as Emma came from the kitchen with tea and biscuits.

"Oh, Miss White," Emma breathed as she nearly dropped the tea tray. "You are incandescent," she stated in disbelief as she looked up the staircase. There was no evidence the tall woman had spent the evening crying or that her hair had been in disarray only an hour earlier.

"Thank you, Emma. I don't know what I would have done without you," Deborah replied.

Emma rolled her eyes as she regarded Deborah. "You two would have been fine. But Deborah," she said before her friend could finish her descent. "I told Mr. Vandermeer what happened. And it doesn't matter to him," she whispered.

Deborah nodded her understanding. "Thank you, Emma," she said again as she continued down the stairs.

"Now, go show Mr. Vandermeer," Emma said as she nodded toward the parlor.

But Todd was already watching Deborah as he leaned against the parlor doorway, his arms crossed and a mischievous smile on his lips. "Emma," he announced as he unfolded his arms, "If I may call you that."

"You can," Emma nodded with a grin.

"Mrs. Vandermeer, if I may call you that," he said to Deborah, a smirk on his face as he gave her a nod.

Mrs. Vandermeer? "You may," Deborah grinned as her shoulders nearly reached her ears. She wasn't about to deny him his fun.

"Mrs. Vandermeer and I are going to take our leave of you now to go to our home to have dinner. We would be most honored if you could join us," he offered graciously. The invitation didn't even sound like an afterthought.

Emma smiled broadly. "Thank you for your offer, Mr. Vandermeer, but I believe I'm staying in for dinner this evening," she replied, knowing she had no gowns as elegant as the one Deborah wore. "Besides, Todd,... if I may call you that," she added playfully.

The broker gave her a grin. "You may," he replied with an enthusiastic nod.

"I do believe you'll be spending your evening watching your bride whilst she tries on all her new clothes," Emma hinted as she batted her eyelashes. "And then you shall return here at eleven in the morning for breakfast and then we shall all go shopping."

Todd blushed and Deborah looked surprised. "New clothes?" she repeated. "Shopping?"

He nodded to Emma. "You're next," he said as he offered his arm to his future bride and led her toward the front door.

"If you would," Emma said as he indicated the tea tray. "Could you please give these biscuits to your driver? He has been most helpful this evening." She wrapped several of the biscuits in a linen napkin and handed the bundle to Todd.

"As have you," he replied with a nod as he regarded the bundle of biscuits. "Good night, Emma," he said as he escorted Deborah through the front door and then closed it.

"Good night, you two," Emma said with a happy sigh.

And I will see you both in the morning.

CHAPTER 39
LOST IN LOVE

*J*une 18, 1802, *Kingly Street*

During the carriage ride back to Grace Park, Todd held his beloved as close as he could and told her the news about his parents. Deborah listened intently and filled in details where he didn't include them or corrected him when he supposed incorrectly.

"Your mother didn't die during childbirth," Deborah explained gently, her hand closing over the top of his. "She died a few weeks after you were born... some kind of illness," she replied when he asked if she knew what happened to his mother. "And then Mrs. Dawes and some other nurses arranged for a wet nurse and took care of you at hospital until you were weaned."

Even though he expected his mother no longer lived, Todd still felt a pang when he heard Deborah's words. "So, you've known about my parents all along?" he asked quietly, his face showing confusion. "And I have known nothing."

Although he felt sadness over his parents' fate, it came with a profound sense of relief. Coupled with meeting the love of his life, Todd Vandermeer found himself in a state of contentment. He sighed as the chaise turned into Margaret Street.

Deborah angled her head so she could better see him and said, "Mrs. Dawes told me about you when I first started working at the Home. You were one of her first live births, so she was rather... *protective* of you."

Todd kissed Deborah's hair. "I do consider her my mother sometimes," he murmured, a smile finally emerging. *My mother may marry my butler*, he thought with amusement.

Deborah moved her head up onto Todd's shoulder and noticed his lighter mood. "We always thought you donated money to the Home because you knew she had delivered you and taken care of you," Deborah said quietly. Sitting up straighter, she eyed him for a moment, her expression one of wonder. "So, if you didn't know, then why *did* you become a patron of the Home?"

Todd shrugged a shoulder. "Until this very evening, I believed I was born in a facility much like Mrs. Dawes' place. Sometime during my youth... I don't remember just when or even why... I decided my mother must have been a lady of the night and that was why I ended up in an orphanage," he explained. He rolled his eyes when he decided his suppositions were founded on very little information. "And instead, I had respectable parents. I probably have living relatives right here in London." He stared off to his right and admired the beautiful landscape before realizing he was seeing the south side of Grace Park's manicured backyard and gardens.

Deborah reached up with a hand and placed it on the side of his face. "We'll find them, then," she said. She kissed him. "Maybe even in time for the wedding."

Todd smiled and nodded. "I simply cannot wait another two weeks to be married, though," he said. "I must take you as my wife tonight," he whispered. "I cannot let you leave again, either. I want you here at Grace Park, safe in your room... here," he said as he pointed toward the house.

The chaise slowed and finally stopped next to the front steps. The coachman jumped to the cobblestone drive to assist his passengers. "You can put the chaise away for the night, Mr. Stevenson," Todd said as he stepped down and turned to lift Deborah from the chaise.

"Very good, sir," the coachman said as he bowed.

Deborah took Todd's arm and handed him his cane. "I won't be going back to the Home tonight," she replied. "Mrs. Dawes isn't expecting me until Monday, even though she says she has a gentleman coming to call on her Sunday afternoon." She lowered her eyes and bit her lip. "I know we must get my gown tomorrow, so I was hoping we could spend these two days together."

Todd gathered her into a hug and kissed her neck. "Then I am the luckiest man in the entire world," he whispered happily. "And

Winston is the second luckiest man because *he* is the gentleman who will be calling on Mrs. Dawes," he added with a big grin.

Deborah smiled, happy to know she shared a secret with Todd. "She told me. She has been most giddy this past week. It's not safe to be around the two of us as we are both so in love," she murmured, somewhat embarrassed by her admission.

Todd was about to kiss her on the lips when a bright light shone on them from above. Winston had opened the front door in anticipation of their entering and was surprised to find they were not yet at the top of the steps. "We'll continue this after dinner," Todd said as he led her up the steps. He turned his attention to the butler. "I'm starving, Winston. Is it still possible to get dinner this evening?" he asked as he escorted Deborah into the vestibule and handed over his cane to the butler. Deborah regarded the packages stacked up against the walls and wondered if they were *all* for her.

"Of course, sir. It's merely eight-thirty," the man replied. "Would you care to dress for dinner?" he asked as he raised his eyebrows. "Miss White, it's good to see you again this evening," he greeted Deborah and turned his attention back to Todd. "She is certainly dressed for dinner," he commented with an appreciative nod toward the lady.

Deborah shook her head. "No, Winston. He is quite fine like this." When she noticed his uncertain expression, she added, "Truly, he is fine."

Todd took her hand and was about to lead her to the dining room when he turned and said, "Winston, could you see to it that all those packages get delivered to Miss White's room, please? And then you are to take tomorrow off." He fished for a coin in his pocket and tossed a guinea to the butler. "And your afternoon with Mrs. Dawes is on me," he said happily.

Deborah's eyes widened. "Those boxes are *all* for me?" she asked in a whisper as she hurried to keep up with him.

Smiling wide, Todd nodded. "And tonight I'm going to watch you try on everything... and I might even let you wear something," he teased as they entered the dining room.

A footman scurried into the kitchen and Todd followed him. "Ladies and gentlemen, I apologize for our tardiness. Please, don't rush on our account," he stated to the very busy kitchen staff. He then returned to the dining room to find Deborah already seated to the right of his carver at the head of the table. At some point, he considered, it would be more proper for her to be at the other end of the table, but until he bought a very short table, he was going to insist she sit next to him.

They dined on thick chicken cream soup and piping hot bread, Cornish game hens stuffed with mashed yams and, for dessert, a bowl of strawberries in cream.

As Deborah regarded one of the strawberries resting in her spoon, Todd noticed her contemplation. "What is it?

"The perfect strawberry," she replied as she plucked it off the spoon and held it up for him to see. "The shape, the color..." She reached over and held it to Todd's mouth. "For you," she offered.

Todd took the strawberry and part of her finger in his mouth, and then carefully bit down. "Mmm," he moaned as she pulled her fingers away. "It was perfect," he said, a mischievous grin forming on his mouth. "I believe I have a perfect one right here, too," he said as he fished one out of his bowl with his spoon and offered it to Deborah. Taking the strawberry with her tongue and lips, she licked his finger as he pulled it away and chewed the sweet fruit. "It was perfect," she agreed, one eyebrow arching up in surprise. Taking a large one out of her bowl, she sat up straight, nested it at the top of her cleavage and merely regarded Todd. He swallowed hard and stared at the strawberry. Glancing around to be sure no one else was in the room, he got up from his chair, pulled Deborah up from hers, and used his lips to engulf the fruit and kiss the space where the fruit had rested.

Deborah gasped at the sensation of his lips on her skin.

Todd looked up at her, thinking he had done wrong. "I apologize, Miss White. Please forgive me," he whispered, a worried expression on his face.

"Not at all," Deborah replied. "It was very sensual," she said as she swallowed. She glanced around and then whispered, "Perhaps we could finish our desserts in the mistress suite?" she suggested as she watched his face closely, hoping she hadn't offended him with the suggestion.

Todd swallowed again. "I'd like that very much," he replied as he reached over the table, dumped all the strawberries into one bowl and quickly snatched it from the table. Deborah grabbed the bottle of champagne and glasses and they hurried out of the dining room and up the steps to the mistress suite.

Candles lit the peach room in a warm, golden glow. Winston had piled the packages near the wall of windows, but Deborah gave them little regard as she set the champagne on the large walnut dresser. The bed was turned down, its decorative pillows stacked neatly next to the bed.

Turning to Todd, Deborah took the bowl from him and set it next to the champagne while he closed and locked the door. She took a strawberry and bit into it, and then offered the rest of it to Todd. He took it with his lips and then kissed her fingers while he pressed one hand against the small of her back and pulled her body against his.

"I love you, Todd Vandermeer," Deborah said quietly, her lips trembling. "With all my heart and all my soul, I love you. Take me. Take me... as your wife... this very night," she pleaded, hoping she hadn't misinterpreted his comments from earlier that evening.

Mrs. Vandermeer, he had said.

Todd held her close. "And I love you, Deborah Vandermeer," he replied as he took a deep breath. "I will love you, and honor you, and keep you in sickness and in health... for as long as I live." Without having the paper on which he had written the vows, Todd knew he had forgotten to say something. But the gold ring he had purchased at Rundell and Bridge was in his pocket.

"And I will obey you, and serve you, and honor and love you as long as I live," Deborah replied before she swallowed hard.

Todd pulled the gold band out of his pocket and held it up. "With this ring, I wed thee," he said, pulling up her left hand and placing the ring on her long, slender fourth finger. *These fingers*, he thought as he finally took a breath.

"And now, you may kiss the bride," Deborah whispered happily as she gazed at the ring, it's three gemstones sparkling in the candlelight.

Although there was a time in her life when she might have dreaded this night, Deborah found herself looking forward to her wedding night with Todd Vandermeer. She had spent the last two years listening intently to the tales whores told over dinner— instructions on how to simply please a client and stories about plea- suring a man so he would return for more. She had spent several hours with Todd reading about sexual intercourse and studying the illustrations in a book he said was a gift from a raj he knew in India. Anxious and excited, Deborah quickly licked her lips and angled her head as Todd took a deep breath and placed a hand along her neck.

Their first kiss was passionate and deep. Breathless, their lips finally parted briefly. Deborah began pulling his shirt from his breeches. Sliding her long fingers underneath and up the sides of his body, Deborah watched as he flinched when her thumbs caressed the hair on his chest, and she grinned as he gasped when she touched his nipples.

Closing his eyes for a moment, Todd took a deep breath and began loosening the cravat from around his neck. Deborah pushed the billowing fabric of his shirt over his head and dropped it to the floor while her lips took purchase on one of his nipples, gently biting and caressing it with her teeth and tongue.

Although a first glance at Todd would suggest a thin man, his arms were well developed from years of using canes to walk. Deborah traced the lines of the muscles with a finger and kissed his biceps and collarbone as he held her and kissed her forehead and temples.

Lifting her arms over her head, crossing them, and reaching down, she grasped the fabric of her gown and pulled it up and over her head. Lost in a sea of blue satin, Deborah waited while an amused Todd pulled the rest of the gown over her head and tossed it onto a nearby chair, sighing as he took in the sight of her.

Corseted and wearing a camisole and pantaloons, Deborah smiled demurely as she turned her body so her back was to him. When he didn't immediately move to untie the corset's bow, she reached for one of his hands and lifted it. Todd's fingers trembled as he finally grasped and pulled the tie, the bow unraveling in his hands. Deborah turned around in his arms and reached for the buttons on his pantaloons, slowly undoing them, aware of his hardened manhood behind the wool fabric.

Bending down to remove his boots, Todd watched as her corset loosened, her breasts slowly appearing through the thin chemise with each breath she took. He removed his stockings while mesmerized by her décolletage.

Deborah reached behind her and used her own fingers to loosen the ties further until her hardening nipples peaked above the edge of the corset. Todd took a deep breath and swallowed hard as Deborah pulled the corset over her head and tossed it onto the chair. Although her camisole covered her torso, its thin fabric revealed her firm, upturned breasts and erect nipples.

Finally free of the corset, she pulled Todd into a hug and drew her fingers slowly down his back and between his drawers and buttocks, pushing the breeches and drawers to the floor.

His entire body vibrating in anticipation, Todd pulled the camisole over her head as she lowered herself, her breasts rubbing down the front of his chest and around his hardened penis and along one thigh while her lips occasionally kissed his skin. He sucked in a breath and held it, uncertain of what he should do next.

Placing his hands on her shoulders, Todd leaned on her slightly as he stepped out of the breeches. His large hands slid under her arms and easily lifted her to her feet. Wrapping his arms around her, he held her tight against his body.

Deborah kissed him, moaning as she guided one of his hands to the underside of a breast and his thumb along the side of a nipple. Her breaths came quicker and her body trembled as Todd leaned down and took the nipple in his mouth, licking it with his tongue and kissing it between his lips.

After a moment, he turned his attention to the other nipple, suckling it and caressing it until it was hard and red. Gasping at the intimate touch, at his careful, almost tentative kisses, Deborah was suddenly emboldened. Reaching down with an open hand, she slid it along the front of his body and around his hardened penis, pressing slightly against it with her palm while tentatively touching the wet head with her thumb. She drew her moistened thumb down the back side, and cupped his balls with her long fingers, all the while watching his tightly controlled reactions, expecting him to make her stop at any moment. "Am I... doing this... right?" she managed to whisper, her heart rate so fast she could hear her pulse in her ears.

Todd managed a nod. "I think so," he whispered, the words sounding labored. Finally, unable to control himself any longer, Todd lifted her onto the bed and climbed atop her. Deborah pushed her pantaloons down as far as she could, and Todd removed them completely.

Wrapping her legs around his back, she felt his body shivering as he hovered over her. When he didn't move to enter her, she slowly slid her hands down his back and around his buttocks, gently guiding him into her. A glimpse of her nightmare, when her vision was gray and she felt panicked, passed through her mind. She forced the image away and concentrated on Todd's face and on the feel of his skin against hers. Arching her back, Deborah gasped as he pushed into her completely, his cock a ramrod.

Todd grunted at the extreme and sudden pleasure, lowering himself onto her so that he could bite her shoulder to stifle his groans.

Leaving her hands on his buttocks, she felt them tighten as a spasm gripped his body and he pressed harder into her. His almost silent moan vibrated through his body when he suddenly stiffened and held himself very still.

Filled with a warm sensation, Deborah let go and slid her hands up along his back, allowing her thumbs to caress the sides of his body. She took delight in his gasps and moans and his shivering flesh. *His seed is in me*, she thought, its warmth permeating her entire body.

Unable to take any more pleasure, Todd took her hands in his and pushed them above her head. His manhood still inside her, he slid his hands down her arms and used one to cup a breast while he kissed and suckled it. With the other, he fondled her other breast and her belly before moving the flat of his hand to where their bodies met. His thumb circled her wet flesh in search of her swollen womanhood, finally caressing it when her breath hitched.

Todd watched in awe as Deborah writhed in pleasure, her head angled back into the pillows and her chest lifting from the mattress. It was only a moment before she arched her back and cried out as the intense pleasure gripped her, held her and finally coursed through her entire body. His own body responded. He felt his manhood harden once again, his lust nearly overcoming his desire to provide pleasure.

Carefully letting go of her breast, Todd pushed into her as hard as he could and felt the grip of her silken haven tighten on him, felt the ripples of her orgasm as her muscles contracted. Unable to hold off his own oncoming pleasure, he let go and lowered himself onto Deborah as his body spasmed once again, his mouth pressed against a breast to muffle his moans.

When the waves of pleasure had finally subsided and his breathing was more normal, Todd slowly pulled out of her and rolled onto his back.

Deborah murmured a sound of disappointment as he did so, but she turned onto her side and pressed herself against him, wrapping her arm across his chest as he wrapped his arm around her shoulders and held her close.

"Did I... did I hurt you?" Todd asked in a whisper while trying to catch his breath. He kissed her hair and smoothed it with a hand.

Deborah smiled and shook her head against his chest. "Not at all. It was ecstasy," she replied quietly, lifting her head to look at him. "You are a very good lover."

Grinning at her remark, Todd closed his eyes and said a prayer of thanks.

"I shall be very jealous of your mistress during the nights you spend with her," she commented sadly, winding a finger in a whorl of black hair on his chest.

"What?" Todd replied in surprise, lifting himself onto one elbow as he regarded Deborah with a frown. "But, I... I don't have a mistress," he replied defensively. "And I most certainly don't have plans to take one. Why ever would you...?"

Deborah's eyes widened. "Oh," she replied as she pushed herself up on one elbow so their eyes were level with one another. She was happy to hear his denial, but worried she had offended him with the remark. "I apologize, Mr. Vandermeer. It's just... I... I thought that all wealthy men had mistresses," she said as she bit her lip. "And when you said your vows, you didn't promise to forsake all others."

Todd sighed and hit his forehead with the palm of his hand. "I knew I missed one of the vows," he whispered, shaking his head in dismay. Turning to her, he took her hand and said, "I promise to forsake all others."

Deborah gave him a brilliant smile and leaned in to kiss him. "As do I," she said happily. After a moment, her brows furrowed. "But you must have had a mistress in the past. You are so... you seemed to know... you knew *exactly* how to pleasure me," she whispered intently, trying to make her point despite her embarrassment.

Somewhat amused, but even more relieved he had succeeded in his first attempt at lovemaking, Todd shook his head and dropped back onto the pillows. "As did you," he whispered, too quietly for her to hear.

When he didn't respond right away, Deborah lowered herself to the bed and saw that tears streamed down the sides of his face. "Did I offend you?" she asked in alarm. "Mr. Vandermeer, whatever is wrong?"

Todd shook his head and smiled. "I'm fine. I am in ecstasy, in fact," he replied happily as he pulled her body onto his and stroked her back with his hands.

He pushed his fingers as far as they could reach to draw circles in the small of her back. Her involuntary reactions told him her skin was once again receptive to sensual touch. "Everything I did with you I learned from that book we've been reading," he whispered with a mischievous grin.

"Indeed?" Deborah replied, biting her lip as she considered his words. "Then you are a very good student of a very good book," she commented, a smile forming on her lips. "And you have been reading ahead of me," she scolded, her lower lip pushed out in a pout. Underneath her, she felt his manhood harden again. She pulled her knees up and lifted her hips so he could enter her as she pushed down onto him, startling him with the move. "This was as far as I read," she whispered as she sat up and arched backwards. She sighed as her fingers raked his chest. Then she reached behind her and pushed against his thighs.

Todd closed his eyes and gasped as she raised and lowered herself on him. Gripped tightly inside her, at first he could do nothing but try to breathe as his hands held her hips, guiding them as she pushed onto him. He moved one thumb to where his manhood disappeared into her. Pressing lightly, he watched as she flinched and gasped in surprise. He felt her push herself against his thumb just as he gripped her hip tighter with his other hand, preventing her from escaping his ministrations. She gasped and cried out his name as an intense, sharp and almost painful sensation coursed through her abdomen.

Tentatively, Todd pressed the thumb in the same spot. Deborah cried out again, curled her body forward, and pressed her breasts against his chest and her head against his shoulder. Panting as she tried to catch her breath, she reached down behind her and cupped his balls with her fingers, triggering a spasm of pleasure he had fought hard to delay.

He grunted and hugged her hard, trying to hold onto the sensation as long as possible. *If only I could have met you years ago*, he thought, and then wondered if he had said it aloud or merely dreamed it. When at last he was spent, he stroked her back with both hands, reveling in the feel of her body pressed so hard against his. Her entire body trembled as he held her. "Are you cold?" he asked in a whisper, not realizing he was shivering as much as she was.

"No, my love," she answered quietly, kissing his shoulder and neck and straightening her legs along the sides of his. "I am bliss-fully warm," she said quietly, her voice almost a sigh. She used one of her hands to caress his chest and the side of his body along his ribs, grinning when his entire body would suddenly stiffen or shiver beneath her.

They lay silent for several minutes until, at last, their breaths returned to a normal rhythm.

Deborah continued to slide the pads of her fingers over the whorls of hair on his chest, occasionally stopping to kiss a particular spot. Amazed she could feel so comfortable while naked and pressed against a man, she realized it was because Todd made her feel safe and loved.

I love this man.

And not just because they had said their vows of marriage. "Will you stay with me tonight?" she asked in whisper.

Todd smiled and gently pulled out of her while he rolled her onto her side. "Last night, tonight, and every night," he murmured as he hugged her to the front of his body.

Deborah lifted her head from the bed and regarded him for a moment. "Last night?" she questioned with a quizzical expression.

Returning the quizzical expression, Todd nodded. "Yes. And you were most welcome in my bed, if I may say," he said in a quiet whisper. "I slept until half-past eight this morning."

Pushing her face into his chest, Deborah smiled to herself. "Do you always sleep without a night shirt?" she asked in a whisper, remembering how she'd found him.

His eyes closed, Todd grinned and whispered, "Last night, tonight, and every night from now on."

It was only a few moments before they drifted off to sleep.

*U*sed to being awakened by crying babies in the middle of the night, Deborah woke with a start to the sound of silence. Todd lay sleeping next to her, a beatific smile on his face. One candle still burned on the nightstand.

Needing to relieve herself, she carefully slid off of the bed and hurried to the bath. During the two nights she had stayed at Grace Park, she had learned of the private bath's many amenities and intended to take advantage of one of them immediately.

The dressing table, nearly as long as one wall, included a very large sink with hot and cold water faucets, bottles of lotions and perfumes, and toiletries the likes of which she had never seen before. Crystal drinking glasses and a large comb and brush set placed next to a hand mirror completed the display.

Lighting a match and then a candle, she saw that Winston had seen to it that the hot water heater was lit. Deborah filled the sink with steaming water and added cold water from the other faucet until the mix was a comfortable temperature. She helped herself to a bath linen from the stack and found a smaller washing cloth.

Climbing into the sink, she reveled in the sensation when her bottom and feet were surrounded by water. A bar of French milled soap, scented with lavender, lay next to the sink. She wet it and rubbed it on herself, delighting in the bubbles left behind on her skin.

In the dimness, she could barely see her reflection in the gilt framed mirror above the dressing table, but she managed to complete her sponge bath and to rinse herself off before stepping off of the table.

Wrapping herself in the large linen, she pulled the plug from the sink bottom and grimaced at the sight of her hair in the mirror. She plucked the pins from her mussed bun and brushed it, the long, dark locks falling to the middle of her back.

Ready to return to bed, Deborah picked up one of the perfume bottles and sniffed it. She was about to squeeze the atomizer when Todd said, "You don't need that, my love."

Surprised, Deborah nearly dropped the bottle. "Oh!" she exclaimed as she jumped, realizing he had been watching her as he leaned against the door frame, his arms loosely crossed against his chest. One knee was bent so a foot rested against the door jamb.

Todd shook his head and reached out to her, wrapping his arms around her shoulders. He pulled her into a hug. "I am so sorry. I didn't mean to startle you," he whispered as he bent down to kiss her. "I missed you. Are you well?"

Deborah thought there was something different about him as he held her. Either he had become more confident in himself as a lover, or he was simply more comfortable with her. Either way, she found the subtle change exciting. "I'm very well indeed. And you, husband?" she countered with a demure smile.

Todd smiled at her use of the word 'husband.' "I am married to a beautiful woman with whom I am deeply in love, so I'm very well," he replied with a sigh. Sniffing her, he whispered, "You smell like milled soap. Whatever have you been doing?"

Deborah pressed her linen-covered belly against him and felt him harden through the soft fabric. "Bathing," she replied slowly. "And you are," she leaned in close and whispered in his ear, "Hard."

Todd closed his eyes as she drew her fingers down his side and used her thumbs to brush against his nipples and chest hair. "Indeed. I believe I have been since the first night I met you," he whispered, grinning as he said it.

Although he had fallen in love with Deborah the first night he had met her, he had not felt *lust* for her until the night before. Now he wondered how he had managed to keep their relationship platonic for an entire week.

"Does it... does it hurt you when it's like this?" Deborah asked as she pressed against him again.

"No," he replied, thinking about the question for a moment before answering. "It's uncomfortable after a time, though, I suppose." He felt his face redden. In all his days, he never expected to be discussing his manhood with a woman.

"Then we shall hurry back to bed and provide you some relief," Deborah suggested with an arched brow as she started to move for the door.

"In a minute," he answered as he held onto her. "I would like to bathe first," he said, nodding at her linen. "I should aspire to be as clean as you."

Deborah grinned and turned to fill the sink with hot water. "May I help?" she asked demurely as she pulled two linens from the stack on the table. She remembered one of the prostitutes from a brothel describing how she would clean a customer before she allowed him into her bed. Although the men usually balked at the requirement, they seemed most pleased at the effect the foreplay had on them.

"Indeed. I believe I would enjoy it very much," he replied, swallowing hard as he remembered the maidens bathing the men in India. He had never indulged in such bathing for he thought it a private affair and much too embarrassing given his very long legs and arms.

Deborah pulled him to the table and dipped the soap in the water before rubbing his shoulders and arms with it. Wetting one linen, she rinsed him off as he moved to lean over the sink.

Todd took great pleasure in the feel of her soapy fingers on his skin and in the gentle caresses as she used the linens to rinse and dry him, alternately working her way down the front of his body and then his back. When only his genitals remained to be washed, she soaped her hands and hesitated for a moment. Her eyes met his, concerned she might have shown too much enthusiasm with her ministrations.

Todd, his breaths coming in shallow gasps, wrapped his hand around hers. He moved it toward his hardened manhood, but gave a start when she tentatively touched him before wrapping her fingers around it.

He gripped her shoulder and leaned over, startled by the sensation as her hand moved up and down and her thumb caressed the head of his manhood. Her other hand cupped his balls, gently massaging the soap around them.

Grunting and breathing in short bursts, Todd tried to pull away, but the Deborah's grip merely tightened, sending a spasm of pleasure coursing through him.

In her hands, Deborah could feel his cock come alive, and after a moment, his seed spurted onto her linen. As she gripped him harder, Todd groaned and placed a hand over hers to still her movement. "Please, stop," he whispered between gasps for air.

Unsure if she had hurt him or pleasured him too much, Deborah released her fingers and slowly pulled away her soapy hands. Immersing them in the water, she rinsed them off.

Still leaning heavily against the dressing table, Todd nodded to her. "Thank you. That was most exhilarating," he managed to say between breaths.

When Deborah moved to rinse him off with the wet linen, he flinched and pushed away the towel. "I think I should do it," he said as he stood over the sink and used a glass to pour water over his member. When he was thoroughly rinsed, he faced her and reached out and removed the linen from around her body. "Now you can dry me," he said with a playful grin.

Startled at being left naked, Deborah inhaled sharply before she bent down and gingerly touched the linen to his nether region, barely making contact as she wiped him dry. When she was satisfied with her work, she kissed the head of his manhood, kissed the space around his navel, and finally kissed his collarbone.

Todd wrapped his arms around her and held her close. "Thank

you," he whispered. Then he picked her up and carried her to bed.

"You are most welcome," Deborah replied as he set her down on the bed. "Are you hungry?"

Startled by the question, Todd didn't need to think long. "I am starving," he replied. He hurried to the dresser to get the bowl of strawberries. "Would you like some champagne? There is most of a bottle here," he remarked as he reached for the bottle.

In the dim light of the one candle, they took turns feeding each other and drinking champagne. "Tell me," Todd requested as he held up a tiny strawberry. "What is the part of a woman that is said to look like this and brings her great pleasure?"

When Deborah frowned and couldn't immediately answer, he added, "I read about it in the book, but I didn't recognize the word to be able to read it or say it."

"Oh, I believe you must be referring to the *clitoris*," Deborah whispered.

"Clitoris," Todd repeated carefully. "Tell me about it," he said quietly, obviously curious.

Deborah sat up and leaned on one arm, uncomfortable at explaining something she knew of only from listening to the prostitutes who lived at the Home. "Well, I hear it is red. It is supposed to grow larger during sexual intercourse. It is very sensitive—it is said to be the source of a woman's pleasure," she paused in her recitation as she tried to remember more. "Oh, it can also be coaxed to cause orgasms from a simple touch or during cunnilingus," she remembered, hoping she had pronounced the Latin word correctly.

"So... I could... touch yours?" Todd asked hopefully.

Debra shrugged one shoulder and blushed. "I believe you already have done so. Several times, in fact." When Todd's look of curiosity turned to consternation, she added, "When you touched me with your thumb. Three times, at least. It was most pleasurable," she assured him, her demeanor once again demure.

Todd swallowed and nodded. "Oh. Good." After a few seconds, he asked what she feared he would. "Would you allow me to touch it with my tongue? I would be most careful," he added quickly, hoping he had not offended her with the request.

Deborah bit her lip and thought for a moment. "If I have just bathed, I would welcome it, I suppose," she replied nervously, aware that her nipples had pebbled as his queries excited her.

And she had just bathed.

Todd set aside the bowl and kissed her lips, lightly at first, and then harder as his passion for her consumed him.

Deborah lay back and slowly spread her legs as Todd pushed his way down the front of her body, stopping to kiss her ribs and belly. His tongue caressed the skin that spanned the hollow space between her hipbones before he moved lower. Once his head was between her thighs, he gently pushed her knees up with his hands and gingerly reached out with his tongue, barely touching her. She flinched, somewhat in anticipation but also at the soft, wet touch. Forcing herself to relax, she took a deep breath and let it out slowly.

How far ahead had he read the book?

His second attempt was more sure as his tongue stroked upwards on her. Deborah gasped in pleasure but didn't pull away. "Yes," she whispered as she moved her arms out to either side of her body. Her fingers clutched the bed linens harder as Todd repeated the stroking, but from a different angle. Her chest rose from the bed as intense sensations coursed through her abdomen. When his tongue stroked the third time, Deborah arched her back, but his tongue kept its purchase on the red fruit, and he suckled it gently with his lips.

Wave after wave of pleasure washed over Deborah, and she found she was totally helpless but to allow it to happen. His lips finally let go, but when he flicked his tongue hard across the engorged bud, she cried out and writhed in pleasure, sure she would faint from the intense sensations. "No more," she whispered and gasped as she shook her head from side to side.

Understanding she had endured as much pleasure as her body would allow, Todd withdrew his tongue and kissed the insides of her long thighs. Moving to the side of her body, he held himself up on one elbow as he watched her expression of bliss. He marveled at how large her nipples had become during his ministrations. He gently kissed both and then her mouth.

Pulling the linens and blankets over their bodies, he carefully cradled her shoulders and rolled her body to rest against the side of his. She moaned and molded her body to fit, wrapping one leg over one of his and an arm over his chest. Still shivering uncontrollably while he rubbed a hand down her arm, she murmured, "I am yours for life, Mr. Vandermeer."

Todd kissed the top of her head and replied, "And I am yours, Mrs. Vandermeer," before falling into a deep, dream-filled sleep.

CHAPTER 40
WEDDING PLANS

June 19, 1802, No. 3 Kingly Street

On Saturday morning, Todd and Deborah joined Emma Fitzsimmons at her townhouse for a late breakfast of eggs, hot rolls filled with cinnamon, and tea before departing for an afternoon of gown shopping. Although most brides simply wore their Sunday best for a wedding ceremony, Todd insisted Deborah have a special gown. Miss Suzanne's, the modiste's shop in Oxford Street, offered an array of ready-made gowns and a comfortable place for Todd to sit and even drink brandy, should he wish while the women tried on gowns. The shop's proprietor was most helpful in finding longer dresses for Deborah and encouraged Emma to try on gowns appropriate for her role as a witness.

Emma wouldn't allow Todd to see Deborah in any gown that might possibly be her wedding gown, though, insisting it was bad luck to the see the bride in her gown before the wedding. Not having heard such a claim before, Todd did his best to sneak peeks as Deborah entered or exited the dressing room.

When he instead caught Emma in a peach satin gown with long sleeves, he stood up and called her over to where he stood. "You must wear this gown at the wedding," he stated as he motioned for Miss Suzanne to join them.

Emma's eyes widened and she held out the price tag pinned to the end of one tapered sleeve. "Mr. Vandermeer, this is more than I make in three weeks!" she whispered as she showed him the 4£ 6s written on the tag.

"I'll buy it for you, of course," Todd replied as he waved off any concern about the price. "As well as shoes and whatever else you will need for the wedding. As Deborah's gift for standing with her," he added in explanation before Emma could put voice to her protest. Turning to the proprietor, he said, "Please wrap this for her and put it on my bill."

Miss Suzanne hesitated as she gave Emma an uncertain glance but finally nodded. "Very good, sir," she replied with a prim smile.

Stunned, Emma could only say, "Why, thank you, Mr. Vandermeer. How very kind of you." When she noticed him looking over her shoulder as Deborah walked out of the dressing room, she put her finger on his nose and pushed it to one side. "No peeking!"

Todd grinned and turned away. "Please tell Deborah the blue one does not suit her." At Emma's gasp, he added, "And we really must see to it that Mr. Wellingham gives you a raise in pay."

Mortified, Emma replied, "You'll do no such thing." When she realized his comment was made in jest, she added, "Now, behave yourself," in mock anger as she returned to the dressing room with Miss Suzanne in tow.

Still grinning, Todd replied in a whisper, "Me thinks you doth protest too much." But he returned to his club chair and honored Emma's request, reading that day's *The Morning Chronicle* as he waited for the women to complete their shopping.

The notice of his betrothal was in a prominent location on the Society page, and he smiled as he read it. Every word was just how he wanted it, just as the writer had assured him it would be.

Todd Vandermeer, son of the late Col. William Vandermeer and his wife, Adelyn Tennison Vandermeer, and a broker with the East India Company, has announced his intention to marry Miss Deborah White, a midwife at Mrs. Dawes' Home for Unwed Mothers. The outdoor ceremony is scheduled to take place Saturday, July 3 in the gardens at Mr. Vandermeer's home in Marylebone and will be followed by the traditional wedding breakfast. Invitations have been sent to a number of friends. Mr. Thomas Wellingham of Wellingham Imports will stand for the groom. Miss Emma Fitzsimmons, a recent graduate of Warwick's Grammar and Finishing School and a personal bookkeeper to Mr. Wellingham, will stand with Miss White. The bride and groom were introduced by Miss Emma Fitzsimmons, who worked with Miss White at the Home as her charity whilst attending Warwick's. A destination for the wedding trip has not yet been set. Upon their return to London, they will oversee the opening of the new location for Mrs. Dawes' Home for Unwed Mothers in the former Cooper Hotel. Mr. Vandermeer, a long-time patron of the Home, purchased the hotel as a wedding gift for Miss White.

When he looked up from reading the announcement, he found Emma and Deborah staring at him. They each had a wrapped package and were smiling nervously. "I found the perfect gown," Deborah stated carefully, occasionally glancing in Emma's direction. "And Miss Suzanne said it could be altered and ready in time for the ceremony."

Todd looked at the two women and shrugged. "That's good news, is it not?"

Emma gazed at Deborah as Deborah bit her lip. "It's more than I could have ever imagined a gown to cost," she whispered, her expression becoming more pained.

Todd sat up straighter. "Is it more than a hundred pounds?" he asked.

"No!" Emma and Deborah replied in unison, shocked that he thought a gown could cost that much. He was an importer, after all.

"'Tis fourteen *pounds*," Emma said with a wince.

"And will it fit properly once the alterations are made?"

Deborah nodded. "The sleeves just need to be tightened a bit, and a ruffle needs to be added to the bottom of the skirt to make it long enough. But it comes with gloves. And a veil for my head."

Todd shook his head and shrugged his shoulders. "Does the veil have one of those little crowns on the front?" he asked, his face lighting up as he watched his two favorite women in the world stare down at him.

Emma exchanged a questioning glance with Deborah and then looked to Suzanne, who nodded. "There's a small pearl-encrusted tiara," the proprietor explained as she held it up for him to see.

Todd glanced at the tiara and looked back at the two women. "Then I shall buy it for you," he said with a mischievous grin.

Excited, Emma and Deborah turned to Miss Suzanne, who had already set aside the gown for alterations.

Todd stood up and handed the newspaper to Deborah. "We're an item in *The Morning Chronicle*," he commented with a sly grin as he walked over to pay for the gown. Emma and Deborah read the notice, giggling and gasping as they took turns reading.

"Come, ladies, and let us have some supper," Todd said as he offered them his arms. They headed for the entrance. As Todd held open the door, an older lady, dressed in a beautiful scarlet morning gown and decorated bonnet, stepped into the shop and thanked him for holding the door for her. When she glanced up and saw his face, her eyes widened as if in recognition.

Deborah and Emma moved out of the woman's path, both admiring her gown while the woman continued to stare at Todd. Uncomfortable, Todd nodded to her and wondered if he knew her from somewhere or if perhaps the woman was merely surprised to find a man in the modiste's shop. "Good day, ma'am," he said as he motioned for Deborah and Emma to pass through the doorway.

"Good day, sir," the woman replied as she recovered her composure. "And thank you," she said with a nod.

The older woman continued to stare at Todd as he and the two younger women headed off down the street. Todd was aware of her gaze until they were finally out of sight.

Who is she?

CHAPTER 41
A LONG LOST RELATIVE
APPEARS

une 20, 1802, Grace Park

About an hour before luncheon on Sunday, Winston answered a tentative knock at the door of the Vandermeer mansion. A woman, who appeared to be in her forties and dressed in her Sunday best, stood holding a newspaper clipping.

"Good afternoon, ma'am," the butler greeted the handsome, dark-haired woman.

Obviously nervous, the woman held up the clipping and said, "I apologize for the interruption, kind sir. I... I'm looking for my daughter, Miss Deborah White. I don't know if she is the Miss White mentioned here, though," she said as she indicated the clipping, "But I shall forever be in your debt if I might be allowed to meet this one."

Winston angled his head, surprised by the request. "Please come in, Mrs...Mrs. White?" he guessed.

"Yes. Thank you, sir," she replied, her eyes widening at hearing the butler's query. She entered the vestibule, her gaze sweeping the entry and what she could see beyond in the great hall. Her expression was a clear indication of how impressed she was by the house.

The butler started for the parlor, and when Mrs. White didn't immediately follow, he said, "This way, ma'am."

The woman took a deep breath and quickly followed the butler to the parlor, where he insisted she take a seat until he could inform Miss White she had a caller.

When he reached the mistress suite, Winston hesitated before knocking on the door. Upon Deborah's reply of, "Come in," he gingerly opened the door and found he had no reason to be concerned. Todd was dressed in breeches and a shirt and sat in the chaise lounge by the large windows eating an apple. Deborah, dressed in one of the new gowns Todd had purchased for her, was sitting with her back against Todd's chest and holding a large book. Todd's free hand was wrapped around Deborah's waist as he read the same book over her shoulder.

"Excuse me, Miss White. There is a Mrs. White in the parlor asking for you," the butler stated formally.

Deborah sat up straight and stared at Winston. "Mrs. White?" she repeated quietly. "*Mama?*" she asked, saying it with a French accent.

"I believe so, Miss White. Shall I bring tea?"

Deborah set aside the book and slowly stood up. Todd followed suit once he was able to get his legs off the lounge. "Yes, thank you, Winston. I'll go down right now." Turning to Todd, she gave him a frightened look. "I have not seen her in more than two years," she whispered. "And I'm not yet one-and-twenty. She could stop the wedding..."

Todd shook his head and held a hand to her face. "She has probably been looking for you for two years. Go to her," he said quietly. He didn't know what he would do if the woman did decide to withhold parental consent for the marriage. He and Deborah were already courting scandal simply because she had moved into the house. "I must finish getting dressed. I'll be down shortly."

With that, Deborah left the room and made her way downstairs. Taking a deep breath, she entered the parlor and stood staring at the woman that was, indeed, her mother. Grayer than when she had last seen her, Emily White otherwise looked the same as the day Deborah had been banished from her parents' home.

"Mama," she said quietly.

The woman stood up from the settee and stared at her daughter. "It *is* you," she said in awe as she took in the sight of her daughter dressed in an elegant gown and slippers. "You... you are very beautiful," she commented as she let out her breath. "Everything here is... beautiful," she added as she waved a hand to indicate the room.

Deborah bit her lip, still not sure of the woman's intentions. "Why... why have you come?" she asked, sure she was going to cry at any moment.

Mrs. White shook her head. "I have been looking for you ever since your father... sent you away," she said, tears pricking the corners of her eyes. "It was wrong of him, and he wouldn't listen to me. He was so sure his mother would stop sending him the monthly allowance if she found out what happened to you that he told her you had gone to work as a servant in a wealthy family's home. *Damn* him," she cursed as she began to sob.

Deborah hurried to her mother and wrapped her arms around the elder woman's shoulders. "Please, don't cry, mama. I am well, and I'm to be married to a most wonderful man with whom I am in love," she said with barely contained excitement.

Mrs. White pulled away from the hug. "And what of the child?" she asked as she met Deborah's gaze.

Shaking her head, Deborah replied, "There is no child, mama. I miscarried shortly after I left home. But I was at Mrs. Dawes' Home for Unwed Mothers, and she took good care of me."

The older woman frowned, tears still streaming down her face. "Then why didn't you come home?"

Deborah stared at her mother, stunned by the question. "Father made it very clear I was not to return," she replied. "I take it *he* didn't want you to look for me?"

Emily White sniffled and pulled a hanky from her reticule. "Your father is *dead*, and so is his damned mother," she said angrily, dabbing at her tears and sniffling quietly.

Deborah winced at the comment, stunned at the news and by her mother's curse. Her eyes downcast, she stared at the carpet near her feet for a moment. "How long ago?" she asked.

"Nearly a year now," her mother replied, her anger abating. "They left me with a comfortable living. Not a happy one without you, I suppose," she said as she sniffled. She wiped her face dry and turned toward the door. As she curtsied, Deborah turned to find Todd standing in the doorway. He was dressed in a scarlet topcoat, a navy brocade waistcoat, wool breeches, Hessians, and a fresh shirt. His cravat, snow white and perfectly tied, displayed an onyx pin. Bowing deeply, he nervously watched his future mother-in-law as the woman took in the sight of him.

"Mama, I'd like to introduce my future husband, Mr. Todd Vandermeer," Deborah stated as she held out her hand to Todd. "Todd, this is my mother, Mrs...." She paused, realizing her mother was now a widow. "Mrs. Emily White."

Todd bent down and, taking Mrs. White's hand, kissed the back of it. "I'm very honored to meet the woman who bore my beautiful bride," Todd stated formally. "I cannot thank you enough. I shall endeavor to be the best husband she could ever have and will honor and cherish her all of my days."

Left speechless by Todd's words, Mrs. White could only nod and watch in awe as the man stood up to his full six-foot-six-inch height. Deborah found she could no longer suppress a smile as she watched her mother's reaction.

Winston carried in a tray filled with tea and cups, Dutch biscuits and scones, and dried fruits. Placing it on the low table in front of the settee, he poured tea and offered sugar and cream.

"Please, sit down and be comfortable," Todd said to Mrs. White. Deborah took her wing chair next to Todd's and thanked the butler for the tea. Her mother did likewise while Todd said, "Please let the cook know we have a guest for luncheon, would you Winston?"

The butler nodded with a smile. "Very good, sir," he replied before leaving the parlor.

"Oh, I didn't mean to intrude," Mrs. White said as she held out a hand to stop the butler.

"Mama, please, you really must stay for Sunday supper. Mr. Vandermeer's cook is the very best in London," Deborah said as she smiled at Todd. He reached over and took her hand in his.

"I would love to, Deborah, truly. But I cannot. I must be at your aunt's house by two o'clock for supper there. I promised her I would come today," she replied, obviously disappointed she had made the commitment.

"So Aunt Katherine is well then?" Deborah asked, referring to her mother's sister.

"Yes, she is quite fine. But I have put her off far too long. Perhaps we can meet at the house this week?" she suggested. "Your room... I have left it the way it was."

Deborah sat up straighter, her brows furrowing with her surprise at hearing her mother's claim. "Thank you," she replied. "I will come by, then. Would..." She paused, considering when she might have an evening available to pay a call on her mother. "Would Thursday evening be acceptable?"

Her mother smiled brightly. "Thursday would be capital." Turning her attention to Todd, she asked, "And could you join us, as well, Mr. Vandermeer?"

Todd smiled and nodded. "Of course, Mrs. White. And please, call me Todd," he said with a grin.

Mrs. White felt a hint of confusion. She knew of Todd Vandermeer from what she had read in the newspapers. Due to his tenure with the John Company and popularity among some of the *ton*, she had assumed he would be a calculating man with a bent toward snobbishness. But there was nothing pretentious about him, and he certainly didn't behave as a person born into privilege.

"Will you be able to attend the wedding, Mrs. White?" Todd asked as he pointed to the clipping she still held clutched in her fingers.

Deborah's mother looked to Deborah and saw her nod her head. "I would be most honored," the woman replied.

"Will you give me away then, mama?" Deborah asked hopefully. "I am not yet one-and-twenty."

The woman nodded, but appeared uncomfortable. "Of course. If that is what you wish."

Deborah studied her mother's reaction. "Is there something amiss?" she asked, hoping her mother wouldn't forbid her to marry Todd.

"No, not at all," Mrs. White answered too quickly. "It's just that, I came here today not even sure if you would be my daughter, and here I am about to gain a son," she said as tears welled in her eyes.

Todd sat up straighter and acknowledged the comment with a nod. "Please know, Mrs. White, that as my wife, Deborah will have this house, and my protection, and my love for the rest of my life. And I'll see to it she is well taken care of after my passing," he added in earnest.

Deborah gasped in surprise at the mention of his dying sometime before she would. "How can you say such a thing?" she asked, allowing her shock to show.

"It is the more likely scenario, my love," he replied as he placed a hand on her arm.

"Please, excuse the interruption," Winston said as he stood at the entrance of the parlor. "Mr. Vandermeer? Your presence is required in the study," he announced formally.

Todd knitted his eyebrows together and frowned. "It seems I have a visitor. Please excuse me, Mrs. White. If you should take your leave before I have completed my business, then please know that I look forward to Thursday evening." He stood up, bowed to the ladies, and left the room to follow his butler.

When he had taken his leave, Mrs. White leaned over and took Deborah's hand. "Does he treat you well?" she asked, her face betraying her worry.

Deborah smiled and nodded. "Like a queen, mama. I fear he is spoiling me," she admitted as she leaned closer to her mother. "We fell in love over dinner. We have much in common, you see ...," she started to explain, but her mother interrupted.

"Does he beat you? Has he forced himself on you?" she asked in a hoarse whisper.

"No!" Deborah replied, mortified her mother would think such a thing. "He is kind, and his servants adore him. He was raised in an orphanage and started his life with nothing, so he treats others with dignity and respect."

Her mother's frown returned. "Then he is a bastard?" she asked quietly, holding the clipping up to reread it.

"No!" her daughter repeated, keeping her voice low. "His father was an officer in the British Army. He died at Bunker Hill in Boston. Then his mother died a few weeks after his birth," she explained in hushed tones. "The woman for whom I work, Mrs. Dawes, was the midwife. She saw to his needs until he was weaned. He is a good man, mama," she insisted, surprised her mother would think the worst of Todd.

Emily studied her daughter, a skeptical look still etched on her face. "What will happen when he finds out you have lost your virtue?" she whispered. "What then?"

Deborah's shoulders fell as she regarded her mother. "He already knows," she finally replied with a sigh. "Miss Fitzsimmons... the woman who will stand with me... we have told him everything. He loves me despite knowing. And maybe he loves me just a bit more because of it," she added in a whisper, trying to provide reassurance. "He is certainly more... protective of me," she said with a small smile.

Mrs. White sighed and leaned her head to one side. "The rags make him out to be a favorite of the *ton*. I thought he would be a snob," she said in her own defense.

Deborah couldn't help but grin. "Not my Todd,... at least, not here at home or among friends," she said as she tried to imagine him behaving like some aristocrats. She found she could not. "I feel affection for him, mama. I may even love him," Deborah said quietly, deciding not to admit her feelings just yet.

Nodding, Mrs. White placed a hand on her daughter's arm, squeezing it gently. She stood up and said, "Well, then. I will see you Thursday. Come for dinner."

Deborah accompanied her out of the parlor. "We will, mama. Please, give my regards to Aunt Katherine," she said as she hugged the older woman.

"I will. She'll be so pleased to know you are well," her mother said as she kissed her daughter on the cheek.

When Deborah had said her 'good-bye' at the front door, she turned to find Todd standing in the great hall, an expectant look on his face.

"Who was here?" Deborah asked as she hurried to him, wrapping her arms around his shoulders and kissing him on the cheek.

He shook his head. "No one. Winston thought I should give you two some time alone," he explained as he took one of her arms and kissed her wrist. "How did I do?" he asked with a worried expression. "Does she think me a rake?"

Deborah's eyes widened. Had he overheard her mother's initial questions about him? "Of course not! You were brilliant. She is most impressed with you, in fact," Deborah replied with a smile. "I'm most impressed with you," she added as she kissed him until the dinner chime sounded. "Thank you for agreeing to the visit on Thursday. And dinner. It means so much to me," Deborah said as they made their way to the dining room.

"It will be good to meet your relatives," he replied, surprised at how much he was looking forward to meeting Deborah's family. "Perhaps we will have an opportunity to meet some of my relatives before the wedding," he added hopefully, his face beaming in anticipation.

Perhaps.

CHAPTER 42
A MAN IN LOVE

une 24, 1802, Grace Park

"You'll stay at Cherrywood after the wedding, of course," Gregory Grandby stated, his tone suggesting there would be no argument. "There's a large guest suite with a very long bed that should suit you two just fine," he added when he noticed Todd Vandermeer's raised eyebrows.

"How very generous of you," the taller man replied happily. "I admit, I've been so concerned with the details of the wedding and the renovations on the Cooper Hotel, I hadn't given much thought to a wedding trip. I accept your offer, of course," Todd agreed with a nod. After a moment, he added, "My Deborah will be most pleased, I'm sure."

Gregory fought the urge to roll his eyes. "She truly has you snared, old man!" he teased as he spread his arms out across the back of the settee. They were seated in Todd's study, Gregory having just arrived at Grace Park from his estate in Derbyshire earlier that afternoon.

The plan was for him to stay at Grace Park and take a room at a London hotel for several days from which he would conduct business meetings. Once his business was complete, he would move to Woodscastle for a two-week stay around the time of the wedding and the Hornsby ball. "Is the young woman here now?" Gregory asked as he noticed a servant quickly pass by the open door.

Todd grimaced and shook his head. "Sadly, no. She's spending today and tomorrow at the Home for Unwed Mothers. There are several babies due this week," he said lightly. "I cannot wait for you to meet her," he added, his expression one of bliss.

"What is it about this woman that has you so completely mad?" Gregory asked in mock disgust. "I've never seen you like this. You have me worried, you must know. You're about to be leg-shackled, and you seem to be looking forward to it."

Todd shrugged and sighed heavily. Crossing his arms while he leaned over his desk, he said simply, "I love her. I have since the moment I met her."

Gregory regarded his friend in silence. He leaned forward as he reached for the pipe poised upright in an ashtray on the low table in front of him. "Indeed?" he replied, his attention on the signet ring he wore on his right ring finger. The large garnet was surrounded by the carefully braided lock of hair his love had sent him, and the same lock wrapped around the gold to form a strawberry blond band.

"Yes, indeed," Todd stated indignantly. When Gregory didn't immediately reply, Todd added, "Why is it that you, with all your experience with women, find it so hard to believe that I have found a woman to love?"

Frowning, Gregory stood up and approached Todd. "Truth be told, I, actually, have very little experience with women, if you must know," he said in a hoarse whisper, keeping his voice down so as not to be overheard by a servant.

Todd regarded Gregory with a raised eyebrow and a look of total disbelief. "*You*. The man who apparently has a girl in every port is now claiming not to have experience with *women?*" he questioned with a half-grin. "You expect me to believe you?" Todd added as he shook his head. His grin slowly disappeared as he took in the sight of a most sober and sad Gregory, and he slowly stood up.

Gregory shrugged and took a brief puff from his pipe. "Yes, if you would be so kind," he answered simply. "But, please, try not to tell the entire town of my situation. I've spent years cultivating an image that has become very important and vital to my business transactions, and I cannot afford to be exposed for the man I truly am. At least, not yet," he added before taking another draw from the pipe.

Todd straightened to his full six-foot, six-inch height and planted his hands on his hips as he considered his friend's words. He tried to sort what they really meant. "You're in love!" he blurted, his face breaking into a huge grin as he realized why Gregory had been so unsupportive of his new-found love. "You *bastard!* You're in love."

Surprised his friend had guessed his secret so quickly, Gregory swallowed hard. "Since Christmastime, yes," he said with a nod, his eyes downcast and his mood sour.

Todd pushed away from the desk and put a hand on Gregory's shoulder. "And yet, you behave as if it's the end of the world. Does the object of your affection not feel the same for you?" he asked in a quiet whisper, his eyebrows drawn together in concern.

Gregory shook his head quickly. "She does, actually," he said as he turned his gaze up to his friend. "She has both written and spoken of her love for me, and I believe her letters to be heartfelt," he explained in a lowered voice. He held up his right hand. "And she sent a lock of hair as proof," he added with a nod.

Cocking his head to one side, Todd regarded the ring with a look of disbelief. "I'd hate to see your mood if she didn't share your affection," he commented lightly. "Whatever is wrong, man?"

Sighing, Gregory scrubbed his face with one hand. "I'm having a bit of trouble figuring out how to tell her family," he hedged before sitting back down on the settee. He put the pipe into the ashtray and leaned back with a sigh. "Like you and everyone else in this country, her brother believes me to be a rake. It's unlikely he'll allow a marriage between the two of us." He picked up the pipe again, his actions a testament to his nervousness.

Todd sat in a tall chair next to the settee and leaned forward. "You... you know this man, then," he said as he watched Gregory contemplate his future.

"Oh, yes," Gregory replied. "Nearly my entire life, in fact. He's as stubborn and as bull-headed as I am, and I'd really rather not have to challenge him to a duel in order to gain his sister's hand in marriage," he commented without the least bit of humor. "Duels are illegal, after all," he added as he took another puff off the pipe. "But then, so is marrying a girl younger than one-and-twenty without her guardian's consent," he nearly shouted as he dropped the pipe back into the ashtray.

Shaking his head from side to side, Todd listened to his friend and realized the identity of the stubborn and bull-headed man at the heart of Gregory's problem. "Oh, my God," Todd said suddenly. "You do have a problem. Thomas Wellingham insists he won't allow Christiana to wed until she is at least eighteen."

Gregory suppressed a frustrated grin as he heard Todd's words. "So, what part of my description of our mutual friend was the tell, eh?" he asked rhetorically.

Todd allowed a huge grin as he leaned back in the chair. "We know many stubborn men, my friend. But you're the one who gave him dueling pistols for Christmas," Todd accused with a raised eyebrow. He regarded his friend for a few moments. "But all is not lost. We just have to accelerate the process," he stated confidently.

Startled by Todd's remark, Gregory shook his head. "And what *process* might that be?" he asked when he realized Todd was having too much fun at his expense. "We cannot make Christiana older than she is."

Grinning, Todd replied, "We need to find Thomas his own woman to love, of course."

Gregory rolled his eyes. "Don't you think I've already thought of that?" he countered with a sigh. "Christiana and I have been trying for months to introduce him to…" He stopped as he realized Todd was still grinning. "You know something, don't you?" he accused as he watched Todd's expression of glee appear. "Some*one*, rather?" he added hopefully.

Todd regarded Gregory and continued smiling as he remembered a conversation he'd had with Thomas Wellingham over a midday meal. "We give the man what he wants," he replied simply.

At Gregory's raised eyebrow, Todd's smile broadened. "And, what, pray tell, might that be?" Gregory asked, somewhat suspicious of his friend's plan.

"A dock. Two, actually. And a refurbished west wing for Woodscastle," Todd stated confidently.

Gregory stared open-mouthed at Todd for several seconds before shaking his head. "Oh. Is that all?" he replied rhetorically. But after another moment, his first smile of the day spread across his face. "Todd Vandermeer, you are a genius," he said triumphantly.

Feeling rather proud, Todd nodded his agreement.

CHAPTER 43
LOST

June 22, 1802, Woodscastle

In the middle of the fifth week of Emma's employment at Woodscastle, Thomas Wellingham returned
home from a longer than usual day at his work. Humphrey greeted
him at the door, as was his custom, and took his master's topcoat
and hat. When Thomas turned to make his way from the vestibule
to the library, that day's newspaper inserted firmly under his arm, he
suddenly stopped and redirected his attention to the round table at
the center of the entry. One of his mother's large vases was situated
at the center of the table and in it was a rather large and ornate
floral arrangement. He stared at it for a moment before glancing at
his butler.

"Miss Fitzsimmons and Miss Wellingham assembled it during
their luncheon today," Humphrey explained with a prim smile,
openly admiring the work of floral art.

Thomas started to say something but then walked around the
table before saying, "I suppose this took several hours to create," as
he motioned with his free hand in a large circular pattern.

His butler shook his head. "About a half-hour, sir. Miss Christiana cut the flowers this morning and Miss Emma helped with the
arrangement when they finished their luncheon in the garden."

Thomas nodded uncertainly. "And are there any flowers *left* in
the garden?" he asked rhetorically, his manner suggesting he was
amused.

Humphrey did his best to suppress a grin. "Oh, yes, Mr. Wellingham. Enough for many more of these, I assure you. Unless you'd rather the flowers stay *in* the garden?"

"No, oh no," Thomas assured him. "This is beautiful, really. It reminds me of..." His voice trailed off as he scrubbed the side of his face with one hand.

"Your mother, sir?" Humphrey prompted. "She used to create a bouquet for that very table at least once a week in the spring and summer."

Thomas nodded. "I remember now," he said quietly, his eyes not quite focused on the flowers but rather on a memory of his mother in his mind's eye.

"If I may say so, 'tis good to have females back in the house," Humphrey commented with a nod, his brows furrowing as his attention was drawn to the top of the stairs.

His master regarded him for a moment, but, lost in thought, he didn't follow Humphrey's line of sight. "Yes. I suppose it is," he agreed before turning to make his way to the library.

*H*aving grown accustomed to her work space in the library, with its thick carpets and heavy drapes helping to insulate the room from the extraneous sounds of the household, Emma Fitzsimmons found she could concentrate for hours on end without interruption.

Mr. Wellingham had been at the office every day the week before as well as the past two days, but he usually returned at four o'clock to spend time with his sister as she practiced the piano. Emma was only slightly aware of his arrival that Tuesday afternoon and merely nodded in his direction when he entered the library a few minutes later, a newspaper folded under his arm.

Following his daily routine, Humphrey brought them both tea. As he set down the cup and saucer for Emma, the butler paused longer than usual. Emma looked up to find him waiting for her to acknowledge him. "Thank you, Humphrey," she said, nervous when Humphrey seemed to hover.

"Miss Fitzsimmons, I'm very sorry to interrupt, but Miss Wellingham is asking for you. She seems to have taken ill," he explained nervously. The man was quite pale and, for a moment, looked like he might be sick.

Emma's eyes widened as she took in the sight of Humphrey's

ghostly face. "Where is she?" Emma replied, pushing her chair out from the desk and standing up before Humphrey could move out of the way.

"At the top of the stairs, miss," he said, biting his lip.

Emma rushed from the room and only then heard the loud whimpering. "Christiana?" she called out, panic rising in her as she rushed up the curved staircase, her skirts bunched into her fists in front of her. Christiana was indeed at the top of stairs, nearly doubled over in pain, the bottom of her gown soaked in blood.

Thomas, made aware something was wrong when he heard Emma call out his sister's first name, ran from the library and saw the two women at the top of the stairs.

"Send for a physician!" Emma shouted as she lifted Christiana into her arms and carried her to her bedchamber.

Humphrey hurried to the front door and called out for Mr. Allen. He returned to the vestibule to let Thomas know the groom was on his way to town, but Thomas was already taking the stairs two at a time, his riding boots making a racket on the runners.

"Thank you, Humphrey," he called out as he disappeared into the corridor. He found the girls in Christiana's room. Emma, who was leaning over Christiana's prone body, had her hand on the girl's forehead. "She's burning up," Emma said to no one in particular. When she realized Thomas was in the room, she added, "I need a compress and some cold water."

"I'll see to it," he replied, moving to the door. At the sight of the blood, Thomas swallowed and looked away. "Are her monthly courses usually this bad?" he asked in a hushed tone.

Emma didn't take her attention from Christiana as a sense of horror filled her. She had seen this before—several times, in fact— at Mrs. Dawes' Home for Unwed Mothers. "This isn't her monthly course," Emma whispered, lifting Christiana's gown and feeling her abdomen. It was hot—Christiana nearly screamed at the slight pressure.

"What kind of pain is it?" Emma asked urgently, trying hard not to allow her fright to show.

Between sobs, Christiana managed to get out a description of cramping and abdominal pain.

"Oh, my God," Emma said under her breath. "Christiana, when was the last time you had your monthly courses?" she asked in a soft whisper. When the younger girl didn't answer right away, Emma sighed and asked, "Can you remember for me?"

Christiana eyes widened and she turned away, her cries strengthening. "March,... I think," she finally admitted between sobs. *How could I not have noticed missing April and May?*

Emma gasped and glanced briefly at Thomas, who had just come back into the bedchamber. She wondered if he had already figured out what was happening.

"I need to get her undressed," Emma said as she rolled Christiana onto her side. Christiana immediately curled into a fetal position and whimpered quietly while Emma undid the row of jet buttons down her back.

Thomas had moved to the other side of the bed, desperately worried and at a loss as to what to do to help. "Mrs. Werthers is bringing some medical items, and she'll see to it we have hot water," he said as he watched Emma work. Only a moment later, the housekeeper entered with a bundle of white cloths and a pail of water. "The hot water will be here in short order," she said, gasping as she saw the blood on Christiana's gown. "But we'll want cold for that."

"Thank you, Mrs. Werthers," Emma said as she dipped a rolled cloth into the water and placed it on Christiana's forehead. She turned back to the housekeeper and whispered, "Sometimes she just has a very *difficult* monthly course."

Mrs. Werthers put her hand on her chest. "Well, is that all?" she replied, the worry lines around her eyes disappearing. "It's a relief to know she'll be all right, Miss Fitzsimmons," she added as she turned to leave the room, her sense of urgency gone.

Emma was sure the housekeeper would pass the information on to the rest of the household staff—it was better they not know the truth. "And Mrs. Werthers, could you please see to it that the blood is cleaned up at the top of stairs? I wouldn't want anyone to slip in it," Emma said quietly, her fingers automatically undoing button after button.

"Miss Dahlia is cleaning it up right now," the housekeeper assured her as she bobbed a curtsy and left the room.

"What is happening to me?" Christiana whispered, her tears subsiding.

"Are you still having cramps?" Emma asked, not sure if she should tell Christiana in the presence of her brother. She desperately fought back her own tears of fright and sadness.

"No," Christiana said quietly. "I think the pain has stopped."

Emma nodded and took a deep breath. At least the bleeding seemed to have stopped, too.

Thomas stared at Emma as she avoided his eyes. "Well?" he finally questioned, his impatience getting the better of him. "Is she going to live?" he asked, his voice harsh. He came around to the other side of the bed and stood as close to Emma as he could without touching her. "What's happening to her?" he asked in a hoarse whisper. When Emma didn't answer right away, Thomas frowned. "You will tell me now," he insisted, his voice rising with each demand.

Inhaling and then covering her mouth with one hand as tears streamed down her face, Emma saw the anger in his eyes. She felt panic. "Please, believe me. I didn't know. I don't even know who ...," she added with a questioning look at Christiana, who refused to meet her eyes.

"Tell me!" Thomas nearly shouted, grabbing Emma's upper arms and shaking her.

Frightened, Emma balled her fists and whispered between sobs, "I'm not yet positive, but I believe she has had a... a... mis... carriage." Her legs suddenly felt as if they were made of rubber. The only thing holding her up was Thomas' grip on her arms.

Startled, Thomas' hold on her lessened and Emma fell against him, sobbing. As her tears penetrated the fabric of his linen shirt, Thomas forced his breathing to slow. Frowning, he held her for a moment and let his face rest against the side of her head until the impact of her words hit him. "She was... she was with child?" he asked in a whisper, not believing what he'd heard. He felt Emma's head nod next to his face and thought for a moment. "For... for how long?" he asked, the anger slowly ebbing from his body as a different emotion filled him.

"At least... at least two months, but I don't know for certain," Emma replied, shaking her head and finally standing on her own. "She has never mentioned a boy or had one call on her."

Thomas leaned over Christiana, one fist shoved into the mattress to support him. "Were you *raped?*" he asked in a hoarse voice, his mind racing with thoughts of what might have happened followed by a need for revenge. Rage built up inside him, and if he had any doubt the day the housebreakers had visited his home, he knew now he was capable of killing another man.

Christiana didn't meet his gaze, but merely shook her head. "No," she said quietly. "He loves me. Please don't ask me who it is." She finally turned to meet her brother's shocked face, saying simply, "I love him, you see."

Thomas' shoulders fell as he collapsed on the edge of the bed, his whole world changed in a matter of moments. He sat with his head in his hands for a moment, occasionally spearing his fingers through his hair while he struggled to breathe.

Emma stared at him, her heart racing as she feared for Christiana. "Please, Mr. Wellingham," she whispered hoarsely. "Do not... do not beat her," she pleaded, her voice breaking as she considered what he might do to his sister. A parade of images raced through her mind as she remembered the girls who had arrived at the Home for Unwed Mothers with bruises and welts or broken bones from having been beaten by their fathers or brothers, some of whom were the very fathers of the babies the girls carried in their bellies. Tears flowed freely down Emma's cheeks as she tried to focus on his boots.

Thomas' eyebrows knit together, and he stared up at her in astonishment. That she thought him capable of such an act hit him like a slap across the face. Shaking his head, he stood up and leaned very close to Emma. "I would *never* beat her," he stated emphatically, his eyes boring into Emma's as he made the vow. "*Never*," he repeated as he turned and glanced down at his sister.

Christiana, who had whimpered through most of their exchange, quieted when her eyes locked on her brother's. It was only a second, though, and she turned her face away, sniffling.

Embarrassed that she thought him capable of such brutality, Emma stepped back. "I am... sorry. I... have just seen... so many..."

Thomas took a deep breath in an attempt to stem his sudden anger. *Not anger*, he realized as he shook his head.

Hurt.

Emma's words had stung him more than he cared to admit. But she had probably witnessed first hand what happened to unwed pregnant girls during her charity work at Mrs. Dawes' facility. Of course she expected him to punish Christiana, he realized. He vowed he would keep his anger in check. "Apology accepted, of course," Thomas said quickly, understanding Emma's concern but still deeply offended she would think him capable of such an act. *She has seen girls beaten quite badly*, he remembered. *But how could she think I would do such a thing?* With a nod, he left the room, his loud footfalls down the hall a testament to his barely controlled emotions.

A moment later, Mrs. Werthers brought in a pail of hot water as Emma continued to undress Christiana.

By the time Dr. Talbot arrived, Emma had cleaned the blood from Christiana's legs and changed the compress several times. At the doctor's insistence, a very sad Emma left the room, went to the kitchen to wash her hands and face, and returned to the library to resume her work.

When the doctor had taken his leave nearly an hour later, Emma closed up the inkwell and set aside the ledger book she'd been trying to sort. Despite the time she had spent on one particular page, she had been unable to concentrate despite knowing something wasn't quite right. Perhaps if she started fresh in the morning, the problem would become clear to her.

As she stood up from the library table, Thomas, no longer wearing his waistcoat and cravat, strode into the library. He stopped short at the sight of her.

"Is she all right?" Emma asked as a wave of weariness took hold. Her eyes, puffy and red from crying, wanted to close and never open. She had never felt so tired, so spent in her entire life. If Thomas had come to relieve her of her duties, she found she didn't have the energy to protest.

"Good Lord, I owe you a new gown," Thomas said, horrified at the sight of Emma's blood-stained gown.

Emma glanced down at the front of her sprigged muslin gown and shrugged. Although it was streaked and smeared with Christiana's blood, but she found she didn't care. "'Tis just a gown," Emma murmured. "Will she be all right?" she asked again.

Thomas nodded as he stepped closer. "Dr. Talbot said she'll be fine," he replied quietly. He took another step closer to Emma, but suddenly uncomfortable, he stopped. "She... she is asking for you. That is, if you can stay longer," he added, realizing only then it was nearly dark.

"Of course. I'll go right up," Emma said as she curtsied, her eyes lowering as she felt the heat of a blush coming over her.

As she was about to leave the room, Thomas reached out and caught her hand, pulling her close to him. "Please, forgive me for the way I treated you earlier," he whispered, finding it hard to look at her as he made the apology. "My behavior was—"

"To be expected, given the circumstances," Emma finished for him, a watery smile crossing her face. She gently kissed his hand. "I know you would only ever do right by her," she whispered. "I am sorry I assumed the worst."

Thomas nodded at the comment, no longer offended. "I assure you again, I couldn't do such a thing to Christiana," he murmured. "Now, to the man who did this to her..." he started to say. He took a deep breath and let it out slowly.

Emma nodded and gave him a wan smile. "If I had been blessed with a brother, I would want him to be just like you," she said in quiet voice. When he finally met her gaze, she released his hand.

All the teasing and comments and questioning that Christiana and Todd Vandermeer had made about her and Thomas came flooding back to her. *They were right*, she thought, her eyes closing in despair. *I want to be with him.*

I may be in love with him, she thought, a bloom of color covering her cheeks.

She couldn't tell him, of course. *He's my employer.* Propriety stilled her voice. Common sense had her giving him a curtsy and taking her leave of the library.

Climbing the stairs as fast as she could, Emma allowed herself to hope Christiana would tell her more than she had that afternoon. After spending nearly two years with the girl, Emma was sure she'd known everything about her, and yet, there was a secret Christiana had never shared with her.

She had a lover I knew nothing about, Emma thought to herself. *At sixteen years old, she is in love and has given her virtue to another. I am nearly five years her senior and have only now fallen in love.*

How can this be?

At the stop of the stairs, where there had earlier been droplets of blood staining the marble floor and balcony rails, everything was clean and neat. Except for the gown she wore, all evidence of the miscarriage had been wiped up or washed out or was in the laundry.

When Emma reached Christiana's room, she knocked on the open door and found Christiana awake and reading in bed by the light of a candle lamp. "Emma!" she said, a small smile showing despite the gloom. "Please, do come in." She patted the edge of the bed to let Emma know it was all right to sit with her.

Emma moved slowly into the bedchamber and sat down. She placed her hand on the side of Christiana's face, glad to see and feel her fever was gone. Christiana almost seemed to glow in the bright candlelight.

"How are you feeling? And what did the doctor say?" Emma asked as she took one of Christiana's hands.

Christiana shrugged, and although she wanted desperately to weep, she didn't. "I'm sad, of course. Sad for myself, because I really did want to have a baby, lots of them, as you know, and sad for Thomas because I know how disappointed he must be in me," she said quietly. "And I'm sad for you because I tell you everything, but I couldn't tell you about this," she added with a shake of her head. Her red-rimmed eyes looked into Emma's, searching for disdain or, worse, indifference from her best friend as she gripped the edge of the counterpane.

"So, you knew you were with child?" Emma asked carefully, surprised Christiana could keep such a secret from her.

"No. Well, I suppose I should have suspected something, but I didn't know. But I meant about my beloved," she said, her face showing happiness for the first time that afternoon. "You have to know, Emma, I really do love him. And he loves me," she added emphatically. "We want to have at least ten children when we are wed."

Emma smiled and had to fight back tears. Christiana had always said she wanted lots of children. "And did the doctor say if you would be able to?"

Nodding, Christiana murmured, "He said I was just too young right now, but that I should be able to have as many as I want after I'm seventeen or so."

Emma shook her head back and forth, still not able to believe her younger roommate had kept her romance from her. "So, how long have you known your... suitor?" she asked, finding it hard to refer to the brigand who had taken her roommate's virtue as anything so polite as a suitor.

Christiana thought for a moment, "Well, I first remember him from when I was five, I believe, but..."

"Five?" Emma repeated, astonished. *She has known the boy for over ten years!* "So, he's not someone from the Blue Coat School?" Emma clarified, referring to the boys' school near Warwick's. A wave of relief washed over her. She doubted a boy from that school would be old enough to accept the financial responsibility for a wife and child.

Christiana screwed her face into a look of disgust. "No! Certainly not," she replied, offended Emma would assume a schoolboy could be her lover. She thought for a moment, her face breaking into a smile as she began listing her lover's qualities. "My beloved is older. He's long been out of school, and he travels a good deal. He has relatives all over England, most of them in Society. He is very rich. And he is a friend of ours. Oh, and I'm most certain you will meet him someday soon," she added, one arm wrapping around her knees as she drew them up to her chest.

Emma fought back tears. "I had better. If I find out you have gone and eloped like Lydia Collins did—"

"I won't elope," Christiana stated emphatically, shaking her head as if offended by the prospect. "I promise I won't. Besides, I want a big church wedding with all the ribbons and flowers and my friends and family and a wedding reception at the Star and Garter at Richmond Hill overlooking the park," she exclaimed happily, one hand flailing around her as she described her big day.

Her demeanor turned serious as she stared at Emma. "And when we do get married, will you stand with me?" she asked quietly. When Emma didn't reply right away, Christiana added, "You can wear whatever color you wish," as if allowing Emma a gown of her choosing would be the enticement necessary to gain Emma's favor.

Emma nodded and let go of Christiana's hand. "Of course, I will," she said with a grin, tears streaming down her face again. "If I ever get married, you must stand with me. And you can wear whatever color you wish. Agreed?" she whispered before a sniffle interrupted her.

Christiana nodded. "Agreed."

Emma sighed and wiped away tears with her damp hanky. "Now, I really must be going," she said, embarrassed by her tears and the subject of Christiana's conversation. "'Tis very nearly dark," she commented as she glanced out Christiana's window. "You get some rest, and I'll see you in the morning."

Christiana frowned. "You're not expecting to go back to town tonight?'" she half-questioned. After the incident with the housebreakers, Christiana couldn't imagine Emma riding her horse on the

Great Western Road, even with a groom as an escort. "Then you must get Mr. Allen to take you, at least," she ordered when Emma indicated she did indeed intend to go home. "Good night, Emma," she said before she returned her attention to her book.

CHAPTER 44
AND FOUND

When Emma left Christiana's bedchamber, she found Thomas at the end of the hall waiting for her.

"Miss Emma," he said quietly as he bowed. Emma curtsied in return, not sure if he had eavesdropped on her conversation with his sister or was merely on his way to visit her. "'Tis awfully late. Perhaps you would agree to dine here and spend the night in the guest bedchamber? I took the liberty of having Mrs. Werthers prepare the room," he said as he motioned to the guest bedchamber door.

Emma suppressed a grin at his mention of the room they had shared when he was so ill.

"I'd hate for you to make the trip back to town after a day like this," he added, afraid if she did leave, she might think too much about the events of the day and never return.

"Oh, Mr. Wellingham, you are very kind to offer, but I have no clothes suitable for dinner..." she said as she indicated her stained gown. Indeed, she had taken home the gown she had worn the last time she'd had dinner and spent the night. She didn't even have a fresh gown for daytime.

"We can find you something," he interrupted, knowing his mother's gowns were still lined up in a wardrobe in the master suite.

Emma considered his offer. "And my horse? 'Tis probably about his feeding time."

"Mr. Allen has already seen to it," Thomas replied, a bit too quickly.

Surprised he wasn't as insistent as he had been the first time he told her she was spending the night, a very weary Emma decided to accept his offer of hospitality. "All right then, thank you," Emma agreed, her heart soaring while part of it still mourned for Christiana's loss.

Thomas took a torch from the hall sconce and led her across the landing at the top of the stairs and to the master bedchamber, where ornate double doors led into a spacious bedchamber. When the firelight illuminated the room, Emma was speechless as she surveyed the richly appointed room. Walls covered in scarlet red moiré fabric, cherry wood moldings and furnishings, and deep, dark carpet made it the most elegant room she had ever seen. Paintings in gilt frames hung on every wall. Drapes made of velvet with satin fobs and chiffon sheers graced the expanse of windows on the far wall. There wasn't a sign of disuse. Mrs. Werthers must have seen to its cleaning on a regular basis.

"What a beautiful room," she breathed. Perhaps one day she would decorate her own bedchamber in such finery, she considered as she walked slowly around the suite. "Who decorated this bedchamber?" she asked in a quiet voice, her fingertips gently gliding over the moldings and fabrics.

Thomas took a quick glance around, noticing, probably for the first time, he realized, the tasteful decor and fine furnishings his mother had arranged so many years ago. As a youth, he hadn't paid the room much attention. Indeed, he didn't remember being allowed in the room. "My mother did this room shortly after my father and she moved into Woodscastle," Thomas replied proudly as he took a look around. He noticed Emma stroking the fabric of the drapes and remembered Todd's comment about long, slender fingers. *Emma has those fingers,* he thought, aware of a tightening in his groin.

"Then this is the master suite," Emma commented as she took in more of the room's beauty. "Why don't you use this room now, Mr. Wellingham?" she asked quietly as she turned her attention to him.

Thomas considered her question and couldn't decide how to answer. "I haven't given it much thought. I suppose I figured I'd move in here once there was a mistress for the house," he said as he shrugged, embarrassed by the situation. He avoided looking down, afraid he might find the front of his breeches tented from his arousal. Instead, he turned and opened the deep, wide wardrobe, an ornate box on curved legs and so tall, it nearly reached the ceiling. Inside was a row of at least twenty gowns. Most were styles from the 1780s or before, but there were two empire gowns—one in deep blue satin and another in a pale green batiste.

"These don't look like gowns from your mother's time," Emma commented as she took one and admired the fabric. Indeed, they were new, she realized as their modiste labels appeared from the folds of the fabric.

Shaking his head, Thomas smiled. "No, these were purchased for Christiana," he admitted with a shrug, "But I didn't know what size to get, and... well, I suppose she'll never be tall enough to wear either of them."

Emma held the blue one in front of herself, trying to decide if it would fit. It was nearly identical to the one Todd had purchased for Deborah, she thought as she realized Thomas was watching her reflection in the cheval mirror across the room.

Thomas nodded. "It suits you," he said, crossing his arms as he turned in her direction. "And 'tis a good color for you, if I may say," he added, his desire for Emma increasing with every move she made in the room.

Emma stepped back and caught her reflection in the cheval mirror. "Thank you, Mr. Wellingham," she said with a smile as she cradled the gown in her arms. "I believe this one will suit" She turned to face him. "How long before dinner?"

Moving the torch toward a large dresser, Thomas made out the hands of a brass clock. "About an hour," he replied. When he turned toward her, he lowered the torch so it hid the growing bulge in his breeches. "I'll show you to your bedchamber."

The two left the master suite and crossed to the corridor with the smaller bedchamber. Emma, already familiar with the guest bedchamber, realized his mother had probably decorated it, as well. With its private bath and ornate walnut furnishings, the room wasn't particularly feminine, but it was certainly comfortable. The room began to glow as Thomas lit several lamps with the torch.

"I'll see you at dinner," he said as he bowed and made his exit.

Given the circumstances that forced Emma to stay in this bedchamber the first time, Thomas seemed almost embarrassed at having to come into it again. Emma could barely get a curtsy in before the door shut behind him.

Emma eyed herself in the looking glass above the dresser and realized she had work to do before dinner. Picking up the hair brush and comb set, probably placed on the dresser as ornaments, she quickly put her hair in order. She took advantage of the private bath to wash up as best she could. The gown went on without a problem, and because of its low v-neck in both the front and the back, there were no buttons to fuss with. However, the chemisette she wore under her empire dresses in the daytime had to go—there was simply too much fabric given the v-neck of the gown.

Pulling it off, she adjusted her corset to better display her décolletage. The sleeves of the gown, which only came to the top of her arms, were tight and could stand to be longer, but overall, the gown fit as well as could be expected. When the dinner bell chimed at eight o'clock, Emma put her feet back into her black slippers and took one last look before heading out the door.

When she arrived in the dining room, Thomas was already seated at the head of the table. He stood and bowed, clearly impressed by the sight of her. She curtsied and then glided to the chair to his right where she sometimes ate luncheon.

"You look lovely tonight, Miss Emma," Thomas said in greeting. Pulling her chair out for her, he noted she wore no earrings. He chastised himself for not bringing the gift he'd purchased for her as a 'thank you' for being his nursemaid the week before.

"You are especially handsome tonight, Mr. Wellingham," she replied. She caught herself, lifting a hand to her mouth. "Oh, my, that wasn't an appropriate thing to say to one's employer."

Thomas' eyebrows went up. "I didn't mind a bit. Perhaps...," he started to say, *We could forget we're employer and employee for one night*, and thought better of it. Despite having shared a bed the night he was so sick with fever and chills, all their daily interactions had been as formal and repressed as they had been the first time they met. "Given everything that has happened today, perhaps we can set aside propriety for this evening," he said instead.

Dahlia brought in steaming bowls of soup and poured white wine from a carafe. When she left the room, they were alone, a crackling fire in the large fireplace supplying the only sound.

"Christiana says she's in love," Emma said quietly.

Thomas angled his head and finished a sip of wine before replying, "You say it as if it's a surprise."

Emma's eyes widened. "Of course, it is," she insisted. Because of his odd comment, she frowned and asked, "Is it not to you?"

Thomas glanced at the table and then returned his attention to Emma. "Yes, I suppose it is," he said quietly. "I just thought she might have shared more of her secrets with you whilst at school," he reasoned, his attention turning to the soup.

Nodding, Emma said, "I thought so, too. You must know, she is very sorry and very sad right now," she said quietly. "You see, she wants to have ten children..."

"*What?*" Thomas blurted out after nearly spraying a mouthful of wine all over the table. "Without benefit of marriage?" he added, trying to keep his voice down.

"No, oh, no," Emma assured him, putting down her soup spoon. "Although that seems to be the way with the girls in London these days," she commented with a raised brow. When she noted his quizzical stare, she added, "Over half of the babies born in town are born to unwed mothers," she explained quickly, knowing that although some were born to prostitutes, most were not. "But, Christiana wants to marry this man she loves. She claims she wants to have lots of children with him," she said with a good deal of concern.

Shaking his head and trying to maintain a state of calm he wasn't particularly feeling, Thomas asked carefully, "And who might this... *man*... be?" hoping Christiana might have shared her secret with her best friend.

Emma leaned in his direction. "She said it was 'a friend,' someone she remembers knowing since she was five years old," she replied as she recalled the details of their conversation.

Thomas gave her a glance of surprise. "But she didn't mention a name? A family name, perhaps?"

Emma shook her head. "I was hoping you might know," she countered. "She refused to identify him, but she did say he was long out of school, that he had many relatives who were in Society, and that he travels a great deal. Oh, and she mentioned he is rich. And she assured me it was not someone from the Blue Coat School," she added with an arched eyebrow.

Thomas snorted at the last comment, saying a, "Thank goodness," under his breath. Sighing, he tried to figure out who could have taken his sister's virtue. "Well, unfortunately, we have several friends who fit the description to some degree," he commented as he mentally pictured friends of his parents and friends he had made since childhood.

"She said I would meet him sometime soon," Emma added. "Is anyone expected to visit? Perhaps in the next few weeks?" she asked, hoping the additional hint would narrow down the possibilities.

Thomas shook his head again. "Well, Gregory Grandby will be here next week, but it cannot be him," he said in an offhand manner. "Although, he could be considered rich. Has a bit of a reputation as a rake, I suppose, but," he shook his head. "He'll probably be a bachelor the rest of his life," he murmured as he stared off into space. "Humph. I have no idea who this mystery man could be."

They sat in silence for a few moments before Thomas placed a hand on the table near her arm. "Miss Emma," he said quietly, "I know she may talk to you in confidence about this at some point. If that happens, could you...?"

Emma placed her right hand over his. "If she should tell me, I will, of course, inform you. But you must promise not to get too terribly angry with the man, or with Christiana, for that matter, when you do find out," Emma insisted quietly. "She is quite sure she loves this man. She assures me they'll marry. You risk estrangement if you insist on keeping them apart."

At first, Thomas bristled at her words. How dare she assume how he would react? But once he gave them more thought, he finally nodded in agreement. "If it is indeed a friend, and he didn't force himself upon her, then I promise." He took a deep breath. "You must know I'm very disappointed in her."

Emma nodded. "Christiana knows that, too. She's very sad for you, but I find she's not regretful in the least," she said with a furrowed brow. "She did promise me she wouldn't elope, though," she added with an arched brow. "She wants a church wedding with flowers and ribbons and all of her friends and family around her."

Putting a spoon into his soup, Thomas stirred it around. "Is that so?" he replied as he shook his head. "I think what makes this so hard for me is that I seem to have lost touch with her this past year. As disappointed as I am in her, I'm more disappointed in myself... that I didn't know what was going on in her life," he added, barely able to get the words out.

Whispering, Emma replied, "I believe I know exactly how you feel. This all had to have happened whilst I was attending classes." She paused for a moment, thinking of the time line. *Sometime in the spring. Sometime during April.* "Or the theatre," she whispered, recalling the evening in April when she made a dinner for Christiana. The girl had said she was ill and didn't want to join the rest of the Delta and Gamma House residents for the play at the Sans Souci.

Thomas' brows furrowed. "What is it?" he asked as he leaned forward, watching Emma's face change as she seemed to recall something.

Dumbfounded, Emma stared at Thomas. "She never told me about a gentleman caller... or a suitor, but I believe he must have visited her the evening in April when the rest of us had to be at the theatre—to see a play—for our theatre arts class," she explained quickly. "We were away from Gamma House for several hours."

Eyebrows raised, Thomas shook his head. "The doctor agreed with your two-month estimate," he said quietly. "So, what else is troubling you?"

Emma regarded her host, not sure she should admit just how Christiana's secret had affected her. "I am hurt she didn't trust me enough to share her secret. And I cannot help but feel jealous that my roommate, who is nearly five years younger than me, has already found the love of her life, and she isn't scheduled to have her come-out until next Season!"

Thomas couldn't help but smile in reply. "Five years, you say?" he said in a teasing tone, hoping to dispel some of the heaviness that hung in the air. A wave of relief washed over him as his estimate of Emma's age was confirmed. "I'm surprised Warwick's accepted you."

Feigning embarrassment, Emma took a sip of wine. "I did have to be a bit vague about my age back then," she admitted. Most girls who started at Warwick's did so by twelve or thirteen—it was expected they would enter Society at fifteen or sixteen and be engaged or married by seventeen or eighteen. Very few actually completed the four-year school.

"You lied about your age?" Thomas asked, his amusement growing as he finally started eating his soup.

"I did not *lie*," Emma insisted, nearly interrupting his comment. "I simply... didn't complete that portion of the application."

Thomas shook his head, a grin on his face. "Indeed," he replied before taking another spoonful of soup.

"Indeed, and I do believe they'll accept anyone who is willing to pay their tuition and board fees," Emma added with a hint of derision as she took a spoonful of soup. It was not particularly good, but she found herself hungrier than she expected.

"Miss Emma?"

"Yes, Mr. Wellingham?"

"I usually take a walk through the back gardens after dinner. Humphrey has assured me there are still some flowers left in the garden after that massive floral display you helped construct. Will you accompany me this evening?"

Emma leaned against her chair back, at first confused and then amused by his reference to the number of flowers that had been used in the vestibule arrangement. She was also surprised by the question. "I assure you, the garden is still full of flowers, and yes, I will," she agreed with a nod and a relieved sigh. "It would be a welcome diversion from having to clean my gown," she added with a grin, remembering that her bloodstained gown was soaking in the bath.

"I have had Mrs. Werthers see to it your gown is ready for you in the morning," Thomas said in reply. "And if it is not, there is always the green one in my mother's wardrobe," he added, taking another spoonful of soup.

Shaking her head, Emma said, "Oh, Mr. Wellingham, I simply couldn't. It was more than enough that you allowed me to borrow this one."

Thomas sat back in his chair and regarded her, his brows furrowing. "Borrow?" he repeated. "No, this is for you to keep. I insist," he said as he barely touched the sleeve of the gown.

There was something in the way he made the statement that had Emma withholding her protest. Despite the fact that an unmarried woman simply couldn't accept a gift of clothing from a man, she realized it would do her no good to remind him of that bit of propriety. His decision seemed quite final, and she really did like the gown. "Oh. Well, then, thank you, sir," she said quietly before returning her attention to her soup.

CHAPTER 45
A WALK IN THE GARDEN

lthough June evenings in southern England could be cool and foggy, or warm and clear, or cloudy and rainy, it didn't seem to matter what the weather held when Thomas escorted Emma through the back doors of Woodscastle. As they walked along a path through the gardens, Emma was amazed at how black the skies could be on a moonless night. Stars crowded the sky—more than she ever saw from her townhouse in London. There the skies were filled with soot and fog, and, at most, one might see the moon.

Thomas interrupted the silence after a few moments of walking. "If you were at home tonight, what would you be doing?" he asked as they strolled, her hand on his bent arm. The heady fragrance of jasmine assaulted his nostrils as they passed under an arboretum covered with vines.

Surprised by the question, Emma nearly stopped walking. "I... I would be kneading dough for the morning's rolls, which for tomorrow would be orange, since I'm out of cinnamon, and then I'd clean the kitchen, do some laundry, read a book, and then be in bed by eleven."

Thomas paused in mid-step. He was about to ask her about the cinnamon, a somewhat expensive spice given the East India Company had exclusive rights to import it from Sri Lanka. Instead, he asked, "You don't have occasion to... go out?" So many Londoners enjoyed shopping or the theatre, since most shops were open until ten o'clock.

Emma shook her head. "Just the one dinner at Grace Park since I finished school," she replied, realizing how little time there was to socialize when one had only borrowed servants. "Sometimes I have dinner with my neighbors, or I host them at my townhouse," she added.

"What about the theatre?" he ventured as they strolled.

"I have been many times," Emma replied with a happy nod. "I enjoy it very much, especially at Sans Souci," she explained, referring to the theatre in Leicester Place. She wondered how busy the theatre might be on such a perfect night, especially after reading of the scandalous behavior of one of the actresses in the current production. "I don't employ a companion, though, so I really must find opportunities to attend with friends. But I find it's an activity best done with others anyway. So you have someone with whom to talk about it afterwards," she explained.

Thomas furrowed his brow at the mention of a companion. "When I hired you, it didn't occur to me you would have to travel here every day and yet you don't have an escort to see you here safely," he commented, his concern evident in his voice. "I do hope Mr. Allen is satisfactory."

"Oh, very much. He always arrives about the time I'm in the mews. Even if he wasn't available to escort me, the Great West Road is well-traveled, Mr. Wellingham, and my townhouse is in the West End. I believe it is quite safe as long as I ride in the daylight," she replied, surprised he was still concerned for her safety after more than a month of her being in his employ. *But then the house-breakers had paid a visit...* Emma shook her head to clear the image of the men who had been left dead on the steps of Woodscastle.

"I cannot imagine riding side saddle for six miles," Thomas murmured.

Emma had to suppress a grin as she realized he had never seen her ride. "My horse is far too large for a side saddle, Mr. Wellingham." When she noted his furrowed brow, she added, "And now you have surmised the most scandalous thing about me."

Thomas issued a 'humph' and replied, "I hardly think riding a horse as it was intended to be ridden could be considered scandalous." He imagined her legs spread over his own horse and then realized what she meant. He coughed to cover his sudden comprehension and ignored the heat he felt in his loins.

"I wear trousers under my gowns when I ride," Emma admitted

quietly, her tone suggesting the wearing of trousers was the scandalous part.

Thomas swallowed and nodded, his expression barely under his control. "That seems most practical, Miss Emma. Indeed, I wonder why more women don't employ such a riding habit," he commented as lightly as he could under the circumstances.

Shocked by the idea, Emma regarded her employer before realizing he seemed to believe what he had just said. "Societal expectations, I'm sure," she answered quietly. As they continued on the garden path, Emma became aware of Thomas' continued gaze in her direction. She dared not look at him, instead turning her attention on the stars above and ahead of them. "If I were not here, what would *you* be doing tonight?" she asked, remembering it was her turn to direct the conversation.

Thomas sighed audibly. "Since I was at the warehouse today, I would have spent the early evening in the library reading posts and the news..."

"*The Gazette*, *The Times*, the *Daily Chronicle*, or the *Daily Mail?*" she queried, insisting on more detail.

"*The Times*, of course," Thomas replied with a grin. "And then I would dress for dinner, eat with Christiana until eight-thirty or nine, depending on our conversation... or lack thereof,... take a walk, as we are doing now, go to the library for a brandy or a glass of claret and a book, and then be in bed by midnight."

Emma paused in mid-step. "You don't... go out?" she asked, parroting his line of questions. They were near a row of rose bushes, and she briefly closed her eyes as she inhaled the sweet scent.

"I somehow knew that might be your next question," Thomas accused with a hint of amusement in his voice. He glanced in her direction just as her eyes opened, her head lifted and her long neck appeared fully exposed as she breathed in the night air. His breath caught at the sight. *She looks like she's just been kissed*, he thought, jealous of whatever god of the night sky had the privilege.

Swallowing hard, he struggled to remember her question. "I sometimes do if I have spent the day at work," he finally got out, realizing he had paused too long. "As you know, I don't always come back to Woodscastle, but rather take a room at a hotel next to Boodles. Spending time at the club gives me a chance to discover what's going on in the world of finance and business," he explained, implying the comment was made in jest. "And I sometimes eaves-drop on our fair city's elders," he added with a sly grin.

Emma raised her eyebrows in mock astonishment. "You are probably in good company then. What about the theatre?"

"Like you, I have been many times, but it is not my preferred source of entertainment."

Something in the way he made the comment, the way his eyebrow arched in a teasing manner had Emma's expression of contentment turning to one of shock.

Had he really just said what she thought he said? And in such a manner as to suggest ...? "Mr. Wellingham!" she admonished him, her free hand moving to cover her mouth.

Thomas stopped walking, wondering what he had said to make her react so. "Oh, you misunderstand, Miss Emma," he said when he realized how what he had said could be misconstrued. "I'm not a rake, I assure you. My preferred source of entertainment is *social* intercourse," he said, emphasizing the 'social'. "Having dinner with friends, either here or in town, where we have the opportunity to discuss all sorts of topics, and share entertaining stories, and drink good wines until at least midnight," he explained as he gently squeezed the hand that held his arm.

Mortified by her comment, Emma felt her cheeks redden and was glad for the cover of darkness. "Oh, please pardon me for imag-ining... something else," she apologized. *Someone else,* she nearly said, a stab of jealousy making it hard to breathe. *Someone who might have been his mistress?*

"Of course," Thomas replied with wan smile, surprised he had been able to shock her without even trying. He had wondered if anything could cause her embarrassment. She seemed rather worldly compared to other women in whose company he had been of late, wives of associates or shopkeepers. But then, Emma had probably helped her father run his shop, and she had been taking the accounting classes in addition to her schooling at Warwick's. Her exposure to young men seeking a means to employment probably allowed her insights otherwise not available to young women who never ventured past the schoolroom or assemblies.

After another long pause, Emma asked, "Are you still planning to attend the Vandermeer wedding?" She knew he was to stand with Todd, but he hadn't mentioned the wedding since their talk about

Todd and Deborah the Monday after Todd had proposed, nor had Thomas said anything over dinner about his friend.

Thomas smiled and nodded. "Oh, yes. I am standing with Mr. Vandermeer, in fact," he answered. "And you?"

Emma nodded, grinning like a schoolgirl. "Of course. I am standing with Miss White," she replied happily. "That is, if I'm not expected to work for you that day," she added as she paused in mid-step, realizing he might expect her to be at Woodscastle that Saturday. He had excused her from work the Saturday past only because of the situation with the housebreakers.

"Oh, I wouldn't expect you to work that day," Thomas replied. After a pause, an amused expression appeared on his face. "It makes you very happy to think about them, does it not?" he half-questioned. A breeze caught a tendril of hair at her temples, and he watched from the corner of his eye as she tucked it behind her ear with two long fingers.

"It does, indeed. Except for last Friday evening, they have been blissfully happy," Emma replied with a nod.

Thomas nearly stopped walking as he regarded Emma. "What happened last Friday?" he asked, his brows furrowing as he grew concerned for his friend. He had lunched with Todd that very day, he remembered, and been with the man as his friend surveyed every available wedding ring in no less than five goldsmiths' shops. He was sure the couple would exchange their vows at some point during the next two days—Todd's lust for his bride-to-be had made Thomas realize just how serious his friend was about taking a wife.

"A bit of a misunderstanding, and a bit of an *overreaction* on Miss Deborah's part is all," Emma replied carefully. "But, it was good in the end," she stated as she remembered the evening's strange events. "Mr. Vandermeer learned who his parents were, and it has been... amazing for him."

Thomas smiled as he recalled a post he had received Saturday from the ecstatic man. There were no details in the letter, just the news that Todd had discovered the identity of his mother and father. "A very important bit of information, since he has spent his entire life believing he was a bastard," Thomas replied sardonically. At that moment, a shooting star streaked through the sky.

"Did you see that?" Emma whispered in awe. Another one, with a much longer tail, disappeared into the black horizon. "This must be a meteor shower," she breathed as she craned her neck to look for others.

"Make a wish," Thomas said quickly.

"What?"

"Make a wish," he repeated. "Christiana always tells me to make a wish when we see a shooting star," he explained as he noticed yet another streak across the sky.

Emma closed her eyes and considered. *I wish for a man like you,* she thought, and then, as she gave it more consideration, she amended it to, *I wish for you to be my man.* Yes, that was much better, she decided.

"What did you wish for?" Thomas asked in a teasing tone as he squeezed her hand again.

Emma had to suppress a gasp. "I cannot say or it won't come true," she replied indignantly, surprised by his question.

Thomas laughed and led her on the path back to the house. "Will you join Christiana and me for breakfast in the morning?" he asked as he opened the back door. "I cannot say if it will be as good as your orange rolls," he warned with a grim expression.

"I'm sure it will be a wonderful breakfast," Emma said with a nod. "I would be delighted. Thank you again for your hospitality," she added as they reached the bottom of the stairs. She bunched the front of her skirt in one hand before turning to take the stairs.

"Thank you for having dinner with me," Thomas replied. When he started up the stairs with her, Emma stopped and frowned. "What is it?" he asked, his brows furrowing to match her expression.

"Aren't you going to the library for a brandy and a book?" she asked, remembering what he had said about his nightly routine.

He nodded his head. "I will, in a few moments. But first, I will see you to your room." He held out his arm for her as Emma continued to climb the stairs.

"That's very kind of you, Mr. Wellingham," she replied, placing her hand on his arm. When they reached the door to the bedchamber, she curtsied as he bowed, and they parted company for the night.

CHAPTER 46
AN ERROR IS REVEALED

June 23, 1802, Woodscastle

At eight o'clock the following morning, Emma, wearing her freshly laundered gown from the day before, took her seat in the library. She scanned the bothersome ledger that had plagued her the afternoon before. What had caused her to think something was wrong?

It only took a moment to notice the source of the error she had found the day before—there, in plain sight, the amount for the beginning and ending inventory journal entry changed from one page to the next, just as they had done in the journal she had worked on the day of the business meeting. The error was small— only a pound—but an error, nonetheless. As she flipped through the pages to the next entries for inventory, she found the same kind of error but for a larger amount—ten pounds.

She was looking for instances of the same error when Thomas strode into the library. He walked purposely to the library table and stood next to her. Startled by his sudden presence, Emma tried to stand up to curtsy, but he placed a hand on her shoulder.

"Please, don't get up," he said quietly. His manner was most formal, but he seemed preoccupied. "I merely came to say 'good morning' and to beg your forgiveness," he began softly. "I just received a post from town. It seems my presence is required at the office as soon as possible. As such, I'll be unable to have breakfast with you this morning," he explained, his words coming quickly. His apology seemed heartfelt, though.

"Oh, of course, Mr. Wellingham," Emma replied with a nod.

"Perhaps Christiana will be well enough to join me," she said hopefully. "She was awake and about to bathe when I came down earlier." When she noticed his hesitation, she asked, "Is something... wrong?"

He nodded, but didn't look at her. "Please, don't think poorly of me. I was wondering if you would do me the favor of allowing me to... to kiss... to kiss your neck before I depart?" he whispered as he held his hands behind his back. "I believe I shall have a much better day should you grant me such a favor."

Stunned by the request—and even more stunned by the impropriety of his request—Emma gasped and considered her options. *He wants to kiss me,* she thought happily.

He wants to kiss me because he thinks he might have a better day?

What an odd request!

"Well," was all she could say at first. "I... I am flattered you believe a simple kiss will allow you to have a better day. I suppose my neck is yours to kiss," she replied with a slight shrug as she held her head up and turned it to the side. Holding her breath, she thought of closing her eyes.

Thomas grinned. If she'd given him an answer regarding the impropriety of his request, he didn't know what he would have done. He took his time as he bent over and allowed his nose to touch the short hairs at the nape of her neck. She withheld a gasp when she felt the sensation of his warm breath on her skin. She struggled to sit still. His lips finally took purchase and gently kissed her skin. Pulling his hand out of his pocket as he ended the kiss, he threaded the wire of an earbob through the piercing in her right ear lobe.

Startled by the weight of it, Emma reached up to feel it, her fingertips gingerly touching the warm metal. Thomas held the mate in his hand.

Emma realized it wasn't one of the earbobs she'd seen in his dresser drawer the night he had been so ill, but rather a gold fob in the shape of a teardrop suspended from a wire. With her thumb and forefinger, she carefully lifted the earbob from his hand just as she realized a matching necklace hung from his other hand. Awestruck, she looked up at him as he reached around her neck and fastened the clasp of the necklace where he had kissed her.

"They're beautiful," she breathed as she held the teardrop that hung from the gold chain. "But... why?" she asked in a whisper as she looked up at him. *First a gown, and now jewelry. What is he thinking?*

"These are not a gift, of course, for it would be wholly inappropriate for me to bestow you with a gift since you are an unmarried woman," he explained quickly, his language stilted as he remembered he had bestowed a gift in the form of a gown only the night before. "They're my 'thank you' for having been the best nursemaid I have ever had," he clarified. Scowling, he glanced away, his attention on something else in the library. "Come to think of it, though, you may have been the *only* nursemaid I have ever had," he murmured, not intending for her to hear his thought.

Emma swallowed and glanced up at her employer. "It was my pleasure, I assure you," she answered automatically as she fingered the earbob, and then realized how her words could be misconstrued.

"I rather doubt that," Thomas replied, his vantage point allowing him a quick glance along the contours of her collar bones and down her cleavage and around the gentle swell of her breasts above the edge of her chemisette.

Opening her mouth to argue, Emma thought better of it and then said simply, "Still, I would hardly be a good employee if I should have allowed my employer to die of a cold and fever when it was within my capacity to at least provide some assistance. If you had died, I, of course, would be out of a job..." She inhaled sharply and covered her mouth with ink stained fingers, the heat of her increasing blush making her ears burn.

Thomas smiled at the comment. "Ah, so it was merely self-preservation on your part then," he teased gently. "I should have guessed."

Emma dared a glance up at him then, realized he was teasing her, and gave a shrug. "And there is the fact that you are my best friend's brother. I wouldn't wish to be responsible for her becoming an orphan," she countered playfully, a hint of a grin turning up the corners of her mouth.

Thomas arched an eyebrow. *She's flirting with me*, he thought, his loins stirring in response. *And I believe I may have started it.* "Then it was rather kind of you to spare her from the orphanage," he countered with a nod. As an afterthought, he added, "Or perhaps it was the orphanage you were sparing?" he suggested, allowing a rueful grin to appear.

Feigning shock, Emma had to suppress a giggle. "Mr. Welling-ham!" she scolded, no longer able to keep a straight face. "How could you think such a thing? For now I cannot tell your sister of this conversation!" At the sound of a throat clearing, the two glanced toward the library door.

"Mr. Wellingham, would you care for tea before you leave?" Humphrey asked from the open library door, his hands holding a silver salver laden with a tea service.

Emma suppressed a gasp of surprise and used the pen to point to one of the errors she'd found on the ledgers. "Right here, Mr. Wellingham," she said in a business-like tone. "I have found several errors just like this in various amounts," she added as she angled her head to look up at Thomas, hoping the butler hadn't seen him actu-ally kiss her neck or place the jewelry on her ear or around her neck.

"Indeed, Miss Emma," Thomas commented as his brows stitched together and he realized she wasn't just covering for his impropriety. He turned his attention to the butler. "Thank you, no, Humphrey. I need to leave now," he said as he returned his attention to the ledger. "How often does this kind of error occur?" he asked in all seriousness as he leaned over Emma's shoulder and peered at the two entries.

"I don't yet know. I found some similar problems in two ledgers last week, and the first one in this book late yesterday, and I have just found two more this morning," she explained with a furrowed brow. "I'll work on this today. If you should return before I leave this evening, I'll give you a full report of my findings."

Thomas gave a cursory nod. The errors seemed rather insignifi-cant to him, but he appreciated her being able to show him some-thing of her progress. "Splendid," he answered. "I'm off, then," he said as he bowed to her, nodded to the butler, and left the library.

Humphrey watched his master take his leave of Woodscastle before he poured a cup of tea. "Good morning, Miss Fitzsimmons," he said as he set a full teacup, saucer, and napkin on the library table.

"Thank you, Humphrey, and good morning to you," she said as she took the cup. Putting it to her lips, she glanced out the window to see Thomas mount a horse and take off at a run down the drive leading to Burlington Road. Meanwhile, Humphrey remained in the library, rearranging pillows and straightening the decanters and glassware on the sideboard.

"Humphrey," Emma said as she turned in her chair. "May I ask you a question about Mr. Wellingham?"

The butler paused as he considered her query. "Of course, Miss Fitzsimmons. If it is within reason," he replied cautiously as he walked to her side of the library. He couldn't help but notice the jewelry she wore on her ears and around her neck. He had seen the pieces while putting away his master's clothes.

"Is Mr. Wellingham courting someone?" she asked, not sure how to put the question in a more subtle form.

Humphrey, a bit taken aback by the question, was tempted to say, "Yes, haven't you noticed?" Instead, he considered how to answer her question. "I don't believe so, Miss Fitzsimmons. He is one of those men of whom they say 'is married to his work'. And I believe it is his intention to look after his sister until such time as Miss Wellingham is betrothed."

Emma nodded, a tooth capturing her lower lip. "'Tis a pity," she murmured. "I believe he would be a good catch for one of London's wealthy daughters," she said matter-of-factly.

Bothered by her comment, Humphrey regarded Emma for a moment. *Wealthy daughter? Whatever gave her the impression Thomas Wellingham would only consider a woman with a large dowry?* He cleared his throat and finally spoke. "If I may?"

Emma raised her eyebrows, noting the butler's expression. "Of course."

"Why do you say 'a wealthy daughter', Miss Fitzsimmons?" he asked.

Straightening in her chair, Emma at first wondered if he objected to her use of the term 'daughter' and then realized it was instead the reference to 'wealthy' that caused him consternation. "Well, at Warwick's, we had discussions about the classes people are born into and with whom they should associate and marry. Members of the aristocracy are expected to marry their own. Wealthy girls are encouraged to marry within their own class, as are wealthy men. Apparently, rich men who marry beneath their class have a harder time maintaining their social status. As a wealthy man, I am led to believe Mr. Wellingham would be looking to marry a girl with a substantial dowry," she explained.

A look of disappointment crossed the butler's face. "You must remember that not all the wealthy of this world were born to it," he said as he moved to stand across the library table from Emma. "Are you not a wealthy daughter?"

Emma shook her head. "Oh, no, not at all." At his quizzical expression, she added, "I certainly wouldn't be allowed to work if I were," she claimed. "I was barely born into the middle class. My father was in trade. He owned a hat shop in Oxford Street."

The butler arched a bushy eyebrow. He originally thought her to be a friend or relative—she shared the maiden name of one of his cousin's wives—who was merely offering her math skills in an effort to assist Mr. Wellingham with some accounting issues. And then he considered her other comment. "George Fitzsimmons was your father?" he asked, surprised by the news that not only was Miss Fitzsimmons not a wealthy woman, but that her father had been his hat maker.

"You knew of him?" she said, surprised to find someone else who remembered her father.

"Well, I bought hats from him, yes," he admitted with a nod, but then he shook his head as he tried to work through the irony in her earlier statement. "And yet you attended Warwick's?" he asked as he returned the conversation to the original subject.

Seeing his point, Emma shrugged and realized an explanation was in order. "It was my father's dying wish that I be educated there. I've no idea why. I used nearly all of the inheritance he left me to pay for the tuition and board. But having no prospects for marriage, I thought it best to take Mr. Stokes' accounting class, as well. At least, now I'm employable should I find an employer who can see past the fact that I'm a woman."

The butler nodded his head. "I believe I can tell you why your father wanted you to attend Warwick's," he said gently. His clasped his gloved hands behind his back as he leaned forward.

With the conversation now about her father, Emma found herself overcome with sadness. A doting father, George Fitzsimmons managed to make hats by day and do the company books at night until such time that Emma was old enough to take them on. After his wife's death, he arranged for his daughter to be cared for by one his sisters. Although the aunt could be trusted to look after Emma during the daytime, her gambling habit kept her out late into the night. George insisted Emma spend the evenings and Sundays with him.

Once he contracted chronic pneumonia and could no longer work, he sold half the business to his younger partner.

George Fitzsimmons had been dead nearly four years now. Somewhere, there was a much younger sister. A sister possibly being raised as a ward or a daughter of Matthew Fitzsimmons, Viscount Chamberlain, and his wife Caroline.

Emma blinked back tears and swallowed hard to stave off a sob. "Please enlighten me," Emma replied as she folded her hands in her lap and leaned forward.

"Certainly," the butler nodded curtly. "It is every father's wish that his daughter have what he couldn't provide," he stated with a good deal of certainty. He made the comment as if he'd had a daughter of his own. "By sending you to a school attended by children of wealth and privilege, he was seeing to it you would meet and associate with the wealthy of this world. In doing so, I believe he thought to increase your chances for meeting a wealthy man you would one day marry."

Emma considered the butler's words. Had her father conspired to see her marry well? She continued to fight back tears. "Is that it, then?" she replied rhetorically, displaying a watery smile.

Humphrey nodded, smiling in return. "And, although you say you had no prospects for marriage when you were in school, I can assure you that it has... that it *will* change," he said confidently. When Emma didn't seem able to reply, the butler took a deep breath and offered a handkerchief. "If there is nothing else, I must return to my duties now, Miss Fitzsimmons," he said with a bow.

A rather stunned Emma nodded as she accepted the linen cloth and dabbed at her eyes. "So must I."

She fingered the gold teardrops on her ears and at her throat. *What can he know about my marriage prospects?* she wondered as she watched the butler leave the library.

CHAPTER 47
HATS AND NUMBERS

When Emma mounted her horse later that afternoon, it was well after six o'clock. She had stayed later in the hopes that Thomas would return from London so she could tell him about all the errors she had found in the ledgers. By the time she had completed her audit of the inventory journal entries, she had found that over four hundred pounds were missing over the course of just five months, yet the overall totals listed for the liabilities and assets were correct.

The money was somewhere—she just had to find it.

A night of rain had helped to smooth out most of the road back to London, but occasionally a deep rut or large body of water forced Emma and Mr. Allen to direct their horses to take a slight detour. As her bay trotted into a pasture to avoid such a puddle, Emma noticed an odd sight in an oak tree up ahead. She slowed down her mount and called out to Mr. Allen. "I'll be but a moment!" She tugged on the reins, directing her bay to stand just under the tree. Perched on a low-lying limb of the oak was a man's black top hat.

Reaching up with her riding crop, she was able to snag it and catch it with her other hand as it lost its purchase on the branch. She flipped it over to look at the label and was surprised to find it was from her father's shop. Although it had obviously been soaked with water, it was now dry, still in good shape, and would be wearable after a good brushing.

She remembered the night Thomas had come home in the rain. He hadn't been wearing a hat.

When she turned her mount to head back to the road, she was surprised to see Mr. Allen and Mr. Wellingham watching her from atop their mounts. Thomas had slowed his horse to a trot when he noticed her and then pulled to a complete halt alongside his groom as Emma rode up through the pasture to meet them.

"Good evening, Miss Emma," he said as he tipped his hat and took in the sight of her holding what appeared to be one of his hats on the end of her riding crop.

"Good evening, Mr. Wellingham," she said with a crooked smile. "Is this, by chance, your hat? I found it in that oak tree over there," she said as she gestured behind her.

Thomas pulled his bay closer and reached for the hat, wincing at the sight of the riding crop on which it was mounted. Looking at the label in the hat, he smiled and shook his head. "Unbelievable," he replied as he studied the inside of the hat. "It is indeed. I lost it the night of that awful rainstorm," he said wistfully. "And 'tis one of my favorites. Thank you for taking the time to fetch it from the tree," he added happily.

"You're very welcome," Emma replied with a nod. "It just needs a good brushing." She watched as he fingered the brim and studied the top. "That style was one my father loved to make. He said it was a hat that made gentlemen," she recalled with a smile.

Thomas angled his head as he gazed at Emma. "Ah, yes. I remember you mentioning George Fitzsimmons was your father," as he recalled the first night he met Emma. "By the way, the deal we have with the new owner..."

"Mr. Smith?"

"Yes," he nodded. "'Tis going quite well. Better than could be expected, in fact," he commented with a firm nod. "I appreciate your bringing his situation to my attention."

Emma smiled and nodded. "I'm glad it worked favorably for the both of you." After a pause, she added, "I have news about the missing money from the inventory account. Would you like me to tell you about it now?"

With a wistful smile, Thomas was still studying the wayward hat. "No. I have had a very good day, thanks to you, I might add," he said as he held the hat up, "And I'd rather not have *you* spoil it with bad news."

Emma feigned indignation. "Well, then we shall be on our way," she said as she gave a nod to Mr. Allen and pointed her horse toward London. "Thank you again for the... use of the gown, and good night, Mr. Wellingham," she said as she nodded in his direction. She had been about to say 'jewelry', but realized Mr. Allen was within earshot.

"And good night to you, Miss Emma," Thomas replied as he tipped both his hats. "I trust you won't be too late this evening, Mr. Allen," he added as he turned to regard his groom.

"I've no plans in town tonight, sir," the groom replied.

"Very good. Ride safe," Thomas said. Then he headed toward Woodscastle, his extra hat perched on the pommel of his saddle.

CHAPTER 48
DINNER AT THE IN-LAWS

*J*une 24, 1802, *Whitechapel*

"My darling, what's troubling you?" Todd asked as the coach rocked over the cobblestone streets toward Whitechapel. The late June evening was clear but humid, and Todd was perspiring more from the heat than from any anxiousness he felt over meeting Deborah's family.

Deborah squeezed Todd's hand tighter as she glanced in his direction. Although they weren't yet married in the eyes of the church, she had honored Todd's request that they behave as if they were. "I'm so nervous," she replied with a hint of a smile. "I haven't seen my aunt in over two years. And although my mother seemed... *amenable* with our arrangements, I fear she may have changed her mind over the course of the past few days," she explained quietly.

Todd wrapped an arm around her shoulder and pulled her close. "You cannot think your aunt would disapprove of our marriage," he said quietly. "Unless ...," he started to say and then stopped. What had her parents told the rest of the family regarding Deborah's two-year absence? "What has your aunt been led to believe about you?"

Deborah shrugged, her nearly bare shoulder rising against the space between his chest and arm. Wanting to impress upon her mother that Todd had the means to support her—if the time she had spent in Grace Park wasn't evidence enough—Deborah wore one of the more formal dinner gowns Todd had purchased for her.

"They told my grandmother I was sent to work as a servant in a

"

wealthy family's home," she replied. "Certainly nothing near the truth," she added in a whisper.

Todd regarded his betrothed—his wife, as he now thought of her—for a moment before pulling her closer. "Will you tell me now what happened to you?" he asked quietly. "I... I must know more about the man who attacked you," he added with furrowed brows.

Sighing, Deborah nodded, knowing he would always wonder if she didn't tell him what she could remember. "I didn't see his face, for his hat brim kept it in shadow," she answered simply. "It was a very... *crumpled* top hat. He was much shorter than me. He wore an old-fashioned cape coat and tattered trousers. All black," she added, her eyes closed so she could more clearly recall the sight of her attacker. "And the odor about him was most foul." Her body shivered suddenly and Todd tightened his hold around her shoulders in response. "He kept calling out, 'Freak. You are a freak,' and he knocked me down and slapped me across the face so hard I couldn't see, and then he ripped my gown and... forced himself..." The last words were spoken so quietly, Todd had to strain to hear them. With each additional bit of description, he pulled Deborah closer to him so she was finally pressed against his chest. But it wasn't her words of what the man had done but rather what the man had said that had his entire body stiffening.

He remembered the man who had called out insults while he and Thomas had been shopping. 'Freak!' the man had called out, apparently following them as they quit each shop. Black cape coat, rumpled clothing, crushed top hat.

It had to be the same man!

Deborah's attacker.

What was it about tall people that could possibly have the man so offended? Offended enough to commit such violence? Had the man made a move against him while he was in Ludgate Hill, Todd wondered how he might have reacted. He carried no weapon, other than his cane, and he hadn't had to use his fists other than to punch his colleague that day at the John Company. He supposed he could have done the same to the strange man. *Should have*, he realized now. Wished he had.

"I promise you, I shall see to it that he is made to pay for what he did to you," Todd vowed in a whisper. He used his hand to cup her cheek so he could turn her face up to look at him. There were no tears there, but he saw the weariness in her eyes. She had relived the scene in her nightmares more times than he could know. "That he would strike you makes my blood boil even more than knowing the rest of what he did," he added with a pained expression. "And then I wonder... how would I have come to know you if this hadn't happened to you? Would we still have met if you didn't work for Mrs. Dawes? If you didn't know Emma?" he asked quietly.

Deborah's eyes widened at his questions. Not having considered the circumstances of how they had come to meet, Deborah merely nodded before sighing loudly. After a moment, she asked, "Are you... *sorry* you know now?"

"No," he replied quickly. "My imagination was far too active, and your telling has tamed it considerably."

Surprised by his words, Deborah swallowed hard. "And you're not angry that I didn't tell you before?"

Shaking his head, Todd kissed her cheek. "No, my darling. As I told Emma, I believe I love you even more, for you have overcome this tragedy." When Deborah gave him a curious look in response, he added, "Well, you didn't throw yourself off a bridge or hang yourself from a tree as some do," he reasoned. "And I'm your protector now," he added with determination.

Deborah couldn't help but smile at his statement. "Perhaps from highwaymen and libertines," she agreed, "But what about members of my family?"

Leaning back in the carriage seat, Todd grinned. "We shall just have to wait a bit more to determine if I can prevail," he said, a bit of cheer coming back into his voice as the horses pulled the coach to the side of the street and jolted to a stop. Before the driver could even jump down from his seat, Todd stepped out of the coach and straightened his dark gray coat. Holding his hand for Deborah, he said, "Thank you, Mr. Stevenson," as Deborah stepped from the coach and stared at the home she had lived in for seventeen years. Except for an additional layer of soot on the dark red brick, it looked the same as the day she left.

The front door opened to reveal Aunt Katherine, a dark-haired, heavyset woman who smiled brightly when she took in the sight of her oldest niece. She held her chubby hands together in front of her bosom and then spread her arms wide as Deborah ran up to hug her. "Deborah!" her aunt whispered as she hugged her close. "You look positively resplendent!" Nearly as tall as Deborah, Katherine's deep blue brocade dinner gown with its fitted waist and wide hips was in sharp contrast to Deborah's scarlet satin empire gown, and it reflected the difference in their ages.

"And you look exactly the same!" Deborah exclaimed with a grin as she stepped back. "Oh! Where are my manners?" she said as she hurried to Todd's side. "Mrs. Katherine Dooley, I'd like you to meet Mr. Todd Vandermeer," Deborah said as she hooked her arm around Todd's elbow. "Mr. Vandermeer, Mrs. Dooley is my aunt."

Todd removed his hat and bowed deeply to Katherine's curtsy. "I am very pleased to meet you, madam," he said as he smiled.

Before he could stand up straight, the woman had him in a bear hug. "I'm so honored to meet you, sir," she replied excitedly. "I have read of your generosity and of your adventures in India. You really must tell us stories from your travels during dinner," she insisted as she turned to the house and motioned for them to enter. "And you, my dear," she added as she addressed Deborah, "You must tell me all about your schooling these past two years. I was so surprised when Emily told me you're a midwife now!"

Stunned by the comment, Deborah remembered to close her mouth. She shared an amused glance with Todd. *My family thinks I have been in school these past two years*, she thought to herself.

Deborah's mother, embarrassed by her sister's behavior and catching only the last of Katherine's comments, greeted them at the door with a curtsy. "Mr. Vandermeer," she said with a nod. "Welcome to my home."

Todd smiled and took her hand, brushing his lips over the backs of her knuckles. "Thank you, Mrs. White. It's so good to see you again," he said, rising from his bow. From the cordial greeting, Todd figured Mrs. White was happy to have him in her home, although she did seem anxious.

When Deborah stole a glance in his direction, he knew she had the same impression. "You're looking well, mama," Deborah offered as they entered the parlor. The light-colored room had changed little since she lived in the house. The settee was more worn, but otherwise, the furnishings were clean and polished, and the drapes were drawn back to reveal the lacy sheers and a view of the lawn and small garden out front. Within moments, a parade of various sized children entered the room, and Deborah's eyes widened in surprise. When her cousin, James Dooley, entered the room and bowed deeply, her smile faltered.

Younger than Deborah but just as tall, James was the next eldest of all the cousins in the Dooley family. He was also the most stubborn and certainly the best looking of the bunch, Deborah realized as she surveyed the group that had assembled in the parlor. Given his age, Deborah formally introduced him to Todd before introducing the rest of the children.

"Mr. Dooley, 'tis good to meet you," Todd said as he offered his hand and afforded the young man a smile.

James would have none of it, though, refusing to shake Todd's hand as he continued to glance nervously at Deborah. "I cannot say the same for myself, sir," he replied with his chin raised high.

Deborah inhaled sharply, as did her mother and aunt. The children in the room seem preoccupied with each other and didn't take notice of the stand-off.

Todd blinked, and then blinked again as he struggled for a suitable reply. "Pardon me. Have I done something to offend you? If so, it wasn't my intention, I assure you," he said quietly.

James glanced at Deborah again, a hint of menace in his eyes. "No," he replied simply. "However, she has if she has accepted a marriage proposal."

It was Deborah's turn to blink. Swallowing, she moved closer to her cousin. "How have I offended *you*?" she asked in a quiet voice. "I accepted Mr. Vandermeer's marriage proposal, yes, but what has that got to do with you?"

The young man turned to her and angled his head. "You were to be *my* wife," he stated evenly, his anger barely in check.

Her mouth dropping open and her surprise evident to anyone watching, Deborah stared at her cousin. "And when did you decide this?" Turning quickly to Todd, she said, "Mr. Vandermeer, this is the first I have heard such a claim, I assure you."

Outwardly, Todd showed no emotion as he tried hard to keep an impassive expression. Inside, though, he feared he would be challenged to a duel, or worse, be asked by her family to renounce his betrothal to Deborah. She was already his wife, as far as he was concerned, and he had no intention of giving her up without a fight.

Emily White stood, as did Katherine Dooley, and the two joined the conclave. Clearing her throat, Katherine said, "James Dooley, you will apologize to Mr. Vandermeer and to your cousin immediately. You have no claim on Miss White."

But James Dooley's face lit up with a huge grin, and he started to laugh. "You should see your face," he said between guffaws as he pointed at his cousin.

Startled, Deborah gasped and reached out to slug him across the shoulder. "James! It wasn't funny!" she shouted, her face ablaze in anger as she realized she and Todd were the victims of one of James' practical jokes.

Mortified, the older women rolled they eyes, and Katherine reddened in embarrassment. "I'm so sorry for my son's poor sense of humor, Mr. Vandermeer," she said with a hand over her chest.

Allowing a smile, Todd nodded. "It's quite all right, Mrs. Dooley. For a moment, I thought I might have to accept a challenge to duel," he said lightly. Would he be able to shoot a gun, or worse, hold his own with a fencing sword? He rather doubted it. He had never held a gun let alone shot one, and he had only tried fencing the one time at a local academy.

"Oh, dear," Emily said quietly as she covered her mouth with her hand. "Would you really have accepted such a challenge?" she asked, startled by his comment.

Todd reached out and pulled Deborah to his side. "If the choice was to duel or lose Miss White, I assure you, I would accept the challenge," he said with conviction. "Illegal or not, I will not willingly give up your daughter to anyone."

"Damn!" James cursed in a whisper. "And I'd be dead, 'cause I can't shoot worth a damn," he added, awestruck.

"James!" his mother scolded as she swatted her fan across her son's arm. "Watch your language," she ordered. "And apologize this instant!"

Rubbing his arm where his cousin and the fan had hit him, James sobered and nodded to Todd and Deborah. "I apologize for my joke. And my language," he said solemnly. "It won't happen again."

Deborah eyed her cousin suspiciously, still embarrassed by his words and for having hit him. "Apology accepted," she said in unison with Todd.

"Well," Emily said as she turned her attention back to the betrothed couple. "I do believe dinner is served." She hung back as the others left the parlor and said, in a sideways manner to Todd and Deborah, "If he were *my* boy, he would be sent to his room without dinner."

Deborah grinned knowingly, and Todd arched an eyebrow when he caught her expression. Todd offered his other arm to Emily, and she took it graciously. As they walked out of the parlor, Todd said, "I take it, then, that, on occasion, you have been sent to your room without dinner?" he teased Deborah.

Startled at the supposition, Deborah leaned forward and glanced at her mother. But the tops of her ears turned pink and she rested her head against Todd's arm briefly. "On occasion," she finally admitted with a nod, her lashes lowered.

When they caught up to Katherine at the entrance to the dining parlor, Emily let go of Todd's arm and ushered several children into the kitchen. Todd was left standing next to Katherine. "Is there a Mr. Dooley?" Todd asked of Katherine as he absently patted Deborah's hand on his extended arm.

The older woman shook her head. "My husband died many years ago, Mr. Vandermeer. Just after my youngest was born, in fact. Consumption, the doctor said," she explained. "'Tis why James is a bit headstrong, I believe," she added, hoping the oldest boy's behavior wouldn't reflect badly on her.

Todd gave a look of concern. "It must have been very difficult for you to raise your children by yourself," he commented, realizing the family probably didn't employ a governess or nannies.

Katherine nodded. "Mr. Dooley left me with a bit of an inheritance, to be sure," she said carefully. "But I take from your comment that perhaps you weren't referring to the financial aspect," she added, sensing a hint of pity in his voice.

"Oh, of course not," Todd assured her quickly, his eyes widening as he made the denial. Although he knew he sometimes offended others with comments he found perfectly acceptable, he did know that discussing another person's finances was verboten.

"They're a handful, to be sure," she admitted of the eight children spread over fourteen years. "But James will be leaving us to join the militia next month, so my cook won't have to go to market as often," she said with an impish grin.

Deborah gasped at the comment. "The militia?" she repeated, trying to imagine her cousin having enough discipline to be a soldier. "James?"

Mrs. Dooley held her head at an odd angle and leaned over towards Deborah. "I told him he could join the militia or go to a workhouse. He chose the militia."

Deborah and Todd both nodded. The idea of sending a child of any age to a workhouse sent shivers up Deborah's spine. She had heard horror stories of the long hours and intolerable conditions suffered in such places of employment. The children may as well have been slaves given their low wages and horrible treatment.

As she walked into the dining room, her hand hooked into Todd's elbow, Deborah was comforted by the familiar sights and scents of the room. Yet the table was set with fine porcelain china, crystal goblets, and silver flatware on a silk tablecloth she hadn't seen before. A candlelit chandelier lent an air of elegance to the room. The sky beyond the single window in the room was nearly dark as the sun set on the other side of the house. The children had been herded into the kitchen, including James, she noticed, as they wouldn't be allowed to eat with the adults.

"What a beautiful table, Mrs. White," Todd said as he admired the sparkling array of dishes and accessories. "I don't believe I have seen such a fine display since my last trip to France."

Deborah's mother blushed and waved her hand in front of her. "Why, 'tis so kind of you to say, Mr. Vandermeer, but I'm sure your table must look finer than this for even your most simple supper."

Todd shook his head. "I assure you, it is nothing compared to this."

Emily White noticed Deborah shaking her head in response to her comment and thought perhaps the man was indeed humble.

"Please, do us the honor of sitting at the head, Mr. Vandermeer. It has been too long since there was a man in the house," Emily said as she indicated the carver at the end of the table.

"Thank you, Mrs. White," Todd replied as he moved in that direction. When he noticed there were no footmen hanging about, he remained standing so he could hold chairs for the three women before taking the carver. He smiled when a dark-haired girl of about twelve brought out bowls of soup and set them carefully at each place setting. Her resemblance to Deborah was startling. Glancing at Deborah, seated to his right, Todd angled his head in the direction of the girl and furrowed his brows.

Deborah smiled and rolled her eyes. When the girl was about to return to the kitchen, Deborah said, "Miss Grace, could you come here, please?"

Startled, the girl first looked to Deborah's mother and then went to stand next to Deborah. Todd immediately stood as the girl approached.

"Miss Grace, I'd like to introduce you to my... betrothed, Mr.

Vandermeer," Deborah said, catching herself before she said 'husband'. "This is my sister, Grace."

Surprised, Todd leaned down and took the girl's hand in his, kissing the back of it. "I am very honored to meet my future sister," he said in amazement as he smiled at the girl.

Visibly blushing, Grace curtsied and finally met his gaze, her neck angled back so she could look up at him. "'Tis very good to meet you, sir," she said, her dark lashes fluttering in embarrassment.

"Do you have any brothers or other sisters?" he asked Grace.

The girl nodded. "Master William, and Miss Sophia, and Master Charles," she said quietly.

Taken aback, Todd looked to Deborah for confirmation. She sighed and nodded her head. "Sophia and Charles were in the parlor with us, but I didn't see William," she replied as she looked to her mother.

Emily smiled as she waved a hand toward the kitchen. Grace excused herself and left the room. "William is now Lieutenant White. He is in the militia," she said proudly.

Todd sat down and replaced his napkin on his lap. "You must be very proud," he commented, remembering how he felt when he found out his father had been in the army.

Deborah shook her head and looked perplexed. "I thought he would still be at school," she said with furrowed brows.

Her mother shook her head. "He was, until your father died. Then he enlisted. His commission has him assigned somewhere near Bath," she added when she noted Deborah's quizzical stare.

Katherine couldn't help but smile as she noticed the expression on Todd's face. "Why, Mr. Vandermeer, you really must share what is amusing you so."

Todd took Deborah's hand and rested it on the table. "I'm an only child, and yet I'm going to have four brothers and sisters!" he said with a huge grin.

Blushing a bright red, Deborah rolled her eyes and regarded him. "I'm glad you are happy about it," she said as she stole an embarrassed glance at her mother.

Emily White merely smiled at her, realizing her daughter hadn't shared any of her family information with Todd. "And eight cousins," Emily offered with a glance in her sister's direction.

"And an uncle," Katherine added with a grin.

"Our older brother, Edward Livingston, lives in Kent," Emily explained with a nod.

"He married one of the Merriweather girls," Katherine offered with a raised eyebrow, hoping the mention of one of the wealthier families in the district would be familiar to her future nephew.

Mortified by her sister's mention of their brother's wife, Emily whispered, "Katherine!"

Todd's eyes widened at the mention of the Merriweather name. "Indeed?" he replied, his soup spoon held in mid-air. "One of my friends, Gregory Grandby, grew up at Merriweather Manor," he said in explanation of his interest. "I suppose the wife is one of his cousins. Or... an aunt, perhaps," he considered, when he realized the probable age difference.

The two sisters exchanged quick glances. "Well, she wasn't one of the better daughters," Katherine started to say, but Emily's dagger-filled stare stopped her from completing the sentence. "Let us just say she didn't receive the same consideration when it came to her inheritance as the rest of her siblings did," she amended carefully. "Which is why our brother was even able to consider her for matrimony. He certainly doesn't have the income to support a typical Merriweather to the degree in which she would be accustomed."

Todd grinned at the comment, realizing to whom they were referring. "Mary Margaret did have her favorites," he said with an arched brow. "But I hear Miss Lucy was the favorite aunt because she was such fun. Mischievous, too, I understand."

Emily, Katherine, and Deborah gasped and stared open-mouthed at Todd. "Oh, damn," he murmured as he covered his mouth with a hand, realizing he had probably offended someone, or all of them, with the comment.

Deborah, failing to suppress a grin, put her hand on Todd's shoulder. "She is my favorite aunt, too!" she said in surprise, and then covered her mouth when she realized what she had said in front of Katherine. But Katherine merely waved a hand in the air to indicate she understood Deborah's meaning.

Emily leaned forward. "She can be a bit... unusual at times, but she is a delightful woman. You would never know she was raised in a wealthy family."

A wave of relief washed over Todd. He took Deborah's hand from his shoulder and kissed the back of it. "I can hardly wait for you to meet Mr. Grandby," he said. "That you two have a common aunt... and an uncle, come to think of it, will truly amuse him. He'll be at the wedding, of course," he added as he turned to the other women. "And will you be there as well?"

Katherine turned to Emily. "Of course, I'll be there," Emily replied with a hand on her chest. "I must admit, I am concerned about a wedding taking place in a... garden, though."

"Mama," Deborah interrupted, "Todd's gardens are simply gorgeous. If the Lord did not wish for a wedding ceremony to take place outside among his most beautiful creations, he wouldn't have made them so divine."

"They're your gardens, too," Todd said quietly as he placed his hand over hers.

Katherine sighed and held her hands together against her bosom. "They are so in love," she whispered in awe. She glanced at her sister, wishing the woman wouldn't object so much to the wedding plans. "I suppose you had to obtain a special license to have the ceremony out-of-doors," she said with a raised eyebrow, the comment made with expectations that a special license did, indeed, have to be obtained.

Todd nodded. "The Archbishop of Canterbury was a bit skeptical about a garden wedding, but agreed with it as long as the ceremony is complete by noon," he explained with a wave of his hand. He didn't mention the bribe he had paid in addition to the license fee. "He seemed more troubled that I wish to have a small orchestra playing music during the ceremony." An extra five pounds had made that concession possible.

Katherine and Emily both gasped at this news. "I have never heard of music at a wedding," Emily replied, looking to Deborah and then to Katherine.

"Me, neither, but it sounds lovely," Katherine stated evenly. "I look forward to attending the ceremony, Mr. Vandermeer," she added with a smile. Indeed, having Mr. Vandermeer as a nephew would be much like having Lucy Merriweather Livingston as a sister, she considered with a grin.

"I'm very pleased to hear it," Todd replied as he finished his soup. "Will your sisters and brother be able to attend?" he asked as he turned his attention to Deborah.

Emily cleared her throat and shook her head. "Apparently not," Deborah answered as she took her mother's meaning. "Not even

Grace?" she asked after a moment. "She's old enough," Deborah commented as, if on cue, Grace entered the room to clear the soup bowls. "Perhaps she could spread the rose petals before the ceremony starts," she suggested, realizing she hadn't yet made the final arrangements with Winston.

"Well, perhaps. We shall see," her mother answered with a curt nod.

The evening continued for another two hours as Grace delivered course after course and the conversation turned from the wedding to the honeymoon, traveling in general, Todd's work, Deborah's work, and finally Todd's trips to India. Before leaving the table, Emily reminded Deborah to visit her room and help herself to her clothes and other belongings. "Grace would like very much to have your bedchamber," she added, hoping Deborah would agree to the arrangement since she clearly had no intention of returning to live in the White household.

"She is most welcome to it," Deborah said with a shrug. "I'm surprised you didn't allow her to move in before now."

Todd followed Deborah up the staircase and into her childhood room. Deborah shook her head as she surveyed the small bedchamber, noting how it felt a bit like stepping back in time. Her mother had said it was the same as the day she left, and indeed, it was. There were two gowns and a pair of slippers in the wardrobe and several pairs of pantaloons and stockings in the dresser, but nothing she didn't already have several more of in her suite at Grace Park. There was an item on a shelf near her bed, though, and she carefully picked it up and held it to her bosom.

"What is it?" Todd asked as he noticed her cradling a small box.

"A music box," Deborah replied as she turned a dial on the bottom and set the box back on the shelf. A minuet played for a few minutes before the dial unwound completely. "It was a gift from my parents for Christmas. I was twelve."

Todd nodded, making a mental note to buy her one. "And that?" he asked as he pointed to the small chest at the end of her bed.

Deborah took a quick breath and hurried to open the hinged box. Inside were layers of linens, a set of silver, a pearl necklace, and pearl earrings. "My dowry, I suppose," she said as she glanced at Todd. "I'd like to take this to your house, if it's all right," she added as she closed the lid on the chest.

"Our house," he corrected her. "And, of course, we can take it with us tonight," he added as he reached down to pick up the box. It was heavier than he expected, but once he had it up and his arms safely under it, he was able to heft it and get it down the stairs and out to the coach. Mr. Stevenson took the chest from his master and loaded it onto the back of the equipage.

Todd returned to the house to find Deborah hugging her mother. The woman's face was wet with tears, and Katherine stood back with a sad expression on her face.

"Is something wrong?" he asked, his brows furrowing.

Katherine shook her head. "My sister is just being a mother," she said with a small grin. "She forgets she's not losing a daughter but gaining a son," she added with a nod to Todd.

Todd suppressed his surprise at hearing the comment, although his ears reddened. "Thank you, Mrs. Dooley. I do believe that is one of the nicest things anyone has ever said to me," he replied as he realized the full impact of marriage to a woman with a large family. "I look forward to seeing you at the wedding."

It was well after midnight when the couple bid their farewells and climbed into the waiting coach for the ride back to Grace Park.

As Todd held Deborah, he leaned over and kissed a tear left on her cheek. "You have a wonderful family," he whispered in her ear.

Deborah wrapped an arm around the small of his back and another around his waist and burrowed her head into the space between his chest and arm. "I do now," she agreed with a sniffle.

I do now.

CHAPTER 49
HEART TO HEART

June 24, 1802, Woodscastle

On the second day after Christiana's miscarriage and after a particularly busy day at the office, Thomas arrived at Woodscastle at four o'clock intending to have tea with his sister. He found her at the piano-forté in the music room, her fingers gingerly pressing the keys as she studied a piece of sheet music.

Humphrey followed him with a tea service and biscuits. Realizing the two weren't yet ready to partake, he took his leave and Thomas sat down next to Christiana at the piano.

He wrapped an arm around her shoulders and pulled her closer to him. She resisted at first, but finally gave in and allowed him the hug.

"Are you feeling any better?" he asked quietly as he held her, his chin resting on the tightly-wound bun at the top of her head. The scent of lavender filled his nostrils, and he closed his eyes.

Christiana's head nodded against his chest. "I'm fine. Truly," she replied. After a long pause, she added. "Please don't be angry with me."

Thomas tightened the hug and shook his head, stunned by the pleading he heard in her voice. "I'm not angry, sister," he assured her, unconsciously rubbing her arm. "I just... I wish to understand *why...*" He shrugged, not exactly sure what he wanted to hear from her.

Christiana inhaled and gave a sigh. "Have you ever been in love,

Mr. Wellingham?" she asked in a whisper, her demeanor very serious.

Thomas had to suppress a smile. Whenever she called him by his formal name, he knew he wasn't in her good graces. "No," he lied, not ready to admit he might have feelings for Emma. "Well, I did have that crush on..."

Christiana rolled her eyes and gave her brother a look of disappointment.

"What does that have to do with—?"

"Do you know what the greatest gift is a woman can give to the man she loves?" she asked as she sat up straight. At that moment, Christiana had no patience for what she was sure to be a lecture on impropriety and loss of virtue.

Thomas let his arm drop to the piano bench, and he found he was at a loss. "Children?" he guessed, not quite sure how to answer. When he saw her look of disapproval, he shrugged. "I don't know," he admitted. I've never given it any thought."

Christiana sighed and rolled her eyes again. "Her virtue!" she said emphatically. "And she doesn't give it with conditions or strings attached. It's a *gift*," she said quietly. "I chose to give my virtue to the man I love. I *chose* to," she repeated in a louder voice. "He didn't ask for it, nor did he expect me to offer it when I did. And, yes, I did give it to him before marriage, but it was my choice to do so," she added as she pointed her finger into his chest. "I don't expect you to agree with it, but you must respect that it was my decision to make."

Thomas stared at his sister, stunned because her words sounded as if they had come from a woman twice her age. Even more stunning was the explanation. She said the words as if she truly understood their implication, as if she believed them.

So a woman's virtue is a gift, he considered as he continued to stare at her. Despite her explanation, he found he still thought of her as ruined. Did the man to whom she had gifted her virtue understood what she had given up?

Thomas nodded finally and said, "I think I understand." When had his sixteen-year-old sister turned thirty? "So, will I like this boy?" he asked with a pained expression. There was nothing more he could say to his sister. There were only four people who knew of her miscarriage, so perhaps her reputation wouldn't suffer.

"He is not a *boy*," Christiana answered, annoyed at his choice of words. "He is a man. A *gentleman*, in fact. And you already do," she added as she straightened. She grinned, happy to keep her secret to herself for as long as possible.

"I know him?" Thomas asked. Emma had made it clear the man was a friend of the family. He swallowed, but he found he was no longer as curious as to the identity of her suitor as he had been before his sister's lecture.

"Yes," Christiana replied shortly. "So, please, promise me you won't challenge him to a duel," she pleaded while she shook her head. "He's a better shot than you, and I wouldn't want to lose you over this."

Thomas' look of indignation had Christiana's impish grin appearing again. After a moment, Thomas warned, "I could have Miss Emma shoot him on my behalf. What then?"

Mortified, Christiana stared at her brother until she realized he was teasing her. "Promise you won't!"

Thomas finally chuckled. "I promise," he replied with a nod. "I might punch him in the jaw, though," he murmured as he quickly stood up from the piano bench in order to avoid Christiana's elbow. "Come, let's have tea," he said, reaching his hand out to Christiana.

Glancing up at her brother, Christiana nodded and accepted his hand, relieved to know they were once again brother and sister.

CHAPTER 50

A RAKE ARRIVES AT WOODSCASTLE

July 1, 1802, Woodscastle

The following week, a team of four Yorkshire Coach horses pulling a black barouche came to a halt in front of Woodscastle. One of the two coachmen opened the door and lowered the steps for its single occupant. The man who stepped out was tall but well built and dressed in Hessian boots, Nankeen pantaloons, a light yellow waistcoat, and a dark green tailcoat. He wore a hat that only exaggerated his height, and he removed it as he very nearly bounced up the steps to the front doors. Once inside, he passed his hat and walking cane to Humphrey.

"Good day, Mr. Grandby," the butler said with a heartfelt smile as he took the man's hat. "Mr. Wellingham is expecting you. I believe he's in the library."

The tall man nodded. "Thank you, Humphrey. I can find my way," he said as he headed down the hall, his polished boots tapping on the marble floor tiles. He entered the library without knocking and nearly called out a greeting to his host when he realized his host was instead a hostess.

Emma, seated at the library table next to the front windows, was in the process of transferring a page of numbers to a new ledger. Having become used to Thomas entering and leaving the library without announcing his presence, she didn't notice the stranger and simply continued her addition.

Until he loudly cleared his throat.

When she looked up, the sight of the tall stranger brought her to her feet immediately. She curtsied quickly and recovered her composure, saying, "Pardon me, sir. I didn't hear you come in."

ithout seeming to do so, Gregory Grandby studied the tall woman with the golden blonde hair and comely figure. *This handsome young woman is a surprise indeed*, he thought as he tried to guess her age and found he could not. There was something familiar about her, but he couldn't immediately remember where he might have seen her before.

"It is I who should ask to be pardoned," he said as he bowed. "I was expecting to find Thomas Wellingham."

"And found him you have, you old dog," Thomas said as he walked up behind Gregory. "I see you've met my accomptant, Miss Fitzsimmons," he added as he motioned in Emma's direction.

"Actually, we didn't get that far," the visitor replied with a raised eyebrow as he vigorously shook hands with Thomas. "Miss Emma, since our host is undeniably rude, I shall introduce myself. I am Gregory Grandby of Derbyshire. I'm very pleased to make your acquaintance." He bowed deeply, and when he was on his way back up to standing, Emma curtsied.

"Likewise, I'm sure," she replied with a nod of her head. She wasn't quite sure what to think of the man, but first impressions told her he was a rake. He was no doubt in the London area for the Hornsby ball, an affair that involved just about everyone in Society within ten miles of London who hadn't vacated the city for the summer. That meant he would be staying for at least a fortnight.

"Breakfast is about to be served. Let's go to the dining room, shall we?" Thomas suggested to his friend.

Gregory regarded his friend and then nodded in Emma's direction, his eyebrows doing a dance that suggested he was flirting.

"Miss Fitzsimmons, would you care to join us for breakfast?" Thomas asked as he tried to ignore Gregory's playful facial expressions.

Emma shook her head. "No, thank you, Mr. Wellingham. I had breakfast before leaving home this morning," she replied with a nod, grateful she wasn't required to spend what would amount to at least an hour of small talk and forced interest when there was so much work to do in the ledger she was currently reviewing.

The two men bowed and Emma curtsied before returning to her work.

When they were out of earshot, Gregory elbowed his host.

"It's quite kind of you to line up my next chit for me," he teased gently. "Unless you have designs on her yourself," he added as he studied Thomas' reaction.

He wasn't disappointed.

"Miss Emma is not your next *chit*, I assure you," Thomas replied. "She is a most proper young lady and would simply not tolerate your behavior," he added as he led his guest to the dining table. Christiana, who was sitting in her usual seat to the left of Thomas, stood up and hurried to the two men.

"Mr. Grandby!" she called out, curtsying before hurrying to his side. "'Tis so good to see you again. Are you well?" she asked politely, careful not to display too much affection for the man while in Thomas' presence.

"Indeed, Miss Wellingham. You're looking splendid this morning," their guest replied as he bowed to her. He took her hand and brushed his lips over her knuckles, taking a bit more time than was usual for the courtesy. He didn't immediately release her hand. "I expect to be entertained by your music the entire time I'm here," he added as he rubbed a thumb over her fingers. "Except when I'm allowing you to beat me at cards," he murmured.

Christiana, a slight blush coloring her cheeks, gave her brother a quick glance. Thomas merely furrowed his brows. "How did you know Christiana played piano?" he asked, allowing an expression of surprise on his face.

Gregory shook his head. "I was in attendance at your sister's last recital in April," he claimed, knowing he could have been there had he stayed in London an extra day. "I was sitting in the back, my dear. You played beautifully," he stated with a nod. "As did Miss Emma. Perhaps she will play for us tonight?" he hinted, watching for Thomas' reaction.

Thomas scratched his head, apparently hearing about the recital for the very first time. "You didn't tell me you had a recital in April," he said by way of a slight scolding to his sister as he made his way to the end of the dining table.

Biting her lip, Christiana stole a quick glance at Gregory. "I didn't wish for you to be there," she countered as she took her seat at Thomas' left. "But why did you attend, Mr. Grandby?" she asked, sure he had left town the day before the recital. She caught him winking at her when Thomas wasn't looking, and she gave him a knowing nod in reply. "Oh, I know why you were there," she said, batting her eyelashes playfully.

Thomas glanced at his sister as he took his seat in the carver at the head of the table. Gregory took the seat to his right. "Do you now?" Gregory replied nervously as he placed a napkin on his lap. What excuse would Christiana come up with on his behalf?

"I can assure you she was not interested in you. In fact, she has already married another," Christiana stated defiantly, her made-up scenario entertaining Gregory to the point he had a hard time keeping a straight, or in this case, a disappointed look on his face.

"No!" he exclaimed as he slapped a hand on his chest in feigned disappointment. "But Miss DeVille seemed so... so perfect for me," he said sadly. "'Tis her loss, of course."

Thomas rolled his eyes. "Indeed."

Gregory regarded his friend and smirked. When Thomas' attention was turned to Dahlia as the maid poured wine, Gregory winked again at Christiana. She blushed but could manage only a shrug in return. "Indeed, because now I have met Miss Emma," Gregory replied with a raised eyebrow, his attention again on Thomas in order to gauge the man's reaction.

Thomas' head turned too quickly. He stared at his guest. "Whatever do you mean by that?"

Raising his chin in the air, Gregory struggled to keep his amusement in check. "I played host to Miss Emma's landlord and lady until just last week," he began in explanation. "It seems Mrs. Simpson is of the opinion that Miss Emma and I would make a most handsome couple. Now that I have met the woman, I couldn't agree more."

Christiana's eyes opened wide until she realized Gregory was only teasing her brother. Her look of shock turned to one of mild amusement.

Thomas, on the other hand, looked positively mortified. "What makes you think Miss Emma would be interested in a rake like you?" he asked as he lifted a forkful of baked eggs and forced them between his lips.

Gregory grinned. "How could she not be?" he teased. "I am five-and-twenty, handsome, educated, borne of a good family, and I am rich," he stated with a wave of his hand. Turning his attention to Christiana, he added, "I can offer a home with beautiful gardens, travel wherever and whenever she chooses, a good deal of children, and my undying love. However could she turn me down?"

Christiana, who knew this last comment was directed at her, blushed and smiled in reply.

"Humph," Thomas grunted. "How, indeed?"

Emma continued to work on ledgers, uninterrupted, until it was nearly four o'clock. At that point, she closed up the books and asked Humphrey for her pelisse. "Was Miss Dahlia allowed to leave early?" she inquired, hoping the maid would already be at her town-house seeing to some of the food preparation for that evening's dinner. Emma had arranged to hire the girl so she would have help with the dinner she planned for her landlords. Although she would make most of the meal herself, Emma wanted Dahlia to serve and clear away dishes as well as help with the table settings and cleanup.

"Indeed, Miss Emma. She took her leave just as soon as luncheon was complete," Humphrey replied. "Good luck with your dinner party," he added with a wink. "I do hope it goes well."

Emma gave him a nod and looked around the vestibule, embarrassed at leaving earlier than usual. The sound of the piano-forté in the music room told her Christiana was still practicing. She hadn't seen Thomas or his guest since they departed the library earlier that day.

"Where do you think you are going?" came a voice from down the hall.

At first, Emma didn't realize the question was directed to her. Gregory, who had apparently run the length of the hall from the music room, stood breathless before her and bowed. Startled, Emma allowed Humphrey to assist her in getting into her coat sleeves. "I'm going home, Mr. Grandby," she replied just as Thomas came around the corner, also breathless.

"Take me with you," Gregory said, his slurred words betraying his drunkenness. For a man as foxed and as tall as he was, staying on his feet had to be a challenge, Emma considered.

"Me, too," Thomas said, his drunkenness also apparent. "She cooks good," he added as he waved in Emma's direction. "And she's a good shot!"

"Indeed?" Gregory swayed, his attention finally falling on his friend. "How would you know that?" he asked as his brows furrowed comically.

Emma smiled despite her initial revulsion at the men's behavior. "I really must be leaving. I'm hosting my neighbors for dinner this evening." She quickly curtsied and grinned as she noticed the butler rolling his eyes. She made her way out the front door.

"Can I be your neighbor?" she heard Gregory call out as she climbed onto the borrowed phaeton and took the reins.

"Good night, Mr. Grandby. Good night, Mr. Wellingham," she called out as she hurried her horse down the curved path to Burlington Road.

For just a few minutes, she was afraid they would follow her home.

CHAPTER 51
DINNER WITH THE SIMPSONS

*J*uly 1, 1802, No. 3 Kingly Street

After leaving the horse and phaeton at the stables, Emma hurried to the kitchen and felt relief when she found Dahlia filling the teakettle. "I am so in your debt, Dahlia," she said as she greeted the maid.

"'Tis my pleasure, Miss Emma," the Spanish woman said in her thick accent. "Mr. Larsen brought me and will be by to fetch me at eleven-thirty," she added as she started filling a pot in which to cook green beans. Emma had invited the Simpsons for dinner at eight, so Dahlia's timing would work just fine given the typical formal dinner schedule.

Emma smiled, sure Mr. Larsen had a tendré for the maid and would do anything to please the woman. "That was very sweet of him," Emma replied as she pulled on an apron. "We shall have to see to a late dinner for him," she said with a wink, her smile growing when Dahlia clearly blushed at the comment.

Emma had baked the rhubarb and strawberry pie the night before, filling her townhouse with the scent of berries. Before leaving for Woodscastle that morning, she had made dough for rolls and found several costermongers from which she bought fruits and vegetables. With Dahlia's help, she cut up potatoes and layered them with butter and dill. The pork chops, bathed in a marinade of vinegar, apple juice, and spices, were already in a casserole in the newly-lit oven. Dough was rolled into small balls and placed in a shallow pan to rise on top of the oven.

Once Dahlia had the beans cleaned, she put them into the steam pot with some diced onion and set it on the stove to heat. The soup, which Emma had started that morning, just needed cream and spices before it would be heated to a slow simmer.

Dahlia cleaned the fruits and artfully arranged them on a platter, adding a small bowl of honey and lemon juice for dipping.

Satisfied the food was under control, Emma climbed the steps to her bedchamber and changed for dinner while Dahlia set the table with china and linens.

When Sophia and James Simpson arrived at eight o'clock with a floral bouquet and a bottle of wine, Emma was dressed for dinner in an aqua empire gown and the teardrop-shaped earrings and pendant Thomas had given her.

Sophia Simpson, striking in a traditional brocade gown of scarlet and gold, moved with the bearing of a woman born to wealth and privilege. Her skin was still luminous, the barest hint of cosmetics applied so perfectly she appeared much younger than her forty-six years. Older than Sophia, James Simpson shared the same regal bearing, but Emma knew his to be learned from his years of service as a butler. His short cropped hair, dark and combed into position, seemed almost too perfect, but then his cravat was tied to perfection, as well.

Exchanging pleasantries before seating the Simpsons in the parlor, Emma offered drinks and excused herself to give the flowers to Dahlia. She returned with a bowl of walnuts for the table in the parlor. As she poured their drinks, Emma asked about the Simpsons' health. James found a wine puller on her service cart and opened the claret for dinner.

"Mrs. Simpson and I have just returned from holiday," James stated as he took his drink and thanked Emma.

"We had a simply lovely time. Goodness knows, I prefer living in town, but I just adore the countryside," Sophia said as she sipped her drink and helped herself to a walnut.

Emma took a sip of her own drink. "Do you have a home in the country?"

James and Sophia exchanged glances and knowing smiles. "My family's estate is in Derbyshire, but my son has taken up residence there. He is very kind to share it with us on occasion," Sophia said wistfully.

At the mention of Derbyshire, Emma sat up straighter. "Mr. Wellingham has a guest who has just arrived from Derbyshire.

Perhaps you know Mr. Grandby?" she asked as she noticed the mantel clock and realized it would soon be time to serve the soup.

"Indeed, we do know Gregory Grandby," James replied with a devilish grin, his eyebrows dancing. "I do believe every unmarried woman in England also knows..."

"James!" Sophia exclaimed, astonished her husband would say something so vulgar in mixed company. James merely winked at his wife and continued to grin.

Emma couldn't suppress a smile and had to cover her mouth with a hand. At least her assessment of Thomas' guest was correct, she realized. She considered telling her guests about the condition in which she had left Gregory Grandby, but decided not to since his host was in his cups as well. "I believe the soup is ready to be served. Shall we move to the dining room?" Emma asked as she stood up and led the way for her guests.

James stopped and bit his lip. "Oh, dear. I forgot to bring the necessarié," he said, referring to the case that held their silverware and cups for dining.

"Oh, there's no need to bring your own, Mr. Simpson," Emma assured him as they entered the dining room. Dahlia had set the table with complete place settings and silverware. "My mother saw to it we always had plenty of pieces," Emma said as she waved at the table.

Her dining parlor was not spacious by any means. Large enough for an antique Rococo sideboard and a table for six, it featured a candle chandelier that provided a comfortable amount of light for dining. The ivory and green silk-covered walls, ivory moldings, and green Aubusson carpet made the room look rich.

"I simply love what you have done to this room," Sophia said as she entered. "Mr. Bronstein lived here for nearly twenty years and did absolutely nothing in the way of decoration."

Emma nodded and thanked Sophia for the compliment. "I take it, then, Mr. Bronstein didn't have a wife?" she queried, remembering how the townhouse looked when she toured it. Referred to the Simpsons by Sir William after she met with him to review her finances, she felt privileged to have been chosen for the townhouse that very day. She assumed there were several interested parties as the location—and townhouse—were excellent.

"A confirmed bachelor, he was," Sophia responded as she moved to one of the place settings. "I never once saw him in the company of a woman."

Having followed the women into the room, James quickly moved to pull out the chairs for both his wife and Emma. Had she been able to afford a footman for the evening, Emma considered he would be seeing to the comfort of her guests and the details of the dinner service. But James took on the task happily, his years of service obviously a source of pride for the man.

"I gathered he was well-educated," Emma replied with a nod. "Excuse me whilst I speak with the maid," Emma said as she went into the kitchen.

James bowed and remained standing until Emma returned. Dahlia followed, carrying a tray with the steaming bowls of tomato and cream soup.

James continued standing until Emma sat down. "Thank you, Mr. Simpson," she said as he pushed in her chair and then took his own seat. "It is so kind of you."

"It is my pleasure, I assure you," James said as he took his seat, his hand brushing his wife's shoulder as he did so. Although Sophia didn't acknowledge the contact, a coquettish grin lit her face, and Emma was sure she saw a slight blush rise in the elder woman's face.

"Mr. Bronstein was a professor at Oxford in his younger years," Sophia continued the conversation as she put her napkin across her lap and picked up her soup spoon. She nodded at James and he poured wine for the three of them. "But he was quiet and paid his rent every year on the day it was due. It was a pity when he died."

James took a cautious sip of wine, nodded his head in approval, and set his glass on the table. "Mr. Bronstein was a scholar, you see," he said as he surveyed the perfectly set table. "Although a Jew, he was most interested in the world's oldest religion and spent many years translating ancient texts."

Emma regarded James Simpson before leaning forward. "Are you perhaps referring to Hinduism?" she asked quietly.

The former butler nodded his head and grinned, glad to learn his tenant was educated enough to know the oldest religion wasn't Judaism. "Indeed. He was well-versed in several languages and worked tirelessly on his books. I believe many of them were from India and written in Sanskrit."

Nodding, Emma took a spoonful of soup and tried not to blush when she remembered the illustrations in *The Kama Sutra*. "I have been careful not to disturb his works," she replied, hoping her guests would believe the comment. "I expect some distant relative might one day wish to take possession of them."

Actually, she had spent hours perusing the late scholar's books, finding the translations neatly printed in tiny type under each line of foreign text. Many of the books were religious in nature, but in a few, their illustrations, if viewed before reading the text, would make one think the books were pornographic in nature. She had certainly thought that of *The Kama Sutra*, her current book of choice at bedtime. Although she was only a few chapters into the ancient text, she marveled at how the topics of kissing and foreplay and lovemaking were written from a sacred perspective. The book seemed to imply the act of making love to a woman was actually a man's means of worshipping a deity. Had the book been available in a translated form in Europe, she was sure its contents would be misconstrued and considered salacious.

"It was most fortunate you came seeking a townhouse when you did, Miss Emma," James commented as he picked up his spoon. "And that you came with such a strong referral. Sir William does not bestow his good opinion on just anyone."

Emma angled her head as she tasted her soup and decided it was acceptable. "I'm so privileged to have had his advice and counsel these past few years," she replied with a nod. "I was afraid he might object to my pursuing an occupation, but it was he who recommended me to Mr. Wellingham for a position, so I'm in his debt in more ways than one."

Turning toward Emma, Sophia held her soup spoon in midair. "The soup is delicious, Miss Emma. Did you make this yourself?" she asked as she sniffed the steaming soup in the bowl of the spoon.

Emma smiled in relief. "Yes. I cannot yet afford to hire a cook," she admitted. "And I've only just borrowed Miss Dahlia from Woodscastle for the evening," she added with a nod in the direction of the kitchen.

"But with your talent as a cook and hostess, why ever would you wish to have a cook?" Sophia replied with a smile. "Now, you really must tell us. How is it working for Mr. Wellingham? Is he treating you fairly? And paying you a good wage, I hope?" she asked, a note of concern in her voice.

"Oh, I like it very much, indeed," Emma replied, surprised by

Sophia's concern and even more surprised she would mention the topic of her wages. "I have my own place to work in Mr. Wellingham's library, time off for luncheon and tea, and I believe the wage he pays me is very fair for an entry-level position," she assured the older woman. "In addition, his grooms see to the care of my horse during the day and one of them accompanies to and from home nearly every day. And I usually have the company of Miss Wellingham for luncheon and her music in the afternoon when she practices piano-forté."

Finishing his soup, James sat back in his chair. "Miss Wellingham was the girl with whom you shared a room at Warwick's, was she not?" he asked with a furrowed brow.

"Yes, for my last three semesters there," Emma replied with a smile, amazed the man would remember such a detail. "She is nearly seventeen and quite different from most of the girls at the school."

Sophia put down her spoon and eyed Emma. "However do you mean?" she asked, a quizzical expression forcing one eyebrow higher than the other.

Her face flushing in embarrassment, Emma wondered how to describe Christiana without offending a woman who could have come from wealth. "Although she is from what appears to be a family of some fortune, she does not flaunt her wealth and is very gracious toward people from all classes. Most of the other girls are ...," Emma paused in her comment, not quite sure what word to use to describe the other girls at Warwick's Grammar and Finishing School.

"Snobs," Sophia finished for her as the older woman began tittering. Putting a hand to her chest, she said, "My dear Miss Emma. I could only hope Warwick's might have changed for the better since my tenure there, but I suppose it is too much to hope that the rich of this world would become a kinder, gentler people," she said as she shook her head. "You are to be commended for helping Miss Wellingham in that regard, I am certain."

Emma's eyes widened at Sophia's admission that she had attended the finishing school. "Was it really like that when you attended?" Emma asked in astonishment, nearly missing the woman's compliment. *She really did come from a family of wealth,* Emma realized with relief, deciding her initial assessment of the woman was correct.

The older woman rolled her eyes and shook her head. "I'm

almost ashamed to admit that it was, yes. But I was only there for three years," she added quickly, as if being spared the additional year meant she was far better for it. "I was part of a marriage contract when I was but five years old, and the betrothal was announced when I turned sixteen. I was married the following year."

James leaned forward. "Unfortunately, not to me," he said sadly, although his face betrayed amusement.

Sophia batted her eyelashes and grinned at his comment. "One must remember I might not have met you had I not first been married to another," she said coyly.

"Indeed," James replied with a sigh, gazing lovingly at his wife.

Emma watched the interplay between the married couple and grinned, almost embarrassed at witnessing their banter. "Please excuse me whilst I see to our next course," Emma said as she started to stand. James followed suit, but Dahlia was already coming out of the kitchen with the tray of fruit. As the maid removed the soup bowls, Emma relaxed and realized she could trust the maid to do what she did every day at Woodscastle.

James took his seat and glanced quickly in his wife's direction, noting her look of approval. Emma caught the exchange and felt as if she were being evaluated by the couple. Her nervousness returned. This was her first time hosting the couple in her townhouse. Their other dinner together had been in their home.

Curls of steam danced over the pork chops and potatoes as Dahlia placed china plates on the chargers in front of each guest. The beans seemed overcooked, but Emma had nothing else to serve in their stead. The odor of hot dinner rolls wafted from the kitchen as Dahlia moved in and out of the dining room delivering various dishes.

"Did you find the weather agreeable when you were in Derbyshire?" Emma asked as she tried her beans, finding them not as overly tender as she had first thought. The fruits were sweet and surprisingly flavorful given the early season. She had to suppress a smile when James reached for a dinner roll even before Dahlia had set the linen-lined basket onto the table.

"We had one night of horrific rain," James replied as he quickly dropped the hot roll on his plate and started cutting his meat, "But it was sunny and warm the rest of the trip. Quite delightful."

Emma realized he referred to the rainy night she had spent at Woodscastle, when Thomas had been so sick with fever and chills.

"That storm was quite bad here, as well," Emma confirmed as she tried a potato.

"Dear, I do hope you didn't travel to work that day," Sophia said, taking a sip of wine. Her demeanor was quite serious, as if she intended to scold Emma if she had made the trip to work that day.

"I did, actually," Emma replied with a nod, realizing she had to be careful in how she described the situation. "But there was no hint of rain when I left for work that morning. I did have to spend the night in the guest bedchamber at Woodscastle, though, and I returned here the following evening."

Sophia took a quick breath. "Well, that's a relief. Your travel out to Woodscastle has always been a source of concern for me."

Emma shook her head. "I assure you, I take great care in my trek to Chiswick. One of the grooms usually accompanies me. Mr. Wellingham, I fear, was not so lucky, though, on that rainy night. He couldn't find shelter in town and had to make the trip to Woodscastle by horseback. He was quite ill when he finally made it home," Emma explained as she unconsciously touched the teardrop pendant at her neck.

James and Sophia exchanged glances, but said nothing at first. "So I do hope you are making use of our old phaeton?" Sophia asked, before setting her glass of wine near her plate.

Emma put down her fork. "Not every day, of course, but it has been a life saver on many a morning, including today. I do thank you for your generosity in allowing me to use it," she said emphatically.

James leaned forward and replied, "It is our pleasure, believe me. We have owned that thing for many years and rarely use it. My fault, really. Once we got the barouche, I found traveling in the phaeton to be too... open."

Sophia rolled her eyes and leaned toward Emma. "My James has become very spoilt since our wedding, I'm afraid," she said with a teasing smile in her husband's direction.

Smiling at her landlord, Emma shook her head. "Mr. Simpson doesn't strike me as being the least bit spoiled," she said in the man's defense.

James beamed at the comment. "Ah, but I am, and I revel in it."

After a moment, Sophia said, "Speaking of matrimony..."

Emma, who had sliced off a bite of pork, stopped her fork before putting it in her mouth. *Matrimony?*

"During our stay in Derbyshire, we had a chance to speak with

Mr. Grandby about his marriage plans," Sophia continued, an eyebrow arcing in a suggestive manner.

"Or lack thereof," James commented as he watched Emma's reaction. "We were... hoping to introduce the two of you," he explained carefully.

Emma put down her fork. "But, I thought..."

"He is not the rake he comes off as, I assure you," Sophia said, giving her husband a quick glance that said volumes about what she thought of his earlier comment. "He is just a very good actor, you see," she started to explain, but was interrupted by James.

"And, although he has actually said the phrase, 'My needs are few. A girl in every port and port after dinner'—"

"James!" Sophia exclaimed, her eyes wide.

"—he actually does not engage in that kind of activity," James continued with a pointed look in Emma's direction. "I assure you," he added with a curt nod, hoping to assuage his wife's anger. He actually reached out and placed a hand over Sophia's arm, giving it a quick rub before returning it to his lap. The sudden anger and tension seemed to drain from her instantly, as if she realized she had overreacted to his jibe.

Emma glanced at both guests, trying to decide what to believe about Thomas' guest. "Isn't Mr. Grandby already... betrothed?" she asked. At their expressions of surprise and the slight shake of Sophia's head, she added, "It would seem a marriage would have already been arranged for a man of his background," she said, surprised they were considering her as a possible mate for the man.

Sophia sighed and shook her head, but didn't immediately reply. She took a quick glance in James' direction before saying, "No marriage has been arranged, but... I suppose it matters not since it seems our efforts were a bit too late," she added with a hint of sadness in her voice.

"Mr. Grandby informed us he has already decided on another young lady," James stated evenly, disappointment evident on his face. "It seems he has been in love with her for a very long time and plans to ask for her hand during his stay in the area," he explained.

"After he arranges it with the girl's family, of course," Sophia added, her face betraying her disappointment as well.

Emma did her best to keep her face impassive. Mr. Grandby's behavior certainly didn't fit a man who had already decided on a wife. Despite James' assertion he wasn't a rake, Gregory Grandby acted the part to such perfection, Emma could hardly believe he could be considering matrimony. "I do appreciate what you tried to do on my behalf," Emma assured the two of them, even though she really didn't mean it. She found the idea of Mr. Grandby as a husband an impossible proposition given his behavior earlier that day. "I would think you two would be happy for him," Emma suggested as she placed a hand on Sophia's. "It sounds as if he will be marrying for love."

Sophia shrugged a shoulder, but Emma could tell the woman was near tears. "You two would have... You would have made a most handsome couple," she said quietly while composing herself.

First, Todd Vandermeer and now Gregory Grandby, Emma thought. *I wonder whom my friends will have in mind for me next?*

James leaned forward. "Sophia, he still may change his mind," he offered in a whisper. "He has only just met Miss Emma, after all."

Taking a deep breath, Sophia sat up and nodded. "I know. 'Tis silly of me, I know, but I just thought I could play matchmaker on his behalf," she said with a small smile. "And yours, of course," she added quickly as she turned to Emma. Her eyes bright with unshed tears, Sophia nodded and pushed back her chair. "Please excuse me. I just need a moment in your privy." Before either Emma or James could react, Sophia was up and out of the dining room, her skirts swishing against the door frame as she made her way out of the room and up the stairs.

James settled back in his chair, closing his eyes for a moment as if he were considering what to do.

Seeing his indecision, Emma said in a quiet whisper, "She just needs a moment," although she was startled the woman would take such an interest in Gregory Grandby's choice of a wife. "I find it quite sweet she cares so much about Mr. Grandby."

Nodding, James took up his fork as if to resume eating. "She has known him his entire life," he offered, as if that were reason enough. "I suppose I have, as well," he added after taking a bite.

Emma smiled, and before she thought too much about the question, she asked, "However did you two meet?"

James beamed as if he had wanted someone to ask the question for a very long time. "I was the butler at Merriweather Manor, very near to Woodscastle," he replied quickly, leaning toward Emma and keeping his voice low. "Sophia was a recent widow. The most beautiful woman my eyes have ever beheld in my entire life," he vowed, his face taking on a faraway look as he related the events that led to their marriage.

Emma gasped at his recitation, her smile widening as he described his wife.

"She found reasons to speak to me nearly every day, as if I were a member of the family rather than a servant. On my days off, she would show up in the same coffeehouse as I was in, claiming she was shopping and merely wanted refreshment. After a couple of years..." He stopped for a moment, as if he couldn't believe he was telling the story. "She came to me... in my quarters, no less, and confessed her love for me. Begged me to bed her. Begged me to take her as my wife. As if I'd ever consider... anyone else."

Emma caught her breath, stunned that a woman of Sophia's ilk could be so forward in her love for a man as to offer herself like that. "How very... *romantic!*" Emma spoke, a hand coming to her mouth as she considered what the two must have gone through to have a marriage of mixed classes. Sophia's family would have certainly opposed such a union.

But, as a widow, perhaps the family at Merriweather Manor was not her own.

Emma's reverie was stopped short when Sophia appeared at the door, her head leaning to one side as she listened to her husband.

"We were married a few months later," he finished, his eyes bright as if tears were forming in their corners. He sniffed the air and a grin broke out on his solemn face. "And I can honestly say I have loved her since the moment I first smelled her sweet scent," he whispered, turning slightly to acknowledge his wife's presence in the room.

Sophia moved to stand behind her husband and wrapped her arms around his shoulders. She bent down and placed a kiss on the side of his temple. "I just think he loves my perfume," Sophia teased gently, allowing James to pull out her chair for her. Once she was reseated, she took a deep breath. "I apologize for having to leave you so suddenly."

Her eyes didn't betray a hint of the tears she must have shed while up in the privy, Emma noted. "There's no need to apologize, Mrs. Simpson. Your husband has just told me the most romantic story. It makes me believe I might one day find a man to call my own."

"Of course you will, my dear," Sophia replied brightly. "You must tell us who is calling on you these days."

At Emma's look of surprise, James put down his fork and seemed to pause before asking, "May I ask how it is you know Mr. Vandermeer? I remember he was here the day after that terrible business with the housebreakers."

Emma resigned herself to having to explain the situation and put down her own utensils. "Mr. Vandermeer has proven to be a very good friend. On that particular day, he was seeing to my wellbeing. He had read the story about the housebreakers in *The Times* and was most concerned."

Setting down her wine glass, Sophia stared at Emma. "It was true, then, what the paper said?" she asked, her eyebrows drawn together. "That really was *you?*"

Shrugging, Emma's face took on a faraway look. "For the most part, yes. But I wasn't hurt, and the sheriff was kind enough not to arrest me," she added with a wan smile.

"Well, I should hope not!" Sophia replied, a bit indignant. "So then, exactly why was Mr. Vandermeer here?" she asked, her look of concern replaced with a hint of mischief.

Emma smiled as she recalled the day. "I met him at Woodscastle when he was there for a meeting with my employer. You see, he had asked me to a dinner party at Grace Park..."

Sophia gasped in happy surprise.

"But with everything that happened the day before the dinner," Emma continued, acknowledging Sophia's reaction with a nod, "I brought along my friend Deborah White to act as a chaperone. We all had a most wonderful dinner."

"I hear he has the best chef in London," James commented lightly.

"He does. And now Mr. Vandermeer and Miss White are engaged and will marry on July the third," Emma finished with a satisfied grin.

James snorted and sat back in his chair, a huge grin on his face. "Mrs. Simpson, we have missed much whilst we away were on holiday," he said happily.

"Indeed!" Sophia answered, realizing the story hadn't turned out quite like she expected.

"But I find it rather hard to believe Todd Vandermeer will marry," her husband added.

Confused by the comment, Emma looked at James and then at Sophia. "But, why?" she asked quietly.

Sophia's face took on a more serious expression. "Yes, James. Why do you find it so hard to believe?" she asked her husband, her words clipped.

His grin disappearing, James sat up and cleared his throat. "I apologize. I didn't mean it as it sounded, I assure you. It's just that..." He paused, not quite sure how to describe the situation. "I have known Todd Vandermeer since my time as a butler at Merriweather Manor. It has always amazed me that an orphan could befriend boys who were of a class well above his own, and then grow up to be one of the more successful brokers for the John Company, if not the best then at least the tallest, and then he buys one of the most magnificent homes in Cavendish Square from that Michael Merriweather—you know, the one that had to sell because of his gambling debts and yet still had to go to prison—and now we find out he is to marry a friend of Miss Emma. The man is charmed. Simply charmed," he finished, still astonished by the news.

Sophia angled her head and allowed a grin. "Why, I think my husband may be jealous of Mr. Vandermeer," she teased gently.

"I am," James stated, his grin belying his words.

Emma covered her mouth with her napkin to hide her amusement. She told them what Deborah had discovered about Todd's parents, surprising both of them with the information. She decided not to tell them she might have been Todd Vandermeer's wife-to-be.

Whatever would they think of her then?

"Now, when will you meet Mr. Grandby's betrothed?" Emma asked in an effort to get the subject back to someone not quite so close to her.

James shook his head. "It will be some time around the Hornsby ball, we're told," he said before he resumed eating. "This pork is most excellent, by the way," he said between mouthfuls. "You must share the recipe. I'm always looking for good ways to prepare meats these days," he commented as he took another bite.

So, he does the cooking, too, Emma thought as she nodded in his direction. "Thank you, Mr. Simpson," she replied, relieved the man seemed sincere in his appreciation. "Will you be attending the Hornsby ball?" she asked, thinking Gregory Grandby was probably planning to propose to his intended that very evening. With a bit of luck and careful questioning, she might discover the name of the girl he planned to ask.

The gentleman looked to Sophia with a raised eyebrow. "Shall we this year?" he asked with a smile. "We've never been, but every year we receive an invitation and say we will."

Sophia blushed and looked uncomfortable for a moment. "Perhaps we will," she replied lightly, although Emma had the impression the comment was not heart-felt.

"And will you, Miss Emma?" Sophia asked as she took a bite of pork on her fork.

"Oh, no. I don't have an invitation nor an escort," Emma replied with a shake of her head.

Sophia and James exchanged glances again. "So, your Mr. Wellingham has not yet asked you?" she asked in surprise.

Emma leaned forward, surprised by the question. "I... I wouldn't expect Mr. Wellingham to invite me," she stammered with a frown. "He's my employer, after all."

Sophia raised her eyebrow. "But will he still be your employer in mid-July?" she countered with a mischievous grin.

Caught off-guard, Emma shook her head. "Well, I don't suppose so," she replied, wondering at Sophia's mischievous grin.

Smiling coyly, Sophia angled her head and regarded her husband. "Perhaps we can be of help in that regard, don't you suppose, James?" she suggested with an arched eyebrow.

James raised his own eyebrows and grinned mischievously. Appearing most devious, he replied, "Yes, I believe we can."

Glancing back and forth between the couple, Emma did her best to keep her mouth shut and her protests to herself. A blush bloomed across her cheeks when she realized just whom they were considering.

If they have Thomas Wellingham in mind for me next, she thought, *then so be it.*

CHAPTER 52
TWO GENTLEMEN IN THE LIBRARY

July 2, 1802, Woodscastle

"You say she's been your sister's roommate for nearly two years, and you've only just met her?" Gregory asked quizzically. "You know, London is only six miles away."

Raindrops streaked down the library windows, clearing the fogginess enough to show more gray clouds in the distance. Thomas had sent Emma home earlier that day with Mr. Allen as an escort, wanting to make sure she made it to Kingly Street before the rain started. Although she had protested at first, he reminded her of the wedding and thought she would have much to do as Deborah's attendant.

Thomas rolled his eyes and dropped the newspaper he was reading to his lap. "It's not as if I was trying to avoid her," he replied defensively. "It's just that whenever I took Christiana to dinner or had dinner with her at the Gamma House, Miss Emma was simply not there." Before Gregory could make a remark, Thomas added, "And I'm sure she wasn't trying to avoid me. She was attending a class. Besides, I did meet her. Last February, in fact."

Gregory took a puff from the pipe he was smoking and grinned. "Indeed. Well, I must say, Christiana has nothing but good things to say about the woman."

Thomas nodded his agreement. "'Tis true. And Christiana's certainly the better for having spent time with an older girl. I must admit, I was pleasantly surprised at how mature she was at Christmastime."

Gregory took another drag on the pipe and then sat in the leather chair next to the library window. "Funny. I rather noticed it last summer."

Thomas, who had returned to his newspaper, gave his best friend a sideways glance. "I'm afraid I wasn't around much during her summer holiday," he murmured quietly. "Shipping season and all," he added with a sigh. He hadn't told his friend about Christiana's plan to marry. He had briefly considered perhaps Gregory was Christiana's mysterious suitor, but given their age and height differences—and Gregory's apparent tendencies toward a rakehell's lifestyle—Thomas decided it was unlikely. Besides, Christiana's behavior toward Gregory since his arrival bordered on ambivalence.

Thunder rumbled in the distance and the rain increased in intensity. Thomas glanced out the window. "I do hope this rain clears up before the morning," he said, concerned for Todd's wedding plans. "We're attending a wedding tomorrow," he said over the top of the paper.

"But not yours, I'll bet," Gregory replied lightly, doing his best to antagonize his host.

"No, not mine. Todd Vandermeer is marrying Deborah White at eleven o'clock tomorrow morning. In the backyard gardens at Grace Park," he added as he glanced out the window again, an eyebrow furrowed in worry.

"I'm quite aware of our mutual friend's plan. I received an invitation to the affair just before I left Cherrywood," Gregory remarked, barely able to hide his boredom. "Our boy Todd seemed most insistent I attend. Have you met the bride?"

Shaking his head, Thomas replied, "No, but she is a friend of Miss Emma. And, I must say, I do believe she has made Vandermeer the happiest man in London," he said as he lifted the paper and resumed reading.

Gregory put the pipe in an ashtray and leaned forward. "Speaking of marriages, have you arranged one for your sister?" he asked quietly.

Thomas dropped the newspaper again. "Are you *daft?*" he replied in disgust. "After what my parents did to me, do you honestly think I would do that to her?" he asked rhetorically.

Thomas thought for a moment about how his parents' arrangements had affected his life. It wasn't as if he'd deliberately avoided the girl to whom he was supposed to be betrothed. He simply had no desire to make her acquaintance. And she certainly hadn't contacted him—nor had her parents—despite the fact that he continued to live at the same house his parents had occupied when the arrangement had been made. He often wondered how many people actually knew about the betrothal. "I have no intention of fulfilling that particular obligation made by my late parents," he glanced upwards. "May they rest in peace." At the same time, thunder sounded again in the distance.

His best friend chuckled. "Even if Lydia Collins is a most handsome girl?"

Thomas gave his friend a withering stare. "Is she?" he asked, not about to take the bait. "I admit, I've never met the chit, but I find I don't have a particular desire to do so."

Gregory's expression of utter disbelief had Thomas curious. "What is it?" Thomas asked, losing patience with his friend.

"She attends Warwick's with your sister! How could you *not* have met her?" he asked, perplexed.

Shaking his head, Thomas didn't recall an introduction nor even a passing comment by Christiana about the girl. He rather doubted his sister even knew about the betrothal. "I just have... not. Just as I hadn't met Christiana's roommate. There must be more than a hundred girls at that school," he reminded his friend.

"She's richer than you," Gregory whispered, leaning toward his friend. "Her father is an officer at Whitehall."

"Who is?"

"Lydia Collins," Gregory answered with a stomp of his foot.

Thomas shook his head back and forth. "I don't care. I certainly don't wish to marry some chit for her dowry. Or lack thereof," he added, annoyed his friend had even brought up the subject.

"But does she know that?" Gregory asked, keenly interested in the subject.

Thomas stared at this friend. "I've no idea," he replied as he finally gave it some thought. "I've never even been in contact with the family since father's death." When he saw Gregory's expression, he jumped to an utterly incorrect conclusion. "You're welcome to her if that's what all these questions are about."

The sudden look of shock on Gregory's face was almost comical. "*I* don't want to marry her," Gregory replied defensively. "She's a snobbish, short, ugly brunette with no figure at all," he claimed before he shoved the pipe back into his mouth.

Thomas straightened in the couch. "You said she was handsome..."

"I was just thinking if you have no intention of marrying her, you really should let her father know so he can make other arrangements... before she becomes an old maid," Gregory argued defensively.

Taken aback, Thomas gasped in surprise. "She's not even eighteen!" But he found he had to agree with his friend's advice. "I'll write a note to Mr. Collins this afternoon," he promised finally, sighing loudly. "Now, is there anything else we need to discuss?"

Gregory smiled conspiratorially. "Why, yes, I thought you'd never ask."

Thomas' face fell. "What is it now?" he asked in surrender.

"Mergers and acquisitions," Gregory said with a grin, his hands planted firmly on his knees.

Feeling as if he were about to be trapped, Thomas leaned back in his chair. "Go on," he replied carefully.

"Do you ever wonder who owns the stock in your company?" Gregory asked quickly.

He didn't allow Thomas time to answer.

"Miss Emma Fitzsimmons owns two percent of Wellingham Imports," he replied to his own question. "Did you know that?"

Nodding his head very slowly, Thomas replied, "Yes. Well, no, actually. It's... it is rather more than I expected, actually." Sir William had mentioned Emma's investment in the company, but in such a casual manner, Thomas thought her stake to be quite small. She had implied her finances were tight since she'd used up her inheritance on room and board at Warwick's.

"Exactly!" Gregory said excitedly. "And how much do you own?"

Furrowing his brows, Thomas thought for a moment. "Well, I gave Christiana twenty-five percent and I kept fifty and Sir William was going to find investors for the remainder."

Stunned, Gregory stood up. "You didn't keep controlling interest of your own company?" he asked in surprise, his demeanor now more serious.

"I have more stock than anyone else," Thomas argued. "What's your point?"

Gregory shook his head. "This will never do," he said as he began pacing back and forth in front of his friend. "You need to acquire Miss Emma as your wife and merge your stocks. That will give you fifty-two percent of the stock and a controlling interest in the company." He turned to face his friend in order to gauge his reaction and was soundly hit in the face by a flying pillow.

"I'm not going to *acquire* Miss Emma just to get controlling interest of my own company," Thomas stated in no uncertain terms, his voice much louder than he meant for it to be. "However," he added, his voice much quieter as he picked up the rumpled newspaper. "I am going to finish reading this newspaper."

With that, he hid behind the pages, leaving an amused Gregory staring out the window at the gray clouds—a rather amused Gregory, who, unbeknownst to Thomas, owned the remaining shares of Wellingham Imports.

CHAPTER 53
WEDDING DAZE

July 3, 1802, Kingly Street

"The rain stopped!" Deborah exclaimed happily as she leaned out Emma's bedchamber window and surveyed the street below.

"Indeed," Emma replied as she brought in a pot of tea and cups on a tray and set them on her dresser. "It appears it will be a beautiful day. Did you sleep well?" she asked, knowing Deborah had to be as nervous as she was, if not more.

Her friend had arrived about nine o'clock the night before and spent the night. Mr. Stevenson was scheduled to pick them up at ten o'clock to take them to Grace Park for the ceremony at eleven. Thomas, Christiana, and Gregory would arrive by carriage sometime before then. All the arrangements for the garden wedding had been made—it was up to Todd's household staff to carry off the remaining details this morning and his cook to prepare the breakfast feast Todd wanted all his guests to enjoy for the rest of the day.

Deborah pushed herself away from the window and bit her lip. "I did, although I must admit, I missed Todd terribly," she commented with a frown. "And I had forgotten what it was like to sleep in a nightrail," she added with a frown as she smoothed out the new but wrinkled nightrail she wore. "'Tis much more comfortable to sleep in the nude," she whispered.

Emma raised her eyebrows but managed to suppress a gasp. "You've already been sharing Todd's bed?" she asked quietly.

Deborah nodded and said, "Mine, actually," and then she

blushed when she realized to what she had admitted. "Please, Emma, don't think poorly of me. When we left here a fortnight ago, Todd insisted he couldn't be without me, so we said our vows after we arrived home. He even gave me the ring," she added as she held up her left hand.

Emma nodded and tried to admire the ring, but she felt her face blooming with color. "I remember his behavior that night. He loves you so much, Deborah," she replied as she poured tea.

Smiling, Deborah fell back onto the bed. "I know. And I do feel affection for him," she said as she sat up straight again. "And what about you, Emma?"

Emma raised her eyebrows. "What about me?" she asked as she handed Deborah a cup.

"Thomas Wellingham?" Deborah replied expectantly. "Oh, you really must tell me. All Todd would say was that one night you had to be Mr. Wellingham's nursemaid."

Open-mouthed, Emma gasped and nearly dropped her own teacup. "Mr. Vandermeer told you about that?" she asked, mortified. "I cannot believe it." She swallowed, trying to calm down when she realized he could only have learned of that night from Thomas.

"Did you make love to him?" Deborah whispered, obviously more excited now that she'd seen Emma's reaction.

"No! I most certainly did not," Emma replied defensively. When she noticed Deborah's expression of disappointment, she moved to sit down on the bed and then composed herself before she spoke. "I... I shared his bed for part of the night, but not in *that* way, the way you mean, and only because he was cold. He was chilled to the bone. He had a terrible fever. And we both wore nightclothes," she insisted, seeing Deborah's mischievous grin reappear, "Deborah, I was so frightened he was going to die. I... I would have done anything for him that night." Stunned by her own admission, Emma swallowed hard and held a hand to her mouth.

Deborah leaned over and hugged her. "So, you do love your Mr. Wellingham," she said happily. "Todd so wants you two to be together," she added as her shoulders nearly touched her ears in excitement. "I look forward to meeting him today."

Shaking her head, Emma sighed. "He's my employer, Deborah. I cannot be in love with him, and no one seems to understand that," she whined.

"Not for much longer," Deborah countered as she took a sip of tea. "You said your work for him would be done soon."

Emma took a deep breath and sighed, not sure how she felt about the end of her assignment. "I know. I shall have to find another position by September," she said. She bit her lip. Feeling Deborah's good cheer, though, she smiled. "Or, I suppose I could marry a rich man like you're doing," she teased. *Thomas Wellingham is rich*, she reminded herself. His company's books were a testament to that fact. But what could she offer as a dowry besides a few pieces of furniture and her name in some hats?

Deborah blushed and drank the rest of her tea. "Emma ...," she stopped for a moment and tried to decide if she should ask what she had in mind.

"Go on," Emma replied, realizing Deborah's mood had turned serious.

"Todd is the best lover, and yet he says I'm his first," Deborah whispered. "I was sure he had a mistress, but he denies it. He told me he learned from the book we've been reading. Can that be possible?"

Emma felt herself blush. She couldn't help but grin as she tried to imagine Todd Vandermeer in bed. "Well, I... I suppose. What's the name of the book?"

Deborah twirled her tea cup on the end of her fingertip. "I don't know. It's Indian, I believe. And it's mostly drawings..."

"Ah, I believe you are referring to *The Kama Sutra*," Emma stated with a nod. "It's an ancient Indian text, an instructional manual, of sorts, about love. It was written by a scholar hundreds of years ago. There's a copy on the top shelf of the bookcase downstairs." When Deborah opened her mouth in apparent shock, Emma added, in her own defense, "The former owner of the townhouse left behind his entire book collection." She didn't mention she'd seen a copy in Mr. Wellingham's library, as well.

Deborah sat down on the end of the bed. "Have you read it?"

Emma poured more tea for herself. "Not all of it," she replied truthfully as she joined Deborah on the end of the bed. "It's quite large. And quite... informative," she admitted, trying to remain dispassionate. "I've read all about kissing and about half of the positions for sexual intercourse," she whispered conspiratorially.

"Would you like to take a look while you're in the tub?" she offered as she grinned mischievously.

Deborah's eyes widened and she bit her lip. "Half the positions?" she repeated. "However many are there?" she asked, her eyes widening even larger.

"Sixty-four," Emma replied with a raised eyebrow. "Eight, really, but apparently there are eight versions of each."

Deborah leaned forward and held her head in her hands. Emma waved a hand in front of her face. "I find it hard to believe that after two years of listening to the tarts at the Home describe their bedchamber antics... that you would need further instruction on how to please a man," she said with a wink. At Deborah's feigned indignation, Emma grinned. "Should I bring it up?" Emma asked again.

"Yes!" Deborah exclaimed.

"All right, but we really must get you ready," Emma replied as she stood. "Mr. Stevenson will be here with the carriage in a couple of hours. In the meantime, I have water boiling on the stove for your bath, and I can do your hair whilst you read."

"Could this be the same Todd Vandermeer I last saw in April?" Gregory asked as he grasped the taller man's hand and shook it vigorously. "You look positively... healthy," he added as he released the groom's hand so Thomas might make his greeting.

"Indeed, Vandermeer, you look as if you have put on another stone since I saw you last," Thomas said in awe. It had only been a few weeks since their business meeting at Woodscastle and a week after that when they had shared a luncheon, but Gregory was right. Todd was the picture of health and happiness as he stood in his morning jacket, breeches, and top hat. For a man about to be married, he didn't display a hint of nervousness.

"All because of the love of a good woman," Todd replied as he shook Thomas' hand and gave him an obvious wink. When he noticed Christiana standing behind her brother, he bent down and kissed her on the cheek. "Miss Wellingham, you are as beautiful as ever," he commented as Christiana, caught off-guard by the kiss and compliment, could, at first, only curtsy in return.

"Thank you, Mr. Vandermeer," she said with an embarrassed smile. "Has Miss Emma arrived yet?" she queried, hoping to spend time with Emma and Deborah before the ceremony.

"Not yet, but their carriage is due here shortly," Todd replied as he glanced around. The taller hedges of the backyard gardens hid Margaret Street from view, but if a carriage pulled into the front curved drive off Chandos Street, it could be spotted from some vantage points. "Apparently, it's bad luck for a groom to see his bride before the wedding, so Deborah spent the night at Emma's townhouse."

Both Gregory and Thomas exchanged surprised glances at Todd's use of the women's given names.

Christiana moved forward to stand between Gregory and her brother. "But didn't you already see her in her gown when you went shopping for it?" she asked, worried that perhaps the bad luck may have already begun.

Todd shook his head and grinned at the question. "They wouldn't allow it," he claimed. "I had to sit in the shop looking the other direction the entire time Deborah tried on gowns!"

Gregory said, "But I bet you had to pay for it."

Mortified, Christiana swung her reticule against his thigh, wishing it had something heavy in it.

Noticing her grimace aimed at Gregory, Todd smiled. "It was my pleasure, believe me, Gregory. I cannot tell you what a relief it is to spend time with a woman who has nothing and expects nothing. She appreciates everything," he explained as he waved at the house and gardens. "She takes nothing for granted, the servants adore her, and she wants to continue to work at the Home for Unwed Mothers when we return from holiday." Although the comment was directed to Gregory, Todd glanced at Thomas several times as he said it.

"You're going to allow her to work?" Thomas asked, somewhat surprised by the news. He figured Todd was much better off financially than he was, but the idea of a wife having an occupation hadn't occurred to him.

Todd nodded. "Of course. I'm a patron of the Home, and they will be moved into their new quarters by the time we return. She won't be paid, of course, but it's her choice to continue her work for charity."

Thomas nodded his understanding and considered the taller man's words. "I look forward to meeting your bride, Todd."

Todd nodded and turned back to Gregory. "And you won't believe this, but you have something in common with my Deborah," he stated with a mischievous grin.

"Indeed?" Gregory replied, his brows furrowing.

"Your Aunt Lucy is married to her Uncle Edward," Todd said triumphantly.

Thomas smiled as he watched Gregory's reaction, fondly remembering the woman to whom Todd referred.

"No!" Gregory replied with a startled expression. "Uncle Ed Livingston is her *uncle?*" he asked rhetorically.

"Brother to her mother and Aunt Katherine Dooley," Todd said with a nod. "They'll both be in attendance today."

Gregory merely shook his head in disbelief as he glanced around the gardens. *Will wonders never cease when it comes to this man?*

The sounds of a small orchestra could be heard tuning their instruments for their performance. Three violins, a three-stringed double bass, a flute, and an English horn were held by musicians all dressed in their finest.

Despite the disapproving glances from the parish clerk and priest when Todd mentioned having an orchestra play during his wedding, Todd had insisted there be music. He had witnessed two weddings in India during his trips there and found the music a valuable addition to the ceremonies.

Christiana excused herself to watch for the carriage in front of the house as Todd, Thomas, and Gregory made their way to the lawn where the ceremony would take place.

Winston found his master laughing heartily with Mr. Grandby and Mr. Wellingham. He cleared his throat and Todd turned to look at him. The butler merely nodded, and Todd returned the nod.

"Gentlemen, 'tis time," Todd announced proudly.

Gregory and Thomas exchanged glances. "Well, I know what I have to do," Gregory said with a big grin, elbowing Thomas. As a witness, he merely had to watch the ceremony from the vantage of one of the chairs set out on the green lawn.

Thomas turned to Todd and nodded quickly. "Will you be all right whilst I'm back there?" he asked as he motioned toward the house. "You're not going to faint or run away on us?" he asked in jest as he regarded his friend.

Shaking his head, Todd replied, "No, Mr. Wellingham. You might faint, though, when you see Emma," he teased, a big grin splitting his face.

"Indeed? Is my cravat straight?" Thomas asked, quickly changing the subject.

"'Tis fine. Now go," Todd said as he reached out to push Thomas' shoulder. "There's a breakfast feast awaiting, and I am starving."

Not quite sure if Todd were being literal or if he was referring to his lust for his bride, Thomas strode off toward the house. Winston met him near the walkway from a side entrance and motioned him inside. Emma and Deborah, both dressed and ready, turned their heads simultaneously as Thomas entered the hall. Stopped short by the sight of them, he stood in awe and forced his mouth shut. Remembering to remove his hat and to bow, he did so, and both women curtsied.

Although he had been warned, he couldn't have imagined just how elegant Emma Fitzsimmons could look in peach satin. The gold teardrop earbobs he'd given her hung from her ears, and the pendant lay against the space between her collarbones. If it had dropped, it would be caught in the deep cleavage hinted at by the bodice of her gown. Although the sleeves were long, they didn't start until several inches below the tops of her shoulders, and the ends were tapered to cover the tops of her hands. Her hair, adorned with tiny flowers, was twisted into a chignon while tiny ringlets cascaded down around her temples. A flat peach hat adorned with the same flowers was pinned to one side of her head.

"Good morning, Mr. Wellingham," Emma said with a smile, admiring how distinguished, almost regal, her employer looked in his gray morning suit and matching top hat. A new pair of Hessians were shined so bright they reflected the domino pattern of the marble floor.

"Good morning, Emma. May I be allowed to say that you look positively incandescent?" he asked, not even realizing he had used her given name.

Emma felt her ears turn pink and her smile widened. "Why, of course, Mr. Wellingham. Thank you. May I introduce you to my friend, Miss Deborah White?" She turned to Deborah and said, "This is Thomas Wellingham."

Thomas stepped forward and nodded at the bride. He had to look up to make eye contact, and he could see why Todd Vandermeer found the woman so perfect for him. Her dark, almost black hair was pinned up in a multitude of curls all over the top of her head, and her veil was held in place by a small pearl-encrusted tiara Thomas was sure Todd insisted she wear. The gown she wore was made from silver satin and featured tiny pearls and exquisite embroidery. Like Emma's gown, the sleeves didn't start until several inches below her shoulders, and her décolletage was well displayed.

A pearl necklace circled her neck and pearl earbobs hung from her ears. With her large dark eyes and pale porcelain skin, she made a most beautiful bride.

"It is so very good to meet the woman who has made my friend so very happy. And healthy," he added with a grin as he looked up at her.

"It is an honor to meet you, Mr. Wellingham," Deborah replied with a nod. "Todd has told me so much about you. He's very blessed to have you as a friend."

Caught off-guard by the compliment, Thomas merely nodded and said, "Thank you." Taking a deep breath, he offered Emma his arm and she took it.

"Emma, will you hold this for me until the priest asks for it?" Deborah queried as she held out an enormous gold and onyx ring. King George the Third's crest was emblazoned in gold in the onyx.

"Of course," Emma replied as she took the ring and slipped it over her gloved thumb.

As they passed the butler, he handed the women their bouquets of peonies and gave Emma a parasol. Thomas donned his hat as Winston stopped Deborah from following too close behind. Thomas and Emma left the house and walked along the garden path to the site Todd had chosen for his ceremony.

"You were right, Miss Emma," Thomas commented as they slowly walked the path. "She seems perfect for Todd. I've known the man since we were young boys, and he looks better than I've ever seen him. Quite healthy, in fact."

Emma blushed. "Thank you for saying so, Mr. Wellingham. He is perfect for Deborah."

Thomas nodded absently. "May I see that ring?" he asked after they rounded the corner of the building and were headed for the clearing in the middle of the garden.

"Of course," Emma replied as she removed the ring from her thumb and handed it to Thomas. He studied it and turned it over, looking for an inscription. "I don't understand," he said as he shook his head. "Did she buy this as some sort of wedding ring?" he asked, handing it back to Emma.

"No. In fact, it belonged to Todd's father," Emma said as she slipped it back onto her thumb, carefully watching Thomas' reaction. She wasn't disappointed when he stopped walking and turned in surprise. "He was an officer in King George's army," she added with a small smile. "I take it then that you didn't see the announcement of their betrothal in *The Morning Chronicle?*"

Thomas stared in awe and glanced across the large lawn to where Todd was standing. "No, I didn't," he said as he shook his head, his attention still on the groom. He thought of the day he and Todd and lunched together and then shopped for jewelry. At no point had Todd mentioned his parents. "He sent me a post saying he knew the identity of his parents, but does Todd know this information about his father?"

Emma smiled and nodded. "We told him two weeks ago," she replied, deciding the details of how Todd learned of his parents could be told later. "His father, Colonel William Vandermeer, died in Boston in one of the first battles in the Colonies. Deborah went to Horse Guards and was able to claim some of his father's effects and a certificate. She also obtained a copy of Todd's record of birth showing his parents' names."

Pausing, Thomas stared at Emma. "Who were they?" he asked, his brows furrowed.

"His mother was Adelyn Tennison, but she died shortly after giving birth to him. Deborah is giving the items to him as a wedding gift of sorts," Emma explained. She glanced toward where the ceremony was to take place and indicated they should continue their walk.

But Thomas stood stock still as he pondered the information. "Tennison, you say?" he repeated.

Nodding, Emma confirmed the name. "Yes, Adelyn Tennison. Do you... know of her?"

Thomas shrugged and then quickly shook his head. "My mother was a Tennison," he said with a faraway look. After a moment, the mirth returned to his eyes. "So the bastard's not a bastard, after all," he said with a huge grin. He leaned over and kissed Emma's temple. "This is wonderful news, Emma. Thank you for telling me," he added as he placed his free hand over hers and they resumed their walk to the gardens.

Sure all the wedding guests had arrived, Winston was about to make his way to the back gardens when he heard pounding at the front door. He hurried to the vestibule and then slowed his pace as he approached the door. Opening it slowly, his eyes had to travel upwards more than usual before they made contact with those of the nattily dressed man who stood before him.

"Good day," the tall man said in greeting. At that moment, a woman appeared at the man's side. Dressed in a morning gown of impeccable cut and quality, she curtsied and threaded her hand through the man's crooked arm.

Had Winston not heard the man's voice, he would have thought he was staring at an older version of his master. The haircut, the facial features, indeed, even the man's choice of clothing were so close to that of Todd Vandermeer that he replied, "Mr. Vandermeer, I presume?"

The older gentleman smiled broadly. "Indeed, I am," he replied with a surprised nod, "And this is my wife Helen. I find myself in an embarrassing situation, you see, I ...," he started to say.

"You have come for the wedding, no doubt," Winston said as he opened the door wider and stepped back so the two might enter. "You are just in time. I'll take you to the garden straight away," he said in haste. He marched through the vestibule and the great hall to the back door.

The startled couple exchanged glances and followed the butler. When he flung open the glass doors to the back garden, Helen Vandermeer gasped. "A wedding... out of doors?" she whispered, not quite sure whether to be shocked or impressed.

"Yes, Mrs. Vandermeer," the butler replied with a nod to the side. "It took some doing and a special dispensation from the Archbishop, but Mr. Vandermeer was quite insistent he and his bride be married in his garden. With music, I might add," Winston explained, making sure he didn't sigh as he was tempted to do.

To his left, he could see Mr. Wellingham and Miss Emma making their way toward the clearing in the garden. He held up a hand in their direction, and although it took a moment for them to notice him, they slowed their gait so the newly arrived guests might be seated before they reached the clearing. "May I inquire as to your relation to my master?" the butler asked the couple as they reached the seating area. "So that I might properly introduce you?" he added when he noted their startled expressions.

The tall man shrugged and gave his wife a brief glance. "I believe I'm his uncle... his father's brother," Mr. Vandermeer said uncertainly, "But I have no proof as I didn't know my brother and his wife had any children," he explained quickly. But, at that moment, his nephew turned his attention from the priest at the front of the clearing and stood staring at the new wedding guests.

"Oh, my!" Helen Vandermeer commented quietly, her hand moving up to cover her open mouth. "He looks just like you did when I married you," she whispered in her husband's direction.

Christiana, dressed in a pastel green batiste gown with multicolored ribbons adorning the top of her skirt and cap sleeves, hurried from the house to sit next to Gregory in the second row of chairs. She buried a white-gloved hand under the folds of her gown and held Gregory's hand while the other held a small parasol over her head. "Emma is simply gorgeous," Christiana whispered, nearly breathless. "If my brother does not agree, then there is simply no hope for him."

Gregory did his best to suppress a grin. "And what of the bride?" he asked in a quiet voice. "She cannot be as beautiful as you."

Blushing, Christiana squeezed his hand. Her strawberry blond hair was styled in a cascade of ringlets and an elegant chignon high on the back of her head. Her freckles began to appear with the noonday sun, and Gregory found it hard not to kiss her nose. "She is exquisite, Gregory. And very tall and very elegant."

Gregory grinned. "To you, my dear, everyone is tall," he remarked as he turned around and spotted Thomas and Emma. They were walking the garden path and heading in their direction. He noticed how they stopped and talked for a moment, and then it appeared as if Thomas kissed Emma on the side of her head. *Either that or he's sniffing her ear*, he considered. Gregory sat up straighter and tried to get a better view. "I do believe your brother just kissed Miss Emma," he whispered, surprised and amused.

Christiana turned in her chair and watched the couple as they approached the clearing. "I think you have taken too much sun," she replied as she studied her brother and best friend. At that moment, Winston appeared from a pair of large glass doors with two more wedding guests. "Oh, my," she remarked as she turned around in her chair and then stared at the back of Todd Vandermeer.

Gregory gave a quick glance over his shoulder and turned around as well. "I do believe I see what you mean," he whispered loudly, wondering how he could get the groom's attention.

Two elderly ladies took seats in the front row. One, dressed in a blue brocade and lace gown with an elegant hat, began crying quietly while the other, in white brocade, tried to console her. Christiana figured one of them to be Deborah's mother. Since

Deborah wasn't yet one-and-twenty, she required parental approval for the marriage to take place.

Other guests, three from the East India Company and several from the Home for Unwed Mothers, including Mrs. Dawes, filled the other chairs. Ribbons blew in the slight breeze, and a young, dark haired woman sprinkled petals along the long carpet that led to the priest and minister who would marry the couple.

Todd stood ready at his spot at the front, turning occasionally to look for his bride. Although a silver cane was propped up against a nearby chair, he didn't use it. When he turned at the sound of Gregory's quiet call, he was astounded to see an older version of himself staring back. It was a long moment before he could find his voice, and by that time, other guests had noticed the couple standing in the middle of the aisle. Todd hurried to join the couple, his right hand outstretched. "I am Todd Vandermeer," he said proudly as he shook his uncle's hand.

"I am Richard Vandermeer, and this is my wife, Helen," the taller man replied with a nod. "We didn't mean to interrupt your... wedding," he said as he noticed the stares of the other guests.

Todd was shaking his head. "You're not interrupting at all," he replied happily. "In fact, I've been hoping a relative might appear in time for this very day, you see, once I discovered I might actually have some relatives," he added as he regarded his uncle, just then realizing the man was even taller than he was. "You're related to my father, are you not?"

Richard nodded. "William was my older brother. He was dispatched to the Colonies only a few weeks after his wedding, and we lost touch with his bride. I'm... very sorry we didn't know of you," he said quietly.

Noticing Thomas and Emma were nearly to the clearing, Todd shook his head quickly. "It's quite understandable," he said in reply. "I only learned of my father's identity two weeks ago. Please, do me the honor of witnessing my wedding," he urged as he motioned to a pair of empty chairs in the front row. "And stay for the breakfast feast, please," he added as he turned to his attention to Helen, realizing he remembered her. She had been the woman who seemed so surprised to see him in the modiste the day he had taken Deborah and Emma shopping. *No wonder she seemed to recognize me,* he thought happily.

His aunt smiled at his enthusiasm and nodded. "Of course we

will stay," she replied as she reached up to kiss him on the cheek. "I look forward to meeting your bride."

Todd beamed when he noticed Deborah appear from around the side of the house. "She is nearly here," he breathed as he nodded in the direction of the house.

The Vandermeers turned in unison to see the bride approaching and then hurried to take their seats.

When Thomas and Emma passed the small orchestra, the music segued to Bach. They slowed their steps even more as everyone turned to look. In the distance, Deborah could be seen walking slowly along the path, and the guests began to murmur even more than they had at the arrival of the Vandermeers.

"Well, this is turning into an interesting event," Gregory whispered to Christiana as he watched the Vandermeers take their seats. He turned his attention back to his best friend. "And you were certainly right about Miss Emma," he added as he admired his best friend and the bookkeeper. "And now I see what you mean about Miss White," he said as he realized just how tall the bride stood. He rose from his seat. Never having attended such an affair, other guests followed his suit and stood watching the bride approach.

As Thomas and Emma took their places on either side of the priest, the music changed, and Deborah slowly moved toward her groom. Although a long veil covered her face, it was sheer enough so anyone could tell she was an elegant beauty.

Todd could barely wait for her arrival. He nearly left the priest to join her halfway down the aisle, but Thomas put a hand on his arm to stop him. "Steady," he said in a hoarse whisper. "Let her come to you." Emma overheard the remark and had to raise her bouquet to hide her grin behind a peony.

When Deborah was nearly to the front, Thomas finally let Todd walk over to join her. Holding his arm for her, he kissed her forehead through the veil. Gasps from the guests could be heard, and although he may have done wrong, Todd simply didn't care. Emma reached over and took Deborah's flowers as the priest began the ceremony.

Except for the odd location of being outdoors in a garden, the ceremony was the same as it would have been in the church. Thomas marveled that his friend had paid twenty guinea to secure a license so the wedding could be in his garden and a week earlier than normally allowed by church doctrine. Had Todd waited, though, his wedding would have been on the same day as the Hornsby ball, and that wouldn't do, Thomas decided. He found his gaze falling on Emma as he heard the priest begin the ceremony.

"Dearly beloved," the priest said in a clear voice, "We are gathered together here in the sight of God, and in the face of this congregation, to join together this man and this woman in holy matrimony; which is an honorable estate, instituted of God in the time of man's innocency, signifying unto us the mystical union that is betwixt Christ and his church; which holy estate Christ adorned and beautified with his presence, and first miracle that he wrought, in Cana of Galilee; and is commended of Saint Paul to be honorable among all men: and therefore is not by any to be enterprised, nor taken in hand, unadvisedly, lightly, or wantonly, to satisfy men's carnal lusts and appetites, like brute beasts that have no understanding; but reverently, discreetly, advisedly, soberly, and in the fear of God; duly considering the causes for which Matrimony was ordained."

Although he appeared to be listening, Thomas allowed his mind to wander. He imagined Emma dressed in the gown Deborah wore, tried to imagine her as Todd's bride and found he could not. What had he been thinking to recommend her to his friend? The thought of the two of them being married, of sharing Grace Park, of dining together, of sharing a bed... Thomas closed his eyes in an attempt to erase the thought and instead imagined Emma in his own bed, naked and ripe and willing, her lush lips forming a come-hither smile while her long fingers moved to caress and stroke and welcome his body atop hers.

Thomas blinked, realizing the priest had turned his attention to Todd and Deborah. "I require and charge you both, as ye will answer at the dreadful day of judgment when the secrets of all hearts shall be disclosed, that if either of you know any impediment, why ye may not be lawfully joined together in matrimony, ye do now confess it. For be ye well assured, that so many as are coupled together otherwise than God's Word doth allow are not joined together by God; neither is their matrimony lawful."

Todd and Deborah glanced at one another but merely shook their heads. Turning his attention to Todd, the priest said, "Todd William Vandermeer, wilt thou have this woman to be thy wedded wife, to live together after God's ordinance in the holy estate of matrimony? Wilt thou love her, comfort her, honor, and keep her in sickness and in health; and, forsaking all others, keep thee only unto her, so long as ye both shall live?"

Todd grinned and nodded. "I will," he said, almost too loudly.

As a smile appeared on the priest's face, a titter passed through those in attendance. Gregory tightened his hold on Christiana's hand. He leaned over and whispered, "I will," before giving her a raised eyebrow.

Christiana gave him a sideways glance, her cheeks blooming with color. "Shh," she replied, holding one finger in front of her lips.

The priest turned his attention to the bride. "Deborah Katherine White, wilt thou have this man to be thy wedded husband, to live together after God's ordinance in the holy estate of matrimony? Wilt thou obey him, and serve him, love, honor, and keep him in sickness and in health; and, forsaking all others, keep thee only unto him, so long as ye both shall live?"

Swallowing hard, Deborah nodded and said, "I will." A tear escaped from the corner of her eye and slowly left a wet trail on her cheek as it fell.

Stepping forward, the minister nodded and then looked out onto the witnesses. "Who giveth this woman to be married to this man?" he asked in a clear voice.

Emily White stood up and took Deborah's hand in hers. "I do," she said quietly as tears streamed down her face. She lifted Deborah's hand and gave it to the minister. He, in turn, took Todd's right hand and placed Deborah's right hand into it. "Say after me," the minister ordered.

Todd shook his head and began the vows without prompting. "I, Todd William Vandermeer, take thee Deborah Katherine White, my wedded wife," he said as he held Deborah's gaze, "To have and to hold from this day forward, for better for worse, for richer for poorer, in sickness and in health, to love and to cherish, till death us do part, according to God's holy ordinance; and thereto I plight thee my troth."

The minister shrugged his shoulders and simply continued the ceremony. He took Deborah's right hand and placed it around Todd's right hand. Before he could say, "Say after me," though, Deborah was speaking her vows in a voice that sounded thready at first, but was soon strong enough to be heard by everyone in attendance.

"I, Deborah Katherine White, take thee Todd William Vandermeer, to my wedded husband, to have and to hold from this day forward, for better for worse, for richer for poorer, in sickness and in health, to love, cherish, and to obey, till death us do part, according to God's holy ordinance; and thereto I give thee my troth."

The minister reached over to separate their hands, and it was a moment before he was able to pry them apart.

Thomas was jolted out of his reverie when the priest turned to him and held out his hand expectantly. Reaching into his topcoat, Thomas pulled out a gold band and gave it to the priest, who in turn gave it to Todd.

The groom, smiling broadly and with no hint of nervousness, slipped it on Deborah's finger and said, "With this ring I thee wed, with my body I thee worship, and with all my worldly goods I thee endow. In the name of the Father, and of the Son, and of the Holy Ghost. Amen."

The priest was about to continue the service when he noticed Emma holding out the army officer's ring. Confused, he took it as he nodded to her and then gave the ring to Deborah. She held it and waited for Todd to raise his hand. When he didn't immediately react, Deborah reached down, lifted his left hand, and slipped the ring onto his finger. Todd stared at it in wonderment, at first not understanding the symbol in the onyx.

"With this ring I thee wed," Deborah stated in a quiet voice. "With my body I thee worship, and with all my worldly goods I thee endow. In the name of the Father, and of the Son, and of the Holy Ghost. Amen."

Gregory furrowed his brows and snorted. "She has no worldly goods to endow," he whispered, mostly to himself.

Christiana, stunned by his comment, elbowed him hard in the ribs. "Neither do I!" she whispered.

The minister, befuddled by the addition to the ceremony, nearly forgot what came next in the ceremony. Todd and Deborah kneeled down in front of him, though, and he announced, "Let us pray." When all heads were bowed, he continued, "O eternal God, Creator and Preserver of all mankind, Giver of all spiritual grace, the Author of everlasting life; Send thy blessing upon these thy servants, this man and this woman, whom we bless in thy Name; that, as Isaac and Rebecca lived faithfully together, so these persons may surely perform and keep the vow and covenant betwixt them made, whereof these rings given and received are tokens and pledges, and may ever remain in perfect love and peace together, and live according to thy laws; through Jesus Christ our Lord. Amen."

Reaching down, the priest joined their right hands together and said, "Those whom God hath joined together let no man put asunder."

The minister stepped forward and addressed the witnesses. "For as much as Todd and Deborah have consented together in holy wedlock, and have witnessed the same before God and this company, and thereto have given and pledged their troth either to other, and have declared the same by giving and receiving of a ring... of rings," he stammered, "And by joining of hands; I pronounce that they be man and wife together. In the Name of the Father, and of the Son, and of the Holy Ghost. Amen."

Holding his arm up, he added, "God the Father, God the Son, God the Holy Ghost, bless, preserve, and keep you; the Lord mercifully with his favor look upon you; and so fill you with all spiritual benediction and grace, that ye may so live together in this life, that in the world to come ye may have life everlasting. Amen."

Todd and Deborah walked hand in hand to the table that had been set up as the Lord's Table and kneeled in front of it, facing the priest. The minister began singing as he, too, moved to the table.

Emma struggled to stand still when she realized Thomas was gazing in her direction—gazing at her. She wondered if something might be wrong with her gown, or if her bouquet had lost some of its blooms, or if her hair had come out of its pins, or if... she inhaled sharply when a frisson passed through her body, a pleasant shiver that had her senses on alert, her breasts swelling with their arousal. It was as if the man's gaze were a hand caressing her entire body, his fingers teasing her skin, lightly tickling her so delightful skitters passed through her flesh, his lips taking purchase on her neck, her throat, her collarbones, her nipples. Another frisson took hold of her body, this one so intense, she was sure it was visible to anyone watching her.

To Thomas, perhaps?

The priest said, "Lord, have mercy upon us."

And me especially, she thought, forcing herself to pay attention to the service when everyone replied, "Christ, have mercy upon us."

The minister said, "Lord, have mercy upon us." Pausing a moment, he led the attendees in the Lord's Prayer.

Although Thomas had been following the service since having to come up with the wedding ring, he once again stole a glance in Emma's direction. *God, she is beautiful*, he thought. Why hadn't he noticed the first night he had met her?

Because I wasn't looking. Not then. Not since Rebecca had seen to it he would probably never again feel lust for a woman. Her insults and bedroom antics, employed on him when he was only twelve or thirteen—he couldn't even remember how old he had been back then—had been quite effective, leaving him emasculated. Leaving him with no desire to bed a woman. *So, I wasn't about to go looking for comfort in a woman's bed*, he thought, remembering how he had simply immersed himself in his work and the duty of raising his younger sister.

But something had changed. Something profound. Something... dare he think it? *Life changing* had come out of that awful night when he thought he had died. A woman had cared for him, fed him, warmed him with her body and probably saved his life. His own body reminded him of what it had felt like to hold her against him, her soft body nestled into his, providing warmth and something to hang onto when he thought he was about to die.

My lifesaver, he thought with a start. *My angel.*

Thomas was brought back to the present when he heard everyone say, "From the face of their enemy."

Well, he supposed Rebecca had been his enemy. But he was back. And the woman who was responsible for bringing him back stood so close, he was sure he could smell the scent of her with every breath he took.

To think, she could be the one standing with Todd, saying her vows and forever being his wife. Or, at least until she was his widow.

Thomas swallowed. Hard. *Could I have waited that long for her?* If Emma hadn't arranged for Deborah to meet Todd, Emma would be saying her vows now. She would be Todd's wife. If he ever had a hope of having her as his own, he would have had to wait until his best friend had died and Emma had completed her mourning period.

Damnation!

Whatever disparaging thoughts he'd had about Deborah evaporated. She was marrying his friend, probably prolonging his life by several years and seeing to it Emma could be his own.

If she'll have me.

Realizing the ceremony was nearly over, Thomas turned his attention back to Todd and Deborah. The minister, having paused a moment, continued the ceremony with, "O God, who by thy mighty power hast made all things of nothing; who also after other things set in order didst appoint, that out of man, created after thine own image and similitude, woman should take her beginning; and, knitting them together, didst teach that it should never be lawful to put asunder those whom thou by matrimony hadst made one: O God, who hast consecrated the state of matrimony to such an excellent mystery, that in it is signified and represented the spiritual marriage and unity betwixt Christ and his Church; Look mercifully upon these thy servants, that both this man may love his wife, according to thy Word, as Christ did love his spouse the Church, who gave himself for it, loving and cherishing it even as his own flesh, and also that this woman may be loving and amiable, faithful and obedient to her husband; and in all quietness, sobriety, and peace, be a follower of holy and godly matrons. O Lord, bless them both, and grant them to inherit thy everlasting kingdom; through Jesus Christ our Lord. Amen."

The priest continued, "Almighty God, who at the beginning did create our first parents, Adam and Eve, and did sanctify and join them together in marriage; Pour upon you the riches of his grace, sanctify and bless you, that ye may please him both in body and soul, and live together in holy love unto your lives' end. Amen."

The priest motioned for the happy couple to stand as he surveyed the witnesses. Much to his surprise, Todd smiled, lifted the veil from Deborah's face, and kissed her for several seconds. When their lips finally parted, Thomas stepped over and kissed Deborah on the cheek while Todd kissed Emma on the forehead. Gregory used Christiana's parasol to hide his kiss with her as the other guests laughed and applauded.

Winston stood from where had taken a seat in the back row and announced that breakfast was served.

In a separate part of the garden, under the shade of several trees, stood a long table filled with foods of every description. A large cake, made of fruits, rum, and sugar, was positioned in the middle. A ham lay ready for slicing at one end and a large pitcher of chocolate, ready for pouring into crystal cups, stood at the other. Towers of hot rolls and platters of breads, buttered toast, and eggs of every variety graced the rest of the table. The guests happily took their places and waited for the bride and groom to take theirs before beginning the feast.

"Excuse me, but might you be Mrs. White?" Gregory asked as he leaned over the table to address Emily White.

Emily regarded the tall, handsome man with a look of surprise. "Why, yes, I'm Emily White," she acknowledged with a nod.

"Gregory Grandby, at your service," he replied with a bow. "I have been told we have relatives in common," he said with a mischievous grin.

Emily smiled broadly and her sister, Katherine Dooley, stood up to curtsy. "Indeed, we do," she said happily. "Our brother is Edward Livingston," she said proudly, nodding as she said it.

Christiana glanced up and watched Gregory interact with the older ladies.

"His wife, Miss Lucy, is my favorite aunt," he was saying in reply. "I must introduce you to my intended," he said, feeling a bit awkward as he turned to take Christiana's elbow. Christiana stood up and curtsied to the women. "This is Miss Christiana Wellingham. Her brother was standing with Mr. Vandermeer," he explained as he held Christiana's hand.

"Oh, so you are engaged?" Emily asked at his use of the term 'intended.'

Christiana looked around nervously, and when she saw her brother and Emma were still out of earshot, said, "Although Mr. Grandby cannot yet ask for my hand, I have assured him I will accept his offer of matrimony," she said with a mischievous grin, hoping word wouldn't get back to Thomas before Gregory could ask his permission to propose.

Katherine's eyes opened wide upon hearing the news, and then her face expressed surprise. "Where are my manners?" she asked. "I'm Katherine Dooley. Miss White, or rather, Mrs. Vandermeer, is my niece," she added by way of introduction.

"'Tis very good to meet you," Gregory said with a slight bow.

As Thomas and Emma joined the guests at the table, Thomas paused to hold a chair for Emma before he took the seat next to her near the end of the table. Gregory introduced them to Deborah's family as Todd motioned his aunt and uncle to join him near the head of the table. Deborah took her seat at the other end of the table.

"I'm very pleased to announce that my newly found aunt and

uncle were able to join us today," Todd said in a raised voice so that everyone might know the identity of the last-minute arrivals.

The couple nodded and smiled as the other guests acknowledged them. "Mr. Vandermeer, you must tell me how you found me," Todd said as they took their seats.

His uncle straightened and indicated his wife with a hand. "Helen read of your betrothal in *The Morning Chronicle*," Richard said, leaning to the side as Winston handed him a glass of champagne and moved down the table, passing out flutes from a tray he held.

"And I've seen your name in the paper before, of course," Helen chimed in, "What with your position at East India and your donations to deserving charities and all," she added with an approving smile. She thanked the butler for the champagne and nodded to a footman who offered her a plate full of toast and eggs.

"She always suspected we might be related, but it wasn't until she saw you whilst shopping that she realized you must be a family member," Richard explained shortly. "Cut short her shopping trip, she did, so she could come home to tell me of the tall man who opened the door for her," he recalled with a smile. "She was positively excited."

Todd rolled his eyes. "I so wish I had introduced myself," he apologized as he shook his head.

"'Tis quite alright. You were quite busy escorting those two," Helen replied with a happy grin as she waved toward Deborah and Emma. "Miss Suzanne said you were there to buy gowns for your wedding, and she told me your name, so then I just hurried home to tell my Richard about you," she added, cocking her head proudly. "When I read the announcement in the Society page, and I could barely breathe!"

Richard reached over the table to pat his wife's hand. "Took some research to find your home, though," Richard said as he leaned toward his nephew. "The announcement in the paper didn't include an address, so it's why we haven't called on you before today."

Shaking his head, Todd grinned as he regarded his aunt and uncle. "I can hardly believe this. Thank you for finding me. Now, you must tell me *your* story," he insisted, glancing around the table to be sure the other wedding guests were being served.

Richard angled his head to one side and replied, "I'm a barrister and spend most of my day at the Old Bailey." He leaned to one side as a footman placed a plate of eggs and toast in front of him. "Your father encouraged me to study law before he left for the war. I have him to thank for my education since it was he who paid for it," he explained, his face taking on a serious expression. "I cannot help but think I took something that more rightfully belonged to you."

Leaning closer to his uncle, Todd furrowed his brows. "Whatever do you mean?"

The older man shrugged. "He obviously didn't have an opportunity to update his last will on the event of his marriage and his assignment to the Colonies. There was no mention of you or his wife," he explained quickly. "I'm so sorry you weren't given your due upon his death," he added, his concern quite genuine.

Todd shook his head and glanced over at his aunt before answering his uncle's comment. "I appreciate your concern, Mr. Vandermeer, but please know I don't resent you for what happened. I only found out the identity of my parents two weeks ago," he explained with a nod.

Helen took a deep breath. "Who was she?" the woman asked as she placed a hand on Todd's forearm. "We never learned of her until the men from the War Office came calling with the news of your father's death. They asked if we knew where they could find her," she said in a quiet voice. "But they had no name or a place to start their search." She looked at her husband with a nervous expression, her eyes darting between Richard and Todd.

Shaking his head, Todd replied, "She died a few weeks after I was born. I only know her name was Adelyn Tennison," he added, hoping one of them might remember the woman.

Richard gasped and Helen inhaled sharply before she had a chance to cover her mouth with a gloved hand.

Todd looked at his aunt and uncle in turn. "What is it?" he asked, his concern increasing as he watched the two of them exchange shocked and then finally happy expressions.

"Well, now we know what became of your sister," Richard remarked, a grin spreading across his face before a more somber expression replaced it.

Helen sighed loudly and nodded. "Indeed," she said before turning to Todd. "Your mother was my sister, so you are my nephew, too!" she said as she patted his arm. "We always wondered what became of her. I used to receive letters from her, and then, once the war started, we heard nothing else. We feared the worst," she explained as she displayed a myriad of emotions.

Todd placed a hand over hers. "So, you didn't know she married your brother-in-law?"

Reaching out to place a hand over his wife's, Richard cleared his throat. "We suspected they might marry, but my brother kept his private business very private," he explained, shaking his head. "I believe he thought your mother might suffer if an enemy discovered she was married to an army officer."

Nodding, Todd considered his uncle's words. "I'm sorry for your loss. For both of you," he said quietly.

Helen smiled and continued to pat his arm. "And we're sorry for you. Please know that, had they lived, your parents would have..."

"Spoilt you rotten," Richard interjected with a grin, clapping Todd across the shoulder.

Todd smiled broadly. "I cannot tell you what a... relief it is to finally know something about them," he said in a quiet voice.

"Thank you, both, for choosing today to find me. It seems I had to get married for my family to find me," he added with a grin.

His uncle and aunt nodded and smiled at his words. "We have taken too much of your time with all this," Helen said as she leaned back in her chair. "This is your wedding day! We can catch up another time."

Grinning, Todd nodded, noticing Deborah sitting at the other end of the very long table. "I am finally married to the love of my life, and now I find myself seated too far away from her," he announced to the entire table in mock despair. Laughter ensued, and before everyone had helped themselves to the ham, Todd excused himself from his aunt and uncle and managed to secure a seat next to Deborah at the other end of the table.

Winston opened several bottles of champagne and refilled the glasses for everyone at the table. Christiana glanced in Thomas' direction, wondering how many she would be allowed to drink. He didn't seem to notice her, though, nor the fact that champagne was being served.

His attention was on Emma and the bride and groom.

Emma removed her gloves before taking the glass of champagne Thomas held for her. When everyone had a glass, Thomas stood up and cleared his throat. The murmurs and conversations ceased as he held his glass in the air. "I'd like to make a toast," he announced, pausing a moment to allow the boisterous conversation to subside. "In the eighteen or so years I have known Mr. Todd Vandermeer, I have never seen him more happy nor as healthy as you see him here today. The source of his happiness is this most beautiful woman, Miss Deborah White. The equally beautiful Miss Emma Fitzsimmons," he said as he indicated Emma, who blushed at his comment, "Saw to it that these two should meet so cupid might take aim and impale their hearts with one of his love-stricken arrows. The arrow was swift and sure and, as you can see," he said with mirth, holding his arm out to indicate Deborah and Todd. "They are dead." Deborah and Todd looked at each other in shock and then feigned being shot by arrows.

Thomas had to wait for a round of laughter to die down before he continued. "They are now as one loving couple, and may they live the rest of their long lives as happy and as healthy as you see them here. Let us all drink to Deborah and Todd!" he said, and he took a long sip of his champagne.

The guests replied with a chorus of "cheers" and drank to the toast. Thomas sat down, leaned over, and touched the rim of his glass to Emma's before she took her drink. She grinned at him, her face still flushed from his comment. "Cheers," she said before taking a sip.

After a few hours of conversation and feasting, Deborah excused herself to change for the trip to Derbyshire. When she descended the steps from the mistress suite, she wore a dark green traveling gown and matching spencer and a poke bonnet adorned with flowers and ribbons. Mr. Stevenson positioned the chaise in the front drive and loaded two trunks onto the back.

Todd said farewell to the guests and made a special farewell to his aunt and uncle before he assisted Deborah into the coach. When they were off for their trip, several guests removed their shoes and tossed them after the departing carriage, applauding and yelling their good wishes.

When the chaise was out of sight, the guests made their way to their own equipage and left the grounds, spreading the news of the unusual wedding to all they knew.

CHAPTER 54
A REVEALING TRIP TO GUNTER'S

Emma sighed and turned to climb the stairs to the house as Thomas moved to offer her his arm. "Thank you, Mr. Wellingham," she said, placing her hand on his sleeve. As they made their way into the house, she turned and couldn't help but notice Christiana seated next to Gregory in the single carriage that remained in the drive.

Thomas noticed her slightly arched eyebrow. "Mr. Grandby and I are taking Christiana to Gunter's Tea Shop for an ice," Thomas explained as he knitted his hands behind his back. "Would you care to join us?" he asked, hoping the invitation didn't sound insincere. "My treat, of course. We've only just thought of it, you see. And the weather is perfect for an afternoon on the square..."

"I haven't had an orange sorbet since my father took me there last. I would love to," Emma replied, interrupting her employer's ramblings while nodding enthusiastically. Her father had treated her to Sunday afternoons at Gunter's on many occasions, but without a proper escort, she found the prospect of visiting the tea and sorbet shop an impossibility these days.

Thomas nodded. "Capital. We can, of course, give you a lift to your townhouse afterwards," he offered as he continued to stand just inside the door.

Emma shook her head. "Actually, I will be staying here at Grace Park this evening. Miss White..." She stopped and took a breath. "Mrs. Vandermeer," she corrected herself with a smile, "She insisted, and I found her offer impossible to decline."

Cocking his head to one side, Thomas wondered what it was about Grace Park that held such appeal and then remembered it was more modern than most houses. "Then we shall return you here to Grace Park," he said with a nod as he once again held out his arm. Returning the smile, Emma managed to grab her bonnet and parasol with one hand as she took Thomas' arm.

Christiana, who seemed to be in deep conversation with Gregory as she sat impossibly close to the older man, gasped when she realized her brother was not alone when he returned to the carriage. "Emma!" she exclaimed, her face brightening. "Are you joining us this afternoon?" she asked as she watched her brother assist her best friend into the carriage.

"It seems I am," Emma replied as she took the seat opposite Christiana, finding the seating arrangement awkward when Thomas was forced to sit next to her instead of next to his friend. Proprietary would have the girls sitting next to one another, but neither Gregory nor Christiana seemed uncomfortable with the arrangement. Emma pulled on her eyelet bonnet and opened the parasol.

"Mr. Larsen. To Berkeley Square, please. We're going for ices," Thomas ordered as he settled into his seat. "With a bit of luck, we'll find a maple tree under which we can enjoy our treats," he added as he turned his attention to the others.

The ride from Cavendish Square to Berkeley Square took longer than it should have given the short distance between the two, but Saturday afternoon traffic, both horse-drawn and pedestrian, made for frequent stops. Emma used her parasol to shield herself and Thomas from the hot afternoon sun while Christiana could do little to include Gregory under her parasol's protection—he was simply too tall to fit under it. The man breathed deeply when Mr. Larsen managed to position their carriage in a large shadow on the east side of the square. "Ah, relief from the sun," Gregory said, dabbing his forehead with a handkerchief as the carriage came to a halt.

A short, stocky waiter strode toward the carriage and bowed before asking, "What may I get you this afternoon?" In the growing heat of the July afternoon, beads of sweat were sprouting on his forehead. "Do you require a list of our flavors?"

Christiana leaned forward to answer but covered her mouth and looked to her brother when Gregory reached over to place a silencing hand on her arm.

"An orange sorbet for the lady, a lemon sorbet for the young miss, and strawberry sorbets for my friend and me," Thomas stated as he leaned toward the edge of the carriage. "What would you like, Mr. Larsen?" he asked as he turned in his seat so the driver could better hear him.

An obviously surprised Mr. Larsen nearly stuttered as he replied, "A lemonade would be most welcome, sir." He smiled in Emma's direction, figuring she was responsible for his employer's sudden concern for his welfare.

Thomas nodded. "Then a lemonade for my driver," he added as he turned back around in his seat to face the waiter.

"Very good, sir. It will just be a few moments," the man responded before bowing. He hurried across the street to the east side of Berkeley Square where Gunter's Tea Shop was located.

Given the shade of a nearby maple tree, both Christiana and Emma put down their parasols and placed their gloved hands in their laps.

"It is a beautiful afternoon," Emma commented lightly as she surveyed the square and noted the increasing number of curricles and carriages pulling into spaces under the nearby trees. Nearly thirty plane maple trees filled the long oval garden in the middle of the square, and a colorful array of flowers bloomed in manicured gardens throughout the space. Waiters scurried about the square taking orders and delivering small dishes of ices and sorbets balanced on large, round trays to the customers who remained in their carriages. Emma was perplexed, though, when she noticed Thomas nod in Gregory's direction and then toward the railing below.

Gregory rolled his eyes and then got up from his seat, stepped down from the carriage, and walked around to the other side of the carriage. Thomas followed him and the two leaned against the railing, both crossing their arms in unison.

"Whatever are you doing?" Christiana demanded as she slid over to the edge of the carriage seat and alternately stared at her lover and her brother.

The two men exchanged glances and Gregory uncrossed his arms. "Preserving your reputations," he answered quietly, leaning forward but maintaining a respectful distance from Christiana's ear.

Frowning, Christiana turned to Emma. "But Thomas has brought me here many times and always stayed in the carriage," she countered in a loud whisper.

Sighing, Emma leaned forward and whispered, "'Tis not usually proper for a lady to be seen eating with a gentleman if she is not related or betrothed to him." Before leaning back, she added, "Mr. Grandby has a rather... poor reputation, you see, although I have been assured by my landlords that he does not, in fact, deserve it."

Overhearing Emma's whispered comment to Christiana, Thomas exchanged a glance with Gregory. The taller man shrugged and pretended to watch a passing barouche, his face devoid of expression.

The waiter arrived with a tray filled with treats for their carriage as well as two others parked nearby. Gregory pulled out a guinea and gave it to the man before Thomas could pay him. "Keep the change," Gregory said as he took two sorbets off the tray and gave them to the ladies.

"Thank you, sir," the waiter said as he pocketed the coin, his eyes wide with surprise. "Yours, sir," he said as he gave a dish to Thomas. "And yours," he added as he took another dish of strawberry sorbet off the tray and gave it to Gregory. The man hurried to other side of the carriage and lifted a glass of lemonade to Mr. Larsen, who gladly took it. Then he was off to the next carriage.

"This is most refreshing," Christiana commented as she finished her first spoonful of lemon sorbet. "It was getting awfully warm at Grace Park."

Emma regarded the younger girl. "I hadn't noticed," she replied as she took a bite of her orange sorbet, smiling as the familiar flavor slid down her throat. "What did you think of the ceremony?"

The question was intended for Christiana, but Gregory replied, "Very unusual but, at the same time, it seemed very normal. I was rather impressed with our friend's arrangements, I must say."

Thomas raised his eyebrows at the comment. "I rather liked it being out of doors. It helps that the man has the nicest gardens in all of Mayfair. And the breakfast was magnificent. I have asked for his cook, but the man won't give him up."

Emma giggled and took another bite of sorbet. "They're a lovely couple. Will they be able to reach Derbyshire this evening, Mr. Grandby?"

Licking his spoon, Gregory contemplated the question. "Possibly. And if not, there is a pleasant inn about halfway there where they can spend tonight," he said lightly. "And 'tis better if they do," he added in a quieter voice.

Placing his spoon into his sorbet, Thomas turned toward his friend. "What are you saying?"

Gregory glanced up at the women and then lowered his voice so only Thomas could hear. "My head housekeeper is a terrible gossip. You know as well as I do there will be no blood in that marriage bed tonight," he spat out.

Frowning, Thomas regarded his friend for a moment before replying. "'Tis true." At Gregory's raised eyebrow, he added, "I encouraged Todd to exchange wedding vows with his bride two weeks ago. He said he couldn't wait until his wedding night, and I rather doubt Miss White would have denied him her maidenhood if they were secretly married."

Gregory made a sound of disgust and rolled his eyes. "Do you honestly believe Miss White still had her maidenhood to give our dear friend?" he asked in disbelief. "She's been living with ladies of the evening, for Christ's sake!"

Overhearing the question, Christiana made eye contact with Emma, who swallowed hard and gave no indication of what she knew to be the truth.

"How dare you?" Thomas countered, a hint of anger in his voice. "Do you know this because *you* took it?" he asked rhetorically, his face reddening as his anger increased. "She's practically family to you!"

Surprised by his friend's response, Gregory backed away. "No. No, I assure you I did no such thing," he claimed in his own defense. "I just... I just find it hard to believe her to be... *virtuous*, is all."

Christiana gasped at Gregory's comment and turned in her seat to stare at him. "Deborah White is a midwife," she stated in a lowered voice tinged with indignation. "Not a prostitute."

Noticing Emma's pressed lips and sudden discomfort, Thomas moved to the edge of the carriage and reached up to place a hand on her arm. "Are you well, Miss Emma?" he asked quietly. "I apologize for Mr. Grandby. His suppositions are no doubt unfounded."

Emma placed a gloved hand over her employer's and nodded. "Christiana speaks the truth," she said with a small smile. "And Deborah loves Todd very much."

Thomas held Emma's gaze for several seconds before pulling his hand away and turning to his friend.

Refusing to make eye contact with Thomas, Gregory stared at the side of the carriage for several seconds before admitting, "I have taken but one, and only because it was given to me. And I assure you, it will be the *only* one I take." After a moment, he stole a glance in Christiana's direction and found her gazing at him, a wan smile on her lips.

Shaking his head at his friend's confession, Thomas said, "All right, then. We'll speak no more of this." He resumed eating his sorbet, but wondered why Gregory would make such a claim. Certainly a man of his reputation would have had more than one virgin in his day. Or did he spend his nights with married women and widows? Cyprians, perhaps? Or did he employ a mistress to be at his beck and call? It was easy to imagine the man bedding any number of women. Except...

Rebecca had treated Gregory the same as she had the other boys of Merriweather Manor, belittling and cajoling and criticizing and bribing them to her bed. Although she claimed she was teaching them how to please a woman, Thomas often wondered if Rebecca could ever be satisfied in bed—or anywhere else, for that matter.

Had Gregory overcome his association with his older cousin? Or had he used the skills he'd learned from her to lure women to his bed for his own enjoyment?

Is that why he had his reputation, 'a girl in every port, and port after dinner'?

Damnation! The man didn't even like port. And when was the last time he had traveled to a port city? Reputations were usually made from some basis in reality. Perhaps he would ask his friend. He would have asked right then except they were in mixed company.

The ride back to Grace Park was quiet and quick, the late afternoon traffic having dispersed with the growing heat. Emma said her 'good-byes' to Christiana and Gregory, making sure her farewell to the rake was as sincere as possible. She didn't want the man thinking she held a grudge against him over his poor opinion of Deborah.

"Have you everything you need, Miss Emma?" Thomas asked as he once again escorted her up the front steps of Grace Park.

"Oh, yes, Mr. Wellingham. Thank you for asking. Deborah—Mrs. Vandermeer—was quite thorough in helping me to pack last evening."

Thomas nodded. "Very good then," he replied as he moved to knock on the front door.

"Mr. Wellingham," Emma said as she held up a hand to block his. "I feel I owe you an explanation," she said in a quiet voice. "I'd rather you keep it in confidence, though, and not tell Mr. Grandby," she added as she glanced in the direction of the carriage.

His brows drawn together, Thomas regarded his bookkeeper with concern. "What is it?"

Swallowing, Emma closed her eyes for a moment and then blurted, "Mr. Grandby was correct. Deborah did lose her virtue, but not by her choice. She was raped a couple of years ago."

The whispered words felt like a blow to his stomach, and Thomas held his breath for several seconds before gasping. "Does Todd know?"

Emma was nodding even before he could ask the question. "He knows. We told him the night they said their vows. *Before* they said their vows," Emma added quickly, realizing she was trembling as she made the confession. "He said it made no difference to him."

Thomas took a deep breath and then swallowed hard. "And why did you feel the need to tell me this?"

"Because Mr. Vandermeer... he came to the same conclusion as Mr. Grandby did." At Thomas' look of confusion, Emma added, "Todd sorted Deborah had come to be at the Home for Unwed Mothers because she was a prostitute with child."

Rolling his eyes, Thomas sighed loudly. If Deborah ended up at the Home for Unwed Mothers, it stood to reason she was with child. "And the baby?"

Emma shook her head, rather glad he had come to the same conclusion as Todd. "Miscarried. A few weeks after Deborah moved into the Home."

Nodding, Thomas looked off into the distance. "And the man who raped her?"

Leaning hard against the front door, Emma shook her head. "She remembers he wore a black cape coat and he called her a 'freak' several times before throwing her to the street. In the market in Cheapside, of all places, right out in the open."

Thomas slowly shook his head as a look of disgust crossed his face. Her mention of the word 'freak' had his brows furrowing.

He remembered the day he had been jewelry shopping with Todd. There had been shouts of 'freak' several times as they exited the shops in Ludgate Hill. The odd man, dressed in a old cape coat and crumpled top hat, would disappear just as they turned to discover his identity.

"So, please, don't be angry with Mr. Grandby," Emma added quietly.

Shaking his head, Thomas took a deep breath. "I have every right to be angry with him. His choice of topic for conversation was most inappropriate. This was supposed to be a happy afternoon—our best friend's wedding day—and he very nearly ruined it with his comments."

Angling her head to one side, Emma allowed a wan smile and said, "But it was a happy day, and I wish to thank you so very much for the orange sorbet. It tasted just as I remembered."

Thomas regarded Emma and allowed a smile of his own. "Thank you for joining us. We shall take our leave now," he said, motioning to the carriage below. "I'll see you Monday," he added and then bowed.

"Monday, yes," Emma replied as she curtsied. "Thank you so very much for a delightful day," she added as she waved to Christiana and Gregory.

When Winston opened the door, Emma entered the vestibule but turned to stand on the threshold to watch as Thomas descended the stairs.

"May I show you to your room?" Winston asked as he regarded Emma.

"Certainly, Winston," she replied, her face brightening as she turned to follow the butler.

"If I may?" Winston said as they started up the stairs.

"Of course," Emma replied.

"He loved you," he said simply. "And he probably always will, even as he now loves another."

Emma nearly stumbled on the steps. "But he cannot," she answered wearily, wondering how the butler had decided such a thing. "He is my employer."

Winston frowned and glanced in the direction of the front door. "I was not referring to Mr. Wellingham."

Emma stared at the butler, her brows furrowed in confusion. "Oh," she replied, not sure what else to say.

CHAPTER 55

CONFESSIONS OF A
COUNTERFEIT RAKE

uly 6, 1802, Woodscastle

On the following Tuesday morning, Thomas set off on horseback for London, his farewell including an apology to his guest and a statement of his intent to put in a long day at the warehouse.

Left behind, Gregory Grandby was at odds. Intrigued by the woman Christiana claimed was her best friend, he wanted desperately to seek Emma's advice. She had seemed level-headed at the wedding and breakfast feast, and surprisingly tolerant of him at Gunter's where he had made the mistake of voicing his opinion of her friend (although, in his own defense, he hadn't meant for either of the women to hear a comment meant for Thomas only). Given the delicacy of his question, he didn't know how he could broach the subject without offending the woman, or, if indeed, he should even try.

Her first impressions of him were no doubt poor, he considered. He knew he came off as dissolute to those who didn't know him personally; indeed, it was a reputation he had taken time and care to perfect. When he attended meetings, he acted bored and nonchalant when he was actually listening intently to everything being said. He appeared to drink to excess when in fact, he rarely drank at all. His reputation as a libertine had been achieved by the simplest of comments; "My requirements are minimal—a girl in every port, and port after dinner." But in reality, for at least the past year, he had loved only one girl.

No one expected him to be one of the richest men in England, nor a cousin to the Earl of Torrington, but that was just part of the enigma that was Gregory Grandby.

When Christiana excused herself to write a letter after breakfast, Gregory entered the library. He wasn't surprised to find Emma deep in concentration as she transcribed ledgers. She'd been in the same chair at the same table most of the day Friday and all of Monday, he considered. He had gained an appreciation of her knowledge of accounting when he spoke with her at length on the topic after the Vandermeer wedding on Saturday. He found he missed her presence when he had spent Monday night in the library writing letters. Had he never met Christiana Wellingham, he might well have considered the woman for his wife. *Mrs. Simpson, you were almost right,* he thought with a smirk.

"Miss Emma," he said quietly as he approached the library table, not wanting to startle the bookkeeper. He bowed as Emma looked up from the ledger and put her pen back into the inkwell.

"Good morning, Mr. Grandby," she said with a polite smile. When the tall man continued standing at the end of the table, she motioned to the chair across from hers. "Would you like to sit down?" she asked, curious as to why he had greeted her so formally.

"Yes, thank you," he said as he pulled out the chair and sat down. "I apologize for interrupting your work. I'm in a quandary and am hoping you can tell me if I have made a mistake."

Emma furrowed her brows. *Is he sincere or merely teasing?* "Go on," she replied, curious as she was cautious.

Folding his hands on the table, Gregory leaned forward and kept his voice very low. "I must preface my story by explaining to you that I do not, in fact, have a girl in every port, and indeed have only ever been in love with one woman my entire life," he stated simply, his confession sounding heartfelt, although a bit rushed.

Emma tilted her head in disbelief. "Indeed?" she replied calmly, adjusting herself in her chair so she faced him. "Then why do you lead people to believe—?"

"It's convenient," he interrupted quickly. "It's necessary to maintain a certain... *reputation* that affords me access to information and to people with whom I wouldn't otherwise be able to gain confidence. As a result, I have been a very successful investor and don't have to find employment in the traditional sense," he explained with a wave of his hand. "But it's a delicate question I must ask, and

I know of no one else to turn to for an answer," he continued, his voice still very quiet.

Intrigued, Emma wondered if Thomas had shared part of their late afternoon conversation with the man after they had left her at Grace Park. "Please feel free to ask," she replied, folding her hands together atop the ledger book.

Gregory swallowed and took a deep breath. "As I said, I have been in love for some time. The girl is from a good home, attends a private girls' school, and has no need to seek a wealthy husband. Although I haven't asked permission to court her, I have called on her several times over the past year." He paused for a moment and considered how to continue. "In every instance except the last one, we merely spent our time together talking in a parlor or over dinner at a public hotel. At no time did I try to kiss her or engage her in any activity that could be considered... improper," he insisted, his voice taking on a lower pitch. He punctuated his comment with a rap of his knuckles on the table, and Emma couldn't help but notice the signet ring on one finger.

"Did you speak of betrothal or matrimony?" Emma asked gently, thinking he had changed his mind about taking her into his confidence. *Is that a lock of red hair?* she wondered, her attention darting back to the ring.

"Yes, of course," he answered quickly, his head bobbing. "We plan to marry, although 'tis doubtful she will be allowed to do so until next year. At the earliest," he added in an off-hand manner. "I have a bit of work to do on the family in that regard," he said with a sigh, his eyes rolling as he did so.

"So, what happened the last time you called on her?" Emma asked as she leaned her head into her crooked hand, still curious as to what the problem could be.

"She... she kissed me," he said in a whisper. The way in which he spoke the words made Emma believe he thought the young lady's behavior scandalous. "And... I," he paused and took a deep breath. "I kissed her back," he admitted quietly, not able to make eye contact with Emma as he made the confession. He took another deep breath and let it out before continuing. "And then," he bit his lip and began breathing heavily. "She... she insisted we go to her bedchamber... and we..." He stopped, and Emma noticed he had tears in his eyes.

"Made love?" she whispered for him. On the one hand, she

found herself rather touched to hear of his heartfelt romance but saddened it had resulted in such conflicted feelings. Then she remembered the comment he had made while standing next to the carriage in Berkeley Square.

I have taken but one.

He nodded. "It was just kissing at first," he said as he recalled the evening. "But she... she said she wanted me... she wanted me to take her virtue. She said it was the only gift she could think of that was valuable enough to prove her love for me," he whispered hoarsely. He shook his head back and forth. "She had *nothing* to prove,... we love each other, and we *will* marry," he said emphatically, "But she... was... *very insistent,*" he finished as he shook his head and sat up straight. "Why did she insist so if we were in love? And was I wrong to oblige her?" he asked quietly. "Was it *wrong* for me to accept her gift?" he asked finally, a heavy sigh escaping him as he leaned over the table, his head held up by his hands. "I have been conflicted over the matter ever since."

Stunned by the man's confession, Emma swallowed and considered how to answer. His plea seemed sincere. She was quite sure he wasn't teasing. There were still tears pricking the corners of his eyes.

Lowering her gaze, she continued to ponder the question. For those living in the country, courtships were almost platonic. The mere touching of hands might be considered scandalous. But in London, where the majority of the citizens were young, courting couples were known to hold hands and to kiss. Although premarital sex was verboten, most men engaged the services of a prostitute now and then, and the richer ones obtained the services of mistresses through negotiations.

But to have a future wife insist on being bedded prior to the nuptials didn't seem the norm for a girl raised in a proper home. *Why ever would a girl do such a thing? A test, perhaps?* If he had simply refused to comply, would the girl feel rejected? Or be so angry she would break off their betrothal?

Emma remembered the story of how the Simpsons had met and married, all because Sophia had pursued the butler. *She begged me to bed her...* And she recalled Deborah's tale of bedding Todd a week before their wedding.

Emma returned her attention to Gregory's signet ring as she

pondered his question, not quite seeing the lock of hair wrapped around the garnet until she noticed the color of the hair.

Strawberry blonde.

She sat up straight. "Oh, my," she gasped as she realized whom he was talking about. "Does she... does she want children?"

Gregory allowed a wan smile and nodded his head. "We both do," he replied with an enthusiastic nod. "We have agreed on ten," he added somewhat proudly.

Mortified, Emma stood up and covered her mouth with a hand. Breathing too quickly and sure she was about to faint, Emma sat back down just as Gregory made to stand up from the table. She stared at Gregory as he slowly lowered himself back into his chair, his brows furrowed in concern as he watched tears well up in Emma's eyes.

Now rather nervous, Gregory leaned back in his chair. "It was wrong, wasn't it?" he said, his anxiousness growing. "But what am I to do now? Is there anything I *can* do?" he babbled, unshed tears still at the edges of his eyes.

Emma composed herself and placed a hand over one of his. "Had it been anyone else, Mr. Grandby, I would have said you did the only thing you could under the circumstances," she began as a sob interrupted her words. Tears started to stream down her face. "But she's only *sixteen*, and..."

Gregory's brows furrowed again as his eyes widened. "She promised she would tell no one," he whispered defensively. Swallowing hard, he placed his head in his hands and scrubbed his face.

"She didn't," Emma replied. "Oh, my God," she said under her breath. "If you had been here two weeks ago, Mr. Grandby, I fear you would be dead by the very hand of your best friend."

Shaking his head, Gregory leaned forward. "How did *he* discover our secret?" And after a pause, he added, "And how is it then I'm still alive?"

Emma lowered her gaze to the ledger, trying to decide how much to tell the man. By telling him, she felt she was breaking a trust. But not telling him seemed wrong as well. "Christiana miscarried a baby about two weeks ago," Emma explained as she wiped away tears with a handkerchief Gregory had stuffed into her hand.

Gregory stared at the bookkeeper for several seconds, as if he either didn't believe her words or couldn't comprehend their meaning. "Oh, Christ!" he whispered hoarsely, pushing back from the table. His head fell into his hands and he began to weep. "No!" he pleaded as he shook his head. "This... this cannot be happening," he whispered, his grief turning into despair.

He looked up at Emma, wondering what she must think of him. Had she judged Christiana harshly? "She is recovered, though?" he asked between sobs. "She has seemed in good health the entire time I have been here," he claimed, still not believing Emma's words. "Will she—?"

"She recovered, rather quickly, in fact, and she is fine, now," Emma assured him, handing the handkerchief back to him. "Mr. Wellingham was most upset, of course, but Christiana refused to tell us enough to determine your identity. She's been very good at keeping you a secret." Emma paused a moment, seeing his distress. She felt sorry for the man. "Unless you have said something to Mr. Wellingham..."

"I have not," Gregory shook his head quickly, dabbing at his eyes. He lowered his head, embarrassed by his show of emotion. "I planned to ask his permission to propose this week," he said with a nod, his head bobbing more as he continued to think on the matter.

Emma nodded and wiped away the last of her tears on a sleeve. Realizing his friend could quickly become a foe, she sat up straighter and said, "Then do so. Be direct, be forceful, remind him that you are his best friend, and... if he should show any anger toward you, tell him what you have just told me."

Stunned, Gregory stared at her from across the table. "The part... about the *gift?*" he asked quietly, a pained expression on his face.

Smiling slightly, Emma nodded. "Thomas Wellingham has great respect for gifts and their meaning," she replied gently. She allowed a heavy sigh in attempt to calm her sobbing.

They sat in silence for several minutes until Gregory finally pushed away from the table. "I must go to her," he said quietly. "I assure you, I won't betray your trust, Miss Emma. I thank you for the time you have spent with me, and I thank you for your advice." He bowed and was about to leave when he turned and said, "Perhaps someday ...," he started to say and then stopped and shook his head. "Never mind."

And with that, he was out the door and on his way to find Christiana.

Still stunned and sad for the man, Emma was left in the library with a completely different impression of Gregory Grandby. How was she ever going to keep her promise to Thomas? She had promised him if she ever discovered the identity of Christiana's lover, she would tell him. But, at that moment, she wanted to keep the couple's secret as long as was possible.

With a great deal of trepidation, Gregory climbed the stairs and walked slowly to Christiana's bedchamber. He knocked softly and entered when he heard her say, "Come in!"

At the sight of him, Christiana's face beamed, and she ran into his arms. He quickly stepped in and shut the door behind him, worried a servant might have seen him.

"I have wanted to hold you like this ever since I last saw you in April," Gregory said as he hugged her. "I've missed you terribly." Christiana seemed so small and fragile as he held her. "Please, you must tell me everything that has happened to you since I last saw you," he added as he lifted her chin with his finger.

Christiana face bloomed with color and she turned away. She hadn't expected Gregory to come to her bedchamber while he was a guest at Woodscastle. Their time together had been stolen moments in the music room while she practiced piano-forté and he pretended to study the art and statuary. They ate dinner with Thomas every night, with Gregory at one end of the table and Christiana to the left of her brother. There was little they could say to one another in her brother's presence, and Christiana found it more difficult each day to keep from seeking him out. "Has my brother gone to town?" she asked, wanting to ensure their privacy.

Nodding, Gregory bent down and picked her up in his arms. Christiana giggled as he sat down in a large overstuffed chair near the fireplace and left her sitting on his lap. She burrowed her head into the crook of his arm, inhaling deeply. The scent of pipe smoke mingled with the odors of wool and musk. "I adore the scent of you," she whispered as she wrapped an arm around the front of his chest.

Gregory snorted and kissed the top of her head. "And I adore all of you," he replied, wrapping his arms around her shoulders. He felt her fingers as they touched the buttons of his waistcoat. Lifting her hand to his lips, he kissed the palm and simply held on to it.

They sat in silence for several minutes, happy to just hold one another. It was Gregory who finally broke the silence. "When I last held you like this, you had just given me a very precious gift," he remembered quietly.

Christiana murmured, "In all my life, it was the best night ever," she replied with a watery smile.

Gregory studied her face, wondering if she really meant what she said. "Oh, dear," he replied. "Then for the rest of my days, how will I ever live up to that night?" He meant the comment to sound amusing, but sadness crept into his voice, and he fought the tears he thought he had under control.

"Every night with you will always be the best night ever," Christiana replied softly. When she looked up to see his face, though, she saw the mixed emotions, saw the red-rimmed eyelids. "I do love you, Gregory," she insisted quietly, touching his face. "That will never change," she assured him as she reached up and kissed his cheek.

He nodded but didn't reply right away. "I cannot help but think I did something wrong that night," he whispered, holding her tighter. "I know 'tis what you wanted, and God knows, I wanted it, too. You must know I want you always," he added as he pulled her closer to him. "But I couldn't help but think I did wrong... what if we had...? If I...What if I had left you with child?" he asked, his face displaying his pain. "Oh, Christiana," he sobbed as he finally let the tears flow.

Startled by his comments, Christiana wrapped her arms around his shoulders and nestled her head against his neck. "I was... but, I lost the baby," she whispered quietly, the breath going out of her as she made the confession. "I'm so sorry. I didn't even know I was with child when it happened," she said shaking her head against his neck.

Gregory let out a strangled cry, the tears coming again to his eyes. "Oh, my love," he whispered.

"But after the miscarriage, I realized how very much I wanted to have a child. Your child, Gregory," she said softly. "Ten, even."

There were no more tears for her to cry. She had already mourned the loss the day it happened and several nights since.

Closing his eyes tightly and covering his mouth with a fist, Gregory emitted a cry of grief, and his body shook as he sobbed. "And you? Are you well? Truly?" he asked hoarsely. "Will you... recover?" Despite Emma's assurances, he wanted to hear it from Christiana, to ensure she was indeed whole again and would be well enough to have children should she still want them.

Christiana placed a hand on the side of his face. "Yes, Gregory, I'm fine," she assured him, her watery smile genuine. "The doctor said I was just a bit too young yet. He said we may have as many babies as we want. But we should wait until after I'm seventeen or so," she added with a shrug. She buried her face into his neck, her lips gently kissing his throat in an effort to console him.

"What if I had lost you?" Gregory whispered as he intertwined the fingers of his left hand with her right hand. "I could never forgive myself."

"Shh," Christiana replied as she placed a finger against his lips. "You won't lose me." Reaching up with one hand, she used her thumb to wipe away a tear and then kissed away another, its salty aftertaste remaining on her lips.

Nodding, Gregory sniffled and held her close. "Promise?" he replied as he watched her study his face.

"I promise," she answered with a smile.

"I think I shall hire a doctor to live with us, though," Gregory murmured. "Just to be sure."

Christiana raised her eyebrows, not sure he was being serious. "Wouldn't that be expensive?"

Gregory shook his head. "No. Not for us," he said quite seriously. At her look of surprise, he added, "My dear, I make over five-thousand pounds a year on my investments alone," he said quietly, "So I think we can afford a doctor on our household staff. Of course, we still have to find a house," he added with a furrowed brow. "Preferably with a staff."

Smiling, Christiana studied her beau's expression. "Five-*thousand* pounds?" she repeated, her face showing shock. "You *are* rich!"

Gregory nodded. "'Tis a burden," he said with a nod, his melancholy mood still evident.

Not quite believing his comment, Christiana studied Gregory's face for a moment. "Wouldn't we live at Cherrywood?" she asked.

Shrugging, Gregory thought a moment. "We could, I suppose. It's a family estate, and I stay there on occasion. But it is mostly a place to go on holiday. It's certainly too far from town," he reasoned as he stroked her arm.

"We could live here," Christiana suggested lightly. "I'm sure my brother would allow it," she claimed, not really believing her words. Her manner sobered, though, when she considered the state of the house. "The entire west wing is still a wreck. Perhaps we could have repairs made and live on that side of the house," she reasoned, imagining a married life with her intended and the ability to stay close to her brother. "There are more bedchambers on that end, all with private baths, and a salon, and a parlor, and a master suite," she claimed, her excitement growing as she considered the possibility. "And a nursery!"

"Indeed?" Gregory replied, at first only half-listening to her idea. Then he remembered his conversation with Todd. "I will give it some thought," he said. Would Thomas agree to such an arrangement?

Why wouldn't he? The man had talked of renovations for years and had done nothing. *To hell with him*, Gregory thought suddenly. *I'll just hire an architect and get the work started.*

With a clear vision of his future in mind, Gregory sat up straighter, mindful of Christiana still clinging to his neck. "In the meantime, my love, I wish to hold you for the rest of my life, or until such time as hunger drives me to the dining room," he said aloud, his mood finally lifting.

Christiana giggled as she relaxed back into his embrace, molding herself against him. They stayed that way until the chime sounded for luncheon.

CHAPTER 56
THE (AUDIT) RESULTS ARE IN

July 7, 1802, Woodscastle

"Mr. Wellingham," Emma called out when there was a break in his conversation with Gregory Grandby. "When you have a moment, there are some things I need to show you," she said as she spread out several ledgers on the library table.

"Things to show you?" Gregory repeated quietly to Thomas as he elbowed his friend.

Emma overheard his teasing remark, but merely grinned. The man really did come off as a rake and a tease, but Emma now knew otherwise.

"'Tis business," Thomas said to his friend seriously. "I must attend to it immediately."

Gregory's demeanor changed drastically. "Trouble in the import industry?" he asked, suddenly all business. "You didn't lose a ship in that storm last week, I hope," he added, referring to a squall along the west coast of Africa.

"No. I know enough to hire ship captains who know what they're doing," Thomas replied. "Ultimately, this could be more serious, though."

Gregory seemed intrigued. "Personnel problem?"

Thomas considered how much to tell his friend. "I'm about to find out. If you decide to listen in, I cannot have you repeating anything you hear to anyone outside of this room."

The tall man nodded, suddenly sober. "Understood."

The two men flanked Emma as she completed laying out the ledgers. "What have you found?"

Emma took a deep breath and pointed to one of the open books. "In the January financials, on this ledger, is the closing balance of assets deemed 'inventory.' On the opening balance for inventory the following week, one pound of assets has been dropped. Two weeks later, ten pounds were dropped from one week to the next. One week later, one pound was dropped but then recovered the following week."

She switched to a different set of ledgers and continued, "But that week started a pattern of ten pounds dropping every two weeks until two months ago.... " She pulled out another ledger and pointed to an entry, "... When the pattern went to one hundred pounds." She pulled out still another ledger and pointed to the same inventory entry. "And last week it was back to ten pounds dropped."

Thomas took a cursory glance at each of the entries to which Emma pointed. "But what journal entry category are the amounts being applied to?" Gregory asked as he leaned over Emma's shoulder.

Given the amount of time she had spent discussing accounting with the man after the Vandermeer wedding, she wasn't the least bit surprised by the question. She answered simply, "Payroll."

Thomas sighed loudly. "I knew it. *Damn!*" Although he expected her to find the problem, he had hoped it wouldn't require the need to dismiss an employee. Realizing he had cursed, he closed his eyes and then turned to Emma. "Please accept my apology for the outburst," he whispered.

"No offense taken, I assure you," Emma replied.

Thomas took a deep breath. "So, with whom are we dealing?" he asked, somewhat afraid to find out the truth about one of his employees.

Emma pointed out each of the handwriting styles on the ledgers in question. "J. Arthur Peabody. The amounts are even included on his payroll cheques, according to these entries. As auditor of these books, it is my duty to have him charged with the crime of embezzlement. I must report my..."

"No!" Thomas said quickly as he moved to the other side of the table. "Not yet. I must speak with Sir William Burroughs first. I promised him I would inform him of my findings."

Emma stared open-mouthed at Thomas and covered her mouth

with a hand. "You spoke to an *investment banker* about your suspicion?"

"Indeed," Thomas replied shortly. "It was a result of our discussion that led to his recommending you for this audit," he stated quietly.

"But he could *ruin* you..." she started to reply.

Thomas shared her concern, but assured her Sir William had promised to keep the information in confidence. "How much more work do you have to do here?" he asked as he waved his hand over the ledgers.

"I'm finished with all the ledgers you have brought me," she replied.

"Finished?" Thomas repeated. "But... but I was told an audit would take three months!"

Emma shrugged and said, "Well, I only did nine months of ledgers. A complete audit would have involved twelve months' worth."

Impressed, Gregory asked, "So, would you be available to do my company's books then?"

Emma looked to Thomas and noticed his eyes rolling. "Grandby has no company, although, if he did, it would probably be the best run company in the British Empire," he stated in an off-hand manner. "I know you might find that hard to believe. I certainly did for many years," the importer stated without a hint of humor.

"Why, thank you, Wellingham, I didn't know you knew," Gregory half-joked.

Thomas shook his head. "If it is agreeable to the lady," Thomas began as he turned his attention back to Emma, "I wish to remove you as auditor of my company and promote you to the position of accomptant beginning a week from Monday. You'll work in the clerking office in the London warehouse with the other accomptants," he stated formally.

It took every ounce of restraint for Gregory not to react to what he had just heard, but he found he couldn't remain completely silent. "Does she get a raise?" Gregory asked as he straightened up from his perusal of the ledgers. He turned to Emma. "Don't accept unless he gives you a raise," he whispered, his demeanor once again changing back to playfulness and mischief.

This is most unexpected, Gregory thought with dismay. *This is not good. This is not what was supposed to happen*, Gregory mused behind his light-hearted manner.

Emma simply stared at Gregory before turning her attention back to Thomas. "You're offering me a permanent position?"

"You shall receive the same pay as Mr. Peabody received. Minus the embezzled amounts, of course," Thomas added. "And, I will pay you for your five days off next week."

Gregory leaned down and whispered, "Make it *six* days and take it!" He knew from Emma's expression of delight that she would accept the offer. She would be a fool not to given she was a woman.

Emma smiled and suppressed the urge to cry out her answer. "I accept your offer, Mr. Wellingham," she said with an enthusiastic nod.

"Since you are in such an accepting mood, would you allow me to escort you to the Hornsby ball Saturday evening?" Gregory asked.

Surprised, Emma nearly choked and couldn't find her voice to answer. The man could be so forthright! And why was he asking *her* to the ball when he should be taking Christiana?

"Miss Emma already has an escort for the ball, you dunderhead," Thomas answered for her, slapping his friend rather hard on the arm as he said so.

Emma started to say, "I do?" but thought better of it. "Thank you for asking, Mr. Grandby. Perhaps you would be allowed to escort Miss Wellingham instead?" she offered as an alternative. She knew Christiana desperately wanted to attend, but Thomas hadn't offered to take her and, after what had happened two weeks ago, Christiana was afraid to ask him.

Thomas snorted, a sound that startled both Gregory and Emma. "He would get her there, but there's no telling how she would get home," he said in a tone that suggested he was serious.

Emma glanced at Gregory, who was watching her reaction. "He's right, of course," the tall man admitted. "I can be terribly irresponsible." But he winked as he said it and then gave Thomas a look of scorn.

Emma grinned at him and winked back, hoping she wasn't overestimating Christiana's beau.

CHAPTER 57
TRUTHS BE TOLD

July 8, 1802, Bank of England

The following morning, Mr. Allen was dispatched on horseback to deliver a letter to Sir William, a letter requesting an audience with the investment banker. The groom was back in under two hours with word that Thomas could come to the bank 'at his leisure'.

"At my leisure?" Thomas repeated when Mr. Allen relayed Sir Williams' words.

"Indeed. And if I may say so, guv'nor, I believe he was expecting to hear from you."

Thomas exchanged a nervous glance with Gregory. He asked that Mr. Larsen bring the carriage around as quickly as possible.

When the two friends departed for London a half-hour later, Mr. Larsen sensed their urgency and saw to it he covered the six miles to the city in short order—it was navigating the crowded streets of London proper that took the greater amount of time to get to the Bank of England, With the city's recent growth, the number of horses and carriages had increased, and traffic often came to a standstill until a constable could be summoned to bring order to the chaos.

Several streets from the bank, Thomas and Gregory disembarked from their carriage, opting to walk the remaining distance along Cheapside to Threadneedle Street. With the warmer temperatures, the soot no longer rained down as heavily as it did during the winter months, but Gregory complained bitterly of the filth in the air.

"I don't understand how you can tolerate this," he remarked as they passed the stock exchange offices.

"I don't," Thomas replied. "That's why I still live at Woodscastle. I can barely tolerate being in the office, and that is far removed from *this*," he indicated with a wave.

"Just why did you buy a building so far from the center of the city?" Gregory queried. "Doesn't your business require you to be on the east end, or at least, closer to the docks?"

Thomas nodded and passed through the outer entrance of the bank as a doorman held open the massive door. "On the contrary. I bought that particular building and built onto it because it was close to the Thames, and far enough upriver that my shipments wouldn't get caught up in the mess down at the docks. Have you seen how many ships try to deliver goods there? I swear you could walk across the river and never touch water."

Gregory shook his head as he removed his hat. "I haven't ventured to the docks in many years. I hear it's much too dangerous."

Thomas removed his hat and gave it to the receptionist. "There is crime, true," he replied. "But mostly 'tis vandals who steal from the ships that cannot move due to the crowded conditions." He turned his attention back to the receptionist. "Thomas Wellingham to see Sir William. I believe he's expecting me."

The receptionist took Gregory's hat, nodding at the man with a good deal of deference. "Indeed. You may go right in," he said as he nodded toward the office, never actually acknowledging the man who spoke to him.

Sir William was indeed waiting for them. He stood in the entrance of his office and greeted them heartily. "Your visit couldn't be more timely. I have excellent news," he boasted jovially as he motioned them to leather chairs in his well-appointed office. To Thomas, it smelled much like the Boodles but lacked the smoky haze.

"You are too kind, as I bring less than good news," Thomas replied, sitting down on the front edge of one of the proffered chairs. Gregory spent a bit more time surveying the rich furnishings, carpet, and paintings adorning the office before finally taking a seat. "Sir William, I'd like to introduce you to Gregory Grandby, a friend of mine for many years."

Sir William chuckled. "Mr. Grandby needs no introduction, Mr. Wellingham. We've known each other since he was but a babe in nappies."

Surprised, Thomas turned and looked at his friend. "I didn't know," he replied simply. Gregory didn't offer a reply, but merely sat in silence and acted bored.

Sir William returned his attention to Thomas. "And how is Miss Wellingham?" he asked politely.

"'Tis very kind of you to ask. She is doing very well," Thomas stated with a smile. "She has recently finished her second year at Warwick's and has become very accomplished on the piano-forté."

Sir William nodded. "Good, good." Changing the subject, he said, "So, did you ever hire the..." He paused, not sure if he could discuss the matter with Gregory present.

"Mr. Grandby is familiar with the situation," Thomas offered. "You may speak freely."

Sitting up as straight as he could, Sir William continued, "When last we spoke in February, I recall making a recommendation. Did you hire an auditor?"

Thomas nodded, his face taking on a solemn expression. "I did indeed, which is why we're here today." He unrolled the ledger sheets he held in his hand. "She presented her findings..."

"She?" Sir William interrupted. "So, you hired Miss Emma?" he half-asked, an amused, and perhaps an excited, expression on his face.

"Yes," Thomas replied, "But—"

"She's a smart woman," Sir William continued. "And how long did it take her to complete the audit?'

Annoyed, Thomas shook his head. "About seven weeks, but she redid some of the—"

"Seven weeks!" the banker replied in surprise. "It would take any other auditor at least three months to do your books," he exclaimed, his hands splayed out over the papers on his desk.

Thomas sighed. "She is good, yes. Now, she completed her audit late yesterday. And it seems I do have an embezzler in my employ."

The banker sat back and placed his hands on his rounded belly, his expression taking on a look of disappointment. "Indeed. Do you know *who?*" His manner suggested he was troubled, but certainly not surprised at the findings.

"An accomptant, of course. Mr. J. Arthur Peabody," Thomas stated firmly.

"And how much are we talking about?"

"Four-hundred and twelve pounds," Thomas whispered hoarsely. "So far."

Sir William jerked his head up, obviously stunned by the amount.

"It started in January, as I suspected, and continues even now," Thomas explained, becoming more anxious and angry as the meeting continued. "Two-hundred of that just occurred a few weeks ago."

"That greedy *bastard*," Sir William said under his breath. "I told him not to exceed one-hundred pounds at a time..."

Thomas and Gregory both sat up straight. Thomas leaned forward and nearly pounced from his chair. "What did you just say?" he asked, his face reddening.

Sir William held out his hands and motioned for Thomas to sit down. "'Tis quite alright," he said quickly, "Please, sit down so I may explain."

Gregory leaned forward, his head tilted sideways. "*Explain?*" he repeated, his voice taking on an edge suggesting he could do violence. "Were *you* behind the embezzlement?"

Looking extremely uncomfortable, the banker sighed and leaned back in his chair. "During the late nineties, we financed several import and export businesses that have since failed. The business in general has been very risky, even for East India. I mean, in one year's time, women wear a different kind of gown and suddenly sales of expensive brocades and tapestries stop and the importers are caught unawares. Those fabrics are no longer fashionable, but they have orders still being filled in India. They're suffering huge losses on just one commodity, and yet they still don't even know it."

Thomas shook his head. "What has unfashionable fabric to do with Mr. Peabody embezzling from my company?" he asked impatiently.

"It was a test, Mr. Wellingham," Sir William replied curtly, his face expressing his obvious discomfort.

The expression on Thomas' face was unreadable.

Sir William continued, "Peabody was not really embezzling," he claimed with a wave of one hand. "Oh, we arranged for him to take the money from inventory and make it look as if he were padding his salary, of course, but the money is actually in an escrow account here at the bank. Earning interest," he added emphatically.

"*Damn* you," Thomas said quietly. "How *could* you?"

Not the least bit insulted, the banker shrugged. "It was necessary. We wanted to be sure you were a safe investment for us—that you were able to run a viable business. You have proven yourself in every aspect. You understand the overland trade routes, the safest time and locations to consign ships, you hire the best captains, and you are making excellent choices as to what you will import. And you can read your ledgers, which is more than I can say for most of the businessmen in this town. You passed the test."

Shaking his head, Thomas suddenly felt betrayed by someone in whom he trusted.

How could Sir William do this to me?

Sir William could tell his explanation didn't go over well with the young businessman, and he added, "We'll see to it you're reimbursed for Miss Emma's salary, of course."

Thomas, still fuming over the news, didn't reply.

Gregory, who had sported a sour expression on his face throughout the entire exchange, spoke up. "I believe you said you had *excellent* news."

The banker nodded, his mood brightening again. "Indeed. The request Mr. Wellingham made to the town to build his own dock just down from his warehouse has been approved. You can start construction immediately. With any luck, you'll have your dock up and running before the end of this year."

It was a small consolation, but Thomas was certainly glad to hear the news. This could mean expediting shipments faster than any other of the other small import and export businesses since ships would be able to dock and off-load their cargo a short distance from his warehouse. He would no longer have to rely on Pudding Dock.

"We'll finance the building, of course," Burroughs said emphatically. "And... we won't charge interest on the loan," he added quickly, hoping to gain back some of the respect he knew he had lost.

Thomas nodded. "That's very kind of you," he replied, not daring to show the least bit of gratitude given what he had just been told. "I'll hire a construction crew this week to get started." He made to get up from the leather chair, but sat back down. "You do know I'll have to excuse Mr. Peabody of his duties."

Sir William nodded sadly. "'Tis perfectly understandable. I would only ask you not speak poorly of him to your associates. He was merely... acting on my orders, and I can assure you he wasn't comfortable doing my bidding. I'll see to it he has a position here at the bank."

Thomas nodded. "Agreed," he said as he stood up. "Sir William," he nodded in the banker's direction, not yet ready to afford the man a proper bow.

Gregory stood up, leaned against the wall, and crossed his arms. "I need to speak with you alone, uncle," he stated in a serious voice.

Startled, Thomas looked first at Gregory and then at Sir William. "*Uncle?* Is he your mother's brother?" Thomas asked quietly.

Gregory nodded, clearly unhappy to be associated with the man at the moment. "Unfortunately, yes. Wellingham, will you excuse us?" Gregory asked, his tone still very serious.

"Of course. I'll be at the front," Thomas said before he left the office and closed the door behind him. He retrieved his hat from the receptionist and waited near the front doors for his friend.

It wasn't long before raised voices could be heard coming from Sir William Burrough's office, and Thomas couldn't help but wonder if his friend was angry with the banker for what he had done.

When at last the door opened and Gregory came out, though, Thomas was surprised to find both his friend and the banker in good spirits. "I'll see you Saturday evening at the ball," he overheard Gregory say to Sir William.

"Indeed, you shall," the banker replied.

The receptionist handed Gregory's hat to him and said, "It's always good to see you, Mr. Grandby."

"Thank you, Mr. Connor," Gregory said as he donned his hat.

As they passed through the bank doors, Thomas was about to ask Gregory what had transpired in his uncle's office when he heard a man shouting the word 'freak'. Thomas froze at the familiar voice.

Gregory nearly walked into Thomas, pulling up just as a group of men surged to their left. A woman began screaming.

A man shouted, and as the two turned to follow the movement of the mob, the unmistakable sound of a gunshot rang out. An eerie silence, punctuated by nothing but a high-pitched scream, descended on the crowd as the movement of the mob ceased.

"Good God, what was that about?" Gregory whispered to no one in particular. Thomas was already past him, hurrying along the wall of the bank to get a better look. Through a break in the crowd, he saw a tall, middle-aged blonde woman standing over a man who lay bleeding on the cobbles. His black cape coat and filthy trousers were familiar, but the crumpled top hat near the foot of the woman confirmed Thomas' suspicions.

A sheriff rode up on horseback, surveying the scene as Gregory joined Thomas. Hurrying to the familiar man, Thomas extended his hand as he greeted him. "Sheriff Morgan," he said, breathless. Before the lawman realized his identity, Thomas pointed to the prone body. "This man is a rapist," he said.

The well-dressed woman, who until that moment had been screaming at the top of her lungs, suddenly stopped and began whimpering. Her bonnet was crushed in one hand and a reticule hung from the other. One of her fingers was looped through the trigger of a small pistol, its barrel still smoking.

Noticing that her pelisse was torn at the shoulder, Gregory went to her side. "Are you hurt?" he asked gently.

The woman shook her head just as another tall gentleman came hurrying to her side. "Victoria!" he called out, wrapping his arms around her. He regarded Gregory with an odd expression before he recognized him. "Mr. Grandby? What are *you* doing here?"

Gregory's brow arch in surprise. "Samuel Morton?" he asked, surprised to see the man anywhere but seated at a gaming table.

"Yes, and this is my wife," he answered, just then noticing the dead man near his wife's feet. He let out a strangled yelp.

The sheriff, having just heard Thomas' story about the rape, approached the woman. "Who shot this man?" he asked of her and the crowd around her. He obviously hadn't seen the gun hanging next to her reticule.

"I did," Victoria Morton answered, her dispassionate gaze finally settling on her husband. Her whimpering had subsided and she surveyed the men standing around her and the scene at her feet. "Bastard tore my coat," she complained then, her posture indicating she had fully recovered her composure. "Samuel, take me home," she ordered then, turning to leave as if nothing had happened.

The sheriff stared after her, his mouth open in astonishment.

What was it about women and guns? A cursory glance at the dead man showed he had been cleanly shot in the forehead. His clothing was clearly torn and dirty, and the stench of him forced Morgan to pull out a handkerchief and cover his nose. As he did, he noticed the warped features of the very short man—a nose that had been broken many times, cheekbones that were far from even, and a scalp with mere patches of gray hairs scattered about.

A victim of disease, perhaps? Or a homeless creature who had been born with deformities and left to live on the streets? Either way, he would have been a perfect addition to the ranks of Bedlam, Morgan figured. He considered going after the retreating couple, but decided not to— the woman had obviously suffered a scare and shot the man in self-defense. And Thomas had given him enough information to decide prosecution wasn't worth pursuing.

With the spectacle ended, the mob of men dispersed, and the dead man was left with the sheriff standing over him.

Thomas and Gregory walked along in silence before Gregory finally spoke. "Who was that... that creature?" he asked, realizing Thomas knew more than he had let on.

Thomas considered what to say, considered that perhaps he should say nothing. But his friend seemed intent on knowing. And providing him with an explanation would certainly set his friend straight about his mistaken impression of Deborah White. Finally deciding to be blunt, Thomas took a deep breath. "Deborah White's rapist," he answered, a hint of anger apparent in his voice.

Gregory stopped in his tracks, a gasp of surprise still caught in his throat. "Oh, Jesus," he finally got out, a surge of nausea overcoming him. He struggled to regain control and gave Thomas a questioning look when he finally caught up with him again.

"He's the one who took Mrs. Vandermeer's maidenhood," Thomas whispered as he stopped walking, aware that his pent up rage made his words sound angry. "He took what rightfully belonged to Vandermeer," he spat out, wanting to be sure Gregory understood. "*He* was the reason she ended up at Mrs. Dawes' place," he added, his voice a bit softer, knowing the explanation would clear up any misconception Gregory held about their friend's wife. He closed his eyes for a moment, allowing a long silence to pass before he continued. "Do you know the very worst of this, Gregory?" he asked as he regarded his friend, his bottom lip caught by a tooth. At Gregory's tentative shake of his head,

Thomas whispered, "Todd would never have met his wife had it not happened."

Gregory stared back at Thomas in horror, holding his breath as he realized the truth in the words. "I see," he said, his voice very quiet. "I should have realized my new-found cousin wouldn't have..." He let his voice trail off, feeling every bit the fool he knew Thomas thought of him that day at Gunter's.

She wasn't a prostitute or a courtesan. Just an unfortunate girl caught by a crazy man who now lay dead at the hands of another Tall Meg.

How appropriate, he thought.

"You didn't know," Thomas finally said with a sigh. He considered what they had just witnessed, glad he could tell Todd he no longer need be concerned about finding his wife's rapist. His face brightened. "And now I finally know why Samuel Morton has never taken a mistress." *He always wanted the hat shop girl,* he remembered, trying to stave off the grin he felt coming to his lips. *He had to have meant Emma.* A pang of jealousy stabbed him.

Gregory smiled at the comment. "Indeed. I would live in fear of my life if I were married to a woman like Victoria Morton," he agreed. Even before Thomas could take a jab, he added, "I assure you, I've never had a mistress, and I have absolutely no plans to take one."

Thomas nodded at him, still not quite convinced his friend wasn't a rake. "Good. It will save your wife a trip to Victoria Morton's," he teased. Despite his attempt at lightening the mood, there wasn't any humor as they continued their walk back to the carriage.

"Please, don't be angry with Sir William," Gregory said with a heavy sigh. "He really didn't want to participate in the bank's pitiable test of you."

"So then why did he?" Thomas asked too quickly. He was still smarting from the news of the fake embezzlement. He had a mind to change banks. The dock was excellent news. The mistrust on the bank's behalf was an insult.

"He didn't tell you some other important news," Gregory went on. "Seems he was able to work out a deal with the board. In exchange for participating, he made them invest a tidy sum into your company, and he is now allowed to recommend your company to other potential investors. You'll have enough working capital to build the dock and another warehouse, if need be."

Thomas paused in mid-step. "Really?" An odd thought crossed his mind. *Hadn't Sir William already recommended his company for invest-ment? Back in February,* Thomas remembered. *He'd said Emma owned stock.*

"I was merely reminding him of his commitment to Wellingham Imports," Gregory continued, unaware of his friend's slower pace. He turned then and allowed Thomas to catch up to him. "And I told him of my intention to start courting a young lady," he added in an off-hand manner.

Thomas completely stopped walking. "Courting? *You?*" he answered in disbelief, his brows drawn together so tightly they appeared as one. "I have always thought of you as the confirmed bachelor. Who has turned your eye and changed your mind so completely?"

Gregory didn't reply, but merely gazed at his friend for a long time, finally taking a deep breath and letting it out slowly.

"No," Thomas said as he shook his head. "You cannot. I... I forbid it... not that she would, but..."

"You don't even know who I'm thinking about..."

Thomas stepped back, his expression unreadable. "Well, you have threatened to ask Miss Emma for her hand several times just this past week," he countered. Who else might Gregory take to wife?

Gregory shook his head, his eyes rolling up. "You can be so blind, my friend," he said sadly. "Of course, I jest about Miss Emma —'tis very easy to tease you when it comes to her. You are madly in love with her, I can tell. But I have had my eye—and my heart—on someone else for over a year now. If pressed, I would have to admit I have probably loved her my entire adult life."

Thomas continued to shake his head as they continued their stroll toward the carriage. "Your cousin Elizabeth?" he guessed, remembering a boyhood crush Gregory had on the older girl the summer he spent with Gregory in Derbyshire. "It cannot be your cousin Rebecca," he added with a stern shake of his head. "Even *I* would forbid that arrangement," he said as he involuntarily shud-dered. The quick flashback to his youth and two afternoons in her bedchamber came unbidden in his mind. *It's no wonder I haven't wanted to court a woman,* he thought sourly.

Gregory grimaced and shook his head as he climbed into the

carriage. "So, you are deaf as well as blind," he said to Thomas as his friend stepped up behind him.

When Thomas finally realized whom Gregory was in love with, it hit him with the force of a punch to the face. "Christiana?" he whispered. "My *sister?*" he said aloud, still in disbelief. "You? *You* are the one she's in love with?"

Gregory nodded, a wan smile on his face. "Will you give me your permission to ask for her hand in marriage?"

Awestruck, Thomas shook his head. Was this the man who had taken his sister's virtue? "She's not even seventeen—"

"She will be next week," Gregory interrupted. "I was hoping to ask for her hand on her birthday."

"You're nearly ten years her senior—"

"She is ten years more mature than me," Gregory countered, a claim he knew Thomas wouldn't argue.

"You are a foot taller than she is!"

"And she is a foot shorter than I," Gregory countered, not able to come up with anything better to say.

"And 'the girl in every port'?" Thomas asked as he leaned toward his friend.

"The only *port* I was ever in was that damned Rebecca Merriweather's," Gregory hissed, having just been reminded of his elder cousin with the penchant for taking advantage of her younger male cousins. "I should probably be grateful she made me so wary of the fairer sex for so long."

Thomas gave him a quizzical stare. "And why would that be?" he asked carefully, his demeanor softening as he watched his friend's face.

Had Rebecca tortured Gregory with the threat of a riding crop if she wasn't satisfied with his performance in her bed, too? Thomas unconsciously rubbed the space under one rib where a piece of his flesh had been torn out by the tip of her riding crop. Despite the haughtiness she displayed when attempting to teach him how to pleasure her, Rebecca had apologized profusely and then nearly fainted at the amount of blood he'd spilled in her bed before he was able to staunch the flow with one of her pillows.

Gregory glanced around to be sure he wouldn't be overheard. "Unlike the other men of wealth in this town, I don't have illegitimate children or a mistress to support. And I don't have any diseases," he added with a raised eyebrow. He stilled his features, hoping his face hadn't turned red with his admission.

Nodding in agreement, Thomas replied, "I'm of the same mind in that regard." He didn't want to admit he had used his sister as an excuse to avoid women and marriage. Ever since the second afternoon he'd spent with the dominating Rebecca Merriweather, he'd been afraid to seek a wife, he realized.

"I love Christiana," Gregory whispered, his lips pursed as he tried to retain his composure.

"Forgive me," Thomas said quietly, "But I'm still finding it difficult to believe my best friend wants to marry my sister."

Gregory shook his head. "No. I think you're having a harder time believing your sister is in love with me."

Thomas stared at his friend. "Is she?" he asked carefully. *How could I have been so deaf?* Her lover was described to him in perfect detail—he remembered Emma's recitation of Christiana's description during dinner.

"Yes. Very much so," Gregory replied without hesitation. "Last year, I wasn't so sure, but these past few months..." He paused and took a breath. "She has confessed her love, she sent me a lock of her hair..." He held out the hand with the signet ring. "She has readily accepted my invitation to the ball, and we've talked of matrimony. At great length."

There was a moment of silence as Thomas considered his sister. She was grown up now. Mostly. Since attending Warwick's, she had learned the art of graciousness, of being a good hostess, and she had refined her skills in music and art. Perhaps she was ready to take on his best friend. "Ten children?" Thomas asked.

Gregory sat up straighter at the accusation. "Why, yes," he replied. "How...how did you know?"

Thomas took a deep breath, trying to decide if he could muster the anger he had felt so recently. He found he could not. *Water under the bridge,* his father used to say about things that couldn't be changed. "A fortnight ago, I could have killed you with my bare hands for what you did to her," Thomas said sadly, his eyes not quite meeting Gregory's. "But now... all I can do is give you my blessing," he finally said with a nod. "I'd just ask that you hold off on the marriage until she is at least... thirty..." He broke off, chuckling when he desperately wanted to weep.

Gregory took his hat off and beat it against Thomas' shoulder.

"Eighteen and no older," he replied with a grin. "It'll take us a while to have ten children."

"Done," Thomas agreed with a nod. "Mr. Larsen, take us home," he called out to the driver.

"Very good, sir."

Gregory resumed his serious tone. "I have a proposal I wish to make to you regarding Woodscastle."

Thomas eyed his friend suspiciously. "And what might that be?" he asked carefully, not sure he wanted to hear it.

"I want to buy the west wing so Christiana and I may live there when we are not traveling," he explained simply.

Snorting, Thomas leaned back in the carriage. "The west wing is a disaster!" he replied, his brows furrowed in disgust. "I'll not have my sister..."

"I plan to refurbish it completely, of course," Gregory interrupted with a nod. "I'll pay you five-thousand pounds directly and hire and pay for all the refurbishing myself," he added, hoping he wasn't too far off the mark as to the value of the estate. The work on the roof was due to start the following day, and he had already hired the contractor and a decorator to redo the rooms. Some of the building materials might have already been delivered to the estate.

Thomas' eyes widened and a look of shock crossed his face. "The entire estate isn't worth but eight-thousand pounds," he argued. "Well, maybe ten," he reconsidered quickly, remembering there were tenants farming the lands beyond the back gardens.

"'Tis what Christiana wants, and it's important to me," Gregory answered evenly.

Taking a few deep breaths, Thomas found he was at a loss. Of course he wanted his sister to remain close, and the west wing was in dire need of repairs. The arrangement would still leave him with the east wing. "What about the music room and the library?" he asked, realizing they could be considered part of the west side of the estate.

"You keep the library, Christiana gets the music room, and we share the stables and grounds," Gregory replied quickly.

Realizing Gregory had given his proposal a good deal of thought, Thomas eyed his best friend with suspicion. He finally said, "Done."

Gregory nodded and held out his right hand. "I'll have the money for you by next Wednesday. On Christiana's birthday," he added as he shook hands with his about-to-be brother-in-law. "If I may make a suggestion?"

Thomas nodded, curious as to what Gregory had up his sleeve now.

"Perhaps you could use the funds to build your dock instead of taking the financing deal Sir William offered," he suggested with an arched eyebrow.

"Are you daft?" Thomas replied. "Sir William said he would finance it and not charge me any interest. I believe I shall take that deal," he said as he turned his attention to the London surroundings.

Gregory nodded, but said, "Just in case you decide to change banks, I hear good reports about Barings." Satisfied he had completed his deals, Gregory leaned back on the carriage bench and watched the London traffic.

Thomas followed suit, agog with all that had happened in such a short amount of time. After a few minutes, though, he turned his attention back to Gregory. "What makes you think I'm madly in love with Miss Emma?" he asked in surprise, just then remembering the comment Gregory made when they were walking to the carriage.

Gregory took his hat off and again beat it against Thomas' shoulder. "Can you deny it, you dunderhead?"

At that moment, Thomas realized he could not.

CHAPTER 58
HONEYMOON INTERRUPTED

July 8, 1802, Cherrywood in Derbyshire
Pulling on a pelisse and matching bonnet, Deborah walked into the library at Cherrywood to find her husband near the fireplace. The library's richly appointed furnishings and amber colored paneling and coffered ceilings made the room a favorite for the tall man, and his wife found its lush seating and natural light comfortable for doing embroidery during the long summer days when they weren't out exploring the Peak District.

Derbyshire had been a perfect choice for a honeymoon locale, and Cherrywood the perfect estate in which to spend the week after the wedding.

As she approached, she realized Todd's attention was captured by the painting over the fireplace. She had noticed the painting the first day they arrived at Grandby's estate home. Although its subject was posed in a provocative manner, it was lovely to look at and seemed right for the warm surroundings.

Leaning against the mantel, Todd was studying the painting closely, and Deborah felt embarrassment when his gaze stayed on the painting despite her arrival in the room.

"She is very beautiful. Do you... know her?" Deborah asked quietly, feeling a hint of envy. The woman in the painting was beautiful, although only her profile, a hint of a bare breast, and her bare back and shoulders were revealed. The rest of her body was teasingly covered with a draped robe that hinted at a bare bottom. An appropriate painting for an *unmarried* man's room, Deborah thought on closer inspection.

Todd tore his gaze away and regarded his wife. His brows were furrowed as if he were troubled by something. "I used to," he replied quietly. "I recall meeting her at least once when I was quite young. She was Mr. Grandby's mother. Disappeared long ago under very mysterious circumstances," he related in clipped tones. He noticed his wife's apparent discomfort at his attention to the artwork and quickly took her hand. "She is not as beautiful as you are, of course," he said, leaning down to kiss her on the lips. "I should think you would be a much better subject for such a painting."

Deborah blushed, afraid a servant might see them or hear her husband's comment. "You're forgiven, then," she said with a smile. "I came to bid you farewell," she added with an angled head.

"You won't be gone long?" Todd half-questioned as he took his wife's hand and kissed the back of it. "I shall miss you terribly, you must know."

Deborah smiled again as she reached up to kiss her husband's forehead, careful to be sure no servants were about. "No more than an hour, to be sure. I'm just going for a walk about the grounds," she assured him as she managed to get her hand back. "The gardens are stunning, and the trees are so beautiful. Are you sure you don't wish to join me?" she asked, hoping the invitation sounded as sincere as she meant it.

Smiling, Todd reached down to kiss her. "I will join you on a walk after dinner, of course," he assured her, "But I wish to keep my knees from aching as long as possible." He settled into a large chair and took a book from the side table. "And I'm going to finish this book."

Foster, the butler, entered the library and loudly cleared his throat. On the other two occasions when he had walked in on the couple, they had been kissing quite happily and been not the least bit embarrassed by his interruptions. On this occasion, he had to step aside and nod as Mrs. Vandermeer made her way out the library door. She greeted him and even curtsied despite his station not requiring such pleasantries. He gave a leg in reply and continued into the library to deliver the sealed letter he brought on a salver. "Excuse me, Mr. Vandermeer. This post just arrived for you," he stated as he held the tray out to the tall man.

Todd looked up in surprise and took the letter, thanking the butler as he did so. Foster bowed and left the library, closing the doors behind him as he did so.

Loosening the seal on the letter without breaking the embossed wax, Todd noted the 'H' in the seal and wondered whom might have sent it. A quick look at the bottom of the scrawled note made him gulp, and it took three tries before he was able to make out all the words.

To My Esteemed Colleague, Mr. Todd Vandermeer, I find myself in Dire Straights and hope you can find it in your Schedule to meet with me post-haste. The Gowns have arrived from France. I have spent days in Negotiations with shops to no avail; despite their Quality manufacture and Beautiful Packaging, I cannot find a suitable shop in which to sell the hideous things. You recommended I import these gowns, and I have done so without question. Surely you had resellers in mind. You must share your knowledge or you can be sure you will share in my Demise at the Company. Yours very truly, Randolph Hughes.

"Damn!" Todd said under his breath. "Stupid man," he added in a whisper as his hand scrubbed his face. *Stupid me for ever recommending such an endeavor.*

Leaning against the back of the settee, he tried to remember why he had even recommended the gowns to Hughes in the first place. He had been annoyed with the man, to be sure, but vengeance wasn't suitable when dealing with a fellow broker at the John Company.

Then he recalled his dinner with Deborah and Emma. They had shared ideas and even the names of some shops where such gowns could be sold.

Moving to the large desk in the corner, Todd took up a pen and began writing down everything he could remember about his conversation with the ladies. Then he recalled the comments Thomas had made with respect to mistresses wearing such gowns should they be bought by their gentlemen. Ideas began forming in his mind, and he continued taking notes.

Once he had his list complete, he created a detailed plan and included several potential customers the women hadn't mentioned, including members of men's clubs and the sister of Mr. Hughes. He knew she attended the theatre on a regular basis. Surely if she were to appear in a transparent gown over one of her more audacious gowns, the overall effect would be of a more suitable, toned-down look. If Emma and Deborah would agree to wear them over their morning gowns, a shopping trip in Oxford Street would certainly turn heads and get female shoppers talking. Perhaps his aunt could be persuaded to do the same in The Strand, he considered. Still writing when Deborah returned, Todd looked up to find her reading over his shoulder.

"Whatever are you doing?" she asked as she tried to make out his erratic handwriting.

"A marketing plan for transparent gowns," Todd replied as he rolled his eyes. "Mr. Hughes has bungled the handling of them and has lain the blame at my feet," he said quietly as he turned over the paper on which he was writing so Deborah could read Hughes's letter.

"Oh, dear," Deborah breathed as she read the note and reread it again to determine if the man wrote in jest or was serious about his threat. "What will you do?" she asked, turning the paper over to read his notes on the back.

"Save him and his position. And myself, I suppose," Todd replied in resignation.

Deborah wrapped her arms around his neck and kissed the back of his head. "Why is he threatening you?" she asked in a whisper, her lips moving down to his ears.

Grinning at the tickling sensation her tongue created, Todd turned his head and kissed her on the lips. "I recommended the gowns as a kind of saving grace for him," he admitted sadly. "I thought he would be able to find buyers and be successful with this —help him to regain his standing in the company, if you will. But the man has no imagination and no head for this kind of business. So I shall do what I can," he vowed before he kissed Deborah again.

"And then what?" Deborah asked as she sat on the desk and faced him.

Shaking his head, Todd looked up and said, "I have been made an offer of employment elsewhere, and I wish to discuss it with you before I accept or decline it."

Sitting up straighter on the desk, Deborah stared at her husband. "You wish to discuss it with... with *me?*" she asked in surprise. Clearly awestruck, Deborah regarded her husband for several seconds before a grin spread on her face. "You are serious."

Todd leaned back in the desk chair and grinned. "Yes, of course. You're my wife," he said as he looked up at her. "It's an important decision, and you're a bright woman," he added, surprised he had to justify his request for her input.

"I am... honored," Deborah replied as she held a hand to her chest. "Whom has made you the offer?" she asked, her heart beating faster as she considered the possibilities. "Would you still work for East India?"

Shaking his head, Todd replied, "Wellingham Imports. Thomas wishes me to join him there as a partner in the business."

Deborah smiled broadly, surprised by the source of the offer. "And you didn't readily accept the position when he made you the offer?" she asked, her eyebrows high on her forehead. The two were the best of friends. The fact that he hadn't simply accepted the offer at the time it was offered seemed somehow ridiculous to her.

Todd continued to grin at her and, still seated, he wrapped his arms around her waist. "I told him I needed to discuss it with you, but now I realize that wasn't necessary," he teased as he lay his head on her lap. "And I said something about wanting to see his books, but I know his business is sound. Emma is auditing his company's ledgers, you must know," he added, lifting his head so he might see Deborah's reaction.

The frown was still on her face as she shook her head. "I didn't know," she countered, her thoughts racing back to the day Emma arrived at the Home for Unwed Mothers with the news of her impending employment for Thomas Wellingham. "I thought she was merely his household bookkeeper," Deborah stated, surprise in her voice.

Todd angled his head to one side. "Me, too, until the day after that awful rainstorm," he replied, annoyance in his voice. "Thomas was still very ill and mentioned I could get the books from Emma, and the secret of her employment was no more."

Deborah furrowed her brows. "You seem... *disappointed* at learning of her position," she observed.

"Only in that she had to lie to me at Wellingham's instruction," Todd replied as he shook his head. "It's all right now, of course, but when he admitted her association with his company, I felt... betrayed, I suppose," he said quietly. "Thomas and I have been friends since childhood, and we speak about many private things.

Why would he feel the need to hide the nature of her employment from me?"

Sighing, Deborah stroked Todd's hair with her fingertips, and he closed his eyes for a moment. "What exactly is an audit?" Deborah whispered.

Todd kept his eyes shut, but his expression told her he was enjoying her fingers in his hair. "A close inspection of the company's accounting ledgers," he said in reply. "To discover and repair any errors or look for poor accounting practices or..." His eyes opened, and he raised his head from her lap.

"What is it?" Deborah asked, pulling her fingers away from Todd's head.

"Look for evidence of embezzlement," Todd said with a faraway look. "That has to be it," he whispered as he absently took one of Deborah's hands in his.

"Embezzlement?" Deborah repeated uncertainly. "Is that where an employee steals from his employer?" she asked as she tried to recall when she had heard the term.

Todd smiled as his eyes met Deborah's. "Yes. And it would certainly explain all the secrecy," he added, his face brightening. "Emma is searching for an embezzler," he said, almost with glee. Biting his lip, the smile disappeared from his face.

Deborah, who followed the line of reasoning and didn't like where it ended, said, "But if someone is stealing from Mr. Wellingham, then the company might not be worth as much," she stated evenly. "But if Mr. Wellingham hired an auditor, then he must know there is an embezzler and is just trying to determine who it is," she added as she looked up to find Todd staring at her.

"And how much has been stolen," Todd added before he kissed the back of Deborah's hand.

"So that he can get the money back," she countered with a hopeful nod.

"Now do you think I should accept the position?"

Grinning, Deborah replied, "Of course! When Emma discovers the identity of the embezzler, there will be a good bit of scandal, don't you think?"

Todd laughed and considered the possibility. "Or even more secrecy," he said quietly, his mood darkening again.

"Or, she could just be determining the value of the company so Mr. Wellingham can decide how much he can afford to pay you,"

Deborah suggested, sitting up as straight as she could on the desk, quite satisfied with her latest conclusion.

"There is that possibility," Todd agreed. Was he allowing his imagination to get the best of him? "So, what am I to do?" he asked, a faraway look on his face.

"I think you shall accept Mr. Wellingham's offer," Deborah replied.

Todd regarded his wife with a stern look. "All right then, I shall," he agreed.

"But, first there is another offer which you must consider," Deborah stated, her lips pressed together and her demeanor more serious.

Concerned, Todd stood. "What is it?" he asked, placing his hands on Deborah's arms.

"You must accept my offer of an afternoon upstairs in our bedchamber," she stated quietly, her manner turning coy.

Todd's mouth opened in shock and he looked around to be sure no servants were within earshot. "I do believe that's the best offer I have heard this entire week," he replied happily, holding out his arm for her and then striding quickly from the library. "Mr. Hughes will just have to wait."

And as they exited the library, Deborah took another look at the painting above the fireplace, memorizing as many of the details as she could.

CHAPTER 59
A GENTLEMAN COMES A CALLING

July 8, 1802, Woodscastle

The day after his meeting with Sir William, Thomas Wellingham found himself at odds. Emma had completed her audit and wouldn't be working for him again until a week after the Hornsby ball.

Damn, the ball, he remembered.

He had meant to ask Emma if he could escort her—she as a companion for Christiana, of course—and somehow, in the midst of the audit results, it was all but forgotten. He supposed Emma was at her townhouse in London, but he had no idea where it was located or even whom to ask for directions. His breakfast, once hot and appetizing, was getting cold.

"Why the sullen mood?" Gregory interrupted his thoughts. "Are you perhaps, missing someone?" he teased, although the tone of his voice didn't hold much humor.

Christiana, who had been reading a letter from a classmate, turned her attention to her brother. "Mr. Grandby is right. Why are you of such poor humor this morning?" She leaned forward and placed a hand on her brother's arm.

Embarrassed, Thomas tried to affect an air of detachment. "I just realized I haven't paid Miss Emma for her last week of work here. I should deliver a cheque to her immediately, but I've no idea where she resides," he explained, putting down his fork in surrender.

"He misses her," Gregory whispered to Christiana, but she was paying him no attention as she sat up very straight in her chair. "I know where she lives," she claimed with her chin up as far as possible. "Would you like me to take you there? Please, brother? I haven't been to town since the end of school, and I need a gown for the ball."

Thomas leaned forward and regarded his sister. "You're sure you can give instructions to Mr. Allen?" he asked, his mood much improved.

"Of course. At least, I can provide directions from Warwick's Gamma House. You see, that's the way she's taken me to the townhouse," Christiana explained, smiling when she realized her brother really was more interested in Emma than he was indicating.

"Then finish your breakfast. Humphrey," he called out, only to find his butler a few feet away. "Could you have Mr. Allen hitch up the carriage, please? We're going to town."

The butler bowed. "Very good, sir," he replied before hurrying out of the dining room.

"May we also go to Birchall's?" Christiana asked as her smile brightened. "I'd very much like to get some new sheet music."

Thomas glanced at his sister with surprise. "Of course." When he considered her request, though, he added, "Have you already learned how to play all the music I bought for you last month?" His noonday trip to the music seller had cost him nearly two pounds for two books of piano music, several sheets of compositions by Bach, and a piece requiring two people to play. Curious as to Emma's ability to play, he had hoped Christiana would ask the woman to play the piece with her. *Perhaps she had while he was in town*, he realized.

Gregory glanced at Christiana before sighing loudly. Clearing his throat, he said, "Yes, she has. And she has played it all at least a dozen times," he added, in a tone that suggested he knew because he had heard it all personally—at least a dozen times. "In fact, I shall buy you whatever music you wish, my dear," he stated as he turned his attention to Christiana.

She beamed and placed a hand on his shoulder. "You are already spoiling me," she whispered demurely.

Thomas overheard the comment and considered insisting he buy the sheet music, but his mind was on other matters. So much so, he didn't notice the sound of a delivery wagon depositing its load of slate shingles on the west side of the house, nor the arrival of several workman already performing demolition work in the west wing rooms.

Spending two consecutive days in London wasn't Thomas Wellingham's idea of a good time, but his mind was distracted from the hustle and bustle of the world's largest city. He was most anxious to find Emma. Once he was assured she was paid and had her agreement to attend the ball with Christiana, then he would see to it Christiana had a new gown.

The driver pulled up in the front of the Gamma House of Warwick's Grammar and Finishing School. In the daylight, Thomas now noticed for the first time why it had been so difficult for his driver to find the building at night. Seven identical brick buildings making up the housing for the school lined Glasshouse Street for its entire length.

Behind the buildings and facing Swallow Street were the buildings housing the classrooms and a chapel. During the school year, nearly one hundred of the wealthiest girls from London and beyond attended classes here, and over half lived in the school's boarding facilities.

"Now turn left into Warwick," Christiana said to the driver as she indicated the next street. The driver hurried the horses along, made the turn and continued to follow Christiana's instructions to turn right on Beak and left onto Kingly. It was a mere quarter mile to the lower part of Kingly Street in which Emma's townhouse was located.

A well-kept neighborhood, there were trees lining the cobblestone street and row after row of closely-spaced two-story brick houses on either side. Most had a few steps leading up to a front door. Some had steps leading down to a below-street door, and some had entrances right off the sidewalk level. Giant pots of flowers were seated next to several doors.

When they were about halfway down the street, Christiana asked the driver to pull over. A scent of cinnamon hung in the air as she announced, "We're here!" She pointed to a red street-level door on the right. Topped with the number '3', the door was flanked by flower urns, one brimming with color and ivy while the other appeared as if its contents had been eaten away.

Gregory sniffed the air. "This cannot be London," he said as he stepped down from the carriage. "It smells too good." He turned to help Christiana. "Are you sure this is where she lives?" he asked, glancing nervously at the front door of the townhouse directly adjacent to Emma's.

"Oh, yes," Christiana smiled as she allowed Gregory to simply lift her out of the carriage and place her gently on her feet. Hurrying to knock on the door, she said, "She's making cinnamon buns."

Thomas' stomach rumbled as breathed in the scent. "I do hope she can spare one," he muttered as he followed his sister and Gregory.

As Emma opened the door and happily greeted them, Thomas' heart soared. She motioned them to enter and stood aside as her guests filed into the small vestibule. Dressed in a simple green empire gown mostly covered with a soiled apron, Emma appeared as any woman might as she went about her morning chores. Her golden hair, although styled with ringlets at the front, was long and loose and hung past her shoulders in the back.

As he removed his hat, Thomas bowed and said, "Please, pardon the intrusion, Miss Emma, but I come bearing your last week's wages."

Emma smiled and curtsied as she took Gregory's hat and cane and stepped over to take Thomas'. "'Tis no intrusion at all, Mr. Wellingham. It's so good to see you. To see all of you. Please, do have a seat," she said as she motioned to the settee and chairs in the small parlor. She placed the hats and cane on an elegant hall tree next to the front door and turned to pull Christiana into a hug. *I haven't even put up my hair*, she thought absently.

"Thomas is taking me to buy a gown for the ball," Christiana whispered excitedly as they hugged each other. "Gregory is going to escort me."

Emma released her shoulders and stepped back. "Could you help me in the kitchen?" She turned her attention to the men. "We will return with tea and buns in a moment." The two hurried to the kitchen and Emma poured hot water into a teapot. "He is the one, isn't he, Christiana?" she half-asked, a hopeful look on her face as she removed the apron. "I admit, I didn't think favorably of him when he first arrived at Woodscastle, but when I see you two together…"

Christiana's face bloomed with color as she heard Emma's words. "I cannot keep it a secret any longer. He is the one," she whispered as she nodded her head.

Emma found herself at odds. She had promised Thomas she would tell him if she found out the identity of Christiana's beau. However, after speaking with Gregory and now with Christiana, she found she wanted to keep their secret. "Has your brother said anything about you requiring a chaperone?" she asked, realizing that for such a large event and given her status, Christiana would require the presence of an older woman to act in that capacity.

"Heavens, no," Christiana replied. "I doubt he realizes I should have one, but he'll be at the ball, and I expect he'll keep me in his sights the entire evening," she claimed as she screwed up her nose in disgust.

Emma hid her disappointment at hearing Christiana's words. She had no prospects for the events of the rest of the summer and upcoming Little Season. She hoped she might fill the role of chaperone for Christiana. At least then she would be able to attend the Hornsby ball.

Thomas' first impressions of Emma's townhouse were quite favorable. The furnishings were beautiful—some of them even antique. The wall coverings were elegant, the colors were tastefully done, the drapes were made of high quality brocade, and the lace sheers were impeccably woven. Thomas took one of the chairs and glanced over at Gregory. Although his expression told him Gregory was impressed with the parlor and the woman in general, Thomas sensed the man wanted to say something while the girls were out of earshot. "Tell me what you're thinking," he stated with a heavy sigh.

To his surprise, Gregory wasted no time. "If you don't ask this woman for her hand in marriage, I shall ask her on your behalf," he whispered hoarsely as he sat down heavily into an overstuffed chair.

Thomas jerked upright, his face reddening with embarrassment. "You'll do no such thing," he ordered, trying his best to keep his voice down.

"I'm at least going to ask her if she'll help decorate the west wing," Gregory countered as he glanced around the room and studied furnishings. Thomas found he couldn't disagree with the idea. "The roof is being replaced this week, by the way," the taller man said, his nonchalant attitude a sudden source of irritation to Thomas.

"Indeed?" Thomas replied, surprised at the news. "I suppose the work on the rooms has already begun as well?"

Gregory merely nodded when he realized the girls were already on their way back to the parlor, Christiana carrying a tea service and Emma carrying a tray of piping hot cinnamon rolls and lemon pastries.

"Did you know, Miss Emma, that one can smell your baked goods halfway down the street?" Thomas asked as he took one of the rolls. "You really must share your receipts with my cook."

"Or just go be his cook," Gregory whispered to no one in particular.

"Indeed, Mr. Wellingham. Thank you," Emma replied with a smile as she offered the tray to Gregory while Christiana saw to serving tea.

"One lump or two?" Christiana asked of Gregory as she prepared his cup.

"Two, please," Gregory replied as he eyed Thomas carefully.

Thomas accepted a cup from Christiana but waved off the sugar. "Thank you, sister," he said with a nod and sat back in his chair. "You have a very lovely home, Miss Emma," he commented as Emma poured tea for Christiana.

"Thank you, sir," she replied as she gave a cup to Christiana and took one for herself. "I adore the neighborhood, and it's really quite safe." She and Christiana took the settee.

Before they had even taken the first sip of tea, Thomas asked, "Miss Emma, will you do me the honor of attending the Hornsby ball with me this Saturday?"

Christiana had to suppress a delighted gasp while Gregory, suddenly snorting tea through his nose, nearly dropped his cup. Even Thomas couldn't believe he had actually said the words out loud. This was the sort of question one asked in private.

Emma was rather restrained in her response. "Why, thank you, Mr. Wellingham. It would be my pleasure," she replied with a nod and a smile. "Perhaps we could discuss details before you depart today," she suggested, noting the reaction of the other couple in the room.

Thomas nodded, trying to retain an air of dignity while he watched as his sister was barely able to keep her seat. "When we take our leave of here, it will be to go shopping for a ball gown for Miss Wellingham. Would you care to join us?"

Emma could barely contain her excitement. "Why, how kind of you to offer," she replied with a smile. "I'd be delighted."

"We wouldn't be keeping you from anything?" Gregory chimed in, reminding everyone he was still in the room.

Emma shook her head. "Not at all. In fact, I was planning to shop for gowns suitable for work. But shopping for ball gowns can be so much more enjoyable," she said as she elbowed Christiana playfully. The younger girl beamed as she sipped her tea, knowing Emma referred to wedding gowns.

"What color gown should we consider for her?" Thomas directed his question to Emma. "I suppose there is a fashionable color for this ball?"

Emma put down her teacup on the small table next to the settee. "All the unbetrothed girls will be wearing white tulle or batiste, of course," she replied with a nod, her enthusiasm waning as she shared a glance of disappointment in Christiana's direction. It was the curse of single girls that bright white be worn. Neither of them preferred to dress in white—it was too severe for their lighter hair and pale skin."But that doesn't mean she couldn't try a very pale yellow or a pink tulle," Emma said as she indicated Christiana, thinking that since Gregory Grandby had made known his intentions to ask for her hand, Christiana was no longer on the Marriage Mart.

Christiana's face brightened. "Pale yellow would do well. Maybe in chiffon?"

Emma glanced back at Thomas. He was watching her and doing nothing to hide the fact. "Would you like a pastry, Mr. Wellingham?" she asked as she indicated the lemon custard-filled triangles.

"If I may, I'd prefer another cinnamon roll," he said as he reached for one of the buns. "I cannot tell you how hungry I was when I arrived at your door. The smell and taste of these is simply divine," he added as he sniffed the still warm roll.

"Please, help yourself to as many as you'd like," Emma replied, blushing at his comment. "I'll wrap the rest for you to take with you. More tea?" she added as she held up the pot.

"Don't mind if I do," he answered as he held out his cup. Gregory cleared his throat, intending to ask for more, but Emma had already turned to refill his cup. "Mr. Grandby?"

"Yes, please," he answered, startled at how quickly she performed her duties as hostess. He also took one of the pastries as she held the tray for him.

"Miss Wellingham tells me you're escorting her to the ball,"

Emma said as she set down the tray. "What will the men be wearing this year?" she queried.

"Black tails, white ties," the two men replied in unison, neither showing much enthusiasm for the formal dress.

Christiana held a hand up to her mouth, trying to suppress a giggle.

"And to whose shop are we going?" Emma asked Christiana, her excitement building as she realized she, too, would be shopping for a ball gown. "There's a nice modiste not too far from here, if you're interested," she suggested, remembering Madame Suzanne's. "'Tis where Mr. Vandermeer bought Miss Deborah's wedding gown and my gown, as well. The clothes are divine, and they have comfortable chairs and brandy for the men to drink whilst they wait."

Gregory sat up straight at this interesting tidbit. "Really?" he replied, deciding that shopping for gowns might not be all bad. "I think this shop sounds like the place to go. Thomas?"

Busy with another cinnamon bun while carefully watching Emma, Thomas hardly noticed the conversation. "Fine," he answered, not even sure to what he had agreed.

When they'd had their fill of tea and pastries, Emma wrapped the remaining rolls in a tea towel and placed the bundle in a basket. She excused herself to pin up her hair and don the white eyelet bonnet William Smith had given her. Picking up her reticule from the hall tree and passing out hats and canes, she waited until everyone else had left before closing and locking the door. With the basket on one arm and the reticule hanging from the other, she found Thomas waiting to help her into the carriage.

"Perhaps Mr. Allen would like a bun?" she asked as she stepped up into the carriage.

Thomas reluctantly nodded. "That's very kind of you," he commented as she offered the basket to the driver. He didn't hesitate to take one of the buns and thanked Emma profusely.

When they were settled into the carriage, the men on one side and the women on the other, Emma gave instructions to Mr. Allen. Within minutes, they were in front of 'Suzanne's,' the rather upscale shop in Oxford, featuring gowns appropriate for dinners and balls.

Gregory was the first to step out of the carriage, making a comment about brandy, but he turned and immediately lifted Christiana out. Emma couldn't help but notice Gregory's protective stance when he was with the girl, and she caught him as he pecked

Christiana on the head while he set her on her feet. Smiling, Emma was about to step out of the carriage on the same side when she felt Thomas' hand reach for hers. She turned to find him ready to assist her, and she smiled. "Thank you, Mr. Wellingham," she said as she stepped down. He held out an arm for her and she took it, her heart soaring as they walked into the modiste.

As Emma had described, the shop featured a large selection of ready-made gowns. Several full-length looking glasses were lined up on one wall next to two changing rooms. Racks of gowns and manikins lined two other walls, and in the middle of it all was a collection of overstuffed chairs and small tables equipped with glasses, a bottle of brandy, a decanter of claret, and a crystal pitcher of water. The modiste herself, Miss Suzanne, stood at a counter near the changing rooms and greeted them with a curtsy. Recognizing Emma, she said, "I do hope the gowns for the wedding were acceptable."

Emma nodded. "They were, indeed." She motioned toward Christiana as she said, "Miss Wellingham and I will be attending the Hornsby ball," she said as she indicated Thomas and Gregory. "So we are looking for suitable gowns."

The men took their seats while Miss Suzanne attended to Christiana and Emma. The girls began their selection process by simply putting anything that might fit into a changing room. Giggling, they took turns displaying each gown while the men sipped brandy and made comments about the gowns.

Thomas took note of Gregory's behavior as Christiana modeled each gown. The man's approach to choosing the best gowns seemed serious, but he had a way of being flippant if a gown was somehow wrong. For those gowns he deemed acceptable, Gregory gave a signal to Suzanne, she nodded, and when the gown was no longer on Christiana, it was placed on the counter for wrapping.

"How much is this going to cost me?" Thomas asked as he noticed the pile of gowns on the counter.

Gregory followed Thomas' gaze. "Nothing," Gregory replied. "These are my gifts for Christiana."

Flabbergasted, Thomas was about to remind Gregory it would be most improper for him to purchase anything for Christiana, but then Emma stepped out from a changing room wearing a butter-colored long-sleeved gown of exquisite design. Layers of chiffon accentuated her height and figure and pale skin. Thomas found he couldn't keep his mouth closed. He glanced at Suzanne and found her watching him expectantly. He nodded and she nodded in return. As Emma walked to the looking glass and saw her reflection, she stepped back and turned to see the back of the gown. A small smile appeared, but when she searched for and found the tag with the price, she merely sighed and returned to the dressing room, obviously disappointed.

Gregory looked at Thomas and Thomas finally turned toward Gregory. "What?" he asked with a hint of annoyance, downing the rest of his brandy in single gulp.

"If you don't buy that gown for her—"

"Shh," Thomas replied as Christiana began modeling another gown. Thomas made a joke about the fit and the fabric, and Christiana shrugged her shoulders, smiled at him, and disappeared into the dressing room. Gregory poured more brandy into Thomas' glass, careful to do so without drawing his attention.

Emma came out wearing a white satin tulle gown, the bodice embroidered with silk and tiny beads. Although it had short cap sleeves, she wore long white gloves that extended beyond the elbow, so very little of her bare arms showed. Even in white, she was a stunning sight to Thomas Wellingham. When she turned to look at her back in the mirror, she noticed him watching her and quickly glanced away, her face coloring up as she did so. Satisfied the gown fit, she took one more turn and then returned quickly to the changing room.

Thomas turned to nod at Suzanne, but she had disappeared into Emma's dressing room, apparently to assist her out of the gown. When the proprietor opened the door to take out the gown, Thomas caught a glimpse of Emma's profile as she began to pull another gown over her head. Her corset was pulled tight, and her pantaloons barely covered her knees. He remembered, as if in a dream, when he'd had that body pulled against him. His loins tightening, he let out a small moan.

Gregory's eyebrows shot up as he gave his friend a sideways glance. "I'm quite sure we could get you a marriage license, and you can be wed within a week," he commented quietly.

Thomas was about to shush him when he realized Gregory was no longer teasing him. In fact, the man seemed downright serious. "I'll take it into consideration," Thomas murmured as he straightened in his chair and took another drink.

"This is the last one," Christiana said as she emerged from the dressing room in a pale green empire gown made of batiste. Thomas recognized it—the taller version hung in their mother's wardrobe. With her strawberry blonde hair and pale skin, it was a stunning gown. Gregory started to nod at Suzanne, but Thomas reached over and put his hand on Gregory's shoulder. "I'll get this one," he said as he nodded at Suzanne.

"Suit yourself," Gregory replied, grinning as he watched Christiana turn in front of the mirror.

Before Christiana had returned to the dressing room, Emma emerged from hers wearing an empire gown of aqua batiste. The smile on her face told Thomas she liked it even before she saw it in the mirror. He tried to motion to Suzanne, but the proprietor had moved to Emma's side to adjust the gathers. In the meantime, Emma saw Christiana's gown and her mouth opened. Turning to Thomas, she pointed at the gown. "That's the same gown you already bought for her," she said quietly, as Christiana returned to the dressing room.

Thomas nodded. "But this one fits her," he replied with a grin.

Emma returned her attention to Suzanne. "I will take this one," she said happily. Confused, the proprietor glanced at Thomas for guidance. He shrugged in reply, not quite sure if buying three gowns for Emma would be considered too many—or too generous. If anyone outside of the four of them found out, it would be scandalous. "I can afford this one, you see," Emma whispered to Suzanne.

"I shall wrap it up for you, miss," the modiste replied. "And may I inquire as to where you found the eyelet bonnet you were wearing when you arrived?"

Emma smiled and nodded. "At *Fitzsimmons and Smith*," she said happily. "Mr. Smith's wife makes them for the shop."

Suzanne nodded. "I shall have to make her acquaintance," she replied with a restrained smile.

Emma grinned at her comment and returned to the dressing room. *If Suzanne carries the bonnets in this shop, the 'Fitzsimmons for Women' label could become quite lucrative.*

Whilst the girls changed back into their morning gowns, Gregory and Thomas waited for Suzanne to wrap their purchases and total their bills. As Thomas paid her for the two gowns and a pair of long white gloves, he asked Suzanne to keep the butter-colored gown in the shop. He would either stop by to retrieve it or send a servant for it later in the day. Confused, Gregory said, "Isn't that supposed to be her ball gown?"

"No," Thomas replied simply as he tucked the parcel with the white gown under his arm. "She'll wear the white satin like all the other unbetrothed women at the ball."

Gregory noticed Christiana leaving her dressing room. "Must I really have to wait until she is eighteen?" he asked, a pained expression on his face. He downed the rest of his glass of brandy and sighed.

Thomas glanced in his sister's direction just as Emma left her changing room cradling the aqua gown. "God, she is more beautiful now than when she went in there," he murmured.

"So, that's a 'no'?" Gregory replied, hoping to catch his friend off-guard.

"I suppose we can discuss an earlier wedding date," Thomas replied, his attention still on Emma.

"A week from Saturday, perhaps?" Gregory suggested, his level of amusement rising as he watched Thomas' concentration.

"Maybe," Thomas replied absently.

Awestruck, Gregory stared at his friend. "Thomas?" he said carefully. "Are you ill?" He waved a hand in front of Thomas' face.

Thomas shook his head. "I am very well, in fact." He motioned toward the counter. "And what are you waiting for?" he asked, a hint of annoyance in his voice. "She has your bill totaled," he said as he swatted Gregory on the shoulder.

"Pardon me," Gregory said as he stepped up to the pile of wrapped gowns. He paid Suzanne and started to pick up as many of the parcels as he could, finally allowing Christiana and Emma to help pile them onto his outstretched arms.

As they left the store, the girls giggling as they watched Gregory carry his tower of packages to the carriage, Thomas pulled Emma aside. "Would you care to take a tour of your new workplace this afternoon? 'Tis not far from here, and I can make arrangements for Mr. Allen to pick us up there in an hour," he suggested quickly.

Taken aback by his hand on hers, Emma thought for a moment. "I'd like that very much, Mr. Wellingham. Could we leave our parcels in the carriage, do you suppose?"

"Of course. Mr. Allen can keep an eye on them whilst Christiana and Gregory continue shopping," Thomas said. Turning to his sister and best friend, he announced, "Miss Emma and I are going for a walk to the warehouse. I wish to show her around before she starts her position there," he said lightly. "Might I suggest you visit the jewelry store just down the street? Mr. Vandermeer found a very good selection of wedding bands," he added, his attention on Gregory. "Mr. Allen. Please be at Wellingham Imports in one hour. Good day."

With that, he offered his arm to Emma and she took it, making a quick shrug in Christiana's direction.

Left speechless, Gregory and Christiana could only stare at Thomas while he walked away with Emma.

"Well, I'll be damned," Gregory muttered under his breath. "He should drink brandy more often."

"What did you say?" Christiana replied as she finally took her eyes off the departing backs of her best friend and brother. "If I didn't know better, I'd think I heard you just curse!"

Gregory finally turned his attention to Christiana. "I did, and I'm not about to apologize for it," he stated, watching Thomas and Emma make their way down toward the river.

CHAPTER 60
A WALK TO A WORKPLACE

July 8, 1802, London

    "'Tis a lovely day for a walk," Emma said as she and Thomas crossed a street and headed toward the river. "And if it's safe enough, I may consider walking to work from my townhouse, at least in the summertime," she added as she realized how cold it might be so close to the river in the winter.

Thomas considered her comment. "I believe it would be safe enough, but I wouldn't want you walking home in the dark. There is a large stable on the north side of the building, though, so you could ride your horse to work should you wish," he explained. Of course she wouldn't walk home—or even to work—unless he was with her.

They strolled in silence while Emma considered how to tell Thomas she knew the identity of Christiana's lover. She had made a promise to tell him should she discover his name, but she didn't want to admit she knew from Christiana. She finally broached the subject, saying, "Remember when we agreed that if I should find out who Christiana is in love with..."

"Gregory Grandby. Yes, I know," Thomas responded with a nod as he slowed his pace. "He plans to ask for her hand on her birthday," he said quietly.

Emma gasped. "So *he* has spoken with you?" she queried carefully.

"Indeed. He asked me yesterday after we visited with Sir William," he added sadly. "He was rather stern about it, actually," Thomas added. "He wouldn't have taken 'no' for an answer."

Yesterday, she considered. *That was just the day after I found out, and I had no opportunity to speak with Thomas about it before I left Woodscastle. Then I suppose I have kept my word as best I could, given the circumstances.*

"And I found I couldn't say 'no'," Thomas continued, adding a sigh to the end of his statement. "Christiana is in love with him, and after our discussion yesterday and our shopping trip today, I guess I must admit he is, indeed, in love with her."

Shaking her head, Emma said carefully, "You must know Christiana will not want for anything."

Thomas angled his head. "Whatever do you mean?" he asked. He noticed a puddle and guided them around it before giving his full attention back to Emma.

"Gregory Grandby's investments earn him five-thousand pounds a year," she said matter-of-factly. "And he was already quite rich before he began investing," she added with a shrug.

Thomas snorted and stopped walking. Leaning toward Emma as she turned to face him, he said, "Did you say *five-thousand* pounds?" he repeated, his face showing complete disbelief.

"Yes," Emma replied, nodding. "You didn't know he was... wealthy?"

Grinning, Thomas resumed walking. "Miss Emma, there is 'well-to-do' and there is 'wealthy' and there is Croesus. I suppose I have always considered him simply well-to-do," he explained in his defense. "He offered me five-thousand pounds to buy the west wing of Woodscastle. This was after I agreed to let him ask for Christiana's hand," he added quickly. "He wants a place where they can live when they're not traveling," he explained, shaking his head as he remembered Gregory's words.

"Five-thousand pounds?" Emma repeated, not sure she had heard him correctly. "For *half* the house?"

"The bad half," Thomas replied as he nodded his head. "The west wing is in dire need of major repairs. And he claims he will pay for those, as well."

When he didn't continue, Emma dared ask, "So, did you accept his offer?"

Thomas grinned broadly. "Of course!" he replied happily. "We share the grounds and the stables, they get the music room, and I get to keep the library and the east wing. Work on the roof has already begun, and I've no doubt there's an army of carpenters already at work on the rooms.

"Oh, and he would like your assistance when it comes time to decorate," he added as he paused at the corner before crossing another street.

"Indeed?" Emma replied, shaking her head in wonderment.

"He rather likes your parlor," Thomas explained. "As do I," he added with a nod.

"Why, thank you," Emma replied with a smile. As Thomas helped her step up onto a stone walkway on Puddle Dock, she remembered the comment he had made about seeing Sir William. "You mentioned you spoke with Sir William. Did you tell him about the ledgers?" When she noticed his stiffened spine, she regretted having brought up the topic. "I'm so sorry. I shouldn't have asked," she said quickly, hoping she hadn't ruined the afternoon.

"No, no," Thomas replied. "As an investor in Wellingham Imports, you have every right to know what the Bank of England was doing behind our backs."

"Oh?" Emma whispered, her heart pounding in her chest. "Whatever do you mean?"

Thomas described his meeting with Sir William and the subsequent good news. "So, in the long run," he stated, his mood lightening, "Wellingham Imports is better off financially. The bank will reimburse the company for your salary and other audit costs, the embezzled money is in an escrow account earning interest, and they will finance the building of our dock and charge no interest," Thomas finished with a shrug.

Emma stood shaking her head. "I'm so sorry, Mr. Wellingham," she said softly. "Does this mean then that Mr. Peabody will be staying on at Wellingham Imports?" she asked, thinking she was now out of a position.

"Oh, absolutely *not*," Thomas replied, shaking his head in earnest. "Sir William will see to it Mr. Peabody has a position at the bank. I still expect you to start your position a week come Monday," he assured her. A thought crossed his mind. "You haven't changed your mind about working with me, I hope?"

Emma shook her head. "Not at all," she assured him, finding his wording rather interesting. "I must have employment after all, and I do have a vested interest in the success of Wellingham Imports," she added with a wan smile.

Thomas smiled in return. "I suppose if every employee had a 'vested interest' in the company, we might do even better than we have been," he commented, a thought crossing his mind.

Emma eyed him closely. "Are you speaking of employee owner-ship, Mr. Wellingham?" she asked curiously.

Nodding, Thomas stared at Emma for a long time before answering. "Sir William was right about you," he said as he stopped at the edge of the walkway. "You are a smart woman."

Standing up straighter, Emma stared back at Thomas in surprise. "He said that about me?" she repeated in awe. "Well, I thank you both, then," she said with a nod of her head.

"There is one more thing I should tell you," Thomas said, his face darkening.

Emma caught the haunted look and turned to face him. "Oh, dear," she breathed.

"The man... the cur who raped Mrs. Vandermeer. He was appre-hended yesterday," Thomas said quietly. He could hear Emma's breath catch and finally met her gaze. "He was an indigent. A Bedlamite," he struggled to get out. "He attacked a Long Meg down near the bank, in front of dozens of onlookers, and he was shot... killed. I thought you should know."

Emma nodded, a sense of relief spreading through her. "Did you... *see* him when you were at the bank?" she asked, her gloved hand splaying out over her chest as she regarded him.

"I only heard him yell, 'Freak'," Thomas admitted. "And then Gregory and I watched as a mob descended on him."

"And the woman who was attacked?" Emma asked, her breath held out of fear for the victim. *Odd how an attack near the bank had such a different outcome than one that took place in Cheapside,* she thought sadly. "Is she...?"

Thomas shook his head quickly. "She was unharmed. Victoria Morton was quite *vocal* and shot the man before others stepped in," he explained carefully. He wondered if Emma knew of Samuel Morton's desire for her.

Emma held her breath for a moment. "Mrs. Morton shot him?" she repeated in surprise.

"He tore her coat, and she was quite displeased," Thomas said, a glint in his eye suggesting he was trying to find some humor in the situation. "Sheriff Morgan was on the scene almost immediately," he added, a muffled laugh escaping his throat. "I told him what I knew."

Nodding, Emma digested the news and allowed a sigh of relief. "Thank you for telling me," she breathed, her eyes closing for a moment. "Deborah will be—"

"Todd knows. I sent word late yesterday," Thomas interrupted her. "You see, that same man yelled at Todd several times whilst we shopped in Ludgate Hill," he explained, his gaze taking on a far away look. "We didn't realize at the time." He stopped for a moment, sorry he hadn't done something about the odd man then.

"How could you if he didn't attack anyone?" Emma countered. "He probably just seemed like an escapee from Bedlam."

Thomas angled his head to one side. "Still, it is a bit of relief to have the matter settled." He wondered if the indigent would have thought Emma too tall. If so, she could have been one of his victims.

What would he have done had she been raped?

The thought nearly made him ill, and he struggled to regain his sense of composure.

"Indeed," Emma replied. Then she remembered something William Smith had said. *Mr. Morton would be dead by the hands of Mrs. Morton should she ever find out he is even thinking about taking a mistress.* "And should I ever come across Mrs. Morton, I shall have to thank her," she added, her smile widening at the thought of Samuel Morton's wife owning a gun.

Looking up at the tall building in front of them, Emma realized they had arrived at Wellingham Imports. "It's so large." she said in awe as she noted the building took up nearly all of the space between four intersecting roads.

"Todd Vandermeer calls it my 'box'," Thomas said. "But my box is paid for, as are the stables and the horses," he added as he motioned to the line of stables directly in front of the building. Large horses were lined up in a few of the pens, and the odor of hay and manure wafted over them.

They continued to the front of the building as Thomas fished a key from his pocket. Opening the door, Thomas waited for Emma to enter first and then was about to follow her in when she stopped, let out a yelp, and backed into him.

Thomas quickly placed his hands around her waist and moved her aside to see what had startled her. Keeping a protective arm around her, he sighed loudly. "Master Overby, you really mustn't frighten people like that."

The young boy stood with his arms crossed in front of his chest and an angry look on his face. "But Mr. Wellingham, I ain't never seen this lady before, and you said don't never allow anyone in who I ain't never seen," the boy insisted.

"It's 'have never seen' and you know me, so please allow us to pass," Thomas ordered as he bowed to the boy.

The boy bowed in return as Emma curtsied. She stared at the familiar boy, trying to place where she had seen him before.

"Miss Emma, this is Master Overby. He is our caddie and some-times a security guard, as well," Thomas said as he motioned to the young boy.

"Pleased to meet you, Miss Emma," Master Overby replied, his Cockney accent apparent. "Wait. I have seen you before," he added as he pointed a dirt-covered finger in her direction. "You were one of ladies at Mrs. Dawes' place."

Emma nodded at the sandy-haired boy and smiled. "'Tis my pleasure, Master Overby," she replied. "And, yes, I used to volunteer at the Home. I remember seeing you there." She couldn't help but notice how filthy the youngster was. Was he a street urchin? Or did he still live at the Home? *Are his mother and younger sister still alive?*

Thomas glanced around the warehouse and didn't see many people working nor much activity on the warehouse floor. "Where is Mr. Bingham?" Thomas asked of the boy.

"He's gone home. They finished up the last of the deliveries this morning, and with nothin' comin' this afternoon, he sent everyone down here home. They have ta be here early tomorrow morning for the coaches," he explained in their defense. "The upstairs people are still here, though," he said as he indicated the open stairway that led to offices along one wall of the building.

"Indeed," Thomas replied as he finally removed his arm from around Emma's waist and instead offered it to her for support. "Miss Emma will be working here as a clerk. You will allow her passage whenever she is here. Do you understand?"

The boy's eye widened. "You hired a *girl* clerk?" he replied, a look of disgust on his face. "I mean, a *lady?*"

Thomas closed his own eyes and took a deep breath. "Yes, Master Overby. She was the top of her class in Mr. Stokes' class," he said as he gave an apologetic glance in Emma's direction.

"Oh, all right then," the boy said as he bowed again.

"You may go home now, Master Overby," Thomas said as he started to lead Emma through the warehouse.

The boy let out a whoop, saying, "Thank you, Mr. Wellingham," before crashing through the front door.

As Thomas shook his head at the departing caddie, Emma watched him run down the street and disappear around a corner. "Does he even have a home to go to?"

"Well, he claims he has a mother and a baby sister," Thomas replied. He watched through the windows as the boy headed north. "But I have no idea where he lives. Seven Dials, probably," he reasoned, thinking of the poorest area of the city.

Emma recalled what Todd Vandermeer had said when she asked him about his employment at East India. "Do you suppose he will go as far with Wellingham Imports as Todd Vandermeer did with East India?" Emma asked as Thomas led her through the storage areas.

"Whatever do you mean?" he replied, pausing in front of one section of the warehouse.

Emma angled her head. "Mr. Vandermeer said he started as a caddie when he was six years old."

Thomas grinned. "I remember him doing it, too. 'Tis what I used to do for my father when I wasn't in school. In fact, that's how I met Mr. Vandermeer," he recalled fondly. "I often wondered how an orphan could have landed his position, though," he said under his breath. "I'm sure bribes must have been paid for him to get into East India. Someone was certainly looking out for him."

Surprised at the comment, Emma asked, "Whatever do you mean?"

Shrugging, Thomas thought for a moment. "To most, the job would seem menial at best, but for a boy who is fast and knows his way around the docks and around town, being a message boy for a company can end up being very lucrative," he explained as he nodded. "Master Overby is good. At some point, I'll probably offer him a job on the dock—now that I'm allowed to build it—or perhaps here in the warehouse. If he learns to read and write, he may end up as a broker or even running the place," he said as his hand waved to indicate the entire warehouse.

"And why the bribes?" Emma asked. "Did Master Overby have to...?"

"No, no," Thomas interrupted her quickly. "He came seeking a job, and I needed a caddie. He claimed to know his way around, and so far, he's proven himself quite capable," he said casually. "When I mentioned the bribes, I was referring to a situation that used to occur when children were seeking jobs in large companies. Someone would have to pay up front in order for the youth to be considered for employment. There are so many who seek the positions, you see, and there are the unscrupulous who take advantage. I rather imagine someone would have required a bribe at the John Company in order to consider an orphan such as Mr. Vandermeer for a caddie position."

Emma shook her head sadly. Had Mrs. Dawes paid the bribe?

"I really must see to it he takes a bath, though," Thomas said in an off-hand manner.

"Indeed," Emma replied with a smile as she continued to look around. "And what is this area here?" she asked as she pointed to a separate room with a single crate pushed into a corner.

Thomas shook his head and sighed. "This is where unclaimed shipments come to be written off, I'm afraid," he said as he took her to the crate.

Emma immediately recognized the name on the crate. "Worthington Fashions?" she said as she read the label. "They used to make gowns. But I do believe Mr. Worthington died last winter," she stated, her face taking on a worried look as she glanced at Thomas.

He nodded and removed the top of the crate. "You have probably seen this inventory on the books for the entire time you were auditing," he said as he pulled out a bolt of brocade. "Two-hundred and fifty yards of this stuff. No one makes gowns from it anymore," he said as he unwrapped the fabric. "About half is this color and the rest is a sort of royal blue."

Gasping, Emma angled the scarlet and gold fabric to see it in the light from a nearby window. "This is beautiful, Mr. Wellingham," she breathed as she studied the design. "It would be perfect for drapes. And perhaps even for wall covering."

Thomas shook his head, not realizing the fabric could be used for something other than making gowns. "I haven't even tried to find a buyer. I was about to have you write it off as a loss," he said as he put the bolt back into the crate.

"'Tis Christiana's favorite color," Emma said wistfully.

Frowning, Thomas replied, "I thought pink was her favorite color." Her entire bedchamber was done in pink, and she owned more pink gowns than any other color.

Emma tried to suppress a smile. "Pink may have been her favorite when she was younger, but she's more mature now, Mr. Wellingham. She prefers scarlets and darker greens now."

Placing the lid back on the crate, Thomas snorted. "Indeed."

Emma pursed her lips. "Did you say there were two-hundred and fifty yards of this?" she asked as she considered a proposal.

"Unfortunately."

"Or not. Perhaps you can sell it to Mr. Grandby for the west wing," Emma suggested with a raised eyebrow. "There is enough here to do drapes, a duvet, and pillows for the master suite and drapes for a parlor, and the blue could be used in a bedchamber or two."

Standing up straighter, Thomas regarded his bookkeeper while he considered her suggestion. Finally smiling, he replied, "You may have saved Wellingham Imports from a rather expensive write-off, Miss Emma."

Smiling coyly, Emma nodded. "If you like, I can present this to Mr. Grandby when Mr. Allen brings the carriage. He may agree to the sale on the spot," she said as she took Thomas' arm.

"If he buys it, I promise you a bonus," he said as he led them to the stairway. They climbed to the row of offices at the top. Heading to the farthest office, Thomas said, "This is where you'll be working, Miss Emma," he said as he opened the door.

Nine clerks sat at desks in various positions in the room, but only a few looked up as their new co-worker stepped into the room. "Gentlemen, I'd like you to meet Miss Emma Fitzsimmons," Thomas announced as he nodded in the their direction and Emma curtsied. All the men rose quickly from their desks and bowed in their direction. "She'll be taking Mr. Peabody's position a week come Monday," he explained quickly. At the sound of several gasps and an overall negative reaction to the news, he added, "Mr. Peabody has accepted a position at the Bank of England."

The murmurs quieted and a few returned to their work. Thomas was surprised when Benjamin Cunningham remained standing.

"It will be an honor to have Miss Fitzsimmons join us," the man said as he smiled.

Recognizing her classmate from Mr. Stokes' class, Emma

grinned and nodded to him. "Thank you, Mr. Cunningham. I'm very honored to be working with all of you," she added.

She glanced around the room to determine where she might work. Finding the empty desk in a corner on the south wall, she smiled. The south wall was almost entirely windows, flooding the room with light and reminding her of her space in the library at Woodscastle. Stepping farther into the room, she realized the windows provided a view of the River Thames below.

"Mr. Bingham sent everyone downstairs home. I do believe you should be entitled to the same consideration," Thomas said as he addressed the room.

The clerks all stared at Thomas in disbelief and then glanced at each other. "Thank you, sir," a few replied uncertainly.

"I'll be here for a while yet," Thomas said as he checked his chronometer. "I wanted to give Miss Fitzsimmons a tour of the place before she starts work."

Emma and Thomas curtsied and bowed and left the room of stunned but happy clerks.

"That went better than I expected," Thomas commented as he stopped at the next office and opened it.

"Indeed," Emma replied. "I'm so glad you hired Mr. Cunningham. He was one of the best students in our class, and I know he has a wife and family to support."

Thomas nodded as he entered the office. "He came highly recommended by Mr. Stokes," he replied. "As did you, come to think of it," he added with a smile.

The warehouse manager's office was as deep as the clerks' office, but not nearly as wide. Paperwork was neatly stacked on the desk, and books of manifests and receipts filled a bookshelf in the back of the room. Besides a window on the south wall, there was also a window in the front wall that allowed a view of the warehouse below.

"This is Mr. Bingham's office," Thomas said with a wave of his hand. He stepped aside as several clerks bade their farewell and headed down the stairs. When they had passed, he left Mr. Bingham's office to go to the next door. Emma pulled Bingham's door shut behind her as Thomas opened his office door. "And this is my office," he said as he allowed her to enter first.

The owner's office was about the same size as the clerks' office and featured a large south window and an even larger desk, although a partition wall separated the desk from the rest of the space. The room was paneled in walnut, the wood gleaming in the afternoon sun. The floor was covered in a large carpet of dark green wool. In the back area, a settee and wing chair were positioned in one corner along with a low table, while the other corner held a small library table and chair. Although spare of other decoration, it was elegant and spacious.

"This is beautiful, Mr. Wellingham," Emma breathed as she stood in front of his desk and admired the furnishings.

Thomas moved to his desk and took a quick look at some notes littering the top of it. "Thank you," he replied with a nod. "It still needs... your touch, I suppose," he commented as he glanced around.

"Indeed?" Emma replied absently as she moved to the window and looked out over the crowded river. "You have an incredible view, Mr. Wellingham."

"And I rarely take advantage of it," he replied in an off-hand manner. "It seems I didn't miss much by not being in today," he added as he finished reading the notes.

"Mr. Allen has just pulled up," Emma said. She turned to find Thomas standing very close.

"Miss Emma, I wanted to thank you again for everything you have done for me," he said quietly. "I don't believe I have ever had such a loyal employee."

Emma felt heat rising over her face and ears. "You're very kind to say so, Mr. Wellingham," she replied with a nod, sure her blush was readily apparent.

"About the ball," Thomas continued, remembering he still needed to give her details. "I'll come by with the carriage on Saturday at seven o'clock. We shall have dinner at The Clarendon Hotel and arrive at the Hornsby's by ten," he added quickly. "I'd be honored if you would return with me to Woodscastle and spend another day there. To keep company with Christiana, of course."

Emma's small gasp and look of surprise worried him at first. "I've never had the pleasure of dining at The Clarendon," she marveled. "The entire evening sounds... perfect, Mr. Wellingham."

"And the rest?" he asked nervously. "You'll stay in the guest bedchamber—your bedchamber—of course."

"Oh, of course. I'll be sure to pack a valise, then," she said as she nodded. "Mr. Wellingham," she added as she took a deep breath.

"Thank you. For everything," she said, her heart beating so fast she thought she might faint.

Thomas offered her his arm and they made their way down the steps as Christiana and Gregory, hand-in-hand, walked cautiously into the warehouse. Christiana smiled when she saw her brother and Emma coming down the stairs. "Did you see your office?" she called out happily.

"Indeed," Emma replied with a smile. "It has a window!"

When Thomas and Emma joined the younger couple, Emma said, "There's something I'd like to show you back here, Mr. Grandby." She pointed to the separate room off the warehouse.

Gregory's eyebrows arched up and he eyed Thomas. "Indeed?" he replied with a mischievous grin.

Thomas hurried ahead of the other three and removed the lid from the crate.

"Mr. Wellingham mentioned you would like some decorating help with the..." She stopped, not sure if the purchase of the west wing was supposed to be a surprise for Christiana.

"West wing?" Gregory finished for her. "She knows," he said as he nodded in Christiana's direction.

"He told me all about it," Christiana said, her eyes bright. "We just picked out a wedding ring," she added in a whisper to Emma. "It's really going to happen, Emma. I'm going to be married!"

Emma bit her lip and hugged Christiana. "Oh, I'm so happy for you," Emma whispered as she knelt down in the front of the younger girl. "I hope you like what I have picked out for your master suite and some of the other bedchambers," she said as she stood up and walked over to the crate. Thomas had pulled out one of the bolts and was unwrapping the fabric. Emma reached in and unwrapped some of the blue fabric from another bolt. Holding it out for Christiana to see, she asked, "What do you think of it? 'Tis very expensive," she warned, "But I just know Robert Chipchase and Son could use this to upholster a settee, chairs, whatever you wish," she added as she fingered the brocade. "And there is enough for drapes, as well."

Christiana's mouth was open, and she finally covered it with a hand. "Gregory! Oh, please, can we get them?" she pleaded as she rushed up to the crate to touch the fabric. "How much is it?"

Emma glanced at Thomas and answered, "Ten shillings a yard."

Gregory walked up behind Christiana, wrapping his arms around her and kissing her head. "Of course, we can get them," he said as Christiana looked up at him.

Smiling, she kissed him, the upside-down kiss proving awkward for her betrothed.

"Here now!" Thomas said harshly. "There will be none of that... just yet," he added with a grin.

Blushing at their public display of affection, Emma wrapped the fabric around the bolt and slid it back into the crate. Thomas followed suit but kept his eyes on Emma. Christiana and Gregory started for the front door. "So, how much was this crate?" Thomas asked as he replaced the lid.

"About ninety pounds," she replied in a hoarse whisper.

Staring at her for a moment, he glanced over at Gregory and then at Christiana. Returning his attention to Emma, he smiled and said, "Congratulations on your first sale."

Blushing again, Emma replied sadly, "'Tis probably not the margin you would have received from another buyer, though."

Shaking his head, he offered her his arm. "It's thirty percent!" he replied happily. "I didn't have another buyer. She is my sister. And it's off the books," he added with a grin.

Emma took his arm and Thomas led her out of the warehouse. After helping her into the carriage, Thomas saw that, with all the parcels and Gregory and Christiana, there was little room left for him and Emma to sit. When he noticed Gregory's suspicious grin, he realized it had been planned that way. He took the seat next to Emma, apologizing for the tight fit.

When they returned to Emma's townhouse, Thomas assisted her from the carriage and turned to pick out one of the parcels from the pile as well as the one containing her aqua gown. Emma unlocked the door. As she opened it, he held out the parcels to her, the one containing the white gown on top. "I'd like to give you this as my 'thank you' for attending the ball with me." He thought a moment. "It's white, so I'll understand if you choose not to wear it for the ball," he added, carefully watching the emotions playing out on her face.

Emma's eyes widened at his suggestion. "But, Mr. Wellingham," she countered, her head shaking quickly. "I cannot accept a gift such as this..." she argued in a lowered voice, her face blushing a shade of pink Thomas found rather appealing.

"Why not?" he asked, his expression showing a mix of surprise and concern. The gown obviously fit her quite well, he thought, and although the stark white was not as becoming on her as was the butter colored gown she'd tried on earlier, it was certainly appropriate for a mid-summer ball. And, despite her age, it was appropriate for a woman who had not yet had her come-out. In fact, he reasoned, she might be the only debutante who would attend a ball with an escort who wasn't her brother, father or an elderly aunt. He glanced away for a moment and then returned his attention to Emma.

"If I may," she said in a quiet tone, her lips pursing as if she was deciding whether to press the claim or accept the gown.

Thomas moved closer to Emma. "Why, pray tell, aren't you allowed to accept the gift of a *gown?*" he asked, his voice betraying a hint of impatience.

"A lady is not allowed to accept any apparel as a gift from a gentleman," Emma answered apologetically. "Even so much as a pair of gloves." She took a quick glance in the direction of the carriage and then turned her attention back to Thomas. "Unless she's your... *mistress*," she mouthed more than whispered.

His mouth dropping in disbelief, Thomas replied, "But, you're not!" Motioning toward his future brother-in-law, he added, "He bought gowns for my sister!"

Emma ducked her head and sent a glance in Gregory's direction. "Do you disapprove? I'm sure Suzanne thought... I'm sure she was under the impression they were *married*," Emma whispered in defense of the modiste.

Thomas took a breath, intending to contradict the modiste's impression, and then he thought better of it. *Am I the only one who has a hard time believing my best friend and sister are to one day wed?* "Indeed," he replied with a sigh. "What are my options with regard to the gown? I certainly don't wish to create a scene or cause undo embarrassment to you, but I must insist you have a suitable gown for the Hornsby ball."

Emma's brow lifted and an approving expression made her seem years younger than she was. The Hornsby ball represented one of the only opportunities for those not of the *ton* to attend a gala event suitable for even the Prince Regent. For Thomas to gain an invitation meant he was someone of quality.

Emma leaned over to whisper conspiratorially, "You can be

assured I would never divulge such a gift, if it were given to me, should you wish to override propriety."

Thomas frowned. "I'm your employer!" he countered, his annoyance evident.

Emma's eyes widened dramatically and she directed her attention to her feet. "I should think it perfectly acceptable for you as my employer to purchase a gown for me, sir."

The gown was a beautiful, and it fit quite well and was long enough to hide her ankles. As much as she wanted to wear it for the ball, she knew it was impossible for her to buy it given her own meager funds. "So I accept it, of course. Happily," she added as she stole a glance at Thomas. Then she blushed when she noted how intently he was watching her. She moved to take the parcel from Thomas, handling it as if it were priceless.

"Thank you," Thomas sighed. "Will you wear it to the ball?"

"Oh, of course I'll wear it!" Emma replied as she hugged the package to the front of her body, still awestruck he had purchased the white satin and tulle gown.

Thomas lifted her free hand to his lips and kissed it. "Thank you, Miss Emma," he replied with a nod. "I'll come for you Saturday." With that, he jumped into the carriage as Mr. Allen waved in Emma's direction.

"Thank you, Miss Emma," the driver called out as he tipped his hat.

Emma waved at Mr. Allen and then at Christiana as the younger girl winked at her. "I'll see you at the ball," she called out as the carriage made its way down Kingly Street.

CHAPTER 61
DINNER WITH THE SIMPSONS

July 10, 1802, Great West Road

When the carriage pulled onto the Great West Road, Gregory wrapped his arm around Christiana's shoulders and pulled her to him. His lips hovered over her forehead, and it was a moment before he touched them softly to her skin. "You look beautiful, as always," he whispered. He kissed her hair. He wanted desperately to hold her closer, to cradle her as he had earlier that week, but proprietary prevailed, and he merely hugged her.

Christiana tilted her head and reached up to kiss him on the lips. "I have been wanting to kiss you all day," she said quietly, glancing nervously at Mr. Larsen's back to be sure the driver didn't see her impropriety.

They had engaged in quiet conversation and stolen kisses throughout the week, sometimes in the music room while Christiana played, once in her room while Thomas was in London and Emma worked in the library, and nearly all of Tuesday afternoon when they shared a sorbet from Gunter's Tea Shop in Berkeley Square. Although Christiana had been without a chaperone, those who took notice of them must have thought them married. No one seemed to have given them a second look, nor did anyone they know approach them. "It's like we're hiding in plain sight," Gregory had said with a mischievous grin.

Christiana had sensed something different in Gregory since his return from London on Wednesday, though. That was the day he and Thomas had visited the Bank of England, and Christiana wondered if he had asked her brother for his permission to marry her. When they spent the afternoon walking through the woods and gardens, Christiana half expected him to propose, and although they didn't discuss marriage at first, Gregory did tell her of his plans for Woodscastle.

"I have made arrangements with your brother to purchase half of Woodscastle," he announced as they strolled along the pond on the west side of the grounds. At Christiana's startled look, he added, "The west wing. For us."

Christiana squeezed his hand and stopped walking. "The west wing?" she repeated, her stare turning into a beaming smile. "Oh, Gregory! Thank you!" she exclaimed, awkward pulling him into a hug.

Gregory laughed and wrapped an arm around her shoulders. "Don't thank me yet, my love. There's a good deal of work to be done before it will be livable, I fear," he reminded her, thinking of the day she had given him a tour of the water damaged and time ravaged side of Woodscastle. The master suite would require the least amount of work, but the rooms on the south end of the wing needed replastering, new moldings, and new floors. "I met with an architect yesterday, and a contractor will begin the refurbishing in a day or so," he promised as he surveyed the surroundings to be sure no one was watching them. "The roofers should be here tomorrow. I've made it clear I want the work to be complete before we're married."

Christiana's smile faltered. "Can the room closest to the master suite be the nursery?" she asked, keeping her arms wrapped around his middle.

Gregory arched an eyebrow, remembering what the room arrangements were like at Merriweather Manor. "I think we shall want the babies in our room for a few months," he replied, "And the older children at the end of hall." He wondered how all those aunts and uncles could have had so many children given their youngest was always in their room with them.

Christiana's arms tightened around him, and she felt his body respond to hers. "I wish we were in our master suite right now," she whispered, turning up her head to gaze at him.

His eyes were closed, but there was a beatific smile on his lips. "Indeed," he replied. "However, the next time we make love, it will be on our wedding night, and not before," he added firmly. "And speaking of our wedding, have you given any thought as to where we should go on our wedding trip?" he asked as he moved them to the trunk of an oak tree and sat down against it. He pulled Christiana down next to him and held her so her head was tucked into the small of his shoulder.

Eyes widened, Christiana considered his question. "I'd dearly love to see Cherrywood again," she said. "I've not been there since I was... twelve, I think."

Rolling his eyes, Gregory kissed her head. "So, we can go to Cherrywood. Is there anyplace *else* you'd like to go?" He was secretly hoping she would request a destination on the Continent.

"Where do *you* wish to go?" Christiana countered as she turned her head to look up at him. "Of all the places you have traveled, which is your favorite?"

Gregory leaned his head against the tree trunk and closed his eyes. "Woodscastle," he finally said quietly.

Christiana sat up straight and stared at him. "*Here* is your favorite place?" she asked, disbelief evident in her facial features.

"Of course. 'Tis close to my childhood home, 'tis close to my mother, but not too close, and you are here," he stated with a grin as he leaned over to kiss her.

Blinking, Christiana considered his words as she stared into the tree trunk for a moment. A line of ants was marching up the bark, following the uneven lines as they made their way to somewhere else. When she finally returned her attention to Gregory, she said, "Your mother? She is near here?" she whispered, incredulous. "But Thomas said..."

Gregory bit his lip. "Despite all the claims that have been made about what might have happened to my mother, or where she might have gone, or who she was secretly in love with, she is alive and well and living in the West End. And she has been since she left Merriweather Manor," he said quietly, ending his explanation in a long sigh.

Christiana stared open-mouthed at her beloved. "She didn't take a lover on the Continent?" That had been her favorite version of the story. Although she had never met Sophia Burroughs Grandby, she knew the woman had been the daughter of a duke. She imagined her in the arms of an Italian count, her lover bestowing her with gifts and a life far better than that of a widow in England.

"No," Gregory replied.

"And she didn't go to the States?"

"No," he repeated.

"And you've known she was in London for...how long?"

Gregory leaned back a moment and sighed. "As long as I can remember," he replied with a watery smile. "She very much wants to meet you, although I should warn you she had someone else in mind for me with regard to matrimony." He didn't know if he would ever tell her Emma was the 'someone else,' but he thought it only fair to warn her.

Christiana swallowed hard. "Indeed?" she answered. She was still flustered by the news his mother wasn't missing—or dead. "Why didn't you tell Thomas?" she asked, wondering how he could keep the whereabouts of his mother a secret from his best friend.

Biting his lip, Gregory's face sobered. "She didn't want anyone to know. I promised I would tell no one," he said. "I honored her request."

Why not? she wanted to ask. Instead, she queried, "So, why are you telling *me?*"

Laughing, Gregory shook his head. "Well, it seems that since I've decided to get married to the girl of my dreams, my mother wishes to meet her. I told her I couldn't make a proper introduction unless I could tell you who she was," he explained matter-of-factly, still grinning as he recalled his mother's delight and dilemma over his choice of a wife.

"Girl of your dreams?" Christiana repeated as her face blushed a pleasing shade of pink. "You said that to your *mother?*" Eyes wide and her face still pink, Christiana looked away in embarrassment.

Gregory laughed again and pulled Christiana to his chest. "Yes, I said it," he admitted, chuckling as he held his intended. "I love you. I... dream about you. About us," he whispered as he leaned over to kiss her on the head. He held her for a long time, his lips pressed against her hair.

Suddenly, he sat up straight. "Now, about the matter of our wedding trip," he said as he waited for her to meet his gaze. "I was thinking of taking you to Rome," he said. He watched her face and waited for her reaction, hoping she would be happy.

He wasn't disappointed.

"Rome?" she whispered in awe, "As in... Italy?"

Gregory nodded. "There is only the one, yes," he whispered in delight.

"That would be divine! Oh, thank you," Christiana replied, not knowing what else to say. Remembering the issue of his mother, though, she added, "When will I meet your mother?"

Gregory's shoulders sank as his good mood dampened. "She has asked us to dine with her and Mr. Simpson before the Hornsby ball on Saturday night," he replied, his demeanor suggesting he didn't necessarily agree with the timing.

Christiana's eyes widened again. "That would be capital. But why aren't you pleased?"

Sighing, Gregory looked away for a moment. "Your brother has forbade me from asking for your hand until your birthday. I was *hoping*... well, I was hoping I could introduce you to my mother and her husband as my betrothed. Now, I cannot."

Grinning mischievously, Christiana said, "I won't tell if you don't."

Gregory sat up straight and regarded Christiana with a hint of surprise. "So, you're saying that you would allow me to introduce you as my betrothed?"

Christiana nodded. "Of course!"

The trip into the West End was quick—the streets weren't nearly as crowded as during the daylight hours. Gregory gave Mr. Larsen directions as they made their way on the cobblestone streets. When he gave the last couple of instructions, Christiana took note of their location and realized she recognized the neighborhood. When Gregory instructed Mr. Larsen to stop the carriage, she looked at first to her right and then down the pavement to her left, sure she had been on the street before.

Indeed, just a couple of days before.

"Isn't this Miss Emma's street?" she asked as he lifted her out of the carriage and placed her carefully on the pavement. She turned and spotted the red door—Emma's front door. The pot with the half-eaten flowers was still next to the stoop.

"Indeed, it is," Gregory replied before he gave instructions to Mr. Larsen in a quiet voice. Then he led Christiana to the door with the number 'four' above it and knocked.

"Your mother lives next door to Emma?" Christiana whispered, her breaths coming faster as she regarded Gregory and then glanced up to Emma's bedchamber window. The room was lit, as was the parlor, and she imagined Emma dressing for the ball.

"Yes. She and her husband are Miss Fitzsimmons' landlords, in fact," he explained quietly. "My uncle, Sir William, recommended Miss Fitzsimmons for the townhouse, and once they met her, they quite agreed to the arrangement."

Before Christiana could react to the information about Emma and her landlords, the door opened. A very handsome man, grinning with recognition, bowed and said, "Good evening, Mr. Grandby, do come in."

Christiana preceded Gregory into the small vestibule.

"Miss Christiana Wellingham, I would like to introduce you to my stepfather, Mr. James Simpson," Gregory said with a nod to the older man.

Performing a deep curtsy, Christiana replied, "I'm very pleased to meet you, sir."

James bowed and took her gloved hand, kissing the back of it. "Likewise, I'm certain."

He took Gregory's hat and Christiana's spencer. "I must say, you will be the most beautiful girl at the Hornsby's this evening. I am disappointed Mrs. Simpson and I won't be in attendance."

Christiana's smile changed with his words. "'Tis very kind of you to say, sir. Thank you," she replied, curious as to why the Simpsons wouldn't be at the ball.

"You're looking well, Mr. Simpson," Gregory said as he reached out and shook hands with his stepfather. "So, you decided not to attend again this year, then?"

James shrugged and gave his stepson a grin. "Next year," he said with a wink, his comment suggesting his response would be the same no matter what year is was.

"And how is Mrs. Simpson?" Gregory asked as he glanced toward the corridor, wondering if his mother was within earshot.

James leaned in toward them and lowered his voice. "She is well, but she is... nervous."

Letting out the breath she had been holding, Christiana said, "She cannot be as nervous as I am at this moment."

James chuckled and turned to lead them to the parlor. "There is no need to be, Miss Wellingham, I assure you," he said calmly.

"Is she in the parlor?" Gregory asked quietly.

James nodded and jerked his head to indicate they should follow him into the plush and elegantly decorated parlor off the vestibule.

Christiana inhaled sharply as she entered the room. Scarlet red walls with gold gilt gimping were the perfect backdrop for the white wood and sage green upholstered furnishings. The large window on the west end of the room was draped with velvet swags and lace panels. Despite the mid-summer warmth outside, a small fire crackled in the fireplace. The portrait above the mantel was of a man who bore a striking resemblance to Gregory, and Christiana glanced up to ask who he was and then noticed their hostess standing in front of them.

"How do, Mother," Gregory said with a huge grin as he wrapped his arms around the shoulders of the handsome woman before pulling back a bit to kiss her on the cheek.

Startled, she slapped him on his back, her delicate hands ineffectual against the tall man's frame. "Gregory! We have a guest," she admonished him, but her nervousness was replaced with amusement, and a smile shown on her face.

"I wish you to meet my future wife, Miss Christiana Wellingham," he said as he pulled Christiana forward.

Christiana curtsied and took in the sight of the beautiful woman who was to be her mother-in-law.

"Miss Wellingham, this is my mother, Lady Sophia Simpson."

Sophia curtsied and stepped forward to take the girl into her arms. "'Tis so good to meet the girl who has captured my son's heart," she said graciously.

If the woman thought otherwise, she was certainly good at hiding it, Christiana thought as she felt the woman's arms squeeze her. The scent of her perfume drifted to Christiana's nostrils. The floral and citrus scent was as sophisticated as the woman who wore it. "I'm so very honored to meet the mother of my beloved," Christiana answered as she returned the hug, not sure what else to say.

Sophia stepped back and studied her future daughter-in-law, keeping one hand on Christiana's shoulder. "My, your resemblance to your mother is *striking*," she said as she studied the girl, her head shaking back and forth in disbelief.

At the comment, Christiana's eyes widened. "You... you knew my mother?"

Sophia angled her head and held out her arm to indicate a nearby settee. "Oh, of course. Please, have a seat. Christina had the same color hair, and your eyes are identical," she added as she continued to study Christiana. When she noticed Gregory pressing his lips together, she said, "James... Mr. Simpson will be bringing coffee and walnuts in a moment."

Gregory waited for Christiana to sit down before joining her on the settee, secretly pleased his mother seemed to approve of his intended simply because she reminded her so much of a woman who had been her friend.

"Your brother and Gregory were friends in their youth, so we were acquainted through them," Sophia explained as she sat down in a patterned chair across from them.

James brought in a tray with a plate of shelled walnuts and a coffee service from which steam curled and disappeared in the dimly lit room. "May I have the honor of serving, Mrs. Simpson?"

The sound of hoof beats on cobblestone made their way into the parlor, but the sound suddenly ceased. Sophia didn't reply and simply listened.

"I'll see if we have a visitor," James offered as he reached over and squeezed his wife's hand. James left the parlor to investigate, but came back shaking his head. "It was nothing but a carriage and its well-dressed rider here to call on our neighbor," he announced with a wicked smile as he returned to the parlor. He poured coffees and passed the plate of walnuts to their guests.

"That would be Mr. Wellingham," Gregory said with a nod as he leaned forward. "He's escorting Miss Emma to the ball. I'm sure he has dinner plans as well."

Sophia sat up straighter in her chair, her eyebrows arching. "What an interesting situation," she commented as James took his seat in the chair next to hers.

"Indeed," James replied with a raised eyebrow. He took a walnut and chewed it slowly.

"We had the pleasure of dining at Miss Emma's townhouse just a fortnight ago," Sophia said as she put down her coffee and nodded to Christiana. "I understand she's been your roommate at Warwick's these past couple of years."

Smiling now that the topic had turned to something familiar, Christiana replied, "Indeed. Miss Emma was a great help to me. She is very kind and generous and quite patient."

Sophia turned to James. When she caught his eye, he picked up the conversation. "When we asked if she was going to attend the ball with her Mr. Wellingham, she said that, as he was her employer, she wasn't expecting him to invite her. Can this mean she is no longer employed by Mr. Wellingham?" Although his question started on a happy note, he realized if Emma was no longer employed, she might have to take her leave when her lease ended.

Gregory angled his head as he considered how well the timing of the audit coincided with the ball and Emma's new position. "She is *on holiday*. She'll resume her employment as an accomptant at Wellingham Imports. A week come Monday, in fact," he said with a wry grin. "A rather convenient situation, I should think," he added as he squeezed Christiana's hand.

"Indeed!" Sophia said happily.

James gave a sigh of relief as he eyed his wife. "Will your brother ask for her hand, do you suppose?" he asked as he directed the question to Christiana.

"I can only hope so," she replied with a smile. "I've been encouraging him in that direction for some time," she said as her face took on a pink blush.

"If he doesn't ask her before Sunday is over, I shall do it on his behalf!"

A collective sound of surprise erupted from his audience, and he stopped trying to suppress a smile. "I assure you, mother, Emma Fitzsimmons is the perfect woman for Mr. Wellingham."

Smiling demurely, Sophia replied, "Then you'll finally have the brother you've always wanted." She batted her eyelashes quickly as if to stave off tears.

Struck by the meaning of his mother's words, Gregory simply nodded, a satisfied grin on his face.

"And I shall have the sister I have always wanted," Christiana said with a happy sigh as her shoulders came up around her ears.

"Come, let us eat dinner," James said as he stood up. "Mr. Wellingham's carriage has just departed, and we want to be sure you're at the Hornsby's before they get there, hmm?"

Gregory gave his stepfather a curt nod. "Indeed. Despite my reputation, I have managed to secure his permission to marry his sister, so I had best be sure I'm where I should be this evening."

Smiling, Christiana shook her head. "And by that, you mean we're in the company of a chaperone at Buttenhoff's now having dinner," she commented in a teasing voice.

Matching her smile, Gregory replied, "Indeed we are," he said with a wave of his hand.

Christiana blushed and shared a wink with her future mother-in-law.

CHAPTER 62
DINNER

July 10, 1802, Woodscastle

At five o'clock on Saturday, Thomas Wellingham adjusted the knot in his cravat for the fourth time. He could no longer hear Christiana singing in her room and figured she had departed for the evening. Smiling, he recalled the sight of her hair tied up with tissues a few moments earlier when she had asked for help with buttoning her gown. She had chosen the pale yellow batiste gown Gregory had purchased for her, but was having a hard time deciding on long or short gloves.

On the one hand, Thomas was relieved she and Gregory would be riding to London in the smaller carriage. Gregory had promised to take her to dinner at Buttenhoff's, keep an eye on her during the ball, and to return home with her.

On the other hand, Thomas didn't know if he could trust them once they were out of his sight. Although Christiana had promised Emma she wouldn't elope, the thought it could happen still bothered Thomas. Had there been time, he would have lined up a chaperone for the couple, but anyone who knew him knew Gregory was a family friend and could act as her protector in his stead.

"Your carriage awaits, sir," Humphrey announced as he entered Thomas' room.

Thomas tried to suppress a sudden grin. "You say that as if you have wanted to say it your entire life," he teased.

The butler bowed and angled his head as he studied his master.

"Perhaps I have. Let me get this for you," he offered as he undid the white cravat and then tied it into a perfect mail coach knot.

"I must speak with you about the household staff," Thomas said as he watched his butler in the reflection from the tall mirror.

Humphrey paused in his appraisal of the waistcoat Thomas wore. "Of course, sir."

"We need to find a manservant for Mr. Grandby, a housekeeper for the west wing, and another servant or two for the household staff," Thomas said quickly. "And if she is available for more work, we should hire Miss Dahlia full-time," he added, pulling on the ends of his sleeves. "Has Mr. Larsen asked for her hand in marriage yet?" he asked then, not allowing the butler to respond to the first requests.

"Sir, he has not. He... he says he must save some money before he marries," Humphrey replied uncomfortably. "Two pounds, I believe he said, since he must arrange quarters for the two of them. The space above the stables is hardly suitable for a woman, you understand."

Thomas nodded. "There will be suitable quarters for them in the west wing when Mr. Grandby's contractor has completed the repairs," he stated. "Mr. Grandby is buying the west wing, you see." At the butler's astonished stare, Thomas added, "I keep the parlor on the east side and we share the library, dining room, the stables, and the grounds." He felt satisfaction as Humphrey's expression turned to one of joy. "See to it Mr. Larsen, and, well, all the servants and yourself are given a two-pound bonus," he commanded with a nod. "And tell Mr. Larsen to make Miss Dahlia a proper proposal," he added, thinking Christiana's favorite servant would be more likely to agree to full-time work if she were married and living in Woodscastle.

"I will do so, Mr. Wellingham," the butler agreed with a nod.

The thought of marriage reminded Thomas of something else. "Has Mrs. Werthers seen to the master suite? I believe I'll be moving in soon," he murmured.

"She has. And I'll see to the other staffing needs right away. Is there... anything else, sir?" he asked as he resumed his straightening of Thomas' waistcoat sleeves.

"I seem to be missing something," Thomas said as he studied his reflection in the mirror again.

"Your hat and cane are in the vestibule. Mr. Grandby and Miss Wellingham are already on their way," Humphrey replied as he brushed invisible lint from Thomas' shoulder.

Thomas rolled his eyes. "I look like one of those birds that live in the cold regions," he complained as he studied his reflection in the oval looking glass.

"I assure you, sir, you are far better looking than a penguin," Humphrey replied with a frown. "May I ask if you're escorting anyone to the ball?" he asked as he walked around his master, ensuring the topcoat and waistcoat were both properly buttoned.

"Miss Emma has accepted my invitation," Thomas replied with a nod as he glanced again into the cheval mirror.

Humphrey struggled not to smile too broadly. "Very good choice, if I may say, sir," he commented as he fussed with Thomas' cuff links. He wanted to say more, but in his position and with the other news he'd been told, he decided it wouldn't be appropriate.

Thomas noticed his butler's hesitation. "And?" he said expectantly. When Humphrey merely returned his gaze, Thomas sighed. "Please continue with what you were about to say," he said, wanting the elder man's advice.

Humphrey took a deep breath. "She would make an excellent mistress for this house, sir," he finally spoke, careful as to how he made his comment. "The staff likes and respects her. Miss Wellingham adores her. And, if I may say so sir, I believe you do as well."

Thomas looked nervous and nodded. "I do, Humphrey," he agreed. "Thank you for your candor." After a pause, he said, "And what about Miss Emma, do you suppose?"

It took every muscle in Humphrey's face to maintain control and keep his impassive expression. "The feeling is mutual, I am sure," he stated in a bored voice.

Nervous, Thomas stared as his butler. "You're sure? Or are you assuring me?" he murmured, a hint of amusement coming to his face. The butler finally allowed a grin but didn't give a reply. Thomas noticed the time on the mantel clock. "I really must leave if I'm to call on her at seven o'clock."

Before leaving his bedchamber, though, Thomas stopped in front of the tall chest of drawers. The multi-jeweled brooch and matching earrings were in the top drawer, he remembered.

Purchased on a whim when he noticed them in the window of a jeweler on New Bond Street years ago, he had squirreled them away thinking they would one day be a gift for his sister. The pieces were far too sophisticated for Christiana, though.

He quickly pulled out the box and opened it, deciding the brooch would look appropriate on Emma's satin and tulle gown. He paused as he considered how improper it might be for him to give her jewelry, though. She wasn't a member of the family, although as a close friend of his sister's, he felt justified in bestowing the bauble on her.

Chastising himself for not having a velvet purse or a ribbon to decorate the box, he stuffed it into his waistcoat pocket and hurried from the room.

In the vestibule, he grabbed his hat and cane and hurried out to the barouche. Mr. Allen tipped his hat and waited until his master was seated before he cracked his riding crop, sending the horse on its way.

It was nearly an hour later when they pulled up to Emma's town-house. Thomas checked his pocket watch and decided it would be acceptable to wait a few minutes before going to the door. He noticed a curtain move, though, and changed his mind. "Mr. Allen," he called to his driver. "I'll require assistance with Miss Emma's valise," he said as he stepped down from the barouche.

The driver jumped down to the street. "Very good, sir," he said with a smile.

"You seem rather pleased, Mr. Allen," Thomas commented as they walked to the door.

"Oh, yes, sir," the driver replied. "If I may say so, I very much like Miss Fitzsimmons. Always bringing me baked goods for taking care of her 'orse," he said, his Cockney accent making it hard to understand some of his words.

"Indeed?" Thomas replied as he pounded the knocker on the door. *No wonder the staff likes her,* he realized. *She's probably been feeding them all.* "I do hope you aren't expecting anything this evening. I'm quite certain Miss Emma has been preoccupied with her preparations for the ball and all."

The door opened and Emma stood to one side. "Good evening, gentlemen. Please, do come in," she said as the two men bowed. She curtsied. When Mr. Allen didn't make a move toward the door, she motioned him to come in.

Thomas gazed at the woman who wore the white satin tulle gown and long white gloves he had given her the day before yesterday. It was another moment before he realized she was also wearing the gold teardrop earrings he had given her for being his nursemaid.

Her hair was arranged in a chignon on the top and back of her head, but several ringlets spilled from the sides. A row of tiny white flowers lined each turn of the chignon and one crossed the top of her tightly wound hair. He was speechless as he took in the sight of her.

"You look like an angel," Mr. Allen whispered as he held his hat in his hand, the words coming out before he could think to censor them.

Thomas' first reaction to his driver's comment might have been one of annoyance, but instead, he nodded in agreement. "Indeed, Miss Emma, you do look like an angel," he said quietly. How was he going to comport himself for an entire evening with such a beautiful woman at his side?

Embarrassed, Emma blushed and nodded at the two men. "Thank you. I really am ready, but I do need to fetch something from the kitchen. Please, have a seat in the parlor," she said as she curtsied and hurried to the back of the townhouse.

The driver remained by the front door while Thomas took a seat in the parlor. On the table next to the chair lay an opened letter and a twenty-pound note. Curious, he tried to find a return address or signature, but couldn't do so without moving the paper. *Twenty pounds!* he thought. *Who would send an unmarried woman that kind of money by post?*

A thought struck him, sending his stomach to the floor. *Is she someone's mistress?* He remembered Samuel Morton's comment about the girl in the hat shop. Twenty, living alone and unchaperoned, it was certainly a possibility, although not for Morton.

The stab of jealousy hurt. Emma had no servants, at least none he had seen, and she hadn't mentioned employing any. As a mistress, she would certainly enjoy the benefits of enough pin money to afford them as well as jewelry and gowns and all manner of frippery.

She doesn't have much jewelry at all, his sister had said the night after the housebreakers arrived.

A mistress would definitely have jewelry.

Remembering the brooch, Thomas removed the box from his waistcoat and opened it. He was staring at it, mesmerized by the multicolored facets and the shards of light reflected from them, when Emma returned from the kitchen with a small basket on one arm and a long length of white tulle and small reticule draped over the other.

Thomas stood up as she handed the basket to Mr. Allen and said, "I wasn't sure if you would have the opportunity to eat a proper dinner this evening. Oh, and my valise is right there," she said as she pointed to a small bag next to the front door.

Mr. Allen smiled broadly as he took the basket. "Much obliged, Miss Emma," he said happily. "I'll be at the barouche, Mr. Wellingham," he said as he proudly took the basket and the valise out the front door.

Emma joined Thomas in the parlor and sat in the chair on the other side of the same table that held the letter. "If I may be allowed to say, you are looking very handsome this evening, Mr. Wellingham," she said as she held her gloved hands together in her lap.

Thomas smiled and nodded, suddenly nervous and at a loss for words. He sat up straight and then leaned an arm on the chair. "I would be honored if you would wear this on your gown this evening," Thomas said as he held out the brooch.

Emma gasped, immediately recognizing the piece of jewelry from when she had seen it in the top drawer of his bureau. "'Tis beautiful, Mr. Wellingham," she breathed. She reached out, her gloved fingers barely touching the brooch as it lay in his hand. "But... shouldn't your sister be wearing this?" she asked in awe, her eyes finally meeting his.

"No. I wish for you to have it," he said simply.

"Have it?" she repeated, her eyes widening in surprise.

At his insistence, Emma finally took the brooch from his hand. As she pulled her arm back, the fabric of her glove snagged the letter and the twenty-pound note, pulling them to the edge of the table. Thomas quickly reached over and repositioned the letter to the middle of the table, noticing the signature of *Mr. William Smith* at the bottom of the letter.

"Oh, thank you," Emma said as she picked up the twenty-pound note with her other hand and held it. After a moment of contemplation, she folded it and slid it into her reticule and then attached the brooch to her gown. "Do I have it positioned correctly?" she asked, angling her head as she tried to see it better.

"Yes, but I think it would look even better if you wore these with it," Thomas commented as he held out the matching earrings.

Emma inhaled sharply and swallowed hard when she looked at the earrings he dangled over the table. "You are far too generous, Mr. Wellingham," she said.

More jewelry! Didn't the man know how truly wrong it was to be giving her baubles?

Knowing better than to argue with Thomas Wellingham, she took the teardrop earrings from her ears and inserted the wires of the multi-jeweled set in their place. Grinning, she turned to find Thomas with an odd expression on his face. "Is something wrong?" Emma asked, her grin fading.

Thomas shook his head and finally said, "I am speechless. I thought my sister might be the most beautiful girl at the ball tonight, what with her yellow gown and those tissues tied all over her head ...," he described in a teasing voice as he waved his hands out on either side of his head.

Emma covered her mouth with a hand as she tried to suppress a giggle. "They're a sight, aren't they?" she agreed. "But her hair looks lovely after they're all pulled out," she assured him with a nod.

"But you," Thomas continued, "You will be the most beautiful woman at the ball."

Emma held her breath a moment, rather stunned by the words. Reaching over with a gloved hand, she touched his arm. "You are very kind to say it, but remember, it was you who bought the gown and jewels." *The kinds of gifts a man bestows on a mistress,* she thought.

Is that what he has planned for me?

Shaking his head, Thomas found his attention returning to the letter. "We should be taking our leave," he said as he stood up and reached out a hand to Emma.

Perched on the edge of her chair, Emma took his hand and held it between her two gloved hands before she kissed the knuckles. "Thank you," she said, her eyes suddenly bright. If a position as a mistress was all he could offer her, Emma knew she would accept it. Gladly, in fact, if it meant being able to spend her nights with the man. A sudden frisson shook her body, its tendrils of pleasure reaching from her breasts to her toes and leaving a blush of pink in its wake.

Thomas stared at her for a moment before nodding. "It's my pleasure," he murmured as he offered his arm. Standing, Emma took his arm and allowed him to lead her to the front door. She took a key off the umbrella stand, locked the door behind them, and slid the key into her reticule.

Situated in the center of the West End, the Clarendon Hotel included a grand dining room featuring large Greek columns, marble tile floors, tables of ebony wood, and upholstered dining chairs of the utmost comfort. The establishment served its specialties on Wedgwood china. Waterford crystal decorated the tables. The waiters, better dressed than some of the patrons, were discrete and attentive, but careful to keep their distance when circumstances required. The chefs, trained on the Continent, prepared game meats and sauces of impeccable taste and texture.

Thomas led Emma through the front doors as they were held open by two liveried footmen. The odors of fresh baking bread and grilled meats hung in the air. A host approached Thomas and spoke softly with him before leading them to a table for two against a marble wall. Stunned by the expensive décor and sheer scale of the place, Emma could only follow the host and try very hard to keep her mouth from gaping.

The host pulled out her chair and she sat down, amazed at how comfortable it was. Thomas sat across from her and took the menu from the host. "We will start with a bottle of champagne, please," he said as he looked over the list of items. "A plate of the fruits, and a loaf of whatever bread it is I smell baking."

The host nodded. "Very good, sir."

Thomas leaned forward as he held the menu. "What do you like?" he asked Emma as he perused the list of entrées.

"Do they have pheasant?" she asked, not really caring what she ate. She was so hungry, she thought she could eat anything.

Thomas nodded. "Of course," he answered, "Although, now that I think of it, we'll probably have that for dinner tomorrow evening," he commented absently.

"Are you hunting tomorrow?" Emma asked as she took a drink of water. A slice of lemon bobbed on the surface.

Thomas seemed surprised by her question. "Of course not," he replied. "Mr. Grandby is, though. I have invited you to spend the next two days at Woodscastle. I would be a poor host to leave you at the house, unless you would care to join Mr. Grandby and me? I rather imagine you could take down a bird or two," he suggested, a hint of tease in his voice.

Emma shook her head. "I'm quite sure Christiana and I can find some amusement in the music room," she countered with a coy smile.

A waiter approached with a bottle of champagne, undid the wrapping, and expertly popped the cork. Foam poured from the bottle and into a white linen as he filled their glasses. "Thank you," Thomas said as the waiter placed the bottle into a bucket of ice. When he left, Thomas held up his glass and Emma copied his action. "To a beautiful night," he said and touched his glass against hers.

They sipped the champagne at the same time, but Emma had to stop as bubbles tickled her nose. "What else do they make here?" she asked as she tried to take another sip.

Thomas studied the list again and tossed the menu onto the table. "Do you trust me?" he asked.

Taken aback, Emma sat up straight in her chair. "Of course," she replied, though her hands gripped the edge of the table.

The waiter approached with the fruits and bread, a display of artistry and color that delighted Emma. "And what may I get for your main courses, sir?" he asked as he set the plates in the middle of the table.

"We'll have the sliced ham, scalloped potatoes, and vegetables," Thomas answered as he glanced at Emma.

The waiter said, "Very good, sir," and disappeared.

Emma was still studying the fruit tray, admiring the shapes of the cut fruit. Removing her gloves, she used her small fork to stab a piece of apple and place it into her mouth. "This is delicious," she murmured. "There is some sort of honey sauce on it." She tried to determine the ingredients from the flavor and found she couldn't immediately make out the recipe. "Boiled sugar and lemon, a bit of cinnamon. I cannot make out what the other flavor is, though," she said.

Impressed she could determine flavors so quickly, Thomas took a piece of pear. "I believe it's some kind of nut oil," he offered.

"Walnut!" Emma announced with a triumphant smile. "I shall have to make this."

Thomas smiled and shook his head. At Emma's questioning glance, he shrugged. "'Tis Christiana's favorite dish," Thomas said as he helped himself to a hunk of bread. "And Mr. Tanner doesn't know how to make it."

Emma leaned forward. "She has never mentioned eating here," she said quietly. How had the girl kept the place a secret?

"Oh, she hasn't had it here," Thomas replied. "Over at Reagan's," he nodded as he indicated with a wave a public house just down the street.

Smiling, Emma said, "That's her favorite place. She talks about the food for days after you take her there," she added as she helped herself to more fruit. "Will Mr. Grandby be taking her there for dinner tonight?"

Thomas shook his head and wiped his mouth with his napkin. "They're going to Buttenhoff 's," he replied. "Are you familiar with it?"

Startled at the name of her father's favorite tavern, she nodded. "Of course. It's just down the street from my father's hat shop," she said, and then added, "Well, *Fitzsimmons and Smith*, I should say." She sat quietly, lost in thought. *It's no longer his shop*, she considered sadly. *Nor mine. Or my sister's, whoever she might be.*

"Is something wrong?" Thomas asked when he noticed she had stopped eating. She seemed, in fact, to be having rather unpleasant thoughts. *What did I say to cause her such consternation?*

Emma sighed. "It's a rather auspicious day, I suppose," she replied, blushing at having been caught in a reverie. "I received the last payment for *Fitzsimmons* today. The hat shop belongs entirely to Mr. William Smith now," she stated, her expression betraying her sadness.

Relieved by the simple explanation for the twenty-pound note, Thomas nodded. "You'll continue to take in some money from the business, though," he reminded her.

"'Tis true. Mr. Smith has agreed to pay me a royalty for the use of the Fitzsimmons name," she said with a nod. After a moment, she shrugged and helped herself to more of the fruit.

Thomas hesitated before deciding it was all right to tell her about his deal with the hat maker. "You should know it could be a substantial amount given his success with the business," he said quietly. Leaning forward, he continued, "As you're aware, I made a deal with Mr. Smith for transporting wool from northern England," he explained as he pulled off a hunk of bread from the loaf. "Those ten coaches we run are now filled—every trip—and most of the ship- ments are wool that is delivered directly to his shop to make felt."

Emma angled her head. "Indeed?"

Thomas nodded. "One of the ship captains whom I employ, Captain Harding, does two trips to the States during the best sailing season each year. We used to just import turpentine from the Carolinas and tobacco from Virginia, but when Mr. Smith mentioned his need for beaver, well, I added that to the shipping request. Captain Harding just returned from the States last week. The next ledger will show a huge inventory for the skins, but every one of them is scheduled to be purchased by Mr. Smith."

Stunned, Emma shook her head. "I'm so happy to hear it worked out for the both of you," she said quietly, still a bit melancholy over the loss of the shop. "It's where I first learned to keep books, you see," she said quietly, realizing even as she said it, the comment would make no sense.

Nodding, Thomas bit his lip. "I thought perhaps there was a woman behind your father's success," he acknowledged with a nod. "And without having been an accomptant, how would you know you wanted to pursue it as an occupation?" he reasoned, helping himself to more fruit.

Emma angled her head to one side and allowed a wan smile. "I do adore numbers," she admitted. Then she remembered to ask about Todd and Deborah. "Do you know if the Vandermeers returned from their wedding trip today? Will they be at the ball?"

Leaning forward, Thomas replied, "I received a post from Mr. Vandermeer yesterday. They do indeed intend to be at the ball tonight, but their return is earlier than expected. It seems a matter at the John Company cut short their time at Cherrywood. Nasty bit of news, I'm afraid," he added.

"Is something wrong?" Emma asked, hoping the problem wouldn't affect Todd personally.

Thomas leaned in and lowered his voice. "It seems one of Mr. Vandermeer's colleagues imported a rather large number of gowns from France, and now he's unable to consign as many as he was led to believe would sell into modistes. The broker claims Mr. Vandermeer encouraged him to make the deal for the gowns, and now he wants Mr. Vandermeer to take the blame for the overbuy."

Covering her mouth with one hand, Emma thought for a moment. "Would they be... *transparent gowns*, by chance?" she asked, a worried look on her face.

Cocking an eyebrow, Thomas regarded Emma. "Yes, as a matter of fact," he replied. "How are you familiar with the deal?"

Emma sighed and put her hand down. "Not the deal, of course, but I remember him asking Miss White and me what we thought of such a fashion when we had dinner with him," she admitted, her face still showing worry.

"Did you...?" Thomas started to ask, not quite sure how to phrase his query.

"He wondered in Society who might wear such gowns and what shops might carry them," Emma said, "and we gave him our thoughts on the topic. I admit, I'm surprised his colleague still went through with the deal. I do hope this problem has not ruined their holiday in the country," she added. Sometimes travel could be hard on a couple, and she hoped they still loved each other as much as they had on their wedding day. "Did Mr. Vandermeer mention if they were both well?"

Thomas recalled the short note. "Todd says his wife is incandescent in the country and his knees have not given him pain for their entire trip," he stated with a grin. "All in all, I think they're doing quite well."

Grinning at the news, Emma remembered the night she had found Deborah on her doorstep and wondered how such simple misunderstandings could lead to such drama.

The arrival of their dinner plates brought her out of her reverie. "Thank you," she said as the waiter positioned the plate on the charger in front of her.

Thomas thanked the waiter as he poured more champagne and refilled the wine goblets. "I don't believe I mentioned it after the Vandermeer's wedding feast, but I had the opportunity to meet the elder Vandermeers," Thomas said, his mouth suggesting he was amused by what he was about to say. At Emma's arched eyebrow, he added, "You were discussing business with Gregory at the time."

Emma nodded as she recalled the conversation and Gregory's insistence that he would be reviewing the accounting practices of all the companies in which he held investments.

"I was sure I recognized Mrs. Vandermeer," he said simply.

Emma smiled. "And?" she prompted when he didn't continue right away.

Smiling, Thomas nodded. "She was Helen Tennison. Adelyn Tennison's sister."

Gasping, Emma covered her mouth with a hand. "How did she not know about Todd when he was born? Surely her sister would have mentioned having a baby!"

Thomas regarded Emma for a moment, his expression unreadable. "I was rather hoping you would first ask why it was I recognized her," he stated congenially, "However—"

"Why did you recognize her?" Emma interrupted, her face blushing as she grinned.

Angling his head to one side, Thomas replied, "She was a cousin to my mother and spent a good deal of time with some of the Merriweather ladies at Merriweather Manor. This was before she was married, of course," he added before falling silent.

When he didn't continue, Emma leaned forward. "And?" she encouraged him, her curiosity piqued.

Thomas frowned and sighed. "It seems Adelyn disappeared after her marriage to William Vandermeer. Helen said they all assumed she eloped and ran off to save the family from scandal, never to be heard from again," he stated evenly.

"Oh, my God," Emma breathed, her amused expression replaced with one of sadness. "One would think Adelyn would have at least written or sent a courier with news. Or that William would have sent word to his brother about their marriage."

Shrugging, Thomas was quiet a moment. "I believe an army officer would have been overprotective of his new wife during a war," he said casually. "I understand life was a bit more chaotic at the time. Especially when he was sent to the Colonies so soon after their wedding." He took a taste of his ham and chewed a moment. "Anyway, Todd is happy to at least know more about her and his father, as well," he said lightly.

"The timing couldn't have been better," Emma commented when she had finished a bite of her ham.

Thomas nodded. "May I inquire as to why you asked if I knew of an aristocrat's wife named Caroline?"

Emma blinked. And blinked again as she considered how to respond. "I have a sister," she finally replied. As Thomas sat back and regarded her with a look of consternation, she added. "I found letters addressed to my father from a woman named Caro. Caroline. She was in love with him. Had an *affaire* with him. Gave birth to a baby girl."

Thomas shook his head, rather stunned at the news. "Caroline

Fitzsimmons?" he whispered. "She's the only one I could find married to a man with a name beginning with an 'M'," he added when he saw her expression of surprise. "I meant to tell you some time ago."

Emma nodded, realizing the woman in question had to be her Aunt Caroline.

"She had the babe before she married Lord Chamberlain. When her sister and brother-in-law died in an accident, she was able to claim the baby was her niece. She and my uncle have been raising her as such ever since," she explained quickly.

Samantha Fitzsimmons. "Have you paid a call on her?" Thomas asked.

Shaking her head, Emma said, "Not yet. Samantha is only eight years old. I thought perhaps—"

"Pay a call on your aunt, at least," Thomas interrupted, realizing the child would be too young to understand. "Take her the letters. Tell no one else what you've told me. Let her decide when it's *appropriate* for you to meet your sister."

Emma's eyes widened at his instructions. "But..."

"She's a *viscountess*," Thomas whispered. "She'll be far more accommodating if you don't create a scandal."

Stunned by his words, Emma realized he had a point. "She may have borne my uncle an heir and a spare," she said with a wan smile. "So I might have cousins now. Perhaps I'll pay a call to meet them," she added as her mood lightened. "Thank you for the recommendation. I shouldn't wish to do anything rash." She returned her attention to her plate, glad to have a plan in place regarding her sister.

Thomas nodded, deciding he needed to change the subject. "I do hope you like the ham," he mentioned as he cut another slice of meat. "I've found myself craving it for several days."

Emma smiled as she tried the potatoes. "I like it, too," she said as she tried to determine what ingredients made up the luscious cream sauce. "Especially for breakfast," she added. "My butcher lets me buy a small portion. Even if I have my neighbors for dinner, I couldn't begin to use up an entire ham," she commented. Taking another bite of the meat, she smiled as she recognized the flavors of molasses and cloves. "This is very delicious," she added.

"Indeed," Thomas replied. "Now, you must tell me about these neighbors of yours. How is it they get the benefit of your good cooking?" he asked, remembering the afternoon of Grandby's arrival at Woodscastle. "We nearly followed you home that night you were hosting them for dinner," he said with amusement.

Emma giggled. "I was rather afraid you might," she admitted, putting down her fork. "I certainly had enough food, as it happened," she recalled. "My neighbors, James and Sophia Simpson, are an older couple. Not something you see of much in town these days. He used to be a butler for an estate west of London. He mentioned knowing Mr. Vandermeer when he was a child. I'm not sure from where Mrs. Simpson came, but she speaks fondly of Derbyshire, and she has the bearing of a woman born to the upper class. Even at forty... perhaps fifty, she is a very beautiful woman," Emma remarked. "Apparently, when the estate owner died, they inherited a fair sum that allowed them to move to town and buy all the buildings on my street," she explained as she returned her attention to her plate and resumed eating.

Thomas paused his fork in mid-air. "Simpson, did you say? Did he work for the Merriweathers, by chance?" he asked, setting his fork on the edge of his plate.

Emma thought for a moment. "Yes, I believe that's correct," she said as she tried to recall the conversation. "I think the name of the estate was Merriweather Manor," she remembered. "I get the impression 'tis very near to Woodscastle, although I don't know in which direction."

"Good Lord," Thomas said. "Do you know who *lived* at Merriweather Manor?" he asked with a huge grin on his face.

Emma shook her head. Other than having heard the name of the matriarch, Mary Margaret Merriweather Grandby—she had been the Countess of Torrington—, Emma didn't know the identities of any of the other Merriweathers or their immediate family. Then she recalled Mr. Simpson's mention of Michael, the one who had to sell his house to Todd Vandermeer in order to pay his gambling debts.

"Grandby," he answered, nearly laughing. "The Merriweathers were his paternal grandmother's family. He spent most of his youth there. As did I, come to think of it." After a moment, he added, "Now I wish we had followed you home. Could you imagine the looks on those poor people's faces when they meet Gregory Grandby as an adult?" he asked rhetorically. "Drunk?" he added in a whisper.

Grinning, Emma placed a hand over her mouth. "And that's how you know him? Because you lived nearby?" Then she recalled just why they had wanted her to meet Mr. Grandby.

You would have been a most handsome couple, Sophia had said.

They already know *Gregory Grandby as an adult*, Emma reasoned, startled by the revelation.

Thomas grinned and nodded. "Yes," he replied. "He had dozens of cousins. I think the countess must have had eight or nine children with Gregory's grandfather—he was the Earl of Torrington, you see—and most of them lived there with their own broods. Including Milton Grandby, the new Earl of Torrington, by the way. He's a cousin to Gregory. As are all the grandchildren of the Duke of Ariley, come to think of it."

He paused to think a moment as Emma displayed a look of surprise at learning Gregory was related so closely to the aristocracy. A thought of *aren't we all?* crossed his mind when he considered that his cousin, Graydon, was the Earl of Trenton. And Matthew Fitzsimmons, Viscount Chamberlain, was Emma's uncle.

"Gregory's father, Roger, was the youngest of Mary Margaret's children. He died when Gregory was... three, I think he was. And then, when we were six or seven perhaps, his mother disappeared rather suddenly. As did her inheritance. It was all very mysterious."

Emma put down her fork. "Was she ever found?" she asked in alarm.

Thomas shook his head. "Never. At least, I haven't heard anything about it since."

"Who was she?"

"Her name was Sophia." He paused for a second as he thought of something. "Sophia Burroughs," he said with a grin of realization. "Yes, that's it," he added, now understanding how Gregory and Sir William were related. He shook his head after a moment and continued, "Many believed she found a lover after her husband died and simply took her inheritance and left England for another country."

Sir William Burroughs, Emma thought. *Sophia's brother?* Shaking her head, Emma said, "But to leave her child behind? That doesn't seem like something a mother would do," she commented sadly.

Shrugging, Thomas took a sip of champagne. "She left him in good company, though," he said in the woman's defense. "Gregory had the best education, and he was with family. A good deal of family. Probably why Mr. Simpson left their employ soon after Sophia disappeared. Poor chap probably couldn't handle another charge," he said with a grin. "Gregory may not have even realized his mother had gone missing," he added as an afterthought.

But he also remembered when Gregory sorted his mother wasn't coming back. After months of telling Thomas about trips his mother was taking, Gregory finally admitted she was either dead or had abandoned him completely. And yet, the boy never seemed bitter or particularly sad over his loss, and Thomas decided perhaps the woman had done his friend a favor.

Emma angled her head. "So, Mr. Simpson *resigned?*" she asked, her brows furrowing again.

Thomas nodded as he remembered the series of events that rocked Merriweather Manor. "Yes, just a couple of months after Gregory's mother disappeared." He paused as he regarded her with concern. "Emma, are you all right?" Then he heard her sudden inhalation of breath.

"Well," she started to say and then stopped. "'Tis just that the way Mr. Simpson tells it, he was still in Mrs. Grandby's employ when she died, and that's why he received an inheritance," she said, still a bit confused.

Thomas shook his head. "I cannot imagine Mary Margaret giving anything to a servant they didn't earn," he replied with a frown. "Besides, most of that estate was probably entailed. And why give anything to a butler when she had eight children? She was a tightwad if there..."

Emma stared at Thomas as he stared back. "Do you suppose...?" she started to ask and then bit her lip.

Thomas shook his head. "It cannot be," he replied as the hairs on the back of his neck stood on end.

"The Simpsons didn't buy the buildings on Kingly Street with *his* inheritance," she whispered.

"You are saying they bought them with *hers?*" Thomas concluded as he sat back in his chair. "You believe the butler married Sophia Burroughs Grandby?"

Emma nodded quickly. "Yes. Yes, I do. It all makes sense, Mr. Wellingham. Mr. Grandby's estate is in Derbyshire, is it not?" she asked, understanding now why Sophia would speak of it so fondly.

Sighing, Thomas leaned forward. "Cherrywood. Yes, it is," he replied, deciding to allow her the line of reasoning.

"And Mr. Simpson said they had just returned from a holiday there, and that they stayed in *her* family's estate," Emma said with a nod.

Thomas finished his champagne. "Well, Cherrywood is one of the Burroughs' family estates," he considered, shaking his head, still in a bit of disbelief. "They go there for the Christmas holiday."

"And she said her son had taken up residence there!" Emma said with excitement. She drained her champagne glass.

Pressing his lips together, Thomas sighed. Gregory hadn't mentioned his mother in twenty years. Perhaps he had known exactly where she was all along.

"But why keep her a secret?" Thomas took a deep breath. "Let us say Sophia Simpson is, indeed Sophia Burroughs Grandby Simpson. Why disappear? And why the mystery?" he asked in dismay. Watching Emma's changing expressions amused him, but his amusement quickly turned to something more serious as he noticed a slight blush, probably from the champagne, color her cheeks and the tops of her breasts. *God, she's lovely.*

Emma stared at her mind's eye for a moment. When she finally focused on Thomas, she leaned forward and said, "Her marriage to Roger Grandby was probably arranged when she was a young girl. After he died, she fell in love. She fell in love with the *butler*," she countered in a hoarse whisper. "And James Simpson told me his wife had begged him..." she paused and shut her mouth, embarrassed by what the man had said.

An eyebrow arched in expectation as Thomas regarded her. "His wife had begged him to do *what* exactly?" he prompted.

"Marry him!" Emma stated, her attention on something far away. "Sophia came from wealth, she'd been in an arranged marriage, but she fell in love with him and begged him to marry her!"

Nodding, Thomas considered her story. He still wondered at some of the details. He finally shook his head. "I suppose it could be her," he said doubtfully.

"What would have happened had her family—had the countess —discovered her marriage? To a butler?" Emma asked, not giving up.

Sitting back in his chair, Thomas angled his head. "I see your point."

"And they were most disappointed during dinner. Especially Mrs. Simpson. They had hoped they could introduce Mr. Grandby to *me* when he was next in London, but while they were in Derbyshire, he informed them he was already in love with another."

Thomas sat up straighter. "Indeed?" He thought for a moment. Gregory had barely acknowledged Christina when he arrived at Woodscastle. Had Gregory hidden his interest in Christiana that first week because the two were keeping their relationship a secret from him? If so, they had certainly done a damned good job of it.

As if they'd had experience.

Well, Gregory certainly did if he'd been keeping his mother's whereabouts secret all these years.

Then Thomas recalled the rest of Emma's comment.

"His very own mother tried to arrange a marriage with *you?*" he repeated as he sighed and shook his head in disbelief.

Offended, Emma's eyes widened. "You don't have to make it sound so *awful!*" She glanced around, wondering if anyone would notice if she took her leave of the dining room.

Blinking, Thomas shook his head. "Awful for *you*. To be married to Gregory, I meant," he said, a pang of jealousy gripping him until he remembered Christiana would be marrying his best friend. The jealousy was replaced with pity on his sister's behalf. "I do hope Mrs. Simpson isn't too disappointed when she meets my sister."

At his clarification, Emma relaxed back into her chair and finally allowed a wan smile. "She won't be, Mr. Wellingham. I was very complimentary in my description of your sister, I assure you."

Thomas was still bothered by the revelation, though. "It seems to me that someone in London would have recognized her by now, don't you suppose? She couldn't have stayed hidden in plain sight all these years," he started to say, and then decided that, well, maybe she could.

Emma's eyes widened, remembering the letters she'd found in the escritoire. Her own half-sister was hiding in plain sight. *She's eight years old*, remembering the date of the letter where Caro mentioned her daughter's age. *Samantha*.

Realizing Thomas expected her to respond to his question, Emma pulled herself out of her reverie. "Oh, dear. I wonder if I said something awful about Mr. Grandby that night?" she asked rhetorically, a look of consternation on her face. When she noticed Thomas' quizzical expression, she continued. "I must admit, Mr.

Wellingham, I wasn't the least bit impressed by him that first day. But the Simpsons described him in a far better light than his reputation would afford. I believe the comment Mr. Simpson made about him was his saying, 'My requirements are few. A girl in every port…'"

"… And port after dinner," Thomas finished for her, sighing and shaking his head. "Yes, yes. And to think, I believed his bunk for all these years, too. Here he is, a wealthy man who has apparently only been with one woman—other than my sister," he quickly amended, unaware his line of conversation was wholly inappropriate. "—His entire life." At Emma's raised eyebrow, he added very quietly as his face flushed, "There was this older cousin who took delight in having her way with the boys in the family."

Smiling to cover her embarrassment, Emma said, "Once Mr. Grandby explained his motives to me, I found… I found I rather liked him. But not in a romantic way, of course."

Thomas nodded. "I must admit that sometimes even I don't know when he's being serious or not. Christiana seems to have him figured out, though, which I suppose is how it should be."

"Especially with ten children," she commented lightly.

Thomas started to grin. "Now I believe I understand why he wants so many."

"Indeed? Why is that?"

"He was an only child. He lived with thirty, thirty-five cousins probably, but he had no brothers or sisters!" Thomas said triumphantly. "I certainly cannot come up with a better explanation."

Emma regarded Thomas for a moment and then leaned forward. "Thank you for considering my theory," she said with a smile. After a moment, she found she couldn't stop smiling.

"What is it?" Thomas asked, his smile as broad as hers.

"This has been a most enjoyable evening, and we haven't yet gone to the ball."

The waiter, who had apparently been waiting for a break in their conversation, stepped forward to pick up their plates and ask about sweets.

"I simply could not," Emma said, realizing she had eaten more than her share of the fruit and most of what was on her dinner plate.

"I will pass, as well," Thomas said in surrender. The waiter gave him the bill and bowed as he stepped back. "Enjoy the ball."

Thomas left a pile of pound notes on top of the bill and assisted Emma with her chair. "Shall we?" he said as he offered her his arm.

"Thank you, Mr. Wellingham," she replied as she took his arm and, feeling just a bit tipsy from the champagne, glided out of the hotel.

CHAPTER 63
AND A BALL

Twilight had turned the sky to an inky blue when Thomas and Emma arrived at the Hornsby residence. Located at the intersection of three streets, the four-story brick home boasted some of the most modern conveniences and indoor gas lighting. Some would argue that the ballroom, which was the entire fourth floor of the house, was not large enough to accommodate a ball as large as this one, but others would say it was necessary to have it there for the intimacy it offered. Emma found she didn't care one way or the other—she found the place divine.

After surrendering his hat and cane and Emma's tulle shawl to one of the footmen in the large vestibule, Thomas led Emma up the grand staircase. A huge chandelier hung over the landing where the stairs split—one set to the left, the other to the right. It didn't matter which set of stairs one took as eventually they all led up to the ballroom.

The ceiling corners of the massive room featured painted scenes of cherubs and angels flanked by gold gilt moldings and cornices. The six twelve-foot windows on the long wall each led to their own balconies, their velvet drapes pulled aside at the level of the doors. The orchestra was seated in a balcony at one end of the room and had already been playing for some time. Footmen weaved between couples as they carried trays laden with glasses of champagne and small finger foods and sweets. A giant fireplace was lit on the other long wall, but there would be no need for its heat when more couples joined the dance.

"Do you see Christiana?" Thomas asked Emma as she surveyed the ballroom.

She shook her head. "Not yet. You mentioned she chose the yellow gown?" she half-asked, hoping she could spot the color amongst the rainbow of gowns.

"Indeed, the yellow one," Thomas replied quickly. "At least, she was wearing that one when last I saw her," he added. "I believe she had a difficult time deciding."

Emma glanced at Thomas and sighed. She could hardly believe she was attending the Hornsby ball. And although Thomas Wellingham might have been her employer—would be her employer again in just over a week,—she was intent on thinking of him as just a man who also happened to be her best friend's brother. A man for whom she had developed feelings of affection, she had to admit.

"There they are," Thomas said as he stepped up his pace and hurried to greet Christiana and Gregory.

"You made it," Gregory said in greeting as he bowed and Christiana curtsied.

"As did you," Thomas said with a raised eyebrow after he and Emma returned the courtesies. "I trust your dinner went well?" he asked.

"It was wonderful," Christiana replied. "Did you like The Clarendon?" she asked, mostly of Emma.

"Very much so," Emma replied with a smile. "Mr. Wellingham was most generous to take me there." She hadn't seen the bill but could only imagine how expensive the meal and champagne had been.

Todd and Deborah Vandermeer stepped up to their enclave and smiled as they curtsied and bowed. "It's so very good to see you all here," Deborah remarked as she held Todd's arm. Her bright blue satin and chiffon gown seemed to float around her as she moved.

Emma reached an arm around Deborah's shoulder and gave the taller woman a hug. "Welcome back to London! You still look like such a happy bride," she whispered.

"I am, oh, Emma. This week has been magical," she said before she reached over and kissed Gregory on the cheek. "Thank you for letting us stay at Cherrywood," she said as her lips nearly touched his ear.

"It was my pleasure," Gregory replied as his face flushed red.

Christiana glanced up at him and smiled at his reaction to being publicly kissed.

Emma hugged Todd as well, and he leaned down to kiss her cheek. "Let me be the first to congratulate you," he whispered in her ear.

Confused, Emma pulled away. "Oh, you mean about the position at Wellingham Imports, of course," she said as she smiled.

Todd's face clouded and he shook his head. "Not exactly," he replied as he glanced at Thomas and rolled his eyes. "I must speak with you later this evening," he said, his demeanor indicating a bit of humor.

"Of course," Thomas replied with a nervous smile. "Have you danced yet?" he asked of Gregory and Todd.

"Two times already," Gregory replied. "Which may be all I'm allowed if I'm to believe the old biddy over there," he murmured as he waved toward an older woman who sat on a nearby chair as if it were a throne. "Your sister has kept me on my toes."

They all laughed at the thought of Christiana dancing with a man so much taller than she. Christiana would have been the one on her toes.

Emma glanced in the direction he indicated and saw that he meant Lady Pettigrew. Although she was a viscountess, Lady Pettigrew was a friend of the Hornsby's, no doubt because her husband's association with Charles Hornsby had helped rebuild their fortunes when Pettigrew's gambling nearly bankrupted the viscountcy.

Seated in an elaborate chair, Lady Pettigrew looked as if she were the hostess of the ball rather than Eleanor Hornsby.

Emma wondered how Gregory had come to speak with the woman. Lady Pettigrew, a good friend of Mrs. Streater, was a gossip of the worst sort. Emma hoped Gregory would know enough to steer clear of her for the rest of the evening—especially if he intended to dance with Christiana again.

The orchestra resumed playing, the strains of music suggesting a waltz. Thomas turned to Emma. "Do you waltz, Miss Emma?"

Emma blushed. "It has been some time, but I believe I still know how," she replied. With that, Thomas said, "Please excuse us," to their party, and led Emma to the dance floor. As he placed one hand around her gloved hand and another on the side of her waist, he said, "I, too, have not done this in a long time. I promise I will try very hard not to step on you," he said as they joined the other couples in the large loop that circled the room.

As they did their turns and reached the fourteenth count of the music, Emma arched, extended her left leg, and looked back over her left shoulder as she'd been taught to do. While the move was meant to display a dancer's elegance and grace, it also accentuated her collarbones, neck, and décolletage. While in that brief moment of extension, she noticed Gregory and Christiana were a few couples behind them in the circle of dancers. She straightened on the one count to find Thomas' face nearly touching her shoulder. He didn't miss a beat, though, and managed to put a respectable distance between them within the next three counts. "I apologize, Mr. Wellingham," Emma said, her face flushing as they continued.

"It was a most elegant move," Thomas replied, nearly breathless. "I will be ready for when you do it again," he said as he held his head up.

And he was. On the fourteenth count, his right leg bore his weight while Emma arched and extended her left leg. On the one-count, they resumed the one-two-three waltz steps. Emma was aware of people watching, especially of Todd and Deborah, and she wondered if she had erred in performing the dance in this manner. The speed of the dancers around the floor made it impossible to watch others as they danced, though, so she merely continued the routine until the music finally ended. When they had come to a halt, she curtsied to Thomas' bow. He reached for her hand, escorted her off the floor, and into an unexpected audience with Sir William Burroughs.

"Beautiful dancing!" the banker exclaimed as he bowed to them. Out of breath, Emma quickly curtsied as Thomas bowed to the banker.

"Sir William, you are too kind," Thomas replied as he stood up.

"Miss Emma, you look magnificent this evening," the banker gushed. "I didn't even realize it was you until just now."

Emma smiled and nodded her head. "Thank you, Sir William. It's very good to see you again," she said, trying to control her breathing. The dance had been most exhilarating.

Thomas glanced around them. "Did Mrs. Burroughs join you this evening?" Thomas asked when he didn't see the man's wife in the immediate area.

Sir William shook his head. "No, not tonight. She's been under the weather for some time now," the elder man explained. "She rarely goes out anymore. As a result, young lady," he said as he turned his attention to Emma, "I expect a dance with you later."

She nodded. "Of course, sir," Emma answered, hoping it wouldn't be a waltz. They were about to beg forgiveness and go for refreshments when Gregory and Christiana joined them, both out of breath.

"Sir William," Gregory greeted his uncle. "I'd like you to meet the lady I am courting," he said with a nod. "Miss Christiana Wellingham, this is my uncle, Sir William Burroughs," he said in introduction.

The banker's eye widened as did his smile. "You do your family proud," he said to Gregory as he bowed to Christiana's curtsy.

Christiana allowed a grin as she watched her beloved interact with her brother's banker. "I'm very pleased to finally make your acquaintance, Sir William," Christiana said with a nod. She had to stop herself from mentioning having met his sister earlier that evening.

A footman stopped with a tray of champagne, and everyone in the party took a glass. Thomas glanced down at his sister and held out his forefinger. "Just one," he mouthed. Disappointed, Christiana rolled her eyes and nodded.

A young man approached Christiana, bowed, and asked for a dance. She looked nervously at Gregory, who nodded. "I expect you to dance the next one with me, though," he said. He took her champagne glass before she was whisked away.

Thomas turned to Emma. "Pardon me, Miss Emma, but I must leave you for a few moments."

"Of course," Emma replied, thinking she should find the ladies retiring room. Gregory took her hand, though, and asked for the dance. "It would be my pleasure, Mr. Grandby," she said as she curtsied.

They merged into the slow moving dance just behind Todd and Deborah, and Emma found Gregory to be a much stronger lead than Thomas had been. "You must forgive me if I pull too hard, Miss Emma," the tall man said as he performed the dance flawlessly. "I'm used to dancing with Miss Wellingham, and she is not as tall as you," he explained with a sly grin.

"You dance very well, Mr. Grandby. Where did you learn?" Emma asked, keeping up her end of the conversation while she studied his face, trying to see if there was a resemblance to Sophia Simpson. Indeed, he had her eyes and her nose, she realized.

"Here in London," he said. "I, too, went to a private school here in town. But that was many years ago," he added as he spun her under his arm. "May I ask for some assistance from you this evening?" he asked, changing the subject.

Surprised, Emma nearly lost the count. "Whatever for?"

Gregory nervously glanced around the room. "I have been given permission to ask for Miss Wellingham's hand in marriage," he stated, watching her closely for her reaction.

Emma nodded. "Yes, Mr. Wellingham informed me last Thursday," she replied. "I must give you my very best wishes," she offered, finding they really were heartfelt.

"I know you realize what this means to me," he said quietly. "It would be an honor if you could help me with my proposal. A rehearsal, if you will."

Stunned, Emma nearly let go of Gregory's shoulder. "Of course," she replied. "But I don't know when we could. I'll be spending the next couple of days at Woodscastle, but I understand you'll be hunting tomorrow."

Before she knew it, Gregory had danced them out of the circle to one of the windowed doorways and onto a balcony. Out of breath, Emma found the fresh air a relief. "Well, I guess now is as good a time as any," she said as she rested against the balustrade.

Gregory fought to catch his breath. "I beg forgiveness, but I couldn't allow Christiana to see us leave," he explained quickly. "Now, what do I do? I take her hand, right?"

Emma shrugged as she considered his best approach. "It's not yet of regular practice here in England, but I understand that on the Continent, a tall man should be below his lady when he asks for her hand. Get down on one knee," she commanded as she pointed to the balcony floor.

Frowning, Gregory glanced down and then back to Emma. "Must I? I would really prefer to do it from up here," he protested.

"But you really must get down on one knee," Emma insisted. "Miss Wellingham is not nearly as tall as you..."

"My dear, except for Vandermeer, no one is nearly as tall as me," Gregory reminded her. "Perhaps if we did it in the garden sitting down on one of the benches..." he suggested.

Emma considered the option. "That might do. Or you could just ask her in the course of conversation like every other man who proposes marriage," she suggested, thinking he was more nervous than he needed to be. It wasn't as if Christiana was going to turn down his proposal!

Gregory sighed loudly. "Oh, if I must." He knelt on one knee and took Emma's right hand. "Oh, bullocks. Now what do I do?" he asked, a look of confusion on his face. "This shouldn't be this difficult."

Emma had to cover her mouth with her other hand to suppress a giggle. "If you have a betrothal ring you plan to put on her finger, you might want to start by taking her left hand," she suggested, pulling her right hand from his grasp and offering her left.

His brows furrowing, he took the proffered hand. "Understood. Now what?"

Emma shook her head. "You say something like, 'Miss Wellingham, I humbly request your hand in marriage' or 'would you do me the honor of...'?"

At that moment, Thomas Wellingham stepped out onto the balcony. As he took in the sight of his best friend proposing to Emma Fitzsimmons, and her apparent happy reply, a wave of anger, jealousy, indeed even betrayal, washed over him. Before he knew what he was doing, he had rushed over to the couple, grabbed Gregory by the shoulder, hauled him to his feet, and punched him across the jaw in one smooth movement that startled even him.

Emma instinctively stepped back against the balustrade, her hands over her mouth. "Stop!" she shouted just as his fist made impact.

Stunned by the blow, Gregory nearly spun around and had to steady himself against the balustrade before standing fully upright. He held a hand to his jaw. "Ouch! What the...?" he complained. Then he realized who had hit him. "*Wellingham?!*" he shouted, smarting from the pain and raising his fist to make a counterstrike. He stepped forward and Emma rushed between the two men.

"Stop it, stop it right now!" she hissed, pushing the men apart, surprised she had the strength to move Gregory.

"Why did you hit him?" she asked Thomas, more confused than angry. "You said you gave your blessing—"

"To ask Christiana for her hand, yes," Thomas interrupted in anger.

"Well, he was merely rehearsing..." Emma stopped in mid-sentence as she sorted Thomas' mistaken impression. "You thought...? Oh, dear!" *Was he jealous, then? Perhaps he feels affection for me.*

Embarrassed, Thomas stepped back and took a moment to collect his breath and his thoughts. At least no one else was on the balcony to witness his attack on his friend. "Grandby, I must apologize. I'm... sorry. I thought... I thought you had misled me about wanting my sister's hand," he said quietly, hoping to excuse his behavior. "Miss Emma," he said as he bowed in her direction, "Please accept my apology for my... outburst."

Emma curtsied in return and said, "Apology accepted, of course."

Gregory burst out laughing. He put an arm around Thomas' shoulder and hugged the surprised man. "I can certainly understand how you might get the wrong impression... Miss Emma, I do believe I must have been doing something right," he added as he pulled her into the hug.

"I do believe it was the bended knee," she said with some spite when he let go of her.

"Indeed," Thomas agreed. "You had me completely convinced. Now, shall we get some champagne? Or something a bit stronger, perhaps?" he asked, holding his arm out for Emma.

She took his arm and glanced over at Gregory. "Are you going to ask Miss Wellingham tonight?"

"Absolutely not," Thomas stated emphatically. "He's not allowed to ask until Christiana turns seventeen."

Emma angled her head. "But, that's less than a week away," she replied with a pout.

"And far too soon for my comfort," Thomas said in response. "Come, sir," he said to Gregory.

The three of them returned to the ball, Gregory's jaw considerably reddened on the one side. Christiana hurried up to them and quickly took Gregory's arm. "Please, don't allow me to dance with anyone else but you tonight," she said to Gregory.

"Was Arthur that poor a dancer?" Gregory asked, a smirk on his face.

Christiana gave a small frown. "No, but he's not you," she said quietly. Turning to Emma, she asked, "Would you join me in the ladies retiring room?"

Emma gratefully accepted the invitation, and the two women excused themselves from their escorts. "I've had to use the facilities since we arrived," Emma whispered as they entered the posh rooms of the ladies retiring room. "Oh, my," she said as she took in the multi-mirrored room and all the beautifully dressed wealthy women of London.

These were not the ladies of the *ton*, of course, but given their husband's positions of importance at various companies in town, they could very well pass if seen strolling in Hyde Park during the fashionable hour. Several were simply resting on the overstuffed settees lining one wall or perched on the dressing table seats in front of candlelit mirrors. A maid handed a linen towel to a lady as she finished washing her hands in a porcelain basin. Another maid came into the lounge with a pitcher filled with hot water.

"This is now my favorite part of the fourth floor," Christiana said in awe as she led Emma to the private rooms, each furnished with a chamber pot on which was a comfortable seat. "'Tis like an indoor privy," she said as she opened a door for Emma, "But so much nicer."

"Indeed," was all Emma could say as she hurried to relieve herself. With the extra amenities, she took care to freshen up and put some powder on what she was sure was a shiny nose.

When she heard Christiana open her door, she joined her outside the privies and went to wash her hands. "How is it with you and Mr. Grandby?" she asked in a quiet voice. "I saw you waltzing."

Christiana smiled. "I think 'tis going well, but Gregory has seemed... nervous, I suppose, all night long," she commented before quickly glancing around the room. "You cannot tell my brother, but I met Gregory's mother tonight," she whispered, excitement in her voice.

Emma shook her head as she finished drying her hands. "Indeed?" she replied in surprise as she pulled on one glove. "And... *where* did you meet her?" she asked in a matching whisper, quickly pulling on her other glove and looping her reticule handle over her arm.

"Her townhouse," she replied, eyeing Emma's reflection in the mirror. "How long have you known?"

Emma turned to look at Christiana directly. "'Tis true, then? Mrs. Simpson is his mother?" she asked, her voice still a whisper.

Christiana stared at Emma. "However did you *know?*"

Shaking her head, Emma nervously glanced around. "I only just figured it out over dinner tonight," she answered in hushed tones.

"When I hosted the Simpsons for dinner, they made comments... your brother doesn't quite believe it, though." She regarded Christiana. "She's a wonderful lady. A duke's daughter, even. Did you... like her?" she asked as she leaned closer.

Nodding, Christiana finally smiled. "She is to the manor born, but not at all snooty," the girl answered carefully. "And I really adore Mr. Simpson," she added happily. Lowering her voice, she said, "Gregory introduced me as his betrothed, but you cannot tell my brother because Gregory isn't allowed to ask for my hand until Wednesday."

Emma led Christiana to the salon end of the retiring room. "Yes, and Gregory will have a bruise on his jaw to prove it tomorrow morning," she warned under her breath. As she stepped aside to allow two older women to enter, Emma realized one of them was Lady Pettigrew. She overheard the ladies discussing an eminent proposal for marriage. "See?" Emma said as she waved at the women. "Even they know."

A look of distress on her face, Christiana said quietly, "Lady Pettigrew was not speaking of *my* impending betrothal."

Emma angled her head and tried to hear the subject of the women's conversation. "Collins?" she whispered to Christiana. "Do you know whom that might be?"

In a hurry to leave the salon, Christiana took Emma's arm and led her out the door. Finding their escorts was easy—Thomas and Gregory stood not ten feet from the entrance to the retiring room while Todd and Deborah stood gazing at one another and sharing a glass of champagne.

"Mr. Wellingham, I hope we didn't keep you waiting too long," Emma apologized as she approached and curtsied.

Thomas shook his head and held out a glass of champagne for her. "Not at all," he replied, his mood even more jovial than it had been earlier in the evening. "We just got our drinks a few moments ago, and some very good news from Mr. Vandermeer," he added with a smile and a nod toward the newlyweds.

Emma took her champagne and turned to look at the Vandermeers. "Good news?" she repeated expectantly.

Todd bowed his head in her direction and said, "I have just accepted Mr. Wellingham's offer of employment at Wellingham Imports."

Beaming, Emma hugged Deborah and congratulated the tall

man. "As I mentioned earlier, I, too, have accepted a position as an accomptant. I'll start a week from Monday," she said to the couple.

Grinning broadly, Todd glanced at Thomas before giving Emma his congratulations. "And is that the only position you have offered her?" he whispered over her head.

Rolling his eyes, Thomas drank some champagne and replied, "At the moment, yes. She'll take the position of payroll accomptant and do her work in the clerks' office with the other accomptants."

Todd looked disappointed but brightened when he found Deborah watching him. "Where will you work?"

Overhearing the question, Thomas leaned in and said, "Mr. Vandermeer has his own office next to mine, of course. He must choose some taller furnishings and decoration, though. The space is rather empty at the moment."

Deborah smiled at the news and leaned her head against her husband's shoulder. "You won't have as far to travel to Wellingham Imports," she murmured before pressing her lips against the sleeve of his topcoat.

"And I'll be closer to the Home for Unwed Mothers," he countered with a raised eyebrow, a hint of amusement in his voice. "Perhaps we could take luncheon together sometime?" he suggested, an eyebrow arching suggestively.

Deborah blushed bright red and glanced around to be sure no one else had heard her husband's comment.

Gregory offered Christiana his arm when he realized she was standing next to him. She beamed as she looked up at him and he offered her a cup of lemonade. "I tried for another champagne, but your brother wouldn't allow it."

"Thank you for trying. This will do fine," Christiana replied with a smile as she took a sip. She watched her brother closely, realizing he must have seen the two older women entering the women's salon just moments before. "Shall we go back to the ballroom?" Christiana suggested, hoping to get the group away from the salon before the older women reappeared.

"Indeed," said Thomas as he studied Emma's profile. "Some ladies might get the impression we are trying to take advantage." He was about to lead their group away when Deborah stepped up.

"May I have a word with Miss Emma?" she asked, hoping they could speak in private.

Emma looked to Thomas, her expression showing she was

surprised at the request. "But, of course," Thomas answered, stepping back and then joining Todd for some conversation.

Deborah nodded toward the ladies salon, and Emma followed her in. They found an upholstered bench on which to sit down and did so, their arms interlocked.

"Oh, how was it, Deborah? I've been thinking of you all week!" Emma whispered excitedly, glad they were able to take time away from the others.

Blushing, Deborah lowered her eyes. "It was a wonderful trip. Cherrywood is simply magnificent."

Emma regarded her friend for a moment, realizing immediately something wasn't quite right. "And?" she prodded.

"I had occasion to feel a bit jealous this past week," Deborah said, her fingers intertwining nervously with Emma's.

"Of whom?" Emma asked, not bothering to hide her surprise at the comment. Todd seemed like the last man in London to show interest in a woman other than his wife.

Sighing heavily, Deborah's eyes finally met Emma's. "A *what*, actually," she stammered. "A painting. Or rather," she shook her head and rolled her eyes, as if embarrassed to admit what had caused her to feel envy. "A woman in the painting. She was draped in satin and... she was almost naked. Todd couldn't take his eyes off of her when we were in the library at Cherrywood."

Breathing a sigh of relief, Emma could only say, "Oh, indeed."

The taller woman squeezed her hand and leaned closer. "As soon as we returned to London, I sent a post to Jean Claude Perot. I've commissioned him to paint the same scene, but with me in it," she said, her eyes bright. "Only my back and arms will be bare..."

Emma stared at her friend, astonished. "The French painter?" she interrupted. "The one who painted you last spring?" Alarmed, Emma held her breath as she considered her friend's plan. She knew Deborah had already posed for the painter several times, but she'd been uncomfortable knowing the artist had done a painting featuring Deborah's face on an unclothed body.

Nodding her head, Deborah explained, "I want to give it to Todd for his birthday."

"Oh," Emma replied, swallowing and smiling with relief. Certainly the man would appreciate such a gift, she considered. He could hang it somewhere private, his study perhaps, away from visitors, and look upon it whenever he wished. "What a very daring wife you are," she whispered in delight.

Deborah's face finally lit up in a smile. "I'm so very glad to hear you say it," she said in relief. "Now I'm vexed as to how I will go through with it!"

Emma and Deborah giggled at the comment as they made their way out of the salon to join their escorts. When their glasses were empty, the men invited the women to dance.

Now that more people were in attendance, the dance floor was much more crowded and required the dancing be done longways. The Duke of Kent's Waltz was being performed as they made their way to the end of the line to join in, but the music ended before they could participate. When the music resumed, they performed the Prince William followed by the Sun Assembly. The Fair Quaker of Deal was about to start when Gregory begged for refreshment, and he and Christiana departed the dance floor.

Thomas pulled Emma aside. "Let us sit this one out," he suggested, and led them through one of the doors to a balcony with a stone bench.

Taking a seat, Emma placed her hands on her lap and breathed deeply. The air was clear and warm for a July evening, and she felt a bit drunk from the champagne.

"Are you having a pleasant time?" Thomas asked as he joined her on the bench.

"I am, indeed," she replied with a smile. "As is Christiana," she added with a nod. "And are you?"

Thomas sighed and smiled. "I am, too," he finally said.

"Did something happen whilst Christiana and I were in the retiring room?" she asked quietly, noticing the change in his good mood.

He glanced at Emma. "I shouldn't have allowed an old lady to have such a foul effect on me," he admitted with a sigh, "But it seems I cannot easily forget some conversations."

Mortified, Emma asked, "Whatever did she say?" She immediately thought of Lady Pettigrew. Why would her talk of an impending betrothal have Thomas so upset?

Thomas smiled, took one of Emma's gloved, hands and kissed the back of it. "It was nothing," he said, his mood brightening. "Dance with me?" he asked as he held his hand out and stood up.

"Out here?"

"There's certainly more room," he replied as Emma stood up and joined him.

"Indeed," she agreed, placing her right hand on his shoulder and her left in his right hand.

Keeping their steps smaller and the space between them closer than proprietary would normally allow, they danced to two entire sets before another couple burst onto the balcony in a fit of giggles and took seats on the stone bench. With their privacy gone, Thomas and Emma returned to the ballroom for refreshment.

Sir William found them at the punch bowl and reminded Emma of her promise to dance with him. She gave Thomas an apologetic glance as she glided off with her banker to join a longways version of The Spring.

As they crossed in the middle and went around one another, Sir William said, "I do hope my recommending you for Mr. Wellingham's position of auditor was acceptable to you."

Emma smiled. "Oh, it most certainly was, Sir William. I cannot tell you what a relief it was to have employment sorted before I finished at Warwick's. It was most kind of you to recommend me." She completed the second turn and they were apart for a few steps.

"I understand you were able to lease the townhouse I recommended?" Sir William said more than asked as they glided by each other. "And have you met your landlords?"

"Indeed," Emma nodded as she turned and realized what he had said. Taking a chance, she said, "I hosted a dinner for your sister and Mr. Simpson just two weeks ago. She's a lovely woman."

Despite the comment, Sir William didn't miss a step nor did his expression change. "Was she well?" he asked.

"Very, I think. They had just returned from a holiday with her son at Cherrywood," Emma commented as they glided by each other.

The banker grinned in amusement. "When do you start your accomptant position at Wellingham Imports?" he asked as they made their turn.

Now, how does he know about that? "A week come Monday," Emma replied carefully. "I'm on holiday until then." She turned and they crossed in the middle.

"And how long has Mr. Wellingham been courting you?" Sir William queried as the dance was about to end.

Startled by the question, Emma lost her step and had to move quickly to recover her place in line. "Is he?" Emma replied, her face betraying her surprise at the question. "He's my employer, after all," she stated firmly, regaining her composure.

"Indeed," the banker huffed as he bowed and she curtsied. "I was sure there was a merger in your future," he said with a wink. "Thank you for the dance."

Uneasy, Emma smiled as best she could and said, "Thank you, Sir William." When she noticed which way the banker was headed, she decided to take a different path. She didn't have to go far, though, as Thomas stood nearby. He had apparently been watching them dance. Already flushed from the exercise, Emma wondered if Thomas had overheard their conversation. She colored at the thought, certain her face was bright red.

"You dance beautifully," Thomas said as she joined him. "You made Sir William look like a king out there," he added as he handed her a glass of champagne.

"Thank you, Mr. Wellingham. You are too kind," she managed in reply as she tried to catch her breath. Trying to sip the champagne, she found her thirst made her drink it too fast. "He knows," she said with a quizzical expression as she leaned in very close to him.

"Knows?" Thomas repeated, not quite understanding.

"I think Sir William must be helping to hide Sophia. Or else..." She paused. "Perhaps he wants to make her come out of hiding in plain sight," she said between gasps for air.

Thomas regarded Emma and thought she might have had too much to drink. "Whatever do you mean?" he asked as he pulled her to the edge of the room.

"Sir William told me about the townhouse. It cannot be a coincidence. He knows who owns the townhouses on my street. The Simpsons said he had provided a recommendation for me. And when I told him I had his sister and Mr. Simpson for dinner two weeks ago, he didn't deny anything. He even asked me about her health!" she whispered hoarsely.

Biting his lip, Thomas remembered the night at the club and wondered if, he too, had been led to do something because Sir William wished it. Sir William had recommended Emma for the job as auditor, if not directly, then at least in an off-hand manner.

She is a smart woman, he had said.

But Emma was also Christiana's roommate. *Could that be just a coincidence, or did Sir William have a hand in that arrangement as well?*

"You have an interesting point. We shall think on this more. Perhaps some other time, though," he said with a nod. He reached into the pocket of his waistcoat. 'Tis nearly two o'clock," Thomas said as he checked his chronometer. "Perhaps we should take our leave," Thomas suggested, hoping she would agree.

"That would be fine," Emma replied, relieved that she could be off her feet for the ride back to Woodscastle.

They found the Vandermeers on a bench on one of the balconies, happily kissing one another. Emma blushed and waved when Deborah finally noticed her. "You must come for luncheon this week," Deborah said as Todd got up to bow to Thomas and Emma.

"Yes, you must. Both of you," Todd agreed as he leaned over and kissed Emma on the cheek. "Thank you again, Emma," he said as he took her hand and squeezed it gently. Turning to Thomas, he clasped his friend on the shoulder and looked him in the eye. "Am I going to have to...?" he started to ask in a teasing manner.

"No," Thomas said with a knowing grin as he shook his head. "I'll do it. I promise," he said shortly.

Thomas bowed and Emma curtsied and they left the couple right where they'd found them.

They glided down the stairs to the first floor vestibule to retrieve their accessories. Wrapping her shawl about her shoulders, Emma took Thomas' arm and they walked out the front door. Thomas spotted Mr. Allen. It only took a wave from Thomas and Mr. Allen was driving the horses to the front of the house.

"Have you seen my sister or Mr. Grandby recently?" Thomas asked.

"No, but I believe they planned to take their leave before midnight," Emma replied. "Christiana cannot stay awake much past eleven."

Thomas grinned as he assisted Emma into the barouche. When they were seated, Mr. Allen hurried the horses on their way.

CHAPTER 64
A RATHER VIVID DREAM

ery early on July 11, 1802, Great West Road
As the barouche bounced down the road toward Woodscastle, Thomas couldn't help but stare at Emma's profile. She positively glowed in the moonlight, and the look of contentment on her features made him wonder what she might be thinking. *That damn Grandby was right*. And so was Todd, of course. He really did feel affection for this woman. He probably had since that night he had met her at Warwick's.

He reached his arm behind her shoulder, careful to rest it on the top of the squabs. "You must tell me what you're thinking about this very moment," he breathed quietly, surprised by the sound of his voice. The last few glasses of champagne had taken affect, and he felt as if he were floating on air.

Emma turned slowly to face him, her mouth slightly apart as her eyes tried to focus. Thomas reached up with his left hand and cupped her cheek, pulling her closer as his thumb ever so lightly followed the lush curve of her lower lip. He leaned in to kiss her. As their lips touched, Emma seemed to come alive, her mouth responding to the gentle touch, inviting him to continue.

Thomas tasted the champagne still on her breath and took in the scent of the roses in her hair as his lips glided over hers. He didn't pull away but was forced to separate from her when the carriage jerked as it rolled over a rut in the road. Despite the sudden movement, Emma continued to gaze in his direction. "Please, tell me," he whispered, wanting desperately to know what she was thinking at that moment.

Emma recovered from her reverie, her mouth forming a perfect "O", as if she'd been caught in the middle of committing a crime. Without looking at him, she replied, "I couldn't, Thomas. It was scandalous," she whispered, a slight shake of her head accompanying the denial. She hoped Mr. Allen was unable to hear their conversation over the running horses and spinning wheels.

At the use of his first name, Thomas grinned. "Was *I* in your thoughts, perhaps?" he asked, his lips nearly touching her ear as he spoke the words.

Feeling his warm breath on her neck, Emma sighed. "Oh, yes," she whispered as she closed her eyes.

I have had entirely too much champagne.

Intrigued, Thomas moved closer. "Now you really must tell me. Then I will tell you what I'm thinking."

Emma, her mouth slightly open as she contemplated her thoughts, replied quietly, "Thomas, I simply cannot. You would think me a... a wanton woman, and you would never look at me with respect ever again."

Thomas straightened. He had never heard her call him by his first name before this night, and he rather liked it, especially couched in such secrecy. "Please, Emma, tell me," he begged, his lips so close to her ear, his nose touched her hair. When she turned to look at him, he placed a hand along her cheek and kissed the corner of her mouth.

By all rights, she should have pushed him away. She should have moved as far away from him as she could. She shouldn't even be with him, considering her status as an unmarried woman with no chaperone. But she was here, with him, and Thomas found he was under her spell.

The barouche pulled into the curved path to Woodscastle. In the moonlight, servants could be seen preparing for their arrival.

Emma inhaled sharply, surprised by the clandestine kiss. "You must promise you won't change your good opinion of me. That you won't change *how* you think of me," she countered, not sure she would even reveal her thoughts if he did agree to her terms.

"I promise," he breathed, his anticipation growing. Then he pulled a glove off of one of her hands and kissed her knuckles as if sealing his promise.

Emma swallowed hard and allowed her eyelids to drop. In a hypnotic trance, she recalled, "I was dreaming that we were arriving here at Woodscastle, and that you had Mr. Allen take my valise to the guest bedchamber. You took me by the arm and led me to my bedchamber, but instead of leaving me at the door, you kissed me and took me to your bedchamber, and we undressed one another, and you carried me to your bed and we made love for..." Her litany ceased when the carriage came to a halt in the drive in front of Woodscastle.

Thomas held his breath through her admission, and now he stared at her. *She must feel affection for me,* he thought, his loins stirring. *She must!* He reached into his pocket before remembering he didn't have the ring with him. *Damn!*

Emma misunderstood his expression, though, and gasped at what she had revealed. Her hand covered her mouth. *This is my employer! How could I admit such a thing?*

Mr. Larsen appeared at the side of the carriage to assist her.

"Mr. Allen!" Thomas called out as Emma decided to accept Mr. Larsen's proffered hand and stood up. "Please take Miss Emma's valise to the guest bedchamber. And where is Humphrey?" he asked of no one in particular.

"Here, sir," his butler replied from the top of the front steps.

"Did Miss Wellingham arrive home safely?" Thomas called out. The coach shook as Mr. Allen removed the small valise from the back of the barouche. Emma stepped down carefully, glad to have Mr. Larsen's support given the state of her knees at that moment.

"Indeed, sir. She has already retired for the evening," Humphrey answered curtly, not bothering to add that Christiana was sleeping when she arrived. Gregory had carried her to her bedchamber and put her to bed with the help of Mrs. Werthers.

Thomas nodded and said, "Thank goodness for small favors," under his breath while trying to keep his head straight when his body wanted to be doing other things. "Due to the lateness of the hour, I believe we can forgo breakfast this morning. Could you please inform the cook?" he called out as he stepped down from the barouche.

"Of course, sir," the butler replied as he bowed and turned to go back into the house.

Emma was already out of the barouche and on her way to the front steps when Thomas ran up to take her arm. "Please, forgive me, Mr. Wellingham. I'm afraid I have flustered you," Emma said quietly, keeping her eyes on the direction of their movement. She dared not look at her host, and was thankful the darkness hid her reddened face. *I cannot believe I actually said it all aloud,* she thought, chastising herself for drinking too much and then chastising herself for having such vivid daydreams.

"Just a bit," Thomas admitted as he tried to slow their pace to a stroll. He couldn't help but notice she addressed him with his formal name. "But if you would indeed wish your dream to become a reality, it is certainly within my... I will... it would be my honor to oblige you," he stammered nervously. "However," he added, his voice taking on a rather foreboding tone, "If we do this, Emma, you will be *mine*. " The last word came out more forceful than he intended.

Emma's breath caught as she considered his words. *Mine?* she repeated to herself. *Does he intend for me to be his mistress?* The repercussions of her words just now forming in her addled mind.

Would it be so very wrong? What would be the harm in agreeing to his terms? She thought of the security she would have, her townhouse, protection. She had always known if she were unable to land a position or arrange a suitable marriage, being a mistress was one way to ensure she would have the funds necessary to live. And if she was to be someone's mistress, who better than Thomas Wellingham? She certainly had feelings for the man.

The cotton haze in her head slowly lifted. An odd sensation swelled in her belly, and she felt her knees weaken as she imagined sharing his bed.

It wouldn't be the first time, she thought, smiling.

They climbed the staircase while Mr. Allen passed them on his way down. "Thank you, Mr. Allen," Thomas said in a normal voice as the coachman descended the stairs.

"You are welcome, sir, and thank you again, Miss Emma. The dinner was delicious."

Somehow, Emma had the wherewithal to nod in the direction of Mr. Allen as he made his compliment, although her attention was entirely on Thomas and what he was trying to say as they climbed the staircase.

"And if you have changed your mind," Thomas continued quietly, "I would request you merely grant me a kiss before I leave you."

When they reached the door of the guest bedchamber, Thomas glanced around to be sure no servants were nearby. He opened the door and led Emma in by one hand, quickly closing the door. He turned to face her.

Dropping her reticule on the floor, Emma moved closer to Thomas as he reached out a hand and cupped her cheek. When she didn't move away, he leaned down and touched his lips to hers. Emma responded by opening her mouth and meeting the pressure of his lips against hers.

She felt his arms encircle her body, his hands on her back pulling her to him as the kiss continued. She inhaled the scent of him, a subtle musk that emanated from his entire body, and she breathed in the scent of the citrus laundry soap from his cravat, the lingering smoke of a cheroot on his topcoat, and the smell of wool in his waistcoat.

And the kiss!

His lips were firm, but he was careful in how he held them against hers, at once tasting hers and pulling away slightly before pushing them against hers again and again.

When his mouth finally moved away from hers, it was to gently kiss her cheek and neck. "I have wanted to kiss you like this all night long, Emma," he whispered just before his lips took her earlobe and a multi jeweled earring into his mouth.

Emma gasped at the sensation his tongue created as it caressed her ear. She was aware of how her body responded to his kisses and his touch, sure her breasts had escaped her corset, and if they hadn't, she wanted them out and in his warm hands.

A shiver passed through her body as his lips moved to her neck and throat. Arching back, she took a deep breath as his tongue made its way down to the space below her collarbone, and his lips hovered over the swell of her breasts.

Her thighs quivered, nearly unable to support her. The heat between them made her very aware of the male that held her up. She could think of nothing but giving herself to this man. "Take me, Thomas," she whispered as she gasped for air.

Thomas lifted his lips from her collarbone and stared at her for only a moment. He placed a hand against her cheek and brushed his thumb over her lower lip, caressing the fullness of it as she wrapped a gloved hand around his wrist and rested another on his shoulder.

He no longer felt the effects of the champagne and wondered if she still did. But his body demanded attention. Taking her by the hand, he crossed to the connecting door that led to his room.

Emma allowed him to pull her along, realizing he really did mean to make her dream a reality. And she would become his mistress, she remembered, finding she wasn't as opposed to the idea as she might have been, when it could have been Samuel Morton or some other married man arranging for her to warm their bed.

A servant had turned down the bedding, the crisp, white linens revealed in the light of two candle lamps. Near the edge of the bed, Thomas turned to face Emma. He placed one hand along her neck, pulling her to him. His kiss was feather light, as if he expected Emma to step away at any moment. Instead, she pressed herself against his body and wrapped her arms around his neck and shoulders. Realizing she wasn't going to change her mind, Thomas moved his hand from her neck to the back of her head. He kissed the woman he had come to love, gently at first, and then harder until he had to breathe once again.

Long fingers unbuttoned his waistcoat and tail coat while he struggled to figure out how to remove her gown. She had his cravat untied and was pulling his shirt over his head when her gown became a puddle of satin and tulle around her feet. Although she knew she should be shocked by her lack of modesty, Emma recalled the night she had played nursemaid to Thomas.

Her wet night gown had been transparent, and although Thomas hadn't said so, she knew he had seen more of her than he let on. And, at the moment, his bare chest was of more importance to her than thoughts of modesty. She had seen it bathed in sweat under the midday sun. Now, it glowed in the candlelight, the light dusting of hair tickling her nose and the pads of her fingers as she kissed the area around his nipples. At his sudden gasp, she moved her lips to his upper arms and slid her trembling fingers to play over his back.

Thomas shuddered at the sensations that coursed through his body. Pulling the bow that held her corset laces together, he worked at unraveling the ties, his fingers shaking as he did so.

Within seconds, her breasts were released from their bondage. The hardened nipples poked through the camisole underneath the corset. He gingerly touched one with a thumb and kissed it through the thin fabric, feeling satisfaction when he heard Emma's breath catch. He let go as he felt her hands pushing down and over his buttocks and the back of his thighs as she removed his breeches and drawers. Boots thumped to the floor and slippers were tossed to the side before they regarded one another in the dim light.

Still in her stockings, garters, pantaloons and a camisole, Emma could feel her entire body trembling in anticipating. Completely nude, Thomas stood before her and kept his eyes locked on hers until she removed the camisole, pulling the cotton fabric slowly over her head to reveal her full breasts.

She is truly giving herself to me, Thomas realized, his gaze traveling the length of her body before he placed his mouth against one of the orbs and suckled the nipple. *Sustenance for the soul,* he thought absently.

Emma gasped in surprise at the sensation his lips and the tip of his tongue created in her. She dropped the camisole onto the pile of clothes at her feet. A shiver of pleasure passed through her, settling just above her thighs, reminding her of the sensation she had experienced when she had seen him chopping wood. A whimper escaped her lips as the throbbing sensation deep within her demanded attention.

Thomas placed one hand on the back of her shoulder, and then drew his other hand down the length of her back and around her milky white bottom, pushing down her pantaloons past her long thighs as he went. *Firm and strong,* he thought as he remembered how she rode a horse. Already aroused, the thought of her thighs wrapped around his torso made him even more so.

Moving his hand to the front of her body, he slowly felt her belly and breasts, his thumb extended so as to brush the tip of her engorged nipples as he continued his caresses. Despite the growing heat of her body, her skin shivered under his touch, and he heard her sudden but quiet gasps. His other arm wrapped around her waist and brought her closer, forcing his hardened manhood to press against her belly. Straightening up, he ran his hands along the side of her body, over to the small of her back, up her spine, and onto her head, where he groped for the pins that held up her hair. Plucking them out as he kissed her mouth, he tossed the pins onto the bench at the end of the bed. In the firelight, her golden hair, still smelling of roses, tumbled down past her shoulders.

Thomas pulled away to look at her, his gaze taking in her entire body before returning to her face. "You're so beautiful," he whispered urgently. Naked except for her stockings and garters, she was the most erotic sight he had ever beheld. Bending down, he kissed her other nipple while Emma slid her trembling hands down the side of his body and then tentatively touched his manhood, her fingers barely making contact until it was pressed into her palm.

The silken skin, tight and already wet at the tip, throbbed against her hand. She marveled at the sight of it, surprised it didn't frighten her as she expected and rather relieved it wasn't as large as those she had seen in the illustrations in the books in her library. Sliding her forefinger down along a pulsing vein, she gingerly touched his balls and then cupped them with several fingertips.

Releasing his grip on her nipple to catch his breath, Thomas closed his eyes and leaned against her, his hand moving down the front of her, across her hips, and down as far as he could reach along one leg and then slowly up to the apex of her thighs.

She inhaled, and she might have backed away, but Thomas held an arm across her back as he slid first one finger and then another between her thighs. The warm moistness spread over his fingers as he felt for the nub that, if rubbed just so, would send her into ecstasy.

Startled by his touch, Emma inhaled and clung to him, her fingernails digging into his arms, branding him with a series of half moons in his skin.

At her instinct to clench shut the opening to the space between her thighs, Thomas coaxed her legs apart as he continued to massage the engorged nub just inside the honeyed folds.

Emma's breaths came faster as a sharp but exquisite sensation gripped her. She cried out, her back arcing so that her breasts were within reach of his mouth. He licked one hardened pebble with the side of his tongue before pulling it into his mouth. She cried out his name as her body convulsed against him.

Realizing she was no longer able to hold herself up, Thomas removed his hand from between her thighs, sliding it behind her knees to lift her into his arms. She pressed a cheek against his chest as he lay her down on the bed. Determined to pleasure her completely before taking his own, he slid his hand slowly down her belly. First one finger and then another slid through her dark curlies to the wetness beneath.

Emma gasped as she felt his slick fingers stroke the tender folds of skin. There was a pause in their exploration as Thomas moved his kisses from her belly to a peaked nipple, his tongue playfully licking the hard pebble. When he finally slid a finger inside, Emma jerked, clenching instinctively around the intruder as she'd done earlier.

Thomas held his breath as he watched her eyes widen, her bee stung lips parting slightly. He covered one of her nipples with his mouth. When he felt her relax, he pushed his finger in further and used the pad of his thumb to circle her swollen sex.

Whimpering, Emma lifted her hips slightly, forcing his finger to bury itself deeper inside her. Her breath catching, she slid a hand down the side of his body, pausing when she was aware his manhood resting against her thigh. She gingerly touched the taut silken skin, smiling when her ministrations elicited the same reaction from Thomas that she had expressed only seconds before.

Thomas closed his eyes, fighting the urge to simply allow the release his body was demanding. Determined to bring Emma to ecstasy before he would allow his own, Thomas slid another finger into her and circled his thumb around the wet source of her impending climax. Emma reflexively gripped his manhood as she allowed her body to experience the intimate assault. Thomas groaned loudly when he could no longer fight off his own impending orgasm. He pushed his open mouth against her breast to muffle the growling sound. Emma tried desperately to stifle her own sudden cry as the orgasm swept though her torso, the waves of pleasure rippling through her entire body, the sensations so profound she simply gave into them and allowed them to wash over her and through her. She was vaguely aware of the pulsing organ she still held, its warm fluid spilling onto her thigh.

Long before the ripples of pleasure had ceased in her body, Thomas experienced a final spasm of pleasure and allowed his body to collapse, most of his weight pressed against Emma's side, his head buried into the space between her neck and shoulder. His hot breath washed over her breast as he hugged her close, his labored breathing the only sound in the room.

Emma trembled uncontrollably, her body suddenly alive with new sensations. She found herself shocked at the intensity of what she'd experienced, surprised Thomas hadn't taken her maidenhood. She was sure he had experienced something, though, given how his body had convulsed and the sounds he had made.

With her free hand, she gingerly felt her wet thigh, rubbing the warm fluid into her skin in small circles that sent out delicious tickles through her skin. Her fingers brushed against his manhood where it still rested on her. Still somewhat erect, the organ seemed to come alive with her touch.

Thomas clamped his hand down over Emma's, a growl escaping his lips as he pressed her hand onto his hardened manhood. Startled at the sudden motion, Emma gasped, her chest rising off the bed. When she didn't pull her hand away, Thomas inhaled deeply as he lifted himself onto one elbow. Through heavy lids, he saw her breasts were still full, their nipples erect as if expecting more. Despite his climax, Thomas realized he wanted more.

As if reading his thoughts, Emma breathed in deeply, her chest rising erotically before she whispered, "I am yours."

Thomas needed no other invitation. Climbing atop her, he leaned down and kissed her fully on the lips. When he sensed her legs spreading apart and felt her thighs pressing against the side of his hips, he held himself over her body, pausing to take in the sight of her.

As she watched him through lowered lashes, the euphoria from her climax still evident on her face, Thomas entered her slowly. He felt her entire body trembling—in anticipation or fear, he didn't know—he merely knew he had to have her. "I rather wish I knew what I was doing," he managed to whisper, pausing when he realized he could go no further without something giving way.

Emma's eyes closed as a giggle burbled forth. "I'm of the same mind," she murmured, the champagne responsible for her giddiness.

Thomas hovered over her, unsure if she meant him or her. Then he grinned as her eyes opened and a look of shock appeared on her face. "I meant *me*, of course," she added, attempting to suppress another giggle.

Satisfied she hadn't meant any offense with her comment, Thomas sobered and kissed one of her nipples. "This may hurt a bit," he whispered, his lips brushing against hers. He was aware of her nod of acknowledgment, and when he lifted his head a bit so he could see her face, he saw desire in her eyes. When his manhood reached her maidenhood, Thomas paused, pulled out, and then thrust his member deep into her.

Emma winced at the sharp pain, but stifled any sound as the warm sensation of fullness filled her lower body.

Attempting to control his motions so as not to hurt her—he pushed into her quickly and then slowly pulled out, repeating his movements rhythmically—Thomas fought the urge to allow the quick release his body demanded. He knew he wanted to make it all last as long as possible.

Emma's lips took purchase on one of his nipples, though, and with the gentle suckling and the stroking of her fingers down the sides of his torso, Thomas could no longer hold back. As he pushed into her as hard and as fast as he could, the release he felt was so intense it seemed to consume his entire body. He nearly yelled out as Emma arched her back in response to his body's wave of pleasure, her thighs gripping him tightly. He forced his mouth onto one of her shoulders to stifle the growl emanating from his throat.

He felt Emma's body shudder under him and he relaxed, all his energy expended and the last vestiges of his climax waning.

Lowering himself onto her and then collapsing in exhaustion, Thomas rested his head on Emma's shoulder as he felt her fingers wind into the hair on the back of his head and lightly stroke his back.

Emma sighed. *I am yours.* Had she really said it aloud? She kissed the top of his head as he continued to lie on top of her. When he finally stirred, it was to kiss her and roll off of her body.

Not knowing what to say, he pulled her against his body and held her head on his shoulder. *This is happiness,* he considered as he kissed her hair. "Thank you," he murmured sleepily.

Emma purred in response. Her body still trembling, her skin still sensitive to touch, she pressed the length of her body against his and reveled in the new warmth radiating from it.

Overcome with fatigue, Thomas fell asleep with his nose in her hair and a slight smile on his face. Emma sighed as she promised herself she wouldn't regret this night before finally drifting off to sleep.

CHAPTER 65
WAKING TO REALITY

*H*earing the sounds of soft snoring behind her, Emma slowly opened her eyes. The warmth pressed against her bottom and the back of her thighs was welcome, comfortable, the soft breaths against one shoulder a source of reassurance. The candle lamps on the nightstand had both burned out, but moonlight lit the room in a soft glow.

The events of the night came back to her in a flood of happy memories, and she smiled, the euphoria filling her. She carefully left the bed to use the chamber pot in the guest bedchamber's bath, stopping to pick up her discarded gown and undergarments on the way to the other room. When she returned, she slipped back into the bed and slowly molded herself to the body that lay there.

"I missed you," Thomas whispered as his arm wrapped around her and pulled her against the front of his body, much like he had the night he had been so sick.

Emma sighed in response as she intertwined her fingers into his and held his hand pressed to a bare breast. *How positively scandalous this all is,* she thought, not the least bit ashamed of herself.

At nearly one-and-twenty, she had no intention of being a maiden spinster, especially since her roommate had given up her maidenhead at the tender age of sixteen. *There's the reason,* she figured as she wondered how she'd had the nerve, the audacity, to admit her dream to Thomas. *I was jealous! So jealous of what Christiana had already experienced with a man,* she realized. *Could Gregory have been as tender and thoughtful as Thomas?* Had Christiana, too, experienced pleasure of such profound force that she was forever bound to the man that took her maidenhood?

The thought made her sigh in exasperation, but she found she didn't regret what she had shared with the man pressed against her. A sense of well-being washed over her as she closed her eyes. *This feels so... right,* she thought happily, deciding that being a mistress might not be such a horrid experience.

Thomas lifted onto one elbow and peered over Emma's shoulder. "You're thinking awfully loud thoughts, my love," he whispered, nibbling Emma's shoulder playfully.

Startled at the sound of his voice, Emma leaned her back into his chest, a beatific smile on her face as she looked at him over her shoulder. His hair was terribly tousled, and there was the beginning of stubble on his face, but he was glorious to behold in the moonlight. She let go of his hand and turned to face him, kissing his chest as she pressed her body against his. "I didn't mean for my thoughts to awaken you," she murmured, resting her head in the small of his shoulder.

"Do you... regret what we...?" he asked in a halting voice, misinterpreting the sound of the sigh he had overheard.

"No," Emma replied fervently, lifting her head from his shoulder so she could look at him as she said it. "Not a bit. I suppose I should, but I find I... I cannot," she whispered as her fingertips played over his skin and hairs, swirling them with one fingertip while using another finger to continue her hand's journey down his body. She could feel tiny ripples under his skin as her touch excited him all over again. "Do you?" She turned her head to gaze at him as her hand moved down one rib and into the space where a piece of his flesh seemed to be missing. Her fingertip circled the divot and she glanced at him with a furrowed brow.

"Only that it didn't happen..." He intended to say, "sooner," but then stopped as he realized what her explorations had found. "No, of course not," he murmured, quite aware of her staring at him. "It's an old wound," he added with a nod in the direction of his rib, deciding that, at the moment, he didn't wish to tell her how it got there. The unbidden memory assaulted him though, and he was forced to review it in his mind's eye.

. . .

$\mathcal{R}$ ebecca Merriweather had been quite indignant with him that afternoon when she claimed he had provided her no pleasure despite his repeated attempts to bring her to some kind of climax, first using his manhood and then his fingers. It was his second time in her room, a bedchamber made famous because Rebecca took it upon herself to train her male cousins in the art of pleasing a woman. As a friend of Gregory's, he'd fallen under her tutelage due simply to his association with her cousin.

His first afternoon with Rebecca had been a surprise. He had arrived at Merriweather Manor with the intention of spending the day fishing with Gregory on one of the nearby estate ponds. Gregory was no where to be found, but Rebecca had spied Thomas from the second floor balustrade above the vestibule and instructed the butler to send him up. He had hurried to her side, expecting her to tell him of Gregory's whereabouts. Instead, she had motioned to her bedchamber's door and had given him a curt nod when she was sure no one was watching. Once they were beyond the threshold, Rebecca had shut the door, turned the key in the lock and whirled around to regard him with an appraising glance. "Undo my buttons, will you?" she murmured as she turned and leaned back so that he could reach the fabric-covered closures on the back of her cambric gown.

Surprised, but aware of what the invitation meant, Thomas reached up and undid the series of buttons, his breaths coming faster as the gown opened up and the back of her corset appeared. He had seen his mother in a corset once, quite by accident, he recalled. She was quite stunning in the snow white undergarment and stockings held up on her thighs with blue ribbon garters. And his body had reacted much as it was doing now.

"Take off your clothes and wash yourself in the basin," Rebecca ordered as she pulled down one of her gown's sleeves to reveal a naked shoulder. With a teasing eyebrow, she disappeared behind a dressing screen.

For a fraction of a moment, Thomas had considered leaving the room. He knew what went on in this girl's room, knew from the whispers of Gregory's cousins that Rebecca was quite free with her favors but demanded much in return. He stripped quickly before washing his hands in the basin.

"There's a linen next to the bowl. Be sure to clean your prick,"

Rebecca called out from behind the screen. Thomas glanced in that direction as he followed her instructions. He nearly gasped as he caught sight of an entire leg clad only in dark stockings, the tops of her milky white thighs completely uncovered. Aroused, he hurried to clean himself and was nearly finished when Rebecca emerged from behind the screen wearing only the stockings and a black corset.

The corset wasn't like the one he'd seen on his mother. Instead of the straight front that had forced her breasts to swell over the top and appear otherwise flat, this one had ruffled cups that seemed to barely contain her breasts.

Aware Rebecca was studying him, Thomas tried to use the linen to cover his member. He could feel a blush coming over his face and chest when he realized she had witnessed his arousal.

"There's no need to hide it from me," Rebecca said in a low voice, gliding to him so quickly he was surprised when she reached out with one hand, leaned down, and rubbed her palm down the length of his manhood, cupping him with her fingers while using her other hand to support herself on his shoulder. His sudden intake of air was cut off when her mouth covered his, her tongue forcing his lips apart as she kissed him.

It was a moment before he could follow her lead, but when he attempted to return the kiss, she pulled away and watched his face as her hand rubbed his hardened manhood. She smiled when she caught him studying the swell of her breasts above the corset. Her thumb caressed the tip of him, spreading a bead of moisture around as her fingers gripped him. His climax was sudden. When he realized what was happening, he jerked and struggled to maintain his feet while attempting to cover himself with the linen.

Rebecca straightened and regarded him with a bemused smile. "Now that you've had your fun, it's my turn," she whispered, her eyebrow arching in a suggestive manner. She motioned him to the bed. "Do exactly as I say, and I'll invite you back for more," she claimed as she sat on the bed and leaned back into a mound of over-stuffed pillows. At Thomas' nod of agreement, she motioned for him to join her on the bed. "Would you like to kiss my breasts?" she asked, studying him with an air of detachment.

Thomas nodded, but instead of moving to kiss her, he lifted a hand to the ruffled cup of her corset and pushed up gently as he had once seen his father do to his mother. Rebecca arched her other eyebrow and regarded him with surprise, her eyes following his as he moved closer and pressed his open mouth over the swell he created with his hand. She purred in response, lifting one arm above her head. As she rested her arm on the pillows, the top of a nipple appeared above the edge of the ruffle.

Hesitating, as if he were seeking permission, Thomas glanced at her before taking the nipple between his lips and sliding his other hand up the stays and over the mound of her other breast. Rebecca inhaled sharply and arced her back. Her breasts pressed against his hand and mouth, and he used his tongue to tease the tightening bud of the nipple. When he realized it was hard and pink, he moved his mouth to the other breast, pulling down the ruffle with two fingers and exposing her entire breast.

Stunned he'd been allowed to uncover such an intimate part of her, Thomas paused. He didn't know what to do next. But Rebecca's eyes were closed, her lowered lids revealing long lashes that swept across the tops of her cheeks. When she didn't open them, Thomas left one hand on a breast as he slid the other down to a naked thigh. She leaned farther back into the pillows and spread her legs, digging her heels into the down mattress. Her hand grasped his, spreading his fingers with her long ones and guiding his thumb to the lush folds between her thighs. He felt her wetness, felt the heat that emanated from the space hidden in an array of dark curly hair, felt a rounded bud that she had led his thumb to press against and then rub in small circles. He watched in fascination as she writhed and moaned with every circle he made with his thumb, her back arcing and relaxing until she pushed against him and cried out, her expression easily mistaken for one of pain.

At some point, his manhood had hardened again, and he was tempted to push into her. As her hand stilled his, he realized how wet his fingers had become while he performed his ministrations. He quickly positioned himself atop her, his shaft pressed against the moist folds that hid her source of pleasure. Rocking gently, he rubbed his member along her sex, his breaths coming faster as his arousal became complete.

Rebecca's eyes opened slowly and she glanced down the front of her body. Her hands traveled the length of his body and gripped his buttocks, the sensation so startling to Thomas that he climaxed, his seed spilling onto the front of her corset.

Sighing in a disgusted manner, Rebecca rolled her eyes. "You'll have to work on controlling yourself," she whispered as she reached for the discarded linen and wiped off her corset. When Thomas didn't move from atop her, she lifted her hands to his chest and pushed. "You can get off of me now," she said in a bored tone.

Embarrassed, Thomas lifted himself to his knees and took a moment to gaze at Rebecca in the waning light of the afternoon. She certainly wasn't pretty in the traditional sense, he considered, but her raven hair and gray eyes made her alluring, and the dark arc of her eyebrows could make her appear sinister or demure depending on the curve of her mouth.

When she noticed him watching her, Rebecca returned his gaze. "I have a riding lesson tomorrow afternoon, so, no doubt I'll be in a foul mood afterwards. Perhaps you could try and improve my disposition?" she suggested, her arched brow indicating her less than demure side.

Thomas considered her invitation. It would be foolish to turn down the opportunity to be with her. "Of course," he nodded, his voice cracking. "When may I call on you?"

"Be at my door at three, and don't keep me waiting," she ordered in a whisper that held as much promise as warning.

Thomas dressed quickly and bowed before leaving her room, excited about his time with her but determined to keep it to himself.

When he arrived at the appointed time the following day and there was no answer at her door, he let himself into Rebecca's room. He couldn't very well wait outside in the hall where any of her cousins or aunts and uncles could see him.

As promised, Rebecca was in a foul mood when she burst into the room, discarding her boots and riding habit as she made her way to the dressing screen, a stream of not-so-ladylike language coming from her flushed lips. When she finally noticed Thomas perched on the edge of a chair, she took a deep breath and regarded him for a moment before stripping off the last of her outer garments in response to his bow. "You had better please me this afternoon," she warned in a husky voice, one hand dropping the coils of her riding crop as she gripped the handle.

Thomas swallowed, not sure what he could do or say to change her mood. "I shall endeavor to do my best, Miss Merriweather."

Rebecca came out from around the screen and regarded him, her hands on her hips. Thomas stared in awe at her daring costume.

The natural colored corset she wore was like nothing he had seen in his mother's fashion journals. There were arcs cut out around her breasts, but no cups or chemise or chemisette to cover the bare breasts. Her hands and arms were covered in matching gloves, and the stockings she wore barely covered her knees. She smelled of horse and a sour odor Thomas couldn't quite place.

"What would you like me to do first?" Thomas asked, realizing then that she wouldn't be pleasuring him as she had the day before. This was clearly a test of his abilities to please her, but he was sure he could repeat his actions of the day before and leave her satiated.

He was wrong.

He kissed her. He fondled her breasts and licked and suckled them. He coaxed her to spread her legs and worked to make her moist. He slid his penis against the folds between her thighs. He entered her, slowly at first and then increased his thrusts, not allowing himself a release. He rubbed her engorged bud, first with his thumb and then with his entire palm, determined to bring her to the same exquisite euphoria he had managed the day before.

With the riding crop in one hand, though, Rebecca seethed with anger and threatened him with it several times. Frustrated when he was unable to please her and frightened by her threats, he finally crushed her engorged womanhood against the palm of his hand.

He didn't know if it was the nearly painful orgasm she experienced or her general rage that caused her to whip him, but the tip of the crop arced through the air and lit on his rib, biting out a piece of his flesh.

That had been the last time he had been in bed with a woman.

*T*homas closed his eyes a moment to suppress the memory of those afternoons with Rebecca Merriweather. It had been a huge boost to his ego to have the girl invite him to her room —to include him in her group of sexual partners, especially when he knew she favored Gregory.

But at what cost?

He had been left feeling frustrated, doubting his ability to please a woman and believing every woman behaved as Rebecca had in her bedchamber. The wound he sported would be with him his entire life. *Why put myself through such an ordeal?*

Then he had seen Emma in her rain-soaked nightrail. Had seen her engorged nipples poking through the thin muslin and had seen the dark space at the top of her thighs. Seen her with her hair down past her shoulders. He had experienced her evening of nurturing and nursing and the hour of being pressed against her with nothing but the fabric of their nightclothes separating their flesh. Ever since that night, he was easily aroused at the thought of her.

Emma had no torture device like the riding crop Rebecca brandished. Her kind of torture was the complete opposite, providing an ongoing night of pure pleasure. At the moment, her long, slender fingers were doing a rather pleasant torturous dance along his hardened manhood.

Thomas could take it no more and rolled her over onto her back. Moonlight streamed into the room from the west window, and its glow gave a surreal feeling to the slow lovemaking. As it illuminated Emma, Thomas willed himself to hold on longer this time.

He watched Emma's face in the faint light as he heard her quickening breaths, watched her body as the waves took her, watched her breasts heave as he pushed into her, over and over again. He reached out his tongue to lick one of her nipples, then pulled it into his mouth with a kiss, and gently bit it until he felt her fingernails dig into his back. He heard her quietly cry out and then reveled at the sensation her moist lips set off when she kissed his shoulder and collarbone. It was when she arched her back and let out a quiet moan that he finally allowed his release—a spasm that sent his entire body into complete and total euphoria.

Suppressing a yell, he buried his face in her bosom and slowly allowed his body to rest entirely on hers. Out of breath and physically spent, he could do nothing more to fend off her gentle, playful touches, and he simply lay there quietly.

When Thomas hadn't moved for several minutes, other than to breathe in what was then a more normal rhythm, Emma whispered, "Are you asleep?"

"I rather hope not," he whispered in reply, his eyes still closed, "Because if I am, then this has all been just a dream."

Emma smiled and held his head in her hand as it rested on her shoulder. "It was a good dream, was it not?' she asked in a quiet voice.

Thomas, realizing his weight was crushing her into the mattress, rolled off of her body but remained pressed against her. "It was indeed," he whispered as he cupped her cheek with his hand.

"And I shall never think of you the same again."

After a short pause, Emma raised herself up on one elbow and let out a gasp, reaching up to remove his hand from her face. "But, you *promised,*" she whispered loudly while a wave of panic swept over her.

What have I done?

Would he continue to employ her knowing she wasn't the genteel woman she once was? For a moment, she forgot she was to be his mistress, and the thought of losing her position and the income she required to support herself was so overwhelming, she thought she might faint.

"I know," Thomas replied with a nod, an eyebrow arcing. Taking her hand, he raised it to his lips and kissed it gently. "I just cannot think of you the same—as if none of this had happened," he reasoned as he shook his head lightly. But in the growing light of dawn, he saw the panic in her face. He pulled her body onto his and slid his hands down her arms, pleased at the sight of her breasts pressed against his chest. *God!* He wanted so much to love her again. "What is it? What's troubling you?" he whispered, his hands pushing a cascade of long golden hair away from her face.

Near tears, Emma looked away before answering. "I cannot... I cannot afford to lose my position. I don't know how long it would be before I could arrange another one. My townhouse... My horse..." *Who could be carrying a foal.* She stopped in mid-sentence when she noticed his amused reaction. "You mock me?" she asked, her brow rising in dismay. Her body shook with a sob and she fought to hold back tears. *How could I have allowed this to happen? How could a dream turn into a nightmare in such short order?*

Thomas shook his head as he repeated "No, no," several times, his grin growing to a wide smile. "You still have your position. You must keep your position, in fact. At least for the time being. I certainly cannot afford to have you leave me now," he said quietly as he pulled her head against his chest and kissed her forehead.

"You're not going to dismiss me?" she countered in disbelief as another sob robbed her of breath.

Surprised by her reaction, Thomas shook his head. "Of course not," he replied. "That's a promise I can keep," he added, stroking her hair and occasionally kissing her. "And what's this about your horse?"

Emma frowned. "Your horse was seen... *mounting* mine," she

answered, her lower lip pushed out in a pout. At Thomas' look of amusement, she huffed. "I cannot afford another horse, Thomas."

He blinked, realizing she was still feeling panicked. "I'm sure I can forego the stud fee, at least," he teased gently. At the sudden flash of anger in her eyes, he grinned. "And settle a suitable payment for the foal when it's born," he added before he kissed her on the corner of her mouth. The tension in her body seemed to flow out of her all at once

"Truly?"

Thomas nodded. When he considered the two horses were both Cleveland Bays, he rather liked the idea of buying the foal. "I promise," he responded, kissing her again on the forehead.

After a few moments, he remembered their quiet conversation in the barouche. Although it had just been a few hours since Emma had described her daydream to him in such a candid confession, it felt as if they had been lovers for weeks. He reckoned a bit too much champagne and the late hour had contributed to her sharing such an intimate secret with him. Had she been sober, he surmised she never would have put voice to her attraction to him, perhaps not even if he had admitted his affection for her first. "In your dream, tell me, what happens next?" he asked in a whisper.

Emma lifted her head from his chest and looked puzzled. "I... I don't know," she whispered back. At Thomas' quizzical stare, she shrugged. "You interrupted my thoughts before I had imagined anything beyond our... lovemaking."

Embarrassed, she only mouthed the last word, but Thomas read her lips and allowed a wan smile. Her fingers started their play over the side of his ribs and down his hips. His sharp intake of breath told her she had succeeded in exciting him. "And you have not yet shared your dream with me," she reminded him. His raised eyebrow gave part of his reply. "Your dream was far better than mine, I assure you," he teased. "But I have one, and I'm hoping you'll help make it come true," he said quietly as he leaned over and kissed her forehead. He was about to say something else, but his hands stilled hers. She returned her attention to his eyes. "What is it?"

He twisted his body so she had to roll back onto the bed. Suppressing the urge to cry out in surprise at the sudden movement, Emma stared at him. His attention wasn't on her, though, as he seemed to listen intently.

Emma finally heard the sound of quick shuffling feet in the

corridor. She was suddenly under layers of linens and quilts as Thomas covered them both and then managed to pull a nightshirt over his head.

A rapid knock at the door was followed by its opening just as he rearranged some pillows to better camouflage the body next to his.

"Thomas!" Christiana cried out as she came skipping into the room. "How was the ball after I left? You must tell me everything," she demanded as she hurried to his side of the bed.

Her brother could only grin at her exuberance as he reached out to hug her with one arm. "And good morning to you, sister," he answered as he pulled her close, kissed her hair, and then let go of her shoulders. For a moment, he was certain his sister would know of his scandalous liaison with her roommate. "Did you enjoy the evening? Were you... nervous, this being your first ball and all?" He knew he certainly was while hoping Emma could remain motionless during the conversation with his sister.

Christiana smiled and studied her brother's flushed face and general disheveled appearance. "Why, Thomas, I do believe you must have enjoyed more amusement than me," she replied as she reached out to smooth his hair. "Did you dance more at the beginning or at the end? Did you dance with Miss Emma the entire night? And how many times? Lady Pettigrew insisted no more than two should be allowed. And when did you leave the Hornsby's?"

"Yes, and yes," he replied with a nod, "And fifteen times, at least." He jerked as he felt a pinch on the side of his thigh. "Well, maybe only nine or ten," he amended his claim. "I don't give a flying fig what Lady Pettigrew thinks, and I left a bit after two, I believe." Changing the subject as quickly as he could, he asked, "What was the name of the young man from Kent I saw you dancing with?"

"Arthur," she replied as her faced reddened. "And you weren't supposed to see me with *him*," she added with a stern look. "I only danced with him as a courtesy. He was the first to ask me after I danced with Gregory," she added with not a hint of enthusiasm. "I wanted you to see me dance with Mr. Grandby. He was simply the best, most handsome man at the ball," she continued as she nearly bounced with renewed energy.

Thomas couldn't help but smile at his sister's excitement. "I did see him dancing with you," he finally admitted. "Far more than was proper, no doubt. So tell me, did you have an enjoyable evening?"

Christiana nodded, her wilted ringlets dancing around her face.

"But I was hoping you would have an even better evening than me," she said as she sat down on the bed and arched an expectant eyebrow in his direction.

"What makes you think I didn't?" he replied, his demeanor sobering as he decided it was absolutely the best night of his life.

Christiana held her hands out and motioned around the room. "You're *home*," she complained. "If you had been having as grand a time as I, you would still be at the Hornsby's, or maybe just now getting into your barouche. The sun is only now coming up."

Emma had to bite her lip to prevent herself from giggling as she struggled to remain motionless under the covers. Thomas had seen to it she had enough air from an opening near the top of the bed covers. She marveled at how he had arranged the bedding so quickly as to hide her and provide for her comfort all while making himself presentable to his younger sister. Even from under the covers, Emma was reassured of the mutual adoration the siblings shared.

Thomas threw back his head and laughed in response to his sister's feigned disappointment. "You forget I am older and tire more easily than you," he said in his defense. Changing the subject back to his sister's potential husband, he asked in a more serious tone, "What do you really think of Gregory Grandby?" He studied her reaction as he realized she could do worse than Gregory, and Gregory did come from an excellent family. There was no telling if Gregory would be the attentive and devoted husband his grandfathers had been, but at least he knew the man.

Christine's eyes opened wide. "Truly?" she asked, incredulous her brother would ask.

Thomas noted her surprise and thought hard. "Yes."

Feeling her face flush pink, his sister looked away for a moment. When she returned her attention to Thomas, she said, "I love him. You know I do."

Nodding, Thomas couldn't help but feel sad. "Enough, truly, to want to marry him?" he half-asked with a quizzical brow.

"Well, of course!" Christiana replied in mock dismay. Under the covers, Emma had to suppress another giggle. She could just imagine her schoolmate's facial expression.

Thomas grinned and reached for his sister's hand. "Are you going hunting with him today?"

Christiana's eyes opened wide. "I will if it's agreeable with you," she replied, breathless.

Nodding, Thomas replied, "Then off you go," as he gave her hand a squeeze. "And you might want to stay quiet for a few hours more," he added with a wave in the direction of the guest bedchamber. "We have a guest, and due to the late hour of our arrival, I promised we would be allowed to sleep late. We won't be down for breakfast, maybe not even for luncheon..."

"A guest?" his sister interrupted, her eyes widening. "Emma?"

Holding herself motionless, Emma couldn't know if Christiana had guessed she was there in her brother's bed or if she had simply guessed she was the guest.

"Of course," Thomas replied, holding his finger to his lips. "And she's in the room next door, so if you could please keep your voice down until she has enjoyed a good night's rest..."

"Oh, but of course," his sister replied in a loud whisper as she backed away towards the door. "Will she stay for dinner? Will you invite her to stay another night... please?" Christiana noticed the look of happy weariness on her brother's face as he nodded his assurance that he would. She forced herself to calm down and asked much more quietly. "And will you ask for her hand?"

Her breath caught and she put a hand up to her mouth, immediately regretting the question and wishing she could withdraw it. Any previous talk of marriage with her brother always ended badly. "Forgive me," she said hurriedly, rushing back to her brother's side and forcing his hand between her two smaller hands. "It's just that... I'd like nothing more than to have her as my own sister," she pleaded quickly, her eyes wide.

When Thomas didn't respond, she continued, "But also please know your happiness is even more important to me."

Thomas smiled in spite of himself. "Thank you," he said finally. He waved his hand toward the door. "Now be off with you so I can get some sleep." Even as he said the words, he knew with the sun fully lighting his window and the naked woman huddled tightly against his thigh, he wouldn't sleep anytime soon, and perhaps not again until late that night.

Satisfied she hadn't angered Thomas with her plea, Christiana curtsied and had nearly left the room when she turned again. "What *would* make you happy, brother?"

Thomas sighed loudly and replied with a grin, "Your immediate departure!" He tossed a pillow in her direction, but she stepped aside and through the door, giving a giggle as she took her leave of the bedchamber, closing the door as quietly as she could. When her footfalls could no longer be heard, Thomas pulled the nightshirt off of his body and the quilts off of his guest.

Startled at the sudden loss of covers and the light in the room, Emma gasped and tried to cover her bare breasts with an arm. At the same time, she only had eyes for Thomas. He was as naked as she, and more handsome of body than any of the Greek statuary that adorned the west hall and music room of the estate. The morning light made his pale skin appear golden—she could only hope it was doing hers the same courtesy.

"By the gods, you are a sight to behold," Thomas breathed as he gently took her wrist and pulled her arm from in front of her bosom. He moved his hand down to where a satin garter was tied at the top of her stockings. He gently pulled the bow until it was untied.

"As are you," Emma countered, her body trembling in anticipation as her free fingers drew down the length of his side. She felt the other garter release as he pulled the bow loose. Her skin quivered as one of his fingers slid under the stocking and pushed it down to her ankle and over her foot. The same hand slid slowly up her other stocking, caressing the exposed skin of her thigh before sliding under the fabric of the stocking and pushing it slowly down her calf and off of her foot.

Her breaths coming more quickly with each touch of his fingers, Emma lightly stroked his chest with two fingers. She felt the ripples under his skin and saw his body tense. His response was quick and forceful. He was on top of her and inside her and kissing her mouth within a few seconds.

This wasn't the slow, deliberate, careful lovemaking from their early morning hours, but the urgent, passionate coupling of two who hungered for one another. Excited and thoroughly aroused, Emma sucked in a breath as her hands took purchase on his buttocks. There the muscles tensed at her touch.

To stifle his groan from the intense sensation, Thomas moved his lips to her hardened nipples, suckling them each for as long as he could hold his breath. Then he stilled as she arched her back and attempted to stifle a cry, his name coming out in a hoarse whisper.

Once her waves of pleasure had settled and Emma's eyes had cleared, Thomas lowered his entire body onto hers, his head landing solidly on her shoulder. He was aware of her fingers in his hair and on his back, but he had no strength to move and was barely able to catch his breath. *If I die this very moment, it will be as a rather happy man,* he thought with a grin.

He wouldn't admit it to his sister, however.

After a moment, he rolled off of Emma and wrapped his arms around her shoulders, again pulling her head onto his chest. She wrapped one leg around his and slid her hand over his chest and stomach. When he no longer reacted to the touch, she whispered, "That was a rather vivid dream."

As sleep overtook him, she heard him murmur in reply, "But that... that... wasn't my dream."

CHAPTER 66
PENDING ENGAGEMENTS

July 11, 1802, Woodscastle

When sleep finally released Thomas from a dream-filled and very satisfying slumber, he was alone in his bed. Other than the slight scent of Emma on the pillows next to him, there didn't seem to be any evidence that she had ever been in the bedchamber.

Startled, he sat up straight and surveyed the room. The afternoon sun was already behind the west side of the house, and the last vestiges of golden light lit the room. He shoved aside all the covers and linens, tossing pillows onto the floor as he looked for Emma in vain. He winced when he noticed a bloodstain on the linens, confirming what he suspected.

I have taken her virtue.

Guilt descended on him. He chastised himself for not first asking her if she had been with another man. Then he chastised himself for thinking she could have been with another man.

Why had he allowed himself to be caught up in her fantasy? To fulfill some dream she had admitted was just that—a dream?

But then again, how could I not?

He had wanted her more than she desired him. *Still want her*, he amended when he noticed his erection.

Faint voices coming from the room next door finally caught his attention. He rang for Humphrey and began dressing, pausing to allow Humphrey to shave his day-old stubble as best he could in the waning light. A comb alone could not begin to put his hair back where it belonged, so he insisted his manservant pour water over his head as he leaned over the copper tub. Towel-drying his hair while standing in front of the low fire, he did his best to look presentable and proceeded to the bedchamber next door by way of the corridor.

The door was open. Inside, Emma and Christiana were sitting close to one another on the bed, happily chatting about the events of the night before. To an outsider, they would have appeared to be the best of friends or the closest of sisters. To Thomas, they were the two women he loved.

"Mr. Wellingham, do come in," Emma called out as she waved him into the room, stepping off the bed to perform a curtsy. She had already dressed for dinner, as had Christiana. The column gown Emma wore, apricot in layers of light chiffon, set off her flushed face and golden hair. The apricot was certainly better suited to her coloring than the white tulle and satin she had worn the night before.

"You're awake!" his younger sister cried out in delight as she turned to see her brother bowing in the hall. His hair was damp, but not as disheveled as when she'd last seen him that morning, and he looked to be in a good spirits. At the moment, that was all that mattered.

In the waning light from the window and a candle lamp that flickered on the nightstand, Thomas was reminded of Emma's appearance in the moonlight the night before. *Why did I decide to wait for Christiana to be betrothed before seeing myself with a woman?* But another memory of Rebecca came unbidden and he was reminded why he had used his sister as an excuse to avoid entanglements.

"Christiana and I were just discussing the ball," Emma explained as she motioned him to a chair near the bed.

As he entered the guest bedchamber, he glanced around. From all appearances, Emma had spent the entire night and day here. The bed was slightly mussed, and her ball gown lay draped over the edge.

"And did you enjoy the ball, Miss Emma?" he asked as he took the chair. He couldn't help but notice her bee stung lips. He wanted desperately to kiss them again. "I've already had the pleasure of hearing my sister's accounts of her dances last evening."

Emma smiled lightly and nodded, "I did indeed. And did you?"

Conscious of his sister's scrutiny, Thomas nodded. "It was a most pleasurable and exhilarating night," he commented, surprised that for once, his account of attending a ball was truthful. "I do believe I exercised more than I ever have in my entire life. I must have. I slept very late," he said as he redirected his gaze to Emma.

Emma's face took on a pinker color, and she was glad Christiana's attention was on her brother. "I myself only woke up a couple of hours ago," Emma said in reply as she nodded in Christiana's direction.

It wasn't really the truth. She'd been awake for hours, her mind whirling with what had happened earlier that morning. Had she really given her virtue to a man to whom she wasn't married? She had promised herself she wouldn't feel any regret, and she didn't. But prior to bedding her, Thomas hadn't said anything about their arrangement. Anything about her being his mistress. Anything about expectations or compensation. Perhaps he planned to broach the subject after dinner.

Did he expect to bed her again that evening? Although she felt sore, she thought she could abide another coupling if Thomas wasn't as passionate as he had been during their last encounter. His thrusts had been so hard, so deep, impaling her over and over, and yet her own body had countered in kind to meet his powerful moves until he seemed to simply meld and melt into her.

The thought of the passion they'd shared caused a frisson to pass through her entire body, its tendrils of pleasure a reminder of all she had experienced that morning.

"Christiana was kind enough to ask me to stay for dinner and spend another night in this glorious bed. I do hope the arrangement is agreeable to the man of the house?" Although Thomas had asked her to spend the next two days at Woodscastle, it was obvious from Christiana's query and invitation he hadn't informed *her* about the invitation.

Going along with the ruse, Thomas replied, "Indeed, I intended to ask you myself." He turned his attention to Christiana. "Where are your jewels, sister?" he chided her when he noticed she wasn't wearing any pendants or rings.

Christiana gasped and hurried out of the room. Thomas rose from the chair and quickly moved to where Emma sat on the edge of the bed. He took her hand in his and kissed the back of it and then leaned over and kissed her temple. "Thank you for last night," he whispered, a sense of urgency in his voice.

Blushing, Emma nodded. When her eyes finally met his, she sighed. "Thank you, Thomas, for everything," she replied quietly.

Thomas held his breath a moment and then leaned down to kiss her quickly on the lips. "Will you join me for a walk after dinner?" he whispered, his mouth moving to her jaw to steal one more kiss.

"Of course," Emma whispered in reply, her heartbeats coming so fast she thought she might faint. Perhaps he would clarify the terms of her employment as his mistress. She wondered if he would insist they only meet at her townhouse or if she would be expected at Woodscastle certain nights of the week.

Hearing Christiana's footsteps in the hall, Emma quickly removed her hand from his and turned her attention to her roommate as the younger girl entered the room. "That pendant is a very good choice," she remarked as Thomas took a quick step away from her.

"Come. Let's go to the library for drinks before dinner, shall we?" Thomas offered as he held out a crooked arm. Christiana took his arm and he offered the other to Emma. As he caught her eye, he gave her a wink. "Indeed, we shall," Emma said as she took his other arm.

"Did Mr. Grandby succeed in shooting dinner for us this evening?" Thomas asked as they made their way down the hall.

Christiana nodded. "He did, indeed," she replied happily. "He shot three pheasants, and I shot one," she added proudly.

Thomas nearly tripped on the top step. "You shot a pheasant?" he asked, his happy expression quickly turning to a frown.

"Mr. Grandby helped me to aim the gun, of course," Christiana replied as they made their way down the steps. "I could barely lift the thing!"

"Oh," Thomas said simply, not sure what to make of a sister who could shoot a gun. It was bad enough Emma could, he considered. "Will we have music tonight?" he asked as they made their way past the vestibule.

"Only if she is playing," Emma replied as she nodded in Christiana's direction. "I've not had an occasion to practice since leaving school," she said in her own defense when she noted Thomas' disappointment.

Christiana sighed loudly. "I'll play, but only a few selections," she said. "Remember, I'm the one who woke up early today."

Thomas and Emma exchanged knowing glances as they entered the library. Thomas prepared drinks for the three of them and then poured one for Gregory, even though he wasn't yet in the room.

"Give this to your betrothed when he arrives, will you?" he said to Christiana as he handed her the glass.

Startled at his reference to Gregory as her betrothed, Christiana stared at her brother. Even Emma raised an eyebrow and then winked at Christiana. "Of course," Christiana replied as she moved to one of the leather sofas and placed the glass on the table next to it. Thomas waited for Emma to sit down in the other leather sofa, and then he took a seat immediately to her left, leaving no room between them. Christiana couldn't help but notice and tried hard to suppress a look of surprise.

"So, Miss Christiana, I understand you no longer wish to attend Warwick's," Thomas stated.

Christiana displayed an even more startled expression. She cast a quick glance at Emma, who appeared just as surprised Thomas would bring up the topic, tonight of all nights.

"I... I would rather not, 'tis true," Christiana admitted finally. "I find the girls there rather vain and pretentious," she said in her defense, "And I do miss being here at Woodscastle."

Thomas absently squeezed Emma's hand, and she wondered if he was waiting for her to chime in with a recommendation. "Perhaps a part-time governess or tutor can be arranged," she suggested weakly. "There's a good deal of work going on here at the house, too, with the reconstruction of the west wing. It would be convenient for Christiana to be available to answer questions and provide her input during the remodeling," she added, hoping it would be reason enough for Thomas to agree to end Christiana's enrollment at Warwick's.

Thomas angled his head to one side. "I'll consider your request, Christiana, but understand I must speak with Mr. Grandby about these matters. He may be expecting to marry a fully educated girl, and should I allow you to take your leave of Warwick's, he may lose interest in you as a wife."

Although the statement was made in a most serious manner, for some reason, Christiana found humor in it and started to giggle, her face brightening as she considered his words. Even Emma had to cover her grin with one hand to hide her amusement.

When Gregory arrived in the library, he stopped short in the doorway, surprised at what he saw. Emma, looking luminous in an apricot evening gown, sat impossibly close to Thomas on one of the leather sofas. His friend held a drink in one hand and Emma's hand in the other, resting it on his thigh. Christiana, who was wearing the green batiste dinner gown he had purchased for her earlier that week, was laughing at something Thomas had just said. Thomas finally noticed his guest's arrival and started to get up.

"Please, stay seated, Thomas," Gregory said as he entered the room, his jaw discolored from where Thomas' fist had made contact the night before. "I certainly don't wish to interrupt the mood in this room," he added with a huge grin as he moved to sit next to Christiana. He paused to kiss her on the forehead before sitting down. Christiana handed him a glass of brandy and he glanced at her in surprise. "Thank you, my sweet," he said as he took the crystal glass and held it up in a toast. "To a very successful hunt," he said as he held up his chin.

"Indeed?" Thomas replied as he started to take a drink.

"What did you get us for dinner, Mr. Grandby?" Emma asked after she had taken a sip of her drink. The liqueur burned her throat as it made its way down, but it filled her with a comforting warmth.

"Christiana managed to shoot a pheasant on only her second try," he started to say.

"We know what she bagged," Thomas interrupted. "What did you shoot?"

Gregory sighed loudly. "Only our dinner for tonight, which Mr. Tanner is currently making into pheasant under glass, I believe. Oh, and a six-point buck," he added in an off-hand manner. "He was eating the roses in the back garden."

Emma and Thomas gasped in unison before Thomas could turn to her and say, "You'll have to be more careful when you cut flowers," he teased. "We don't want you getting shot."

Christiana was giggling before Emma caught the humor. "Congratulations on your successful hunt, Mr. Grandby," Emma said with a tip of her glass in his direction.

"Thank you, Miss Emma," Gregory replied as he lifted his brandy in her direction. "By the way, my stepfather wanted me to tell you he thought you looked most lovely last night," he added before he took a drink from the glass.

Thomas and Emma exchanged knowing glances. "It was very kind of *Mr. Simpson* to say so," Emma answered carefully.

Christiana smiled as she eyed her beloved. "He said that about me, too."

"And how is Mr. Simpson these days?" Thomas asked nonchalantly as he completed pouring another drink. He picked up the glass of brandy and a glass of claret for Emma and moved to the sofa.

Gregory sat up straight in his chair and regarded his friend. "He is... he is probably the best thing that could have happened to my mother," he finally replied.

"I don't believe you'll find two people more in love with one another than they are," Emma commented lightly. "Well, except for the Vandermeers," she added with a grin. "Has Mrs. Simpson met Miss Christiana then?" she asked carefully, remembering what Christiana had said the night before.

Thomas sat down next to Emma and handed her the glass of wine. They tapped the rims of their glasses and then both turned their attention back to Gregory and Christiana.

Christiana smiled and nodded. "Gregory introduced me to the Simpsons last night. We had dinner with them," she said carefully, relieved she no longer had to hide the truth. "And, I do know what you mean about them being in love," she said as she blushed bright red, noticing that, once again, her brother held Emma's hand in his.

"Mother... Mrs. Simpson... is most pleased with my choice of wife," Gregory assured the two of them as he turned his gaze onto Christiana. "However, Thomas, I feel I must tell you her first choice for me was none other than..."

"Dinner is served," Humphrey announced from the doorway.

Interrupted from his completing his statement, Gregory stood up and offered his arm to Christiana.

"Emma," Thomas said on his behalf.

Gregory's eyes widened as he stared at Thomas, and Christiana gasped as she looked to Emma for confirmation.

"While you were having dinner with the Simpsons, we were including them in our dinner conversation last evening," Thomas explained as he stood up. He offered his arm to Emma and she took it, concerned by Christiana's expression. "Don't worry, sister. Emma wouldn't have agreed to marry your Gregory," Thomas added as he led Emma to the door.

It was Gregory's turn to take umbrage, and he halted in mid-step to consider his friend. "And just why do you say that?" he asked with a frown.

"Because, she doesn't love you," Thomas replied with a smile as he led Emma out of the library.

"Thomas, I saw Lady Pettigrew speaking to you last night," Christiana commented when she had finished her first bite of the pheasant, "And I thought perhaps ...,"

Still admiring the rich spread of pheasant, potatoes, vegetables, and rolls on her plate, Emma glanced at Thomas. She wondered how Lady Pettigrew knew him. Her eyes widened as she watched his face redden and his demeanor darken.

Gregory sat up straighter and paled.

"Excuse me for making this most unflattering statement," Thomas said in measured tones, nodding in the direction of both women, "But Lady Pettigrew is a fastidious, gossipy, old busybody who should mind her own business."

"... But, I think you should know, or perhaps Lady Pettigrew should be told ...," Christiana tried to continue.

"Whatever did she say to make you so uncomfortable?" Emma asked, interrupting Christiana's quiet words. Emma, who knew of Lady Pettigrew through her association with Mrs. Streater, had heard similar comments voiced by others.

Christiana's comment irked Thomas, but he tried to maintain an air of calm. "It seems that whilst I was a child, my parents, who are no longer of this earth, made an arrangement with another family, who are barely still of this earth, that I should become engaged to their as-yet-unborn daughter upon her eighteenth birthday," he explained in an almost mocking tone to his audience of three. "It seems the occasion of her birthday is upon us, and Lady Pettigrew..."

The clatter of a dropped fork on a china plate brought his attention directly onto Emma, whose look of shock and dismay surprised him. Christiana nearly jumped from her chair at the clanking sound, and Gregory gave Thomas a withering stare.

"You are... *betrothed?*" Emma whispered hoarsely, her already flushed face turning red with embarrassment. The events of the previous evening and that morning played through her mind again. At no point had Thomas said anything to indicate he was otherwise promised to another woman.

"No, Miss Emma, I can assure you that I am not," Thomas replied as he held a hand just a few inches above the table, "Yet," he added quickly as he reached out the hand and placed it firmly on her arm, fearing she might flee the table.

Christiana's eyes widened, and she straightened. During their entire tenure together, she had never seen her roommate react in such a manner

Gregory looked down at Christiana and rolled his eyes. "I told him to send a letter....," he whispered as he took Christiana's hand under the table.

"*Yet?*" Emma repeated, again in a hoarse whisper. She was barely able to breathe, and the dining room suddenly seemed very warm. She couldn't help but notice Christiana's reaction. She could only manage a slight shake of her head in Christiana and Gregory's direction followed by an apologetic glance.

"Meaning that I am not yet engaged to anyone, nor will I be engaged to this creature on her eighteenth birthday," Thomas explained quietly. "It would seem I need to dispatch *another* letter to this chit's father to let him know his daughter can be safely married off to a man far more worthy than me."

"Oh, so he did send the letter," Gregory whispered to Christiana.

Emma sat very still for a moment and took a deep breath.

A man far more worthy? Or a man worth more money?

But given the recent successes of Wellingham Imports, she thought perhaps Thomas was worth more than most men involved in trade. She had just completed the audit and knew the value of his company, after all. Christiana had mentioned her own share in the family business would see to her comfort for the rest of her life, even if she didn't marry well. "I am... I am so sorry. Please forgive me," Emma pleaded finally, embarrassed by her outburst.

"It is I who should apologize," Thomas replied quickly, casting another glance in the direction of his sister.

But Emma continued as if she didn't hear him. "Had I known, I surely wouldn't have attended the ball with you, nor accepted your invitation to stay here... how untoward of me..."

"But, why ever not?" Thomas interrupted, his attention now fully on Emma.

Mortified, Christiana slumped in her chair, chastising herself for bringing up the topic of Lady Pettigrew in the first place. She had only meant to explain something to her brother. She had no way of knowing Emma would react so violently.

"If Lady Pettigrew knows of this arrangement, certainly others in town do, too. Others who were at the ball last night," Emma added in a whisper. "They saw you with me. They, too, believe you are betrothed to another."

Thomas nodded as he realized the point she was making. "I appreciate your concern." He moved the hand down her arm to her hand and squeezed it gently. "And, I assure you, I have made it very clear in social circles I never intended to honor my late parent's arrangement," he stated in his own defense.

"'Tis true," Gregory chimed in. "He told me the very same thing last week when I reminded him." He felt a kick in the shin and shot Christiana a look of surprise.

Thomas gave Gregory a look of annoyance. "I have actually never even met the girl in question, nor seen her family since I was five, for that matter, nor do I desire such a meeting," Thomas said in an exasperated voice.

Emma nodded in reply and took another deep breath, attempting to calm her racing heart. "Thank you," she stated quietly, "I'm so sorry for my outburst."

"You are forgiven," Thomas replied with a relieved sigh as he squeezed her hand again.

Taking a drink of wine, Emma noticed a look of guilt on Christiana's face. "What is it?" she asked, worried for Christiana when she remembered who had started the uncomfortable conversation.

Christiana leaned forward, but hesitated before answering. "He doesn't know her, but *we* do," she said in a conspiratorial tone.

It was Emma's turn to slump in her chair. "We *do?*"

Thomas, on the other hand, nearly smashed his wine glass into the table. His sister might be on the verge of betrothal herself, but sometimes her younger age and occasional immaturity could be most annoying.

"Lydia Collins," Christiana stated simply. "From school. She lived in the Delta House."

Emma's mouth opened in surprise, and she found herself unable to breathe. "Lydia Collins?" she cried in dismay, pushing her chair away from the table and covering her mouth with a hand. "The most beautiful girl...?" She paused, trying to remember if during the past three years—the years she and Lydia Collins had attended Warwick's at the same time—the girl had said anything about her marriage arrangements, anything about being engaged, indeed, anything at all to do with marriage.

Thomas was now out of his seat and had moved to Emma's side.

"Christiana," he said in an angry tone, intending to order his sister to her bedchamber.

"No!" Emma blurted and placed her other hand on Thomas' chest. "It is quite all right, Mr. Wellingham," she said. When she recalled her last encounter with the girl, she smiled, and in fact, nearly broke out in laughter. "It really is... quite... all right," she assured Thomas as he gave her a quizzical stare.

Christiana, too, was smiling broadly, happy Emma remembered the same incident as she did. "'Tis what I have been trying to tell you all night, Thomas," Christiana said in a quiet voice.

"Actually," Emma said as she sat up straighter in her chair, "As Miss Collins' intended, you should be most... offended."

Relieved, Christiana began to giggle. Gregory was simply befuddled as he sat watching the show.

"I do believe you could demand some sort of... compensation from her father, Colonel Collins," Emma added, her smile broadening and tears of relief openly flowing down her cheeks.

Thomas, completely flummoxed by the women's behavior, glanced between Christiana and Emma. "Whatever do you mean?" he demanded.

"She eloped the last day of school."

Thomas' eyebrows rose in unison. "Eloped?"

"Lydia Collins eloped?" Gregory echoed, more surprised than even Thomas.

Emma nodded, trying hard not to be amused at his expense.

"With an army officer," Christiana added, the smile now erased from her face.

"The militia was in town that last week of school. I don't believe we saw Lydia during that entire week, at least, not until she came to get her things," Emma added more seriously, sniffling and dabbing at her eyes with her napkin. "I'm surprised Lady Pettigrew didn't know."

Thomas, deep in thought, returned to his chair and sat down—hard. "Perhaps she did know," he said quietly, "And she simply wanted to stir up trouble."

That was it, of course, he realized. The old biddy was trying to determine if he knew of the elopement when she had found him outside the retiring room. She had made a comment about him being seen in Society with a girl from Warwick's. A *different* girl than one would expect.

So Lady Pettigrew had noticed him spending most of the evening in Emma's company. The old woman had been with Mrs. Streater for most of the evening, their heads bent together in ongoing gossip. Hopefully they realized the elopement of his promised bride was of no concern to him when they saw he had moved on, so to speak.

At that moment, he vowed Christiana wouldn't attend another semester at Warwick's. He wasn't about to pay another pound to an institution that employed such a woman as the headmistress.

And what was it Emma had said?

"'Most beautiful girl' did you say?" Thomas spoke quietly, a teasing smile on his face. The smile broadened as he watched Emma's back become more erect. He struggled to stop the smile, though, as he watched her squirm.

Emma's reply was curt. "The most beautiful girl in *Delta House*," she clarified, which sent Christiana into a fit of giggles and Gregory into loud laughter.

CHAPTER 67
PROPOSING A MERGER

July 11, 1802, Woodscastle

"I wish to apologize again for what happened during dinner," Thomas said in a quiet voice as he offered his arm to Emma. She placed her hand on his sleeve, and they walked through the back door to the gardens. Thomas knew they would be watched by Christiana and Gregory and probably by some servants, so he wanted to be as far from prying eyes as possible. "My sister can sometimes be a bit of a troublemaker." He paused in mid-step and shook his head. "Well, not a troublemaker so much as...."

Emma gave a slight smile and nodded in agreement. "She means well, Mr. Wellingham. She hasn't yet learned to be subtle."

Thomas stiffened at her use of his formal name and stopped in mid-stride. "Please, call me Thomas," he insisted in a quiet voice. "Not everything must go back to the way it was."

Emma regarded her host for a moment before replying, "If that's what you wish."

I've offended him, she thought, surprised Thomas wanted such informality in their relationship. *I'm his mistress now,* she remembered. *I must do what he wishes.*

They strolled in silence, the moon rising in the east and casting its eerie glow over the gardens. When they were well hidden from the house, Thomas stopped and then faced Emma. "I would very much like to kiss you now," he struggled to say between nervous breaths.

"And why is that?" Emma replied, the words out before she remembered she probably had no right to ask them.

Taken aback, Thomas didn't have the opportunity to think about his response and said simply, "Because I love you."

It was Emma's turn to be taken aback. "You... you do?" she asked in a whisper. Recovering her composure, Emma placed her hands on his shoulders and allowed him the kiss.

His lips were tentative, their touch featherlight before he pressed a bit harder. Forced to open her lips against his, Emma returned the kiss and wondered if her knees would continue to hold her up. After a moment, she pulled away. "When did this happen?" she asked quietly, her heart racing. Perhaps he truly did feel affection for her. Or perhaps he only felt lust for her after what had happened the night before. He had made it quite clear if he bedded her, she would be his mistress.

You will be mine, he had said.

Thomas glanced away for a moment and then led her to a stone bench surrounded by rose bushes. "I think it started the night I met you at Warwick's," he said as they sat down. He stretched his legs out and leaned forward, his hands clasped together on this knees. "And then, there was something Sir William said at Boodles later that night. And the days you were working here... well, I missed you terribly when you weren't here on Sundays. You defended my home. And there was the night I was so sick," he paused as he pressed his lips together, remembering how much he had wanted her that night. "The day you found my hat in a tree. I almost kissed you then.

"When Gregory arrived, well, damn him, he knew it the moment I introduced you two. Then, last night, at the ball, when you were with him on the balcony, I... I was so *jealous*. I was sure he had misled me about being in love with Christiana and was professing his love for you before I had a chance to do so, and I just couldn't abide the thought."

Awestruck, Emma simply stared at Thomas. When she realized she had been staring too long, she averted her gaze to an old rose bush just beyond the clearing. "And last night?" she asked as she turned to look at him again.

Thomas straightened and took her hands in his. "Last night was all just a dream," he replied quietly, a hint of mischief in his eyes. "Well, except for the part when I was about to ask for your hand in marriage, and Christiana interrupted—."

"Thomas… Oh, my," Emma replied as she pulled one hand away to cover her mouth.

Seeing her look of disbelief, Thomas angled his head to one side. "I thought I was very clear when I told you that if we spent the night together, you would be mine," he reasoned, his voice very quiet.

Emma's breath caught as she recalled her mistaken assumption. "I thought you wanted me to be your *mistress*," she whispered.

Thomas angled his head and regarded her with a look of amusement. "I would take you as my mistress in a heartbeat," he said with a wink. "But I think I'd prefer you as my wife. May I have your hand in marriage?" he asked. He kissed the back of the hand he still held. "I promise you this home, a life together, protection, children if you want them, a sister who adores you very much, and my love."

Tears freely streamed down Emma's face. "But you cannot marry me," she countered as she sniffled. "I have very little in the way of a dowry. You're a wealthy man, born and bred into an aristocrat's family—"

"I wasn't born to a wealthy family, Emma," Thomas interrupted as he shook his head. His brows knit together as he frowned. "Why does everyone think a man can only be rich by inheritance?" he asked in exasperation.

Although it was a rhetorical question, Emma remembered what Humphrey had said that day in the library.

You must remember that not all the wealthy of this world were born to it.

"Well, how…?"

Thomas sighed before speaking. "My father might have been an earl's brother, but he eschewed the aristocracy, much like your father did, and was, at best, a man of middle class. He married a woman who was better off, I suppose, but my mother didn't really come from wealth, either. At least, I don't have any reason to believe she did."

Emma shook her head and gestured toward the estate house. "Then how…?"

Sighing again, Thomas regarded the back of the house and then returned his attention to Emma. "Well, my parents were given Woodscastle as a wedding present," he admitted. "It used to be part of the Trenton holdings. Unentailed, of course. I think a past earl used it for trysts," he added with a roll of his eyes.

"Who was your maternal grandfather?" she asked, sure there was probably another aristocrat in his background.

"Arthur Tennison," he added with a raised eyebrow, knowing she would recognize the name.

Emma gasped, remembering the maiden name of Todd's aunt. "Was he...?" She paused to think of what relation the man might be to Todd Vandermeer's mother.

Thomas shook his head. "Cousin by marriage only and uncle of some sort to Helen," he replied quickly. "There's a connection to the Everly earldom in there somewhere, but I haven't bothered to look it up.

"This entire estate was in utter disrepair when my parents took possession. When it rained, it rained on the inside. The grounds were an overgrown mass of weeds. The west wing is still in a shambles," he claimed as he shook his head. "My father spent the first two years of his earnings from the business just trying to make the place livable. I was eight years old before we had a single servant, and when my mother died giving birth to Christiana..."

Emma's breath caught. She hadn't known what happened to their mother. Christiana had only told her about her father's protracted illness and death.

"... We hired a wet nurse and then a nanny for her. But my father was careful with the business. He didn't take the risks that some other importers did, so there was a business for me to inherit when he died."

Thomas remembered Sir William's comment about the number of importers that had gone out of business at the end of the last century. Perhaps the banker had a good reason for testing him, if for no other reason than to ensure Wellingham Imports stayed in business.

"So, if you didn't come from a wealthy family, then how did you come to be part of an arranged marriage?"

Thomas snorted loudly, hoping he had heard the last of his betrothal to a now-married woman. "In some circles, 'tis common for friends to make promises to other friends when it seems unlikely that the promise will have to be kept," he stated quietly, taking both of her hands in his and gently rubbing the knuckles with the pads of his fingers.

"Whatever do you mean?" Emma asked, puzzled by his comment.

Surprised she didn't understand what to him was obvious, he explained, "Last night, I made you a promise I honestly didn't expect I would have to keep." He paused a moment and carefully considered his words. "If I had known making that promise was going to involve your virtue and the guilt I'm feeling... "

"My virtue was mine to give to you," Emma interrupted as she squeezed one of his hands. "You have no cause to feel guilty for accepting a gift freely given," she assured him, sincerity tingeing her voice.

Remembering Christiana's comments about the gift of her virtue to her lover, Emma's statement made it all clear for Thomas. As the one who usually gave the gifts, he hadn't learned how to graciously accept one.

When he finally nodded his understanding, he felt as if a burden had been lifted. "Still, I never would... well, I might not have... I probably wouldn't have made you that promise in the first place," he said quietly, not really sure what he would have done now that he thought more about it.

In her mind, Emma replayed the scene in the barouche the night before. "But, then, I wouldn't have... at least, I don't think I would have told you my dream," Emma reasoned, her head shaking back and forth. "And then where would we be?"

Thomas chuckled, realizing how simple this all could have been. "You would have spent the night in the guest bedchamber, we would have been up in time for luncheon, and perhaps we would have come out here to the garden during the afternoon." He got up from the bench, turned, and then lowered himself onto one knee as he had seen Gregory do the night before. Placing her hands between his, he said, "But we would still be here with me asking for your hand in marriage.

"Emma, will you marry me?"

Emma smiled broadly, tears still streaming down her face. "Yes, I will marry you, Thomas," she said in a whisper. Leaning forward, she kissed him and continued to do so while he moved up to sit with her on the bench. Somewhere nearby, they heard a squeal of delight.

Startled, their lips parted. "That would be my sister," they both whispered in unison, and then continued to kiss for several minutes.

"After we're married, do you suppose we could sleep in the master suite?" Emma asked hopefully as they started back to the house. "I simply adore that room."

Thomas paused so he could kiss her once more before going around the last of the tall yews. "Of course. I've already asked that it be made ready, in fact," he replied with a mischievous grin.

Emma tilted her head to one side. "And when did you do that?" she asked as she smiled, finding she wasn't at all surprised.

Thomas kissed her again. "A couple of weeks ago," he replied, kissing her temple. "After you commented on how beautiful you thought it was." His lips moved to her jaw line.

"So, you have been thinking about asking me to marry you for... for a *fortnight?*" Emma asked, realizing then that the proposal wasn't a hasty decision on his part. *He's been considering this for a while*.

"Uh, huh," he nodded as he kissed her again and then nuzzled her neck.

"What did I do?" Emma whispered as he kissed her throat. She was finding it hard to concentrate on the subject at hand when his kisses were so delightful.

"It wasn't really anything you *did*," Thomas started to reply as he moved his lips to her earlobes. "It was actually a recommendation from Grandby," he whispered in her ear. "Well, more of a threat, really," he said as he moved his lips onto her bare shoulder.

Emma pulled away to look at Thomas. "How did he threaten you?"

Thomas pulled her into a hug, caressing her hair with one hand while holding the back of her waist with the other. "It seems, my sweeting, I do not own a controlling interest in my own company."

Emma looked up at him as she pulled her head from against his shoulder. "Because you only own fifty percent of your company?"

He chuckled. "Ah, yes, I sometimes forget you know my books better than I do," he murmured as he held her close.

Wrapping her arms around his shoulders, Emma kissed Thomas and then suddenly pulled her lips away. "My dowry!" she said. "Two percent of fourteen-thousand, three-hundred, twenty-five pounds is... is two hundred... uh... eighty... six pounds," she said as she did the multiplication in her head. Her shoulders dropped, though, and she sighed heavily. "'Tis not much," she added sadly, shaking her head as she tried to make out his expression in the dark.

Thomas hugged her closer and chuckled. "Is my company truly worth over fourteen-thousand pounds?" he asked, remembering he hadn't yet reviewed the ledgers from the spring months.

Nodding, Emma studied his face. "Well, it was at the end of May, at least," she said.

"Well, it matters not what it's worth. But just half your stock means all the world to me," he teased as he hugged her harder and grinned "For you see, if you and Christiana and the other major investors in the company were to form an alliance, you could hold a board meeting and have me ousted as the head of the company," he explained.

His impish grin told Emma he hadn't taken the threat seriously. Laughing, she held her head back and placed a hand along the side of his face. "Other major *investors?*" she repeated in delight, placing special emphasis on the plural word.

Thomas shook his head, his brows furrowing. "Yes. Many, apparently. What do you find so amusing?"

Emma's amusement turned to one of confusion when she realized Thomas didn't know that there was but a single major investor in his own company. "How could you not know who owns the other twenty-three percent of your company?" she asked, incredulous.

Shrugging, Thomas shook his head. "Sir William just said he would find investors. And, apparently, he did," he said with a shrug. "He found you," he whispered, leaning in to kiss her hair.

Emma couldn't suppress her smile any longer. "He told me that, at one time there were, indeed, several other investors, but then one of them bought up everyone else's shares for a good deal more than they were worth at the time." She held up her forefinger. "He said the man was his nephew," she added in a quiet voice. "Do you know to whom he was referring?" she teased, remembering Gregory was Sir William's nephew.

The look on Thomas Wellingham's face went from adoration to befuddlement to astonishment to anger to disbelief. "Grandby!" he whispered hoarsely. "Grandby owns twenty-three percent of my company?" Thomas half-questioned in amazement, his voice rising to a yell. And then he burst out laughing and pulled Emma back into a hug. "We are getting married as soon as possible," he said suddenly. "I won't allow a coup on my watch," he claimed with a grin.

Emma regarded his outburst with an amused expression. "Then we shall have to get a special license," she teased, her smile replaced with a small frown. "Which means you'll have to pay a visit to the Archbishop of Canterbury. And don't you have to be at the warehouse tomorrow?" she added. Just how serious was he about a quick wedding?

Thomas shook his head. "Not if we're planning our wedding," he said with a grin as he considered scenarios for the next couple of days. "We can go to town, arrange for the license, see the Vandermeers, and spend the night at the Sablonniere Hotel on Leicester Square," he suggested. "They would certainly have rooms available on a Monday night. Then, if we're allowed, we can get married the following morning."

"The Sablonniere?" Emma repeated in awe. The hotel was elegant and expensive—she'd only been in the lobby when she and her father met friends there from Kent. "Can you afford that?" she asked, incredulous.

Thomas laughed and regarded her for a moment. "You should know better than I," he replied, as he touched his finger to her nose.

"We'll have to go to my townhouse. I'll need to get some clothes and a gown," she said softly, wondering what she could wear for the wedding.

"We shall do that," Thomas replied as he started to pull the pins out of her hair. "But your wedding gown is already up in the wardrobe," he said with a satisfied grin.

"Wedding gown?" Emma asked, not immediately noticing Thomas' mischievous behavior.

"The one you said you adored when we were in the modiste," he replied simply. "The one that was the color of butter. I believe you said it was 'delicious'," he recalled as he continued to pull pins from her bun.

Stunned, Emma tilted her head to one side, and locks of hair began tumbling from the roll on the top of her head. "But when—?"

"The day we went shopping," he answered quietly. "I had Miss Suzanne set it aside whilst you were changing. And then I simply picked it up later that day." He led them to a nearby stone bench and sat down, one hand still clasping one of hers.

Emma regarded him with an awkward smile as she stood over him. "Did you now?" she said in awe.

Reaching into a waistcoat pocket, Thomas nodded, "And I almost forgot to give you this," he said as he pulled out a chatelaine and held it for out her. The ornament already had several keys dangling from one hook, a watch from another, a vinaigrette, a thimble and tiny scissors attached to long chains. A purse filled with coins was attached to another hook. Hanging in the middle was a seal with the letter 'W' engraved in it.

Emma gasped as she studied the chatelaine. "For me?" she breathed as she reached out to touch the ornament. She sat down next to Thomas as he held it in the flat of his palm.

"As mistress of the house, you should have the keys and some pin money, of course," Thomas explained as he noted her surprised expression. "It was my mother's," he added as he placed it in her hand.

Swallowing hard, Emma nodded as she studied the chatelaine. The metal work was intricate, especially where the short chains were attached, and the hooks at the ends of the chains had been closed shut so the keys and purse couldn't be easily removed. A ring at the very top was large enough for a ribbon to be threaded through so it could be worn even if a gown didn't have a pocket. "Thank you, Thomas," she said quietly. "I cannot believe I'm really getting married." Lacing her fingers into the hand that held hers, she squeezed it gently.

"And I cannot help but wonder what would have happened had Mr. Vandermeer asked for your hand in marriage," Thomas commented as he squeezed Emma's hand tighter. His mood sobered, the playfulness gone at the mention of his friend.

Emma sighed. "I probably would have accepted his offer," she admitted, recalling her thoughts at the time she realized Todd's intentions. "But I thought of Deborah long before it came to that," she added quickly, hoping to lighten the mood again. "I was very flattered by his attentions, I must say. But in my heart, I knew I wasn't the wife for him."

Nodding, Thomas swallowed hard. "That day Vandermeer was leaving here as I was arriving... my heart broke just a bit when he said you had accepted his invitation to dinner," he admitted sadly. "And... and it broke a bit more when he said he intended to ask for your hand," he added more quietly. "Of course, I was happy for him, but at that instant, something happened. 'Tis why I was so upset, I suppose, when I heard my sister trying to make a bet with you." Again, he squeezed her hand and swallowed hard.

Remembering Christiana's stunned reaction to her brother's outburst, Emma set the chatelaine on the bench and put her other hand over the one that held hers. "Whatever did you say to Christiana that evening? I do hope you weren't too cross with her."

Cocking his head to one side, Thomas smirked. "I didn't even discuss it with her," he said quietly, shaking his head at the recollection of that evening. At Emma's expression of surprise, he added, "It wasn't as if I disagreed with her assessment of Mr. Vandermeer. Everything she said about him was true to some extent."

Emma inhaled and made a 'tsk' sound. "Christiana was always dreadfully afraid you would arrange for *her* to marry Mr. Vandermeer," Emma said with a grin. "She spoke of it often at school."

Thomas shook his head as a smile broke his melancholy. "And I very nearly did that very day!" he exclaimed loudly. The lighthearted exchange left Emma with a smile on her face as they sat quietly for a few moments, the chirping of crickets the only sound in the garden.

"Did he... did he ever kiss you?"

Emma sat up straighter and stared in surprise at Thomas, her face flushing red. "Why, yes, you know he did," she admitted with an embarrassed grin.

At the hint of anger that crossed Thomas' face, she quickly put a finger on her cheek. "Here, and," she moved the finger to the back of the hand that Thomas held. "Here, and here," she added as she moved her finger to her forehead, "And here." she said as she pointed to her temple. "You saw that one at the wedding ceremony, of course," she whispered.

Thomas smiled at the recollection. "Ah, yes. The moment I knew you were free of the man," he said lightly.

Gasping, Emma wasn't sure how to take the comment.

"Until I met his bride, I thought he might change his mind and decide he wanted you instead," Thomas said in his defense, the teasing smile still on his face.

Emma shook her head and matched his smile. "You had no reason to be concerned, I assure you," she replied, ending her comment with a sigh. "I promised Christiana I would stand with her at her wedding, and she said she would do the same for me. It would be lovely if Deborah and Todd could be there."

Thomas smiled and kissed her on the forehead. "We can write out our invitations and deliver them as soon as we confirm the date with the church. I'll ask Grandby to stand with me," he stated as he pulled out the last hair pin and ran a hand through her long hair, unwinding the last vestiges of its bun. "That way I can keep an eye on him and prevent the coup," he said with feigned enthusiasm. "There," he said proudly as he stroked her hair and rested his cheek against the side of her head. "I like it better this way," he murmured.

Giggling, Emma wrapped her arms around her man. "I love you," she said quietly.

Smiling, Thomas hugged her until she was pressed against him. "And when did this happen?" he teased, still stroking her hair.

Emma thought for a moment. "Well, I think it started the night I met you at Warwick's and you offered me a position," she said, a wistful expression crossing her face. "I could have kissed you that night."

Thomas pulled away and gasped. "Scandalous!" he said with a teasing grin.

"The first night I spent here, Christiana wanted me to like you enough to marry you."

Thomas squeezed his eyes shut. "Sisters!" he whispered as he shook his head.

"And the days I was working here... well, I missed you terribly on Sundays when I wasn't here," she said wistfully. "There was the night you were so sick. I was so afraid for you. The night of the shooting stars. And the morning you gave me the necklace and earrings." She stopped and angled her head. "Why... why the teardrops?" she asked, curious about their meaning.

Thomas shook his head. "Mr. Vandermeer didn't understand the symbolism at first, either. They're supposed to be rain drops."

Emma bit her lip and swallowed. "Oh, of course."

"You were saying?" Thomas whispered as he kissed her hair again.

Emma grinned and continued her list. "At the warehouse, when you asked me to spend a few days at Woodscastle. Then, at The Clarendon Hotel, you ordered champagne! And when you punched Gregory on the balcony last night, then I just knew I loved you."

Thomas listened to her list and smiled. "I forgot about the night of the shooting stars," he said sadly. He had spent most of that afternoon thinking Emma would leave and never return to Woodscastle. And then, after their walk through the garden, he realized that perhaps she didn't despise him as he had expected. "What did you wish for that night?" he asked as he continued to kiss her hair. "My demise, I suppose," he added under his breath.

Emma smiled and sighed. "Oh, no. I wished for you to be my man," she remembered as she bit her lip. "And it's come true!" she added in an excited whisper, her eyes wide. Her arms wrapped tightly around his chest, she hugged him. After a moment, she leaned her head back and asked, "What was your wish?"

Thomas shook his head. "Oh, no," he replied, straightening on the bench. "You'll think me a libertine. It was scandalous," he teased as he continued to shake his head. "You would never think the same of me again," he added with a mischievous grin.

"I promise that whatever you say, I won't change the way I think of you," Emma whispered, teasing him with a kiss.

Smiling at first, Thomas regarded Emma in silence. After a long moment, his demeanor turned serious. "I wished that we could spend every night together," he said softly. He pulled her into a long kiss, a kiss full of promise and passion.

When at last their lips parted, Emma whispered, "I can make that wish come true."

Thomas kissed her forehead and held her against his shoulder. "Do you still think of me the same way?" he teased.

"A libertine, you mean?" Emma replied, her teasing smile lighting her face.

Thomas chuckled.

Several minutes later, they returned to the house and made their way to the library. Christiana was sound asleep on Gregory's lap, her head nestled into the small space between his arm and his chest. "I would get up, but ...," Gregory said by way of an apology.

"It must be past eleven," Emma said with a knowing grin as she took a seat on the leather sofa. "She simply cannot stay awake long after dinner."

Thomas poured drinks for the three of them and regarded his best friend as he took notice of his sister. "She can be a burden," he said by way of warning as he gave Emma and Gregory glasses of sherry.

"One I am more than willing to bear," Gregory replied as he took the glass. "Thank you," he added with a nod. He was surprised Thomas didn't appear upset at finding his sister in such a compromising position.

Thomas took the last drink and sat down next to Emma. She tipped her glass in his direction and he touched the rim of his glass to hers. "To us," he said with a smile. They both took sips from their drinks before returning their attention to Gregory.

The man was grinning at them, but directed his comment to

Emma. "You really must excuse my friend for having taken so long to ask for your hand."

Emma smiled and leaned forward. "Considering he couldn't ask me whilst I was his employee, I rather think his timing was perfect," she countered, her hand reaching for Thomas'.

"Now see, that's where things got a bit off," Gregory replied, holding his glass in the air. "You were never supposed to be his employee, you must know," he said, his brows furrowed and a rather indignant expression on his face.

Thomas stared at his friend and then glanced at Emma. Her brows were raised in shock.

"Well, why ever not?" she asked, unsure of his meaning.

Gregory regarded Thomas and then turned his attention back to Emma. "Did you ever wonder why you attended Warwick's?" he asked as he absently stroked Christiana's arm with the hand that held her.

Feeling defensive, Emma sat up straight. "Sir William said it was my father's dying wish I attend Warwick's," she replied, her lower lip quivering. "He left me enough money to pay for it, so I didn't think to go against his wishes."

Gregory nodded, although from his demeanor, Emma had the impression he didn't believe the reason. "How did you come to own two percent of Wellingham Imports?"

Sighing, Emma replied, "Sir William recommended the investment just before I started the accounting class."

Gregory shook his head. "Did you ever wonder how it was Christiana Wellingham ended up as your roommate?" he asked, his brows nearly into his hairline as his voice increased in volume.

Emma sighed and angled her head. "Well, as I recall, she was rooming with an older girl who got married during Christmas holiday and didn't return to school for the spring semester. I didn't have a roommate, so Mrs. Streater asked if I would be willing to take her as my roommate, and of course, I agreed," she explained calmly. She was suddenly aware of Thomas. He had placed one hand firmly on her knee and was leaning forward as if he intended to pounce on his best friend.

Gregory frowned as he considered her answer. "What do you mean, 'of course'? Why did you agree?"

"I found her attitude refreshing," Emma started to say, "She wasn't a snob like so—"

"Why are you asking these questions?" Thomas interrupted as he leaned farther forward, a frown firmly aimed at his best friend.

But Gregory ignored Thomas' question to ask, "Why did it take you so damned long to meet Thomas?" waving his glass toward his friend.

Emma sat up straighter and regarded her inquisitor, surprised at his curse. "Well, I was already in Mr. Stokes' class when Christiana moved in, so I wasn't at the Gamma House when Mr. Wellingham called on her," she replied defensively. "But had he come for her on a Wednesday night, I would have been home to meet him. I finally did meet him when he came for dinner on a Wednesday last February," she said. "The same night he hired me to be his auditor."

"At whose recommendation?" Gregory countered, directing the question to Thomas. "And why did you need an auditor?"

"Sir William's," Thomas replied coolly, not appreciating his friend's odd manner. "And, as I thought you understood, I believed an accomptant was embezzling money from my firm," he added as he tried to recall exactly when he had noticed something was amiss in the books. "And someone was, just not how I was expecting it to turn out. You know about that, of course," he spoke quietly, a tinge of anger coming to his voice.

Shaking his head from side to side, Gregory sighed. "Do you really think the Board of Directors of the Bank of England would authorize a scheme to fake embezzlement just to determine if a business owner could read his own books? When Sir William already knew you could?" he asked rhetorically. His exasperation was readily apparent. His face was a bright red and perspiration dotted his forehead.

Mortified, Thomas and Emma stared at Gregory as realization struck them. If not the Bank of England, then it could have only been one man.

Sir William, they realized in unison. *But why?*

Her face flushing bright red, Emma stole a glance in Thomas' direction. She wondered why Gregory seemed so upset.

"And just how did you end up in a townhouse right next door to my *mother?*" Gregory asked Emma, his question more of an accusation.

Emma looked surprised at that, but realized what he was implying. "Sir William suggested I look for a space in the West End. He said he knew the owners of a townhouse where a tenant had recently died, and he said it would be available just before I was due to finish school."

Gregory shook his head in disbelief. "Did you even have to *interview* for the townhouse?" he asked, asking the question as if he already knew the answer.

Offended by the tone of the question, Emma sat back in the sofa. "Well, yes. I had tea with your mother and Mr. Simpson. Although, it wasn't really an interview, come to think of it. More like... an introductory tea," she said as an afterthought. "I believe they had already made up their minds to allow me to lease the townhouse," she continued, her comment coming out slower as she considered Gregory's line of questioning. "I think that must have been when Mrs. Simpson decided she wanted me to be your *wife*," she added with an arched eyebrow, hoping the comment might put her on more equal footing with him.

Gregory's ears turned bright red, and he rolled his eyes. "That... that was unforeseen," he admitted, waving his glass.

"Indeed," Emma replied as she exchanged glances with Thomas. "Are you saying Mr. Wellingham and I are together because of Sir William? Because he played matchmaker for us?" she asked in a quiet voice. "Because, if you are, you must also know several others were working toward the same match."

Thomas gave her a sideways glance but didn't ask for names. Todd Vandermeer had certainly been working on him, and he knew Christiana had been working on Emma. Had Deborah also been involved?

Gregory stared at the opposite wall, trying to decide how to best explain his position. "You were supposed to meet and fall in love a year ago!" he said crossly. "Sir William did everything he could to get you two together, and every step of the way, you... you *bungled* it! I was so vexed, I started buying up stock in Wellingham Imports just so I could stage a takeover and force you two to get married, only to find out I couldn't get enough stock unless I married *you!*" he said in dismay, his attention on Emma.

Emma gasped and turned to Thomas. "You were right about the coup!" she exclaimed, her face brightening in delight.

Smiling, Thomas took Emma's hand in his and kissed the back of it. "All this, just so you could marry Christiana?" he asked his friend.

"And to get me out of Warwick's," Christiana added sleepily, her head still resting against Gregory. She sighed deeply.

Thomas shook his head and took a long drink from his glass. "Why... Why didn't you just ask me for her hand when you knew you wanted to marry her in the first place?"

Gregory sat up straight at that, causing Christiana to quickly wrap her arms around his neck in order to hang on or be dumped onto the floor. "And what would you have said if I had asked permission to marry Christiana a year ago?" he demanded to know, his face darkening in frustration.

Emma straightened in the sofa and placed her hand on Thomas' knee. "*I* would have said 'no'," she replied firmly. "Christiana was my roommate and far too young to be considering matrimony a year ago," she explained with a firm nod in Gregory's direction.

Christiana tilted her head to look up at Gregory. "She's right, you must know. I was too young then," she admitted quietly.

"Well... well, what about at Christmas?" Gregory asked Christiana, surprised at her admission.

"I would have said 'yes'," Christiana replied with a nod. "I knew... I was falling in love with you then."

"I suppose then it might have been all right," Emma said slowly, remembering Christiana's gradual maturity.

"If anyone is asking *me*," Thomas interjected, "I would have said 'no'." At Emma and Gregory's surprised looks, he added, "If you had married then, how would I have met Emma?" he asked in his own defense.

"Oh, but you would have," Gregory countered with a wave. "At our wedding, certainly. Or Sir William would have scheduled an investors' meeting. Or planned to have you come to the bank when Miss Emma was there. Or *something*," he added lamely, despite remembering nearly every other attempt to get them together had somehow failed.

Emma and Thomas regarded one another as they interlocked their hands. "You know, a simple 'best wishes' would have been perfectly acceptable," Emma said before finishing her drink. "Perhaps we should ask the Vandermeers to stand with us at our wedding."

Thomas grinned at her suggestion and caught Gregory and Christiana both shaking their heads. "Oh, no," Gregory said as he set his drink down on the table next to him. "*We* are standing with you," he insisted. "I want to sign that document that says I witnessed you getting married."

Emma squeezed Thomas' hand and he glanced at her. When she only smiled at him, he arched a brow, questioning her meaning. "What about a double wedding?" she whispered as she tilted her head in the direction of Gregory and Christiana.

Thomas shook his head. "Remember, Christiana wants a large wedding, with all our family and friends in attendance," he said in a quiet voice. "And she shall have it."

Christiana, now wide awake, overheard her brother's remark and smiled. "Thank you, Thomas." After a short pause, she added, "Oh, and best wishes to you both."

CHAPTER 68
PILLOW TALK

July 12, 1802, Very early in the morning, Woodscastle

Despite being deep in sleep, Emma was aware of being watched. The sensation startled her nerve endings, forcing her to slowly come out of the depths of a dream and then more quickly out of her slumber and into consciousness.

Leaving her eyes closed, she listened intently. When she recognized the scent of the man next to her, she remembered where she was and smiled.

Slowly opening her eyes, she found Thomas gazing at her, his head resting in his hand as he supported himself on one elbow. With just one candle lamp still lit in the master suite, his face was in shadow but still recognizable.

He leaned over and kissed her forehead. "I didn't mean to wake you," he whispered as he drew the back of his forefinger down her cheek.

"Is it already morning?" she whispered in reply, turning her head so as to kiss his finger.

Thomas shook his head.

"Are you well?" She stirred and started to get up.

"Shh," he replied as he placed a hand on her shoulder and gently held her down. "I'm very well," he said quietly as he leaned over and kissed her mouth. Returning the kiss, Emma wrapped an arm around his shoulder and pulled him toward her. When their lips parted, he whispered. "What were you dreaming? You had a most happy look about you."

Emma smiled and closed her eyes. "We were making love... "

"Indeed?" Thomas whispered with a grin.

"But it wasn't here," Emma continued as she opened her eyes and looked around the room, struggling to remember the details of the dream before it slipped away. At Thomas' raised eyebrow, she whispered, "We were... outside... near where you chop wood."

Chuckling, Thomas leaned in and kissed her neck. "And why ever would we be out there?" he teased as he moved his kisses to her collarbone.

Emma sighed and brought her hand up to her head, running her slender fingers through the loose cascade of hair that lay on the pillow. "It was my first time with you," she answered dreamily as she remembered the afternoon she and Christiana had lunched on the back terrace. She remembered the wave of incredible pleasure that had passed through her body, leaving her flushed and feeling uncertain.

"Whatever do you mean?" Thomas asked as he stopped his gentle kisses.

"I saw you chopping wood and felt the most incredible sensation inside me," Emma whispered, still lost in the dream, her hand unconsciously touching his biceps. "It was the most incredible pleasure," she whispered, barely saying the last words as she took a deep breath.

Watching her relive the scene, Thomas remembered the day and felt a wave of excitement pass through him. "Just from watching me chop wood?" he whispered, not quite convinced of her claim.

"Mmm," Emma nodded and smiled. "I was in love with you, but I couldn't admit it to anyone, not even myself," she said quietly. "You were my employer, after all," she whispered as she rolled to her side, placing her lips on his chest and kissing him.

Thomas rested a warm hand on her shoulder. "I shall have to chop wood more often," he murmured before he kissed her neck. "Are you comfortable?" he asked, his lips finally coming to a rest on the top of her shoulder.

"Mmm. Very," she replied, turning her head so her nose poked his sternum.

"I mean, with me?"

Emma kissed the space between his ribs and turned her head to look at him, her brows furrowed as she considered the odd question. "Quite," she said with a nod, and then returned her attention to his chest. After a pause, she turned to look at him again. "Are you comfortable with me?" she asked, her heavy-lidded eyes opening wider.

A grin broke out on Thomas' face. "I am. It feels as if I have known you far longer than just a few months," he murmured. "And I believe I can tell you anything and know you would hold it in confidence."

Her eyes half-closed, Emma nodded her agreement. "I know of what you speak." She nestled her face against his chest and then added, "Would it be different, do you suppose, if we had met last year? Or the year before?"

Thomas closed his eyes a moment, remembering Gregory's recitation of the plan for the two of them to meet far earlier than they had. "I don't know," he finally replied. "I'm quite sure I would have eventually felt affection for you," he admitted quietly. At her raised eyebrows, he added, "I probably would have had more opportunity to eat your good cooking," he explained, his manner quite serious. "And you?"

Emma shook her head. "I was deathly afraid to meet you," she whispered, recalling Christiana's early assessments of her brother. At his expression of shock and guttural response, she added, "Your sister made you out to be some sort of spoiled rotten rich man who always got his way!"

Thomas smiled despite the description. "I am. And I do," he claimed with a chuckle, ignoring the sting of hearing his sister's harsh opinion of him. "She wasn't pleased about being sent to boarding school," he said after a long pause. "Although she was better about it after she moved into your room."

Sighing, Emma closed her eyes. "I almost didn't have the patience for her those first few weeks," Emma whispered, wrapping an arm around his waist and pulling herself closer to him.

"You had more than I did, I'm sure," he whispered in reply, his lips finding the top of her head. "She could speak of nothing else but you the first few times I took her to dinner," he remembered, his fingers absently stroking her bare arm and shoulder.

Opening her eyes, Emma rolled them and try to suppress a grin. "Oh, dear," she said with an embarrassed grin.

"Oh, yes," he replied playfully. "You were tall and golden blonde and had a figure better than the goddess Diana," he recalled dreamily.

"I am. And I do," Emma heard herself replying before she burst into a fit of giggles.

Tracing a lock of her hair across the pillow, Thomas regarded her face for several moments, the candlelight making it appear golden. "When... When did you... *want* me?" he asked as he placed his lips against the top of her breast and rolled her onto her back.

"When did I *not* want you?" she replied with a happy grin, putting her hand against his head and spearing her fingers through his tousled hair.

He lifted his head from her bosom and looked at her intently. "When, really?" he asked, kissing her raised arm.

Emma rolled her head to the other side and thought about his question. "The night of the shooting stars, I suppose," she replied as if back in her dream.

Taken aback, Thomas studied her face for a moment. "I thought you... I thought you despised me that night, after what I'd said to you, what I'd done... I was sure I had left bruises on your arms, I was so... I was so very scared for Christiana." His face darkened as he recalled that afternoon. "You thought I would be a brute and beat her," he accused in a sad whisper. "I was sure you would leave here and never return..."

Emma shook her head back and forth. "No... no... I told you before it was one of the times that made me love you," she whispered dreamily. "You were so apologetic, and you insisted I spend the night, and you brought me to this room, and you gave me that beautiful gown... I *wanted* you that night," she remembered as she continued to stroke his hair.

Just a fortnight ago?

They lay in silence for several minutes before Emma inhaled. "When did you want me?" she asked, her grin returning.

"When did I *not* want you?" Thomas replied quickly, teasing her with kisses on her nipples and belly.

Smiling, Emma jerked away from him and placed her hands on either side of his face, her thumbs stroking his sideburns and cheeks. "When, really?"

Thomas' face darkened, and he shook his head. "The night I was so sick," he whispered, his brows furrowing as he remembered what he had told Todd the day after. "I wanted you so badly. Emma, if I had... if I had been able, I swear... I would have taken you,... even against your will, I fear... I wanted you so badly," he whispered, the memory frightening him. He looked away from her expression of surprise and slumped into his pillow.

Emma lifted herself onto an elbow and stared at him. "It wouldn't have been against my will, I assure you," she whispered and then bit her lip. "In fact, had you... been able, I might have had my way with you when we were in bed together that night," she teased gently.

Thomas opened one eye and considered her words. "Indeed?" he asked quietly, not completely convinced. "We were in bed together that night?" he repeated, unable to keep a playful grin from his face.

Emma smiled at his comment and sighed. "Whatever did I do to make you want me so?"

"Besides undressing me and feeding me and keeping me warm?" he replied with a snort. But he watched her face and knew his answer wasn't enough. Closing his eyes a moment, he thought of the conversation he'd had with Todd about women. "When I got home that night, I saw you at the top of the stairs. I thought you were an angel, Emma. I thought I was dying, and you were coming to take me to heaven," he whispered, his eyes still closed. "When I finally realized it was you, well, you were naked, and..."

"I was not *naked*," Emma interjected, her voice a hoarse whisper and her expression one of shock.

"You appeared naked to me," Thomas amended, opening his eyes and watching her as he continued. "Your nightrail was wet, and I could see through it," he recalled, remembering the curves of her body and her breasts and her hardened nipples poking through the thin, wet fabric. "And it was then I realized you were the perfect woman, Emma. You could be pure and virginal,... angelic, if you will, and yet, you could also be... a... a wanton in my bed... you could satisfy my every immoral desire," he finished, swallowing as he did so.

Emma considered his words. "But we hadn't yet made love... however could you know I would *satisfy* you?" she whispered, frowning as she watched him.

Thomas shook his head from side to side. "Are you joking?" he half-asked in reply, his expression one of surprise. At Emma's blank look, he grinned. "You allowed me to kiss you on the neck in the library, you wanton woman."

"You said you would have a good day," Emma countered quickly.

"And you sat with me under that quilt when I wasn't wearing a stitch."

"You were chilled to the bone!"

"You let me pull you into my bed, and then you slept with me with your bum pressed..."

"You were freezing," she interjected in a hoarse whisper.

"And then you insisted I sleep in *your* bed when the sheets were too mussed..."

"You must not have been as sick as you implied."

"I think... I believe you would've done anything to keep me alive that night," Thomas said simply.

Emma stared at him for several seconds before she finally swallowed and replied, "'Tis true."

"And you allowed me to kiss you at the Vandermeer wedding... twice!"

"But that was... appropriate." After a moment, she added, "Do I?"

Thomas regarded her with a raised eyebrow. "Do you...?"

"Do I satisfy your every immoral desire?" she whispered intently, studying his face in the dark.

Taking a deep breath, Thomas grinned and reached over to pull her toward him. "Considering we aren't yet married and we're sharing a bed and have made love at least a dozen times... I would say you are indeed a wanton!"

"Half a dozen," Emma corrected him, allowing a grin. "Not that I'm counting."

"Then let's make it seven," he suggested playfully.

Emma leaned in and kissed him on the lips, soft and long, before nibbling on his ear and replying, "Yes, let's."

CHAPTER 69
SECRET NO MORE

July 12, 1802, #4 Kingly Street

"Good morning, Mother," Gregory said as he bowed before Sophia Simpson.

Sophia smiled broadly and reached for her son's hand. "Oh, Gregory, do come in," she said as she pulled him over the threshold and into a hug. "'Tis so good to see you," she added, finally releasing the startled man from her hold.

Since his mother had opened the door instead of her husband, James Simpson was not in residence. Given it was his stepfather's custom to meet friends at the Crown and Anchor for lunch on Mondays, Gregory had counted on James to continue the tradition this day.

Smiling at her enthusiasm, Gregory kissed his mother's cheek. "And you, of course," he replied, noticing his reflection in the oval mirror that hung adjacent to the door. He quickly smoothed his windblown hair as he read the printing on a card secured in the frame of the mirror.

Lunching with the boys. I love you.

"You didn't bring your future wife?" Sophia asked, looking out into Kingly Street before closing the door.

Gregory shook his head. "No, mamma. I wanted to spend some time with you, if that's agreeable with you," he replied, holding his hat in one hand while he regarded his mother. She was, as usual, luminescent. How had she managed to remain such a handsome woman despite her age? She wore a stunning green morning gown in a design more modern than usual for her. "You look very beautiful. May I take you to luncheon?"

Sophia stepped back, her smile faltering. "Whatever is wrong?" she asked as she took her son's hand and led him in the direction of the parlor. "Oh, and I'm being a dreadful hostess," she added as she turned and reached for his hat. She placed it on a shelf in the vestibule. "James usually answers the door," she said in her own defense.

"Nothing is wrong, I assure you," Gregory said as he rolled his eyes. "I would just like to dine with you," he explained lamely. "And I... I have news."

Indicating a tall chair in the parlor, Sophia whirled to stare at her son. "News?"

Gregory moved to take the chair but waited for his mother to be seated on the settee before doing so. "Mr. Wellingham has proposed marriage to Miss Emma," he said with a nod. "And she has accepted. They may, in fact, be married by the end of the week," he added, hoping Thomas really could arrange a special license so they could be married in just a few days. Thomas Wellingham could be most demanding when circumstances required it, but Gregory wasn't sure if Emma was old enough to marry without a guardian's consent.

Sophia took a deep breath and tried hard not to look disappointed. "I expected as much, from what Sir William said at dinner last night. Her lease doesn't expire for at least eight months, but I suppose—"

"Oh, they plan to keep the townhouse," Gregory interrupted as he leaned forward. "I was hoping you would agree to Mr. Wellingham using it when necessary. In cases of inclement weather, for example," he explained.

Sitting up straighter in the settee, Sophia considered the request for only a moment. "Of course, that would acceptable," she said as her demeanor brightened. "I cannot tell you what a relief it is we won't have to find a new tenant," she claimed as she stood up and headed out of the parlor.

Gregory could barely get out of his chair before his mother was out of the room.

"Well, are you coming?" she asked as she reappeared in the doorway carrying a parasol and a reticule.

Shaking his head, Gregory suppressed a grin and said, "Right away," and joined his mother in the vestibule. As he took his hat from the shelf, he asked, "Will you leave a note for Mr. Simpson?"

Sophia nodded and pointed to the card propped up in the frame of the oval mirror. *Lunching with my son. I love you*, it read.

Gregory smiled and opened the door for his mother. "We'll have to do this more often, you must know," he said as he stepped out and held his arm for her.

"Indeed, we shall," Sophia agreed as she locked the door and took his arm. "With you living so much closer to London, we can," she said happily.

He helped her into the carriage and ordered the driver to take them to Berkeley Square. "At some point, you'll be recognized," he said quietly. "I won't be able to keep you a secret much longer." He smiled, remembering the conversation he had with Christiana. *Why, indeed, should I keep secret the women in my life?*

Sophia waved a dismissive hand. "Oh, you no longer need keep me a secret," she said as she regarded her son. "In fact, I'll be visiting with the society reporter for *The Morning Chronicle* this week," she explained when she noticed Gregory's look of surprise.

"Society reporter?" Gregory repeated. "Whatever for?" he asked in surprise. What did his mother have in mind?

A mischievous smile crossed Sophia's lips. "Why, to submit the announcement about my son's betrothal, of course," she replied demurely. "Mr. Vandermeer may have been the first to have such an article written about an upcoming wedding, but he won't be the last."

His brows furrowing, Gregory regarded his mother. "What if he recognizes you?" he countered. "He may end up writing an exposé on you."

Sophia shook her head. "'Tis doubtful the reporter will even know anything about my so called disappearance, but if he's older and remembers and asks me, I'm prepared tell him everything."

Gregory swallowed hard as he watched his mother's face. "Are you certain about this?" he asked, worried about the effect the news might have on his other family members.

Sophia shrugged and regarded her son with a smile of resignation. "'Tis time. It's been over twenty years, after all," she replied with nod. "And 'tis time your uncle be relieved of the burden of keeping me a secret, too. It was never fair to William. He had to hide the leftover money in multiple accounts in my husband's name for several years after our marriage," she said as she absently twirled the parasol.

Gregory leaned to one side as he considered her words. "Just where and when did you two get married?" he asked, wondering how they had avoided the reading of the banns and exposing her identity at the time of their wedding.

"In Scotland, of course," Sophia replied happily. At Gregory's quizzical stare, she added, "They don't do a reading of the banns," she explained wistfully. "Oh, I wish you could have been there, Gregory. It was a beautiful ceremony at St. Laurence Church in Forres," she recalled with a faraway look.

"Way up there?" Gregory interrupted, startled. "You couldn't marry in Edinburgh, or someplace a bit closer to England, perhaps?"

Surprised by his reaction, Sophia angled her head to one side. "St. George's Church didn't exist until several years after our wedding," she countered. "And James' family lived near Forres, so we had his family for witnesses," she explained, sounding defiant.

Rolling his eyes, Gregory sat silent for a few moments as the carriage bounced over the cobblestones of Oxford Street. "And Sir William knew of your elopement?" he asked, remembering what his mother had said about Sir William having to hide her money.

Pulling her fan from her reticule and flipping it open, Sophia tittered at her son's comment. "I didn't *elope*," she stated with a demure grin. "And, yes, your uncle knew of my plans. We had to take him into our confidence because of the money. And he helped broker the purchase of the buildings on Kingly Street," she added as she fanned herself. "So I made sure he was handsomely rewarded for his help, and the bank was quite good about promoting him for his participation in the real estate transaction," she said with a mischievous grin.

Gregory hit himself on his forehead with an open hand. "He brokered a deal to purchase real estate with the very same money you removed from the bank just a few weeks prior?" he asked in awe. "Brilliant. Just brilliant," he said as he shook his head from side to side.

"It was more like ten days, but, yes," Sophia corrected him, a rather pleased expression on her face.

Gregory regarded his mother for a moment. He had never questioned how she came to own the townhouses along Kingly— she had simply owned them for as long as he could remember.

"And all because... why, exactly?" he asked. "Why couldn't you just tell everyone you were marrying James Simpson?"

Sophia's mouth opened in shock as she stared at her son. "Can you imagine what Mary Margaret Merriweather Grandby would have done had she learned of my plans to marry the *butler?*" she countered, surprised her son would even suggest such a plan. "She would have seen to it our inheritance was rescinded, and she would have slandered the Burroughs name at her every opportunity!" she exclaimed in horror. The look on her face mirrored the comment. She quickly raised her fan to hide her disgust.

"Oh, of course," Gregory replied, remembering how vindictive his grandmother could be when family and societal events were out of her control. He leaned over and kissed his mother on her cheek. "You had to change your entire life to marry that man," he said quietly. For the first time, he truly appreciated the lengths to which his mother had gone for the man she loved. A simple affair of the heart required she give up so much and yet, he realized, she had everything she wanted and more.

"I did. It was hard, at first, especially because I had to leave you behind. But I didn't lose you. I never would have left Merriweather Manor if I thought for a moment I would lose you," she said as she dropped the fan in her lap and grabbed his hand. "And, I didn't do it without help," she added in a quieter voice.

Gregory eyed her as his hand wrapped around hers. "From Sir William, you mean," he said as he watched her.

"Not at first, no," she replied as she shook her head. "From Christina Wellingham. Mrs. Wellingham," she amended as she returned his gaze. "She was my best friend and confidante through it all."

His brows furrowing, Gregory tried to comprehend her meaning. "I... I don't understand," he replied. "Are you referring to the mother of Christiana and Thomas?"

"I am," she acknowledged. "I did exactly what Christiana's mother did," she said quietly. "She took me into her confidence and described to me how she left a very wealthy family to marry Graham Wellingham. Do you know what Mr. Wellingham was doing for a living before he started his import business?" she asked carefully, wondering if Gregory might already know anything of his best friend's family history.

Gregory arched an eyebrow. "Wasn't he an earl's brother?" he asked. Having left Merriweather Manor to attend Eton, he barely remembered Christiana's father.

"An *estranged* brother of an earl," Sophia countered. "He and the earl had a falling-out, so he worked in a warehouse for the East India Company," she said in a whisper. "And he continued to work there even as he was trying to start his own import company. Can you imagine what life must have been like for them?" she asked, her brows furrowed as she watched for Gregory's reaction.

Gregory's eyebrows shot up at the news. "You're saying Christiana's mother was... *wealthy?*" he whispered in surprise, just then understanding his mother's earlier comment.

His mother nodded and squeezed his hand. "But not after she married Graham, of course. It made it possible for me to believe I could do the same thing. But I had the benefit of an inheritance. Except for Woodscastle, which was almost uninhabitable, Christina had almost nothing when she married Graham," she explained in a quiet whisper. "If she could do it, I decided I could most certainly do it, too."

Shaking his head, Gregory considered his mother's words. *She married for love, as will I*, he thought. Mary Margaret Merriweather was long since dead, and those left from the family were all contemporaries of his and his mother's.

Perhaps it was time for her to come out of hiding.

"Besides, it's not as if I've been *hiding* all these years," Sophia stated as if she could read his mind. She opened the fan again. "I go out in public nearly everyday. I attend the theatre with James. I shop in Oxford and The Strand. James and I have even strolled in Hyde Park during the fashionable hour," she claimed with a raised eyebrow.

Gregory chuckled at his mother's comments. "Indeed," he answered. "And at no time have you encountered any of my relatives?"

Sophia laughed at the question. "But, of course," she replied as she watched her son's surprised reaction. "Your cousin Rebecca and I have even spoken in a modiste, and, if she recognized me, she didn't let on."

Bristling at the mention of his promiscuous cousin Rebecca Merriweather, Gregory squeezed his eyes shut.

"She's not like that any more," his mother said when she noticed his reaction. "When James told me about her, I admit I reacted in a very unladylike manner."

Gregory's eyebrows nearly hit his hairline. "Indeed?"

Sophia nodded. "I believe I used the term 'she-bitch,' which, when you think about it is rather redundant, but I was horrified at the time," she explained. "But now Rebecca has found a man who shares her proclivities."

"Poor man," Gregory mumbled, his discomfort passing as he realized his cousin was no longer a threat to him.

The carriage lurched to a halt in front of Reagan's. As Gregory assisted his mother from the carriage, he heard a familiar voice call out from behind him. "Mr. Grandby, is that you?"

Gregory turned and was surprised to find his cousin, William Merriweather, exiting Reagan's.

"William?" he replied, startled to see his eldest cousin in public and apparently doing quite well for himself. The last he knew of William, the man had squandered his inheritance on gambling and women and was in debtors' prison.

"Indeed, it is," the older man admitted as he rushed to shake Gregory's hand. The man immediately extended his left hand to assist Sophia. She took both gentlemen's hands and stepped down from the carriage to stand between them. William bowed formally.

"How do you do, Mr. Merriweather?" she said as she curtsied to her son's cousin. She knew him to be about ten years older than Gregory, but he looked much older than her own husband. If Gregory hadn't addressed him as 'William,' she wouldn't have known it was him. "You're looking well," she commented as she regarded the man, not sure what else to say given the circumstances. She knew of his fate from having read about it in *The Morning Chronicle*, so she was as surprised as Gregory to see him out of prison.

William seemed to study her face, not quite recognizing the pretty woman. "Milady, you have me at a disadvantage, I'm afraid," the man said. "You seem familiar—"

"Cousin, may I reintroduce you to my mother, Sophia Simpson," Gregory interrupted, curious as to how the man would react to meeting the long lost Sophia Burroughs Grandby.

Recognition passed over William's face and he smiled broadly. "Oh, of course," he said as he rolled his eyes. "You're as beautiful now as when you lived at Merriweather Manor," he commented lightly.

Sophia visibly blushed at the compliment and stole a glance at Gregory before replying, "You're too kind. My son was about to take me to supper. Would you care to join us?" she asked, hoping the invitation seemed sincere and that Gregory wouldn't mind.

"Thank you, Mrs. Simpson, but I've just broken my fast," William replied with a wave of his hand.

Sophia's left eyebrow shot up. "Keeping late nights now, are you, Mr. Merriweather?" she asked, her amused expression a hint she might be teasing the man.

"Actually, yes," William replied with an embarrassed grin. "I recently took control of the Sans Souci Theatre on Leicester Square, and I find I don't get home much before four o'clock in the morning these days," he explained as he rocked on the balls of his feet.

Gregory and Sophia both expressed surprise at the news of William's occupation. "However did you land such a position?" Gregory inquired as he regarded his cousin.

William bobbed his head back and forth. "As you both must know, I used to be a bit of a gambler," he said with a sly grin, "One of my bets had to do with a certain actress and the man she was..." His face reddening, William sputtered and gave Sophia an apologetic glance. "Well, let's just say I eventually won the bet, and besides winning enough money to secure my release from prison, I was granted the position of manager over the theatre in which said actress regularly performs," he explained as his face returned to its normal coloring.

"How fortunate for you," Gregory commented as he wondered about the details of the bet. "I suppose this means your luck as a gambler has changed for the better?"

William looked surprised. "Oh, not at all," he replied. "I haven't gambled since before I was in prison, you see," he claimed, his eyes as wide as they could be. "I'm quite content to earn an honest living these days, I assure you. And the theatre is doing well enough that I'm considering seeking a wife," he added happily.

Sophia and Gregory exchanged glances. "How fortunate for

you," Sophia said with a genuine smile. "Do you have someone in mind, perhaps?"

Arching an eyebrow, the tall man leaned over and said, "As a matter of fact, there is a woman by the name of Miss Charlotte Hughes who has caught my eye," he admitted with a nod. "She attends the theatre regularly and seems a most proper lady," he added, trying hard to keep his excitement in check.

Recognizing the woman's name from Todd Vandermeer's description of his afternoon tea with her, Gregory smiled. "I understand she is sister to a rather well-placed broker at the John Company," he commented with a raised brow.

William nodded and seemed surprised Gregory knew of the woman. "Yes, I have heard that, too. Do you have any other information I could use to help in my pursuit of the lady?"

Gregory shrugged as he recalled Todd's tale of woe regarding the afternoon he had spent with the lady garbed entirely in pink. "I would suggest you not wear new leathern breeches, and do be careful in your use of words that can be misconstrued."

Glancing at Sophia, William raised one eyebrow. "Humph," he replied as he considered his cousin's suggestions.

"Do you have an apartment or... perhaps a house?"

William shrugged. "For now, I live in an apartment at the theatre, but I plan to purchase a house when I find a wife, of course," he acknowledged.

"Then let Miss Hughes take care of arranging its decoration," Gregory said firmly. "I understand she can be quite particular in that regard."

William smiled in appreciation. "Thank you for the information. I'll be sure to consider it when I begin courting Miss Hughes," he said happily. "I must take my leave of you two. Please, enjoy your luncheon," he said as he bowed and hurried off.

Sophia curtsied and Gregory returned his cousin's bow before they turned to go into the public house. "He didn't seem the least bit surprised when I introduced you," Gregory commented as they waited for a host to seat them.

"I told you," Sophia replied as she followed the host.

"Yes, you did," Gregory agreed as he smiled and followed his mother.

CHAPTER 70
ARRANGING A WEDDING

July 12, 1802, Knightrider Street

Thomas Wellingham had never had a reason to visit Doctors' Commons and the office of the Archbishop of Canterbury. At least, not until he decided he had to marry quickly. Besides having thoroughly ruined Emma Fitzsimmons, he was feeling guilt as well as a good deal of possessiveness. In an effort to ensure no one else could claim her—who knew how many others were playing matchmaker on her behalf?—he was determined to make Emma his wife as soon as possible.

Although Emma had assured him they could wait the three weeks or more required to have the banns read in their respective parishes, Thomas had no intention of waiting any longer than was legally necessary. They could marry later that day if he could secure a special license. The minister at St. James had agreed to perform the ceremony at four o'clock if they could get the license and line up some witnesses. If not, a regular license would do if Thomas might want to wait until Saturday morning. However, another twenty guinea would be required so that a private baptism could be rescheduled.

Thomas was sure Todd and Deborah would be willing to pay witness to their vows—they would simply make Grace Park their next stop after securing the license and ask the couple to join them later at the church.

His bride-to-be sat next to him as they waited for his appointment with the Archbishop, her eyes darting about as her nervousness grew. "I'm not yet one-and-twenty," she whispered, her hand squeezing his. "Perhaps we should send word to Sir William. He would be willing to speak on my behalf, given his role as my guardian."

Thomas straightened, stunned at her words. *Guardian?* The idea of having to wait for the banker to respond to a request for his presence set his teeth on edge. "You, my sweeting, are one-and-twenty," he countered. "I'll swear to it," he whispered, using his other hand to unwrap her fingers from around his hand. "And, unlike you, I cannot write with both hands. I need this hand to write," he murmured, hoping to assuage some of her nervousness with some humor.

One of Emma's brows arched up in surprise, but she gave up her death grip on Thomas and instead grabbed the front of the bench on which they sat. She was about to bring up the matter of where they would spend the night, but his name was called and he stood up. "Come with me," he said as he held out his arm. Emma took it and followed him to the office of the Archbishop.

While submitting his application, Thomas answered a few questions. Within moments, a payment of twenty guinea was demanded along with another four pounds to cover the stamp duty. Thomas paid the 25£ in Bank of England notes, and their marriage license was granted.

Gripping the paper, Thomas gave Emma a nod of satisfaction and offered his arm. "We should pay a call on the Vandermeers," he said as they made their way along Knightrider Street. "Invite them to witness our vows."

He grinned as he considered how Todd would respond to hearing the news. *Probably something along the lines of, "What took you so long?"*

Thomas waved to Mr. Larsen, who was feeding apples to the impatient horses in front of his ancient coach. The equipage, although in good repair, looked as if it were older than Thomas. "To Grace Park, Mr. Larsen," he called out.

Thomas handed Emma up and followed her in, settling into the squabs. He reached an arm around her shoulders and pulled her against him. "If I haven't yet said it today, I should like you to know I love you," he said, his voice nearly breathless. Reaching over, he kissed her on the mouth, his lips warm and inviting.

Surprised by his public display of affection, Emma returned the kiss until the coach lurched forward, and she was forced away from him. Her bonnet askew, she undid the ribbons and removed it.

"I apologize," Thomas whispered. "I'm behaving like a *rake*." He straightened his waistcoat and glanced out the window, attempting to think of something other than Emma and what they might be doing if they were at Woodscastle or in the bedchamber at her townhouse.

They rode in silence until the next intersection. "What is it?" Emma asked, noting his frown.

Thomas took her hand in his. "As you know, I told Gregory he could propose to Christiana on her birthday," he said quietly. "But, I also told him he couldn't marry her until she's at least eighteen. At first, I said thirty," he added, but there wasn't any amusement in his voice nor was there any on his face when he made the comment.

Emma watched as Thomas' inner battle played out on his face. For a moment, she thought he might cry, and for another, she thought he appeared angry. "If I may?" she whispered.

Thomas glanced at her and placed a hand on top of hers. "Please," he replied simply, feeling the responsibility of his sister's future a larger burden than he could handle at the moment—especially knowing what Gregory Grandby had put himself through just to see to it Christiana would one day be his wife.

"After we visit the Vandermeers, we can go to the townhouse, and you can write a letter to Mr. Grandby," she suggested. "Let him know of our plans and let him know he is free to marry Christiana whenever they wish to marry. Mr. Larsen can take the letter to Woodscastle on your behalf. If they're in a rush to wed, they can come to town sometime this week and arrange for a license. We'll simply meet them at the Archbishop's office so you can give your permission for Christiana to marry." It was a risky plan to suggest to the man, but Emma decided he could do no worse than say 'no.'

"You've given this a great deal of thought, haven't you?" Thomas asked as he regarded her. He gave no indication if he agreed with her plan or not.

"Your sister wants desperately to be married," Emma whispered in his ear, her lips barely brushing his earlobe. "She no longer wants to attend Warwick's. Perhaps it's time for Mr. Grandby to become her protector," she said quietly. "And she'll still be living at Woodscastle."

Closing his eyes, Thomas nodded his head. "I love you, Emma," he said quietly, wrapping an arm around her shoulders. In a daring move, he kissed her on the lips while the carriage negotiated the busiest section of Oxford Street.

Emma was reminded of Todd's behavior with Deborah, and she couldn't help but smile when his lips released hers. Blushing, she lowered her lashes. "I love you, too," she whispered as she placed her head on his shoulder.

They rode in silence for several minutes. "Is it true?" Thomas asked then, keeping his lips close to her hair, occasionally kissing it as the carriage jerked over the cobblestone streets.

"Is what true?"

"Is Sir William your... guardian?" He didn't know how he would react to either answer, he realized. On the one hand, he was still offended by what had transpired at the bank, despite the reason behind it, and on the other, the man was Gregory's uncle and brother to Christiana's future mother-in-law.

"Only in matters of finance," Emma replied with a sigh. "Lord and Lady Chamberlain should *probably* be my guardians, but..." She allowed the sentence to trail off, her attention on her gloved hands.

Thomas took her hands. "But?" he whispered, remembering she had a sister living with the Fitzsimmons.

Emma's shoulders slumped. "My father left his family a long time ago. It seems he was always finding fault with the hats he owned as a young man, and so he learned how to make them. He wanted to have his own shop, but his family simply couldn't abide his desire to work in trade."

Thomas regarded Emma for a few moments, remembering their discussion about aristocrats her first day of work and then again over dinner before the ball. "I know we spoke of Matthew and Caroline Fitzsimmons and your sister," he said carefully, wondering how best to explain what more he knew of the family. Thomas raised his head, his eyes scanning the ceiling of the coach. "We have relatives in common," he murmured, wondering if she knew of Charity and Graydon Wellingham. He almost hoped not, as he'd heard awful things about his cousin, the earl. "Your father's sister, Charity, is married to my cousin, Graydon Wellingham, Earl of Trenton," he explained.

"You mentioned you were related to Trenton," Emma replied,

remembering their discussion about aristocrats on her first day of work. She also remembered how her father talked of his younger sister. The man had felt sorry for Charity because she had married a man he claimed was violent, while their cousin, Temperance Fitzsimmons, had married Stanley Harrington, Earl of Mayfield, a man who was Trenton's exact opposite in every way. And yet Graydon Wellingham might have married either cousin—it was never quite clear who he favored more.

"I have met Trenton, of course," Thomas said as if he were still lost in thought. "But we don't socialize. We certainly don't attend the same club." Graydon, he knew, was a member of White's.

Did he regret not having kept ties with his late father's family? "I've never met Charity," Emma finally admitted.

Thomas furrowed his brows. "So, why didn't *you* become a ward of Lord Chamberlain's?" he asked. "If Lady Chamberlain knows of you—"

"I was already committed to attend Warwick's," Emma interrupted. "Since I had a place to live, having a guardian didn't seem very important."

Thomas suppressed a grin as he regarded his betrothed. "You lied to go to Warwick's, didn't you?" he whispered, trying hard not to chuckle.

"I suppose so," Emma replied, catching his amusement. "But then, you lied when you claimed I was one-and-twenty," she accused, her head straightening as she regarded him. "And whatever made you tell him your 'passion could not be contained'?"

"*That* was not a lie," Thomas replied defensively. "How was I to know he would be so serious? '*You must overcome your passion, young man*'," he said in imitation of the Archbishop's declaration. "As if he has any idea what 'tis like to have you around," he complained in a low voice.

Until this last statement, Emma found his tirade amusing. "Do I really incite that much passion in you?"

Thomas lowered his head and whispered, "I thought perhaps you would have noticed by now," he replied quietly. He was grinning as he said it, and Emma felt a wave of relief wash over her.

"So... are you?" Emma asked, her expression turning serious again.

"Am I what?" Thomas countered.

"Are you going to overcome your passion?"

"I've absolutely no intention of doing so, and since we're about to be married, I have no reason to," he said defiantly, his chin thrust out and his arm pulling her hard against him.

Emma grinned in response, rather liking how defiant he could be when pushed too far.

The coach slowed and stopped in the half-circle drive of Grace Park. "We're here," he said as he took a deep breath, remembering the last time he had walked up the front steps with Emma.

The day of the Vandermeer wedding.

Thomas thought of how much had happened in the nine days since then. Of the discoveries that had changed his business. Of the decisions that had changed his life. His sister's life. The life of the woman with whom he walked up the steps. The promises he would make to her later that day. The promises she would make to him.

"Are you well?" Emma asked, her brows furrowing with concern.

Thomas slowly smiled. "I am, indeed," he said with a nod.

Thomas and Emma were welcomed by the newlyweds shortly after arriving at Grace Park. Todd and Deborah had been in the study opening wedding gifts and reading notes, the silver salver still littered with correspondence from their time spent honeymooning.

After nearly an hour in the parlor hearing tales of Todd and Deborah's escapades in Derbyshire, they were invited to have luncheon with them. Knowing just how good the cook was, they gladly joined the two newlyweds in their dining room. Quite different from when Emma had dined there with Deborah the month before, the room now featured a much smaller table than the long one that could seat twenty-four. In its current state, the new table could, at most, seat six.

"This is the same size as the one I have in my townhouse," Emma commented as she entered the room. "Whatever have you done?" she asked as she gazed at Deborah.

The brunette woman beamed, her complexion clear and her eyes bright. Emma considered a week at Cherrywood had done the woman a world of good. "Todd wanted us to sit closer to one another during dinner, so he bought this Imperial extending dining table at Gillow's Furniture," she explained with a shrug. "It has lots of extra pieces that allow it to be very long when we host more people. Please, have a seat," she said as she indicated the chairs on either side of the table.

Ever the gracious host, Todd served his best wine and then asked why neither Thomas nor Emma were at work.

Emma blushed and glanced at Deborah to her right. Thomas sat up straighter and picked up his wine glass. "I have asked Emma for her hand in marriage, and she has agreed to be my wife," he said solemnly. "We have come today to invite you to pay witness to our wedding. Either this afternoon at four o'clock or Saturday at eleven o'clock at St. James Church," he said with a nod. "Or both," he added when he noticed Todd's expression of shock.

Todd leaned back in his chair, his face finally splitting in a huge grin. "Finally!" he shouted happily.

Embarrassed at his friend's outburst, Thomas could hardly suppress a grin as he glanced at Emma, who had the same embarrassed expression on her face. Deborah was holding one of Emma's hands while she displayed a radiant smile.

Todd stood up, leaned down over Emma, took her hand in his, and kissed her on the cheek. "Let me be the first to wish you the very best. May your marriage be as happy as ours," he added as he nodded to Thomas and winked at his wife.

"Thank you," Emma replied, her face bright pink.

Thomas nodded to Todd. "You can remove your hand from my betrothed now," he said with a perturbed look.

"Of course," Todd replied, still grinning as he returned to his seat. "And will we soon hear similar news for your sister?" he asked of Thomas. "From what I could see at the ball..."

Thomas' grin lessened, but his mood was still upbeat. "Indeed. If Gregory can get through the marriage proposal on Wednesday," he said in jest.

"You must all come here after the wedding. For the breakfast feast," Todd insisted. "I'll have the cook make you a cake, and we shall have all the foods we had for our wedding breakfast," he added, becoming more excited as he spoke of the plans.

Emma bit her lip and noticed Thomas considering the offer. The Vandermeer wedding breakfast had been a fun affair, with food and conversation that lasted for hours before Todd finally carried Deborah off to their carriage for the trip to Derbyshire.

"Oh, you must agree," Deborah pleaded. "I want so much to host my first party here. It would be an honor for it to be for your wedding feast," she said as she held onto Emma's hand.

Thomas finally nodded. "Thank you. I do believe we shall accept your most generous offer," he said quietly, watching Emma as she smiled.

So much for marrying today, he thought with dismay.

Their luncheon was as filling as it was entertaining. When the men went to the study for a cheroot and brandy, Deborah took Emma to the mistress suite, presumably to show her the gowns and jewelry Todd had purchased for her.

Emma hurried Deborah to the chaise lounge and asked her to sit. "You look positively radiant, Deborah," she said as they sat down. "I didn't have a chance to ask you at the ball, but how is marriage for you? Really?" she asked, a worried expression crossing her face.

Deborah bit her lip and smiled. "I love him now, Emma. You cannot know how wonderful this past month has been," she insisted. Placing a hand over her abdomen, she added, "I think I may be with child."

Emma's eyes widened, but the news didn't really surprise her. Deborah was simply beautiful in the way expectant mothers could be when they were well fed and happy. "I'm so thrilled for you," Emma said as she took her friend's hands. "I was so concerned. I introduced you, and if, for some reason this marriage wasn't going well for you, I would feel just terrible."

Beaming, Deborah leaned closer. "Jean Claude Perot has started the painting," she whispered. "He was in the parlor most of yesterday painting the background and other details, and I'll start posing for him this afternoon!"

Shocked at how quickly Deborah had arranged for her portrait to be painted, Emma shook her head. "I thought you were keeping it a secret from Todd," she replied.

"I am," Deborah assured her. "Todd has an appointment at his office at three o'clock and will be gone for some time. Then, tomorrow, I'll pose whilst he's at work."

"And how will you pay Mr. Perot?" Emma asked, immediately regretting the question.

"My pin money, of course," Deborah replied happily. "Todd has given me far too much to spend on fripperies."

Emma smiled then, her bottom lip caught in a tooth. "So all is well? Truly?"

Deborah's shoulders came up around her ears as she considered

Emma's words. "I cannot tell you how... *passionate* Todd is," she whispered conspiratorially.

Emma eyes widened at Deborah' use of the word 'passionate', and she fought not to smile.

"And how...how I look so forward to making love to him every night, sometimes we don't even wait until after dinner," Deborah continued as she covered her mouth with a hand. "And, sometimes, we don't make love, but merely talk quietly and hold one another."

Emma considered her friend's comments. "Like you," she started to say and then stopped, wanting to share her experiences with Thomas. "We decided to say our vows before the wedding," she said carefully. "We made love after the ball and again last night," she whispered, not bothering to mention that the vows hadn't actually been exchanged just yet. Before she could continue, Deborah hugged her.

"Isn't it amazing?" Deborah asked. "I was so hoping you could find out for yourself just how *amazing* being in love can be."

Emma nodded, but struggled with her questions for the newly-wed. "How did you... What did you do to... to make him never want to take another woman into his bed?"

Sitting up straighter, Deborah considered Emma's question and finally angled her head. "Before I tell you, I must first explain some-thing about Todd," she said quietly. "Mr. Wellingham may not... he may not react in the same manner."

Considering her words, Emma nodded. "Go on."

Taking a deep breath, Deborah looked away for a moment before returning her attention to Emma. "The night you introduced me to Todd, he... he treated me as if I were a goddess. It was as if he placed me on a pedestal, and he wanted to worship me— make me untouchable—even to him," she explained quietly. "But he also wanted me in his bed. He *wanted* me," she repeated, her eyebrows rising suggestively. "I had to make him understand that to be his wife meant I had to share his bed, that he couldn't hold me to some impossible standard as a goddess. So, for the first time we made love, I invited him to *my* bed." She paused for a moment, noticing Emma's flushed face.

Emma swallowed. "After the ball, I told Thomas I wanted to make love to him," she whispered, unable to keep the secret to herself.

Deborah's eyes widened, but she grinned. "And, he, of course, agreed," she said as her eyebrow arched in amusement. At Emma's quick nod, she kept her eyes focused on her friend. "A few nights before our wedding, Todd told me something very..." Taking a deep breath, Deborah paused before continuing, "He told me I was his *wanton*."

Emma inhaled sharply, remembering Thomas had used that very word the night before! *You could also be a wanton in my bed.*

"And as such," Deborah continued, "I should have my way with him. He says he has no intention of taking a mistress, but... I realized then I could make him mine."

Emma nodded, hanging on her every word. "What... how did he mean?" she asked, her brows furrowed. "What did you do?"

Deborah lowered her eyes and leaned toward Emma, supporting herself with her arms on the chaise. "Remember when I told you we have been reading *The Kama Sutra?*" she replied, one eyebrow arched. "I skipped ahead and read the translation about *fellatio*," she said in a whisper. "Remember how the harlots would talk about it at the Home?" she continued, reminding Emma of the pregnant prostitutes at the Home for Unwed Mothers and their colorful discussions about various sexual practices. "Todd had already learned about *cunnilingus* and, well..." Deborah shrugged a shoulder.

Having read most of the translated passages in the version of the book in her townhouse library, Emma raised an eyebrow in reply.

"So, when he said that, I... I turned into a wanton, and I took him into my mouth, and I did what the book said to do. I made him *mine*," she said with a great deal of pride. "He'll not seek another woman's company in bed, I've been assured." Although it was Deborah's turn to blush, she did not, and, in fact, seemed quite pleased with herself. "He begs me to come to bed with him, and, of course, I do," she said with a devilish grin. "I don't believe I would ever turn him down. But once in a while, I am sure to beg *him* to come to bed with *me*," she indicated the room with a wave of her hand, "Here in my bedchamber."

Nodding, Emma bit her lip and slowly smiled. "Thank you," she said simply. She frowned, though, when she remembered their plan to marry later that afternoon. If Deborah was posing for the painter, she would be unavailable to witness their wedding, and from what had been said over luncheon, it seemed quite certain she and Thomas would instead wed Saturday morning.

"Where are you staying tonight?"

Emma pursed her lips, not wanting to admit they were headed for her townhouse. "Well, we were planning to take a room—"

"Take him to your townhouse," Deborah suggested. "Your bedchamber. *Your* bed."

Open-mouthed, Emma nodded, understanding Deborah's meaning. "I will," she agreed. "I will, indeed."

CHAPTER 71
LANDLORDS AND LOVERS

*D*isappointed the Vandermeers had other plans and deciding they would rather wait for their friends than say their vows in front of strangers, Thomas and Emma decided to forego the original arrangement at St. James Church. The minister wasn't surprised when they stopped to give him the news and assured them he would still do the ceremony on Saturday.

Spending the night in the townhouse, and possibly the following day, seemed the wisest course. "Should anyone ask, we simply inform them we are wed," Thomas said quietly. "For as far as I am concerned, we are," he added before planting a kiss on Emma's forehead.

She allowed a wan smile. "We'll simply do things a bit backward this week," she answered quietly.

His eyebrows tweaked up. "Go on," he said, an amused expression replacing his scowl.

"Let us start our honeymoon today and get married on Saturday," she said in a loud whisper. "And, in the meantime, if you should need to go to the office, I won't mind."

Thomas' eyebrows climbed higher. "I rather like how you think," he replied, wondering what was scheduled at Wellingham Imports that week. "We should be at Woodscastle for Christiana's birthday on Wednesday, though," he added as his frown returned.

"Of course," Emma nodded. "But until then," she began and then stopped. She smiled as she remembered Deborah's comments. *Perhaps now is the right time to make Thomas my own.*

Thomas was about to ask Emma what she was thinking when their coach pulled up in front of No. 3 Kingly Street and the front door of No. 4 opened. Sophia and James Simpson, smiling at one another, emerged. From their smart outfits and Sophia's parasol, it appeared they were out for a late afternoon of shopping.

"Good afternoon," Emma called out. James Simpson hurried to the coach and assisted her as she stepped down. She curtsied and turned to introduce Thomas as he stepped down. "Mr. and Mrs. James Simpson," she said, winking in Sophia's direction, "I would like you to meet my husband, Thomas Wellingham." Although it wasn't yet the truth, the words came easily, and Emma found herself playing the part of the blushing bride with ease.

Thomas stared at the former Merriweather Manor butler, amazed that the man had not changed much from what he remembered of him when Thomas was but a young boy.

"'Tis so good to meet you, sir," James said as he grabbed Thomas' right hand and shook it vigorously. "My stepson has told me so much about you," he added as he bowed.

"Can this really be Master Thomas?" Sophia breathed as she looked him over, remembering him as a small boy playing with her son.

"Mrs. Simpson, you are as beautiful today as you were when I first met you," Thomas said as he reached for her gloved hand and kissed the back of it.

Sophia beamed at him and then turned her eyes on Emma as she opened her arms and took her into a hug. "So, I was right about him, wasn't I?" she said happily.

Emma nodded, her face coloring up. "Indeed. I finished my work for him last week, he proposed, we married, and I start a new position for him again next Monday," she said as she held the woman's gloved hands. She paused a moment and then decided to ask about Christiana. "I understand you've met your future daughter," she whispered carefully, hoping the woman had changed her mind about her son's choice of a wife.

Smiling sheepishly, Sophia nodded. "We have, indeed. She is a joy," the woman admitted with a nod. "So much like her mother, who I just adored. She was my very best friend." She turned her attention to Thomas. "Mr. Wellingham, I must commend you on raising such a beautiful girl for my son," she said, her compliment heartfelt. Reaching out, she pulled him into a most unexpected hug.

"Thank you, Mrs. Simpson," Thomas replied when she released her hold on him. *She knew my mother enough to be close friends?* he thought in surprise. Sophia was from a much higher class, a member of the *ton*, given she was the daughter of a duke. "I cannot tell you how... *relieved* I was when Emma told me about you. I feared the worst when you went missing, I'm afraid to admit," he explained with a nod. "Gregory kept your secret safe from even me."

Surprised, Sophia exchanged a quick glance with James and then turned her attention to Emma. "But... how did *you* know?" she asked, her perfect brow furrowing despite her good mood.

Angling her head to one side, Emma remembered the hint that had tipped her off to Sophia's real identity. "You did," she replied with a small smile. "Only a mother would be so concerned about her son's choice of wife," Emma reasoned when she noted Sophia's look of disbelief. That hadn't really been what made her suspicious, she knew, but to explain all the steps she and Thomas had used to figure it out would make her sound like a busybody. And she didn't want to be considered in the same league as Lady Pettigrew when it came to gossip.

"I was that obvious?" Sophia replied with an embarrassed grin.

"Yes, you certainly were," James stated with amusement as he regarded his wife. He took her hand and put it on his arm. "We should let these newlyweds get on with their honeymoon," he said with an arched brow aimed in Thomas' direction.

Emma blushed bright red while Thomas bowed to her landlords. "Would you do me the honor of attending Christiana's birthday dinner this Wednesday evening?" Thomas asked. "She'll be seventeen, and I expect Mr. Grandby will have some good news for her."

When Emma noticed Sophia's quizzical expression, Emma quickly added, "Mr. Grandby is buying half of Woodscastle for her as a betrothal gift. He is proposing... proposing a plan to refurbish and then live in the west wing when they're not traveling," she stammered.

James and Sophia exchanged surprised looks. "They really will be close to town!" Sophia said happily. "We'll be able to see the grandchildren!"

Thomas furrowed his brows, but continued to smile as he watched his best friend's mother. *My sister's in-laws,* he considered with a grin, realizing they hadn't responded to his invitation.

The four bade their farewells, and Emma unlocked the front

door. "Please accept my apology for telling them about Woodscastle," she pleaded as they entered her townhouse.

Displaying an expression of surprise, Thomas asked, "Whatever do you mean? It was perfectly fine for you to tell them," he replied happily. "I already guessed from her comment that Gregory had introduced my sister as his betrothed," he explained when he saw the look of relief on Emma's face. He turned his attention to Mr. Larsen, asking the groom to unload their trunks and to wait while he composed a letter.

Sitting at the desk in the parlor, Thomas wrote his letter to Gregory, even stamping Emma's 'F' into the melted wax to seal the page, and grinned as he did so.

Giving the letter to Mr. Larsen, he explained he would be spending the next two evenings in town and no longer required the groom's services. He asked him to give the letter to Mr. Grandby.

Emma gave Mr. Larsen a linen filled with Dutch biscuits for his journey back to Woodscastle, and the man was off.

Turning to Thomas, Emma took a deep breath and kissed him. He returned the kiss immediately, his mouth hungry for hers and his arms pulling her hard against his body. "If milady would allow it, I would very much like to take you to bed," he whispered urgently, his breath hot against her cheek. "However," he paused to kiss her neck, "I find I'm at a disadvantage," he murmured as he sucked gently on her earlobe. He was pulling pins out of her hair and tossing them toward the hall tree.

Emma was about to suggest he take her right there in the vestibule or perhaps the parlor before she considered their comfort. "Indeed?" she replied, undoing the buttons of his topcoat. "And why might that be?" Her hair fell down from its bun and began unwinding as she tilted her head back to regard him.

Thomas had moved his kisses to her décolletage, using his lips to push aside the ruffles of her bodice so he could kiss the tops of her breasts. "I don't know where the bed is," he said as he reached to pull off his coat, and, as she finished unbuttoning it, his waistcoat.

Blushing, Emma pointed toward the staircase. "'Tis upstairs," she said, breathless, remembering how Todd had behaved the night he came for Deborah wearing only a shirt, breeches, and boots.

Thomas wrapped one arm around her shoulders and reached down to behind her knees to lift her up. Surprised, Emma let out an

"Oh!" as she clasped her hands around his neck. He took her up the steps, his manner most serious.

Once in her room, he let her down and began undressing her. Although he had already done it twice by the light of a fire, today he did so by the light of the afternoon sun. With her gown off, he could see what he had only glimpsed in the modiste the Thursday before.

Emma pulled his shirt over his head and touched her fingers to his bare chest. Reaching around to her back, Thomas pulled the ties that held the corset in place. "I saw you like this last week," he whispered, just before the corset loosened and her breasts were released to the touch of his hands. He ran one hand down the length of her torso and around one of her buttocks, lifting it gently.

"Indeed?" Emma answered, her face taking on a worried look when she wondered when that could have been. She loosened and then pulled the corset over her head, dropping it to the floor. He slid his hands up the sides of her body, forcing the camisole over her breasts and up over her raised arms.

"In the modiste. God, I wanted you. And, now, I want you even more," he whispered hoarsely. He kissed her on the mouth while he undid the buttons of his tented breeches and removed his boots.

"You didn't mention the modiste the other night," Emma whispered, teasing his nipples with her tips of her fingers.

Lifting her in his arms again, he placed her on the bed and removed her pantaloons. "At the time, it seemed a bit much to add to the already long list," Thomas countered, his expression quite serious. "You're not the least bit modest, are you?" he questioned, regarding her mostly naked body with an arched eyebrow. He reached down and untied her garters.

Emma languidly stretched her arms over her head as Thomas removed his breeches, but she halted her movements at his comment. "Should I be?" she asked in alarm, ready to cover herself with the counterpane.

"No!" he replied. He slid her stockings down her legs, his fingers fumbling in their haste. Mounting her, his manhood hard and the tip already wet, Thomas waited while she spread her legs for him and then entered her slowly.

Hungry for her and knowing he couldn't hold on long, Thomas' movements turned urgent as he pounded into her several times, felt her legs wrap tightly around his body and his balls press hard against her before he grunted loudly and allowed his release. His eyes closed tightly as he spasmed, and Emma watched in delight as his face betrayed the pleasure he was feeling.

When he had recovered enough that he could open his eyes, he caressed her breast and nipple with the thumb of one hand, sending Emma into ecstasy a few moments later. As she writhed, he suckled her other nipple and she cried out, her body trembling uncontrollably. Her body shook hard under his, and he finally relaxed on top of her.

Breathing hard for several minutes, they said nothing and merely held each other. When, at last, Thomas pulled his body off of her, he landed on his side facing her. Having no energy to do anything else, he lay there, his head on a pillow while he sleepily watched her watch him. At some point, he fell asleep, and Emma sighed as she continued to gaze at him.

She was startled when she awoke to the sensation of his fingers on her nipples.

"Are they *always* like this?" Thomas asked as he gently pinched one of them between his thumb and the knuckle of his forefinger. Emma grinned and wrapped her hand around his probing fingers.

Long, slender fingers, Thomas thought with a smile.

"Only when I'm thinking of you," she replied coyly. "Or when you're touching them, I suppose," she added, her face flushed. Emma bit her lip, deciding it was time to make him hers and hers alone.

Thomas saw the lust in her eyes and started to lift himself on one elbow. Very firmly, Emma reached out her hand and used her long, slender fingers to push his shoulder down onto the pillow, forcing him onto his back. Startled, Thomas frowned but said nothing.

Lifting herself on top of him and straddling him, her knees on either side of his hips, she reached down with her lips and gently kissed and then bit his lower lip. When he tried to cradle one of her breasts in his hand, she grabbed his wrist and held it against the bed for a moment as she moved her lips down his neck. Occasionally stopping to kiss a particular spot, she held her body suspended over his so only her hardened nipples and golden hair made contact in the whorls of hair on his chest and belly. When he didn't make a move to stop her and his wrist finally went slack beneath her hand, she held herself up with both arms and slowly crawled backwards, catlike, down his body, allowing her nipples and hair to drag over his skin as she continued to kiss him.

A memory crashed into Thomas' mind as he realized what was happening.

You could also be a wanton in my bed!

The thought excited him.

The reality frightened him.

Wanting desperately to pull her down onto him, Thomas started to reach out, but Emma's hand blocked his arm and pushed it down to the side of his body. He tensed, and she felt the rise and fall of his chest as he took shallow, short breaths.

Her lips took purchase on the skin around his navel just as his hardened manhood made contact with the space between her breasts. Gasping, Thomas tensed again and seemed to try and sit up. Emma reached an arm above her head and shoved his shoulder down, then slowly drew the hand back down his body, allowing the pads of her fingers to barely make contact with his skin. She circled them around his navel, barely pressing them against his flesh as they completed the circuit.

His manhood, wet and hard against her sternum, slid between her breasts. He growled, still tensing his entire body. Lowering her head, Emma took his manhood in her mouth, stroked it with her tongue, and then began sucking as hard as she could.

Stunned, Thomas could do nothing. The sensation of her tongue and lips was intense and almost more pleasure than he could endure. At once, he wanted to end her grip on him, and yet, he couldn't bring himself to do so. And then, finally giving up, he couldn't stop the oncoming rush of intense pleasure he knew was about to take him to a blessed oblivion.

Stroking one hand over the curly hairs above his groin, Emma continued her hold on him until her fingers pressed hard at the base of his manhood. Thomas jerked and grunted loudly as the intense sensations gripped him, tossed him, took him. In reflex, he placed his hands on either side of Emma's head, cradling it as he yelled out his ecstasy.

Emma swallowed as his seed spilled into her mouth, but she kept her lips gripped tight to the top his manhood. Another jerk and she allowed her tongue to sip and sup as his release finally subsided. She gently stroked him with her tongue a few times, tasted him, and reveled in the power she had over his body.

Still groaning and breathing in short gasps, Thomas whispered urgently, "Please,... stop!"

Emma froze in place and waited for a moment, not sure what to do. When Thomas gently tugged on her head, she let go of him and allowed him to slide out of her mouth. She kissed the head of his manhood quickly, causing Thomas to gasp and jerk in reflex.

Raising herself on her arms, she pushed her breasts against him as she crawled back up his body, gently kissing his skin as she did so. Lowering her head into the space between his chest and arm, she relaxed against his body and molded herself to fit.

"You really can satisfy my every immoral desire, you wicked woman," Thomas whispered, a note of amusement in his voice. "Wherever did you... learn to do *that?*" he asked, not quite certain he wanted to know.

"The book," Emma answered as she tilted her head to look up at him.

He was staring at the ceiling while one arm was crooked and resting on his chest. Relieved to hear the simple explanation, he extended his forefinger and brushed her nose with it as he turned to look at her. The side of his face was wet, and his body still trembled. "Promise me... please promise me you will *never* leave me," he pleaded, swallowing hard.

Emma regarded him for a moment, realizing at once he was serious. "Promise me you'll never take a mistress," she countered, wanting to hear him say it.

A tear slid down the side of his face, and he placed the heel of his hand against his forehead. "I promise I'll never take a mistress," he assured her, the arm around her shoulders pulling her tighter against his body. "I cannot imagine such an arrangement when I have you," he added quietly, his other arm reaching around to cradle her head. Lost in thought for a moment, Thomas stared at her, remembering something his father had said not long before he died.

"What is it?" Emma whispered as she noticed his faraway look.

Thomas shook his head. "A long time ago, my father told me something. About having a wife, about keeping a wife, about love. And I... I didn't understand what he was trying to say," he murmured, his gaze taking on that faraway look again.

"What did he say?"

Thomas started to reply, faltered, and then swallowed hard. "Please don't think me a fool," he said as he considered what he was about to say. He raised himself on one elbow, still holding her head with the other hand. "I have been with only one other woman in my life, and it was not a... pleasant experience for me... or any of her others, I'm sure," he whispered as he looked down on Emma.

Emma's eyebrows shot up, nearly into her hairline. "Indeed?" she replied, not sure what else to say to such a comment. She had supposed he'd had lovers over the years, presuming so because men of his means were known to employ whores or to keep a mistress.

Shaking his head, Thomas explained, "One of Grandby's cousins. Rebecca. The one I mentioned at dinner the other night. She preyed on all the younger male cousins in the family. I believe she... deflowered, if you will, every boy at Merriweather Manor. Took delight in scaring us all to death when it came to sexual intercourse," he said, his face darkening as he remembered his two encounters with Rebecca Merriweather. His eyes glanced down to his torso and he angled his body so that the scar next to one of his ribs was visible. "So I wasn't very... *interested* in what my father had to say on the subject a few years ago. But he was ill and a few weeks from his death, and it seemed important to him, so I... listened,... but I didn't understand."

Placing a hand along the side of his face, Emma reached up and kissed him on the lips. "Tell me."

"He said when I found a woman I *loved*, I would need to treat her like the rose she was. That if I were to love her and nourish her, her thorns wouldn't hurt me... can this be right?"

Emma suppressed an urge to smile. "Did he say something about a bud blooming into a rose, perhaps?" she whispered, her breasts swelling and her nipples hardening. *Thorns, though? Did he mean angry words, perhaps?*

"Yes!" Thomas replied. "And that if I cared for my rose, if I took her rosebud and made it bloom often, I would have the pleasure of her garden for the rest of my days," he finished, his hand absently moving from behind her head to the side of her breast. His thumb caressed the nipple and Emma inhaled sharply. "Is that... silly?" he whispered as he realized what his hand was doing and stopped it.

"Not at all," Emma whispered as she shook her head. "Tell me about your mother, though," she said quietly. What had he said when he proposed?

My mother didn't really come from wealth.

And what had Sophia Simpson said earlier? *Your mother was my best friend.*

So, maybe Christina Wellingham *had* come from wealth. Maybe she had given up that life to be with the man she loved, or the man who could love her like no other man.

Thomas' eyes glazed over as he remembered his mother. "She was beautiful. Christiana will look just like her, I think, although mother's hair was darker," he recalled. "And she was regal, but not snobbish. She got along well with all the Merriweather women, I remember. But there were times I caught her weeping and wondered why she seemed so sad," he explained, his voice cracking. "I know there were things she wanted, things father simply couldn't give her. He couldn't afford the finer things, of course," he added in a whisper.

"Did she say angry things to him? Hurtful things? Raise her voice to him?" Emma asked softly.

Thomas' attention was still faraway. "Oh, yes. She could be so cruel in that way," he replied slowly, his brows furrowing.

"Thorns," Emma whispered with a nod.

"But, later in the day, or the next day, she would be so loving, so happy. She would dote on my father. She would do anything for him," he continued, as if he hadn't heard her comment. "Why was she like that, do you suppose?"

Emma placed a hand alongside his face and waited for his eyes to clear. "I think your mother may have given up far more than you think to be with your father. There were times she resented having to give up what she had been born to and grown accustomed to... to be with him. But, your father knew how to please her, how to love her so that she wanted him enough to stay with him. He didn't allow her thorns to do more than scratch him."

Thomas regarded Emma for a moment as he considered her words.

"Does Christiana know how her mother died?" Emma asked carefully.

Shaking his head, Thomas replied, "No. I've never told her."

Emma nodded, thinking he had done his sister a favor in keeping the information from her. It would have done her no good to live with the guilt. "Other than the one time when I thought you might beat your sister, have I ever said anything hurtful to you?" Emma asked quietly. She remembered the look on his face, like he'd been slapped hard by his best friend. If only she could take it back.

"No," he answered after he gave her question some thought. He watched her face for another moment and then noticed her swollen breasts. "You understand what my father said then?" he asked uncertainly, swallowing as his attention was drawn to her nipples and the smooth flesh of her belly and hips.

Emma nodded. "I believe the rosebud to which your father was referring is down here," she said as she took the hand that rested next to her breast and moved it down to between her thighs. She rolled onto her back and spread her legs slightly. "I don't know what it looks like in full bloom, but I assure you it has been in bloom at least a few times these past few nights," she added lightly, her lashes lowering over her eyes as she gave a watery smile. "You've been a most excellent gardener."

Thomas flung the covers aside and slowly moved down until he was between Emma's legs. Instinctively, she closed her thighs. "Be careful," she whispered, feeling vulnerable.

"I will. I promise," he said as he gazed up at her.

Very slowly, Emma spread her legs and lifted her knees. Her thighs, still moist from their last lovemaking, felt the heat from his quick breaths. She forced herself to relax and willed the center of her very being to emerge from its hiding place.

Supporting himself on his elbows, Thomas reached out with a finger and gingerly touched the pink bud. "It's as you say," he whispered in awe. "Like a rosebud." He touched it again with the tip of his finger, remembering this was how he had pleasured Rebecca the first day she'd had him in her room.

Emma inhaled sharply and arched her back], but the pink bud didn't disappear.

Placing his hand on her belly, he moved closer and gently stroked the bud with the tip of his tongue. He pulled away and watched with satisfaction as the bud grew larger and reddened. Kissing the rose, he was aware of Emma's gasps. He looked up to find she had lifted herself on her elbows. Her fingers clutched the bed linens and she gasped, her head dropping to the pillow as her arched back kept her chest high.

Impossibly large and tipped with hardened nipples, her breasts were rounder than he had ever seen them. Excited, he wrapped his lips around the engorged rose, suckled it lightly, and used his tongue to lightly stroke it. He felt more than heard the sudden waves of pleasure crash through her body. Her entire being shivered as his tongue completed its journey around the rose. He was finally aware she was crying out, her body writhing above and under him. Reluctantly, he allowed his lips to let go but used the blade of his tongue to stroke her one more time.

"No more!" he heard her pleading, aware of her hands around his head, pushing him away. He watched as the red bloom quivered, and he placed a hand over it lightly, protectively. Emma gasped again, her back arching in another spasm of pleasure as her heels dug into the mattress. The movement forced the engorged bud hard against his hand, and she cried out again as another wave of pleasure coursed through her.

When the shivers under her skin had subsided, Thomas tentatively pressed his hand against her, feeling the moistness of her, the pads of his fingers gently massaging the bud. Once again, he took satisfaction in being able to feel the sensations he set off with just the touch of his fingers.

At some point, her hands had released their grip on his head, and they now lay limp on the bed as she lay back, struggling to catch her breath.

When he was sure she was satiated, he kissed the insides of her thighs and moved up her body. He found her face wet with tears and her body quivering at his every touch. She rolled onto her side and melted into the front of his body, her arms wrapping around him. "I... I promise... I'll never leave you, Thomas" she whispered against his chest. "I am... yours."

Thomas placed a hand along the side of her face and kissed her, hard at first, and then more softly as he felt the shivers in her body fade. When he felt only the beating of her heart, he reached down and pulled the quilts over their bodies. Holding her against his body for several minutes, he occasionally kissed away the tears on her temples and stroked one hand down her spine. When it reached the small of her back, he circled one finger around lightly until her body shivered again.

"I love you, Mrs. Wellingham," he whispered in her ear.

Emma smiled and opened her eyes. "And I love you, Mr. Wellingham," she replied sleepily.

Thomas' eyes widened. "The vows," he said. "We haven't yet said our marriage vows." He rolled over and disappeared from the bed for a moment.

Lifting her head from the mattress, Emma watched as Thomas checked his waistcoat pockets. After a moment, he was back on the bed, holding Emma in his arms and a piece of parchment in his hand. Once he had situated himself so Emma could see him, he cleared his throat.

"Emma….," he started to say and then stopped. "Do you have middle names?"

"Elizabeth Anne," Emma replied carefully, not quite sure why he wanted to know.

Thomas resumed his vows. "Emma Elizabeth Anne Fitzsimmons, I promise to love you, comfort you, honor you, keep you in sickness and in health, and forsake all others for as long we both shall live," he said solemnly.

Emma blinked back tears. "Thomas Edward… do you have other names?" she asked after a pause, only knowing the one from having seen it in the ledgers.

Thomas shook his head. "No," he replied, surprised she knew his middle name.

"Thomas Edward Wellingham, I promise to obey you, serve you, love and honor you, and keep you in sickness and in health, and forsake all others for as long as we both shall live," she replied, tears streaming down her cheeks.

"With this ring, I wed thee," Thomas said as he held out a gold band. Emma inhaled sharply as she studied the ring and watched as he pulled her left hand to him and slid the ring onto her fourth finger.

"You may… kiss the bride," she said happily as her lips met his. And he did so, for several minutes as they lay with their arms wrapped around one another.

CHAPTER 72
A RESIGNATION IS TENDERED

July 13, 1802, Commerce Street, London
Carrying two wax-sealed rolls of papers, Todd Vandermeer strode into the office of his superior at the East India Company. "Sir Charles," he said with a nod as he approached the man's ornate desk. Bowing, he waited to be acknowledged before stating his business.

"Mr. Vandermeer," Sir Charles said in surprise, the ringlets of his powdered wig bouncing. "What brings you here today? I thought you were still on your wedding trip," he said as he stood and held out his right hand. "No trouble, is there?"

Todd shook his head. "The marriage is going quite well, actually. But the trip was interrupted by a missive I received from Mr. Hughes."

The elder man at first frowned and then his eyes found the ceiling. "Is this about those damnable transparent gowns?" he asked in disgust as he walked around his desk to a decorative bar cart. "I say, I don't understand why that man would think he could find a market for those fripperies here in England," he added with a frown. He poured two drinks from a crystal decanter and offered one to Todd.

Sighing, Todd thanked him for the drink and they both sipped the brandy before Todd held up one of the scrolls he carried. "If I may explain, sir," he offered as he handed over the rolled up papers to Sir Charles.

"Go on," the man replied as he set down his drink and then broke the seal and unrolled the papers.

"Mr. Hughes came to me last winter looking for a unique product he could sell in this country. Seems he had a string of bad luck when it came to choosing the next profitable product. I suggested the transparent gowns." Todd paused as he noted the shocked expression on Sir Charles' face. "But I explained to Mr. Hughes they would require a certain degree of care in their marketing. The gowns would not sell themselves. Discriminating women and a few others would first need to be convinced of their *value* before modistes and other shops might be convinced to carry them for sale," he explained carefully. "The document you hold in your hand is a detailed plan that, if followed, should provide the means for The Company to rid themselves of all the gowns and to make a profit on them before the year is complete."

Sir Charles looked up from scanning the marketing plan, one eyebrow arching at hearing the news. "Why didn't Mr. Hughes follow the plan?" he asked as he returned his attention to the detailed pages.

Sighing loudly, Todd at first didn't reply, and he didn't make eye contact with his superior. "I believe the extent of his research into the matter involved asking the opinion of a prostitute on the London Bridge," Todd finally stated while he tried very hard not to blush.

"Oh," Sir Charles said, swallowing the rest of his drink before crossing his arms. "He dropped the ball on the follow-up, then?" he asked rhetorically. "As usual, it would seem," he added under his breath.

Glancing at the papers again, Sir Charles leaned against the front of his desk and regarded Todd. "This isn't your fault—you have obviously done the work necessary to see to it this would be a successful endeavor—so why the long face?"

Todd held out the other sealed roll. "I wish to tender my resignation from East India. I can continue here for a few more weeks if you require my services," he offered with a nod, "Or I'm prepared to leave today if you should wish it."

The elder man straightened, his mouth open in surprise and his brows becoming one. "My God, what has happened?" he asked as he stepped forward and looked up at Todd. "Why have you decided to leave *now?* You've worked here for ...," he paused a moment, trying to remember when Todd Vandermeer had been a caddie for him and his colleagues.

"Twenty-three years, sir," Todd said with a nod, barely able to make eye contact. "I wish to thank you for each and every one of them. But it's time I move on," he stated firmly. "There's no future for me here. I'm not a political man, and I believe politics will become more and more important to this company. More important than monopolies on products and shipping lanes and docks," he added, hoping he wasn't offending his superior with his insights.

Sir Charles grunted before scrubbing his face with his hand. "As usual, you have the seen the future, Mr. Vandermeer." He shook his head, a disappointed look on his face. "I don't expect you to stay, although perhaps you would wish to see Mr. Hughes' upcoming departure when I tell him he has been relieved of his duties?" he suggested with a raised brow and a cunning expression.

Todd shook his head. "I don't believe I would find amusement in such a thing, Sir Charles."

The elder man shook his head. "You've more than earned your keep here, Vandermeer. I'll see to it you get the bonus you are entitled to as well as your commission from your last venture. And if this plan works on these gowns, you can have that commission, as well," he said with a grunt.

Eyes wide at the generous offer, Todd bowed his head. "I thank you, sir," he said, humbled by the man's words.

"Where will you go? Not to the Colonies, I hope?" Sir Charles asked, a stern look coming over his features.

Todd smiled at the suggestion he might leave England. "No, although I expect I'll be doing more business in the West than in the East. I've decided to accept a position at Wellingham Imports," he replied quietly. "Thomas Wellingham and I have been friends since we were both caddies, and he has made me a most intriguing offer."

Sir Charles smiled broadly. "You dog! You'll be up to your neck in domestic products and whatever you can get from the States, won't you?" he teased as he slapped Todd across the arm.

"I expect so, sir," Todd replied with a grin. He paused a moment, uncomfortable. "I'll take my leave now. Good day, sir." The two men bowed and Todd walked to the ornate door. "Thank you again, sir. You've been a most patient and wise mentor."

Giddy with joy, Todd bounded out of East India's offices and into his phaeton, determined to hurry home to tell Deborah of his new plan. When he had left that morning, it was only to propose the plan and agree to see it through should Sir Charles accept it. But once he was in his own office, he realized how uncomfortable being there had become. Packing up his personal belongings, he had loaded them into his phaeton, written a letter of resignation, and headed for Sir Charles' office with a new plan.

Despite the heavy traffic in the eastern areas of London, Todd made it home in under two hours. Hurrying to the parlor where he figured Deborah to be embroidering in the middle of the day, he quietly opened the door.

And stared in disbelief at what he saw.

Determined not to be seen, he quietly closed the door and stepped back. His joy having turned to confusion and uncertainty, he rushed back out of the house and intercepted his groom before the man could unhitch the horse from his phaeton.

"I'm off again," he said as he took the reins from Mr. Stevenson.

Without another word, he headed out of the half-circle drive toward Oxford Street.

CHAPTER 73
THE ANATOMY OF A
PORTRAIT

*T*odd Vandermeer felt as if his heart were breaking. He found it hard to breathe. And all he could think about was where he could find Emma.

Her townhouse, he remembered, hoping she would be there, and if not, he would head to Wellingham Imports to look for Thomas.

His imagination ran wild with what he had seen in the parlor, and he was nearly at wit's end by the time he had reached No. 3 Kingly Street.

"May I have a word?" a surprised Todd asked as a robe-clad Thomas Wellingham slowly opened the door. Todd thought a moment about whom he expected to answer the door and shook his head, as if to clear it.

"Of course. What is it?" Thomas asked, noting the taller man's distress. "Good God, Todd, whatever is the matter?"

Todd continued to look distressed as Thomas motioned him to a chair in the parlor. He slowly sat down, realizing he must have interrupted something between Thomas and Emma. But Thomas didn't seem the least bit perturbed. "Where is Emma?" he asked, his brows furrowing.

"Upstairs," Thomas replied, embarrassed. He was also curious as to why Todd Vandermeer would visit Emma at her townhouse. The man had obviously expected her to answer the door. "We've been... shopping, and I was trying on my new clothes," he lied. "Aren't you supposed to be back at the John Company today?"

Todd ignored the question. "What... what would you do if you found your wife, *nude*, in the parlor with a strange man?" His face turned a bright red. "Or, perhaps she was merely scantily clad," he amended.

Thomas stared wide-eyed at him, his mouth making strange movements as he tried to decide how to respond. "Was... Is the man... naked... or scantily clad as well?" he stammered, trying to determine if the scenario Todd described was real or imagined.

The taller man shook his head. "No. Fully clothed, actually. Oh, and he is sitting in front of some kind of standing board, and he's holding a small brush..." He held up his left hand and pantomimed the motion he had seen the man making.

Continuing to stare, Thomas straightened. "So, he's painting a portrait of your... my wife, perhaps?" he half-questioned, wondering if Todd were referring to his own wife.

Todd angled his head. "Is he?" he replied uncertainly, his brows furrowing. "Oh." His breaths shortened, and he appeared in even more distress as he considered his own question.

"Todd, did you find Deborah in the parlor with a portrait painter?" Thomas asked as he noticed Todd was breathing far too fast. He feared he was about to hyperventilate.

Shaking his head and shrugging his shoulders at the same time, Todd's eyes filled with tears. "I... I don't know. I only saw them from the doorway. I didn't... I did *not* make my presence known as I was... I was so... *shocked*."

Thomas stood up abruptly and said, "Stay here." Leaving the parlor for only a moment, he returned with a startled Emma in tow. She had obviously dressed quickly, and her hair was still loose around her shoulders.

Emma regarded the two men, knowing something was amiss when she noted Todd didn't stand and give a leg upon her arrival. "What has happened? Is there something wrong?"

Sighing loudly, Thomas said in a low voice, "Do you know if Mrs. Vandermeer has arranged to have her portrait painted?"

Emma glanced sideways at her husband-to-be and licked her lips. "She spoke of the possibility. At the ball," she replied. "And then she mentioned it again yesterday."

Todd looked up from his hands. "Is she having an *affaire*?" he whispered, his eyes bright with unshed tears.

Eyes wide, Emma gasped. "She is most certainly *not*," she replied, the look of shock on her face enough to convince the man she spoke the truth. "How *dare* you?" When her arm lifted from her side, Thomas moved between the two, afraid his wife might slap the heartsick man.

"All right!" he stated firmly as he captured the hand that looked like it might strike out at any moment. "Mr. Vandermeer has just seen his wife in a compromising state and is simply wondering what to do," he tried to explain as Emma turned her look of contempt on him.

"And having her portrait painted is somehow *wrong?*" Emma countered, her voice rising.

Holding a finger in front of his lips to indicate she needed to quiet down, Thomas said in a whisper, "She was *nude*."

Emma stared at Thomas. Just the day before, Deborah had mentioned she would be posing for the painter from France, the same painter for whom she had modeled in order to earn money for a pair of shoes.

She turned her attention back to Todd. "Was the painter a Frenchman? Monsieur Jean-Claude Perot, perhaps?" she asked, her head angled to one side. She knew Deborah was posing for a painting for her husband—as a gift—and not because the painter had requested her to model again for his client in France. Some-where on the Continent was a painting of Deborah White wearing very little in the way of clothing.

Todd sat up straight, his eyes darting back and forth. "I... don't know," he replied, relief coming to his features. "But I'm about to find out," he stated as he stood up, bowed, and left the parlor. He returned a moment later. "One more thing, Thomas," he said as he bowed his head again. "I tendered my resignation from East India earlier today. I'll be available to start at Wellingham Imports when you're ready for me to do so," he said quickly.

Astonished, Thomas stared at his friend. "Would this Monday be too soon?" he asked when he recovered his composure.

"Monday would be capital," Todd replied, bowing again to the Wellinghams before leaving the townhouse.

The sound of his boots on the vestibule floor faded before Emma turned to Thomas with a mixed look of surprise and concern on her face.

"Good news, that was," Thomas said as he reached out for Emma's hand.

"Indeed," Emma replied, still shocked by the announcement. "Didn't he say it could be *years* before he left East India?"

Shrugging, Thomas smiled. "I recall it was barely six months ago he announced he was looking for a wife," he countered lightly. His expression turned more serious. "Now, what do you know about this portrait?" Thomas asked as he pulled Emma closer.

Emma took a deep breath and then let it out slowly. She hadn't expected Thomas would ever find out about the painting in question, and she'd had no intention of telling him when Deborah described her plan. Deborah had told her about the painting in confidence, after all. "There is a particular painting in the library at Cherrywood. Apparently, the woman in the painting is... mostly naked," she said in a whisper, "And posed very seductively."

Thomas nodded, remembering just such a painting from his visits to Gregory's estate home.

In the library.

Above the fireplace.

Probably to help keep her warm, given her lack of suitable clothing. "I'm quite aware of it," he admitted, mostly so he could see Emma's reaction. "Gregory's mother, in fact," he added with a raised eyebrow as his head tilted in the direction of the Simpson's townhouse next door. He wasn't disappointed when both of Emma's eyebrows shot up and her mouth formed an 'o'.

"Well. Deborah found Todd staring at it several times during their stay there," Emma continued, once she had recovered her composure. "She was... envious of it, I believe," she explained in quiet tones.

Taken aback by the explanation, Thomas thought for a moment. "So, she's having the same painting done of herself for Todd?" he half-asked, watching Emma's reactions very closely.

"I believe so, yes," Emma nodded, her face taking on a deeper flush. She swallowed hard and tried to avoid Thomas's gaze.

"And how do *you* know this Jean-Claude... Frenchman?" he asked gently.

Gasping, Emma stared at her husband-to-be. "I *don't!*" When she realized Thomas didn't appear convinced, she sighed and sat down hard in the chair Todd had been in. "'Tis not my story to tell, Thomas," she said sadly.

"Perhaps not, but you *will* tell me," he insisted. "Never in all my days would I expect to have Todd Vandermeer asking *me* about his wife's fidelity," he added with a hint of annoyance.

Emma sighed. "He came here looking for me, I'm sure," she replied, wishing she had been the one to open the door. "He has nothing to be concerned about when it comes to Deborah's fidelity, I assure you," she said. She sat quietly for a moment. "Last winter, Dr. Talbot told Mrs. Dawes that Deborah had to have a decent pair of shoes."

"Shoes?" Thomas interrupted as he sat down in the opposite chair. "This is about *shoes?*"

Emma sighed again. "As I said, this isn't my story." When Thomas pulled his chair closer to hers, he motioned for her to go on. She continued, "There was no money for shoes, or coal, or anything else, for that matter. The Home for Unwed Mothers was always very tight on funds, especially in the winter. And Dr. Talbot knew of this French artist who was looking for a very tall woman to model for him. Seems he had a client in France who had commissioned him to do a painting, and the client wanted the woman in the painting to be an Amazon."

"I think I know where this is going," Thomas murmured, his face taking on a scowl.

Ignoring his comment, Emma continued. "So a meeting was arranged—and, I assure you, it didn't go well, according to our dear Deborah—but she agreed after much persuasion to pose for the artist in exchange for enough money to buy the shoes. She posed for him three or four times. Monsieur Perot completed the painting, and Deborah was able to buy the shoes. Rather *ugly* shoes, if you must know," she added with a wrinkled nose.

"Was she nude for that painting, too?" Thomas asked, trying hard not to visualize the tall beauty in all her glory. Todd had already described several aspects of her in vivid detail.

Emma furrowed her brows. "No, actually, but apparently it looked as if she had, for the painting was of a nude woman when it was complete. But the modeling was always done during the day and at the Home, so there was no impropriety..."

"*Impropriety?*" Thomas interjected angrily. "There is a painting out there of Todd's wife—"

"The face in the painting was a close likeness, but the *body* was not hers."

Thomas' mouth gaped open. "He has that beautiful woman pose

and then he doesn't paint her *body?*" he countered, his brows furrowing as he considered the irony.

Sitting up straight, Emma regarded Thomas as her lower lip protruded into a pout. "The client wanted a more voluptuous body," she said meekly. After a pause, she sat up straighter. "So, now you find Deborah to be *beautiful?*" she asked, feeling a sudden pang of jealousy.

Aware of his comment's effect on his wife, Thomas stood up from his chair and crossed to stand in front of her. He cupped her cheek with one hand and lifted her right hand with the other. "Emma, my sweeting, she *is* beautiful," he stated before kissing the back of her hand. "But you... you are far more incandescent," he said with a calculating grin, "And, therefore, far more appealing to me." Leaning down, he kissed her on the lips and took time to allow his tongue to explore her teeth and her tongue. After a moment, she responded in kind, and he pulled her up from the chair and pressed hard against her to continue the kiss. It was a very long time before he allowed her to pull away, and then only because they both needed to breathe.

"That was... most exhilarating," Emma whispered before she kissed him again.

Thomas pulled away briefly to look upon his intended. "We should move to a more comfortable seating arrangement," he whispered with a sly grin. Emma gasped in surprise but allowed him to lead her to the only armless chair in the parlor. Thomas opened his dressing gown and sat down while Emma hiked up her gown. Straddling him, she was aware of how aroused they both were. "Why Mr. Wellingham," she whispered in a teasing tone, "You are a hard man..." She gasped as she felt his fingers spread apart the opening in her pantaloons and his thumb press against her. He entered her at the same moment and planted his lips firmly on her bosom to stifle a groan. A sharp, intense pleasure coursed through her, forcing Emma to arch her back and cling to his shoulders for support.

"I'm afraid you have me at a disadvantage," Thomas whispered between deep breaths. "I won't last long," he started to say before using his hands to push her hips down as hard as he could.

Emma felt the warmth of them through the fabric of her pantaloons and moaned as she realized one of his thumbs was exploring. Quite sudden and very intense, the spasm of pleasure gripped her as she wrapped her arms around his back and held on.

His thumb, circling and pressing where they bodies were joined, accomplished its mission, and she rode the wave of pleasure as Thomas began showering her décolletage with butterfly kisses. Pushing into her again, Thomas allowed his release, his quiet groans lost against her dewy skin.

Emma finally relaxed her hold on his back when she felt his breathing returned to normal. They shared a deep kiss before Thomas leaned back in the chair and smiled at his wife. "You are a wanton woman, Mrs. Wellingham," he whispered with a grin.

Smiling at the premature title, Emma returned the gaze. "And you, Mr. Wellingham, are a very naughty man."

Todd Vandermeer climbed the steps of Grace Park and considered how to enter the parlor knowing he would probably find his wife in a state of undress near another man. He had been gone less than an hour, but it was possible the artist was still there and that Deborah still stood with a silk robe draped low across her bare backside.

How many men have seen her without her clothes on?
Don't be ridiculous.

Winston opened the door before he was at the top of the stairs and greeted his master with a nod.

"Good day, Winston," he said as he passed his hat and cane to the butler. Todd strode through the Great Hall, passing the closed door to the parlor. He made his way to the music room.

Adjacent to the parlor, the music room was sparsely furnished and adorned with only a few paintings and a sculpture of the goddess Aphrodite. The thick carpet absorbed the sound of his boots as he made his way to the paneled wall that separated the two rooms. He placed a palm on the wall near the fireplace and moved it slowly until he found the seam of a hidden door connecting the music room to the parlor. Composing himself, he took a deep breath and slowly pushed on the door.

Deborah, clad only in a drape of low-slung silk covering her nether regions, was standing near the paneled wall with her head turned to her right, as if she were looking over her shoulder. A floral silk robe hung from her lowered arms, leaving her breasts bare in his direction but only her shoulders and back bare from the painter's perspective. Her beautifully coiffured hair, with its large curls loosely piled on the top and back of her head and several ringlets resting on her shoulders, was entirely different from how she usually styled it. The setting in which she stood was familiar somehow, though. A low table adorned with a vase of tall flowers and an ornate hairbrush stood next to her, and the fireplace was in the background.

The painter, mostly hidden behind a canvas panel and easel, was busily mixing paint on a palette and muttering something in French. Moving quietly to stand to Deborah's left, he said in a low voice. "Do not move."

Gasping, Deborah nearly fell backward as her head swung around and she took in the sight of her husband.

"Shh!" Todd motioned with a finger in front of his lips as he cupped her cheek and moved her head back to the position she had been holding it for the pose. Her eyes tried to stay on him, though, and he couldn't help but notice the fear in them.

"I... I can explain," Deborah whispered, her breaths coming faster as her nervousness increased. Todd's expression might have been one of mischief or menace—she couldn't tell.

"In a moment," he replied, moving to her right. Cupping her cheek with his hand again, he kissed her lightly on the lips, smiling when he pulled away. His hand lightly traced the contours of her neck and collarbone before dropping to a breast. Fondling it gently, he watched her inhale in surprise and attempt to avoid his gaze. "I've never seen you like this in the light of day," he whispered, kissing her temple as she inhaled sharply. He could tell from the expression in her eyes that she was still fearful of what he might to do her. "How much longer must you pose like this?" he asked, his lips moving from her temple to her earlobe.

"I... don't know. Monsieur Perot hasn't said," she replied in a nervous whisper, tears coming to her eyes. "Please, Mr. Vandermeer," she breathed as a tear escaped and dropped down her cheek. "Don't be angry with me," she pleaded in a barely audible whisper. She gasped again as Todd leaned down and kissed both her breasts, grinning as he watched the nipples respond to his touch.

Standing to his full six-foot, six inch height, he regarded his wife with a look of satisfaction before kissing her hard on the lips. "Never, my love," he whispered before gently turning her head back to its pose.

"Ah, your lips are now perfect, *mon cherié*," the painter called out happily, seemingly oblivious to Todd's presence. *"Mademoiselle!"* the artist then cried out in disgust. "No tears. Your eyes will be *rouge*," he protested before returning his attention to the palette.

Monsieur Perot painted her lips on the canvas before a shadow crossed in front of his light. Looking up, and up some more, he found he was the subject of a very tall man's scrutiny. The intruder continued to move around him so he stood behind him, facing the canvas.

The painter put down his palette and brush and hopped off the stool on which he had been mostly seated. Rotund and short, he waddled quickly towards Todd, holding out his right hand as he did so. "Monsieur Vandermeer, I presume?" he said in his thick accent. "I am Jean-Claude Perot," he added with a nod, grabbing Todd's hand and shaking it vigorously.

Todd's brows furrowed as he regarded the man who stood in front of him. At barely five feet in height, the artist appeared nearly as wide as he was tall. Surprised at the man's nonchalant attitude, Todd nodded. "Yes. *Oui*," he amended. "Indeed, I am Todd Vandermeer, at your service," he replied, relieved when the Frenchman released his hand. "May I inquire as to what's going on in my parlor?" he asked quietly, keeping his voice low so Deborah wouldn't overhear him. "I see you have my *wife* in state of undress," he said. He returned his attention to Deborah, who, from this angle wasn't showing anything more than her bare back and shoulders, although she still looked as if she wanted to run away. Remembering the night they had said their wedding vows, Todd was determined to keep her in the room. She couldn't run far in just a satin robe.

"Why, I am painting your wife, *monsieur*," the artist replied, the thin mustache over his lip dancing in amusement. "She's a most perfect model. Very... willowy," he stated with a wave of a hand as he glanced back at Deborah.

"And whose idea was it to paint *my wife?*" Todd asked, allowing his voice to take on a menacing tone.

The Frenchman took a step backward, his expression indicating he had taken offense at the question. "Why, your *wife's*, of course. She has commissioned me to paint her in this particular pose. As a gift," he added in his defense. The sounds of weeping could be heard, and the artist turned around. "No *crying, mademoiselle*. I have not yet finished your eyes!" he called out.

"A gift?" Todd repeated, his brows furrowing.

The painter sighed when he realized the tall man wasn't going to take his leave until he had a satisfactory explanation for what was happening in his parlor. "Mrs. Vandermeer, I fear your secret is revealed," he called out sadly. "There will be no surprise birthday present for your husband this year."

Todd's brows furrowed at the odd comment, and he looked to Deborah for some kind of explanation. "What does he mean?" Todd asked, walking up to Deborah. He moved to stand directly in front of her.

Not able to make eye contact, Deborah sniffled. "I... I wanted to give you this painting for your birthday... as a surprise," she stammered quietly.

Todd shook his head. "My birthday?" he repeated. "But, I don't even know the date of my birthday," he said in disbelief.

"August third," Deborah countered, having been told the date by Mrs. Dawes. "It's on your record of birth," she added as her eyes finally met his.

"Oh," Todd replied with a raised eyebrow. He smiled then and wrapped his arms around her, kissing her forehead as he did so. Pulling the robe up and around her shoulders, he closed the front of it and Deborah gripped the edges together in one hand, as if she were embarrassed to be naked in front of her husband.

"Ah," Jean-Claude cooed as he watched the tall man comfort his wife. "I come back next year and paint your family portrait," he said with a grin, his pencil-thin mustache spread out across his upper lip. "By then you will have a *bebe*," he added with a nod.

Smiling, Todd took a deep breath. "May I see what you've done?" he asked as he nodded toward the tall easel.

The Frenchman glanced at his subject, and when Deborah merely shrugged, he motioned for Todd to follow him. Keeping one arm around Deborah's shoulder, Todd led her to stand in front of the oil painting.

Todd recognized the scene immediately. Except for its almost nude subject, a near perfect rendition of Deborah as she had been standing, the painting was a copy of the one that hung in the library at Cherrywood.

"I saw the way you looked at that painting in the library," Deborah began in explanation. "I was jealous of Mrs. Grandby, I suppose," she stammered.

Todd smiled broadly, remembering at once why he had stared so long at the painting. "Yes, I did look at it quite often. But only because I thought it rather odd," he said as he pulled her closer to him.

"Odd?" the painter and Deborah replied in unison.

Todd nodded. "*Oui*. Although the woman in the painting is pretty, she is Gregory Grandby's mother, you see. I've never been able to look at her in the painting without feeling a hint of discomfort, you see. She's one of my friend's mothers, and to see her in such a state of undress is rather embarrassing," he admitted casually. "It was painted when her husband was still alive—before she disappeared—so it's of a happier time for Gregory, no doubt," he added with a nod. "But, you see, the painting at Cherrywood is odd because the flowers in the large vase are all wrong."

Deborah furrowed her brows. "The *flowers?*" she repeated, stunned at the comment. "How so?" Had she even noticed the flowers in the painting? She took a quick glance at the floral arrangement Winston had created in the tall vase near the fireplace, thinking it looked close enough to the one in the painting.

"There are tulips and daffodils all around the one side of the bouquet, and then there are those large mums mixed in with a few red roses. But everyone knows tulips and daffodils are long gone before the roses and mums bloom," he stated with an arched brow. "How could the painter have made such an error?" he asked as he glanced in Jean-Claude's direction, as if seeking an explanation.

The painter rolled his eyes and made a huffing sound. "It is called *artistic license*," Jean-Claude claimed with his chin in the air. "A painter can do what he wishes with the background details of a painting as long as the subject is rendered truthfully." He paused for a moment, his brows furrowing. "Or it could be the flowers were from a hot house," he suggested with a shrug.

Todd regarded the painter for several seconds before he nodded, glancing again at the painting of his wife. "I see you have rendered my wife quite truthfully," he commented while he also studied the other details. "And the flowers and hairbrush, as well," he added, quite liking the painting now that he studied it.

The painter had captured the arc of Deborah's neck and the hint of a breast hidden behind a long arm bent just enough to suggest she was about to pull up the robe to cover her back. "How much longer do you require my wife to pose for you?" he asked, thinking the painting was nearly finished.

Jean-Claude shrugged. "Fifteen, perhaps twenty minutes," he

guessed with a wave. "Then I will work another two hours or so on the finishing touches," he added with his thumb and forefinger pressed together.

"You can have her for thirty minutes, but then she is *done*." Turning to Deborah, he said, "And then, *mademoiselle*, I will have you the rest of the evening." he said in a quiet voice. "Come to my... *our* bedchamber, and do not change your attire before doing so," he commanded gently.

Deborah swallowed hard but saw the mischief in his eyes. "Yes, Mr. Vandermeer," she replied with a curtsy. She hurried to take her place in the tableau and immediately positioned herself in the pose she had held all afternoon.

Todd bowed to the artist, who returned the courtesy, and then left the parlor through the regular door to the Great Hall. "Winston," he called out as he made his way to the stairs.

"Here, sir," the butler replied as he emerged from the dining room.

"Let the cook know Mrs. Vandermeer and I will be dining in the master suite this evening," he said with a mischievous grin. He bounded up the stairs before the butler could give a reply. "Oh, and I'd like a hot bath," he called out, curious if both he and Deborah would fit in the copper tub at the same time.

*U*ndressing quickly, Todd cursed at having allowed the painter another thirty minutes. But the painting was nearly finished, and it *was* beautiful, he considered. He wondered where Deborah intended to hang it given it would be inappropriate in the parlor or even the music room. Remembering the drab walls of the office he would inhabit at Wellingham Imports, Todd smiled at the thought of seeing Deborah whenever he wished.

Winston was busy filling the tub, adding the very hot water from the small water heater to the cold water from the faucet. He announced the bath was ready and then left the room. Passing Deborah on the stairway, he greeted her with a nod, and silently wondered why she wore such odd attire. He knew she had been locked in the parlor the entire afternoon with the French artist.

"The painter said he will continue his work until he is completely finished," Deborah said to the butler. "But the canvas must remained untouched for several days so it may dry," she added over her shoulder. "No peeking!"

The butler's brows knit together. "Of course, Mrs. Vandermeer," he said, no longer perplexed by her attire.

Deborah held the edges of the silk robe in both hands and hurried up the stairs. "Thank you," she answered before she entered the master suite.

Before she was even in the bedchamber, Todd had his arms around her and his mouth on hers, kissing her hard and deep. Closing the door with her foot, she allowed him to press her against it as his hands found their way through the robe and all over her skin. It was then she realized he was completely naked.

"I have never seen you like this in the light of day," Todd whispered between kisses. "As you were in the parlor," he added, his fingers working to remove the short drape of fabric from around her hips. "I wanted to take you right there," he breathed, kissing her neck and shoulder, "On the floor, even," he whispered quickly, "I would have but for that damned painter," he added as his hands cupped her bottom and lifted her up, pinning her against the door.

A single finger found its way to the wet spot between her thighs, pressing and probing until Deborah, gasping in surprise at the sudden assault and the sharp pleasure it generated, wrapped her legs around his hips and her arms around his shoulders. She inhaled sharply as his mouth took her breasts, his tongue her nipples. Before she could catch her breath, his manhood impaled her, hot and hard, pushing and pulsating in a rhythm much faster than their usual lovemaking.

The ecstasy was sudden and searing, white hot energy flowing through them both as Deborah arched her back and cried out, and Todd bit down on her shoulder to stifle his moans.

Exhausted and breathing too hard, Todd leaned heavily against Deborah's body while her hands and lips caressed his head and neck. When she felt him pull out of her, she whimpered as she lowered one leg and made sure she could touch the floor before lowering the other leg to stand on her tiptoes.

Relieved of her weight, Todd relaxed but held her close, not willing to allow any space between them. "I'm so sorry," he whispered between gasps for air.

"Whatever for?" Deborah replied, still breathing in short pants. She tried to pull away enough to see his face. He kept her pinned against the door, though, and she could only continue stroking his arms and the sides of his face.

"I... I've become a barbarian," he whispered, using a hand to scrub his wet face. At Deborah's arched eyebrow, he added, "This was a most improper—"

"Very passionate—" Deborah interrupted.

"Rather uncomfortable—"

"Exciting..." Deborah breathed.

"Barbaric—"

"And a rather pleasurable way to make love," Deborah finished for him, her expression suggesting she didn't mind a bit.

"Passionate, then," he repeated with a nod. "But later, I'll be more gentle with my passions," he vowed. When he could breathe well enough, Todd kissed her with light touches, teased her face with his tongue and lips and finally lifted her in his arms and carried her to the bath.

Deborah gave him a questioning glance before she dipped a toe in the water. She waited for Todd to sit down before she folded herself up and eased her body into the hot water. Her back against his chest and her head on his shoulder, she closed her eyes and moaned softly.

The soreness in her neck and back eased with the warmth of the water and Todd's body heat. The scent of French milled soap filled the air as Todd rubbed the bar over her wet skin and followed the trail with his hands.

"So, if you were to come home from work and find me nude and posed as I was in the parlor today, would you ravish me as you did a few moments ago?" Deborah teased in a hoarse whisper.

Todd slid his hands down her soap-slick arms and onto her thighs. "Would the painter be there?" Todd replied, his teasing voice matching hers.

Shaking her head, Deborah said, "Of course not."

There was a long pause before Todd said anything. "How many times have you posed for Perot?" he asked, his hands slipping over her knees and down the front of her legs. He felt her body tense and stopped moving his hands.

Deborah turned her head in an attempt to look at his face. "Twice for this painting," she replied quietly. "And thrice for a painting he did last March," she whispered, feeling ashamed of what she had done. She felt his body tense and was aware his breathing had stopped.

"Were you... nude then, too?"

She shook her head and tried to turn in the tub. "I wore a gown. He didn't paint my body, only my height and likeness," she explained quickly, hoping she could stave off what she supposed was anger. "I needed a pair of shoes," she added in a whisper, tears dripping down her face. "But I had no money."

Todd regarded her, his brows furrowing. He sighed. "Shoes?" he repeated. His arms wrapped around her shoulders. He kissed her temple and sighed loudly.

Nodding her head, Deborah sighed. "Dr. Talbot said I needed better shoes, and that he knew a painter who required a Long Meg to model for him. I used my earnings to buy the shoes."

Not speaking for a few moments, Todd sighed again. "Did Perot ever..." He stopped and took a deep breath. "Did he ever touch you?"

"No!" Deborah interrupted, shaking her head. "He said he didn't find me pleasant to look upon in the least," she said before twisting her mouth. "In fact, he said he preferred his women much shorter and... rounder," she added with a wave of her hands to indicate a more voluptuous, hourglass figure. "But his client in France wanted a painting of an Amazon with the face of an angel and brunette hair."

Todd made an odd sound in his throat. "You speak as if you were offended," he said, trying to sound amused. Inside, he felt a sense of relief and guilt. He hadn't made his usual contribution to the Home for Unwed Mothers in March but, once he realized his oversight, he had his butler make a larger contribution in April on his behalf.

This is all my fault.

"I truly only felt relief when he no longer required me to model," she replied quietly.

"And yet you hired him to do this portrait," Todd commented, trying hard not to sound as disgusted as he felt.

Deborah shrugged. "He's the only painter I know," she countered, a defensive tone in her voice.

"How did you pay him?" Todd whispered hoarsely, his brows furrowed as if he dreaded the answer.

Pressing her lips tightly together, Deborah swallowed. "With the pin money you gave me last week," she finally whispered in reply. "It

678

was far more than I would've spent shopping," she added as she tried to angle her head so she could see his face. "Please, don't be angry with me," she begged again. "I'm very sorry I misunderstood your interest in the painting at Cherrywood."

Todd let out the breath he'd been holding, a sense of relief washing over him. He hugged her and kissed her temple again. "You're forgiven, my love." After a few moments of silence, he whispered, "I tendered my resignation from the John Company today."

Gasping, Deborah tried to turn around in the tub, but his arm stayed wrapped around her midriff and held her back firmly against his chest. "Did it go poorly then?" she whispered in reply, not sure why he said it so quietly.

"It went quite well, actually," he replied as he slowly released her, his hand sliding down her slick body. "Sir Charles was rather generous. I'll receive my bonus and the commissions that are due me, and Mr. Hughes is to be relieved of his position."

Deborah's sharp intake of breath was one of surprise and delight. "Congratulations, my love," she said happily. "When will you start at Wellingham Imports then?" she asked, half turning in the tub so she could finally look at him.

"Monday," Todd replied, kissing her hair. "I have all my things from the old office packed and ready to move into the new one," he murmured softly. "I should warn you. I plan to hang my birthday present in my office at Wellingham Imports so I may look upon you whenever I wish. I'm sure to return home with a keen desire to ravish you daily," he teased.

Stunned, Deborah sat up straight in the tub and let out a gasp. "In your *office?*" she repeated, her eyes widening in horror as she turned to look at him. A wave of water sloshed over the edge of the tub with her sudden movement.

Todd smiled and kissed her quickly. "Yes, my love." At her continued look of shock, he added, "Where only *I* can look upon it, of course." Gripping the edge of the tub, he pushed until he was standing and then reached down to help her up. As he lifted her out of the tub and into a linen, he sighed. "I would say that at this very moment, you look just like Venus stepping out of the sea on her clamshell, but I believe we've had enough of copied paintings today."

Smiling coyly, Deborah realized to which painting he was referring. "You have seen that Botticelli masterpiece in Italy?" she asked in awe, thinking he would have seen it on one of his many trips to the Continent.

Todd stared at his wife. "Only a color plate in a book," he replied with a raised eyebrow. "What? Did you model for him, too?" he asked, his eyes wide.

Shaking her head as she tried to suppress a smile, Deborah replied, "No, my husband. Sondro Botticelli died three hundred years ago."

Allowing a broad smile, Todd removed the linen from Deborah's body. "A shame," he said as he studied her naked form in the late afternoon light from the nearby window. "You would have been a perfect model for Venus," he whispered.

He lifted her in his arms and took her to the bed where they continued their lovemaking—in a more gentle manner—for the rest of the evening.

CHAPTER 74
CELEBRATING A BIRTHDAY

July 14, 1802, Woodscastle

Mr. Tanner watched as Gregory Grandby picked up the tray laden with plates of toast, eggs, coffee, and chocolate. "You sure you got that all right?" the cook asked as he regarded the rather tall house guest. It was apparent Gregory had no experience in such matters, and Mr. Tanner wondered if he should send for the butler to help the man lest the tray full of food end up on the floor.

"Indeed, Mr. Tanner. Thank you again for your assistance," Gregory said as he backed out the kitchen door and hurried to the stairs leading up to the east wing of Woodscastle. He had arranged for Mr. Tanner to make the morning meal earlier than usual so he could surprise Christiana with breakfast in bed on her birthday. As he negotiated the stairs, he tried keeping his footfalls as quiet as possible.

As he passed Thomas' bedchamber, he wondered if Thomas and Emma had returned from London. Thomas certainly wouldn't miss his sister's birthday, he considered. Nor the payment for the west wing. The five-thousand pounds was safely tucked away in his trunk.

When he reached the door to Christiana's bedchamber, he paused and carefully balanced the tray as he used his elbow to push down the door handle. He gave the door a gentle push.

Peeking around the corner as he held the tray in front of his body, he smiled when he saw her. She was still asleep on her back, wearing a bright white muslin nightrail, the fabric so thin it was nearly translucent. Curls of her strawberry blond hair were splayed out around her face. Most of the bed covers had been tossed aside due to the heat from the night before. Now, in the early morning light and cool air, her nipples were silhouetted in the gown, and there was a hint of the triangle of dark hair just above her thighs.

Gregory had to resist the urge to simply drop the tray and climb into bed with her. He placed the tray on the dressing table, felt in his waistcoat pocket for the small velvet wrapped box, and hurried to close the door.

Moving to the side of the bed, he watched as his beloved slept. Leaning over her, he kissed her on the forehead while he lowered one hand so it barely touched her nightrail and then swept it lightly over her entire body to where her leg disappeared beneath a blanket. Christiana stirred, her eyes finally opening.

"Happy birthday, my love," Gregory whispered.

A beatific smile appeared on Christiana's face. "Good morning," she replied, nervously glancing around the room and then back at her beau. "Is this still the dream?" she whispered, her eyes darting about.

Gregory regarded the girl and raised an eyebrow. "That depends, I suppose," he replied with a mischievous grin. "What were you dreaming?"

Embarrassed, Christiana lowered her eyes as if to recall the images from her dream. "You were making love to me," she whispered. "In your suite at Cherrywood," she murmured, her eyes closing completely as she tried to recapture the dream.

Chuckling, Gregory climbed onto the bed and, leaning on one elbow, used his other hand to cup the side of her face. "You must have been dreaming of our honeymoon," he said quietly, trying hard to suppress the teasing smile that came unbidden. He kissed her on the lips while he moved the hand down around her shoulder and over her breast, cupping it gently while his thumb pressed on the hardened nipple. "Will I be allowed to wake you like this every morning after we're wed?" he whispered in her ear, his lips brushing her earlobe.

Christiana inhaled sharply and opened her eyes. "It would be a most wonderful way to wake up," she murmured happily, the last vestiges of the dream faded from her memory as she took in the sight of Gregory staring down at her. "'Tis a wonderful way to wake up. How long have you been here?" she asked in sudden alarm as she glanced around the bedchamber.

Sighing, Gregory got down from the bed. "Several minutes, at least," he answered with a grin. "Happy birthday," he said as he turned to lift the tray from the dressing table. "I've brought you breakfast in bed."

Sitting up, Christiana smiled while Gregory positioned the tray over her legs. "I fear the eggs are probably cold by now, but I assure you, they were hot when Mr. Tanner made them a few moments ago," he said as he handed her a fork and a napkin and helped himself to a piece of toast and one of the cups of coffee. "Do you still take sugar with your coffee?"

Christiana nodded, her gaze taking in the sight of eggs and Yorkshire toast. "This is a wonderful surprise," she said as her attention returned to him. "And, yes," she added with an amused expression, "You can wake me like this every morning." She started eating as Gregory finished his toast and regarded her. Removing the velvet box from his waistcoat, he placed it on the breakfast tray. "Happy birthday," he said with a grin.

Eyeing the box suspiciously, Christiana took a drink of chocolate and set the cup on the tray. "May I open it now?" she asked, gingerly picking up the small box. It was the same size as a box he had given her for Christmas—the one that had held a locket on a gold chain in which he had hidden several strands of his hair.

"Of course," Gregory replied, his excitement barely contained.

Christiana abandoned her breakfast in favor of the box, slowly unwrapping the velvet and pulling the top off. Inside, on a bed of crumpled velvet, was a single sapphire mounted on a gold ring. Even before she could take the ring out of the box, Gregory asked, "Will you marry me?"

Gasping, Christiana smiled and angled her head in delight. "Yes, I will marry you," she replied, returning her attention to the ring almost immediately. Gregory took the ring from her and slid it on the fourth finger of her left hand. "When we're wed, I'll give you another gold ring—one of my grandmother's," he said as he tested the fit and then lifted her hand to his lips. Kissing the back of it, he added, "But, for now, I want to be sure there's no question you're betrothed."

Christiana leaned over the tray and kissed Gregory. "I do believe everyone will know without even looking for a ring on my finger, 'tis so large a stone," she commented happily, holding her hand out in front of her as she admired the sapphire. "What do you suppose my brother has bought for Emma?" she asked, her eyes still on the sapphire.

Shaking his head, Gregory could only shrug. "I don't know. Mr. Vandermeer told me he was with him when Thomas bought some tear-shaped baubles for Miss Emma. Vandermeer was shopping for a wedding band at the time. Knowing Mr. Vandermeer as I do, I'm sure your brother probably saw at least a hundred wedding rings that day."

Smiling at the comment, Christiana nodded. "He's not as horrible as I imagined," she murmured quietly. At Gregory's raised eyebrow, she added, "Mr. Vandermeer, I mean. I used to think he was awful, especially when I thought he was going to ask Emma to marry him," she explained with an embarrassed grin. "And that was just six weeks ago!"

Frowning, Gregory straightened and stared at Christiana. "What did you say?" he replied, surprise evident in his voice.

Christiana angled her head, amused Gregory didn't know about Todd's interest in Emma. "If Emma hadn't introduced him to Deborah White, Mr. Vandermeer would have asked Emma for her hand. And Emma would have accepted!" Christiana explained in mock horror. "Can you imagine?"

At first, Gregory shrugged his shoulders, not quite under-standing Christiana's point. Then he realized if Emma had married Todd, then whom would Thomas marry?

And *when?*

Gregory regarded his betrothed and sat up straight. "I see your point," he conceded with a frown. Thinking about the turn of events, he shook his head. "I do see your point."

At the sound of horses galloping up to the front of the house, Gregory got up from the edge of the bed and pushed aside the drapes. "They're home," he murmured as he allowed the fabric to settle back into place.

"Do they look married?" Christiana asked with a mischievous grin. She took a bite of eggs and watched Gregory as he pulled the drapery fabric away from the window again.

"I'm not quite sure what being married is supposed to look like," he commented with a grin as he watched Thomas and Emma get down from a yellow bounder while the postillion took their bags from the back of the rented chaise. "But I assure you, I've thought of them as such for most of a year," Gregory added as he let go of the fabric.

Christiana's eyes widened. "You mentioned that the other night, and I found it hard to believe then. How could you know they would end up together when they hadn't even met?" she asked, finishing her eggs and starting on a slice of toasted Yorkshire bread.

Shrugging, Gregory returned to sit on the edge of the bed. He heard the front door opening and Humphrey's voice greeting his master. "Because Sir William said so," he replied with a grin. "My uncle has a way of getting what he wants."

Christiana smiled at the comment. "So he's much like my brother then?" she replied as she regarded her betrothed.

Leaning over, Gregory kissed her on the forehead. "I suppose you could say that. Now, I should go down and greet your brother and his wife before he finds me in your bedchamber," he said as he got up from the bed.

"I'll be down shortly," Christiana said with a smile. "Thank you for breakfast. And for the sapphire," she added, holding her hand out in front of her as she admired the deep blue stone on the gold band. "I can hardly wait to show Emma."

"Best wishes, Mr. Grandby," Emma happily called out as she watched her future brother-in-law descend the steps from the east wing. Thomas had carried her over the threshold and still had her in his arms when they turned to greet Gregory. "She did say 'yes', I hope," she added as her expression turned serious.

Gregory nodded as he bounced from the last step, crossed the hall, and slid into the vestibule. "Indeed, she did," he answered with a satisfied grin as he took in the sight of Emma and Thomas.

Emma giggled as Thomas set her down and allowed her to lean against him until she had her feet firmly beneath her. As they gave their coats to Humphrey, Gregory made a point to look for a ring on Emma's left hand, smiling when he saw the gold band. "And I didn't even have to get down on my knee," Gregory added with a raised brow. Leaning over, he kissed Emma on the cheek. "Congratulations," he said quietly.

"Thank you, Mr. Grandby," Emma replied as she blushed. She watched the tall man turn his attention to Thomas.

"And how is married life treating you, Mr. Wellingham?" Gregory asked in a teasing voice.

Thomas tried desperately to keep his sudden embarrassment from coloring his face. "Exhausting, I must admit," he replied as he thrust out his chin. "And troubling. I don't know that I have the stamina required to satisfy my demanding wife. Nor do I have the funds. I had no idea how expensive marriage can be! And the requirements on my time..."

Emma gasped in surprise at her husband's comments, but his quick wink in her direction made her realize they were all made in jest.

A startled Gregory glanced at her, though, not quite sure if *he* was being teased. Emma shrugged one shoulder in response to Gregory's upturned brow before he returned his attention to Thomas.

"... And I do wish I had done this at least a year ago because 'tis the best thing that's happened to me in my entire life," Thomas finished, his expression still rather serious. He wrapped his arms around Emma's waist and pulled her against him.

Emma let out a startled, "Oh!" as her body collided with Thomas', but her impish grin betrayed her amusement.

Gregory pointed a finger at his friend and bit his lip. "You had me..."

"You have my permission to marry my sister whenever you are legally able," Thomas interrupted as he wrapped a hand around Gregory's extended finger and shoved it aside. "Emma and I are going to do it again this Saturday at eleven o'clock at St. James Church, in fact," he added happily. "After which, the Vandermeers will be hosting our wedding breakfast at Grace Park. Would you care to join us?"

A breathless voice sounded from the top of the stairs. "Oh, could we?" Christiana called out as she hurried down the stairs. She had changed into a green morning gown, but her hair was loose and hung in ringlets to the middle of her back. Gregory caught her in his arms and swung her around, carefully lowering her feet to the floor of the vestibule. When he let go of her, she turned and hugged Emma and then her brother. "I have given it a great deal of thought, and if it's all right with you, Gregory, I really would like to get married at the same time as Emma," she pleaded, her hands holding one of Gregory's.

Gregory smiled and cast a glance in Thomas' direction. "If we can get a marriage license, then, yes, we can get married Saturday," he agreed. "We'll have to go to town right away, though." He looked at Thomas with an apologetic face. "You'll have to come to give permission, if you would," he added. "And we'll have to write and deliver invitations..."

"I can help Christiana with that," Emma interjected. "And we'll let the Vandermeers know, of course. Deborah will be ecstatic to know she'll be hosting even more guests."

Thomas shrugged and regarded his sister. "I was hoping I could take you to Gunter's for a sorbet later today," he said. "Happy birthday."

Christiana's eyes lit up and she reached up to hug her brother. "That would be delightful!" she exclaimed, standing on her toes as she kissed his cheek. "I just need to pin up my hair, and then we can be on our way."

Emma exchanged glances with Thomas. "Shouldn't we wait until after breakfast?" she asked of no one in particular.

"Oh, I had mine," Christiana replied happily. "In bed," she added.

Emma noticed the ring on her finger and reached out to take Christiana's hand. "'Tis beautiful, Christiana," she said quietly as she regarded the dark sapphire.

Christiana reached out her right hand and touched Emma's wedding ring. "So is yours," she sighed as she glanced at her brother. "Did you choose this, Thomas?"

Arching an eyebrow, Thomas nodded. "Yes. I had a most enthusiastic tutor when it came to ring shopping," he commented lightly. "It seems Mr. Vandermeer managed to visit every goldsmith in London before deciding on a ring for Mrs. Vandermeer, so he made sure to inform me of everything he knew about them while we shopped for Emma's raindrops."

Gregory clasped his hands behind his back. "So, does that mean Todd picked out your wife's ring?" he asked quietly. Emma overheard the query and rolled her eyes.

"No, indeed," Thomas replied, rolling his own eyes in disgust. "Had he done so, Emma would be wearing a most audacious collection of multicolored baubles in gold filigree requiring no fewer than three fingers to wear," he answered with a hint of disgust.

Emma smirked. "Deborah's ring is not *audacious*," she commented quietly. "It only has three stones set on a gold ring, and there's no filigree," Emma added.

"That was the ring he picked out for Deborah," Thomas said carefully. "Someday I'll have to show you what he picked out for you."

Emma's mouth dropped open. "Oh," she said before closing her mouth. "Oh, my."

CHAPTER 75
DOUBLE WEDDING DAZE

July 17, 1802, Grace Park in Cavendish Square

Deborah Vandermeer tossed a large lace tablecloth across the long trestle table and Anna caught it on the other side. "Three more to go," she said happily as they moved to the next trestle and repeated the table preparation. Two other maids followed them by placing chargers and place settings in front of the chairs arranged around each trestle table.

"There are a good many more people coming for this wedding, Mrs. Vandermeer," Anna commented as the tablecloth flew over the next trestle.

"Indeed. A double wedding means double the number of guests, I suppose," Deborah said with a grin. She stopped before the last trestle to survey the gardens behind Grace Park and smiled broadly. Her best friend was getting married in a few hours, and she could hardly contain her enthusiasm. Roses were in bloom in the south garden and the lilies were still holding their own along the north side of the property. If the breeze blew in just the right direction, the scent would be heaven for everyone attending the wedding feast for the Grandby-Wellingham weddings.

Todd Vandermeer surveyed the preparations from his vantage point in the study, his grin broadening as he watched his wife help decorate the scene. He would be hosting the season's most anticipated mergers, he figured, with a guest list that included some of the most important Londoners in the trade and import and banking industries. His cook, if he could pull it off, would be forever remembered as the chef that created two wedding feasts in less than a month's time.

The wedding cake was even larger than the one he had built for the Vandermeer wedding, and the ham and towers of bread rolls and the plates of eggs and toast and the platters of kippers and the crystal bowl of chocolate would surpass the spread he had prepared for the July third wedding.

This would go down as *the* summer wedding feast. Todd Vandermeer couldn't be more pleased with himself or his household staff.

"Mighty proud of yourself, aren't you?" a familiar voice called from the doorway.

Todd turned in surprise to find Gregory Grandby grinning in his direction. "You dog! Whatever are you doing here at this time of the morning? Shouldn't you be at St. James?" he asked as he moved to shake his friend's hand in greeting.

"I was on my way, but detoured here to make sure you hadn't changed your mind," Gregory replied in a teasing tone.

Todd regarded his friend with a doubtful glare. "The only person who is considering changing her mind is your betrothed," he replied as he punched Gregory's shoulder. "How is she?"

The groom-to-be shook his head. "I've no idea. I was refused entrance to her bedchamber this morning and told I couldn't see her until the ceremony," Gregory replied. "I spoke with her through the door, but..."

A knowing grin spread across Todd's face. "They mean to make you suffer, you must know," he said with a nod. "I wasn't allowed to see Deborah for the entire night and morning of our wedding. I was ready to elope by the time Winston showed up to dress me."

Gregory watched his friend as he described his wedding day. "Any regrets?"

Shaking his head, Todd replied, "Only that I didn't meet her years ago."

Nodding, Gregory took a deep breath. "All right. I think I know what you mean by that. I'd best be getting to the church, then. Will I see you there?""

Laughing, Todd reached into his pocket and held out the wedding band Gregory had given him to keep until the appointed time. "You should hope so," he countered. "And Emma had better count on me, as well," he added as he pulled out a ring from his other pocket and held it up. "I'll be there shortly. I promise."

Gregory nodded and left the study, his mood greatly improved. His morning hadn't begun so well. When he'd gone to Thomas' bedchamber to seek assurance and advice, he'd found the room empty. It was only after Humphrey had nodded toward the master suite that Gregory had knocked and then entered the suite to find his best friend kissing Emma's collarbones and who knew what else before he could retreat quickly to the corridor with an embarrassed shout of apology.

Could the man not contain himself on his wedding day? It was as if Thomas was flouting his quick marriage to Emma and their marital bliss at Gregory's expense. *But at least Thomas had taken the bait,* he considered. He couldn't imagine having to wait another year to marry Christiana Wellingham.

His loins stirring at the thought of his bride preparing for him, he left Grace Park and directed Mr. Larsen to take him to St. James for the wedding.

"How very rude of us!" Emma whispered as she rolled atop Thomas and pinned his wrist to the bed.

"Of *us?*" Thomas repeated in surprise before taking one of her hardened nipples between his lips. "He's the one who walked in on us!" he countered with a mischievous grin.

Giggling, Emma rolled off of her husband and stretched her arms above her head, her body writhing as she enjoyed the afterglow of their early morning lovemaking. "You've teased him mercilessly all week, and now he finds us enjoying what he cannot yet have," she whispered with a sigh. *Marital bliss, indeed.* "Are you happy, Mr. Wellingham?" she asked after a long pause.

"Indeed, Mrs. Wellingham. Would you care to join me in a bath?" he answered, his mind coming to grips with the day of the week and the thought that they would be getting married, for real and in the eyes of the church, sometime that morning.

"That would be glorious," Emma answered with a grin. She reached out and pulled the bell that would summon Humphrey. Within a minute, the butler entered their suite and assured them that bath water was on its way up from the kitchen.

"I can hardly wait to see you in your gown again," Thomas murmured as he climbed out of bed and pulled on a robe. Emma moaned as his naked body was covered in the fabric. "Not that I prefer you in clothing, of course," he added in a teasing voice before he disappeared into the bath and started to shave his two-day old beard.

Emma followed him and purred as she kissed the back of his neck. She stood next to him at the dressing table. "This has been the most interesting honeymoon," she murmured happily. "I cannot believe I must return to the office on Monday," she added with a frown, eyeing his careful shaving technique as she watched his reflection in the large looking glass.

"Me, neither," Thomas replied between strokes. "Seems like we were just betrothed a week ago."

Emma regarded her husband's reflection and grinned at his joke. "You wicked man," she replied, brushing her hair into a long, golden mass before twisting it, rolling it, and expertly pinning it into a chignon on the back of her head.

Watching her perform the hair styling, Thomas dropped his razor into the basin and stared at her in the mirror. "You are so beautiful," he whispered. "And I shouldn't be seeing you like this on our wedding day," he added with alarm in his voice. "Isn't it supposed to be bad luck?"

Emma gave him a sideways glance. "If you believe that, I suppose. But we've been married for nearly a week," she added, allowing her comment to hang in the air as he continued to look at her with uncertainty.

"All right. I see your point," he murmured as Dahlia, Mrs. Werthers, and Humphrey all arrived with steaming pails of water. Emma poured soap bubbles into the copper tub as the pails were emptied and another pail of cold water from the pump was added.

"Madam, your bath is ready," Humphrey stated formally before he ushered the other servants from the room.

Emma gave a nod to the butler and waited until the man had taken his leave before stepping into the tub. A moment later, Thomas joined her. "Happy wedding day," he whispered.

"Did my brother see you this morning?" Christiana asked as she checked her reflection in the cheval mirror before turning to regard Emma. The older woman stood in front of Dahlia as the abigail hooked the buttons up the back of her butter-colored gown.

"He did, indeed," Emma replied as she smoothed the fabric of the skirt in front and straightened the sleeves. "Did you?"

But Christiana had turned to face Emma and gasped. "You

allowed him to see you before the wedding?" she asked in exasperation. "How could you?"

Emma felt her face flush before she turned to nod at Dahlia. "Thank you. That will be all," she murmured before returning to face Christiana. "Your brother and I have been wed for nearly a week," she countered in a whisper, reaching out to straighten a flower in Christiana's elaborate rolled and braided hair. "I don't believe it will matter that he saw me this morning. Did Mr. Grandby see you?"

"No!" Christiana replied quickly, surprised Emma would even consider the idea. "I was quite careful to be sure we wouldn't see one another this morning."

Emma smiled at her superstitious roommate. "He looked very smart in his gray morning suit and top hat," she claimed as she threaded one of the multi-jeweled earrings into a pierced ear. "As did Thomas, in fact," she added, putting in the other earring. "Do you think the brooch would be too much on this gown?" she asked as she regarded her reflection.

"'Tis probably better without it," Christiana replied, still unsettled by the morning's events.

Emma noticed her future sister-in-law's expression and sat down on the dressing table's bench. "What's troubling you?" she whispered, reaching out to take Christiana's hand.

Christiana turned away quickly and swallowed. "It'll be all right," she answered as she shook her head. "I'm just nervous, I think."

But Emma could see the brightness in Christiana's eyes and knew the girl was on the verge of tears. "Come here," she said as she took the girl in her arms. "This is supposed to be the happiest day of your life..."

"I think Gregory is having second thoughts," Christiana blurted, a tear escaping and leaving a trail on her cheek.

Emma gasped and pushed Christiana away from her body so she could look at her directly. "You cannot be thinking he's having second thoughts about getting married to you!"

Christiana glanced up at Emma and returned a worried look. "I don't know, Emma, but at the moment, my heart is very heavy, and I know it shouldn't be. Not on this day."

"Why do you say that?" she replied, concern in her voice and her face. "Whatever did he say?"

Christiana shook her head and took a hanky from the dressing table. "He didn't say anything exactly, but last night..." She paused to wipe her eyes. "He seemed very... distant and, when I asked him about the renovations in the room that is to be our bedchamber, he said it probably wouldn't be done before we leave for Rome." Christiana sniffled as another tear flowed down her cheek.

Emma bit her lip. The renovations hadn't gone quite to plan, it was true, but she knew the roof was complete, and two rooms were well under way. The master suite was only lacking the furniture and the decorator touches, that with a bit of luck, would be delivered and installed later that day.

Amazed at the speed at which Gregory Grandby had been able to line up contractors and crews for the west wing renovation, Emma soon realized Gregory's ready money was the reason. He could demand nearly anything and it was delivered within a day or two. When she had suggested certain fabrics or colors for a room, they seem to magically appear the following day. *The man can't be that disappointed in the progress,* she reasoned.

Emma gave Christiana a reassuring squeeze on one shoulder and finished pulling up her glove. "I'll go speak to your brother right away. He should be the one to ask Gregory." She hurried out the door and down the hall to the master suite. Now dressed in the gown and gloves Thomas had purchased for her, *for this day,* she considered with a slight grin, she paused at the master suite door and decided to knock before entering. The thought that she shouldn't allow Thomas to see her was struck down when she remembered they planned to ride together with Christiana in Gregory's barouche. Gregory had left the estate earlier, not telling anyone his plans other than he would meet them at St. James Church.

Emma pushed open the master suite door and peeked in, finding Humphrey fussing over the cuff links on Thomas' shirt. The groom looked up and gave her a grin and motioned for her to enter. As Emma did so, she smiled and moved toward him. "Stop right there," he said sternly, his tone causing even his manservant to look up in alarm and turn to regard Emma.

Emma froze in place, a look of surprise on her face. Thomas held out a finger and made a twirling motion with it, his facial expression quite serious.

Nervous, Emma took a step back and then pivoted slowly until she faced him again.

The serious look on Thomas' face became a beaming smile and his butler relaxed as he continued his work on his master's cuffs. "You are positively incandescent!" Thomas remarked as he motioned for her to join him. "I do believe you're more beautiful in that gown today than the day I first saw you in it."

Taking a huge breath and letting it out slowly, Emma allowed a small smile. She moved to stand next to Thomas, leaning over to kiss him on the cheek. "And you are looking most handsome, as usual," she whispered. "I wondered if I might have a word with you. It's about Mr. Grandby. Christiana is..."

Thomas turned to gaze at her. "Worried?" he interrupted, a grin threatening to break out on his face. "Nervous?"

"Very sad, I think," Emma said as she bit her lip. "Gregory left earlier, and he didn't seem in a good mood last night," she said.

Sighing heavily, Thomas shook his head.

"Is he having second thoughts about marrying Christiana?" Emma asked, her face betraying her sudden worry.

Humphrey audibly cleared his throat. When they turned to regard him, he murmured, "If I may, sir?"

A relieved Thomas nodded. "Please, do."

The butler sighed. "Mr. Grandby is most displeased with the lack of progress on the west wing—"

"Displeased?" Thomas interrupted. "The progress has been amazing. The roof, the front hall, how many rooms...?" he turned to Emma, his expression expectant.

"At least two are nearly complete, but not the master suite," she offered.

Thomas stared at her and the breath seemed to go out of his lungs. "Oh," he replied as disappointment settled on his features. "Oh, dear," he sighed, shaking his head. At Emma's concerned expression, he added, "He had... plans... for this evening," he started to say before a flush of red colored his face.

"The contractor assured him the suite would be ready, Mr. Wellingham," Humphrey spoke quietly. "Perhaps he'll be able to complete the work today, and all will be well."

Emma nodded and allowed an encouraging grin. "I'll go see for myself. I saw workers arrive earlier..."

"Dressed like that?" Thomas asked as he waved at her gown.

"It's not that dusty up there anymore, darling," she replied with a wave.

As she headed for the door, Thomas stood up straight. "Are you forgetting something?" he asked, a grin teasing the edges of his mouth.

Emma turned and regarded him. "Oh, of course," she replied quickly, hurrying back to him to give him a quick kiss. Humphrey turned away as if embarrassed by the open display of affection.

Once she'd left the room, Humphrey returned his attention to Thomas and held out a waistcoat. "If I may, sir?" he asked quietly.

Thomas regarded the butler. "You may."

"She's nothing like your mother," he remarked with a grin as he began buttoning the coat.

"No, she's not. Thank the gods," Thomas agreed with a grin.

Emma climbed the stairs to the west wing and paused at the top of the stairs. A cadre of well-dressed men were hurrying in and out of a room at the end of the hall, bolts of fabric and yards of drapery trim disappearing through the open door. A young boy carrying a bolt of fabric passed her in the hall saying, "Excuse me, ma'am," as he made his way to the same room. The fabric was familiar—it was the royal blue brocade originally intended for Worthington Fashions.

As Emma stepped aside, she noticed several maids cleaning the first room she passed—Christiana's salon, she remembered. A beautifully appointed room that was now fully carpeted and furnished, the salon featured scarlet and dark greens and cherry furniture Gregory had managed to purchase on short notice from Chippendale's shop. Emma smiled as she gave the room a quick glance and nodded at the maids. It would certainly be ready when the newlyweds returned from London that evening.

Moving to the next room, she found another group of uniformed women outfitting a bath with linens. When she reached the master suite, she bit her lip as she took in the elegant blue velvet and brocades that dressed the walls and furnishings.

"It will be done by this evening, I assure you," a nattily dressed middle-aged man stated as he approached Emma, evidently admiring her gown as his gaze swept from the floor to her face. He bowed deeply and then reached for Emma's gloved hand to kiss the back of it. "William Argyle, at your service," he added, his mustache twitching as his eyebrows lifted.

"Mrs. Wellingham," Emma replied, surprised as she managed a curtsy. "I've no doubt. The progress has been impressive," she said happily, her attention occasionally captured by the work of so many decorators and carpenters working on the room.

"You're pleased, then?" the decorator asked, his wandering gaze still taking in her manner of dress and her elegant hair style.

"Very much. But I'm not the beneficiary of your beautiful work, Mr. Argyle," Emma replied, her attention again on the room. "My soon-to-be sister-in-law will be most pleased, I assure you," she murmured. "But I'm led to believe her husband-to-be is…"

"Concerned," the man interrupted, a scowl replacing his smile. "Yes, we had a *discussion* this morning. There's no need for him to be upset, however. All is in hand, and the room will be ready for his wedding night," Mr. Argyle stated with a curt nod.

"He was upset?" Emma repeated, "About the progress, then?" she added, hoping it really was this that had Gregory behaving strangely and not second thoughts about getting married.

The decorator rolled his eyes. "I was a bit late arriving this morning," he whispered, his shoulders sagging. "My beautiful mistress wouldn't allow me to leave, you see," he commented lightly, causing Emma to take a sudden breath and fight the flush she felt creeping over her face. "And, of course I had to see to the church decor before I could make my way out here to the country," he said with a wave of hand.

"Oh?" Emma replied, an eyebrow arcing in surprise. "You decorated the *church?*" she asked. *What has Gregory been up to this week?* Her regard for the man grew with each revelation.

"I found him in here… he wasn't pleased," Argyle admitted with a roll of his eyes. "And all of my assurances couldn't assuage his concern. He is a most… *nervous groom*," he added as he leaned toward Emma and lowered his voice.

Emma grinned and lowered her eyes. "I'll speak with him before the ceremony begins," she said with a nod. "Which I must be getting to, I think," she said, a hint of alarm in her voice. "'Tis my wedding day, too!"

Argyle furrowed his brows. "Oh, dear!" he claimed, a hand going to his snowy white cravat. "You mustn't divulge what you know to the other bride!" he ordered. "'Tis to be a surprise for Miss Wellingham. She's not to know until she's walking to the altar!"

Emma stepped back in alarm. "I won't say a word. I promise!" she vowed, a smile finally replacing her look of surprise. She regarded the decorator for a moment and then leaned forward. "Do you think my gown will look all right with your arrangements?" she asked, curious as to the colors the decorator might have chosen for the church.

"Indeed, my lady," Argyle replied with a nod. "You'll look positively delicious!" His hand waved to one side as if to emphasize his assessment, and he was about to say something else when a dresser interrupted him to ask a question.

Emma took the opportunity to escape. She curtsied quickly and left the room, grinning when she found Thomas looking up at her from the bottom of the stairs.

"If we don't leave this very instant, I'll have to send my sister to the church by herself and take you to our bedchamber so that I might have my way with you," he intoned gravely.

"*Again?*" Emma teased as she hurried down the stairs, lifting her skirts so her slippered feet and ankles were showing. When she was on the last stair, she stopped and leaned down to kiss Thomas.

"You wicked woman," he breathed, continuing the kiss until his sister's impatient sigh could be heard from behind them.

"We really must leave or Gregory *will* marry someone else," Christiana complained.

"We can leave right now," Emma agreed, taking Thomas' arm. "My reticule is on the vestibule table, Mr. Allen has our trunk loaded on the barouche, and our flowers are... oh, dear," she said as she nearly stopped walking.

"Right here," Christiana stated with a exasperated sigh as she held up the two small bouquets of white and yellow roses from the back garden. "Miss Dahlia made these for us this morning," she said as she held out one to Emma.

"They match your gown perfectly," Thomas commented as he nodded in the direction of Humphrey near the vestibule. The butler held out a gray top hat and a yellow rosebud.

"Your carriage awaits," Humphrey stated, the edge of his mouth twisted up.

Thomas eyed the butler as he allowed the man to pin the yellow rosebud onto his topcoat. "That's two times in a week you've been able to say that," he murmured with amusement.

Humphrey stepped back and regarded his master. "Yes, sir. And I look forward to saying it often, if I'm allowed."

Nodding, Thomas held out his elbows and led his ladies out the front door. "You're allowed," he answered with a grin. "Mrs.

Wellingham and I will be back in the morning, but do take the day off as you're supposed to, won't you?"

The butler raised eyebrows showed his surprise. "Very well, sir. I shall see you Monday morning," Humphrey replied before shutting the door.

Emma tittered at her husband's use of her new title. "Do you like saying that?" she asked as she allowed Mr. Allen to assist her into the barouche.

"I do," Thomas replied as he helped his sister climb in behind Emma. "I do hope you like it, since it's your name now," he added. He sat across from the two girls. The barouche jerked as the horses took off for Burlington Lane.

"Oh, I do," Emma insisted with a nod.

"She does," Christiana agreed, nodding. For a bride-to-be, though, her face held little joy.

Emma took her hand and squeezed it. "I have good news," she said quietly. How she was going to keep the news of the church a secret for the entire trip?

Christiana turned to look at her. "Then tell me, please, for I could use some right now," she begged, her brows furrowed. Miss Dahlia had braided and rolled her hair into an ornate top knot and ironed tight spiral curls into the strawberry blonde hair at her temples. She looked much older than her seventeen years, and her frown only made her appear older.

"I just spoke with Mr. Argyle, the decorator Mr. Grandby hired to do your master suite. He's assured me that the room will be ready this evening," Emma stated as she clasped Christiana's hand in hers. "I've seen it, and it is *divine*," she added with a reassuring nod of her hand.

Christiana relaxed and nodded. "Thank you," she said simply. When she turned her attention back to her brother, she found him grinning at her. "What is it?" she asked.

Emma glanced at Thomas and did a double-take as she found his expression at odds with the situation. "Yes, what is it?" she repeated as she regarded her husband. "You look like a cat that's swallowed a canary!"

Thomas tried hard to rein in his grin. "I... I'm merely... happy, is all," he replied lamely. "My sister is getting married, and we're getting married... again. You're looking lovelier than I've ever seen you. And it's a beautiful day," he added for good measure. Even as he listed his reasons, he knew Emma wasn't convinced.

"What have *you* been up to, Mr. Wellingham?" she asked as she leaned to one side and angled her head.

Shaking his head, Thomas sighed and rolled his eyes. "Nothing. I've been up to nothing, I promise," he replied defensively.

Emma realized he spoke the truth. It was Gregory who had been the one to arrange the decoration of the church as well as all the other work that had been done at Woodscastle since he made his offer to buy half the estate.

Christiana smiled and leaned forward in her seat. "What has my betrothed been up to, then?" she asked, her face brightening more. For the first time since they'd left Woodscastle, she looked the part of the happy bride.

"Yes, what *has* he been up to?" Emma repeated, eyeing her husband with anticipation.

Thomas shook his head and leaned back in the carriage seat, a satisfied expression on his face. "I'm not saying another word," he said as he crossed his arms.

Gregory regarded St. James Church from his curricle. Feeling nervous, a sensation he was only familiar with when it came to matters of the heart, he was slow to give the reins to his tiger and step down from the equipage. He hoped all had gone to plan. With all the arrangements he had overseen for the renovations at Woodscastle during the past few weeks, it was the readiness of the church he was truly most concerned about.

Argyle had assured him all was well. Over the past few days, the decorator had split his time between the master bedchamber and the church. He assured his current employer that all was in readiness and that his bride would be very pleased with the display of ribbons and flowers that graced the sanctuary. Yards of satin had been rolled out down the central aisle, ending only a few feet from the altar. From the end of every pew hung a spray of colorful greenery and three yellow roses tied with a huge satin bow.

Gregory had been to Harding, Howell and Company so many times during the past week, there were rumors he was buying the draper. *And why not?* he considered. He had certainly dropped enough coin there to justify the gossips. His only concern was that Christiana not discover his arrangements until she was walking down the aisle to meet him. And given her brother, his cohort in the surprise, was seeing to a late arrival for both the brides, everything was going to plan.

Entering the church through the main entrance, Gregory noticed the satin runner before his nostrils were filled with the scent of roses. He actually gasped as he took in the sight. There must have been a thousand white and yellow roses in the sanctuary. And satin—yards and yards of the stuff made into bows and bunting that graced the pews and floral bouquets. Several guests were already seated. He nodded to those who turned to see who had just entered and acknowledged even more who were pouring through the front door for the eleven o' clock ceremony, many gasping in delight at the decor.

Gregory caught sight of the priest and hurried to meet the man, his nervousness gone. Everything had been done according to plan. There was nothing he could do to change anything at this point. From somewhere nearby, his stepfather moved forward to shake his hand, and his mother, looking radiant in a light green gown, reached up to kiss him on the cheek. "Best wishes, my son," she whispered in his ear. Sir William nodded to him, a bright gleam in his eye. Several business partners watched him from their seats, nodding in turn as he noticed them. At least three cousins, including Michael Merriweather, waved at him as he took in the sight of all the guests.

"The brides have arrived," someone said from nearby. Gregory was ushered to his place at the front of the church where Thomas was already standing. They shook hands and Thomas hugged him hard. "You old dog. You've really outdone yourself," he said, his attention turning to the satin-clad aisle. "I hear you had to buy a draper," he teased, his grin the only tell he wasn't serious.

"And the queen is most displeased by all the roses that seemed to have disappeared from her gardens this past week."

"Stuff it," Gregory replied, trying his best to keep a solemn face as he watched the brides enter the sanctuary. Their faces lit up in surprise at the sight of the roses and satin, and Gregory allowed a smile as he watched Christiana's reaction. He would remember her expression of delighted surprise for the rest of his days. He could only hope he would see it again and again as he took her to all the places in the world he wanted to revisit. Before he was even able to complete that thought, Christiana was standing beside him, her lightly freckled face covered with a thin lace veil.

Turning up to meet his gaze, she smiled. "It's all so beautiful," she breathed. "It's perfect. Thank you."

Gregory let out the breath he'd been holding for too long. He was aware of Emma, resplendent in the butter-colored gown he had seen her in at the modiste, her collarbones set off as beautifully as they had been hours earlier when he had caught her and Thomas in their bed.

There was Todd, somehow taller than usual in his gray morning suit—no walking cane in sight—and Deborah beaming as if she were the bride, her light blue gown glittering with the reflected light from a stained-glass window. Before he knew it, he was repeating vows, Todd was giving him his grandmother's ring, and he was turning Christiana around as they were presented to the guests. "It's already over?" he stammered, looking to his left to find Thomas nodding at him with an amused expression.

Christiana gripped his arm, nearly bouncing in place as she smiled at all the guests. "It felt as if it would go on forever," she countered in a whisper.

Emma and Thomas simply nodded and smiled at their guests, occasionally glancing at one another and sharing knowing looks. When Gregory didn't make a move to leave the church, Thomas did so, hurrying Emma past the phalanx of well-wishers to their barouche. "Do you feel married?" he asked as he helped her into the carriage.

"Of course," Emma answered as she took a seat, leaning back into the leather squabs and taking a deep breath. After a moment of shared silence, she sat up. "Do you?"

"Very," Thomas replied, taking a seat next to her and kissing her hair. "I have felt married for... it seems like ages," he said. His expression changed as he regarded his wife.

"What is it?" Emma asked, worry tinging her voice.

"Christiana is married now," he stated evenly. "She belongs to Gregory now."

Emma squeezed his hand, the new wedding band gleaming as it reflected the late morning light. "And?" she asked, sure there was more to his thought than what he had spoken.

"I'm so very *relieved*," he finished, a huge smile splitting his face.

Emma giggled and turned to watch the other newlyweds as they climbed into a curricle, several dozen wedding guests cheering and waving as Gregory took up the reins and Christiana tossed her bouquet into the crowd. Then they were off for the wedding breakfast at the Vandermeers.

"It was a perfect wedding," Deborah was saying as she hugged Emma and then kissed Thomas on the cheek. The surprised groom caught sight of their host and shrugged as he noticed Todd's shocked expression.

"Thanks to Gregory," Emma whispered in reply. "He made all the arrangements."

Deborah pressed her lips together. When Emma caught the look, she pulled the taller woman aside. "Didn't he?" she added, wondering at Deborah's reaction.

"There were several gentlemen involved in this," Deborah confided, an eyebrow arching suggestively.

Emma gasped and was about to ask for details when Christiana and Sophia Simpson appeared to thank their hostess. "You have managed a remarkable achievement," Sophia said to Deborah, placing a small hand on Deborah's arm.

"The breakfast was amazing, the garden is beautiful, the tables are dressed so perfectly... thank you," Christiana said brightly. Tears of gratitude threatened to spill from her eyes.

Deborah beamed, bending over to kiss Christiana on the cheek. "Your husband has quite a lot of clout in this town," she said in reply. "And your brother and my husband and Sir William, and your husband are a force to be reckoned with when they put their minds to something," she added, giving all three women a glance as she made the comment.

Emma considered Deborah's words. "Just what did Thomas have to do with the arrangements?" she asked, keeping her voice low.

Deborah glanced around, apparently making sure the men were out of earshot. "The church wasn't supposed to be available for a wedding today," she replied, an eyebrow arcing up in mischief. "I heard he bribed a priest to reschedule a private baptism."

Her eyes widening, Emma remembered their conversation with the parish priest just the week before. "Oh, yes," she admitted in reply, her face flushing. Christiana gave her a quizzical expression.

"And your husband?" Sophia directed her query to Deborah, her eyes darting to the cluster of men pretending not to watch them.

Grinning in delight, Deborah whispered, "He was able to appeal to our cook's ego. The man agreed to do the breakfast *and* a wedding cake. The second one in a fortnight!" All the women smiled in reply, impressed by the news.

"How did Mr. Simpson have a hand in all this?" Emma asked as she turned to Sophia.

Sophia stole a glance at her husband, smiling when she noticed him smiling at her. "He talked his tailor, Jeffrey Garth, into making their suits. The man did them in only two days!"

"And Sir William?" Christiana chimed in, wondering how the banker had been involved.

Deborah straightened and thought carefully before answering. "He... he was the matchmaker."

Emma, Christiana and Sophia all grinned. "We already knew that," they said in unison, and then burst into a fit of giggles.

"What do you suppose they're chatting about over there?" Todd asked as he and the two grooms took fresh glasses of champagne from a passing footman's tray. James Simpson stole a glance in the ladies' direction as Sir William declined a glass and instead lit a cigar.

"All those flowers in the church, no doubt," the elder man said with a satisfied grin. "Are there any white or yellow roses left in all of England?" he asked rhetorically.

"No," Gregory replied off-handedly.

"Gossip, I wager," James offered. "I hear one of our grooms bought a draper this week."

"I did no such thing. But I could be persuaded to buy their stock," Gregory replied as he shook his head. "They're speaking of gowns, I should think," he said as he slid a hand into his pocket. He watched his wife as she grinned in delight. "And all manner of frippery."

Thomas simply shook his head. "You dunderheads," he said in no uncertain terms. At their surprised expressions, he added, "They talking about *us*."

When the men all turned in unison to stare at the ladies, they were greeted by the sight of all the ladies looking at them. Bursting into giggles, the four women called out, "Thank you" in unison.

Surprised, the men merely bowed and then regarded one another. "As I said," Thomas commented lightly, downing his champagne in one satisfied gulp.

CHAPTER 76
A COUSIN COMES A CALLING

July 18, 1802, Woodscastle

On Sunday morning, having spent their actual wedding night at the Sablonniere Hotel, Emma and Thomas returned to Woodscastle in a yellow post chaise. With the servants off for the day and the house quiet, they retired to the master suite, undressed one another, and climbed into bed together.

Although they had made love very early that morning, enjoying the comfort of a large bed and soft linen sheets and goose down pillows, Emma found herself overcome with passion for Thomas. They were barely in the master suite when she insisted he make love to her again. Not waiting for him to undo the new corset he had purchased for her at Nicole's that week, Emma lay on the bed and spread her legs for him.

In the morning light, Thomas smiled as he climbed onto the bed and spent a moment admiring her. Using the tips of his fingers, he gently pulled the cups of the corset down so her hardened nipples, and indeed, the rest of her breasts, were free of their bondage. She inhaled sharply as his fingers drew circles around her nipples, and then gasped louder as his fingers left her breasts and moved slowly down the busk of the corset to the space between her thighs.

Gingerly touching the swollen folds between her thighs, he found the center of her womanhood already engorged and wet. He stroked up on it, his motion hard and quick. Emma arched her back in response, her intake of breath louder. "Come into me," she pleaded, her breaths coming quicker as she reached out for his arm.

Thomas shook his head, a mischievous smile on his face. "Not yet," he whispered as he stroked the red bud again. Her reaction was sudden and sensual to watch as she straightened her legs and moved her hand to cover his, her long, slender fingers splayed as they pressed his hand against her.

"Now," she pleaded as her knees started to draw up to her body, hitting his back as he sat on the edge of the bed. Very slowly, he removed his hand from under hers, making sure to rub it back and forth across the source of her pleasure. Moaning in response, Emma writhed on the bed, exciting him enough that he knew he could wait no longer.

He pulled his legs up onto the bed and straddled her, his arms held out straight in front of him as he lowered his body on top of hers. Reaching out with his tongue and lips, he touched each nipple, suckling and biting them until Emma spread her legs again and wrapped her ankles around his back. Slowly, he entered her. Her hands clasped his buttocks, pulling him into her as far as possible. He felt his sac nudge against her wetness, his cock surrounded by her warm cocoon.

Pushing into her again and again, he felt her hands press on him, the fingertips seeking places that would pleasure him as they circled and stroked. Even before he was aware of it, a fingertip pressed against the back of his manhood and stroked with his movement. His release was more sudden and more intense than any he had experienced. He winced and struggled to breathe as the pleasurable sensation gripped him and passed through him, finally releasing him when he was sure he would pass out. Exhausted, he lowered his body slowly onto her, his head collapsing into the space between her breast and shoulder.

When he awoke, he found Emma wide awake and listening intently. "What is it?" he whispered as he noticed her nipples still exposed above her corset. Reaching out with his tongue, he touched the nearest one.

"I think I hear a carriage coming up the lane," Emma whispered, ignoring his attempt to pleasure her.

After a moment, Thomas heard the same noise and rolled off of Emma, struggling to sit up on the edge of the bed. "Whatever did you do to me?" he asked rhetorically as he tried to stand and found his legs too weak. Sitting back down, he watched as Emma gracefully got off the bed and hurried to the window, adjusting the corset as she did so. She still wore her stockings, their tops held up on her thighs with blue satin ruched ribbons. Thomas found he was quite aroused as he watched her bend over to peer out the window. "You must know how erotic you look... like that," he managed to get out, his voice husky.

"I cannot be sure, but I think it may be Deborah," Emma murmured, apparently unaware of the effect she was having on her husband. "Something must be wrong, or maybe she's just out for a Sunday drive," she considered, a worried look crossing her face. Hurrying into the bath, she cleaned up as best she could and then grabbed her dressing gown from the valise, wrapping it around herself as she headed down the stairs to the vestibule. Thomas stared after her, moaning as he realized he wouldn't be bedding her again anytime soon.

Emma opened the door to find it wasn't Deborah Vandermeer who had come calling, but rather a woman who only bore a striking resemblance in features and hair. Not nearly as tall as Deborah, the woman was of a wealthy upbringing and stood as tall as possible as she regarded the robed-clad Emma.

"I rather expected a servant to answer," the woman stated uncertainly before Emma could greet her.

Embarrassed that she had opened the door and not been properly dressed, Emma curtsied and replied, "Please excuse my manner of dress. Sunday is our butler's day off. I'm Emma... Wellingham," she managed to say, almost using her maiden name. "May I be of assistance?" She admired the woman's smart spencer, matching poke bonnet and reticule, and her morning gown of pastel green lawn. The gown was impeccably made, obviously tailored specifically for the woman by a very talented modiste.

"I am Miss Merriweather," the woman nodded, not offering a curtsy. "I understand Gregory Grandby is a guest here. I wish to speak with him."

Alarm bells were going off in Emma's head as she regarded the woman—late twenties, early thirties, perhaps? *Merriweather?* Definitely one of Gregory's cousins, she realized. "Please, do come in," Emma offered as she opened the door and led the visitor through the vestibule and into the parlor. She indicated a damask-upholstered settee. As the woman sat down, Emma noticed she carried a newspaper clipping in her gloved hand. "I believe Mr.

Grandby was about to leave for church," Emma guessed as she

noticed the clock on the fireplace mantel. "I'll let him know you're here," Emma said, with as much graciousness as she could muster given the woman's ill mood.

Hurrying out of the parlor, she noticed Thomas coming down the stairs dressed in his robe and slippers. "Is Mrs. Vandermeer all right?" he asked as he joined Emma at the bottom of the stairs and kissed her on the temple.

"'Tis not Deborah," Emma whispered, her heart beating faster as she wondered about the woman's motives for calling on a Sunday morning. "I think it's Rebecca Merriweather," she said when she saw his quizzical brow.

"Oh, dear God," Thomas replied under his breath as his face went white.

Emma remembered his description of one of the Merriweather cousins. *She preyed on all the younger male cousins in the family. I believe she... deflowered, if you will, every boy at Merriweather Manor. Took delight in scaring us all to death when it came to sexual intercourse.* "Is *she* the one who preyed on the young boys of Merriweather Manor?" Emma whispered as they hurried to the west wing stairs.

Sighing, Thomas finally nodded. "Yes," he replied quietly. "Did she say why she's come?" he asked, hoping the woman wouldn't remember him. *Although, how could she not?* He was Gregory's best friend for all those years and spent more time at Merriweather Manor than he had at Woodscastle. And he had bled a great deal when her riding crop connected with his rib. At least she'd seemed suitably frightened and genuinely sorry for what she had done.

"She asked for Gregory," Emma replied as she stopped in front of the door to the just-completed master suite in the west wing. The other newlyweds had taken up residence the night before and were presumedly still there. Emma knocked hard on the door as she noticed the odor of sawdust and new plaster work. "It seems the renovations are really moving along quickly," she said quietly as she turned her attention back to Thomas.

Gregory Grandby, dressed smartly in a dark wool topcoat, scarlet brocade waistcoat, and tan breeches, opened the door. He held a brushed beaver top hat in one hand and Christiana's hand in another. Dressed for church, she wore a pastel yellow muslin morning gown and matching spencer. The ribbons from a yellow eyelet bonnet hung in her free hand. "Good morning," Gregory said as his face displayed that of a man whose hand had been caught in the cookie jar. "We're about to leave for church," he explained when he noticed Thomas' raised eyebrow at finding the newlyweds awake and dressed on the morning after their wedding.

"Rebecca Merriweather is in the parlor and has requested an audience with you," Emma announced evenly. She watched as Gregory's eyes widened and his face paled. *They're both scared to death of the woman,* she realized.

"Whatever's wrong, Gregory?" Christiana asked as she noticed the transformation in her husband. "And who is Rebecca Merriweather?" she added as she noticed the same look on her brother's face.

Thomas and Gregory exchanged knowing glances. "She's my cousin," Gregory finally replied as he pushed between Emma and Thomas as he muttered, "Pardon me." He descended the stairs as fast as he could, nearly ran the length of the hall to the parlor, and entered it at a near run.

"Miss Merriweather," he said as he bowed to his cousin and tried to catch his breath. "'Tis been far too long. I hope this day finds you in good health. You look... *stunning*," he said as he realized he meant it. For some reason, he had imagined his cousin to be so much older than him that he half-expected her to be an old crone by now. Instead, she was more comely than he remembered and certainly more *dressed* than he had occasion to remember her.

"Thank you, Mr. Grandby," Rebecca replied with a nod, a watery smile touching her lips. "Are you well?" she asked, attempting to be civil while at the same time trying to keep up her courage.

"I am, indeed," he replied, stepping farther into the parlor. "To what do I owe the honor of your visit?" he asked, trying to be as cordial as possible.

Rebecca lifted her chin and held out the newspaper clipping. "I'm hoping you can refute this, if this is, indeed, you in this article," she said haughtily. "And just who is Mrs. James Simpson?" she asked crossly as she regarded the cousin she hadn't seen in over five years.

Furrowing his brow, Gregory took the clipping from her. It was the betrothal announcement from *The Morning Chronicle*, last Wednesday's edition. Gregory sighed as he perused the words, surprised by his mother's insistence that an announcement was her right. No other betrothals warranted such announcements—only weddings.

Mrs. James Simpson is pleased to announce the betrothal of her son, Mr. Gregory Roger Grandby II of Derbyshire, to Miss Christiana Wellingham of Chiswick. Grandby, the son of the late Roger Grandby, graduated cum laude from Eton in '98. Miss Wellingham, the sister of Mr. Thomas Wellingham of Wellingham Imports and a niece of the Fifth Earl of Trenton, attends Warwick's Grammar and Finishing School. A wedding date has not yet been set.

Gregory looked up from reading the announcement and regarded his cousin. "'Tis me, yes, and I cannot refute the information," he said carefully, curious as to why the woman had come to see him. He sat down in an adjacent chair and leaned forward. "Mrs. James Simpson is my mother."

Rebecca's eyes widened at the mention of his mother, but Gregory could tell from her haughty behavior that her visit had nothing to do with his mother. "Why have you come, Rebecca?" he asked quietly.

His cousin took a deep breath, and her features took on a severe look. "When will the banns be read and at which church?" she asked.

Gregory sat back in his chair and sighed. "There will be no reading of the banns," he replied quietly. "Miss Wellingham and I were married at St. James Church yesterday morning," he said, carefully watching his cousin and her reaction. "By special license. Did you intend to challenge the wedding?" he asked, knowing she could have done so at any of the three readings of the banns had he not purchased the special license.

He also knew Rebecca could challenge the wedding, and for good reason. He had bedded her, although it had been many years ago. But it was more that *she* had bedded him—and every other male cousin at Merriweather Manor over a period of several years.

Emma walked into the parlor carrying a tray laden with a tea service and breakfast rolls and pastries, all the while silently thanking Mr. Tanner for having the foresight to make them. He apparently knew she and Thomas would be returning from their very short honeymoon that morning.

"Do you take sugar or milk?" Emma asked as she poured a cup for Rebecca.

The older woman seemed surprised by the hospitality. "Yes,

both, please," she replied as she gave a nervous glance in Gregory's direction.

"Have you met Mrs. Wellingham?" Gregory asked as Emma handed Rebecca her cup and saucer.

Emma suppressed the urge to gasp at Gregory's poor choice of words, hoping she didn't outwardly display the nervousness she felt on the inside.

"Yes, we did, although I didn't realize she was *Mrs.* Wellingham," Rebecca replied, ice in her voice.

Emma held out the plate of pastries to the woman. "For about a week now," she said as she angled her head and gave Gregory a look that warned him not to contradict the statement.

"A house full of newlyweds, then," Rebecca commented, her resolve softening. She returned her attention to Gregory, who looked as if he were in physical pain. "Well, cousin, what would you do in my place?" she hissed, on the one hand wishing to make him uncomfortable, but on the other, not wanting to anger him to the point of wrath.

"I am not you, but in your place, I would most certainly not cause heartache for one of my relatives," he said, an expression of concern appearing. "I must take my leave now," Gregory announced as he stood and bowed to Emma and Rebecca.

"But, where are you going?" Rebecca asked, stunned he would leave in the middle of their conversation.

"To church, cousin," he said with a nod. "Would you care to join my wife and me?" he offered, knowing full well she would decline the offer.

"No, thank you, Mr. Grandby," Rebecca replied. The woman swallowed hard as she sat back in the settee and finally regarded her hostess.

Emma had finished pouring a cup of tea for Gregory, but with his sudden departure, Emma took the cup herself and sat down in the chair in which Gregory had been sitting.

"Whatever is the matter?" Emma asked as she leaned toward the older woman, realizing Rebecca was close to tears.

*O*ut in the hall near the vestibule, Thomas intercepted Gregory. "And just where the hell do you think you're going?" he asked in a hoarse whisper. "You cannot just leave with her still in the house!"

Gregory shook his head and pursed his lips. Christiana stood waiting in the vestibule, angling her head around the corner so she could watch her brother and husband.

"She wants to challenge the wedding, I think," Gregory whispered. "But I cannot understand why. I haven't seen her in *years*," he said quietly, his face contorting as he considered the ramifications if she did challenge his marriage to Christiana.

"Shh!" Thomas held up a finger to his lips. He was out of sight from the parlor, but he could hear some of the women's conversation. "We're about to find out."

*R*ebecca took another deep breath, trying hard to keep herself from breaking down into a puddle of tears. "Tell me, Mrs. Wellingham. Do you enjoy the company of a man in your bed?" she asked with a raised eyebrow, daring her hostess to take umbrage at her shocking question and order her out of the house.

*T*homas' eyes widened, as did Gregory's. Christiana moved in to stand next to Gregory but she stayed out of sight of the parlor doorway.

*E*mma knew from Rebecca's demeanor she was being baited and decided she would have none of it. "Why, yes, Miss Merriweather, I do. I find it rather... *exhilarating*," she replied as she held her head at a suggestive angle, an eyebrow arching to accentuate the reply.

Surprised by Emma's answer to her question—that she had even answered at all—Rebecca straightened and stated, "I thought I smelled the scent of recent coitus about you."

Placing her cup and saucer on the low table in front of the settee, only because she was sure that by holding onto them her shaking hands would become evident, Emma replied, "Why, of course you do. I rather like to *take* my husband first thing in the morning," she said. "You see, the day seems to go so much better when I do."

. . .

*O*ut in the hall, Gregory turned to stare at Thomas, his mouth opened in shock.

"Do *not* say a word," Thomas ordered in a low whisper as he struggled to hear Rebecca's reply. Emma was certainly holding her own against the witch, he considered.

*R*ebecca sat up even straighter, swallowing hard. A hint of respect crept into her voice as she stated, "I rather like it in the afternoon. I think it makes the perfect appetizer before dinner."

One of Emma's eyebrow arched up. "Indeed? I shall have to try that," she answered with a hint of enthusiasm, deciding she didn't need to admit that she and Thomas had engaged in afternoon lovemaking at least a few times in the last week. And that, yes, it was the perfect aperitif.

Gregory elbowed Thomas, and Thomas stuck his chin up. Christiana glanced up at the men in her life and merely shook her head, rolling her eyes as she finally pieced together just what was going on in the parlor.

"*M*ay I ask, Miss Merriweather, is there a *mister* Merriweather? I only ask, because if there is, he must be the happiest and most *satisfied* man in all of London," Emma said, arching an eyebrow as she made the comment.

"There is not, although I... I thank you for thinking there might be," Rebecca replied, her eyes downcast. "Part of the reason for my visit today was to discover if there was a possibility Mr. Grandby might have *feelings* in that regard. Of all of my cousins, Mr. Grandby was my favorite, you see, he being an only child and his mother abandoning him as she did. However, from our brief *conversation*, I can surmise he does not have feelings for me. And it would behoove me to let my claim to him..." She stopped then as tears welled up in her eyes.

Emma took a handkerchief from the table next to her chair and moved to the settee. Sitting down next to Rebecca, her brows furrowed in concern, she offered the linen to Rebecca. "Do you love him?" she asked gently, not sure if the woman even knew the emotion.

"No," Rebecca answered quickly as she took the handkerchief, her head shaking from side to side. "I mean, I do because he is *family*, but not in a romantic way, no," she admitted, dabbing her eyes as she said it.

Gregory took a deep breath and sighed. He noticed that Christiana stood next to him and was doing the same thing.

"And he does have that *reputation*," Emma said carefully, pressing her lips together.

Thomas allowed a mischievous grin to cross his face, and he glanced at Gregory.

"Do *not* say a word," Gregory ordered in a hoarse whisper.

Rebecca raised her eyebrows at Emma's comment. "Oh, the 'girl in every port', you mean?" she said as she sniffled. "That is a bit of a problem, I suppose."

Emma leaned her back against the settee. "I find it very hard to believe a woman as comely and as young as you has not yet married. Did your parents not arrange a marriage for you?" she asked carefully, not wanting to upset the woman but curious as to how she could have remained unmarried. She was a Merriweather, after all.

"Young?" Rebecca repeated with a hint of disgust in her voice. "I am eight-and-twenty."

"She's thirty-two if she's a day," Gregory whispered angrily.

"Thirty," Thomas countered as he did some addition with his fingers.

. . .

"And I... I refused the man my parents arranged for me to marry," Rebecca was saying, her head shaking side to side. At Emma's questioning glance, Rebecca added in disgust, "He was ten years *older* than me! I prefer my men *younger*," she explained as she lifted her head again.

Emma regarded the woman for a moment. "Did you receive an inheritance?" she queried, knowing all of the cousins received something when Mary Margaret Merriweather finally passed away.

"But, of course," Rebecca replied, surprised by the question but apparently not offended by it.

"You've not squandered it on expensive clothing or lost it at the gambling tables?" Emma asked gently. She had already decided that Rebecca might be a she-devil, but she did seem to have some sense about her.

"Of course not!" Rebecca replied, indignant and cross that her hostess would even think such a thing.

"So, you could afford to marry for love?" Emma continued, ignoring the rebuke.

Rebecca sat back at that and considered the query. "Yes. Yes, I suppose I could," she admitted as her demeanor softened.

"Is there someone you enjoy *satisfying?* Someone for whom you ache in the middle of the afternoon? Someone who can... pleasure you? Someone... you *love*, perhaps?" Emma hinted, hoping Rebecca would admit there was someone. If not, she didn't know what she would do with the woman.

"Well, of course," Rebecca replied, her chin jutting out defiantly. She lowered her head and added, "But Mr. Garth is... he's a tailor," she said, barely saying the word aloud. "He's very good at what he does for his clients, and he sews women's clothing on occasion." Her wave of hand across the gown she wore indicated he had made the outfit.

"What did she say?" Gregory whispered, missing the occupation of his cousin's lover.

"Shh! I didn't hear it, either," Thomas replied, trying hard to hear.

"He's a *tailor*," Christiana whispered. "James Simpson's tailor.

The one who made your wedding clothes," she added with an arched eyebrow.

The two men glanced at one another and screwed up their faces. "Poor man," they said in unison.

*E*mma furrowed her brows and gazed at Rebecca for a moment. It was true that tailors were not held in high regard in London society, but at least the man was employed. "He does beautiful work," she said as she admired the gown. "But what if he had been... let us say, a butler?"

"*W*hat? How dare she?" Gregory whispered angrily. "Shh!"

"*W*ell, I certainly cannot imagine falling in love with a *butler*. Or any servant, for that matter. Why ever do you ask?" There were occupations that were beneath even Jeffrey Garth's status as a tailor.

Emma swallowed and chose her words carefully. "Do you remember the butler named Simpson?"

Rebecca furrowed her brows and turned to stare at Emma, stunned by the question. "Of course. He resigned, though, when I was... about eight, I think," she said with a nod. "Why do you ask?"

Emma bit her lip and then reached for the newspaper clipping. Pointing to the first name in the article, she said, "Sophia Burroughs Grandby is *Mrs.* James Simpson. A very happily married woman, I might add."

Open-mouthed, Rebecca stared at the clipping and then at Emma. "She married our *butler?*" she asked in disbelief. Staring at Emma for several seconds, Rebecca sat very still. "She didn't have a lover on the Continent?"

Emma shook her head. "And she didn't take a ship to the United States, and she didn't die mysteriously," Emma said as she continued to shake her head. "She fell in love with Mr. Simpson, and he with her. She used her inheritance to buy a street of townhouses in

London. She and Mr. Simpson have been living happily together ever since. They make their living as landlords."

Tears began to flow freely from Rebecca's reddened eyes.

"Is Mr. Garth over the age of twenty-one?" Emma asked quietly as she reached over to place a hand on Rebecca's shoulder.

Rebecca nodded. "He is... he's three-and-twenty," she said between sobs.

"So, you could marry without requiring permission from anyone," Emma stated matter-of-factly.

Rebecca nodded in agreement. "We... we could, yes, but he's a *tailor...*"

Leaning closer to the woman, Emma whispered, "If you can afford to support the two of you, no one need know what he does, or rather, *did*, for a living, Miss Merriweather. As a tailor, he's probably always impeccably dressed—"

"Indeed. Always," Rebecca nodded with assurance.

"So anyone seeing the two of you together would assume he comes from wealth," Emma reasoned for her.

"'Tis true," the older woman agreed, dabbing her eyes again with the hanky.

"No one need know the truth. You can devise a suitable explanation for him when you introduce him as your husband," Emma encouraged, hoping she wasn't moving things along too fast.

"We can create a suitable lineage for him, yes, of course," Rebecca said as a faint smile appeared, her head nodding as she considered Emma's words. She balled the hanky in her fist and sat straighter.

"Do you have a ring you could use for the ceremony?" Emma asked.

Rebecca continued nodding. "Yes. Yes, I have my grandmother's ring," she acknowledged, her tears drying as she ran scenarios through her head.

Out in the hall, Christiana glanced up at Gregory. "Isn't *this* your grandmother's ring?" she asked, holding up her left hand and eyeing the ring Gregory had placed on it the day before.

"My grandmother Grandby's, yes," Gregory assured her. "I certainly wouldn't want to burden you with one of Mary Margaret's," he added quickly.

"Shh!"

"*T*hen you have all you need to marry the man you love," Emma said with a small smile.

"I do," Rebecca said as she wiped the tears from her face and got up to her feet. Turning to her hostess, she said, "However can I thank you?" she asked as she sniffled and pulled her gloves back on her hands. "You have been so kind when I was... *not*," she added. "My favorite cousin must just despise me," she added, biting her lip hard as she closed her eyes tightly.

"*S*he's right about that," Gregory whispered, knowing his cousin would be leaving the parlor at any moment. "Come, my love, we really must leave now," he said as he took Christiana's elbow and walked quietly to the vestibule.

Thomas remained in the corridor, thinking perhaps he would at least greet the woman as she left. It was hard not to feel sorry for her, and he wondered what was wrong about loving a tailor. Of all the professions in which a man could be employed, why was a tailor considered so beneath people of wealth?

*E*mma regarded the woman and shook her head. "I'll explain the situation to Mr. Grandby when he returns from church. Now, you must go and propose marriage to the one you love, Miss Merriweather," she said with a happy grin.

"I will," Rebecca assured her with a nod. The woman left the parlor and nearly walked into Thomas as he stood waiting for her.

"Miss Merriweather!" he said with a genuine smile. "'Tis so good to see you again."

Rebecca regarded the man before her. With him dressed only in his robe and slippers, she found she couldn't place him. "Do... Do I know you?" she asked as she curtsied to his bow and gave a quick glance in Emma's direction.

Emma drew up alongside their visitor. "This is my husband, Thomas Wellingham," she said by way of introduction.

Shaking her head, Rebecca seemed to study Thomas for several seconds before saying, "Oh, you were Gregory's friend. Now I remember you, Mr. Wellingham. 'Tis very good to see you again," she said with a nod. She continued to walk to the vestibule but angled her head toward Emma. "Do not be concerned, Mrs. Wellingham. He was *not* one of my lovers," she whispered.

Emma grinned at that, wondering if the woman had forgotten or was merely protecting Thomas for propriety's sake. "They have to learn from someone," Emma replied with an arched brow, her eyes showing a hint of mischief. "Have a safe trip back to town, Miss Merriweather."

"Thank you, Mrs. Wellingham," Rebecca replied as Mr. Allen assisted her onto her phaeton. With a crack of her riding crop, the horse took off down the drive.

Leaning against the front door, Emma regarded Thomas as he came to take her into his arms. "You were brilliant," he whispered and then kissed her on the lips.

When their lips parted, Emma angled her head to one side. "Did you overhear *everything?*" she asked, her eyes widening as she recalled the details of the conversation she had just had with Rebecca Merriweather.

"If not everything, then certainly enough," Thomas said as he nodded, a glint in his eye.

Emma bit her lower lip. "And you're not cross with me for what I said?" she asked, noticing the hint of amusement on his features.

Angling his head to one side, he asked, "Are you referring to the comment about you 'taking me in the morning'?'"

Emma eyebrows drew together as she barely nodded.

"Oh," he replied quietly. "That was positively the best part. You should have seen the look on Grandby's face!" he said with a happy grin. He kissed her on the nose. "You can take me whenever you want to," he said before kissing her again. "Well, perhaps not when we're at the office, though," he added when he pulled away.

Emma arched an eyebrow. "We shall see about that," she countered mischievously.

Thomas sighed audibly and tried his best not to smile. "And for that, I shall take you back to bed this very instant, Mrs. Wellingham," he said in reply, his arm wrapping around her shoulders as they headed up the stairs to the master suite.

EPILOGUE - AN EARL AND A BANKER CONVERSE

July 20, 1802, Boodles

Sir William settled into his regular chair at Boodles and gave the footman who appeared at his side a nod. The young man acknowledged him with a bow and hurried off, knowing from the elder man's past visits exactly how to prepare his brandy.

Pulling a cheroot from his waistcoat pocket, Sir William reached over a candle lamp and was about to light it when a familiar figure appeared in the doorway.

"I see they'll let just about anyone into this club these days," the younger man drawled as he stepped over and gave the banker a nod.

Sir William grunted. "Are you already in your cups?" he asked, giving the interloper a thorough glance.

Milton Grandby, Earl of Torrington, took the seat across from Sir William and sighed. "Unfortunately, not. I haven't yet been to White's," he commented, looking about the richly furnished men's club. "Just how long have you been a member here?" he asked, his brows furrowing.

The clientele of Boodle's tended toward gentleman from the outskirts of London, the landed gentry whose homes were large and whose estates were much larger. As a banker living in a small manor home in Mayfair, Sir William hardly met the criteria.

"Since the beginning, I suppose," Sir William responded, not explaining why he favored the more sedate environment provided by Boodle's. "I appreciate you coming on such short notice. I admit, I half-expected to receive a note saying you wouldn't," he hedged.

Sir William regarded the young man who had inherited an earldom at the tender age of sixteen. Although there had been concerns as to his youth and propensity for enjoying practical jokes and pranks, the man had been raised to be the Earl of Torrington. He had attended Eton and Cambridge and understood politics far better than most in Parliament. But Milton Grandby sometimes still behaved as if he were merely the son of an earl, his nightly entertainments centered around faro tables, brandy and courtesans —not necessarily in that order.

Grandby seemed offended by the comment. "I always make time for a relative," he replied. His eyebrow arched before he amended his statement, "Or almost relatives." Sir William was the brother of his late uncle's wife, which for Milton meant he was family.

It didn't hurt that Sir William was also the son of a duke.

"Unlike most Merriweathers, I have an appreciation for family. In fact, I have just today consented to be a godfather again," he said with what might have been pride.

"Again?" the banker replied, sitting up as straight as his rounded belly would allow. "How many godchildren do you have now?" he asked, incredulous.

The earl considered the question but didn't provide a response. Meanwhile, the footman had returned with Sir William's brandy. "I'll have a brandy," he said when the footman turned in his direction and gave him a bow. The servant hurried off.

"Grandby! You do realize you may end up with the responsibility of actually having to *raise* one or more of those godchildren," Sir William admonished him. The banker didn't even realize he had called the earl by his family name rather than by 'Torrington'.

The earl's brows arched up with amusement. "I do. And I... I will, should it come to that," he assured the banker. "And in answer to your question, I am now a godfather to twenty-one baby girls," he added happily. "And some ...," He paused to consider how many boys he might have consented to godfather. "Ten boys, at least. My secretary keeps a list."

Sir William arched a bushy eyebrow. "Good God!" he whispered, taking a long drink from his brandy. There was something in the way the earl spoke of his godchildren that had the banker thinking a bit differently about Milton Grandby. If the earl ended up having to take on the responsibility of actually *raising* any of his numerous godchildren, he would probably do so with aplomb, the banker considered.

Milton regarded the older man for a long time. "I rather like how you called me 'Grandby' just then," he said quietly. At Sir William's quizzical expression, he added, "I'm not particularly fond of '*Torrington*'," he explained. "I find myself looking about for my father whenever I hear it," he said, his manner most sober. "Can't say I'm comfortable in his shoes. Don't know that I'll ever be. Can't claim I ever *wanted* to be an earl, in fact. It would have suited one of my cousins far better," he continued with long face.

Sir William finished his brandy and set aside the balloon glass on a side table. "'Grandby' it is, then," he said with a nod. "As such, you'll be interested to learn your aunt Sophia has decided to come out of hiding in plain sight." He watched the earl's face, curious as to how the young man would react to the news.

"Your sister?" Grandby replied, one eyebrow furrowing so his entire face appeared crooked. "Whatever do you mean? Speak plainly, old man!" he ordered. The footman appeared with his brandy, and Grandby took it with a murmured, "Thank you," his manner more agreeable.

Finally lighting his cheroot, Sir William regarded Milton with surprise. "There's the earl I knew you could be," he said with a grin. "And no, Gregory Grandby wouldn't have made a better earl," he stated. "He's too good at trade."

"Makes money hand over fist, if my ears have heard correctly," Grandby said. "Without gambling. Heard he bought a draper."

"Indeed on the first point, but no on the second," Sir William responded. "But he's just gone and gotten himself leg-shackled—"

"No!" Grandby interrupted, leaning forward to regard the banker with a look of astonishment.

"To a Wellingham," the banker said, his eyebrow arching up again.

"Wellingham?" the earl repeated. "But... there aren't any Wellingham daughters in the Trenton household," he argued.

Sir William shook his head. "She and her brother, Thomas, are cousins of Trenton's. Their father, Graham, was the black sheep, the one who went off and started his own import company. Married a Tennison girl the year you were born."

Grandby considered the news, finally allowing a 'humph'. He straightened when he remembered something Sir William had said just moments earlier. "Aunt Sophia. She's alive then?" he queried, a look of concern making him appear older than his seven-and-twenty years.

The banker leaned back in his chair and allowed a smile. "Indeed. Alive and well, married to the love of her life, and living in Kingly Street," he murmured, rather satisfied at how his involvement in the couple's life had resulted in such an agreeable match.

Grandby angled his head to one side. "Love of her life?" he repeated, his brows furrowing. "And who might that be?" he asked, taking a sip of the brandy. He savored the fortified wine, allowing it to slowly make its way down his throat.

"James Simpson," Sir William stated.

The earl regarded the banker for a very long time, his face screwed up as he considered the name. "Simpson? As in... the butler at Merriweather Manor?" he asked finally, his head shaking from side to side. Although he was very young when the butler quit his employment, Simpson was generally considered one of the best to have ever held the position. Despite employing a replacement who was an adequate butler, Merriweather Manor fell into a state of disrepair within only a few years of Simpson's departure. Most of his aunts and uncles left the household to move into town or to their own country estates.

"Indeed," Sir William replied. "They own an entire street of townhouses in Kingly Street. Have since just a month after her disappearance from Merriweather Manor," he added before he took a long draw on his cheroot. "I thought you should know, seeing as how you might come across Mrs. Simpson whilst shopping or in your travels. Wouldn't do for you to appear too terribly surprised."

Milton Grandby drained his liquor in one gulp and set the glass down on the table next to his chair. "You're telling me James Simpson is now my *uncle?*" he half-asked as he slumped in his chair.

The banker's eyebrows lifted, a sign he hadn't considered that particular aspect. "He has been for over twenty years," he replied.

"The butler?"

Sir William nodded, a smile slowly spreading across his face.

"The butler is the reason my Aunt Sophia left Merriweather Manor?" the earl half-questioned. He got to his feet, his own smile slowly replacing his look of puzzlement. "Do you realize what this means?"

The banker's bushy eyebrows furrowed into a single caterpillar.

"What?" he asked, aware their discussion had drawn the attention of several other patrons.

"Well, we now know the answer to the greatest whodunit mystery the *ton* has known for the past twenty-some years," Grandby stated as his arms swept out in a broad gesture. He turned and made his way to the door.

"*Whodunit?*" Sir William repeated, not immediately comprehending the term.

The Earl of Torrington turned. "Why, the butler did it, of course!" he said before giving the banker a slight bow and a big grin. He turned and took his leave of the men's club.

Sir William sat back down, hard, his moan of disgust audible to everyone else in the room. "Indeed," he whispered, rolling his eyes. "Indeed."

EXCERPT

Read on for an excerpt from Linda Rae Sande's
The Pride of a Gentleman
Book II of The Cousins of the Aristocracy

The arrival of anything in a crate was always cause for excitement at Woodscastle. In the past, it meant new furnishings or accessories for the recently renovated east wing or an elaborate toy for Ariel.

The wooden crate that rested on a table in the library had just been delivered in the back of a dray cart. Gregory had managed to pry open the lid and was removing the straw-like padding from around his recent acquisition when his wife joined him.

"Whatever is it?" Christiana asked as Gregory proudly pulled the instrument out of its protective packaging. He set the small crate to one side and removed the bits of shredded straw and paper that clung to the sides of the object.

"This, my dear, is a microscope," he announced as he peered through a hole in the top and looked straight down. "Somewhere, there should be small glass slides," he muttered as he turned his attention back to the crate and rummaged around inside. "Ah! Here," he said excitedly as he pulled out a package and began undoing the wrapping.

"What is this for?" Christiana asked as she looked through the hole she had seen Gregory look through. Not seeing anything but a blurry image, she stepped back so that Ariel's groping hands couldn't reach the instrument.

"It allows you to look at very small things and see them in fine detail," Gregory explained as he held a rectangular glass slide up to the window. Picking a piece of lint off of his vest, he carefully placed it on the slide and then put another slide on top of it, sealing the lint between the two slides. Placing it under the tube and securing it in place with two movable arms attached to the base of the instrument, he positioned his eye over the tube and began turning a geared knob on the tube. "Amazing," he breathed as he stood up and indicated that Christiana should take a look.

Handing the baby to Gregory, she leaned over and looked through the lens. Startled at what she saw, she let out a small shriek and jumped back and into Gregory, who wrapped an arm around her waist and laughed.

"What did you see?" he asked as he leaned over and looked again. His reaction was nearly the same, but he gingerly approached the instrument and noticed the source of the frightening sight; a gnat had dropped onto the slide and was skittering across it. "This is capital!" he exclaimed as he watched the bug through the microscope, careful to keep Ariel's busy fist from hitting it.

"What is it?" Christiana asked, not sure she wanted to know.

"A gnat!" he said proudly, finally pulling away so that she could take his place.

Christiana eyed him doubtfully and peered through the tube again. "Eew!" she said as she forced herself to watch the magnified movement of the insect. Once she recovered from her initial revulsion, she continued to watch the bug with more interest. "Are those the *eyes?*" she asked, awestruck.

"Let me see," Gregory insisted as Christiana stepped aside and let him take her place. "Indeed," he said. "What an odd shape," he whispered, absently giving Ariel back to Christiana. Offering a forefinger for the baby to grab onto, Christiana gave her a quick kiss when she did so. The toddler grinned, her two front teeth gleaming. At the sound of horses, though, Ariel's attention turned to the windows and she pointed. "Orse!" she cried out excitedly.

Christiana looked out the window to see Thomas and Emma dismount and give their reins to Mr. Larsen, who had run out to meet them. They were having an animated discussion, and when Christiana heard Humphrey open the front door, their conversation continued over in the vestibule.

"Have you asked him recently?" Emma was saying as she

removed her riding cloak. "He may be waiting for you to ask him."

"No, not since... not since he's been working there," Thomas answered. Their voices got louder as they approached the library.

"I should probably not say this," Emma mentioned in a quiet voice, "But Deborah said he is less pleased with his work these days. She doesn't know if something has changed or if Todd is just... bored, but she feels it would be good for him to travel. And soon," she added as they headed down the hallway to the library. "He used to travel all the time for the John Company," she added. "And since he is experienced in traveling, and since you do not wish to make the trips to the Continent, it only makes sense that he be the one to go."

Thomas thought for a moment. "And Deborah won't mind if he is gone for a fortnight now and then?"

Emma considered the question. "Not if she's with him," she answered with a gleam in her eye.

He sighed audibly while he rolled his eyes at his wife's logic. "Then I will speak with him on the morrow," Thomas countered as he and Emma entered the library. They both stopped short when they took in the sight of Gregory and his family standing next to the microscope.

"Good heavens, is that what I think it is?" Thomas asked as he approached.

"'Tis a microscope," Christiana replied as she reached up to kiss her brother on the cheek. Ariel's fist pounded on her uncle's shoulder and Thomas took it absently.

"Indeed?" Thomas answered, his interest piqued.

Emma reached over for Ariel, who had let go of her mother in favor of her aunt's arms. "What is it for?" she asked as she walked around to the other side of the library table and studied the instrument.

"It allows you to look at very small things and see them in very great detail," Gregory explained again, glad he would not have to explain it again now that they were all in the library. "I bought it for me, of course," he added. "But I'm hoping our children will take an interest in the sciences. I must admit, I think I will get more enjoyment out of it than they will for a few years at least."

Thomas raised an eyebrow and glanced over at Emma. "Well, as long as you don't allow your kids to experiment with gunpowder...," he said with a wry grin.

"Oh, dear," Emma whispered, looking from Gregory to Thomas and back. "Which one of you did that?" she asked in a louder voice.

"He did," they both said in unison as they pointed to one another, and then turned to look at each other in amusement.

Christiana stared open-mouthed at her husband and brother. "And what did you destroy in the process?" she asked, mortified.

"He launched a glass bottle into the sky," Thomas said as he indicated Gregory. "The thing flew up at least thirty feet."

"After he blew up the dog house," Gregory accused as he nodded in Thomas' direction. At Emma's surprised gasp, he added, "Well, the dog wasn't in it. We were supposed to be dismantling it to build a new one," he explained with a shrug.

"The explosion just sort of hurried the project along," Thomas added with a wave of his hand, his expression showing no humor and certainly no sign of guilt.

Christiana stared at the two men. "Oh!" And with that, she hurried out of the room.

Gregory rolled his eyes and excused himself as he hurried to follow his wife. As he passed Emma, he brushed his hand against the hand that wasn't holding onto Ariel's. Her fingers felt the small parcel he held for her, and she took it, carefully hiding it in her palm.

With her parents suddenly taking their leave of the library, Ariel begged to be let down and crawled out of the room after them. "Bye-bye," she waved, not giving her aunt and uncle another glance.

Emma watched her niece take her leave and smiled broadly. When she turned to face Thomas, she shook her head. "I do not think Christiana was very happy to learn of your experiments," she said as she wrapped her arms around his waist and hugged him.

"I'm quite sure I mentioned that incident to her in the past," Thomas replied as he grinned and returned Emma's hug. "Are you all right?" he wondered in a quiet voice, kissing her temple.

"Mmm," Emma murmured as she buried her face in the small of his shoulder. "I am just a bit tired is all," she admitted. "Perhaps I'll take a nap before dinner."

Thomas kissed her temple again. "All right. In the meantime, I am going to write a letter to Mr. Vandermeer," he said with a nod. "How much more can we afford to pay him, do you suppose?

Emma cocked her head and considered the situation. "If we offer too little, he may be offended. But I still have no idea how much he made at East India," she replied as she continued calculations in her head. "I remember Deborah once implied that he could have left his position at the John Company if they moved to a smaller house, so he must have some income from somewhere else," she reasoned. "Investments, perhaps?"

Thomas nodded. "He has investments in many of the same ventures as Gregory," he said as he pursed his lips. "On a smaller scale, of course."

Biting her lip, Emma took a deep breath. "What about a raise to sixteen-hundred pounds plus some kind of commission on the amount of business he manages on the Continent?" she suggested.

Thomas visibly winced. "Can we afford that?" he asked, his brows furrowing.

Smiling, Emma leaned back in his arms. "Yes. In fact, you can go as high as two-thousand if you think it necessary, but it would be a poor example to set for yourself."

Furrowing his brows, Thomas replied, "Whatever do you mean?" he asked, his expression turning to one of worry.

"I pay you seventeen-hundred-and-fifty a year," Emma replied, surprised he didn't seem to know his own salary.

Startled, Thomas released his hold on Emma and stepped back. "You do? Since when?" he wondered, giving her a look of disbelief.

"Well, since I started doing the payroll. Right after I married you," she replied with an arched brow. "Your articles of incorporation say that you are entitled to a compensation commensurate with the profit from the company. So, that is how I determine how much to pay you, as well as all the employee owners, each month."

He cocked his head and smiled. "And how much do you pay yourself?" he asked mischievously.

Emma rolled her eyes at his implication. "I receive the same salary as Mr. Peabody did—"

"Which was two-hundred, twenty-five per annum as I recall," Thomas interrupted as he crossed his arms and regarded his wife.

"And fifty extra for my share in the company," Emma added happily. "Which I plan to use to buy exquisite gifts for Christmas."

Thomas stared into space for a few moments as he considered the information. "So we could afford—"

"To travel, yes," Emma said with an enthusiastic nod, but her smile waned when she realized that travel was not really on her husband's mind.

ABOUT THE AUTHOR

A self-described nerd and student of history, Linda Rae spent many years as a published technical writer specializing in 3D graphics workstations, software and 3D animation (her movie credits include SHREK and SHREK 2). Getting lost in the rabbit holes of research has resulted in historical romances set in the Regency-era as well as Ancient Greece.

A fan of action-adventure movies, she can frequently be found at the local cinema. Although she no longer has any tropical fish, she follows the San Jose Sharks and makes her home in Cody, Wyoming.

For more information:
www.lindaraesande.com
Sign up for Linda Rae's newsletter:
Regency Romance with a Twist
Follow Linda Rae's blog:
Regency Romance with a Twist